2011 不求人文化

2009 懶鬼子英日語

I'm 我識出版集團
I'm Publishing Group
www.17buy.com.tw

2005 意識文化

2005 易富文化

2003 我識地球村

2001 我識出版社

2011 不求人文化

2009 懶鬼子英日語

I'm 我識出版集團
I'm Publishing Group
www.17buy.com.tw

2005 意識文化

2005 易富文化

2003 我識地球村

2001 我識出版社

地表最強
英文單字

不想輸，就用「格林法則」
背10,000個英文單字

　　猶記十多年前，我在台灣師範大學英語系上大三必修課——「英語語言史」，初次邂逅格林法則，內心甚是激盪。李櫻教授講述英語史，旁徵博引，從語言歷史和語用觀點解釋國內文法教學的諸多盲點，全班同學聽得如癡如醉。課程教科書是經典書籍—— Albert C Baugh, Thomas Cable 寫的《A History of the English Language》，書中提到希臘字根、拉丁字根和英語字根存在巧妙的語音對應現象。李櫻老師解釋說，格林法則是格林童話兩位作者中的哥哥——Jacob Grimm（雅各布 · 格林）觀察日耳曼語和其他印歐語，所提出來的系統性語音對應現象。教授又給我們幾十題練習題，完成後真是意猶未盡。爾後拜讀莫建清教授的大作——《從語音的觀點談英語詞彙教與學》，看到許多系統性的語音對應例子，從此沉浸於語音對應的研究中，樂此不疲。

　　這幾年，台灣陸續有老師講述格林法則，運用語音對應現象幫助學生記憶單字，讓單字學習者有機會初窺格林法則堂奧與實際應用。我也嘗試將格林法則應用於單字教學，力求不失真，且恪遵考據，嚴謹分析，破除穿鑿附會，同時著手蒐集語料。約兩年前，我有幸參加謝忠理老師的《字彙方法學》公益課程，獲益甚多。編寫此書時，我以古印歐詞根為源頭，考據單字之間的關聯，深信詞彙在歷史演進過程中，音變及形變乃是語言發展的必然趨勢。

　　本書著眼於語音對應的學習效益，透過語音、語義串聯單字，以簡馭繁、從已知推未知，提供讀者大幅擴充單字量的良方，既符合乎學理、又饒富趣味。放眼望去，國內格林法則教學大多用在公職或留學考試單

字教學，尚未全面推廣，殊為可惜。莫建清教授為國內的格林法則單字記憶學習開創一條康莊大道，而本書的目標是將格林法則轉化成為適合教學或自學的嶄新元素，結合生動例句、搭配詞語、相關字彙、記憶法則，讓學習者可以藉由多元面次親近詞彙。衷心盼望本書所播下的格林法則種子，能在這條英語教學新路上開花結果，吸引更多人來一睹風采。蘇秦老師和我花了將近一年時間考據、撰寫，這本以學習為導向的格林法則單字書於焉誕生。

　　本書分成兩大單元，透過單字和字根、字根和字根的轉音現象，引導讀者快速掌握單字之間的關係，輕鬆記憶單字。Part 1 格林法則概述是本書的關鍵核心，讀者若能用心體會、反覆琢磨，當可打通字彙學習的任督二脈，日起有功。

　　本書得以完成，需由衷感謝許多師長，尤其是李櫻教授、莫建清教授、謝忠理老師，先進們的教導指正充實了本書內涵。寫作過程，我也參考了摩西的《英語單詞聖經》、黃自來教授的《英語語言史導讀》、張勇先教授的《英語發展史》等書，英語教學前輩們的研究成果，甚是欽佩。最後也要特別感謝我識出版社編輯團隊的辛勞努力，大幅增加本書價值。

　　寥寥數語，仍不足以表達心中的感謝之萬一。

楊智民

2017 於國立員林家商

（旁註：中之部首。←高度相近←意相近）

單字一直都是英語學習的首要課題，更是英語學習者的首要任務，有些人從字卡到字典，見字即背，無所不背，毅力令人難望項背；有些人則是追尋記憶技巧，不論正門巧門，縱使五花八門，只求入門。近年來，「字根字首」四字宛如單字殿堂上的牌坊，令人肅然起敬，卻又如池塘蓮花，可遠觀，不可褻玩焉，因為單字難，字根更難，以字根記憶單字，難上加難，雖不致災難一場，但肯定是一遭夢魘。

→ 字根字首，準確地說，就是詞素，如同中文部首一樣，都是單字的構成成分。詞素拆解合乎構詞原理，結果怎麼會是受益的少，受苦的多，甚至視為畏途呢？未能以簡入繁，化繁為簡是主要原因，也就是不能以已知單字引導學習未知新字。

首先，我們先看一下英語單字演進的一些橋段：

任何語言的字彙都會增加，但是，創新字的方式各具特色。例如中文的一些器具名稱常成為使用該器具的動作，例如漆、刷，英文的功能轉換詞也有異曲同工之妙。英語源自拉丁文及希臘文，一些古代的字彙因現代生活而賦予新意，例如：phone，希臘文是聲音，現代英文是電話；又如 photo 是光，現代英文則是相片。字源與單字的差別道出古今生活經驗的演進。一些古字的演變則是拼字或唸音稍微改變，但是字義相關，例如：foot / fetter、blind / blunder、shade / shadow 等。一些古字傳至現代英語時，不可獨立存在，必須黏接字首或字尾才能成字，例如 octo-pus = eight + foot、re-im-burse = back + in + purse、popul-ous = people + ous。

音相近．義相連
同源字義相近（字義轉換）

湖源－轉音辨字．

　　那麼，英語單字練功房裡的借力使力拳法是什麼呢？從以上可以看出，「音相近，義相連」是以古習今，新舊相扣的橋樑。單字與字根，單字與單字，若是同源，音義必然相近。因此，藉由簡單字與困難字或是字根之間的語音轉換，便能輕鬆掌握兩者關聯，達到借力使力、舉一反三的學習效果。轉音辨字，以英語歷史而言，是事實，而這事實就是格林法則，善用格林法則，以單字學習而言，既是溯源，更是創新。

　　早年曾追隨一位猶太籍美國美南浸信會希臘文博士修讀新約希臘文，深刻體驗希英辭彙關聯，也曾於英國劍橋大學校園聽到來自歐亞交界的塞浦路斯人以希臘文交談，深切感受到希臘文字的優美神韻及語法的嚴謹精確，從而將賞析希臘文視為人生一大雅趣，查閱英希字典，課堂上隨手露兩字，希臘文對個人而言，如同海明威心中的巴黎。

　　時值本書付梓出版之際，由衷感謝共同作者楊智民老師詳實的字源考據及語料蒐集，使本書具有忠於史料、承先啟後的立言價值；感謝何采芝老師及新北市馬修書房美語機構羅曉翠老師協助例句中譯審訂，讓本書能以精湛的品質，將格林法則這段重要的英語史實流傳遍地，宛如一席流動的筵席，成為各地英語學習者的祝福。

2017 初春曾文溪畔

經典美語創辦人 | **謝忠理**

　　一七八六年二月二日，英國東方學家兼法學家 Sir William Jones（威廉瓊斯爵士）在印度加爾各答的亞洲學會發表演講，其中他說道：「Sanskrit（梵文）的結構令人讚嘆，比希臘還完美，比拉丁文還豐富，比這兩者都還精緻洗鍊。不過，梵文與希臘、拉丁兩種語言之間卻具有強烈的關聯性，在動詞的詞根以及文法的形式上皆如此，這其間的關聯性絕非意外所能產生。任何語言學者，在檢驗過這三種語言，發現其強烈關聯性，定會認為這三種語言應該有個共通的始祖，儘管這共同的濫觴或許已經不復存在。」

　　這席話，咸被認為是 Indo-European（印歐語）研究的起源。爾後，經過歷代學者不斷從斷簡殘篇中，將橫跨歐亞大陸的數十種語言交互比較，逐步重建起這個應該存在過，但卻已經消蝕在歷史洪流中的語言。時至今日，印歐語已經公認是包括希臘語、拉丁語、梵文，以及其他從日耳曼語到斯拉夫語的共同始祖。當然其中也包含了目前全球通行無阻的英語。

　　學習英語，首重字彙；瞭解印歐語，對於英語字彙的學習，有莫大的幫助。我個人從事英語教學 30 年，長期協助有志出國留學的同學準備 GRE, GMAT, TOEFL 等考試。在教學中，大量使用印歐語詞根協助同學快速了解英文字彙的源起以及記憶方式，成果顯著。

　　智民學棣學識淵博，深入研究印歐語詞根、格林法則有成，立志戮力推廣，而與蘇秦老師共同撰寫此書，內容鞭辟入裡。個人與智民學棣有緣共同切磋，此書之成，與有榮焉。華人世界的英語教學，因本書的出版而向前邁進了一大步。

2017.04

English4Formosa 創辦人 | 蔡沂霖 Lance

　　個人研究字首字根字尾近 10 載，學生時代，字首字根單字學習法讓我在 GRE 及 TOEFL 考試中拿下遠超預期的高分，目前教授 GRE 及 TOEFL 課程，持續運用該學習法輔助記憶單字，常見學生快速進步，因此，對於單字發展邏輯系統甚是著迷。2012 年起，著手逐字拆解字典單字，並儲存電腦資料庫，不斷研究分析。目前拆解約莫五萬單字，其中約 75% 包括高頻字首根尾，衍生字至少五個，約 10% 是雙單字，約 15% 包含低頻字首根尾，衍生字不足五個，或無法拆解單字。熟練此書所述語音轉換法則，不但有助於深入了解高頻字首根尾的變形轉化，更是能夠將似乎無法拆解的單字和原本核心的字首根尾連結記憶。

　　閱讀此書時，建議讀者先瀏覽經考據的同源字變化，以建立單字延伸系統邏輯，並熟悉語音轉換規則。而後瀏覽考據上雖非同源字，但可藉語音轉換規則輔助記憶的相關字群以擴增單字。最後是綜覽全部內容，徹底融會貫通。研讀書中單字時，除了音標、字義及例句必須熟悉之外，記憶技巧更需熟稔，藉此了解單字詞素拆解，以及詞素黏接還原單字的過程。

　　最後，個人極力推薦此書給所有想要徹底了解英文單字學習方法的學生及老師，學生可以快速累積單字，老師可以在教學上增加靈感。

2017. 04

學好英文的首要條件是能快速記憶單字並且能運用單字。 記憶單字的方法有很多種， 而字根字首字尾記憶法是可以讓我們以理解聯想的方法迅速記憶單字並急速累積單字量。 但如何有效率地快速記憶字根以擴增字彙量？如果你想達成此目的，請參考本書《地表最強英文單字：不想輸，就用「格林法則」背 10,000 個英文單字》。

本書是根據格林法則 6 大轉音公式，介紹字根記憶的技巧及列舉單字詞素的解析。格林法則公式的來源是基於發音部位相同或相近的子音意義相同；至於母音則不具意義，只有拼音功用。譬如本書介紹第一個字根 burs 的記憶技巧是以已知的單字 purse 來記，書中說明 purse 本指皮革製的囊袋，主要用途是裝錢，由於 b 和 p 發音部位相同可互換，所以 burs 這字根也具有相同概念，可指袋子、囊、付錢等概念。舉例的單字有：

bursa（囊）、bursectomy（粘液囊切除術）、bursar（財務主管）、bursary（財務辦公室，大學獎學金）、disburse（支出）、reimburse（償還）

書中對舉例的單字有詳細字根字首字尾分析解釋，再加上英文例句及中文翻譯，讀者可以系統化快速記下這一串的單字並運用。

處於資訊爆炸的時代，快速學習是我們必須擁有的生存技能。本書是英文學習者快速記憶英文字根及單字的必備葵花寶典。

Grace 何采芝

2017. 04

目 錄
Contents

Part ❶ 格林法則概述

Part ❷ 單字對應字根（含少數字首、字尾）

Chapter 1 雙唇音、唇齒音轉換 ……………………………… 037

目 錄
Contents

Chapter 5 子音對應相同 ·········· 245

目錄
Contents

Chapter 6 〔h〕變化 ⋯⋯⋯⋯⋯⋯⋯⋯⋯⋯⋯⋯⋯ 355

Part ① 格林法則概述

Grimm's Law

運用格林法則學習英語單字，當然得了解格林法則是何物？與英語之間有何關聯？以及學習的方式有何奧妙？因此，第一章先將時空溯及兩千多年前的不列顛群島，略述英語語言各時期的歷史，而後進入印歐語系，接著駐足生於斯，長於斯，出土亦然的格林法則──本書主題，詳述英語單字語音轉換及音相近、義相連等格林法則，隨後跨過歷史，邁向現代英語，格林法則英語單字學習及教學兩條康莊大道，引領讀者朝向成功目標前進。

Section 1

英語的濫觴

源起

明朝音韻學大家陳第有言：「蓋時有古今，地有南北；字有更革，音有轉移，亦勢所必至。」，此言揭示語言可消亡，語音可變遷，詞彙可增減。英語學習者無須考據歷史，然若能掌握語音變遷規律，即可運用「格林法則」記憶單字。

英語詞彙數量繁多，來源甚廣，外族入侵和統治，英美兩國與不同文化交流頻繁，英語詞彙於時空交織間一再擴增。巡禮英語發展歷史，耙梳詞彙來龍去脈，鋪陳單字學習圖騰，既是正統，又是創新。

英語語言簡史

1. 歐陸日耳曼時期（西元 449 年以前）

這個時期 Great Britain（大不列顛群島）原住民為 Celtics（凱爾特）民族，使用的語言不是英語。西元前 55 年及 54 年 Caesar（凱撒）兩次帶領羅馬大軍入侵不列顛，但直至西元 43 年才順利征服，使之成為羅馬帝國統治的一個行省。西元 410 年，為了防止 Goths（高德人）侵犯羅馬，羅馬軍隊開始自不列顛撤離。約莫 400 年期間，不列顛與歐陸因著英吉利海峽相隔，不利於羅馬化，因此兩種語言共存，統治者（羅馬人）使用拉丁語，被統治者（凱爾特人）則使用凱爾特語。凱爾特人的國家雖亡，但是民族仍然存在，今日的 Irish（愛爾蘭人）、Scottish（高地蘇格蘭人）、Welsh（威爾斯人）皆其後裔。

羅馬帝國崩解之後，凱爾特人遭受北方及西方民族攻擊，於是向歐陸日耳曼民族中的 Saxons（薩克遜人）求援，豈料反而招致 Anglos（盎格魯人）、薩克遜人及 Jutes（朱特人）等 Germanic peoples（日耳曼民族）入侵。一般都以西元 449 年 Anglo-Saxon Invasions（盎格魯薩克遜入侵）作為古英語的肇始，另一方面，盎格魯撒克遜人將凱爾特人驅趕至西部及北部後，在不列顛島上建立七國聯盟，此為英國歷史上的 the Heptarchy（七國時代）。

2. 古英語時期（西元 449 ～ 1066 年）

張勇先教授於《英語發展史》一書提及英語的形成主要受到三次入侵和一次語言文化革命的影響。三次入侵分別為始於西元 449 年的 Anglo-Saxon Invasions（盎格魯薩克遜入侵），始於西元 787 年的 Viking Invasions（北歐海盜入侵）及西元 1066 年的 Norman Conquest（諾曼征服）。一次語言文化革命則是西元 597 年，St. Augustine（聖奧古斯丁）於英國傳播基督教所引發的語言文化革命。古英語是古日耳曼人的語言，不列顛經歷多次外來入侵，雖瀕臨滅亡，但頻繁接觸外族，英語因而吸納眾多外來詞彙。

▌古英語受三大外來語的影響

Celtic 凱爾特語

眾所周知的 King Arthur（亞瑟王）和圓桌武士都是凱爾特人，也是抵禦薩克遜人入侵的英雄。凱爾特人遭到盎格魯薩克遜人驅趕，僅少許詞彙存留，除了地名，例如：London / Kent / Ledes；河流名稱，例如：the Thames / the Can / the Avon；表示深山峽谷的 -cumb 或 Thor- 為首的地名。凱爾特語對古英語詞彙影響甚微。

Latin 拉丁語

此時期輸入的拉丁語大多是專業術語。西元 597 年聖奧古斯丁帶領 40 名傳教士從羅馬帝國前往大不列顛傳教，基督教徒日益增多，大約轉借 410 個拉丁字彙，例如：pope / priest / minister / epistle / monk / legion / window / school / verse 等。

Old Norse 古北歐語

西元 787 年北歐海盜 Vikings（維京人）開始入侵。看過電視卡通北海小英雄的人對維京人應不陌生，因為主角小威就是維京人。Alfred the Great（艾爾弗雷德大帝）擊退北歐海盜後，雙方達成協議，讓他們於英國東北部建立 Danelaw（丹麥法地區），而北歐海盜使用古丹麥語。北歐語言對英語最大的貢獻是 sk- 開頭的單字，例如：sky / skirt / skill 等，另外，are / they / their / them / take / want 等生活詞彙也來自北歐語。

古英語詞彙大多消失，而留下的都成為現代英語的基本詞彙。張勇先教授考據英語最常用的前 100 單詞，其中 96 字源自古英語，而且幾乎都是單音節。最常用的前 100 個單詞可見下方圖表。

The First Hundred				
the	at	there	some	my
of	be	use	her	than
and	this	an	would	first
a	have	each	make	water
to	from	which	like	been
in	or	she	him	call
is	one	one	into	who
you	had	how	time	oil
that	by	their	has	its
it	word	if	look	now
he	but	will	two	find
was	not	up	more	long
for	what	other	write	down
on	all	about	go	day
are	were	out	see	did
as	we	many	number	get
with	when	then	no	come
his	your	them	way	made
they	can	these	could	may
I	said	so	people	part

▶ 此表取自：http://www.duboislc.org/ED-Watch/Words/1-100.html

3. 中古英語時期（西元 1066 ～ 1489 年）

　　西元 1066 年諾曼地 William the Conqueror（公爵威廉一世）揮軍入侵英國，史稱 Norman Conquest（諾曼征服），這一年被視為中古英語時期的開端。諾曼法國人取代英國人成為地主或教會要職，政治、法律、軍事、飲食等領域的法語詞彙大量進入中古英語。諾曼人建立封建社會，上層貴族使用法語，下層平民使用英語，宗教人士使用拉丁語。諾曼法國人口不多，卻擁有英國絕大部分財富，造成貧富差距，我們所熟知的 Robin Hood（羅賓漢）故事即是英國底層窮人對抗上層講法語富人的故事。

　　然而，諾曼法國統治者與英國人生活在同一土地上，一定會受到英國人的影響。因此，一些上層貴族逐漸學習英語，尤其是 14 世紀 Hundred Years' War（英法百年戰爭）之後，諾曼法國人重新思考自己的歸屬，開始主動學習，英語的地位逐漸提升。中古英語時期，牛津大學學者 John Wycliffe（威克里夫）翻譯聖經，引進 1,000 多個拉丁詞彙，而素有「英語詩歌之父」之稱的 Chaucer（喬叟）將古典拉丁文譯成英語時，也引進許多拉丁字。

　　古英語詞彙在這時期大量消失，取而代之的是成千上萬的拉丁和法文借字，數量眾多，例如：pork / beef / barber / foul / tailor / carpenter / government / majesty / religion / judge / clergy / baptism / chamber / art 等字來自法文；pauper / legal / testimony / recipe / collect / admit / include / subjugate / lucrative / temperate 等字則來自拉丁語。

4. 現代英語時期（西元 1489 年迄今）

　　西元 1489 年英國議會停止使用法語，一些學者將這一年視為現代英語的開端。1489 年迄今，橫跨 500 多年，有些學者又將這段時期分成早期現代英語（西元 1489 ～ 1801 年）及現代英語（西元 1801 年～）兩階段。早期現代英語受到 The Renaissance（文藝復興運動）、印刷術傳播、聖經翻譯、Shakespeare（莎士比亞）創作及 British Empire（大英帝國）拓展海外殖民等影響，引進大量外來詞彙，包括拉丁文、希臘文、法文及其他語言。

❶ Latin（拉丁語）或 Greek（希臘語）的等古典語言

agile / anonymous / anachronism / catastrophe / climax / delirium / capsule

❷ French（法語）

progress / vogue / shock / moustache / comrade / grotesque

❸ Italian（義大利語）

ballot / opera / solo / sonnet

❹ Spanish（西班牙語）或 Portuguese（葡萄牙語）

armada / desperado / hurricane / Negro

❺ Dutch（荷蘭語）

yacht / landscape

❻ Turkish（土耳其語）

coffee / yogurt

❼ Persian（波斯語）

bazaar / caravan

另外，15 世紀初期，英語發生「the Great Vowel Shift（母音大變遷）」——「長母音」從低至高依序提升，請參考右圖。「母音大變遷」只有語音改變，拼字沒有調整，因此造成拼字及發音對應不一致，不少人看到母音字母不知道怎麼正確發音，例如，現代英語「child」的 i 唸〔aɪ〕，「children」的 i 唸〔ɪ〕，child 經歷「母音大變遷」，母音從長音的〔i〕變成〔aɪ〕，而 children 的 i 則趨向現代英語的〔ɪ〕。相關規律可參看右圖的 ❶。其他例如右圖 ❷ 的「heal」經歷母音大變遷，但「health」沒有；右圖 ❸ 的「nature」經歷母音大變遷，但「natural」沒有；右圖 ❹ 的「house」經歷母音大變遷，但「husband」沒有；右圖 ❺ 的「lose」經歷母音大變遷，但「lost」沒有；右圖 ❻ 的「joke」經歷母音大變遷，但「jocular」沒有，因而造成母音的差異。值得一提的是，此圖呈現 15 ～ 17 世紀長母音變化，和現代英語的發音仍有差異。

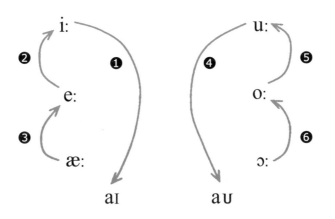

▶ 母音大變遷，取自王旭教授 *"Wonders of the English Language"* 一書

　　西元 1801 年，英格蘭、威爾斯、蘇格蘭、愛爾蘭組成 United Kingdom of Great Britain and Ireland（大不列顛及愛爾蘭聯合王國），一般視為現代英語的開端。這時期不斷湧入借字及創新詞，至今仍未見停歇，美國 Merriam-Webster Dictionary（韋氏字典）曾估計英語約莫 1,000,000 單字，英語儼然成為 lingua franca（國際語言）。

　　總結：超過 75% 的英語單字都是借字，其中以拉丁語、希臘語、法語為大宗。English（英語）屬於 Germanic（日耳曼語族），而 Greek（希臘語）屬於 Hellenic（希臘語族）、Latin（拉丁語）屬於 Italic（義大利語族），French（法語）也是，但這些語言推到源頭，老祖宗都是同一位—— Indo-European（印歐語），請參考印歐語系圖表（第 026-027 頁）。重新建構印歐語的概念始於 1786 年，William Jones（威廉‧瓊斯）爵士在印度的一場研討會所發表的一段話，說明梵語、希臘語、拉丁語、歌德語、凱爾特語、古波斯語有非常相似的語法形式及動詞詞根，之後許多語言學家開始進行跨語言比較，重新建構印歐語語族。這些語言既然出自同一源頭，那其中是否具有系統性的相似特質呢？鼎鼎有名的格林童話作者，格林兄弟中的哥哥 Jacob Grimm（雅各布‧格林）觀察到日耳曼語和印歐語言之間的子音有系統性的對應，此對應稱為 Grimm's Law（格林法則）或第一次日耳曼子音推移，發生時間約是 600 B.C. 到 100 B.C. 之間。

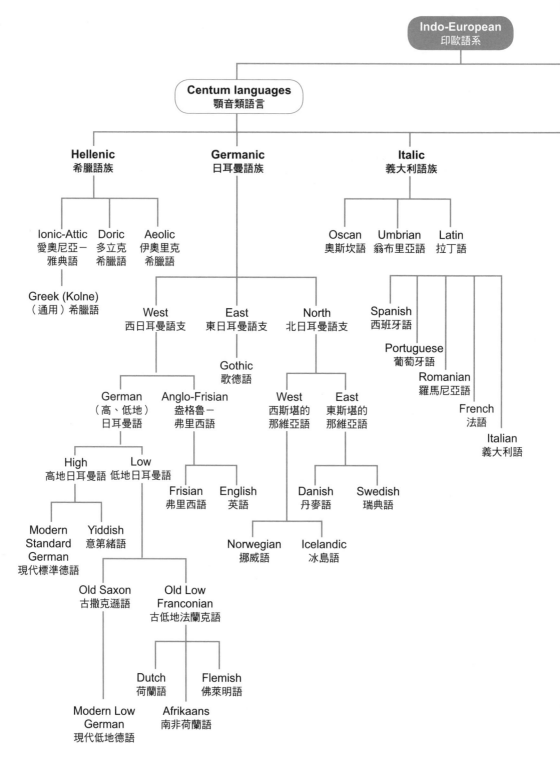

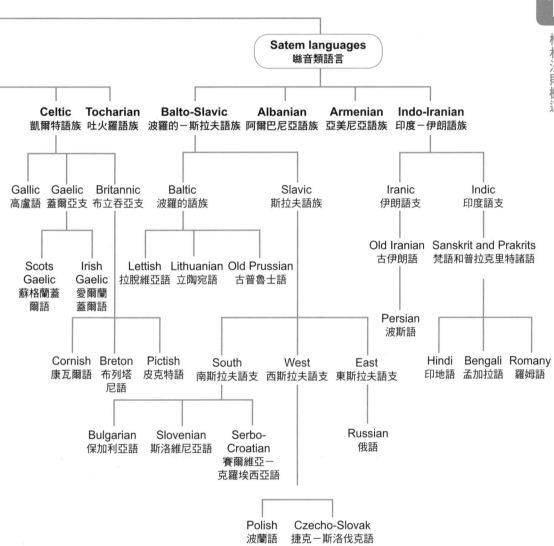

```
                    ┌─────────────────────────┐
                    │   Satem languages       │
                    │   噝音類語言            │
                    └─────────────────────────┘

Celtic    Tocharian   Balto-Slavic      Albanian      Armenian    Indo-Iranian
凱爾特語族  吐火羅語族   波羅的－斯拉夫語族  阿爾巴尼亞語族  亞美尼亞語族  印度－伊朗語族

Gallic  Gaelic  Britannic    Baltic          Slavic        Iranic        Indic
高盧語  蓋爾亞支 布立吞亞支   波羅的語族       斯拉夫語族     伊朗語支       印度語支

                                                          Old Iranian   Sanskrit and Prakrits
                                                          古伊朗語      梵語和普拉克里特諸語

   Scots       Irish     Lettish  Lithuanian  Old Prussian
   Gaelic      Gaelic    拉脫維亞語 立陶宛語    古普魯士語
   蘇格蘭蓋     愛爾蘭
   爾語        蓋爾語                                      Persian
                                                          波斯語

   Cornish  Breton   Pictish   South      West    East    Hindi   Bengali  Romany
   康瓦爾語  布列塔   皮克特語   南斯拉夫語支 西斯拉夫語支 東斯拉夫語支 印地語  孟加拉語  羅姆語
            尼語

      Bulgarian  Slovenian   Serbo-        Russian
      保加利亞語  斯洛維尼亞語 Croatian      俄語
                             賽爾維亞－
                             克羅埃西亞語

              Polish    Czecho-Slovak
              波蘭語     捷克－斯洛伐克語
```

▶ 印歐語系圖表，取自黃自來教授《英語語言史導讀》一書

Section **2**

什麼是「格林法則」？

　　從印歐語系圖表（第 026-027 頁），我們知道拉丁語、希臘語、英語同屬印歐語族，拼字及語音理當彼此接近，但事實上存在許多差異。舉例來說，表示「腳」的英文單字是「foot」，與源自拉丁文的「ped-（腳）」及希臘文的「pod-（腳）」拼字有所差異；表示「心」的英文單字是「heart」，與源自拉丁文的「cord-（心）」及源自希臘文的「card-（心）」拼字也有差異；表示「牙齒」的英文單字是「tooth」，與源自拉丁文的「dent-（牙齒）」及源自希臘文的「dont-（牙齒）」拼字差異明顯。從拼字來看，拉丁文和希臘文頗為相似，但與英文差異很大，為什麼呢？因為英語曾經歷子音改變，子音轉變形成一個 drag chain（拉力連鎖），帶動系統性的音變，請看下圖語音轉換三大系統：

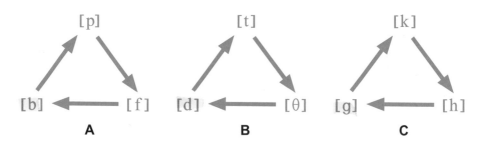

▶ 語音轉換三大系統

　　英語「腳」這單字的拼字，原本應該像「ped-（拉丁語）」或「pod-（希臘語）」以子音〔p〕開頭，但經歷子音轉變，〔p〕變成〔f〕（上圖 A）；〔d〕變成〔t〕（上圖 B），母音也改變，最後形成「foot」的拼寫形式。「心」字原本應該像「cord-（拉丁語）」或「card-（希臘語）」以子音〔k〕開頭，也是經歷子音轉變，〔k〕變成〔h〕（上圖 C）；〔d〕變成〔t〕（上圖 B），母音也改變，最後形成「heart」。「牙齒」原本應該像「dent-（拉丁語）」或

「dont-（希臘語）」以子音〔d〕開頭，同樣經歷子音轉變，〔d〕變成〔t〕（上圖B）；〔t〕變成〔θ〕（上圖B），母音也改變，最後形成「tooth」。這樣系統性的語音改變稱為「格林法則」。格林法則不是深奧的學問，在日常生活中常見，也常發生。通常我們談的格林法則涉及英語九個子音的改變，但實際生活例子中，語音改變的數量遠遠超過九個音。首先，我們透過生活實例來了解語音轉變。

從聽覺的經驗來說，聽錯常是轉音的一個原因，而最容易聽錯的是發音部位相同或相近之間的音，例如北門地區盛產的養殖魚類── milkfish（虱目魚），台語稱作「sat-bak-hî」，相傳約三百多年前，延平郡王鄭成功在安平沿岸向正在採捕魚苗的漁民以閩南語問「什麼魚」，漁民誤認為鄭成功賜名為「什麼魚」，而後便以「什麼魚」流傳。鄭成功用的閩南語、今天的閩南語、白話文等三種語音唸的「milkfish」是不是非常相近？

外來借字也常呈現相近音轉換，母音通轉的情況。「casino」這個字的字源，有人說是義大利文的「casa（房子）」，也有人說是當年到美國舊金山及澳大利亞新金山淘金的人潮有許多來自福建、廣東地區，他們常常聚在一起賭博，吆喝著：「khai-sí-lah（開始啦）」，閩南語進入英語就變成「casino（賭場）」一字，不僅母音不同，子音也不同。「fans」這個字進到中文就成了「粉絲」，母音及子音都改變了。Regan 譯成「lei-gen（雷根）」，〔r〕和〔l〕通轉。「radio」進到日語及台語，狀況一樣，唸成「la-jí-oh」。

一些中文破音字也體現了相近音互換的情況，例如：「bian（方便）」、「pian（便）宜」是雙唇音〔b〕和〔p〕互換，「子 dan（彈）」、「tan（彈）回來」是齒齦音〔d〕和〔t〕互換，「kuai（會）計師」、「一 hui（會）兒」則是軟顎音〔k〕和喉門音〔h〕互換及母音通轉，「是 fou（否）」、「pi（否）極泰來」則是唇齒音〔f〕和雙唇音〔p〕互換及母音通轉的結果。

另外，因著發音錯誤或發音偏好，有些人「river」唸得像「liver」、「rice」唸得像「lice」，發不出〔r〕的音，只好以相近音〔l〕替代。有些人則是〔n〕、〔l〕不分，唸通訊軟體 Line〔laɪn〕時，常誤唸成近似 nine〔naɪn〕

的音，「好 leng（冷）」則唸成「好 neng（冷）」。有些字正腔圓的新聞主播唸新聞的「wen（聞）」時，刻意唸成「ven（聞）」，這是「v（唇齒音）」取代「w（雙唇音）」的例子。

當然，大多數轉音的真正原因在語言歷史中已是不可考，不可妄下定論，但是近似音之間的轉音現象卻是明顯而常見。唇齒音與雙唇音發音部位相近，常出現轉音的同義字，而且跨越語種。例如：白話文（現行的國語）的「浮」唸音是〔fu〕，河洛語（閩南語，也就是台語）是〔pu〕，唇齒音〔f〕及雙唇音〔p〕轉音。又如高雄市區十大路名──一心、二聖、三多、四維、五福、六合、七賢、八德、九如、十全，白話文及河洛語的唸音之間不難發現子音發音部位相近而造成的轉音現象。福斯汽車的德文（古英文與古德文相當接近）名稱「Volkswagen」，發音是〔`folksvægən〕，〔v〕及〔f〕轉音，雙唇音〔w〕及〔v〕轉音，意思是 folks wagon，也就是國民車的意思。

本田汽車「HONDA」的日文發音是〔honda〕，在美國卻唸成〔handa〕，因為英語不接受子音之間的字母 o 唸〔o〕，這也是同一字彙的轉音現象。

believe 及 belief 這類字組是唇齒音〔f〕與〔v〕之間的轉音，而且對稱於名詞及動詞之間。believe 及 belief 之間的唸音差異是同義字之間的轉音現象，不僅存在於英語，也存在於中文、台語，乃至其他語言中，若能細心察覺，應可增添語言學習樂趣，一掬觸類旁通的意外收穫。

Section **3**
語音轉換
Sound Switching

> **音相近，義相連**

　　知道語音轉換的原因之後，我們以格林法則為本，將格林法則三大系統（第028 頁）加以擴充，羅列更多語音。掌握語音轉換系統，便可掌握 400 多個英語字根（教育部公布的 7,000 字表即包含大約 400 個字根），10,000 多個單字，同時掌握單字記憶的學習脈絡。

1. 母音轉換

所有的母音皆可轉換，無一定規律

　　不少單字的母音轉換，但是核心字義相同，例如：「run / ran / run（跑）」等不規則動詞變化，「hot / heat（熱）」等詞性轉變。有些母音轉換的單字雖然字義不同，但是關聯緊密，易於聯想，例如：「linger（徘徊）」表示「走動的時間 longer（較長久的）」、「bat（短棍）」是用來「beat（打）」；大家都知道「foot / feet」都是腳，但不知道「fetch（去拿來）」及「fetter（腳鐐）」都是「foot / feet」的同源字；「bite（咬）/ bait（誘餌）/ abet（引誘）」都是同源字。許多同源單字「母音轉換，字義不變」，儘管母音轉換不像子音一樣規律分明。

2. 子音轉換三大系統（參考下頁口腔發音位置圖及發音部位、方式表）

雙唇音、唇齒音轉換

〔b〕、〔p〕、〔m〕、〔f〕、〔v〕

　　「wife」到「wives」的單複數變化可以看到〔f〕和〔v〕的轉換，「paternal」和「father」可以看到〔p〕和〔f〕的轉換。〔b〕、〔p〕、〔m〕、

〔f〕、〔v〕等五個子音可能互相轉換。

▌齒間音、齒齦音、齒齦後音轉換

〔d〕、〔t〕、〔n〕、〔l〕、〔ʃ〕、〔r〕、〔z〕、〔s〕、〔θ〕、〔ð〕、〔ʒ〕

「send」到「sent」的不規則動詞變化可以看到〔d〕和〔t〕的轉換，「potion」和同源字「poison」可以看到〔ʃ〕和〔z〕對應，〔n〕和〔l〕不易區分，以〔l〕取代較發音較難的捲舌音〔r〕等都說明這些音常見互換。另外，英文單字常見母音之間的〔s〕會唸成〔r〕（r 音化），例如：字根「rus-」意思是鄉村，「rustic」表示鄉下的，「rural」原該拼成「*rusal（農村的）」，但〔s〕在母音中間，轉變成〔r〕，於是拼寫為「rural」。〔d〕、〔t〕、〔n〕、〔l〕、〔ʃ〕、〔r〕、〔z〕、〔s〕、〔θ〕、〔ð〕、〔ʒ〕等 11 個子音可能互相轉換。

▌硬顎音、軟顎音、喉門音轉換

〔g〕、〔k〕、〔h〕、〔dʒ〕、〔tʃ〕、〔ŋ〕、〔j〕

「cool / chill」、「cook / kitchen」、「card / carton / cartoon / chart / charter」等同源字都顯示〔k〕和〔tʃ〕的對應，「young」和同源字「junior」顯示〔j〕和〔dʒ〕的對應。〔g〕、〔k〕、〔h〕、〔dʒ〕、〔tʃ〕、〔ŋ〕、〔j〕等 7 個子音可能互相轉換。

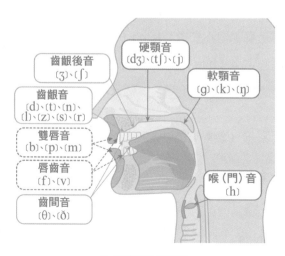

▶ 口腔發音位置圖

發音方式 \ 發音部位		雙唇	唇齒	齒間	齒齦	齦後	硬顎	軟顎	喉門
塞音	有聲	b			d			g	
塞音	無聲	p			t			k	
摩擦音	有聲		v	ð	z	ʒ			
摩擦音	無聲		f	θ	s	ʃ			h
塞擦音	有聲						dʒ		
塞擦音	無聲						tʃ		
鼻音		m			n			ŋ	
流音	舌邊音				l				
流音	捲舌音				r				
滑音		w						j	

▶ 發音部位、方式表

3. 字母對應的兩大規律

雙唇音、唇齒音、母音轉換

wid
vid

`u / v / w 字母通轉`

　　u / v / w 字母息息相關，w 唸 [ˋdʌb‚ju]，double u 的意思，字形上是 v 的重複，英語 26 字母中依序相鄰，可見三者關係緊密。舉例來說：「widow（寡婦）」和「divide（劃分）」、「individual（個人的）」都是同源字，核心字根都是「分開」；widow 中的「wid-」就是「vid-（分開）」：取寡婦失去丈夫，永遠分離的意思。

4. 希臘文字母與拉丁文或英文字母的對應

h 對應 s

　　希臘字母 h 常對應英文或拉丁文的字母 s，例如：「hedon-」、「suad-」、「sweet」都表示「甜」；「hedon-」是希臘字根、「suad-」是拉丁字根，而「sweet」則是英語單字；「helio-（太陽）」是希臘字根，對應拉丁字根「sol-」及英文單字「sun」。

Section **4**

教學建議

格林法則短文閱讀

　　不少人認為格林法則只適用於記憶艱澀困難的單字，其實透過語音對應來記憶 2,000 單字，成效更為顯著，除了語音對應，還能連結語意相近的單字以形成語意群組（即「音相近、義相連」）。以下的兩篇文章用字簡單，適合初學者閱讀。另外，轉音大多發生於音節 onset（首子音），常形成 alliteration（押頭韻），例如：row, row, row your boat。因此，運用格林法則字群編寫短文或韻文，從閱讀中賞析英語音韻之美，充實語言教育中的情意內涵，不失為閱讀創新教學！

練習題
exercise

○　**請閱讀以下短文，讀後請列出與提示字發音及語意相近的單字：**

○　Today is the first day of the Chicken year.

○　There is a chicken family in the kitchen.

○　The hen is cooking biscuits.

○　The cock is baking cream corn.

○　Their chickens are eating grains.

○　They will say "congratulations" to you!

答案：1. cock—chicken　2. cook—kitchen, biscuit　3. corn—grain

　　了解母音通轉也是記憶單字的一大利器，以下教材設計吻合 Differentiated Instruction（差異化教學）的教學概念。

練習題
exercise

1. 請將以下 sing 的相關單字填入正確空格中：

singing / sang / sung / singer / songs

Cindy is a female _____*er*_____ in Singapore. She is good at ___*ing*___ romantic songs, and her voice sounds like messages from Heaven. She is popular with a lot of locals. Last Sunday, Cindy had a concert in Sentosa Island, Singapore, where she attracted a crowd of fans. She ___*sang*___ many songs touching their hearts. Several were classics which have been ___*sung*___ for more than fifty years. She chose ___*songs*___ which were well-known to all.

2. 從短文中找出五個與 sing 押頭韻的單字（不含 sing 的相關單字）。

答案：1. singer / singing / sang / sung / songs
2. Singapore / sounds / Sunday / Sentosa / several

　　格林法則可以為單字教學注入強力動能，為教案設計增添創新元素，舉凡桌遊、紙牌遊戲、心智圖、閱讀、兒歌韻文等都是施展介面。上述例子只是拋磚引玉，教學者可以發想創新，一同為台灣英語教學盡心力。

Part ② 單字對應字根
（含少數字首、字尾）
Grimm's Law

何謂詞素記憶工法？簡單字當槓桿，四兩撥千金，困難字根便輕易置入大腦深層記憶中。

Chapter 1
雙唇音、唇齒音轉換

〔b〕、〔p〕、〔m〕、〔f〕、〔v〕

Section **1**

〔p〕對應〔b〕

purse - burs

purse 本指皮革製的囊袋，主要的用途是裝錢，burs 這字根也具有相同概念，可指袋子、囊、付錢等概念。

---

bursa

[`bɝsə]

n 囊

bursiform
囊狀的

bursitis
滑囊炎

burst
膨裂.

相關字彙
體內生成物

The patient will have a surgery to remove the bursa in the affected area.

病患將開刀移除感染部位的囊腫。

記憶技巧　burs- 本意是袋子，引申為外形相似的囊。

- abscess 膿瘡
- acne 青春痘
- fibroids 纖維瘤
- polyp 息肉
- rash 疹

---

bursectomy

[bɝ`sɛktəmɪ]

n 粘液囊切除術

經瘡

My aunt underwent arthroscopic bursectomy for chronic bursitis.

我阿姨因慢性粘液囊炎而動關節內視鏡粘液囊切除術。

記憶技巧　burs- 表示囊；ec- 等同於 ex-，表示外面的意思；-tomy 表示切；bursectomy 即為粘液囊切除術。

---

bursar

[`bɝsɚ]

n 財務主管，司庫

Mr. Smith is a lecturer in English as well as a college bursar.

史密斯先生是英語講師，兼任大學財務主管。

記憶技巧　burs- 是錢包、付錢；bursar 是管錢的人，例如帳房、會計等。

---

bursary

[`bɝsərɪ]

n 財務辦公室，大學獎學金

The school only awarded bursaries for the study of law and related fields

學校只提供法律相關領域學生獎學金。

記憶技巧　burs- 是錢包、付錢；bursary 是提供求學所需的獎學金。

---

disburse

[dɪs`bɝs]

v 支出

The organization annually disburses a certain amount of money on rural education.

該組織每年投注一定金額在偏鄉教育。

記憶技巧　dis- 表示 away；disburse 表示從錢包拿錢出來支付。

� [rɪɜ aɪ]

相關字彙 經費	• allowance 津貼 • balance 結餘 • budget 預算	• compensation 賠償 • cost 成本 • expenditure 支出	• penalty 罰款 • pension 退休金 • subsidy 津貼

reimburse

[͵riɪmˋbɝs]

v 償還

＊reimbursement

The company reimbursed me for the amount I had paid above the amount required.

公司償還我的溢繳金額。

記憶技巧　re- 表示 back；im- 表示 in-；burse 是錢包；別人把錢放回你的錢包，不就是償還的意思嗎？

相關字彙 借貸	• foreclosure 查封 • loan 貸款 • commercial paper 商業本票	• mortgage 抵押 • detention 扣押 • provisional seizure 假扣押	• collateral 擔保品

purse

[pɝs]

n 皮包

隨倒

The passenger was asked to tip the contents of her purse out onto the counter.

旅客被要求將皮包裡的物品全部倒在櫃台上。

記憶技巧　purse 是 burs- 的轉音。

相關字彙 隨身攜帶物品	• wallet 皮夾子 • shoulder bag 肩袋 • hand bag 手拿包	• hand warmer 暖暖包 • cosmetic bag 化妝包

polemic - bell

Bellona 是古羅馬神話中的女戰神，戰神 Mars 之妻，代表戰爭中的殘忍和血腥，其形象廣泛出現在相關文學和繪畫之中，英語中的字根 bell- 即和戰爭有關。

belligerent

[bəˋlɪdʒərənt]

a 好戰的，好鬥的

The loud music really put me in a belligerent mood.

鬧哄哄的音樂挑起我的好鬥情緒。

記憶技巧　bell- 是戰爭；ger- 是攜帶；-ent 是形容詞字尾；belligerent 表示帶來戰爭，引申為好戰的。

bellicose

[ˋbɛlə͵kos]

a 好戰的

The autocrat frequently made bellicose statements threatening other countries.

獨裁者經常發表恫嚇他國的好戰言論。

記憶技巧　bell- 是戰爭；-ose 是形容詞字尾，表示充滿、具有某特質；bellicose 表示愛好戰爭的。

相關字彙 好鬥	• combatant 戰鬥的 • pugnacious 好鬥的 • truculent 兇狠的

rebel
[ˋrɛbḷ]
a 反叛的

The rebel troops have launched an attack on the army base near the border.
叛軍對邊境附近的軍事基地發動攻擊。

記憶技巧 re- 表示 opposite 或 against；rebel 是發起戰爭、叛變的人，形容詞的意思是反叛的。

rebellion
[rɪˋbɛljən]
n 反叛

The Prime Minister used to be faced with a backbench rebellion against his leadership.
首相曾遭受後座議員反抗其領導。

記憶技巧 -ion 是名詞字尾；rebellion 是反叛的名詞。

相關字彙
反叛和抗議

- boycott 聯合抵制
- defect 背叛
- demonstrate 示威
- foment 煽動
- march 遊行示威
- protest 抗議
- revolt 反叛
- sit in 靜坐示威

rebellious
[rɪˋbɛljəs]
a 反抗的

The juvenile hated to be labelled as a rebellious and trouble-making teenager.
青少年厭惡被貼上叛逆、滋事的標籤。

記憶技巧 -ous 表示充滿，rebellious 是反抗的形容詞。

---

pale - blac

blac 即 blank（空白），和 black（黑）是同源字，最初的意思燃燒，燃燒產生焦黑的木炭、灰燼，亦產生光亮，在黑夜中燃燒，耀眼如白晝，故此一字根雖為白色之意，但和黑也密不可分，可用 pale（灰白的）來聯想。

---

bleach
[blitʃ]
v 將～漂白
(n.) 漂白水

The cloth was bleached white with chemicals.
化學藥劑將布料漂成白色。

記憶技巧 用單字 blank（空白）聯想記憶，k 和 ch 兩音通轉。

相關字彙
改變物體的顏色

- color 著色
- paint 油漆
- dye 染色
- brighten 變明亮
- fade（顏色）褪去
- tint 給～著色

bleak
[blik]
a 荒涼的，
遭受風吹雨打的

It is expected that the economic outlook will be bleak again next year.
一般預期明年經濟前景仍是低迷。

記憶技巧 用單字 blank（空白）聯想記憶；bleak 表示景色荒涼、眼前白茫茫一片。

lip - lab

母音通轉，雙唇音 p 和 b 互換。

bilabial

[baɪˋlebɪəl]

a 雙唇音的

相關字彙
口腔部分

The child seems to have difficulty pronouncing bilabial sounds.

這孩子發唇音似乎有困難。

記憶技巧 bi- 意思是 two；lab- 是 lip；bilabial 表示雙唇音的。

- alveolar 齒齦音
- palatal 上顎的
- tongue 舌頭
- tooth 牙齒
- velum 軟顎

labiaplasty

[ˋlebɪəˌplæstɪ]

n 唇整形

It took the vet a while to perform labiaplasty for a Labrador Retriever.

獸醫花了老半天才做完一隻拉不拉多犬唇部整形。

記憶技巧 lab- 表示唇；-plasty 表示塑形；可用單字 plastic（塑膠）聯想記憶；labiaplasty 就是嘴唇塑形。

slip - lubric

單字 slip 中的 lip，即字根 lubric 中的 lub，母音通轉，雙唇音 p 和 b 互換，兩者皆源自古印歐詞根「sleubh-（滑）」。

lubricant

[ˋlubrɪkənt]

n 潤滑油

The technician added some lubricant to help the engine move more easily.

為讓引擎運轉更順暢，技術員加入一些潤滑油。

記憶技巧 lubric- 表示滑；-ant 是名詞字尾，表示物品；lubricant 即是潤滑之物。

lubrication

[ˌlubrɪˋkeʃən]

n 潤滑，加油

In general, a centralized lubrication system may be referred to as an automatic lubrication system.

一般而言，中央潤滑系統可以稱為自動潤滑系統。

記憶技巧 lubric- 表示滑的；-ation 是名詞字尾。

Section 2

〔f〕對應〔b〕

furnace - bust / bur

雖 furnace 火爐一字和字根 bust / bur（燃燒）並無明確字源關係，但可將火爐和燃燒做聯想，並善用子音 f 和 b 轉換來記憶。

combustible [kəm`bʌstəbl] **a** 可燃的， 易於激動的	No combustible substances are allowed to accumulate in the refinery. 煉油廠不得堆積任何可燃物。 記憶技巧 com- 表示加強語氣；bust- 表示燃燒；-ible 表示能夠～的。
combustion [kəm`bʌstʃən] **n** 燃燒	Spontaneous combustion caused fire to destroy hay crops. 自燃引發起火，燒毀乾草作物。 記憶技巧 -ion 是名詞字尾；combustion 是名詞。

相關字彙 火
- fire 火
- blaze 火焰
- wildfire 野火
- conflagration 大火災
- inferno 熊熊烈火
- ignition 著火
- flame 火焰

fine - bene

兩者之間無明確字源關係，但可藉由子音 f 和 b 互換來記憶 bene（好的）這個字根的意思。

benefit [`bɛnəfɪt] **v** 獲益	All the exchange students will benefit from participating in the advisory program. 所有交換學生將從參加輔導計畫中獲益。 記憶技巧 bene- 表示好；fit- 意思是做；benefit 表示做有益的事。

相關字彙 好處和利益
- advantage 好處
- merit 功績
- privilege 特權
- bonus 紅利

beneficial

[ˌbɛnəˋfɪʃəl]

a 有益的

Bifidobacteria are bacteria which are beneficial to digestive-system health.

比菲德氏菌是有益消化系統健康的菌種。

> 記憶技巧　bene- 表示好；fic- 表示做；-ial 是形容詞字尾；beneficial 就是給人利益的。

Part 2

CH 1

雙唇音、唇齒音轉換

beneficiary

[ˌbɛnəˋfɪʃɛrɪ]

n 受惠者，受益人，收款人

The beneficiary underwent surgery to remove vocal cord polyp this morning.

受益人今早作聲帶息肉切除手術。

> 記憶技巧　-ary 是名詞字尾，表示人。

benediction

[ˌbɛnəˋdɪkʃən]

n 祝福，祝禱

The tribal chief pronounced a benediction over all the teenagers at the ceremony.

酋長向所有參加典禮的青少年發表祝禱。

> 記憶技巧　bene- 表示好；dict- 表示說；-ion 是名詞字尾；benediction 意思是說好話。

beneficence

[bɪˋnɛfəsəns]

n 善行，饋贈

The vegetable vendor's beneficence is known to the nation.

菜販的善行舉國皆知。

> 記憶技巧　-ence 是名詞字尾。

benefactor

[ˋbɛnəˌfæktɚ]

n 恩人，捐助者

The orphanage has a number of generous benefactors from many countries.

孤兒院有數名來自不同國家的慷慨捐助者。

> 記憶技巧　bene- 表示好；fact- 表示做；-or 表示動作產生者；benefactor 就是做好事的人。

> 相關字彙
> 慈善機構和行善者

- charity 慈善團體
- foundation 基金會
- fundraiser 資金籌集人
- raise 募款
- patron 贊助者
- philanthropist 慈善家

benevolent

[bəˋnɛvələnt]

a 仁慈的，慈善的，親切的

The local government received a benevolent donation from an entrepreneur.

當地政府收到一名企業家慈善捐款。

> 記憶技巧　bene- 表示好；vol- 就是 will（意志，願望）；-ent 是形容詞字尾；benevolent 表示善意待人的。

benign

[bɪˋnaɪn]

a 親切的，良性的，溫和的

A benign tumor does not spread to other parts of the body.

良性腫瘤不會擴及身體其他部位。

> 記憶技巧　ben(i)- 表示好的；gn- 表示出生、產生，可用 generate（產生）聯想記憶；benign 意思是產生好的事物、效果等。

Section **3**

〔v〕對應〔b〕

fever - febr

子音 v 和 b 互換，表示發燒、發熱之意。

febrile [ˋfibrəl] **a** 發燒的，發病的	The orchestra conductor is a musician with a febrile imagination. 交響樂團指揮是一名想像力旺盛的音樂家。 記憶技巧 febr- 表示發燒、發熱；-ile 是形容詞字尾。
febrifuge [ˋfɛbrɪˏfjudʒ] **n** 退燒劑	Febrifuge is a medicine serving to dispel or remove fever. 退燒藥是一種解熱驅熱藥物。 記憶技巧 febr- 表示發燒、發熱；fug- 表示逃、消散，可用 fugitive（逃亡者）聯想記憶；febrifuge 意思是發燒消退。

febri fuge

Fugitine 逃亡

have - hab

兩者雖無字源關係，但可藉由子音 v 和 b 互換來記憶，hab- 表示握、拿、擁有，後引申為居住之意。

habit [ˋhæbɪt] **n** 習慣，體型	Hank makes it a habit to spin his pen with his fingers while studying. 漢克讀書時習慣用手指轉筆。 記憶技巧 habit 是經歷長時間培養，而 have（擁有）的行為，一時不易改變。
habitual [həˋbɪtʃuəl] **a** 平常的，習慣的	Previous habitual drug use may put the patient at risk for dialysis. 病人先前習慣用藥可能導致洗腎的風險。 記憶技巧 -al 是形容詞字尾。

habitat
[`hæbə,tæt]

n 棲息地，聚集處，居住地

相關字彙
野生動物居住地

The endangered species is losing its natural habitat in the wild.
瀕臨絕種動物的野外天然棲地不斷流失。

記憶技巧 「棲息地」表示動物擁有的居住地。

- burrow（兔、狐等的）洞穴
- den（野獸的）洞穴
- lair（野獸的）窩
- molehill 鼴鼠丘
- nest 巢
- warren 野兔洞

inhabitant
[ɪn`hæbətənt]

n 居民，居住者

The aborigines are the native inhabitants of this island.
土著是島嶼的原住民。

記憶技巧 in- 表示在～內部或在～上；hab- 表示居住；-ant 表示人。

exhibition
[ˌɛksə`bɪʃən]

n 呈現，展覽會

相關字彙
展覽、表演

The decorative artwork will be on exhibition until the end of this week.
這件裝置藝術品將展示至本周末。

記憶技巧 ex- 表示在外面；-ion 是名詞字尾；exhibition 就是把東西拿出來展示。

- show 展出
- fair 商品交易會
- roadshow 巡迴演出
- exposition 展覽會
- trade show 商展

inhabit
[ɪn`hæbɪt]

v 居住，棲息

This remote island is inhabited only by tribes practicing agriculture.
偏僻島嶼只住著務農部落。

記憶技巧 in- 表示在～內部或在～上的；hab- 表示居住。

inhibit
[ɪn`hɪbɪt]

v 抑制，約束，禁止

This drug can inhibit the growth of hepatoma cells.
該藥能抑制肝腫瘤細胞生長。

記憶技巧 hib- 是 hab- 的轉音；inhibit 原意是因為握、拉著，使某對象出不來，引申為約束、抑制的意思。

prohibit
[prə`hɪbɪt]

v 禁止，妨礙

相關字彙
不允許、禁止

Container trailers are strictly prohibited from driving downtown.
貨櫃車嚴禁行駛市區。

記憶技巧 pro- 表示往前；hib- 表示握、拉；prohibit 意思是拉住使之無法往前走，引申為禁止。

- forbid 禁止
- decline 謝絕
- ban 禁止
- bar 中止
- clamp down 嚴格限制

deliver - liber

deliver 是傳送、運送的意思，可透過子音 v 和 b 互換來記憶 liber 這個字根，liber- 表示自由、不受限制之意。

liberal
[ˈlɪbərəl]

a 心胸寬闊的，開明的，自由的

Some people have liberal attitudes towards pre-marital sex.
一些人對婚前性行為態度開放。

記憶技巧 liber- 表示自由；-al 是形容詞字尾。

libertine
[ˈlɪbərˌtin]

n 放蕩者，玩樂者

相關字彙
風流人物

Leo appears like a libertine enjoying life to its fullest.
里歐一副放蕩不羈，盡情享樂的德性。

記憶技巧 libertine 原指自由民、被解放的奴隸，現指不受拘束的放蕩者。

• Don Juan 放蕩者
• Casanova 大眾情人
• womanizer 玩弄女性者

liberty
[ˈlɪbərtɪ]

n 自由，自由權

The spokesman is not at liberty to illustrate the corresponding measures.
發言人未獲授權說明配套措施。

記憶技巧 -ty 是名詞字尾。

move - mobil

子音 v 和 b 互換，表示移動之意。

mob
[mɑb]

n 暴民，民眾

相關字彙
幫派組織、成員

This mob violence has caused 10 deaths and over 30 injuries.
群眾暴力造成十人死亡，三十多人受傷。

記憶技巧 mob- 原意是易變（動）的人，後引申為行為失序的暴民。

• scam 詐騙集團
• gangster 幫派分子
• juvenile offender 少年犯
• mobster 暴民
• organized crime 組織犯罪

mobile
[ˈmobɪl]

a 活動的，機動的

The mobile medical unit can be dispatched to provide caring medical services in communities.
機動醫院可派往社區進行醫療服務。

記憶技巧 -ile 是形容詞字尾。

mobilize
[ˋmoblˏaɪz]
v 動員，使流通

The authorities concerned have mobilized all the rescue resources.
有關當局已動員所有救援資源。

> 記憶技巧 動詞字尾 -ize 表示 make（使）；mobilize 意思是使～動起來。

momentum
[moˋmɛntəm]
n 動力，動量

Opposition to pension reform has been gaining momentum.
年金改革反對力量一直在增強。

> 記憶技巧 momentum 表示移動的力量。

momentary
[ˋmomənˏtɛrɪ]
a 瞬間的，暫時的

The suspect had a momentary hesitation before he replied.
嫌犯回應前遲疑了一下。

> 記憶技巧 moment（移動）引出立即、片刻的概念；-ary 是形容詞字尾。

momentous
[moˋmɛntəs]
a 極重要的

The association president handing-over ceremony is a momentous occasion.
協會理事長交接典禮是一重要場合。

> 記憶技巧 moment（移動）引申出重要、重量的概念；-ous 是形容詞字尾。

相關字彙
重要的近義字

- major 主要的
- key 重要的
- vital 極其重要的
- crucial 決定性的
- significant 重大的
- great 重大的

prove - prob

子音 v 和 b 互換，表示測試、檢驗的意思。

probe
[prob]
v 用探針探測，調查

The prosecutor probed deep into the suspect's criminal motivation.
檢察官深究嫌犯的犯罪動機。

> 記憶技巧 probe 表示測試、試探。

approbate
[ˋæprəˏbet]
v 認可，批准

The review panel approbated the tender documentation for the construction project yesterday.
審議小組昨天批准營建工程招標文件。

> 記憶技巧 approbate 和 approve 同源；ap- 表示 to；prob- 表示試驗；-ate 是動詞字尾；approbate 表示同意試驗。

approbation
[ˌæprəˈbeʃən]
n 核准，認可，讚許

The committee has finally indicated its approbation of the proposal.
委員會終於核准提案。

記憶技巧 -ation 是名詞字尾。

---

approve
[əˈpruv]
v 批准，贊成，
證明為

The CEO thoroughly approved of the resolution proposed by the consultant.
執行長完全贊同顧問所提的解決方案。

記憶技巧 ap- 表示 to；prove 表示試驗；approve 表示同意試驗。

---

approval
[əˈpruvḷ]
n 批准，贊成

相關字彙
相關語詞

The new minimum wage policy didn't meet with the management's approval.
新最低薪資政策未獲資方認同。

記憶技巧 -al 是名詞字尾。

- consent 同意
- agree 同意
- thumbs-up 贊成
- seal of approval 正式認可

---

proof
[pruf]
n 證據，證明

Remember to retain your receipt as proof of purchase.
記得保留收據作為購物證明。

記憶技巧 動詞 prove 字尾子音變化而衍生名詞 proof。

---

reproof
[rɪˈpruf]
n 責備，申斥

The trainee got a sharp reproof for her carelessness.
實習生粗心，遭到嚴厲譴責。

記憶技巧 動詞 reprove 字尾子音變化衍生名詞 reproof。

---

airproof
[ˈɛrˌpruf]
a 不透氣的，密封的

相關字彙
防止～

To achieve the damp-proof effect, the plumber used airproof material to fill the gaps in the wall.
為了達到防潮效果，水管工人採用防水材料填補牆縫。

記憶技巧 air- 表示空氣；proof 表示試驗；airproof 就是禁得起考驗、空氣跑不進來。

- soundproof 隔音的
- bulletproof 防彈的
- fireproof 防火的
- waterproof 防水的
- rainproof 防雨的

---

prove
[pruv]
v 證明，檢驗

Working holiday in that country has proved to be a very rewarding experience.
在那國家打工度假證實是非常值得的經歷。

記憶技巧 prove 原意是檢驗、試驗，衍生出證明的意思。

reprove
[rɪ`pruv]

v 責備，非難

The manager reproved the sales specialist for not achieving his performance goal.
經理責難銷售專員，因為他未達業績目標。

記憶技巧　re- 表示和先前情況相反；prove 是證明有價值的；reprove 是證明無價值，既然無價值，遭譴責也就再自然也不過了。

disapprove
[ˌdɪsə`pruv]

v 不贊成，不同意

The board of directors disapproved the budget proposal for the coming financial year.
董事會不贊同新財務年度預算提案。

記憶技巧　dis- 表示反方向；approve 表示同意；diapprove 就是不同意。

probability
[ˌprɑbə`bɪlətɪ]

n 可能性，機率

Sam is trying to figure out the probability of winning the game.
山姆試圖算出贏得比賽的機率。

記憶技巧　prob- 表示測試；-ity 是名詞字尾；probability 表示測試後可信的機率。

Section **4**

〔b〕對應〔p〕

---

bear - par

parent
培

兩者雖無明確字源關係，但子音 b 和 p 可以互換，母音通轉，可藉由 bear（生小孩）這個字來記下 par-（生產）的意思。

parenting
[`pɛrəntɪŋ]

n 親職

The association is aimed to promote and improve parenting education.
協會以推廣及提升親職教育為目標。

記憶技巧　par- 表示生產；-ent 表示人，生產小孩的人就是為人父母者；parenting 表示親職。

相關字彙
父母親

- custodial parent 監護父母
- empty nester 空巢老人
- single-parent family 單親家庭
- tiger mother 虎媽
- full-time mother 全職媽媽

biparous

[ˋbɪpərəs]

a 產雙胎的

The biparous animal brought forth two young at a birth.
雙胎動物一次生下兩隻小動物。

記憶技巧　bi- 表示二；par- 表示生產；-ous 是形容詞字尾。

---

multiparous

[mʌlˋtɪpərəs]

a 一胎多子的

The syndrome is very common in multiparous pregnancy.
這是一胎多子非常普遍的懷孕症狀。

記憶技巧　multi- 表示許多；par- 表示生產；-ous 是形容詞字尾。

---

oviparous

[oˋvɪpərəs]

a 卵生的，產卵的

Birds, reptiles, amphibians and most fish are oviparous animals.
鳥類、爬蟲類、兩棲動物及大多數的魚類都是卵生動物。

記憶技巧　ovi- 表示 egg（卵）；par- 表示生產；-ous 是形容詞字尾。

相關字彙　卵、蛋
- broody 孵卵的
- clutch 一窩蛋、一窩小雞
- egg 卵
- eggshell 蛋殼
- incubate 孵卵
- lay 產卵
- spawn 產（卵）

---

burglar - plagiary

兩者雖無明確字源關係，但透過子音 b 和 p 轉音，r 和 l 轉音，用 burglar（偷盜）這個字可以記憶 plagiary（剽竊）這字根，「剽竊」即「偷取他人創作」。

---

plagiarism

[ˋpledʒəˌrɪzəm]

n 抄襲，剽竊

The freelancer was accused of plagiarism by a writer earlier this year.
自由作者今年稍早遭一名作家控告抄襲。

記憶技巧　-ism 是名詞字尾。

---

plagiarize

[ˋpledʒəˌraɪz]

v 抄襲，剽竊

A couple of plagiarized passages were found in the columnist's article.
專欄作家的文章被發現有幾處抄襲橋段。

記憶技巧　-ize 是動詞字尾。

相關字彙　複製
- fake 假貨
- simulation 模仿
- imitation 贗品
- reverse engineering 逆向工程
- duplication 複製
- clone 複製人

dis 翻閱
de

disport 以…自娛 v. sport
休息 n.

deport 放逐

bear - port

兩者雖無明確字源關係，但可利用 b 和 p 互換、母音通轉的概念，來記憶 port 這字根，port-表攜帶的意思。

portable
[`portəbl̩]
a 可攜帶的

The cellphone number is portable. I can transfer it to a new mobile company.
手機門號可移機，我可以將它轉到新手機公司。

記憶技巧 port- 表示攜帶；-able 表示可～的。

portfolio
[port`folɪo]
n 紙夾，文件夾，公事包

The photographer showed the guests a portfolio of his photos.
攝影師向來賓展示一組照片作品集。

記憶技巧 port- 表示攜帶；folio- 表示葉子、紙張；portfolio 原指便於攜帶紙張的盒子。

相關字彙
事物聚集

- arsenal 軍械庫
- assemblage 裝配藝術
- bundle 捆
- collection 收藏品
- compilation 編輯
- constellation 薈萃
- hodgepodge 雜燴菜
- paraphernalia 設備
- stockpile 儲備物資

deport
[dɪ`port]
v 放逐，舉止

The illegal immigrants were deported back to their country of origin.
非法移民遭驅逐回到自己國家。

記憶技巧 de- 表示離開；port- 表示攜帶；deport 表示帶走。

important
[ɪm`portn̩t]
a 重要的，有權力的

The CEO has to make important decisions about business development.
執行長必須做出攸關公司發展的重大決策。

記憶技巧 im- 表示裡面；port- 表示攜帶；-ant 表示形容詞字尾；值得帶進來的一定是「important（重要的）」。

purport
[`pɝport]
v 意圖

The video purports to show the young man pledging allegiance to the international terrorist organization.
錄影帶要秀出這名年輕男子宣誓效忠國際恐怖組織。

記憶技巧 pur- 表示往前；port- 表示攜帶；purport 表示帶出想法或念頭。

report
[rɪ`port]
v 報導

The financial institution is reported to have got involved in money laundering.
據報導，該金融機構曾涉入洗錢。

記憶技巧 re- 表示回來；port- 表示攜帶；report 表示帶回來的新聞，引申為報導。

sport
[sport]
n 運動，運動比賽

Playing extreme sports is an exciting way to war with nature.
從事極限運動是與自然博鬥的刺激方式。

記憶技巧　sport 和 disport 同源，**dis-** 表示離開；port- 表示攜帶；disport 原意是離開嚴肅的工作，並藉由娛樂來放鬆，15 世紀末才出現藉由運動來娛樂放鬆的意思。

相關字彙
運動競賽

- championship 錦標賽
- curtain raiser 正戲前的開場戲
- decider 決勝局
- final 決賽
- Grand Prix 國際長距離賽車
- grand slam 滿分全壘打
- Olympiad 國際奧林匹克運動會
- outing 體育比賽
- play-off 延長賽
- showdown 攤牌
- war of nerves 心理戰

sportsmanship
['sportsmən‚ʃɪp]
n 運動員精神

The excellent sportsman takes defeat with true sportsmanship all the time.
優秀運動員總是以運動家精神面對挫敗。

記憶技巧　-ship 表示特質、情況；sportsmanship 表示運動家特質。

support
[sə`port]
v 支援，贊助，扶養

The majority of the residents in the community strongly support the plan to build an activity center.
大多數社區居民強力支持活動中心興建計畫。

記憶技巧　sup- 是 sub-（在～下面）的變體，受到 port- 首字母 p 的同化而變成 sup-；support 指在下面提著，引申為支持幫助。

Section **5**

〔f〕對應〔p〕

flat - plat
子音 f 和 p 互換，兩者皆表示平坦的。

platform
['plæt‚form]
n 平台，台

All northbound trains will depart from Platform Two.
所有北上列車從二號月台開出。

記憶技巧　plat- 表示平坦的；form 就是形狀；platform 意指平台。

platitude

[ˋplætəˌtjud]

n 平凡，陳腐，陳詞濫調

Many panelists mouth platitudes about the former president's scandals.

許多名嘴一直扯前總統醜聞老梗。

記憶技巧 plat- 是平坦的；-tude 是抽象名詞字尾，類似於 -ness 的概念；platitude 即平凡無奇的言語。

相關字彙 評論

• afterthought 事後的想法
• aside 私語
• backchat 回嘴
• barb 帶刺的話
• feedback 反饋的信息
• hashtag 社群網路話題標籤（#）
• remark 談論，評論
• witticism 妙語，俏皮話

platypus

[ˋplætəpəs]

n 鴨嘴獸

The platypus is a mammal, but it lays eggs.

鴨嘴獸是哺乳動物，但會下蛋。

記憶技巧 plat- 是平坦的；pus- 是腳；platypus 即腳有蹼，類似鴨子的扁平喙動物。

push

father - pater

子音 f 和 p 互換，th 和 t 互換，兩者皆表示父親。

paternal

[pəˋtɝnḷ]

a 父親的

My paternal grandparents came from Quanzhou, while my maternal grandparents came from Hangzhou.

我父親那邊的祖父母來自泉州，母親那邊的祖父母來自杭州。

記憶技巧 pater- 是父親；-al 是形容詞字尾；paternal 表示父親的。

patriot

[ˋpetrɪət]

n 愛國者

The leader of the student movement is considered to be a fervent patriot.

一般認為這位學運領導人是狂熱愛國主義者。

記憶技巧 patriot 字面上是愛父親，引申為愛祖國。

patron

[ˋpetrən]

n 資助者，保護人

The entrepreneur is a regular patron of several charities.

企業家是數家慈善機構的固定資助人。

記憶技巧 patron 是像父親一樣，保護、支持你的人，後來才引申出資助人的意思。

expatriate

[ɛksˋpetrɪˌet]

v 驅逐

The dissident was expatriated out from his country by the autocracy.

異議分子被獨裁政府驅逐海外。

記憶技巧 ex- 是離開；patr- 是父親之國；-ate 是動詞字尾；expatriate 表示驅逐某人離開自己的土地。

deport.

相關字彙	• immigration 移居	• refugee 難民
遷移到其他國家	• asylum 政治避難權	
	• exile 流亡	

---

repatriate
[rɪˋpetrɪͺet]
v 把～遣返回國

The foreigner was repatriated to his country of origin soon after imprisonment.
老外服刑期滿隨即遣送回國。

記憶技巧　re- 是回來；patr- 是父親之國；-ate 是動詞字尾；repatriate 表示把一個人送回自己的國家。

---

compatriot
[kəmˋpetrɪət]
a 同胞的

In the multinational corporation, the trainee is working with several of his compatriot colleagues.
跨國企業中，實習生與數名祖國同事一起工作。

記憶技巧　com- 是一起；compatriot 是和你一起生活在同一塊土地上的同胞，形容詞的意思是同胞的。

---

foot - ped

子音 f 和 p 互換，兩者皆表示腳。

---

pedal
[ˋpɛdl̩]
n 踏板

You should put your foot fully on the pedal when operating the machine.
操作機器時，你腳要整個踩在踏板上。

記憶技巧　ped- 表示腳；-al 為名詞字尾；pedal 是放腳的踏板。

---

pedigree
[ˋpɛdəͺgri]
n 族譜

Last week, I read a book about the pedigree of the royal family of Great Britain.
上星期我讀一本有關英國皇室族譜的書。

記憶技巧　pedigree（祖譜）源自法文，指的是「ped de gru（鶴腳）」，family tree 長的像鶴腳，因而得名。

---

pedestrian
[pəˋdɛstrɪən]
n 行人，步行旅行者

The pedestrian was hit by a vehicle when crossing the road.
行人過馬路時遭到一部汽車撞擊。

記憶技巧　ped- 表示腳；-an 表示人；pedestrian 指徒步走行的人。

---

impede
[ɪmˋpid]

v 阻止，妨礙

Progress on rebuilding the bridge was impeded by continuous rain.

重建橋樑進度因連續下雨而受阻。

記憶技巧 im- 和 in- 表示在～裡面；ped- 表示腳；impede 為腳被銬住，引申為受阻。

expedite
[ˋɛkspɪˏdaɪt]

v 迅速執行，發送

In order to expedite the process, all the employees will be required to work overtime.

為了加快進度，所有員工將被要求加班。

記憶技巧 ex- 表示外面；ped- 表示腳；字面意思是擺脫腳銬束縛，引申為加速。

octopus
[ˋɑktəpəs]

n 章魚

Oven roasted octopus is a popular summer Italian dish.

爐烤章魚是人氣義大利夏季佳餚。

記憶技巧 octo- 表示八；pus- 表示腳；octopus 就是八爪章魚。

podium
[ˋpodɪəm]

n 講台，指揮台

The athlete won a tempest of applause as he stood on the winner's podium.

運動員站上領獎台時獲得如雷掌聲。

記憶技巧 pod- 表示腳；-um 表示地方；podium 就是放置腳的地方。

podiatrist
[poˋdaɪətrɪst]

n 足科醫師

相關字彙
醫療從業人員

The podiatrist moved the wounded boy's leg gently.

足科醫師輕輕挪動受傷男孩的腳。

記憶技巧 pod- 表示腳；iatr- 表示治療；-ist 表示做～的人；podiatrist 意思是治療腳部的人。

- anesthetist 麻醉師
- cardiologist 心臟病科醫師
- chiropractor 脊骨神經醫師
- flying doctor 乘飛機出診的醫生
- gynecologist 婦科醫生
- obstetrician 產科醫師
- pediatrician 小兒科醫師
- surgeon 外科醫生
- acupuncturist 針療師
- pharmacologist 藥理學家

centipede
[ˋsɛntəˏpid]

n 蜈蚣

Centipedes catch and eat their prey with two large special legs.

蜈蚣用兩隻特殊大足抓食獵物。

記憶技巧 cent- 表示百；ped- 表示腳；百足動物就是蜈蚣。

nephew - nepot

子音 ph 和 p 互轉，兩者皆表示姪兒。

nepotism
[`nɛpətɪzəm]
n 偏袒（或重用）親戚

Nepotism is considered to be one of the typical family corporate cultures.

一般認為偏袒親戚是傳統家族企業文化之一。

記憶技巧 -ism 表示一種知識體系或主義；nepotism 字面上是偏袒姪兒，後來衍生出偏袒親戚的意思。

相關字彙
偏袒與不公

- favoritism 偏袒
- bias 偏見
- partiality 偏袒
- injustice 不公正

fish - pisc

子音 f 和 p 通轉，兩者皆表示魚。

Pisces
[`paɪsiz]
n 雙魚座

One of the negative traits of a typical Pisces person is being oversensitive.

過於敏感是典型雙魚座的一項負面特徵。

記憶技巧 pisces 是 piscis 的複數形，所以稱為雙魚。

相關字彙
占星術

- Aquarius 水瓶座
- Aries 牡羊座
- Cancer 巨蟹座
- Capricorn 摩羯座
- Gemini 雙子座
- Leo 獅子座
- Libra 天秤座
- Sagittarius 射手座
- Scorpio 天蠍座
- Taurus 金牛座
- Virgo 處女座
- horoscope 占星術

piscary
[`pɪskərɪ]
n 魚場

An amendment to the bill for the preservation of the offshore piscary was agreed.

一項維護近海漁場修正法案已通過。

記憶技巧 pisc- 表示魚；-ary 表示作為～用途的地方；piscary 就是魚場。

原來如此！

dig 意思是挖；挖出來的壕溝—— ditch 是同源字。

fee - pecu

↑〔pɛkjʊ〕.

子音 f 和 p 互轉，表示牲口（古人的財富是用牲口多寡來計算）或財富。

impecunious
[ˌɪmpɪˋkjunɪəs]
a 沒有錢的

The impecunious intern could not afford to rent this apartment.
口袋空空的實習生租不起這間公寓。

記憶技巧 im- 表示否定；pecu- 表示財富；-ous 是形容詞字尾；impecunious 意思是沒有錢的。

peculate
[ˋpɛkjəˌlet]
v 挪用，盜取

The engineer has been accused of peculating someone else's IP address.
工程師曾被控盜用他人 IP 地址。

記憶技巧 -ate 是動詞字尾；peculate 原意是盜走別人的牲口，後來引申為挪用、盜取。

相關字彙
竊取、盜用

- thief 賊
- burglar 破門盜竊者
- robber 搶劫者
- mugger 偷襲搶劫者
- pickpocket 扒手
- bandit 土匪

pecuniary
[pɪˋkjunɪˌɛrɪ]
a 金錢的，錢財方面的

Dumping untreated sewage into water is a pecuniary offense.
排放未處理廢水至水中可處以罰鍰。

記憶技巧 -ary 是形容詞字尾。

peculiar
[pɪˋkjuljɚ]
a 奇怪的，乖癖的，罕見的

The documentary on the slaughter made me feel rather peculiar.
大屠殺紀錄片令我相當不適。

記憶技巧 pecu- 表示牲口；-ar 表示附屬於；peculiar 本指專屬於某人的牲口，後來才有不尋常的意思。

fire - pyr

子音 f 和 p 互換，母音 i 和半母音 y 互換，兩者皆表示火。

pyretic
[paɪˋrɛtɪk]
a 熱病的

Dengue fever is a fatal pyretic disease in tropical areas of the northern hemisphere in the summer months.
登革熱是北半球夏令月份的一種致命熱病。

記憶技巧 pyr- 表示火；-ic 為形容詞字尾；pyretic 意思是火熱的。

| pyromaniac
[͵paɪrə`menͺæk]
n 縱火狂 | The pyromaniac failed to resist impulses to start fires again.
縱火狂無法克制再次縱火的衝動。

(記憶技巧) pyr- 表示火；-maniac 表示狂熱的人；pyromaniac 就是縱火狂的意思。 |

---

fear - peri
子音 f 和 p 互轉，母音通轉，原始意思皆是冒險、危險，另有嘗試、試驗等意思，在冒險過程中，會產生「fear（恐懼）」。

---

peril [`pɛrəl] **n** （嚴重的）危險，冒險	The sudden thunder shower will put the mountain climbers in great peril. 突如其來的雷陣雨會使登山客陷入極大危險。 (記憶技巧) peri- 表示危險。
perilous [`pɛrələs] **a** 危險的，冒險的	Crossing the river by ropeway is quite perilous. 搭流籠過河相當危險。 (記憶技巧) peri- 表示危險；-ous 為形容詞字尾。
imperil [ɪm`pɛrɪl] **v** 危及	Drift gill nets will significantly imperil numerous species of marine life. 流刺網嚴重危及眾多海洋生物。 (記憶技巧) im- 表示內部；peri- 表示危險；imperil 指讓人陷入危險之中。
experience [ɪk`spɪrɪəns] **n** 經驗，體驗，經歷	I had a pretty unpleasant experience during my last trip to India. 上次到印度旅行時，我經驗一件非常不愉快的事。 (記憶技巧) ex- 表示外面；peri- 表示試驗；-ence 為名詞字尾；experience 是出去嘗試之意。
experiment [ɪk`spɛrəmənt] **n** 實驗，試驗	The research team will carry out a series of experiments in the high-tech laboratory. 研究團隊將於高科技實驗室進行一系列實驗。 (記憶技巧) ex- 表示外面；peri- 表示嘗試；-ment 為名詞字尾；experiment 指拿出來試驗看看。

expert

[`ɛkspɚt]

n 專家

An expert on immigration issues will deliver a lecture at the auditorium tonight.

今晚一名移民議題專家將於禮堂發表演說。

記憶技巧 ex- 表示外面；per- 表示嘗試；expert（專家）要經歷無數嘗試才有資格稱專家。

相關字彙

飽學之士、專家

- walking encyclopedia 學識極為豐富淵博的人
- specialist 專家
- consultant 顧問
- professional 專業人士
- intellectual 知識分子
- pundit 博學（或自稱博學）的人

Part 2 CH 1

雙唇音、唇齒音轉換

first - proto

子音 f 和 p 互換，母音通轉，兩者皆表示第一。

protocol

[`protəˌkɑl]

n 草案，議定書

The diplomatic protocol is aimed to enhance bilateral relationship through trade and investments.

這份外交協議的目標是藉由貿易和投資加強雙邊關係。

記憶技巧 proto- 表示第一；protocol 為第一份文件。

prototype

[`protəˌtaɪp]

n 原型，模範

A prototype of an in-car entertainment system will be displayed on this booth.

攤位將展示一組車內娛樂系統的原型。

記憶技巧 proto- 表示第一；type 表示類型；prototype 意思是原型。

first - prim

子音 f 和 p 互換，母音通轉，兩者皆表示第一。

primary

[`praɪˌmɛrɪ]

a 首要的，主要的

The primary cause of the air crash is the pilot's improper operation.

空難主要原因是機師操作不當。

記憶技巧 prim- 表示第一；-ary 為形容詞字尾；primary 字面意思是第一的，引申為首要的、主要的。

prime

[praɪm]

a 最初的，原始的，基本的，原有的

The correspondent refused to reveal the prime source of information.

通訊記者拒絕透露消息最初來源。

記憶技巧 prime 表示第一的，引申為最初的、原始的。

primitive
[`prɪmətɪv]
a 原始的，遠古的，早期的

The documentary showed the primitive living conditions of the early settlers in the island.
紀錄片顯示早期島嶼居民的原始生活狀況。

記憶技巧 prim- 表示第一；-ive 為形容詞字尾；primitive 字面意思是第一的，引申為原始的、早期的。

subprime
[sʌb`praɪm]
a 次級的

The interest rate on subprime mortgages is always higher than conventional ones.
次級抵押利率高於一般利率。

記憶技巧 sub- 表示在～之下；prim- 表示第一；subprime 字面意思是在第一之下的，引申為次級的。

相關字彙 銀行業務
- balance 結餘
- bank rate（國家中央銀行的）貼現率
- base rate（清算銀行作為貸款基礎的）基本利率
- collateral 擔保品
- deposit 存款
- interest rate 利率
- mortgage 抵押
- passbook 存款簿
- unsecured 無擔保的
- withdrawal 提款

feel - path
兩者雖無字源關係，但可藉由子音 f 和 p 互換，母音通轉來記憶這個字根，兩者皆表示感受。

apathetic
[ˌæpə`θɛtɪk]
a 冷漠的，缺乏感情的

Many young people feel apathetic about public issues, particularly politics.
許多年輕人對公共議題冷漠，尤其是政治。

記憶技巧 a- 表示沒有；path- 表示感覺；-ic 為形容詞字尾；apathetic 意思是無感的。

antipathy
[æn`tɪpəθɪ]
n 反感，厭惡

My husband has a deep antipathy against direct selling model.
我先生非常厭惡直銷。

記憶技巧 anti- 表示反對；path- 表示感覺；-y 為名詞字尾，表示情況、特質；antipathy 有反感的意思。

pathos
[`peθɑs]
n 悲愁

The story was narrated by an experienced voice actress with great pathos.
故事由資深配音員講述，聽起來令人動容。

記憶技巧 patho- 表示情感。

pathetic
[pə`θɛtɪk]
a 悲愁的

It was pathetic to see the stray dog's nose cut away.
看到流浪狗的鼻子被削掉,真慘。

記憶技巧 path- 表示感覺;-ic 為形容詞字尾;pathetic 原表示有感覺的,至於可憐的、令人同情的等衍生語意,最早的紀載可追溯到 1737 年。

food / feed - pan
子音 f 和 p 互換,d 和 n 互換,母音通轉,兩者皆表示食物。

pantry
[`pæntrɪ]
n 配膳室

The patient's daughter-in-law cooked instant noodles in the pantry.
病患媳婦在配膳室煮泡麵。

記憶技巧 pan- 表示食物;-ry 為名詞字尾,表示地方;pantry 指儲存食物的地方。

company
[`kʌmpənɪ]
n 夥伴,公司

The Japanese animator has been working in the transnational company for three years.
日籍動畫家在跨國公司工作三年了。

記憶技巧 com- 表示一起;pan- 表示食物或麵包;company 意思是一起吃麵包的人,引申為夥伴,而公司的意思,始見於 1550 年代。

相關字彙
各類公司

- agency 經銷處
- chain 連鎖店
- corporation 股份(有限)公司
- dealer 業者
- enterprise 企業
- firm 公司
- franchise 經銷權(或公司名稱使用權等)
- limited company 股份有限公司
- parent company 母公司
- shell company 空殼公司
- zombie company 僵屍企業

accompany
[ə`kʌmpənɪ]
v 陪伴

Children must be accompanied by adults when riding the escalator.
搭乘電扶梯時,孩童必須由成人陪伴。

記憶技巧 ac- 即 ad-,ad- 接黏 company 而發生同化現象。

companion
[kəm`pænjən]
n 夥伴,同行

The guide dog has been the blind man's constant companion for over three years.
導盲犬持續陪伴眼盲男子三年多。

記憶技巧 com- 表示一起;pan- 表示食物或麵包;-ion 為名詞字尾;companion 和 company 同源,皆可表示伙伴的意思。

few - pauci / paup

子音 f 和 p 互換，母音通轉，兩者皆表示少的意思。

---

paucity
[`pɔsətɪ]
n 少數，少量，缺乏

There was a paucity of heavy metal left in the liquid.
液體殘留少量重金屬。

記憶技巧　pauc- 表示少；-ity 為名詞字尾。

---

pauper
[`pɔpə]
n 窮人，貧民，乞丐

The rich and famous entrepreneur used to be a pauper before.
名利雙收的企業家以前是窮光蛋一個。

記憶技巧　paup- 表示少，和 poor（貧窮）同源；-er 為名詞字尾，表示人；pauper 即是窮人。

---

flow - pluv

子音 f 和 p 互換，母音通轉，flow（流動）和 pluv（下雨）是出自同一來源。

---

pluvial
[`pluvɪəl]
a 雨的，多雨的

The average amount of rainfall in the pluvial season for this region is only 10 inches.
此地區雨季平均降雨量僅十英寸。

記憶技巧　pluv- 表示雨；-ial 為形容詞字尾；pluvial 的意思是雨的或多雨的。

---

foul - putre

子音 f 和 p 互換，母音通轉，皆表示腐爛的意思。

---

putrefy
[`pjutrə,faɪ]
v 化膿，腐敗

The corpse has already putrefied beyond recognition.
屍體腐爛，已經無法辨識。

記憶技巧　putre- 表示腐爛；-fy 為動詞字尾，表示使～；putrefy 是腐爛的意思。

相關字彙
腐爛、分解

- biodegrade 生物降解
- curdle 凝結
- decay 腐爛
- decompose 分解
- fester 化膿
- spoil 腐壞
- rot 腐爛
- sour 酸腐的
- turn 使變質

putrid
[`pjutrɪd]

a 腐敗的，
放出惡臭的

Several vultures are pecking the putrid body of a dead wart hog.
幾隻禿鷹啄食疣豬腐屍。

記憶技巧 putri- 表示腐爛。

feel - palp
子音 f 和 p 互換，母音通轉，兩者皆表示觸摸，palp 另有顫動、輕觸等意思。

impalpable
[ɪm`pælpəbl]

a 無法感觸到的，
無形的

Joy is a state of mind with an impalpable spiritual quality.
喜悅是一種有著無形心靈特性的心理狀態。

記憶技巧 im- 為否定字，表示相反；palp- 表示觸摸；-able 為形容詞字尾，表示可以～的；impalpable 是無法觸摸的到的意思。

palpitate
[`pælpə,tet]

v 悸動，撲撲地跳

The lady's heart was palpitating with terror at that moment.
那時候，那女子的心臟因恐懼而顫動。

記憶技巧 palp- 表示顫動；-ate 為動詞字尾；palpitate 是顫抖的意思。

相關字彙
上下、前後移動

- swing 搖擺
- bounce 彈回
- rock 使搖晃
- sway 搖擺
- vibrate 顫動
- flutter 顫動
- oscillate 擺動
- shake 搖

fold - ply
兩者雖無字源關係，但透過子音 f 和 p 互換，母音通轉概念，藉由 fold 來記憶 ply（摺）的意思。

apply
[ə`plaɪ]

v 申請，應用，敷

The intern would like to apply for the position to the foundation.
實習生向基金會申請職務。

記憶技巧 ap- 為 ab- 的變體，表示朝～方向，因接黏 -ply 產生同化作用，由 b 轉 p。-ply 表示摺，apply 原表示對摺讓兩端、兩面接觸、相黏，引申為把自己能力放到適當的任務或工作上，直到 1851 年才有申請工作的意思。

replicate themselves

imply
[ɪmˋplaɪ]

v 暗指

The press release implied a lack of trust between labor and management.
新聞稿暗示勞資雙方缺乏互信。

記憶技巧 im- 表示內；-ply 表示摺；imply 本意是往內摺，到 1580 年代才有暗示的意思。

multiply
[ˋmʌltəplaɪ]

v 增加，乘

Such cases could be multiplied indefinitely.
這樣的案例可能會不斷增加。

記憶技巧 multi- 表示多；-ply 表示摺；multiply 本意是不停對摺，造成數目上的增加，至於數學乘（法）的意思，要到 14 世紀後半葉才產生。

相關字彙 計算
- calculate 計算
- count 數
- estimate 估計
- reckon 計算
- assess 對～進行估價
- compute 計算

reply
[rɪˋplaɪ]

v 回覆，反應

The management refused to reply to the requirement of the labor union.
資方拒絕回應工會要求。

記憶技巧 re- 表示回去；-ply 表示摺；reply 本意是摺回去，引申為回覆、反應等意思。

replicate
[ˋrɛplɪˏket]

v 臨摹，複製

These computer viruses will replicate themselves and occupy more and more space.
這些電腦病毒會自行複製，然後佔據愈來愈多空間。

記憶技巧 re- 表示再一次；-ply 表示摺；replicate 意思是再摺一次，衍生為重複、複製的意思。

complicate
[ˋkɑmpləˏket]

v 複雜

Domestic economic conditions have been complicated by the impact of globalism.
國內經濟景況因全球化衝擊而趨於複雜。

記憶技巧 com- 表示一起；plic- 表示摺；complicate 本意是把東西摺在一塊、糾纏在一起，難以分開。

simplicity
[sɪmˋplɪsətɪ]

n 簡單，樸素

The retired couple led a life of great simplicity.
退休夫婦過著很簡樸的生活。

記憶技巧 sim- 表示一或相同，可視為 same 的變體；plic- 表示摺；-ity 為名詞字尾；simplicity 的意思是摺的方式單一、無虛飾的，引申為簡單、樸素。

deploy skills
art on display.

epidemic situation
complex structure
explicit directions

explicit
[ɪk'splɪsɪt]

a 明確的

The manager offered his assistant explicit directions about how to deal with the case.
經理明確指示助理如何處理這件案子。

記憶技巧 ex- 表示外面；plic- 表示摺；explicit 意思是把東西往外摺、往外翻（給別人看），引申為清楚、不含糊的。

supplication
[ˌsʌplɪ'keʃən]

n 懇求，祈禱

膝而下摺.

The believer turned to the idol in humble supplication with her eyes closed.
信徒轉向神像，閉眼膜拜。

記憶技巧 sup- 是 sub- 的變體，因接黏 plic- 而同化為 p，表示在～下面；plic- 表示摺；-ation 為名詞字尾；supplication 是屈膝跪拜、彎腰膜拜的意思。

complex
['kɑmplɛks]

a 複合的，錯綜的

相關字彙
複雜難以理解的

The criminal organization has a complex structure.
犯罪組織結構複雜。

記憶技巧 com- 表示一起；plex- 表示摺；complex 和 complicated 意思相近。

• complicated 複雜難懂的
• difficult 困難的
• confusing 令人困惑的
• incomprehensible 難懂的
• involved 複雜的

perplex
[pɚ'plɛks]

v 使混亂，使困窘

The epidemic situation has continued to perplex epidemic prevention experts.
疫情持續令防疫專家頭疼。

記憶技巧 per- 表示穿透；plex- 表示摺或纏繞；perplex 表示摺過來、摺過去，全糾纏在一塊，引申為使混亂、使困窘。

display
[dɪ'sple]

v 展覽，顯示

Without prior approval, works of art on display cannot be moved.
未經事先允許，展示藝術品禁止移動。

記憶技巧 dis- 表示分開；-play 表示摺，本意是把對摺的東西打開，引申為顯示、展示等。

deploy
[dɪ'plɔɪ]

v 展開，佈署

My first job allowed me fully to deploy my graphic design skills.
我的第一份工作讓我充分發揮平面設計技術。

記憶技巧 de- 等同於 dis-，表示分開；-ploy 表示摺，本意是把對摺的東西打開，引申為展開等。

Part
2
CH 1

雙唇音、唇齒音轉換

ford - port

子音 f 和 p 互換，d 和 t 互換，母音通轉，兩者皆表示通過的意思，ford 當名詞是淺灘的意思，port 當名詞是港口的意思。前面提過 port 字根另一個意思是攜帶（carry），意思雖不同，但實則系出同源，都是印歐字根 per- 的變體。

---

port
[port]
n 港口，機場，舉止

The hotel will be sited with a good view of the port area.
飯店將坐落於港口視野良好的區域。

記憶技巧 port- 表示通道，船隻、飛機進出的地方。

---

export
[ɪks`port]
v 出口，排出

These technology products have been exported all over the world.
這些科技產品已出口至全世界。

記憶技巧 ex- 表示外面；port- 表示港口；export 是出口。

---

import
[ɪm`port]
v 輸入，進口，表明

The business imported coffee beans from Colombia and Sumatra.
公司自哥倫比亞及蘇門答臘進口咖啡豆。

記憶技巧 im- 表示裡面；port- 表示港口；import 是進口。

相關字彙
國際貿易

- balance of payments 國際收支平衡（表）
- balance of trade 貿易的差額
- embargo 禁運
- fair trade 公平貿易
- free trade 自由貿易
- trade deficit 貿易逆差
- trade surplus 貿易盈餘

---

importune
[ˌɪmpɚ`tjun]
v 一再要求，糾纏

The management has been importuned for a raise in pay for working overtime.
資方一再被要求調高加班費。

記憶技巧 im- 等同於 in-，表示 not 的意思；port- 表示港口，字面意思上是沒有港口，難以通行，因此造成麻煩、困擾，衍生為被～糾纏著。

---

opportune
[ˌɑpɚ`tjun]
a 及時的，合宜的

It would be opportune to review contract terms and conditions.
檢視合約條文及條件應該正是時候。

記憶技巧 op- 等同於 ob-，表示朝向；port- 表示港口；opportune 本意是風向有利於船隻進港，引申為時機適宜的、合適的。

contract terms

leafy vegetables
took a plentiful supply   specific team
accomplish the task.

opportunity
[ˌɑpəˋtjunətɪ]
n 機會

You should grab this golden opportunity for financial gain.
應該抓住這掙錢的大好機會。

記憶技巧 opportunity 是 opportune 的名詞，表示時機合宜、大好機會。

porch
[portʃ]
n 走廊，門廊

After dinner, Tom usually sits out on the porch to cool off.
晚餐後，湯姆經常坐在外面走廊乘涼。

記憶技巧 porch 等同於 port，表示出入口或門廊。

full - ple
子音 f 和 p 互換，母音通轉，兩者皆表示滿的意思。

plenty
[ˋplɛntɪ]
a 豐富的

There is plenty more cheese in the refrigerator.
冰箱還有更多起司。

記憶技巧 plent- 表示滿；-y 為形容詞字尾；plenty 有充滿的、很多的等意思。

plentiful
[ˋplɛntɪfəl]
a 豐富的，充分的

The farmer naturally took a plentiful supply of green leafy vegetables.
農夫當然大量供應葉菜類蔬菜。

記憶技巧 plent- 表示滿；-ful 為形容詞字尾；plentiful 表示充滿的意思。

accomplish
[əˋkɑmplɪʃ]
v 完成，達到

The specific team accomplished the task earlier than scheduled.
專案小組提前完成任務。

記憶技巧 ac- 等同於 ad-，表示朝～方向；com- 表示加強語氣；pl- 表示滿；-ish 為古法語動詞字尾；accomplish 本意是充滿，引申為完成的意思。

complete
[kəmˋplit]
v 完成

The administrative assistant has not completed the application form yet.
行政助理尚未完成申請書。

記憶技巧 com- 表示加強語氣；ple- 表示滿；complete 是完成的意思。

complementary
[ˌkɑmpləˋmɛntərɪ]
a 補充的，互補的

Complementary colors are those colors directly opposite one another on the color wheel.
互補色是色盤上位置相對的顏色。

記憶技巧　com- 表示加強語氣；ple- 表示滿；-ment 為名詞字尾
-ary 為形容詞字尾；complementary 意思是補充的。

compliment
[ˋkɑmpləmənt]
v 稱讚，恭維

Everyone complimented the hostess on her dinner suit.
大家讚美女主人的晚禮服。

記憶技巧　com- 表示加強語氣；pli- 表示滿；-ment 為名詞字尾；compliment 的意思是用言語去填補別人的虛榮、滿足感等。事實上，這個字的語意以前是包含在 complement 意思當中，直到 1650 之後才獨立出來。

相關字彙　• praise 讚揚　　　　　　• acclaim 讚賞
稱讚　　　• admiration 欽佩
　　　　　• respect 尊敬

supplementary
[ˌsʌpləˋmɛntərɪ]
a 補遺的，追加的

The supplementary reading program is aimed to motivate teenagers to read extensively.
課外閱讀計畫的目標是激發青少年廣泛閱讀的動機。

記憶技巧　sub- 等同於 sup-，表示在～下面；ple- 表示滿；-ary 為形容詞字尾，supplementary 指從下面補充上來。

feather - pet

子音 f 和 p 互換，th 和 t 互換，母音通轉，兩者皆表示羽毛、翅膀、飛等意思，衍生意思有追尋、要求、懇求（給予）、攻擊、向前衝、往前走等。

petition
[pəˋtɪʃən]
n 請願，訴狀

The residents submitted a petition asking the police to reinforce community security.
居民向警方遞交請願書，請求加強社區治安。

記憶技巧　pet- 表示懇求；-ion 為名詞字尾；petition 本意是向神明懇求，大約在 15 世紀才出現向比自己地位高的人請願、懇求的意思。

相關字彙　• certificate 證明書　　　　　　• consent form 同意書
各類文件　• charter 特許狀　　　　　　　• document 文件
　　　　　• confidentiality agreement 保密協議　• dossier 檔案

competitive
[kəm`pɛtətɪv]
a 競爭的，
有競爭力的

The young guy is working hard to survive in the highly competitive society.
年輕人在高度競爭社會中努力求生存。

記憶技巧 com- 表示一起；pet- 表示追尋；-ive 為形容詞字尾；competitive 本意是為共同目標一起努力，引申為競爭的。

competent
[`kampətənt]
a 稱職的，合法的

My colleague, Judy, proved to be a very competent fund manager.
我同事裘蒂證實是非常稱職的基金經理人。

記憶技巧 com- 表示一起；pet- 表示追尋；-ent 為形容詞字尾；competent 表示適合一起追尋目標的，引申為稱職的。

incompetent
[ɪn`kampətənt]
a 不熟練的，
無資格的

The jury consistently considered the document to be incompetent evidence.
陪審團一致認為文件不具證據力。

記憶技巧 in- 表示 not 的意思；incompetent 指不稱職的。

impetuous
[ɪm`pɛtʃuəs]
a 衝動的，猛烈的

A hurricane is an impetuous wind sweeping all around the region.
颶風是橫掃整個地區的強風。

記憶技巧 in- 表示往內、往～上面；pet- 表示向前衝；-ous 為形容詞字尾；impetuous 即是衝動的。

相關字彙
缺乏深思熟慮及判斷能力

- shallow 淺薄的
- foolish 愚蠢的
- impulsive 易衝動的
- unthinking 欠考慮的
- undiscriminating 無鑑別力的
- hasty 輕率的

repeatedly
[rɪ`pitɪdlɪ]
ad 一再

The company repeatedly stressed its support for employee benefits.
公司一再強調對員工福利的支持立場。

記憶技巧 re- 表示一再；peat- 表示向前走；-ed 為形成過去分詞的字尾；-ly 為副詞；repeatedly 的意思是重複、一再。

repetition
[ˌrɛpɪ`tɪʃən]
n 重複，模仿

The student was asked to avoid endless repetition of redundant expressions in his writing.
學生被要求避免文章中一直重複贅詞。

記憶技巧 repeat 的名詞形式。

fasten - pact

雖兩者並無字源關係，但透過 f 和 p 子音互換，母音通轉，可以輕易記下 pact 的意思，兩者皆表示穩固、牢固、綁緊，pact 另有協議等衍生意思。

pact
[pækt]
n 協議，公約

The cease-fire pact will come into effect as soon as it is signed.
停火協議簽訂後立即生效。

記憶技巧 pact 即協議。

相關字彙
協定、協議
- contract 契約
- bargain 協議
- accord（國家之間的）協議

compact
[kəm`pækt]
a 密集的，結實的，簡潔的

The compact style of writing is a main feature of this collection of essays.
簡潔文體是這本散文集的主要特色。

記憶技巧 com- 表示一起；pact- 表示穩固的；compact 意思是把東西緊密擺放在一起。

impact
[`ımpækt]
n 衝擊，影響

The low birth rate has caused a dramatic impact on higher education.
少子化已嚴重衝擊高等教育。

記憶技巧 im- 即 in-，表示內部或上面；pact- 表示緊密；impact 字面上意思是把東西強壓，使之固定到某物上面，到 1935 年才有強而有力的影響力等語意衍生。

fight - pugn

兩者雖無字源關係，fight 原始意思是用力拉、拔，pung 原始意思是戳、刺，但現今都有戰鬥、打的意思。因此不妨藉由子音 f 和 p 互轉，母音通轉的概念，來記憶 pugn（戰鬥）這個字根，也可用閩南語打的發音來幫助記憶。

pugilist
[`pjudʒəlıst]
n 拳擊手

The victorious pugilist spent his childhood in the slums.
獲勝拳擊手在貧民窟度過童年。

記憶技巧 pug- 表示戰鬥、打；-ist 表示人；pugilist 即打鬥的人、拳擊手。

相關字彙
拳擊、摔跤
- arm-wrestling 腕力賽
- boxing 拳擊
- featherweight（拳擊）次輕量級選手
- fighter 拳擊手
- heavyweight 重量級拳擊手
- kickboxing 跆拳道
- shadowboxing 空拳訓練
- sumo【日】相撲
- wrestler 摔角選手

impugn
[ɪmˈpjun]
v 抨擊

The chairperson usually impugns my competence as a professional photographer.
會長常質疑我身為專業攝影師的能力。

記憶技巧　im- 即 in-，表示上面或裡面；pugn- 表示打；impugn 即打在某對象上，引申為攻擊的意思。

pugnacious
[pʌgˈneʃəs]
a 好鬥的

Many people found the new supervisor arrogant and pugnacious.
許多人覺得新任督導傲慢又好鬥。

記憶技巧　pugn- 表示打；-acious 為形容詞字尾，表示充滿；pugnacious 的意思是愛打鬥的。

repugnant
[rɪˈpʌgnənt]
a 討厭的

Bait and switch is a morally repugnant behavior.
偷樑換柱是道德上難以接受的行為。

記憶技巧　re- 表示回去；pugn- 表示打；-ant 為形容詞字尾；repugnant 本指不相容、抗拒的，到 1777 年才有討厭的意思產生。

office - oper / opus

office 是辦公室的意思，其中的 of- 事實上就是 op- 的變體，皆表示工作的意思，不妨利用 office 來記憶 oper 和 opus（工作）這兩個字根。

opera
[ˈɑpərə]
n 歌劇，歌劇院

The Phantom of the Opera is a well-known musical.
《歌劇魅影》是一部知名音樂劇。

記憶技巧　oper- 表示工作；opera 本指作品，後來特指歌劇作品。

相關字彙　歌劇

● aria 詠嘆調　　　　　● kabuki 歌舞伎
● diva（歌劇的）女主唱者　● libretto 歌劇劇本
● intermezzo 插曲　　　● operetta 輕歌劇

operate
[ˈɑpəˌret]
v 操作，動手術，生效，經營

The sealing machine is not operating properly.
封口機運作不太正常。

記憶技巧　oper- 表示工作；-ate 為動詞字尾；operate 的意思是工作、運轉等。

operation
[ˌɑpəˈreʃən]
n 工作，管理，手術

The patient had an emergency operation on his gallbladder last night.
昨晚病患膽囊緊急開刀。

記憶技巧　-ion 為名詞字尾；operation 是 operate 的名詞。

cooperate [ko`ɑpə͵ret] **v** 合作	We should cooperate with each other to overcome difficulties. 我們應當相互合作以克服困境。 記憶技巧　co- 即 com-，表示一起；operate 表示工作；cooperate 的意思是一起工作，即合作。
cooperation [ko͵ɑpə`reʃən] **n** 合作，協力， 合作社	Both parties should practice mutual sincere cooperation. 雙方應當相互誠摯合作。 記憶技巧　-ion 為名詞字尾；cooperation 是 cooperate 的名詞。

Section 6

〔v〕對應〔p〕

savor - sap

唇齒音 v 和雙唇音 p 可以互換，母音通轉。兩者皆表示品嚐，源自於印歐詞根 sep-，有兩個核心意思，一個是品嚐、一個是覺知或理解，這也就說明為什麼 sapid 意思是美味的，而 sapient 意思是睿智的。

sapid [`sæpɪd] **a** 美味的，有趣的	The hostess provided a sapid meal for all the guests at the party. 女主人提供宴會賓客佳餚美食。 記憶技巧　sap- 表示品嚐；sapid 是美味的意思。
sapient [`sepjənt] **a** 睿智的	Smartphones are a sapient invention of technology. 智慧型手機是睿智的科技發明。 記憶技巧　sap- 表示覺察或理解；-ent 為形容詞字尾；sapient 表示覺察能力高、理解能力高的，引申為睿智的。
相關字彙 形容人具有聰明才智	• intelligent 有才智的　　• clever 聰明的　　　　• clear-sighted 有眼光的 • brilliant 才華橫溢的　　• brainy 腦筋好的 • bright 聰穎的　　　　　• discerning 眼光敏銳的

insipid

[ɪn`sɪpɪd]

a 枯燥無味的

相關字彙
嘗起來味道不好或無味

A tiresome person usually has an insipid personality.
沉悶的人通常個性較乏味。

記憶技巧 in- 表示不～；sip- 是 sap- 的變體，經過雙重弱化（a-e /
e-i）而來，insipid 表示無味的。

- stale 不新鮮的
- rancid 腐臭的
- sour 酸腐的
- unpalatable 味道差的
- bland 淡而無味的
- tasteless 乏味的

insipient

[ɪn`sɪpɪənt]

a 愚昧的

I was being insipient when deleting the files on my cell
phone by mistake.
我誤刪手機檔案的當下真是愚昧。

記憶技巧 in- 表示不～；sip- 是 sap- 的變體，經過雙重弱化（a-e /
e-i）而來；insipient 是不聰明的、愚蠢的，要避免和
incipient（起初的）混淆。

> ### seven - sept
> 子音 p 和 v 互換，兩者皆表示七。

September

[sɛp`tɛmbɚ]

n 九月

My husband and I were both born in September.
我和我先生都是九月出生。

記憶技巧 sept- 表示七，September 是舊羅馬曆法中的七月，但在
儒略曆（現代公曆的前身）中往後移兩個月，變成九月。

septet

[sɛp`tɛt]

n 七重奏

Mr. Suzuki will recite a septet poem in which all
stanzas have seven verses.
鈴木先生要朗誦一首各節都是七句的七行詩。

記憶技巧 spet- 表示七；septet 是七重奏。

septuagenarian

[ˌsɛptʃʊədʒə`nɛrɪən]

n / a 七十幾歲的（人）

相關字彙
老年人

The septuagenarian monk breathed his last breath at
dawn.
七十多歲的和尚清晨圓寂。

記憶技巧 sept- 表示七；genari- 表示十倍；septuagenarian 指七十
多歲的人。

- centenarian 百歲的（人）
- Methuselah 非常高壽的人
- nonagenarian 九十多歲的（人）
- octogenarian 八十歲到八十九歲的（人）
- sexagenarian 六十至六十九歲的（人）
- senior 較年長者

Part 2 CH 1 雙唇音、唇齒音轉換

Section 7

〔b〕對應〔m〕

black - melan

兩者雖無字源關係，但透過雙唇音 b 和 m 互換，藉由簡單的 black（黑）可輕鬆記憶字根 melan（黑）的意思。

melancholia
[ˌmɛlənˋkolɪə]

n 憂鬱症

The retired president is suffering from melancholia.
退休大學校長遭受憂鬱症之苦。

> 記憶技巧　melan- 表示黑色；chol- 表示膽汁；-ia 表示疾病；melancholia 是黑膽汁過多所導致的憂鬱症。事實上，西方的「Humorism（體液學說）」，從希波克拉底以降到公元 19 世紀現代科學研究的誕生這段期間，主宰著西方的哲學和醫學界，認為人體內的四大體液多寡、平衡與否皆會影響一個人的性情和健康。四大體液會因飲食習慣或生活型態彼此消長，若黑膽汁過多會造成憂鬱。

melancholy
[ˋmɛlənˌkɑlɪ]

n 憂鬱

Nancy is sentimental, and she usually falls into a state of profound melancholy.
南西多愁善感，經常陷入深度憂鬱。

> 記憶技巧　melan- 表示黑色；chol- 表示膽汁。

bad - mal

兩者雖無字源關係，但可透過雙唇音 b 和 m 互換，齒齦音 d 和 l 互換來記憶，兩者皆表示錯誤的、壞的、不好的。

maltreat
[mælˋtrit]

v 虐待

The girl with self-mutilation scars used to be badly maltreated.
留有自殘疤痕的女孩以前遭受嚴重虐待。

> 記憶技巧　mal- 表示不好的；treat 表示對待；maltreat 是虐待的意思。

malpractice
[mæl`præktɪs]
n 誤診，瀆職

The plastic surgeon was accused of medical malpractice.
整形醫師被控醫療疏失。

（記憶技巧） mal- 表示壞的、錯誤的；practice 是醫師執業；malpractice 是醫生誤診的意思。

相關字彙
經濟犯罪

- black market 黑市
- bribery 行賄
- cyberfraud 網路詐騙
- forgery 偽造
- insider dealing（尤指股票的）非法內部交易
- racketeering 敲詐勒索
- trafficking 非法交易（尤指毒品買賣）
- bootlegging 非法製造（或運輸、販賣）私酒
- embezzlement 盜用公款
- misappropriation 侵吞
- swindle 詐騙

Part 2
CH 1
雙唇音、唇齒音轉換

malcontent
[`mælkən͵tɛnt]
a 不滿的

The man got a reputation for being malcontent because he complained so much.
男子抱怨連連，大家都知道他有所不滿。

（記憶技巧） mal- 表示不好的；con- 表示一起；tent- 表示握；content 的意思是把東西握住、包含某物，引申為滿意的；malcontent 即不滿意的。

malformation
[͵mælfɔr`meʃən]
n 畸形

Malformation of the embryo results from the effects of constant exposure to radiation.
胚胎畸形是持續暴露於輻射的影響所致。

（記憶技巧） mal- 表示不好的；form- 表示形式、樣貌；-ation 為名詞字尾；malformation 指不好的樣貌，引申為畸形。

malfunction
[mæl`fʌŋʃən]
n 機能不全，故障

A malfunction of the navigation system caused this accident.
導航系統故障導致本次意外。

（記憶技巧） mal- 表示不好的；funct- 表示使用、執行；-ion 為名詞字尾；malfunction 是無法執行，指故障的意思。

malaria
[mə`lɛrɪə]
n 瘧疾

Malaria used to be particularly prevalent in Europe.
瘧疾曾經在歐洲大流行。

（記憶技巧） mal- 表示不好的；-aria 即 air，表示空氣，古人認為 malaria 是由沼澤地帶的瘴癘之氣引起的疾病，現代醫學證實瘧疾是透過蚊子傳播的一種疾病。

malady
[`mælədɪ]
n 疾病，缺點

Many of the villagers are suffering from a strange malady.
許多村民正受一種怪病之苦。

（記憶技巧） mal- 表示壞的、不好的；ady 是 habit 變體，表示「have（有）」，字面上的意思是具有不好的狀況，引申為疾病。

malicious
[mə`lɪʃəs]
a 惡意的，狠心的

The suspect raised her head with a malicious look in her eyes.
嫌犯抬起頭，眼神兇狠。

記憶技巧　mal- 表示壞的；-ous 為形容詞字尾；malicious 是惡意的意思。

---

vol
will

malevolent
[mə`lɛvələnt]
a 惡意的

Everyone could feel the man's malevolent gaze as he walked over.
男子走過來時，大家都感受他兇惡的眼神。

記憶技巧　mal- 表示壞的；vol- 表示「will（意志）」；-ent 為形容詞字尾；malevolent 是惡意的意思。

---

malediction
[ˌmælə`dɪkʃən]
n 誹謗，詛咒

The clerk left the office, uttering maledictions against her director.
職員離開辦公室，嘴巴詛咒著主管。

記憶技巧　mal- 表示壞的；dict- 表示說；-ion 為名詞字尾；malediction 是說壞話、詛咒的意思。

---

malign
[mə`laɪn]
v 誹謗

The candidate has been unfairly maligned by the press.
候選人遭受媒體不公平誹謗。

記憶技巧　mal- 表示壞的；gn- 表示生；malign 是出生即具有邪惡、壞的本質：當形容詞用是邪惡的；動詞是中傷、毀謗的意思。

---

malignant
[mə`lɪgnənt]
a 有害的，惡意的

The division of abnormal cells will bring about a malignant tumor.
不正常細胞分裂將誘發惡性腫瘤。

記憶技巧　mal- 表示壞的；gn- 表示生；-ant 為形容詞字尾；malignant 通常用以表示疾病是惡性的。

原來如此！

medal 是獎牌（金屬製成），與 metal（金屬）同源。metal 常與 mental（心理的）混淆，分辨的方式除了以單字 mind 聯想字根 ment-，辨識拼字相似的 metal，金屬獎牌一詞也強化與 mental 的差別。

big - mag

兩者雖無明確字源關係，但可透過雙唇音 b 和 m 互換、母音通轉的概念來記憶，兩者的意思皆是大。

magnify
[ˋmæɡnəˏfaɪ]
v 放大，擴大

The airbrushing staff pressed the button to greatly magnify the photos.
修片人員按下這個鍵，照片隨即大幅放大。

記憶技巧 magn- 表示大；-fy 表示做；magnify 是放大的意思。

magnifier
[ˋmæɡnəˏfaɪɚ]
n 擴大者，放大鏡

The man with severe nearsightedness has difficulty reading without a magnifier.
重度近視的男子不用放大鏡會有閱讀困難。

記憶技巧 -er 表示主事者名詞字尾；magnifier 是放大鏡。

magnificent
[mæɡˋnɪfəsənt]
a 莊嚴的，動人的

All the guests were very impressed by the magnificent occasion.
所有賓客對華麗排場留下深刻印象。

記憶技巧 magn- 表示大；fic- 是 fac- 的弱化，表示做；-ent 為形容詞字尾；magnificent 字面上意思是做大事的，引申為高尚的、崇高的。

magniloquent
[mæɡˋnɪləkwənt]
a 誇張的

The street performer performed rolls and somersaults in a magniloquent gesture.
街頭藝人以誇張姿勢翻跟斗。 *翻筋斗*

記憶技巧 magn- 表示大；loqu- 表示說；-ent 為形容詞字尾；magniloquent 是說大話的意思。

magnanimous
[mæɡˋnænəməs]
a 心胸寬大的，心地高尚的

The athlete was magnanimous in victory and praised his opponent.
選手勝不驕，還稱讚對手。

記憶技巧 magn- 表示大；anim- 表示心；-ous 為形容詞字尾；magnanimous 是心胸寬大的意思。

相關字彙
能原諒人、有包容心

- forgiving 寬容的
- understanding 能諒解的
- indulgent 縱容的
- merciful 仁慈的
- clement 厚道的

Section **8**

〔f〕對應〔m〕

form - morph

有學者認為兩者系出同源，皆表示形體的意思。可藉由唇齒音 f 和雙唇音 m 互換來記憶。另外，古羅馬詩人奧維德在《變形記》中提到夢神「Morpheus（摩耳甫斯）」，他是睡神許普諾斯的兒子，可以幻化成不同人的形象出現在夢中。因此 morph- 表示形體，但因與睡眠和夢境有關，故產生像「morphine（嗎啡）」這樣的字。

---

morphine
[`mɔrfin]
n 嗎啡

Injected with morphine, the patient felt relief from sharp pain.
注射一些嗎啡，病患的劇痛獲得紓解。

記憶技巧　morph- 和夢神相關；-ine 為名詞字尾，表示化學物質；morphine 和希臘神話中的夢神「Morpheus（摩耳甫斯）」有關，因嗎啡有讓人睡著的傾向，故用夢神的名字來命名。

---

morphology
[mɔr`falədʒɪ]
n 結構，形態學

The core task of morphology is to study the morphemic structure of the word.
構詞學的核心任務是研究單字的詞素結構。

記憶技巧　morph- 表示形貌；-logy 表示學；morphology 是形態學、構詞學。

---

morphological
[͵mɔrfə`ladʒəkəl]
a 形態學的，構詞學的

Morpheme, affix, prefix and suffix are basic terms for morphological analysis.
詞素、綴詞、前綴及後綴是構詞分析的基本用語。

記憶技巧　-ical 為形容詞字尾；morphological 是 morphology 的形容詞。

---

metamorphosis
[͵mɛtə`mɔrfəsɪs]
n 蛻變，變形

The metamorphosis from pupa to adult is incredible!
從蛹到成蟲的蛻變真是不可思議。

記憶技巧　meta- 表示改變；morph- 表示形貌；-osis 為名詞字尾，表示狀態、過程等意思；metamorphosis 是蛻變、變形的意思。

Section 9

〔b〕對應〔f〕

brain - fren / phren

雖兩者並無明確字源關係，但可透過雙唇音 b 和唇齒音 f 互換、母音通轉概念來記憶 fren-、phren-，兩者皆表示腦或想法。

phrenitis
[frɪˋnaɪtɪs]
n 腦炎，精神錯亂

Phrenitis may be an inflammation of the meninges of the brain.
腦炎可能是一種腦膜發炎。

記憶技巧 phren- 表示腦；-itis 為名詞字尾；phrenitis 表示因發炎所產生的疾病。

schizophrenia
[ˌskɪtsəˋfrinɪə]
n 精神分裂症

Paranoid schizophrenia is one of the common mental illnesses.
偏執型精神分裂症是常見的心理疾病之一。

記憶技巧 schizo- 表示分裂；phren- 表示腦；-ia 表示疾病；schizophrenia 即精神分裂症。

相關字彙
心理疾病

- agoraphobia 曠野恐怖症
- bipolar disorder 躁鬱症
- claustrophobia 幽閉恐怖症
- dementia 痴呆
- depression 沮喪

- hypochondria 疑病症
- kleptomania 竊盜癖
- megalomania 誇大狂
- melancholia 憂鬱症
- paranoia 偏執狂

frantic
[ˋfræntɪk]
a 發狂似的

The woman was frantic with grief at the loss of her only son.
婦人失去獨子，傷心欲絕。

記憶技巧 是由 phrenitis 變化來的，-ic 為形容詞字尾，表示發瘋的。

frenetic
[frɪˋnɛtɪk]
a 狂熱的

There was frenetic trading in the crude oil forward market two days ago.
兩天前原油期貨市場交易熱絡。

記憶技巧 frenetic 和 phrenitis 同源，名詞表示瘋子，形容詞有精神錯亂、狂熱的等意思。

compound.
fracture.

phrenology
[frɛˋnɑlədʒɪ]
n 顱相學

Phrenology is the science which studies the relationships between a person's morphology of the skull and personality.
顱骨學是研究一個人顱骨型態和性情關聯的科學。

記憶技巧 phren- 表示頭顱；-logy 表示學；phrenology 是顱骨學。

break - frag / fract
子音 b 和 f 互換、g 和 k 互換，母音通轉，兩者皆表示破裂。

fraction
[ˋfrækʃən]
n 碎片，片斷，分數

Only a fraction of the residents attended the community year-end party.
只有一些住戶出席社區尾牙。

記憶技巧 fract- 表示破裂；-ion 為名詞字尾；fraction 是碎片的意思。

fracture
[ˋfræktʃɚ]
n 裂痕，挫傷，骨折

The orthopedist performed an operation on a compound fracture in the man's injured part.
骨科醫師為男子受傷部位的複雜性骨折動手術。

記憶技巧 fract- 表示破裂；-ure 為名詞字尾；fracture 特指骨頭裂掉。

fragile
[ˋfrædʒəl]
a 易碎的，虛弱的

Workers carefully packed the fragile ceramic vessels into humidity control boxes.
工人小心翼翼地將易碎陶皿打包到防潮箱。

記憶技巧 frag- 表示破裂；-ile 為形容詞字尾；fragile 是易碎的。

相關字彙
易碎的
- brittle 易碎的
- flimsy 輕薄的
- crumbly 易碎的
- friable 易碎的

fragility
[frəˋdʒɪlətɪ]
n 脆弱，虛弱

Financial fragility usually brings about a financial system's susceptibility to large-scale financial crises.
財政脆弱常導致金融體系易受大規模金融危機影響。

記憶技巧 -ity 為名詞字尾。

fragment
[ˋfrægmənt]
n 碎屑，破片

The forest was covered with fragments of the wreckage of the airplane.
樹林散佈飛機殘骸碎片。

記憶技巧 frag- 表示破碎；-ment 為名詞字尾；fragment 是碎片的意思。

frail

[frel]

a 脆弱的，虛弱的，
意志薄弱的

The pavilion is a frail wooden structure.

涼亭是一易損的木造結構。

記憶技巧 frail 是 fragile 法語化的拼寫形式。

port 芽 港.遍

bear - fer / pher

子音 b 和 f 互換，母音通轉，兩者皆表示攜帶的意思。

conference

[`kɑnfərəns]

n 協商，會議

The annual climate change conference attracted a number of environmentalists from around the world.

氣候變遷年會吸引許多世界各地環保人士參加。

記憶技巧 con- 表示一起；fer- 表示攜帶；-ence 為名詞字尾；conference 是把大家的意見聚在一起討論，引申為會議的意思。

defer

[dɪ`fɜ]

v 延緩，延期，順從

The representative was informed to defer his departure for three days.

代表收到行程延後三天的通知。

記憶技巧 de- 表示分開；fer- 表示攜帶；defer 有帶走的意思，和 differ 是同源詞，到了 15 世紀在拼字上、發音上才有了差異，學者推估可能是受 delay 的影響，才有此改變。

different

[`dɪfərənt]

a 不同的，
各式各樣的

The couple are evidently different from each other in some ways.

這對夫婦彼此在某些方面明顯不同。

記憶技巧 dis- 表示分開；fer- 表示攜帶；-ent 為形容詞字尾；different 字面上的意思是分開，引申為不同的。

indifferent

[ɪn`dɪfərənt]

a 漠不關心的，
中性的

The supervisor tended to remain indifferent in the dispute.

督導在爭端中傾向保持中立。

記憶技巧 in- 表示不、相反；dis- 表示分開；fer- 表示攜帶；-ent、indifferent 字面上的意思是不分開，直到 15 世紀時才有冷漠的意思產生。

ferry

[`fɛrɪ]

n 渡船，渡口

The ferry service has been temporarily suspended.
渡船服務已暫時中斷。

記憶技巧　fer- 表示攜帶；ferry 是渡船可把遊客帶往各處。亦有學者提出這個字和「port（港口）」是同源字。

相關字彙
各類型船隻

- barge 駁船
- boat 小船
- bowser【英】加油艇
- cabin cruiser 有艙房的汽艇
- canoe 獨木舟
- cruiser 巡洋艦
- dugout 獨木舟
- gondola（用於義大利威尼斯運河的）平底狹長小船
- hydroplane 水上飛機
- lifeboat 救生艇
- raft 木筏

fertile

[`fɝtl]

a 肥沃的，豐富的，能生育的

The islanders grow and cultivate wheat on the fertile and productive land.
島上居民在肥沃多產的土地上種植小麥。

記憶技巧　fer- 表示攜帶；-ile 為形容詞字尾；fertile 的意思是可以攜帶大量、豐富的事物，引申為肥沃的、豐富的。

fertilizer

[`fɝtlˌaɪzɚ]

n 肥料

The farmer spread synthetic organic fertilizer out evenly on the surface of soil.
農夫在土壤表面灑合成有機肥料。

記憶技巧　fertile 表示肥沃的、豐富的；-ize 為動詞字尾；-er 為名詞字尾；fertlizer 是使～肥沃之物，亦即肥料。

相關字彙
土壤肥沃度

- compost 堆肥
- desertification 沙漠化
- humus 腐質土壤
- manure 糞肥
- nitrate 硝酸鹽類化肥
- top dressing 頂肥
- sterility 不毛

infer

[ɪn`fɝ]

v 推論，臆測，暗示

I inferred from the manager's remarks that he disagreed with my decision.
從經理的談話臆測，他不同意我的決定。

記憶技巧　in- 表示內；fer- 表示攜帶；infer 表示把～帶進來，在邏輯學中解釋為推論。

offer

[`ɔfɚ]

n 提供，提議，奉獻

The antique dealer made an offer of 100,000 dollars for the celadon vase.
骨董商開價十萬美元買下青瓷花瓶。

記憶技巧　of- 等同於 ob-，表示往～方向；fer- 表示攜帶；offer 是攜帶往～方向，引申為提供、提議、報價等意思。

prefer

[prɪ`fɝ]

v 較喜歡，提出，建議

More westerners prefer a vegetarian diet to meat.
相較於葷食，愈多西方人偏好素食。

記憶技巧　pre- 表示前面；fer- 表示攜帶；prefer 的意思是把東西攜帶到前面，因此有提出（控告）、偏好等意思。

refer

[rɪˋfɝ]

v 參考，涉及，
交付，歸因於

In the press conference, the event was referred to as a main issue.

記者會中，該事件被視為主要議題。

記憶技巧 re- 表示後面；fer- 表示攜帶；refer 的意思是往後帶，指的是溯本求源，引申為歸因於、參考或交付。

---

referential

[ˌrɛfəˋrɛnʃəl]

a 參考的

The referential database serves as a benchmark for evaluation.

參考資料庫做為計量的基準。

記憶技巧 reference（參考）加上 -al（形容詞字尾）。

---

suffer

[ˋsʌfɚ]

v 遭受，忍耐，患病

The chain-store franchise system is suffering from a severe brand crisis.

該連鎖加盟體系遭受嚴重品牌危機。

記憶技巧 suf- 等同於 sub-，表示下面；fer- 表示攜帶；suffer 字面意思是往下帶，引申為壓抑、忍耐的意思。

---

blow - flat   *inflation 通膨*

子音 b 和 f 互換，母音通轉，兩者皆表示吹的意思。

---

conflate

[kənˋflet]

v 匯集

The editor conflated the two versions to produce a new work.

編輯將兩個版本合併成一新作品。

記憶技巧 con- 表示一起；flat- 表示吹；conflate 的意思是把～吹到一起，引申為匯集。

---

deflate

[dɪˋflet]

v 緊縮，削減

The patient will aspirate the moment we deflate the tracheostomy cuff.

氣切管氣囊的氣一洩掉，患者馬上吸氣。

記憶技巧 de- 表示往外或往下；flat- 表示吹；deflate 意思是洩氣，財經用語是通貨緊縮。

---

deflation

[dɪˋfleʃən]

n 通貨緊縮

The purchasing power of gold will rise during economic deflation.

通貨緊縮期間，黃金購買力道上揚。

記憶技巧 -ion 是名詞字尾。

inflate
[ɪn`flet]
v 使膨脹，通貨膨脹

Any raw materials that are in demand will inflate in price.
任何有需求的原物料價格都會膨脹。

記憶技巧 　in- 表示內；flat- 表示吹；inflate 意思是往內吹氣，使膨脹，財經用語是通貨膨脹。

inflation
[ɪn`fleʃən]
n 膨脹，通貨膨脹

In the long run, they caused economic inflation.
最後，導致通貨膨脹。

記憶技巧 　-ion 是名詞字尾。

相關字彙
經濟學

- austerity 嚴格的節制消費
- boom and bust 大繁榮後緊接著發生嚴重的不景氣
- buoyancy 價格回升
- downswing 衰落
- downturn 衰退
- gross domestic product 國內生產總值
- gross national product 國民生產總值
- macroeconomics 總體經濟學
- national debt 國債
- stagnation 不景氣
- supply and demand 供求關係

flute
[flut]
n 直笛

My niece can play the flute fast and beautifully.
我姪女長笛吹得輕快優美。

記憶技巧 　子音 b 和 f 互換，母音通轉，「flute（直笛）」需藉由「blow（吹氣）」來發出聲音。

black - flam

black 是黑的意思，乍看之下和 flam- 沒什麼關係，但兩者原始意思皆是燃燒，燃燒產生焦黑的木炭、灰燼，也帶來光亮、火焰。可透過子音 b 和 f 互換，來記憶 flam（火焰、燃燒）這個字根。

flame
[flem]
n 火焰

The convertible car was in flames after a crash at the intersection.
敞篷車在十字路口撞擊起火。

記憶技巧 　flam- 表示火焰或燃燒。

flammable
[`flæməbl̩]
a 易燃的，可燃的

Highly flammable substances should be stored correctly.
高度易燃物應該正確儲存。

記憶技巧 　flam- 表示燃燒；-able 為形容詞字尾，表示能夠～的；flammable 是易燃的、可燃的。

相關字彙
易燃和不易燃

- combustible 可燃的
- non-flammable 不易燃的

inflammable material

aflame
[əˋflem]
a 燃燒的

The desperate pyromaniac set the ticket booth aflame.
窮途末路的縱火狂放火燒了售票亭。

記憶技巧 a- 即介系詞 on 的概念，功能是加在名詞前面，形成副詞和形容詞。aflame 即 on flame，指著火、燃燒的意思。

inflammable
[inˋflæməbḷ]
a 易燃的，易激動的

The use of inflammable material should be prohibited near electrical machinery.
電力機械附近應禁止使用易燃材料。

記憶技巧 in- 表示導致的意思，這個字和 flammable 意思完全相同；其相反字是「non-flammable（不易燃的）」。

flamingo
[fləˋmingo]
n 紅鶴

Wlid flamingos gather in great flocks in Lake Nakuru in Kenya.
大批野紅鶴群聚於肯亞那庫魯湖。

記憶技巧 flam- 表示火，火鶴因其顏色火紅，故以 flam- 來造字。

flagrant
[ˋflegrənt]
a 公然的，
惡名昭彰的

The implementation of coercive abortions is a flagrant violation of human rights.
施行強迫墮胎是公然侵犯人權。

記憶技巧 flagr- 表示火或燃燒；-ant 為形容詞字尾；flagrant 指燃燒，明亮耀眼的意思，引申為明顯的、惡名昭彰的。

effulgent
[ɛˋfʌldʒənt]
a 燦爛的

The clerk replied to me with an effulgent smile on her face.
櫃台人員回應時面帶燦爛笑容。

記憶技巧 ef- 等同於 ex-；fulg- 表示發光；effulgent 是燦爛的意思。

Part **2**

CH 1

雙唇音、唇齒音轉換

---

bottom - fund
子音 b 和 f 互換，t 和 d 互換，母音通轉，兩者皆表示底部。

fund
[fʌnd]
n 基金，專款

The NGO set up a special trust fund to support the project.
此非政府組織設立一特別信託基金，要來支持這項計畫。

記憶技巧 fund- 表示底部，財經用語解釋為基金。

fundamental
[ˌfʌndəˈmɛntḷ]

a 基礎的，重要的，初級的

The fundamental cause of obesity is an energy imbalance between calories consumed and calories expended.
肥胖的主因是熱量攝取及熱量消耗之間的能量失衡。

記憶技巧 fund- 表示底部；-ment 為名詞字尾；-al 為形容詞字尾；fundamental 的意思是基礎的、重要的。

foundation
[faʊnˈdeʃən]

n 基礎，根據，基金會

The garden party marked the anniversary of the foundation of the charity group.
園遊會紀念慈善團體創立周年慶。

記憶技巧 found- 等同於 fund-，表示底部；-ation 為名詞字尾；foundation 指基礎。

profound
[prəˈfaʊnd]

a 深遠的，深奧的，深厚的

The stimulus measure had a profound effect on overall economic development.
振興方案對整體經濟發展影響深遠。

記憶技巧 pro- 表示向前；found- 表示底部；profound 是底部深的意思，引申為知識底蘊深厚。

相關字彙
概念複雜不易理解

- complicated 結構複雜的
- elaborate 詳盡的
- incomprehensible 難懂的
- intricate 複雜精細的

profundity
[prəˈfʌndətɪ]

n 深奧

The writer's novels are considered to be a mixture of the profundity of his philosophy.
這位作家的小說被視為他深奧哲理的集合。

記憶技巧 -ity 表示名詞字尾，profundity 是 profound 的名詞形式。

---

blossom - flor
子音 b 和 f 互換，母音通轉，兩者皆表示開花、花。

---

flora
[ˈflorə]

n 植物群，植物區系

The gut flora in the digestive tracts of humans protect against invaders and modulate the immune system.
人體消化道內的腸道菌叢能抵抗入侵物質及調節免疫系統。

記憶技巧 flor- 表示開花；-a 為名詞字尾；flora 指的是開花的植物，引申為植物群。

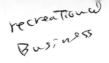
recreational
Business

floriferous
[flɔˋrɪfərəs]
a 開花的

The shuttle bus is heading towards a floriferous resort.
接駁車正開往一處繁花盛開的渡假勝地。

記憶技巧　flor- 表示開花；fer- 表示攜帶；-ous 為形容詞字尾；floriferous 是帶來花的，指的是開花的（植物）。

florist
[ˋflɔrɪst]
n 花匠，花店

My niece has been a florist for two years.
我姪女從事花匠工作兩年了。

記憶技巧　flor- 表示花；-ist 表示人；florist 指的是花匠。

flourish
[ˋflɝɪʃ]
v 茂盛，繁榮

My godfather's recreational business is flourishing.
我教父的休閒事業欣欣向榮。

記憶技巧　flour- 等同於 flor-，表示開花；-ish 為動詞字尾；flourish 引申為茂盛。

flower
[ˋflauɚ]
n 花

Bees gather nectar from flowers and turn it into honey.
蜜蜂從花蒐集花蜜，而後轉變為蜂蜜。

記憶技巧　flower 等同於 flor-，表示花。

---

brew - ferv

brew 的意思是因煮沸而冒泡，ferv- 則是燃燒、發熱，兩者系出同源，可藉由子音 b 和 f 互換來記憶。

fervid
[ˋfɝvɪd]
a 灼熱的，熱情的

The sociology professor is a fervid supporter of same-sex marriage.
這名社會學教授是同性婚姻的熱情支持者。

記憶技巧　ferv- 表示燃燒；-id 為形容詞字尾；fervid 字面意思是燃燒的，引申為熱情的。

fervidity
[fɚˋvɪdətɪ]
n 熾熱，熱情

The girl could not control her fervidity when meeting her favorite celebrity.
遇見最心儀的名人時，女孩控制不住自己的熱情。

記憶技巧　-ity 為名詞字尾。

fervent
[ˋfɝvənt]
a 熱烈的，強烈的

The athlete has a fervent desire to beat the challenger.
選手強烈想要擊敗挑戰者。

記憶技巧　ferv- 表示燃燒；-ent 為形容詞字尾；fervent 字面意思是燃燒的，引申為熱烈的。

grant
finde

fervor
[ˋfɝvɚ]
n 熱忱，熱情

In that era, a wave of religious fervor stirred the West.
那年代，一股宗教狂熱席捲西方世界。

記憶技巧 -or 為名詞字尾；fervor 表示熱情。

相關字彙
充滿能量與熱情

- enthusiasm 熱情
- zeal 熱忱
- vitality 活力
- zest 熱心
- go 精力

effervescent
[ˌɛfɚˋvɛsn̩t]
a 沸騰的，興奮的

My director attracts everyone with his self-confidence and effervescent personality.
我的主管自信，個性活躍，吸引了每個人。

記憶技巧 ef- 等同於 ex-，表示外面；ferv- 表示燃燒、冒泡；-escent 表示變成、開始；effervescent 的意思是開始冒泡的，引申為興奮的。

bound - fin

兩者雖無字源關係，但可透過子音 b 和 f 互換、母音通轉的概念來記憶，兩者皆表示界線，字根 fin 亦有結束的意思。

fine
[faɪn]
v 罰款

The truck driver was fined 1,800 dollars for running a traffic light.
卡車司機闖紅燈遭罰 1,800 元。

記憶技巧 fin- 表示結束；fine 的意思是藉由繳清罰款來免除被處罰。

final
[ˋfaɪn̩l]
n 期末考

The exchange student failed his final in Chinese literature history.
這名交換學生的中國文學史期末考沒過。

記憶技巧 fin- 表示結束；-al 為形容詞字尾；final 本當形容詞用；當名詞用時是結局、期末考的意思。

finale
[fɪˋnɑlɪ]
n 終場，終曲

All the stage actors reappeared briefly during the grand finale.
大結局時，所有舞台劇演員再次短暫登台。

記憶技巧 源自義大利語。

相關字彙
表演

- bill 節目單
- curtain call 謝幕
- encore 要求加演
- intermission 幕間休息
- interval 休息時間
- repertoire 個人（或團體）的曲目（或戲目）

clearly
define

finalize
[`faɪnḷ͵aɪz]
Ⅴ 完成，做最後決定

The task force needs to finalize the project as soon as possible.
專案小組必須儘速完成任務。

記憶技巧 -ize 為動詞字尾；finalize 指的是做最後決定。

financial
[faɪˋnænʃəl]
ａ 財務的，金融的

It is essential for your organization to establish sound financial management.
建立健全財務管理對貴機構至為重要。

記憶技巧 fin- 表示結束；-ance 為名詞字尾；-ial 為形容詞字尾；finance 本來的意思是解決財務上的糾紛，要到 1770 年才有籌集資金和運用資金的概念。financial 現今意思是財務的。

finite
[`faɪnaɪt]
ａ 有限的，限定的

There is a finite amount of natural resources on Earth.
地球上的天然資源有限。

記憶技巧 fin- 表示界線；-ite 為形容詞字尾；finite 的意思是被界線限制住，引申為有限的。

infinite
[`ɪnfənɪt]
ａ 無限的

It usually takes infinite patience to take care of a pet.
照顧寵物經常得花費極大耐心。

記憶技巧 in- 為否定詞；infinite 即無限的。

confine
[kənˋfaɪn]
Ⅴ 限制，使侷限

The chairperson confined the discussion to the issue of same-sex marriage.
主席將討論限於同性婚姻議題。

記憶技巧 con- 表示一起；fin- 為界線；confine 意思是限制。

define
[dɪˋfaɪn]
Ⅴ 立界限，下定義

Evaluation criteria need to be clearly defined.
評鑑標準應該清楚界定。

記憶技巧 de- 表示完全地；fin- 表示界線；define 即立界線，引申為下定義。

definite
[`dɛfənɪt]
ａ 明確的

The entertainer made no definite reply to the rumour about her pregnancy.
關於她懷孕的謠傳，藝人未明確回應。

記憶技巧 -ite 為形容詞字尾；definite 表示立了界限的，引申為明確的。

refine

[rɪˋfaɪn]

v 提煉，改善

The chemical liquid is refined from crude oil.

化學液體是原油提煉而成。

> 記憶技巧 　re- 為加強語氣；fin- 表示界線，亦作精緻解釋；refine 即把品質精緻化，引申為提煉、改善。

refinery

[rɪˋfaɪnərɪ]

n 煉油廠

The refinery will be relocated to the oil industry area in the west.

煉油廠將遷往西邊的石化專區。

> 記憶技巧 　-(e)ry 表示地方。

相關字彙 工業建築或結構	
• blast furnace 鼓風爐	• mill 製造廠　　• smelter 精鍊廠
• boatyard 製造或修理小船之工廠	• plant 工廠
• foundry 鑄造廠	• power plant 發電廠

---

brother - frater

子音 b 和 f 互換，th 和 t 互換，母音通轉，兩者皆表示兄弟。

fraternal

[frəˋtɝnl̩]

a 兄弟的，友好的

We will send our fraternal greetings to the special delegation.

我們將友好問候特使團。

> 記憶技巧 　frater- 表示兄弟；-al 為形容詞字尾；fraternal 的意思是兄弟的。

fraternity

[frəˋtɝnətɪ]

n 兄弟關係（會友，同行）

The alumni association included several members of the legal fraternity.

校友會包括幾位法律界的同僚。

> 記憶技巧 　-ity 為名詞結尾。

---

bore - for

子音 b 和 f 互換，母音通轉，兩者皆表示鑽孔。

perforate

[ˋpɝfəˌret]

v 穿孔於，打眼於

The hood of the stolen car was perforated by bullets.

贓車引擎蓋被多枚子彈穿透。

> 記憶技巧 　per- 表示穿過；for- 表示鑽孔；-ate 為動詞字尾；perforate 是穿孔於的意思。

imperforate
[ɪm`pɝfərɪt]
a 無洞的，無孔的

The pediatrician performed imperforate anus surgery on the child.
小兒科醫師對孩童做肛門閉鎖手術。

記憶技巧 im- 表示否定；per- 表示穿過；for- 表示鑽孔；-ate 為形容詞字尾；imperforate 的意思是無孔的。

basket - fisc
basket 是籃子的意思，字根 fisc 指的是裝錢的籃子，後引申為國庫、政府歲收，兩者雖無明確字源關係，但可藉由子音 b 和 f 互換，母音通轉來記憶。

fiscal
[`fɪskl̩]
a 財政的，會計的

A fiscal year, an accounting period, does not necessarily correspond to the calendar year.
財政年度也就是會計年度，與日曆年度未必相符。

記憶技巧 fisc- 表示政府歲收；-al 為形容詞字尾；fiscal 指的是財政的意思。

confiscate
[`kɑnfɪsˌket]
v 沒收，將～充公，徵收

The property of the corrupted official will be confiscated.
貪汙官員財產將遭沒收。

記憶技巧 con- 表示一起；fisc- 表示裝錢的籃子；-ate 為動詞字尾；confiscate 字面上意思是將錢收集放到籃子中，引申為徵收。

相關字彙
各種懲罰
- banish 放逐
- detain 拘留
- fine 罰款
- waterboarding 水刑

barrow - fort
barrow 是土堆、小丘、古墳，fort 是要塞、堡壘，兩者系出同源，皆是指高起來的地方，藉由子音 b 和 f 互換、母音通轉可以記憶 fort 這字根。fort 除了堡壘的意思外，亦有強壯、穩固等意思。

fort
[fort]
n 要塞，堡壘，市集

Soldiers defended the fort against enemy's heavy attack.
士兵堅守要塞，抵抗敵軍猛烈攻擊

記憶技巧 fort- 即堡壘。

| 相關字彙
防禦建築 | • battlements 碉堡上的城垛
• castle 城堡
• chateau 城堡 | • citadel（護城）城堡
• drawbridge 吊橋
• dungeon（城堡內的）土牢 | • fortress 要塞
• moat 護城河
• turret 塔樓 |

fortify
[`fɔrtəˌfaɪ]
v 加強，設防

The marine corps fortified the coast against the sudden invasions.
海軍陸戰隊防守海岸，以免遭受奇襲。

記憶技巧　fort- 表示穩固；-fy 表示做；fortify 的意思是使～穩固，引申為加強。

comfortable
[`kʌmfɚtəbḷ]
a 舒適的，安逸的

Another comfortable day for outdoor relaxation!
又是一個適合戶外休閒的舒適日子！

記憶技巧　com- 等同於 con-，表示加強語氣；fort- 表示強壯、堅強；comfort 即鼓舞～人，使人堅強；-able 為形容詞字尾；comfortable 表示舒適的，為衍生意思。

effort
[`ɛfɚt]
n 努力，努力的成果

The patient is making an effort to get through the hardship of living with cancer.
病患正在努力渡過與癌症共存的苦楚。

記憶技巧　ef- 等同於 ex-，表示外的意思；fort- 表示堅強力量；effort 的意思是展示堅強力量，引申為努力。

force
[fors]
v 強迫

Employees are forced to accept the unequal severance conditions.
員工被迫接受不公平資遣條件。

記憶技巧　force 和 fort 同源，指堅強的力量，動詞的意思是強迫。

| 相關字彙
軍事武力 | • battalion 營
• brigade 旅
• cavalry 騎兵
• command 指揮 | • company 連
• corps 兵團
• division 師
• garrison 駐軍 | • headquarters 司令部
• paratroops 傘兵部隊
• platoon 排
• vanguard 先鋒 |

forcible
[`forsəbḷ]
a 強有力的，
有說服力的，
強迫的

The hostage rescue team made a forcible entry into the house where the kidnappers had been hiding.
人質救援小組強行進入綁匪藏匿的屋子。

記憶技巧　force（力量）+ -ible（形容詞字尾）= forcible（強而有力的）。

enforce
[in`fors]
v 執行，強行

The provisional government decided to enforce the curfew.
臨時政府決定實施宵禁。

記憶技巧　en- 等同於 in-，表示內的意思；force 表示力量；enforce 即表示把力量施加在某處，引申為執行。

diffusive light.

reinforce
[ˌriɪnˋfɔrs]

v 加強，增援

The old temple is reinforced with steel girders.
古寺以鋼樑強化結構。

> **記憶技巧** re- 等同於 again，表示再一次；inforce 等同於 enforce；reinforce 表示再執行一次，意指加強和增援。

Section 10
〔p〕對應〔f〕

pour - fus

兩者雖無字源關係，現今意思皆表示（傾）倒，可藉由子音 p 和 f 互換、子音 r 和 s 互換、母音通轉來記憶。

fusion
[ˋfjuʒən]

n 熔解，融合，合併

The metal case is formed by the fusion of copper and tin.
這個金屬外殼是銅錫融合成形。

> **記憶技巧** fus- 表示倒；-ion 為名詞字尾；fusion 的意思是將東西倒一起，引申合併、熔解的意思。

confuse
[kənˋfjuz]

v 使混亂，使困窘

Many students confused Austria with Australia.
許多學生將奧地利和澳大利亞混淆。

> **記憶技巧** con- 表示一起；fus- 表示倒；confuse 即是把東西倒一起，混淆不清。

diffusive
[dɪˋfjusɪv]

a 散佈的，普及的

The reflection of light from a surface generates diffusive light.
表面的光反射產生散光。

> **記憶技巧** dis- 等同於 dif-，表示離開；fus- 表示倒；-ive 為形容詞字尾；diffusive 的意思是把東西倒出去，引申為散佈的。

infuse
[ɪn`fjuz]
v 注入，使充滿

The factory infused chemical liquid into underground pipes.
工廠將化學液體注入地下管線。

記憶技巧 in- 表示內；fus- 表示倒；infuse 的意思是倒進去，即注入的意思。

---

perfuse
[pɚ`fjuz]
v 灌入，使充滿

The wounded man's spleen is perfused with blood.
受傷男子的脾臟都是血。

記憶技巧 per- 表示完全地；fus- 表示倒；perfuse 的意思是完全倒滿的意思。

---

profuse
[prə`fjus]
a 奢侈的，充沛的

相關字彙
大量

The mountain climber was profuse in his appreciation for the rescue team's efforts.
登山客再三感謝搜救隊的努力。

記憶技巧 pro- 表示往前；fus- 表示倒；profuse 字面上是往前倒的意思，引申為奢侈的。

- substantial 大量的
- considerable 相當大的
- enormous 巨大的
- extensive 大量的

---

refuse
[rɪ`fjuz]
v 拒絕，推辭

The District Court refused to release the arsonist on bail.
地方法院駁回縱火犯保釋申請。

記憶技巧 re- 表示回去；fus- 表示倒；refuse 的意思是倒回去，引申為回絕。

---

transfuse
[træns`fjuz]
v 注入，輸血，注射

The pregnant woman was transfused with the wrong type of blood.
孕婦輸入的血型有誤。

記憶技巧 trans- 表示跨越；fus- 表示倒；transfuse 的意思是把～從甲處倒到乙處，在醫學上做輸血、注射解釋。

原來如此！

paste 是漿糊、麵糊；pastry 是油酥麵團；pasta 則是義大利麵，三字同源，可以糊在一起學習。

speak - fam

兩者雖無字源上關係，但皆表示說的意思，不妨透過子音 p 和 f 互換、母音通轉，來協助記憶此字根。

---

fame
[fem]
n 名聲，聲望

The young man moved to Hollywood in pursuit of fame and fortune.
這名年輕人為了追求名利而移居好萊塢。

記憶技巧 fam- 表示說；fame 即大家口耳相傳產生的聲望、名聲。

---

defame
[dɪˋfem]
v 誹謗

The mayoral candidate claimed the gossip had defamed her.
市長候選人聲稱小道消息已對她造成毀謗。

記憶技巧 de- 等同於 dis-，表示離開，引申出暗示毀損的意思；fam- 表示說；defame 的意思是說～來詆毀～，即毀謗。

相關字彙
說謊欺騙

- deceive 欺騙
- concoct 捏造
- fabricate 杜撰
- mislead 誤導
- bend the truth 扭曲事實

---

famous
[ˋfeməs]
a 有名的

The area is famous for the abundance of wildlife species.
該地區以野生物種繁多聞名。

記憶技巧 fam- 表示說；-ous 為形容詞字尾；famous 的意思是大家都在說的，即有名的。

---

infamous
[ˋɪnfəməs]
a 可恥的，不名譽的

The man guilty of the infamous sexual assault was sentenced to life in prison.
可恥的性侵犯被判終生監禁。

記憶技巧 in- 表示不；fam- 表示說；infamous 的意思是大家都在說你的不好，表示聲名狼藉的、惡名昭彰的、不名譽的。

---

fate
[fet]
n 宿命，死亡

It is a cruel twist of fate that the man lost his wife and three children on the same day.
是殘酷的命運讓男子一天失去妻子及三名子女。

記憶技巧 fate 本意是神所說的話，引申為宿命。

---

fatal
[ˋfetḷ]
a 致命的，嚴重的

The pregnant woman has a fatal disease with no symptoms observed.
孕婦患有察覺不出症狀的致命疾病。

記憶技巧 fate 表示宿命；-al 為形容詞字尾；fatal 的意思是和命運相關的，15 世紀時才衍生出致命的意思。

Part
2
CH 1

雙唇音、唇齒音轉換

infant

[`ɪnfənt]

n 嬰兒

This website gives advice on feeding newborn infants under six months.

該網站提供六個月以下新生兒的養育建議。

記憶技巧　in- 表示否定的意思，表示相反；fan- 表示說話；infant 指不會說話的人，引申為嬰兒的意思。

相關字彙
嬰幼兒

- foundling 棄兒
- neonate（未滿月的）嬰兒
- newborn 新出生的
- suckling 乳兒
- test-tube baby 試管嬰兒

---

speak - fess

兩者雖無字源上關係，但皆表示說的意思，不妨透過子音 p 和 f 互換、母音通轉，來協助記憶此字根。

---

confess

[kən`fɛs]

v 自白，承認

The suspect falsely confessed to having committed a notorious crime.

嫌犯虛偽自白犯下滔天大罪。

記憶技巧　con- 表示一起；fess- 表示說；confess 的意思是開誠佈公、大家一起說出來，引申為承認。

---

confession

[kən`fɛʃən]

n 自白，承認

The murderer refused to make a confession of his crime.

兇手拒絕認罪。

記憶技巧　-ion 為名詞字尾。

相關字彙
向警方或有關當局吐露訊息

- denounce 檢舉
- finger 告密
- frame 陷害
- inform on 告發
- snitch 打小報告

---

profession

[prə`fɛʃən]

n 職業，宣布

The young man intends to make photography his profession.

年輕人打算以攝影為業。

記憶技巧　pro- 表示往前；fess- 表示說；profess 的本意是對著前方說話，引申為公開宣稱；profession 是名詞形式，15 世紀時才有職業的意思。

---

professional

[prə`fɛʃənl]

a 專業的

The man finally became a high-earning professional photographer.

男子終於成為一名高所得的專業攝影師。

記憶技巧　profession 表示職業；-al 為形容詞字尾；professional 是職業的，引申為專業的。

professor

[prə`fɛsɚ]

n 教授

The lecturer is a professor of law at the University of Baltimore.

講者是巴爾的摩大學法學教授。

記憶技巧　profess 表示對著前方說話；-or 表示人；professor 是對著前方說話的人，引申為教授。

speak - fa

兩者雖無字源上關係，但皆表示說的意思，不妨透過子音 p 和 f 互換、母音通轉，來協助記憶此字根。

fable

[`febl̩]

n 寓言，神話，傳說

The news sounds like a mere fable.

消息聽起來只是無稽之談。

記憶技巧　fable 指的是說出來的內容、故事，寓言是衍生意思。

affable

[`æfəbl̩]

a 友善的，和藹的

The tour guide smiled an affable smile to every group member.

領隊和藹地對每一位團員微笑。

記憶技巧　af- 等同於 ad- 和 to；fable 表示說；affable 的本意是某人很好說話，引申為和藹可親的。

相關字彙
和藹可親

- amiable 和藹可親的
- bubbly 快活樂情的
- friendly 親切的
- good-natured 和藹的
- genuine 真誠的
- pleasant 令人愉快的（宜人的）
- welcoming 款待的
- warmhearted 慈愛的

fabulous

[`fæbjələs]

a 虛構的，荒謬的，傳說的

The gallery has a fabulous collection of contemporary African art.

美術館的當代非洲藝術作品典藏十分豐富。

記憶技巧　fabul- 等同於 fable；-ous 為形容詞字尾；fabulous 是充滿寓言、傳奇的意思，引申為虛構的、很棒的。

preface

[`prɛfɪs]

v 作為～的開端

The man prefaced his friend's wedding with a congratulatory message.

男子致賀詞為朋友的婚禮揭開序幕。

記憶技巧　pre- 表示前面；-face 表示說；preface 的意思是事先說，引申為序言，動詞意思是作為～的開端。

相關字彙
事件開端

- prelude 前奏
- precursor 前導
- antecedent 前事
- preamble 開場白

> ## speak - phon
> 兩者雖無字源上關係，但皆表示説的意思，不妨透過子音 p 和 ph 互換、母音通轉，來協助記憶此字根。

---

microphone

[`maɪkrəˌfon]

n 麥克風，擴音器

A multi-channel wireless microphone system will offer more than one microphone simultaneously.
多頻道無線麥克風系統同時提供多支麥克風。

記憶技巧　micro- 表示小；-phone 表示聲音；microphone 的本意是給有聽覺障礙、只能聽見微小聲音的人所配戴的喇叭狀助聽器，至於擴音器這個語意最早可追溯到 1929 年。

---

megaphone

[`mɛgəˌfon]

n 擴音器，話筒，大聲公

The coach raised the megaphone to his lips and spoke into it.
教練拿起擴音器到嘴唇說話。

記憶技巧　mega- 表示大；-phon 表示聲音；megaphone 的字面意思是大聲的，因此有大聲公、擴音器等意思。

---

symphony

[`sɪmfənɪ]

n 交響樂，交響曲

The typical symphony orchestra consists of four groups of musical instruments.
典型的交響樂團包括四組樂器。

記憶技巧　sym- 等同於 syn-，表示一起；phon- 表示聲音；-y 為名詞字尾；symphony 指的是搭配在一起的和諧聲音，引申為交響樂。

相關字彙　各類型音樂

- andante 徐緩調
- allegro 快板
- cantata 清唱劇
- chorus 合唱曲
- concerto 協奏曲
- fantasia 幻想曲
- medley 混合曲
- oratorio 清唱劇
- rhapsody 狂想曲
- sonata 奏鳴曲

---

euphonious

[ju`fonɪəs]

a 好聽的，悅耳的

The composer is trying to create euphonious effects for his new song.
作曲家努力創造新歌的悅耳效果。

記憶技巧　eu- 表示好；phon- 表示聲音；-ous 為形容詞字尾；euphonious 的意思是聲音好聽的、悅耳的。

---

cacophony

[kæ`kɑfənɪ]

n 噪音，聲音異常

There was a cacophony of screams from the fans when their favorite singer showed up.
最喜愛的歌手一現身，粉絲掀起一陣尖叫聲。

記憶技巧　caco- 表示壞的；phon- 表示聲音；-y 為名詞字尾；cacophony 的意思是難聽的聲音，衍生出噪音和不協和音的意思。

saxophone

[ˋsæksəˌfon]

n 薩克斯風

The manager played the saxophone at the year-end party.

經理在尾牙宴吹奏薩克斯風。

記憶技巧 saxophone 是由比利時人阿道夫・薩克斯（Antoine-Joseph Adolphe Sax,1814-1894）於 1840 年發明的，並用自己名字來命名這種新樂器。

---

appear - phan

兩者雖無字源關係，但兩者現今皆可表示出現、顯露，可藉由子音 p 和 ph 轉換、母音通轉，來記憶 phan 這個字根。

---

phantom

[ˋfæntəm]

n 幽靈，幻影

The sales manager was involved in a phantom accident at Christmas break.

業務經理耶誕假期遇上假車禍。

記憶技巧 phantom 指的是現身的鬼魂。

相關字彙
鬼魂精靈

• demon 惡魔
• devil 魔鬼
• doppelganger 酷似活人的幽靈
• ghost 鬼
• specter 幽靈
• spook 幽靈
• spirit 靈魂

---

diaphanous

[daɪˋæfənəs]

a 半透明的，朦朧的

The woman wears a diaphanous veil all the time.

那名女子總是披著半透明絲質面紗。

記憶技巧 dia- 表示穿透；phan- 表示出現或顯示；-ous 為形容詞字尾；diaphanous 的意思是視線穿透某物，隱約可見內部的東西，引申為半透明的、朦朧的。

---

phenomenon

[fəˋnɑməˌnɑn]

n 現象，奇跡，症候

Typhoons and tornadoes are both natural phenomena.

颱風及颶風都是自然現象。

記憶技巧 phen- 等同於 phan-，表示出現；phenomenon 的意思是現象。

---

fantastic

[fænˋtæstɪk]

a 空想的，怪異的，極大的

It is such a fantastic idea to raise a lion at home.

家裡養一頭獅子的想法好怪。

記憶技巧 fan- 等同於 phan-，表示出現；fantastic 的意思是出現在想像中的，引申為空想的。

fancy [ˈfænsɪ] **n** 幻想，嗜好	My nephew took a fancy to one of his classmates. 我姪子迷戀他的一位同學。 記憶技巧 fancy 是 fantasy 縮減形式，皆表示出現在想像中的事物，引申為幻想。
fanciful [ˈfænsɪfəl] **a** 富於想像力的， 幻想的，奇異的	There are several fanciful architectures in town. 鎮上有幾棟奇特建築。 記憶技巧 fancy 表示幻想；-ful 為形容詞字尾；fanciful 指幻想的。
emphasize [ˈɛmfəˌsaɪz] **v** 強調	The instructor emphasized the importance of risk management. 講師強調風險管理的重要。 記憶技巧 em- 等同於 en- 和 in，表示內部；phas- 等同於 phan-，表示顯現；-ize 為動詞字尾；emphasize 的意思是讓內部的重點顯現出來，引申為強調。

Section 11

〔m〕對應〔f〕

make - fac

兩者雖無字源關係，但皆表示做的意思，可藉由子音 m 和 f 轉換，母音通轉來記憶。

factory [ˈfæktərɪ] **n** 工廠	The poisonous gas was emitted from the chemical factory. 有毒氣體自化學工廠排出。 記憶技巧 fact- 表示做；-ory 表示地方；factory 是製作東西的場所，即工廠。

雙唇音、唇齒音轉換

facile
[`fæsl̩]

a 容易的，流暢的，溫和的

The consultant offered a facile solution to the complex problem.
針對該複雜問題，顧問提出一個簡易解決方式。

記憶技巧 fac- 表示做；-ile 為形容詞字尾；facile 的意思是容易做的，引申為容易的、流暢的。

facilitate
[fə`sɪlə,tet]

v 使容易，助長，促進

Expanding domestic demand may facilitate economic recovery.
擴大內需可加速振興經濟。

記憶技巧 facile 表示容易的；-ate 為動詞字尾；facilitate 的意思是使容易。

facilities
[fə`sɪlətɪs]

n 設備

The horse riding academy offers exceptional medical facilities to its students and staff members.
馬術學校提供學員及工作人員完善的醫療設施。

記憶技巧 facile 表示容易的；-ity 為名詞字尾；facility 的意思是容易、簡易；facilities 指的是可以帶給人們生活便利的設備、設施、工具等。

facsimile
[fæk`sɪməlɪ]

n 複製，傳真

The facsimile of the original manuscript is freely available to art majors.
藝術主修生可任意取得真跡複製。

記憶技巧 fac- 表示做；simile 和 similar 同源，表示相似；facsimile 的意思是做出相似的東西，指的是複製、傳真等。

faculty
[`fækl̩tɪ]

n 才能，機能，教職員

The gifted student has a great faculty for reasoning.
這名資優生推理能力很強。

記憶技巧 fac- 表示做；-ty 為名詞字尾；faculty 的意思是能輕易做完某項工作，引申為才能。

相關字彙
教職員工

- coach 教練
- headmaster 美國私立學校校長
- instructor 指導者
- principal 校長
- relief teacher 救援老師
- supply teacher 代課老師（英）
- substitute teacher 代課老師（美）
- teaching assistant 教學助理

affect
[ə`fɛkt]

v 影響，感動，假裝

The veteran was deeply affected by the documentary.
紀錄片深深感動了這位退伍軍人。

記憶技巧 af- 等同於 ad-，表示去；fect- 表示做；affect 表示去做某事使之發生作用，引申為影響、感動等。

affectionate
[ə`fɛkʃənɪt]
a 摯愛的，親切的

The preschool principal is affectionate with children all the time.
幼稚園園長對孩子的疼愛無片刻停歇。

> 記憶技巧　affection 指的是受外物影響，心中有所喜好；-ate 為形容詞字尾；因此，affectionate 有摯愛的意思。

confection
[kən`fɛkʃən]
n 蜜餞，糖果

The main ingredients of the confection are chocolate and milk.
糖果的主要成分是巧克力及牛奶。

> 記憶技巧　con- 表示一起；fect- 表示做；-ion 為名詞字尾；confection 的意思是添加各種材料製成的食物，如：蜜餞、糖果。

counterfeit
[`kauntɚ͵fɪt]
n 偽造物，冒牌貨

The counter used to sell counterfeit jewellery branded as Cartier.
專櫃曾販售冒牌卡地亞珠寶。

> 記憶技巧　counter- 表示相對；feit- 表示做；counterfeit 的意思是與正版物品相對立的贗品。

相關字彙
不法的

- illegal 不合法的
- unlawful 不合法的
- unauthorized 未被授權的
- illicit 不法的
- underhand 不正當的
- clandestine 祕密的

defect
[dɪ`fɛkt]
n 缺點，弱點，過失

Impatience is the trainee's chief defect.
急性子是實習生的主要缺點。

> 記憶技巧　de- 表示往下或離開；fect- 表示做；defect 的字面意思是愈做愈少，引申為缺點、過失。

deficient
[dɪ`fɪʃənt]
a 缺乏的，有缺點的

The couple's first child is mentally deficient.
這對夫婦的第一個孩子智力有缺陷。

> 記憶技巧　de- 表示往下或離開；fic- 等同於 fac-，表示做；-ent 為形容詞字尾；deficient 的意思是愈做愈少，引申為缺乏的、有缺點的。

difficult
[`dɪfə͵kəlt]
a 困難的，頑固的

It's difficult to persuade my parents to change their mind.
說服我父母改變心意很難。

> 記憶技巧　dif- 表示離開；ficul- 等同於 facile，表示容易的；difficult 的意思是不容易，即困難的。

efficiency
[ɪˋfɪʃənsɪ]
n 效能

The energy efficiency ratio is used to measure a room air conditioner's efficiency.
能源效能比率被用來測量房間空調效能。

記憶技巧 ef- 等同於 ex-，表示出來；fic- 等同於 fac-；-ency 為名詞字尾；efficiency 的意思是做出來，引申為效能。

efficient
[ɪˋfɪʃənt]
a 有效率的

The company managed to develop an efficient distribution network.
公司設法發展高效率的經銷網絡。

記憶技巧 -ent 為形容詞字尾。

infectious
[ɪnˋfɛkʃəs]
a 傳染的

Tuberculosis is an infectious disease caused by bacteria and most often found in the lungs.
結核病是細菌引起的傳染疾病，常見於肺部。

記憶技巧 in- 表示內；fect- 等同於 fact-，表示做；-ous 是形容詞字尾，infectious 的字面意思是在某對象的內部做了一些事，通常都指壞、負面的事情，因此衍生出汙染的、弄髒的等意思，後指傳染的。

相關字彙
描述疾病症狀的形容詞

- acute 急性的
- benign 良性的
- clinical 臨床的
- chronic 慢性的
- communicable 會傳染的
- congenital 先天的
- degenerative 退化的
- epidemic 流行病（的）
- inflammatory 炎症性的
- malignant 惡性的
- traumatic 創傷的

official
[əˋfɪʃəl]
a 正式的

The Prime Minister will pay an official visit to New Zealand.
總理即將正式訪問紐西蘭。

記憶技巧 of- 等同於 opus，表示工作；fic- 等同於 fac-，表示做；-ial 為形容詞；official 字面上的意思是做工作的，因為是工作，並非休閒娛樂，因此又衍生出正式的等意思。

perfect
[ˋpɝfɪkt]
a 完美的，熟練的

The weather is perfect for hiking on natural trails.
這天氣到大自然小徑健行再適合不過了。

記憶技巧 per- 表示完全地；fect- 等同於 fact-，表示做；perfect 的意思是完全做到好，引申為完美的。

proficiency
[prəˋfɪʃənsɪ]
n 熟練，精通

The district manager is trying to attain a high level of proficiency in Japanese.
區經理不斷努力達到日文精熟程度。

記憶技巧 pro- 表示往前；fic- 等同於 fac-，做；-ency 為名詞字尾；proficiency 的意思是可以很順暢往下做，引申為熟練、精通。

Part **2**

CH 1

雙唇音、唇齒音轉換

profit [ˋprɑfɪt] **n** 利益	My landlord made a profit of one million NT dollars on her apartment. 我的房東賣掉公寓，賺了一百萬元。 記憶技巧 pro- 表示往前；fit- 表示做，即一直做所產生的結果，引申為獲利。
sufficient [səˋfɪʃənt] **a** 足夠的，充分的	There isn't sufficient evidence to convict the suspect. 罪證不足，無法將嫌犯定罪。 記憶技巧 suf- 等同於 sub-，表示到達；fic- 等同於 fac-，表示做；-ent 為形容詞字尾；sufficient 的意思是做到足夠的程度，因此有充分的、足夠的意思。

Section **12**

〔v〕對應〔f〕

love - phil

兩者並無字源關係，但皆表示愛。我們可將 phil 倒過來拼字，形成 liph 的組合，和 love 相對照，藉由 v 和 ph 互換、母音通轉的概念，來記憶 phil 的意思。

philosophy [fəˋlɑsəfɪ] **n** 哲學，人生觀，宗旨	High school students should be encouraged to read widely in philosophy. 應鼓勵高中生廣泛閱讀哲學領域書籍。 記憶技巧 phil- 表示愛；-sophy 表示智慧；philosophy 即愛智之學，哲學是一門愛智之學。
philosopher [fəˋlɑsəfɚ] **n** 哲學家，思想家	Socrates and Plato were both Greek philosophers. 蘇格拉底及柏拉圖都是希臘哲學家。 記憶技巧 -er 表示人；philosopher 指哲學家。

philanthropist
[fɪˋlænθrəpɪst]
n 慈善家

The philanthropist donated a substantial sum of money to the charitable institution.
慈善家捐一大筆錢給慈善機構。

記憶技巧 phil- 表示愛；anthrop- 表示人；-ist 表示者；philanthropist 指愛人者，引申為慈善家。

bibliophile
[ˋbɪblɪəˏfaɪl]
n 愛書人，藏書家

The classic bibliophile amasses a large and specialized collection.
典型愛書人累積大量專業藏書。

記憶技巧 bibio- 表示書；-phile 表示愛〜的人；bibiophile 即愛書之人。

相關字彙
熱愛各類型活動的人
- aesthete 審美家
- amateur 業餘從事者
- Anglophile 親英派的人
- bookworm 書呆子
- night owl 很晚睡覺的人
- masochist 被虐待狂者

philharmonic
[ˏfɪləˋmɑnɪk]
a 愛好音樂的

The manager is philharmonic, and he attends concerts very often.
經理是愛樂人士，經常出席音樂會。

記憶技巧 phil- 表示愛；harmony 表示和諧的音樂；-ic 為形容詞字尾；philharmonic 的意思是愛好音樂的。

Section **13**

〔b〕對應〔v〕

---

belly - ventri

兩者雖無字源關係，但皆表示腹部，可藉由子音 b 和 v 互換，l 和 n 互換，l 和 t 互換，母音通轉來記憶。

ventriloquist
[vɛnˋtrɪləkwɪst]
n 腹語表演者

A couple of ventriloquists particiapted in the national talent contest.
有幾位腹語表演者參加全國才藝競賽。

記憶技巧 ventri- 表示腹部；loqu- 表示說；-ist 表示者；ventriloquist 的意思是表演腹語的人。

Section 14

〔p〕對應〔v〕

pull - vuls

兩者雖無字源關係，但皆表示拉、拔，可藉由子音 p 和 v 互換，母音通轉來記憶。

---

avulsion
[ə`vʌlʃən]
n 撕裂，裂片

There is an avulsion fracture in the region of the wrist joint.
肘關節處有一撕裂骨折。

記憶技巧　a- 等同於 ab-，表示離開；vuls- 表示猛力拉；-ion 為名詞字尾；avulsion 的意思是猛力拉，引申為撕裂。

---

convulsion
[kən`vʌlʃən]
n 動亂，痙攣，抽蓄

The athlete's feet went into convulsions and he was pulled out of the competition.
運動員因腳抽蓄而退出比賽。

記憶技巧　con- 表示一起；vuls- 表示猛力拉；-ion 為名詞字尾；convulsion 的意思是大家一起猛力拉，引申為動亂。

相關字彙
身體（部位）不受控制

- fidget 坐立不安
- jerk 痙攣
- shiver 發抖
- shudder 發抖
- twitch 使痙攣

---

evulsion
[ɪ`vʌlʃən]
n 拔出

The patient was injected with narcotics before nerve evulsion.
抽神經前，病患注射麻藥。

記憶技巧　e- 等同於 ex- 表示外面；vuls- 表示猛力拉；-ion 為名詞字尾；evulsion 的意思是往外拉出，引申為拔出。

原來如此！

plus 意思是加上，加上之後成了複數—— plural；plus 與 plural 同源。plus 的相反詞 minus 意思是減去，也就是變小；menu（菜單）上寫的是菜餚說明及價格等細節，同樣有小的意思，因此與 minus 同源。

Section 15

〔m〕對應〔p〕

many - poly

兩者雖無字源關係，但皆表示多，可透過子音 m 和 p 互換、子音 n 和 l 互換、母音通轉來記憶。

---

polygon

[ˋpɑlɪˏɡɑn]

n 多角形

相關字彙
各種形體

Triangles and rectangles are polygons.

三角形及長方形是多角形。

記憶技巧　poly- 表示多；gon- 表示角；polygon 的意思是多角形。

- cube 立方體
- cuboid 立方形的
- diamond 菱形
- flare 呈喇叭形展開
- lozenge 菱形
- pyramid 角錐（體）
- trapezium 不規則四邊形
- trapezoid 不規則四邊形

---

polyhedron

[ˏpɑlɪˋhidrən]

n 多面體

The pyramid is a polyhedron.

金字塔是多面體。

記憶技巧　poly- 表示多；-hedron 表示基座或面；polyhedron 的意思是多面體。

---

polyandry

[ˋpɑlɪˏændrɪ]

n 一妻多夫

Polyandry is so much in practice in Tibet.

一妻多夫在西藏非常盛行。

記憶技巧　poly- 表示多；andr- 表示男人；-y 為名詞字尾；polyandry 的意思是多個男人，引申為一妻多夫。

---

polygamous

[pəˋlɪɡəməs]

a 一夫多妻的
（或一妻多夫的）

相關字彙
婚姻關係

Men are not limited to a single wife in a polygamous society.

男子在一夫多妻社會不限擁有一名妻子。

記憶技巧　poly- 表示多；gam- 表示婚姻；-ous 為形容詞字尾；polygamous 的意思是結過多次婚姻，引申為一夫多妻或一妻多夫。

- antenuptial 結婚前的
- civil union 民事結合
- conjugal 結婚的
- connubial 夫婦的
- matrimony 夫婦關係
- marriage of convenience 有企圖的（政治）婚姻
- mixed marriage 異族通婚

mold - plas

兩者雖無字源關係，但皆表示塑形，可透過子音 m 和 p 互換、子音 d 和 s 互換、母音通轉來記憶。

plasma
[`plæzmə]

n 血漿，原生質

| 相關字彙 |
心臟、血液、循環

Plasma forms 55% of the total volume of human blood.
血漿佔人類血液容量 55%。

記憶技巧 原指塑形的意思，到 1845 年才有血漿的意思。

- aorta 主動脈
- artery 動脈
- blood clot 血栓
- blood pressure 血壓
- blood sugar 血糖
- cardiac arrest 心搏停止
- coronary 冠狀動脈的
- corpuscle 血球
- heart failure 心臟衰竭
- pulse 脈搏

plaster
[`plæstɚ]

n 灰泥，
（黏貼的）膏藥

I applied a plaster on a cut on my ankle.
我在腳踝割傷處抹上藥膏。

記憶技巧 原指塑形，後來才有灰泥和膏藥的意思。

Section **16**

〔f〕對應〔v〕

---

folk - vulg

兩者雖無字源關係，但皆有群眾、通俗等意思，可藉由子音 f 和 v 互換、k 和 g 互換、母音通轉來記憶。

vulgar
[`vʌlgɚ]

a 粗俗的

The former president is leading a vulgar life in his hometown.
前任總統在家鄉過著平民的生活。

記憶技巧 vulg- 表示通俗的；vulgar 的意思是粗俗的、平民的。

vulgarian

[vʌlˈɡɛrɪən]

n 粗俗的富人，
暴發戶

The customer talks and acts like a vulgarian.
客人談吐舉止像個暴發戶。

記憶技巧 vulg- 表示通俗的；-ian 表示人；vulgarian 的意思是有錢而財大氣粗的人，引申為粗俗暴發戶。

different - var

兩者雖無字源關係，但字根 var 即表示改變、不同，透過子音 f 和 v 互換，母音通轉，用 different 來記憶 var 的意思。

vary

[ˈvɛrɪ]

v 變化，多樣化，
不同

The financial statement forms vary greatly in layout.
財務報表版面編排大不相同。

記憶技巧 var- 表示改變；vary 指變化。

variable

[ˈvɛrɪəbl̩]

a 可變的，易變的

The business currently has a loan for ten million US dollars at a variable interest rate.
目前該公司以可變利率貸款一千萬美元。

記憶技巧 vary 表示變化；-able 為形容詞字尾；variable 的意思是易變的。

various

[ˈvɛrɪəs]

a 不同的，多樣的

The bio-tech company went bankrupt for various reasons.
由於諸多原因，生技公司破產了。

記憶技巧 vary 表示變化；-ous 為形容詞字尾，various 的意思是變化多樣的。

variety

[vəˈraɪətɪ]

n 變化，多樣化，
品種

Crops provide a wide variety of foods for the human population.
穀物提供人類種類繁多的食物。

記憶技巧 vary 表示變化；-ty 為名詞字尾；variety 的意思是變化、多樣化。

相關字彙
差異

- difference 差別
- contrast 對比
- distinction 差別
- diversity 差異
- contradiction 矛盾
- divergence 分歧

variform

[ˈvɛrɪˌfɔrm]

a 多種形態的

The variform creature was found in the bottom of sea.
海底發現多種形態的生物。

記憶技巧 vary- 表示改變；form- 表示形狀；variform 的意思是多種形態的。

---

brief - brev

子音 f 和 v 互換，母音通轉，兩者皆表示短、小、淺等意思。

---

abbreviation

[əˌbrivɪˈeʃən]

n 省略，縮寫，約分

Pop is the abbreviation for the word population.
Pop 是人口的縮寫。

記憶技巧 ab- 表示往～方向；brev- 表示短；-ation 為名詞字尾；abbreviation 的意思是縮寫。

---

brevity

[ˈbrɛvətɪ]

n 簡潔，短暫

Effective statements should have clarity and brevity.
有效陳述應該明確而簡短。

記憶技巧 brev- 表示短；-ity 為名詞字尾；brevity 的意思是簡潔。

---

brief

[brif]

a 簡短的

The president-elect delivered a brief speech to thank voters for their support.
總統當選人發表簡短演講，感謝選民支持。

記憶技巧 brief 等同於 brev-，表示短的。

---

briefly

[ˈbriflɪ]

ad 簡潔地，短暫地

The trade mission stopped off briefly in Singapore on their way to Australia.
貿易訪問團前往澳洲時在新加坡短暫停留。

記憶技巧 -ly 為副詞字尾。

---

abridge

[əˈbrɪdʒ]

v 削減，縮短

The mayor will abridge his stay in Europe and return as soon as possible.
市長將縮短歐洲停留時間，盡快回國。

記憶技巧 a- 等同於 ab-，表示往～方向；-bridge 等同於 brief，表示短；abridge 是縮短的意思。

相關字彙
編輯、改編、校對

- bowdlerize 刪節
- censor 審查
- condense 濃縮
- interpolate 竄改
- proofread 校對
- expurgate 刪去（不當處）

lift - lev

lift 是提的意思，lev- 是輕、升起，兩者雖無字源關係，藉由子音 f 和 v 互換，母音通轉，可聯想為東西輕，容易提起或上升。

---

leverage

[ˈlɛvərɪdʒ]

🔵 槓桿作用，手段

With leverage, the investor purchased futures contracts in agriculture products.

透過手段，投資客買進農產品期貨。

記憶技巧 lev- 表示輕；-age 為名詞字尾；leverage 的意思是藉由槓桿作用，輕鬆移動重物。

---

levity

[ˈlɛvətɪ]

🔵 輕浮，輕率

After the solemn meeting, Tony finally got a brief moment of levity.

嚴肅會議結束，湯尼終於得以片刻喘息。

記憶技巧 lev- 表示輕；-ity 為名詞字尾；levity 是輕浮的，缺乏莊重、嚴肅的感覺。

---

levy

[ˈlɛvɪ]

🔵 徵收，徵稅

The unoccupied housing tax will be levied on real estate investors.

房地產投資客將被徵收空屋稅。

記憶技巧 levy 原意是提起，引申為徵稅。

相關字彙
稅務

- audit 查帳
- deductible 可減免的
- duty-free 免關稅的
- overtax 對～課稅過重
- tax dodge 逃稅
- tax shelter 減免所得稅的合法手段

---

alleviate

[əˈlivɪˌet]

🔵 減輕痛苦，緩和

Some vegetables can help alleviate dysmenorrhea.

一些蔬菜有助於舒緩經痛。

記憶技巧 al- 表示朝～方向；lev- 表示輕；-ate 為動詞字尾；alleviate 的意思是減輕（痛苦）。

---

elevate

[ˈɛləˌvet]

🔵 舉起，提升，鼓舞

The clerk has been elevated to the position of section chief.

該職員已擢升為科長。

記憶技巧 e- 等同於 ex-，表示外；lev- 表示提起；-ate 為動詞字尾；elevate 的意思是提起某物，使之離開原本的位置。

---

elevator

[ˈɛləˌvetɚ]

🔵 升降機，電梯

The entertainer's luxury house has both elevators and escalators.

那名藝人的豪宅配備電梯及電扶梯。

記憶技巧 elevate 加上 -or 成為 elevator，指升降梯、電梯，可使人和物移動位置。

relevant [ˋrɛləvənt] **a** 有關的，中肯的	The applicant's work experience is highly relevant to this position. 申請者的工作經驗與該職務非常相關。 記憶技巧 re- 表示加強語氣；lev- 表示輕；-ant 為形容詞字尾；relevant 的字面意思是使～變輕的，引申為中肯的、有關的。
relief [rɪˋlif] **n** 救助，解除， 減壓，安慰 相關字彙 捐錢、救助	After annual inventory, the manager felt an incredible sense of relief. 年度盤點告一段落，經理大大鬆了一口氣。 記憶技巧 re- 表示加強語氣；lev- 等同於 lief-，表示輕；relief 的意思是減輕、減壓。 • alms 救濟（品）　　　　• endowment（基金、財產等的）捐贈 • community service 無償服務　• patronize 贊助 • donation 捐贈　　　　　• sponsor 贊助
relieve [rɪˋliv] **v** 解救，安慰，減輕	The patient was given a shot of analgesic to relieve the pain. 患者挨了一針止痛劑以舒緩疼痛。 記憶技巧 relieve 是 relief 的動詞形式。

原來如此！

else 意思是其他的，同源字 alien 意思是外國人、外國的，語意易於聯想；另一同源字 alibi 可表示不在犯罪現場的證明，也就是當時人在其他地方，與犯罪事件無關。

Chapter 2
雙唇音、唇齒音轉換

〔w〕、〔v〕（含 w / u / v 字母通轉）

Section 1 〔w〕對應〔v〕

Section 2 字母「w」對應字母「u」

〔w〕對應〔v〕

wall - vall

子音 w 和 v 互換，母音通轉，兩者皆表示牆。

interval
[ˋɪntɚvl̩]
n 間隔，距離

The attending doctor will make a ward round at variable intervals.
主治醫師將不定時巡視病房。

(記憶技巧) inter- 表示介於～之間；val- 等同於 wall，表示牆；interval 的意思是介於兩道牆之間的距離，引申成間隔。

will - vol

子音 w 和 v 互換，母音通轉，兩者皆表示決心、意志。

voluntary
[ˋvɑlən͵tɛrɪ]
a 自願的，自動的，故意的

The jury found the suspect guilty of voluntary manslaughter of the woman.
陪審團判決嫌犯蓄意殺害婦人有罪。

(記憶技巧) vol- 等同於 will，表示意志；-ary 為形容詞字尾；voluntary 的意思是自願的、故意的。

involuntary
[ɪnˋvɑlən͵tɛrɪ]
a 無心的，非本意的

The new operating regulation will significantly decrease the risk of involuntary injury.
新操作規則將大幅減低意外傷害風險。

(記憶技巧) in- 為否定字首；involuntary 表示非出自本意的。

volunteer
[͵vɑlənˋtɪr]
n 志願者

My niece signed her name on the list of volunteers.
我姪女在義工名單上簽名。

(記憶技巧) vol- 等同於 will，表示意志；-er 為名詞字尾，表示人；volunteer 表示志願者。

volition
[vo`lıʃən]
n 意志，意欲

The singer left the idol group of her own volition.
歌手自願離開偶像團體。

記憶技巧 vol- 等同於 will，表示意志；-ion 為名詞字尾；volition 表示意志。

volitional
[vo`lıʃən!]
a 意志的，意欲的

The behavior is believed to be under volitional control.
一般相信這是意志控制下的行為。

記憶技巧 -al 為形容詞字尾。

worm - verm
子音 w 和 v 互換，母音通轉，兩者皆表示蟲。

vermicide
[`vɝmɪͺsaɪd]
n 殺蟲劑（藥）

The doctor used vermicide to get rid of roundworms in the boy's intestines.
醫師使用除蟲劑清除男孩腸子裡的蛔蟲。

記憶技巧 verm- 等同於 worm，表示蟲；cid-，表示殺；vermicide 指殺蟲劑。

vermivorous
[vɝ`mɪvərəs]
a 食蟲的

Some species of snail are vermivorous and eat small insects.
一些種類的蝸牛是食蟲性，會吃小昆蟲。

記憶技巧 verm- 等同於 worm；vor-，表示吃；-ous 為形容詞字尾；vermivorous 表示吃蟲的。

wine - vin
子音 w 和 v 互換，母音通轉，wine 現今的意思是酒，vin- 是藤、葡萄樹，兩者系出同源，原始意思皆是酒。

vine
[vaın]
n 藤蔓

Winter jasmine is a type of vine in the olive family.
迎春花是木樨科中的一種藤蔓植物。

記憶技巧 vin- 表示藤蔓。

vinegar

[ˋvɪnɪgɚ]

n 醋

The garlic has been dipped in vinegar for three days.
蒜頭在醋裡浸泡三天了。

記憶技巧　vin- 表示酒；-egar 表示酸。其緣由是工人在釀造葡萄酒時，不小心將葡萄酒遺留於橡木桶，等他發現時，葡萄酒已經發酸。

相關字彙
調味品

- broth（清淡的）湯
- dip 調味汁
- dressing（拌沙拉用的）調料
- gravy 肉汁
- ketchup 調味番茄醬
- mayonnaise 美乃滋
- soy sauce 醬油

---

wagon - veh

子音 w 和 v 互換，母音通轉，兩者皆表示藉由交通工具運輸、移動。

---

vehicle

[ˋviɪkl̩]

n 車輛，傳播媒介

Air is the vehicle of sound.
空氣是聲音的傳播媒介。

記憶技巧　veh- 表示運輸；vehicle 指車輛。

相關字彙
交通、運輸工具

- amphibian 水陸兩用車
- boneshaker 要散架似的破車
- carrier 航空母艦
- escort 護航艦
- flyer（快車、快速巴士等）高速交通工具
- hybrid vehicle 混合動力車輛
- racer 比賽用的汽車
- three-wheeler 三輪車
- two-seater 雙座汽車（或飛機等）

---

convection

[kənˋvɛkʃən]

n 對流

The sun transfers the energy from the core towards the outermost region in the convection zone.
太陽將能量從對流層核心傳送到最外層。

記憶技巧　con- 表示一起；vect- 表示運輸；-ion 為名詞字尾；convection 表示把東西運輸過來聚在一起，在物理學上有對流的意思。

相關字彙
自然科學、物理化學

- air resistance 空氣阻力
- attraction 引力
- chain reaction 連鎖反應
- centrifugal force 離心力
- centripetal force 向心力
- condensation 凝結
- diffraction（光線、電波等的）衍射
- elasticity 彈性
- equilibrium 平衡
- impetus 衝力
- irradiation 輻射
- magnetism 磁力
- surface tension 表面張力
- velocity 速率
- evaporation 蒸發

---

invective

[ɪnˋvɛktɪv]

n 辱罵

The woman uttered a stream of invective against her neighbor.
婦人對鄰居一陣謾罵。

記憶技巧　in- 表示相反、對抗；vect- 表示運輸；-ive 為形容詞字尾；invective 指帶東西來對抗～，引申出攻擊的、謾罵的意思，名詞的意思有辱罵、咒罵等。

waste - vast

子音 w 和 v 互換，母音通轉，字根 vast 的意思是大量的、荒涼的、空白的，waste 現今的意思是浪費，原始意思是留大量空白沒運用，而造成浪費。

vast

[væst]

a 廣闊的，浩瀚的，廣大的

The vast majority of the residents attended the marathon competition.
大多數居民參加馬拉松比賽。

記憶技巧　vast 即大的、廣闊的。

devastate

[ˋdɛvəsˌtet]

v 使荒蕪，破壞，蹂躪

The earthquake devastated a large part of the historic spot.
地震毀損歷史景點的一大部分。

記憶技巧　de- 表示完全地；vast- 表示大量的、廣闊的；-ate 為動詞字尾；devastate 的意思是使～完全留白，引申出使荒蕪、破壞的意思。

wish - vener

子音 w 和 v 互換，母音通轉，兩者皆表示渴望。vener- 另有愛、美、慾望的意思，可藉由愛神、美神 Venus（維納斯女神）來記憶。

venerable

[ˋvɛnərəbḷ]

a 可尊敬的，神聖的，珍貴的

The venerable tradition can be traced to medieval times.
神聖傳統可追溯至中古時期。

記憶技巧　vener- 表示愛；-able 為形容詞字尾；venerable 的意思是值得被愛的，引申為可尊敬的。

venerate

[ˋvɛnəˌret]

v 尊敬，崇敬

Winston Churchill was a publicly venerated politician of the twentieth century.
溫斯頓‧邱吉爾是二十世紀眾所敬重的政治家。

記憶技巧　vener- 表示愛；-ate 為動詞字尾；venerate 的意思是去愛～，引申為崇敬、尊敬。

venereal

[vəˋnɪrɪəl]

a 性愛的，引起性慾的

The young man is suffering from the venereal disease.
年輕人正受性病之苦。

記憶技巧　可藉由 Venus 愛神、美神，執掌生育的概念來記憶性愛的、引起性慾的等意思。

(for) ward - vers

forward 的意思是往前轉，vers- 是轉，透過子音 w 和 v 互換，母音通轉來記憶 vers- 轉的意思。

---

version

[ˋvɝʒən]

n 翻譯，譯本，版本

The Revised Version of the New Testament was published in 1881.
修訂版新約聖經出版於 1881 年。

記憶技巧　vers- 表示轉；-ion 為名詞字尾；version 指的是轉換成另一樣式，引申為譯本、版本。

---

versatile

[ˋvɝsətl]

a 多才多藝的，
多方面的

My uncle is a very versatile entertainer.
我叔叔是一位非常多才多藝的藝人。

記憶技巧　vers- 表示轉；-ile 為形容詞字尾；versatile 的意思是能夠周旋在各種任務、主題之間，引申為多才多藝的。

---

vertical

[ˋvɝtɪkl]

a 垂直的，直立的，
頂點的

相關字彙
直的

The X-axis is vertical with the Y-axis.
X 軸與 Y 軸垂直。

記憶技巧　vert- 表示轉；-ical 為形容詞字尾；本意是轉到頭頂上方的，因此有頂點的、直立等意思。

- straight 筆直的
- upright 挺直的
- perpendicular 垂直的
- erect 垂直的

---

avert

[əˋvɝt]

v 談論，轉移

The Ministry of Labor has endeavored to avert the strike.
勞動部竭力化解罷工活動。

記憶技巧　a- 等同於 ab- / away，表示離開；vert- 表示轉；avert 的意思是轉開。

---

aversion

[əˋvɝʃən]

n 嫌惡，嫌惡對象

The editor has a deep aversion to plagiarism.
編輯極度厭惡抄襲。

記憶技巧　a- 等同於 ab-，表示離開；vers- 表示轉；-ion 為名詞字尾；aversion 字面上是轉開，亦即因厭惡而轉開。

---

adverse

[ædˋvɝs]

a 逆的，不利的

The anti-cancer drug continued to receive adverse publicity about its side effects.
抗癌藥物副作用的負面報導持續發酵。

記憶技巧　ad- 表示朝向；vers- 表示轉；adverse 是轉過去面對著面，表示面對逆境、或遭逢不利處境。

adversary

[`ædvɚˌsɛrɪ]

n 對手

Sam and his mother-in-law became adversaries after he divorced his wife.

和太太離異後，山姆與岳母之間的關係勢同水火。

記憶技巧 ad- 表示朝向；vers- 表示轉；-ary 在此當名詞字尾；
adversary 是逆境中所面對的對手。

adversity

[əd`vɝsətɪ]

n 逆境，災難

The mentor told me not to be impetuous in times of adversity.

導師要我逆境時不要躁進。

記憶技巧 -ity 為名詞字尾；adversity 是 adverse 的名詞。

advertising

[`ædvɚˌtaɪzɪŋ]

n （總稱）廣告

The consultant suggested that the annual expenditure on advertising be reduced.

顧問提議削減年度廣告經費。

記憶技巧 ad- 表示朝向；vert- 表示轉；-ise 為動詞字尾；advertising
即是將某人注意力導至某對象上，引申為廣告。

相關字彙
各類型廣告

- banner 橫幅廣告
- billboard 廣告牌
- classified ad 分類廣告
- commercial（電視、廣播中的）商業廣告
- flyer（廣告）傳單
- junk mail 垃圾郵件
- poster 海報
- trailer 電影預告片
- want ad（報紙上）
  徵聘廣告

convert

[`kɑnvɝt]

n 改變信仰者

Ted, a recent convert to Judaism, took a trip with his wife to Jerusalem.

最近改信猶太教的泰德跟老婆同遊耶路撒冷。

記憶技巧 con- 表示一起；vert- 表示轉；convert 是宗教信仰上轉變
的人，即改變信仰者。

controversial

[ˌkɑntrə`vɝʃəl]

a 爭論的，好爭論的

Students are encouraged to express opinions on the controversial issue.

學生受鼓勵針對爭論議題表達意見。

記憶技巧 contro- 表示對抗；vers- 表示轉；-ial 為形容詞字尾；
controversial 是轉過來對抗的，引申為爭論的。

conversation

[ˌkɑnvɚ`seʃən]

n 會話，談話

Hank got into a conversation with his previous colleague at the party.

漢克在派對和前同事聊起來。

記憶技巧 con- 表示一起；vers- 表示轉；-ation 為名詞字尾；
conversation 的原始意思是每天一起打轉，即每天一起生
活，直到 1570 年代才有聊天的意思。

Part
2
CH 1
CH 2

雙唇音、唇齒音轉換

diverse

[daɪ`vɝs]

a 不同的，
多種多樣的

London is a very ethnically diverse metropolis.
倫敦是一個種族非常多樣的大都會。

記憶技巧 di- 等同於 de-，表示離開；vers- 表示轉；diverse 的意思
是轉開，因此有分開、不同等意思。

---

diversion

[daɪ`vɝʒən]

n 轉向，娛樂

The baby-sitter created a diversion to distract the child's attention.
保姆製造機會轉移小孩的注意。

記憶技巧 di- 等同於 de-，表示離開；vers- 表示轉；-ion 為名詞字
尾；diversion 的意思是從工作中轉開，引申為娛樂。

相關字彙
休閒娛樂

- amusement 娛樂
- distraction 娛樂
- entertainment 娛樂
- frolic 嬉戲

---

divorce

[də`vors]

n 離婚，分離

The former beauty queen's marriage ended in divorce.
前選美皇后的婚姻以離婚收場。

記憶技巧 di- 等同於 de-，表示離開；vorc- 等同於 vers-，表示轉；
divorce 的意思是丈夫、太太轉身離開，引申離婚、分離。

---

extrovert

[`ɛkstrovɝt]

n 外向的人

My partner is a nice guy with an extrovert personality.
我的夥伴是個外向性格的好人。

記憶技巧 extro- 等同於 extra-，表示外面；vert- 表示轉；extrovert
字面上的意思是在外打轉的人，亦即外向的人。

相關字彙
有自信或自大傲慢的

- know-all 假裝或自稱無所不知的
- prig 自命不凡的人
- prima donna（尤指女性）自負的人
- snob 自負傲慢的人
- tin god 自大專橫的人
- wise guy 自命不凡的人

---

introvert

[`ɪntrə,vɝt]

n 內向的人

My nephew is an introvert.
我姪子是個內向的人。

記憶技巧 intro- 表示內部；vert- 表示轉；introvert 是指想法都在腦
內打轉的人，亦即內向的人。

---

reverse

[rɪ`vɝs]

a 相反的，倒轉的，
反面的

The plumber turned the handle in the reverse direction to close the valve.
水管工反向轉手把，關掉活門。

記憶技巧 re- 表示後面；vers- 表示轉；reverse 的意思是轉到後面，
引申為相反的、反面的。

wag - vibro

兩者雖無字源上關係，但可藉由子音 w 和 v 互換、母音通轉來記憶，兩者皆表示搖擺。

vibrate

[ˋvaɪbret]

v 振動

The fraud victim's voice vibrated with agitation.

詐騙受害者激動到聲音顫抖。

記憶技巧　vibr- 表示搖擺；-ate 為動詞字尾；vibrate 即擺動或震動。

vibration

[vaɪˋbreʃən]

n 振動，激動，猶豫

We could feel the vibration on the floor from loud pop music.

我們感覺到熱門音樂造成地板震動。

記憶技巧　vibration 是 vibrate 的名詞。

weave - veil

兩者雖無字源上關係，但可藉由子音 w 和 v 互換，母音通轉來記憶，兩者皆表示編織，veil 另有面紗的意思。

reveal

[rɪˋvil]

v 展現，顯露出

The manager's assistant revealed the trade secret by accident.

經理的助理意外洩露商業機密。

記憶技巧　re- 表示相反；veal- 等同於 veil-，表示面紗；reveal 即揭露面紗，引申為展現、顯露出。

相關字彙
給予他人訊息

- announce 宣布
- broadcast 廣播
- disclose 透露
- disseminate 宣傳
- put out 發表
- reveal 揭露
- spread 傳播
- trumpet 大聲宣告（或說出）

unveil

[ʌnˋvel]

v 除去～的面紗，揭露

The memorial to those who had died in the air crash was unveiled by the governor.

空難往生者紀念碑由州長揭幕。

記憶技巧　un- 表示相反；veil- 表示面紗；unveil 即除去面紗，引申為揭露。

相關字彙
公開或正式宣布

- announce 宣布
- address 對～說話
- bring forward 提出
- declare 宣告
- issue 發布
- proclaim 宣告
- pronounce 宣稱

word - verb

子音 w 和 v 互換，母音通轉，兩者皆表示説、文字。

---

verb

[vɝb]

n 動詞

Linking verbs are followed by phrases which offer extra information about the subject.

連綴動詞後面是與提供主詞的額外訊息的片語。

記憶技巧 verb 14 世紀從古法文進入英語，特指動詞這一詞類。

---

verbal

[ˋvɝbl̩]

a 言語的，口頭的，逐字的

The clerk kept a copy of the verbal translation of the document on record.

書記員保留一份逐字翻譯文件作為紀錄。

記憶技巧 verb- 表示説；-al 為形容詞字尾；verbal 的意思是口語的。

---

nonverbal

[ˌnɑnˋvɝbl̩]

a 非言語的

Body language and tone of voice are both forms of nonverbal communication.

肢體語言及聲調都是非言語溝通形式。

記憶技巧 non- 表示否定字；verbal 表示語言的；nonverbal 即非語言的。

---

verbatim

[vɝˋbetɪm]

a 逐字報告的

The secretariat provided a verbatim account of the proceedings of the conference.

祕書處逐字記錄大會議項。

記憶技巧 verb- 表示文字；-atim 為形容詞字尾；verbatim 即逐字的。

---

adverb

[ˋædvɝb]

n 副詞

An adverb is a word which modifies a verb, an adjective, another adverb or a sentence.

副詞修飾動詞、形容詞、另一副詞或句子。

記憶技巧 ad- 表示朝～方向；verb 表示動詞；adverb 字面上的意思是添加到動詞上的字，即副詞，因副詞可修飾動詞。

---

proverb

[ˋprɑvɝb]

n 諺語，箴言

"An apple a day keeps the doctor away" is an old proverb.

「一天一蘋果，遠離醫生不用愁。」是一則古老諺語。

記憶技巧 pro- 表示前；verb- 表示話語；proverb 即大家常説出來的話，引申為諺語、箴言。

相關字彙

慣用語和常用表達法

- adage 格言
- aphorism 警句
- axiom 格言
- catchphrase 標語
- cliché 陳詞濫調
- idiom 慣用語
- saying 格言

wade - vad

子音 w 和 v 互換、母音通轉，兩者皆表示走。

---

invade
[ɪn`ved]

v 侵略，侵襲

The famous entertainer's privacy has been invaded by paparazzi.

知名藝人的隱私已遭狗仔侵犯。

記憶技巧　in- 表示內；vad- 表示走；invade 即走進來，引申為侵略。

---

invasion
[ɪn`veʒən]

n 侵略

相關字彙
侵略佔領

There will be an annual invasion of tourists in this resort next month.

下個月該度假勝地將出現一年一度的觀光熱潮。

記憶技巧　-ion 為名詞字尾；invasion 為 invade 的名詞。

- occupy 佔領
- suppress 鎮壓
- seize 奪取
- conquer 攻克
- annex 併吞
- besiege 圍攻

---

invasive
[ɪn`vesɪv]

a 侵入的，侵略性的

Joint replacement surgery is an invasive treatment with attendant risks.

關節置換術是有風險的侵入性治療。

記憶技巧　-ive 為形容詞字尾；invasive 為 invade 的形容詞。

---

evade
[ɪ`ved]

v 逃避

To evade taxes, many businesses choose to set up an offshore company.

為了避稅，許多企業選擇設立境外公司。

記憶技巧　e- 等同於 ex-，表示外；vad- 表示走；evade 即往外走，引申為逃避。

---

evasive
[ɪ`vesɪv]

a 逃避的，難以捉摸的

By the time the rock fell down from the mountain, it was too late for the tour guide to take evasive action.

岩石自山上落下之前，領隊要疏散就來不及了。

記憶技巧　-ive 為形容詞字尾；evasive 為 evade 的形容詞。

---

pervade
[pɚ`ved]

v 遍布

There is a smell of fresh durian pervading the atmosphere in the market.

市集空氣彌漫新鮮榴槤的氣味。

記憶技巧　per- 表示穿透；vad- 表示走；pervade 字面意思是走透透，引申為遍布。

Part
2
CH 1
CH 2

雙唇音、唇齒音轉換

pervasion
[pə`veʒən]
n 遍布

Social media has driven pervasion of the business world.
社群媒體趨使商業活動蔓延。

（記憶技巧） -ion 為名詞字尾；pervasion 為 pervade 的名詞。

相關字彙
散布

- disperse 驅散
- distribute 散布
- diffuse 普及
- fan out 作扇形散開
- permeate 彌漫
- spread out 散開
- sprawl 蔓生

---

wake - vig / veg
子音 w 和 v 互換，母音通轉，兩者皆表示活力、醒著。

---

vigor
[`vɪgə]
n 精力，活力

Meditation is said to increase the vigor of the mind.
據說靜坐能夠活化心思。

（記憶技巧） vig- 表示活力；-or 為名詞字尾；vigor 即活力。

---

vigorous
[`vɪgərəs]
a 精力充沛的

The vice president made a vigorous speech to the freshman students.
副校長對新生發表一篇有力的演說。

（記憶技巧） -ous 為形容詞字尾；vigorous 是 vigor 的形容詞。

---

vigilant
[`vɪdʒələnt]
a 不睡的，警戒的

The bodyguard kept a vigilant eye on the celebrity no matter where she went.
無論名人到哪裡，私人保鑣都緊盯著她。

（記憶技巧） vig- 表示醒著、警戒；-il 為名詞字尾；-ant 為形容詞字尾；vigilant 即警戒的。

相關字彙
專注的

- attentive 留意的
- alert 留神的
- concerned 關心的
- focused 集中精力的
- observant 注意的

---

vegetable
[`vɛdʒətəbl]
n 蔬菜，植物人，沒有生氣的人

The young man has been a vegetable since the accident.
意外發生後，年輕人就一直是植物人。

（記憶技巧） veg- 表示活力；-able 為形容詞字尾；vegetable 指像植物有活力生長的，名詞可當蔬菜解釋。但 1921 後，也可以表示過著枯燥、生活單調的人。

way - via / voy

子音 w 和 v 互換、母音通轉，兩者皆表示走、移動、道路。

---

via
[`vaɪə]
prep 經由，憑藉

The CEO will leave Taipei for Seattle via Tokyo.
執行長將從台北經東京前往西雅圖。

記憶技巧 via- 表示走過，衍生經由、憑藉的意思。

---

voyage
[`vɔɪɪdʒ]
n 航行，旅行，航程

The voyage from London to Australia will take almost 24 hours.
倫敦到澳洲的航程幾乎要一天時間。

記憶技巧 古法文字：voy- 表示走、移動；voyage 引申為航行、旅行。

---

convey
[kən`ve]
v 輸送，傳達，傳導

An electric current can be conveyed by the electrolyte in the form of lithium ions.
電流可以鋰離子形式藉由電解液傳送。

記憶技巧 con- 表示一起；vey- 表示走；convey 字面意思是帶著一起走，引申為輸送、傳達。

---

convoy
[`kɑnvɔɪ]
n 護衛，護航

The oil tanker was sailing under convoy of a patrol craft.
油輪在巡邏艇護航下航行。

記憶技巧 con- 表示一起；voy- 表示走、道路；convoy 是和～一起走的意思，引申為護衛、護航。

---

deviate
[`divɪet]
v 脫離，違背

Due to a road closure, cars have to deviate from their usual route.
道路封閉，汽車必須繞道。

記憶技巧 de- 表示離開；via- 表示道路；-ate 為動詞字尾；deviate 指的是偏離軌道，引申為脫離、違背。

---

obvious
[`ɑbvɪəs]
a 明顯的，明白的

The revisor will see if there are any obvious mistakes in the writing.
校正者將檢視文章中是否有明顯錯誤。

記憶技巧 ob- 表示抵抗；via- 表示道路；-ous 為形容詞字尾；obvious 字面上的意思是擋在路中間，引申為明顯的。

Part **2**

CH 1
CH 2

雙唇音、唇齒音轉換

invoice
[`ɪnvɔɪs]

n 發票，裝貨清單，貨物托運

The bookkeeper must submit invoices by the 25th of every month.
會計必須每月 25 日以前繳交發票。

記憶技巧 in- 等同於 on，表示在～上；voi- 等同於 voy-，表示道路；invoice 的字面意思是「on the way（東西已在運送途中）」，引申為運送貨物的明細。

相關字彙 票據
• estimate 估價單
• pro forma invoice 估價發票

previous
[`privɪəs]

a 以前的

I got to know the entrepreneur on a previous occasion.
我在之前的場合結識該企業家。

記憶技巧 pre- 表示前；via- 表示走；-ous 為形容詞字尾；previous 的意思是走在～前的。

impervious
[ɪm`pɝvɪəs]

a 不能滲透的，不受影響的

The candidate is impervious to criticism and defamation.
候選人不受批評及誹謗的影響。

記憶技巧 im- 等同於 in-，表示不；per- 等同於 through，表示穿透；via-，表示道路；-ous 為形容詞字尾；impervious 的字面意思是無法穿透的。

trivial
[`trɪvɪəl]

a 瑣細的，淺薄的，無價值的

Sexual discrimination in the workplace is never a trivial matter.
職場性別歧視絕非小事一樁。

記憶技巧 tri- 等同於 three，表示三；via- 表示道路；-al 為形容詞字尾；trivial 本指的是三叉路口的，亦即公開的，後來才有瑣細、無價值等引申意思。

wander - vag
兩者雖無字源上關係，但可藉由子音 w 和 v 互換，母音通轉來記憶，兩者皆表示漫遊、遊蕩等意思。

vague
[veg]

a 含糊的，茫然的

The sales representative should not have made vague promises.
銷售代表的承諾原本就不該含糊。

記憶技巧 vag- 表示遊蕩；vague 指遊蕩無定點，引申為含糊的、茫然的。

vagary
[`vegərɪ]

n 異想天開，
怪異行為

Retail investors cannot control the vagaries of the stock market.
散戶無法掌控股市起浮。

記憶技巧 vag- 表示遊蕩；-ary 為名詞字尾；vagary 指的是想法遊蕩、天馬行空，特指異想天開。

vagrant
[`vegrənt]

a 流浪的，無賴的

The city has food handouts for vagrant beggars.
城市會發放食物給遊民。

記憶技巧 vag- 表示遊蕩；-ant 為形容詞字尾；vagrant 即到處遊蕩、居無定所的。

vagabond
[`væɡə,bɑnd]

a 流浪的，無賴的

相關字彙
無家可歸之人

After imprisonment, the man is living a vagabond life.
出獄之後，男子居無定所。

記憶技巧 vag- 表示遊蕩；vagabond 的意思是流浪的。

- bag lady 露宿街頭無居所的拾荒女人
- bum 流浪漢
- dosser 流浪者
- tramp 流浪者
- waifs and strays 流浪兒及動物

extravagant
[ɪk`strævəɡənt]

a 奢侈的，放縱的

Many people had extravagant expectations about the global economic prospects.
許多人有全球經濟展望過高的期待。

記憶技巧 extra- 表示外面；vag- 表示遊蕩；-ant 為形容詞字尾；extravagant 字面意思是遊蕩到外面，引申為奢侈的、放縱的。

---

wind - vicar

兩者雖無字源上關係，但可藉由子音 w 和 v 互換、母音通轉來記憶，vicar- 是改變、替代等意思，可用「wind（風）」無定的概念來協助記憶。

vicarious
[vaɪ`kɛrɪəs]

a 代理的，替代的

I took a vicarious pleasure in Tom's promotion.
我為湯姆的晉升感到高興。

記憶技巧 vicar- 表示替代；-ous 為形容詞字尾；vicarious 的意思是代理的。

vicissitude
[və`sɪsə,tjud]

n 變化無常，變換

The pension reformation will be marked by vicissitudes.
年金改革變數頗多。

記憶技巧 viciss- 表示改變；-tude 表示抽象名詞字尾；vicissitude 的意思是一直改變。

Part
2
CH 1
CH 2
雙唇音、唇齒音轉換

wound - vulner

兩者雖無字源上關係，但可藉由子音 w 和 v 互換，母音通轉來記憶，兩者皆表示傷口。

---

vulnerary

[ˋvʌlnəˌrɛrɪ]

n 外傷藥

Nancy applied some vulnerary to a fresh cut on her finger.
南希抹一些外傷藥在手指新傷口上。

記憶技巧　vulner- 表示傷口；-ary 為名詞字尾；vulnerary 即外傷藥。

---

vulnerable

[ˋvʌlnərəbl̩]

a 易受攻擊的，易受責難的

Small and medium enterprises are vulnerable in an economic recession.
中小企業在經濟衰退時期易遭波及。

記憶技巧　vulner- 表示傷口；-able 為形容詞字尾；vulnerable 的意思是容易受傷的。

相關字彙　處於險境

- at risk 有危險
- exposed 易受攻擊的
- insecure 有危險的
- unprotected 無保護的
- undefended 無防備的

---

vulnerability

[ˌvʌlnərəˋbɪlətɪ]

n 易受傷，易受責難

The testing program is able to examine every single vulnerability of the system.
測試程式能夠檢視系統每一漏洞。

記憶技巧　-ity 為名詞字尾。

wear - vest

子音 w 和 v 互換，母音通轉，兩者皆表示（穿）衣服。

---

vest

[vɛst]

n 背心

Thanks to his bulletproof vest, the anti-riot policeman survived the gunshot.
幸虧穿上防彈背心，鎮暴警察躲過槍擊。

記憶技巧　本意是穿，另有寬鬆外衣的意思，現今的意思是背心。

---

divest

[dəˋvɛst]

v 脫衣，剝奪

The shareholder decided to divest himself of his shareholding.
股東決定出脫持股。

記憶技巧　di- 等同於 dis-，表示離開；vest- 表示衣服；divest 即是脫衣的意思。

invest
[ɪn`vɛst]

v 投資，使穿上，授予

The company invested significant amounts of money in the project.
公司投資巨額資金在該計劃。

記憶技巧 in- 表示進入；vest- 表示衣服；invest 本指套在衣服之內，1610 年代才有投資的意思。

investment
[ɪn`vɛstmənt]

n 投資，資金

The high-tech company made a large investment in a new wafer foundry.
高科技公司大筆投資一座晶圓代工廠。

記憶技巧 -ment 為名詞字尾。

相關字彙
投資理財

- annuity 年金
- bond 債券
- fund 基金
- futures 期貨
- hedge fund 投機性的投資團體
- margin 利潤
- mature（票據等）到期的
- stake 股份
- speculator 投機者

---

wit - vid / vis

子音 w 和 v 互換，母音通轉，兩者皆表示看、知道。看跟知道常藉由同一單字表達，如：see。

---

visit
[`vɪzɪt]

n 訪問，參觀

It is not advisable to see every exhibit in the museum in one visit.
不建議一次看完博物館每樣展覽品。

記憶技巧 vit- 表示看；it- 表示 go。

visible
[`vɪzəbl̩]

a 看得見的，明顯的

Micro-organisms are not visible to the naked eye.
微生物是肉眼看不到的。

記憶技巧 vis- 表示看；-ible 為形容詞字尾；visible 的意思是可以看得見的。

visual
[`vɪʒuəl]

a 視覺的，光學的，看得見的

These audio-visual aids in teaching require projectors and interactive whiteboards.
這些教學視聽輔具需要投影機及互動式電子白板。

記憶技巧 vis- 表示看；-al 為形容詞字尾；visual 表示視覺的。

vista
[`vɪstə]

n 展望，回想，前景

Now, there appears exciting vistas of business expansion and global cooperation.
現在，擴展業務及全球合作的大好前景出現了。

記憶技巧 vis- 表示看；vista 表示展望、前景。

Part **2** CH 1 CH 2 雙唇音、唇齒音轉換

advice
[əd`vaɪs]

n 忠告，建議，診察

I'll take your advice and have a check-up to make sure everything is right.

我會聽從你的建議去做身體檢查，以確保一切安好。

記憶技巧　ad- 表示朝～方向；vice 等同於 vis-，表示看；advice 的意思是看法，引申為意見、忠告等。

revise
[rɪ`vaɪz]

v 校正

The author managed to revise the manuscript to make it shorter.

作者成功修潤手稿，使它縮減。

記憶技巧　re- 表示再一次；vis- 表示看；revise 指再看一次，引申為校正。

vision
[`vɪʒən]

n 視力，景象

A leader needs to create a clear vision of the future.

領導者必須創造清楚的未來願景。

記憶技巧　vis- 表示看；-ion 為名詞字尾；vision 即視力。

supervisor
[ˌsupɚ`vaɪzɚ]

n 監督人，主管

相關字彙
公司企業管理

The district supervisor needs to be responsible for directing the operation in an assigned district.

區域督導需要負責指導指定區域的運作。

記憶技巧　super- 等同於 over，表示在～上面；vis- 表示看；-or 表示人；supervisor 字面意思是在上面看著的人，引申為監督人、主管。

- administrator 管理人
- baron 巨頭
- boss 老板
- CEO 執行長
- CFO 財務長
- COO 營運長
- director 董事
- director general 處長
- tycoon（企業界的）大亨
- wantrepreneur 懷抱創業夢，但卻沒行動的人

provide
[prə`vaɪd]

v 提供，預備，規定

The government will provide poorer families with health care at lower rates.

政府將提供貧困家庭優惠醫療照顧。

記憶技巧　pro- 表示前面；vid- 表示看；provide 的意思是往前看，表示未雨綢繆，引申為預備、提供等意思。

provision
[prə`vɪʒən]

n 預備，條款

We have to make provision against any natural disasters that may cause deadly accidents.

我們必須預防可能引發致命意外的天然災害。

記憶技巧　-ion 為名詞字尾。

evident

[ˋɛvədənt]

a 明白的，明顯的

It's perfectly evident from the newcomer's change in her performance that she's competent.

新員工表現的改變明顯看出她的能力很強。

記憶技巧　e- 等同於 ex-，表示完全地；vid- 表示看；-ent 為形容詞字尾；evident 的意思是可以完全看清楚，引申為明顯的。

---

review

[rɪˋvju]

v 審查，評論，複習

Each staff member's salary will be reviewed annually.

每位員工的薪水將每年審查。

記憶技巧　re- 表示再一次；view 表示看；review 指再看一次，引申為複習。

---

preview

[ˋpriˏvju]

v 試演，預展，預習

The movie is due to be previewed the day after tomorrow.

影片排定後天試映。

記憶技巧　pre- 表示前；view 表示看；preview 指事先看，引申為預習。

---

interview

[ˋɪntɚˏvju]

n / **v** 面談，面試，訪問

相關字彙
求職

During the job interview process, the employer asked me a couple of inappropriate questions.

面試過程中，雇主問了我幾個不適當的問題。

記憶技巧　inter- 表示在～之間；view 表示看；interview 指兩者之間面對面的會議，引申為面談、面試。

- applicant 申請人
- curriculum vitae 簡歷
- reject 被拒之人
- résumé 簡歷
- screening 選拔
- vacant 空著的

---

survey

[ˋsɝve]

n 調查，測量

The manufacturer will make a market survey among their distributors next quarter.

製造商將於下一季針對經銷商進行市調。

記憶技巧　sur- 等同於 super-，表示在～之上；vey- 表示看；survey 指的是在上面看，引申為調查。

---

envious

[ˋɛnvɪəs]

a 羨慕的，忌妒的

Tom is envious of his brother's ability to afford the luxurious house.

湯姆羨慕他弟弟買得起豪宅。

記憶技巧　en- 等同於 in- / on，表示在～之上；vi- 表示看；-ous 為形容詞字尾；envious 指的是直盯著～看的，引申為羨慕的、忌妒的。

Part
2
CH 1
CH 2

雙唇音、唇齒音轉換

new - nov
子音 w 和 v 互換，母音通轉，兩者皆表示新。

---

novel
[ˋnɑvl]
a 新穎的，異常的

The head chef will present a novel way to process leftovers.
主廚將提出新的廚餘處理方式。

記憶技巧　nov- 等同於 new，表示新；novel 指新穎的。

---

novelty
[ˋnɑvḷtɪ]
n 新奇，新奇物品

The advertisement has raised my desire for novelty contact lenses.
廣告挑起我配戴新奇隱形眼鏡的念頭。

記憶技巧　-ty 為名詞字尾。

---

novice
[ˋnɑvɪs]
n 初學者，新手

相關字彙
沒經驗的人、初學者

The new employee is a novice at studio lighting.
新員工是攝影棚燈光的新手。

記憶技巧　nov- 表示新；novice 指新手。

- apprentice 學徒
- protégé 門生
- initiate 新加入者
- newcomer 初學者

---

innovate
[ˋɪnəˏvet]
v 創始，革新，改革

Cultural and creative industries are always desperate to innovate.
文創業一向極力創新。

記憶技巧　in- 表示內；nov- 表示新；-ate 為動詞字尾；innovate 指帶進新的東西，引申為革新、創始。

---

innovative
[ˋɪnoˏvetɪv]
a 革新的，創新的

Next week, there will be an international conference on innovative methods of soil fertility restoration.
下周將有一場關於土壤回復肥沃創新方法的國際會議。

記憶技巧　-ive 為形容詞字尾，是 innovate 的形容詞。

---

renovate
[ˋrɛnəˏvet]
v 革新，修補

The government is planning to renovate the old train station downtown.
政府正規畫翻修市中心的舊火車站。

記憶技巧　re- 表示再一次；nov- 表示新；-ate 為動詞字尾；renovate 的意思是革新。

Section 2

字母「w」對應字母「u」

water - und

子音 w 和 u 互換，母音通轉，兩者皆表示水。

---

abundant
[ə`bʌndənt]
a 豐富的

The border areas are relatively abundant in natural resources.
邊疆地區天然資源相對豐富。

記憶技巧　ab- 表示離開；und- 表示水；-ant 為形容詞字尾；abundant 的意思是水滿到跑出來，引申為豐富的。

---

abundance
[ə`bʌndəns]
n 豐富，大量

There is an abundance of marine fishery resources in this area.
這區域海洋漁產資源豐富。

記憶技巧　-ance 為名詞字尾。

---

redundant
[rɪ`dʌndənt]
a 多餘的，豐富的

The redundant power supply unit will supply power to devices the moment they fail.
儀器斷電時，冗餘供電設備將立即供電。

記憶技巧　re- 表示一再；und- 表示水；-ant 為形容詞字尾；redundant 的意思是水一再滿出來，引申為多餘的。

相關字彙
不需要或不想要的

- dispensable 可有可無的
- superfluous 多餘的
- unnecessary 不必要的
- unwanted 無用的
- uninvited 多餘的
- unsolicited 未經要求的
- unlooked-for 非尋求的

---

abound
[ə`baund]
v 充滿

The capital city abounds with financial institutions and multinational corporation headquarters.
首都遍佈金融機構及跨國公司總部。

記憶技巧　為 abundant 的動詞形式。

相關字彙
充滿

- brim with 充滿
- bulge with 裝滿
- bristle with 充滿
- overflow 充滿
- run over 溢出
- seethe 使浸透

sweet - suad

子音 w 和 u 互換、母音通轉，兩者皆表示甜的、愉悅的。

persuade [pəˋswed] Ⅴ 說服	My financial advisor persuaded me to invest emerging markets funds. 我的理財顧問說服我投資新興市場基金。 記憶技巧　per- 表示完全；suad- 表示甜的；persuade 的意思是給人甜頭，以說服人。
persuasive [pəˋswesɪv] ā 勸誘的， 有說服力的	The victim's mother presented persuasive argument for gun control. 受害者母親提出槍枝管制的有力論述。 記憶技巧　-ive 為形容詞字尾。
dissuade [dɪˋswed] Ⅴ 勸阻	Mrs. Lin dissuaded her husband from drinking and driving again. 林太太勸她先生不要再酒駕。 記憶技巧　dis- 表示離開或相對；suad- 表示甜的；dissuade 的意思是給人甜頭，說服人不要去做某事。

one -uni

one 發 [wʌn]，子音 w 和 u 互換、母音通轉，兩者皆表示一。

unite [juˋnaɪt] Ⅴ 聯合，團結，合併	The chief appealed to unite to fight aggression from across the border. 首領呼籲團結抵禦外來侵略。 記憶技巧　uni-表示一；unite 的意思是合而為一的，表示聯合、團結。
unity [ˋjunətɪ] ⁿ 團結，統一，聯合	You should work together with your partners in unity to complete the project. 你應該和伙伴們團結一致完成工作。 記憶技巧　-ty 為名詞字尾。

unify
['junə͵faɪ]

v 統一，使一致，使成一體

The combination of the single market and currency will form a unified economic area.
單一市場及貨幣結合將形成統一的經濟區域。

記憶技巧 -fy，動詞字尾。

---

union
['junjən]

n 聯合，聯盟，公會，工會

相關字彙
勞工組織及其成員

The negotiation between management and labor union has been a success.
資方與工會的協商成功。

記憶技巧 -ion 為名詞字尾。

● chapel 印刷工會　　　　　● syndicalist 工團組織主義者
● labor union 工會

---

unison
['junəsn̩]

n 和諧，一致

All the committee members rejected the extemporaneous motion in unison.
全體委員一致反對臨時提案。

記憶技巧 uni- 表示一；son- 等同於 sound；unison 的意思是單一聲音，引申為和諧、一致。

---

unique
[ju`nik]

a 獨特的

Fingerprints are known to be unique to every individual.
大家都知道每個人指紋都是獨一的。

記憶技巧 uni- 表示一；unique 的意思是單一的。

---

uniform
['junə͵fɔrm]

a 規格一致的

The male employees were required to get uniform styles of haircuts to conform with company policy.
男員工被要求髮型一致以符合公司規定。

記憶技巧 uni- 表示一；form- 表示形式；uniform 的意思是形式一致的。

---

unicorn
['junɪ͵kɔrn]

n 獨角獸

I don't believe there exists unicorns in the world.
我不相信世界上存在獨角獸。

記憶技巧 uni- 表示一；corn- 等同於 horn，表示角；unicorn 即為獨角獸。

---

unanimous
[ju`nænəməs]

a 意見一致的，全體一致的

It turned out that the senior member was elected as convener by a unanimous vote.
結果是資深會員獲得一致投票當選召集人。

記憶技巧 un- 等同於 uni-，anim- 表示心、精神；-ous 為形容詞字尾；unanimous 的意思是心思齊一的，引申為意見一致的。

Part **2**
CH 1
CH 2

雙唇音、唇齒音轉換

universal

[͵junəˋvɝsl̩]

a 一般的，宇宙的，
（全體的，普遍的）

The proposal of issuance of common stock for cash has met with universal approval within the board of directors.

發行普通股以現金增資的提案已獲董事會一致通過。

記憶技巧 un- 表示一；vers- 表示轉；-al 為形容詞字尾；universal 字面的意思是轉變合而為一的，引申為普遍的，一般的。

原來如此！

老張年初四帶法籍友人到鄰居家泡茶。

友人：the 好喝！（法文茶字像 the）

鄰居：哇！法國人會講台語的茶！

老張：不是啦！法語和台語的茶同音！

鄰居又是一臉狐疑！

老張：法國人很能接受我們的東西，法式料理和中餐世界齊名！

友人：是啊！台南有一位法國道士是紅頭的，不是黑頭的！

鄰居：對了！台南後壁菁寮天主堂神父是法籍的，我有他寫的書法春聯！

老張：法國人喝茶很有中國味，不像英國人要加糖和奶精！

鄰居：日本人會把茶葉磨粉變抹茶！

小哲：台灣人喝茶要加糖、加奶精、加珍珠！

小琪：有的還加塑化劑！

Chapter 3
齒間音、齒齦音、
齒齦後音、硬顎音轉換

〔d〕、〔t〕、〔n〕、〔l〕、〔ʃ〕、〔r〕、〔z〕、〔s〕、〔θ〕、〔ð〕、〔ʒ〕

〔t〕對應〔d〕

two - di

子音 t 和 d 互換，母音通轉，兩者皆表示二。

---

diploma

[dɪˋplomə]

n 執照，文憑，公文，畢業證書

The mediator has recently gained a diploma in labor laws and welfare.

調解委員最近獲得勞工法律與福利文憑。

記憶技巧   di- 表示二；pl- 表示折；-oma 為希臘文名詞字尾；diploma 本指將紙對折的意思，後來才有執照、文憑、公文等意思。

---

diplomat

[ˋdɪpləmæt]

n 外交官，善於交際者

The career diplomat has been delegated abroad to London for two years.

外交官已派駐倫敦兩年。

記憶技巧   diplomat 是由 diplomatic 逆向構詞（back formation）產生的，diplomatic 字面上的意思是和文件相關的，到了 1787 年有國際關係的意思，到 1826 年才有善於交際的意思。

相關字彙
外交人員

- ambassador 大使
- attaché 專員
- chancellery 大使的地位
- chargé d'affaires 代辦
- consul 領事
- embassy 大使館
- envoy 外交使節

---

diplomatic

[ˌdɪpləˋmætɪk]

a 有外交手腕的，外交的

The country decided to break off the diplomatic relations with Turkey.

該國決定中止與土耳其的外交關係。

記憶技巧   diploma 是公文的意思；-ic 為形容詞字尾。

---

dioxide

[daɪˋɑksaɪd]

n 二氧化物

There is an efficient way to reduce the release of carbon dioxide into the atmosphere.

有一減少二氧化碳排入大氣層的有效方式。

記憶技巧   di- 表示二；ox- 等同於 oxigen，氧；-ide 表示化學物質；dioxide 的意思是二氧化物。

dilemma

[də`lɛmə]

n 進退兩難

The manager is clearly in a dilemma over how to deal with these cases.

經理很明顯正為如何解決這些案子進退兩難。

> 記憶技巧　di- 表示二；-lemma 表示拿；dilemma 字面上意思是兩個都想拿，表示難以抉擇、進退兩難。

two - duo

子音 t 和 d 互換，母音通轉，兩者皆表示二。

dual

[`djuəl]

a 兩層的，二重的，二元的

The country encourages its citizens to utilize their status of dual or multiple nationality.

該國鼓勵公民善用雙重或多重國籍的身分。

> 記憶技巧　du- 表示二；-al 為形容詞字尾；dual 的意思是二重的、雙的。

duplicate

[`djupləkɪt]

n 謄本，副本

The settlement has to be completed in duplicate.

和解書必須一式兩份。

> 記憶技巧　du- 表示二；plic- 表示折；-ate 為形容詞字尾；duplicate 的意思是對折、複製，當名詞用時，引申為副本。

two- de

雖非同源字，但可藉由子音 t 和 d 互換，母音通轉來記憶。de- 是分離的意思，分離是一分而為二。

defuse

[di`fjuz]

v 拆去～的雷管

The bomb squad was summoned to defuse the bomb found in the MRT station.

防爆小組被召來拆除地鐵站發現的炸彈。

> 記憶技巧　de- 表示分離；fuse 表示引信；defuse 是拆除引信的意思。

dehydrate

[di`haɪˌdret]

v 脫水，使乾燥

Salt is used to dehydrate the meat to keep it from spoiling.

鹽可用來將肉脫水以避免腐壞。

> 記憶技巧　de- 表示分離；hydr- 表示水；-ate 為動詞字尾；dehydrate 的意思是脫水。

delirium [dɪˋlɪrɪəm] **n** 精神錯亂，說胡話	The patient had a high fever accompanied by delirium. 患者發高燒，又神智不清。 記憶技巧 de- 表示分離；lir- 表示犁溝；-ium 為名詞字尾；delirium 的意思是犁田犁歪了，引申為精神錯亂。
derail [dɪˋrel] **v** 使出軌	The northbound train was derailed by mudslide. 北上列車因土石流而出軌。 記憶技巧 de- 表示分離；rail 表示軌道；derail 即出軌。
desalt [diˋsɔlt] **v** 除去鹽分	The chemical factory is equipped with a desalting device. 化學工廠配備一套除鹽設施。 記憶技巧 de- 表示分離；salt 表示鹽；desalt 指去除鹽分。

two - dis / di

雖非同源字，但可藉由子音 t 和 d 互換，母音通轉來記憶。di- 是分離的意思，分離是一分而為二。

discard [dɪsˋkɑrd] **v** 拋棄，解雇	The pedestrian discarded the plastic wrapper into an open recycling container on the sidewalk. 行人將塑膠包裝丟棄在人行道上的開放式回收桶。 記憶技巧 dis- 表示分離；card 表示卡片；discard 本是紙牌遊戲中把牌丟掉的意思，後來語意擴大，有拋棄的意思。
discernible [dɪˋsɝnəbl̩] **a** 可識別的	There is no discernible reason why the client declined to sign the contract. 客戶拒絕簽約真是令人費解。 記憶技巧 dis- 表示分離；cern- 表示過濾；-ible 表示可～的；discernible 本意是可篩選的，引申為可識別的。
discourse [ˋdɪskors] **n** 談話，交談，會話	The linguistics professor will give lectures of discourse analysis next semester. 語言學教授下學期將開言談分析課。 記憶技巧 dis- 表示分離；course 等同於 cur-，表示跑；discourse 的意思是～跑出來，引申為談話、交談。

discrepancy

[dɪ`skrɛpənsɪ]

n 不一致，不符，差異

The financial manager is displeased with the discrepancy in financial statements.
財務經理對於財務報表不符非常不高興。

記憶技巧　dis- 表示分離；crep- 表示發出咯咯聲；-ancy 為名詞字尾；discrepancy 的意思是聲音嘈雜、不一致，引申為差異。

---

dislocate

[`dɪsləˌket]

v 使移動位置，使脫臼

相關字彙
身體受傷

The boy fell off his bicycle and dislocated his shoulder.
男孩自單車摔下，肩膀脫臼。

記憶技巧　dis- 表示分離；loc- 表示地點；-ate 為動詞字尾；dislocate 的意思是使～離開某處，引申為使脫臼。

- injure 使受傷
- harm 傷害
- wound 創傷
- cut 切
- burn 燙傷
- strain 扭傷
- break 斷裂
- bruise 青腫

---

dispel

[dɪ`spɛl]

v 驅散，消除

The minister made an official statement to dispel doubts about the construction project.
部長發表一份正式聲明，以消除興建計畫的疑慮。

記憶技巧　dis- 表示分離；pel- 等同於 push，表示推；dispel 的意思是推開，引申為驅散、消除。

---

ten - deca

子音 t 和 d 互換，母音通轉，兩者皆表示十。

---

decade

[`dɛked]

n 十年

相關字彙
宗教歷史

Communications technology has advanced tremendously over the past decade.
過去十年來，通訊技術進展驚人。

記憶技巧　dec- 表示十；-ade 為名詞字尾；decade 即十年。

- Decalogue 摩西十誡
- The Decameron 十日談

December

[dɪ`sɛmbɚ]

n 十二月

Kelly and her fiancé were both born in late December.
凱莉和未婚夫都是十二月下旬出生的。

記憶技巧　dec- 表示十；December 是羅馬舊曆十月，新曆十二月。

decapod
[`dɛkəˌpɑd]
n 十腳類動物

California freshwater shrimps are a decapod crustacean.
加州淡水蝦是十腳甲殼動物。

記憶技巧 dec- 表示十；pod- 表示腳；decapod 是十腳類動物。

teeth - dent / dont
子音 t 和 d 互換，母音通轉，兩者皆表示牙齒。

dental
[`dɛntl̩]
a 牙齒的，齒科的

The wounded man will undergo a major dental operation.
受傷男子將進行牙齒重大手術。

記憶技巧 dent-表示齒；-al 為形容詞字尾；dental 的意思是牙齒的。

dentist
[`dɛntɪst]
n 牙醫師

The dentist specializes in tooth whitening and dental implants.
牙醫師專精於牙齒美白及植牙。

記憶技巧 dent- 表示齒；-ist 為名詞字尾，表示人；dentist 的意思是牙醫師。

denture
[`dɛntʃɚ]
n 假牙，牙齒

The patient had been asked to remove his dentures by the time he entered the examination room.
病患進入檢驗室前被要求取下假牙。

記憶技巧 dent- 表示齒；-ure 為名詞字尾，當假牙解釋。

相關字彙
牙齒部分和類別

- enamel 琺瑯質
- false teeth 假牙
- incisor 門牙
- fang 犬齒
- molar 臼齒
- pulp 牙髓
- root 根部
- tusk 長牙，獠牙
- wisdom tooth 智齒

indent
[ɪn`dɛnt]
v 縮排，訂購

The secretary usually forgets to indent the first word of each paragraph.
祕書經常忘記縮排每一段的第一個字。

記憶技巧 in- 表示內；dent- 表示齒；indent 可以聯想成用牙齒咬出凹痕，縮排是每段第一行空幾個字母，產生凹陷的感覺。

orthodontics
[ɔrθə`dɑntɪks]
n 牙齒矯正術

The dental clinic is famous for the most advanced techniques of orthodontics.
牙醫診所以最先進牙齒矯正技術著稱。

記憶技巧 ortho-表示正；dont-表示齒；orthodontics 即牙齒矯正術。

tame - dom

子音 t 和 d 互換、母音通轉，tame 是馴服的，dom- 是家，有一派字源學家推測 tame 和 dom-同源，像狗、貓這樣的動物是經馴服，才能養到家中。

domestic
[də`mɛstɪk]

a 家庭的，本國的

The public construction expansion program will cause a substantial influence on the domestic market.
擴大公共建設方案將對國內市場產生實質影響。

記憶技巧 dom- 表示家；-ic為形容詞字尾；domestic即家庭的意思。

domesticate
[də`mɛstəˌket]

v 馴服

These domesticated animals were food sources for the nomads on the plateau.
這些馴養動物是高原游牧民族的食物來源。

記憶技巧 domestic 表示家庭的；-ate 為動詞字尾；domesticate 的意思將動物馴服到家中。

talk - dic

兩者雖無字源關係，但可藉由子音 t 和 d 互換、母音通轉來記憶，兩者皆表示說。

addict
[ə`dɪkt]

v 沉溺於，熱衷於

My brother-in-law used to be addicted to gambling.
我姊夫曾經沉迷賭博。

記憶技巧 ad- 表示朝～方向；dict- 表示說；addict 的字面上意思是持續說，後來才有使熱衷於的意思。

benediction
[ˌbɛnə`dɪkʃən]

n 祝福的祈禱

The chief pronounced a benediction over the worriors before they started.
頭目在戰士出征前為他們祈福。

記憶技巧 bene- 表示好的；dict- 表示說；-ion 為名詞字尾；benediction 即說好話，引申為祝福的祈禱。

malediction
[ˌmælə`dɪkʃən]

n 誹謗，詛咒

Gina muttered maledictions against her previous boss, who treated her differently because of her ethnicity.
吉娜詛咒她的前老闆，她因為種族關係而遭到差別待遇。

記憶技巧 male- 表示壞的；dict- 表示說；-ion 為名詞字尾；malediction 即說壞話，引申為誹謗、詛咒。

Part 2

CH 1
CH 2
CH 3

齒間音、齒齦音、齒齦後音、硬顎音轉換

contradict
[͵kɑntrə`dɪkt]

v 反駁，否認

The new evidence directly contradicted earlier testimony from the defendant.
新證據直接駁斥被告稍早的證詞。

> **記憶技巧** contra- 表示相對；dict- 表示説；contradict 的意思是説相反的話，引申為反駁、否認。

dictionary
[`dɪkʃən͵ɛrɪ]

n 字典，辭典

I've just ordered an etymology dictionary which explains the history of English words.
我剛訂一本解釋英文字歷史的字源字典。

> **記憶技巧** dict- 表示説；-ion 為名詞字尾；-ary 為名詞字尾，表示集合的概念；dictionary 即收集文字的字典。

indict
[ɪn`daɪt]

v 控告，起訴

The prosecutor indicted the former minister for corruption.
檢察官以貪汙罪起訴前任部長。

> **記憶技巧** in- 表示內；dict- 表示説；indict 的意思是説某人所做的壞事，引申為控告、起訴。

verdict
[`vɝdɪkt]

n 判決，辯解

The jury brought in a verdict of guilty against the accused man.
陪審團判決被告男子有罪。

> **記憶技巧** ver- 表示真的；dict- 表示説；verdict 即説真話，特指法庭上説真話，引申為判決。

相關字彙
意見與態度

- viewpoint 觀點
- stance 立場
- opinion 意見
- stand 立場
- attitude 態度

jurisdiction
[͵dʒurɪs`dɪkʃən]

n 司法權，管轄權

The federal court has no jurisdiction over domestic relations cases.
聯邦法院無家庭關係案件司法權。

> **記憶技巧** juris- 表示法律；dict- 表示説；-ion 為名詞字尾；jurisdiction 作司法權解釋。

unpredictable
[͵ʌnprɪ`dɪktəbl̩]

a 不可預測的

The outcome of this kind of experiment might be rather unpredictable.
這類實驗的結果可能難以預測。

> **記憶技巧** un- 表示否定字；pre- 表示前；dict- 表示説；-able 表示可以～的；unpredictable 是無法事先説的，引申為不可預測的。

tow - duc

子音 t 和 d 互換，母音通轉，兩者皆表示拉。

---

abduct
[æb`dʌkt]

v 綁架，誘拐

The diplomat was abducted from the official car by a couple of antiwar activists.

外交官遭反戰激進分子自公務車綁架。

記憶技巧　ab- 表示離開；duct- 表示拉；abduct 的意思是（強行）把人拉走，引申為綁架。

---

conductor
[kən`dʌktə]

n 領導者，指揮者，車長

The orchestra conductor raised his baton and started the orchestra performance.

交響樂團指揮舉起指揮棒，開始交響樂演奏。

記憶技巧　con- 表示一起；duct- 表示拉；-or 為名詞字尾，表示人；conductor 的意思是帶著其他人一起走的人，引申為領導者、指揮者。

---

deduction
[dɪ`dʌkʃən]

n 扣除，扣除額，推論

The remaining balance has been deducted after the deduction of national insurance.

扣除國民保險之後，未繳餘額已扣除。

記憶技巧　de- 表示往下；duct- 表示拉；-ion 為名詞字尾；deduction 字面意思是往下拉，引申為扣除。

---

induction
[ɪn`dʌkʃən]

n 歸納法，誘導，（電磁）感應

An induction coil was the first commercially produced voltage transformer.

感應線圈是最先製造的商業用途電壓變電器。

記憶技巧　in- 表示內；duct- 表示拉；-ion 為名詞字尾；induction 的意思是從眾多事例中拉出規則或主軸，即是歸納法。

---

education
[ˌɛdʒu`keʃən]

n 教育

Parents with a higher education background are able to provide their children with more educational resources.

高學歷家長能夠提供孩子較多教育資源。

記憶技巧　e- 等同於 ex-，表示外面；duc- 表示拉；-ation 為名詞字尾；education 的意思是往外拉，教育的內涵首重引導，引出學生的潛能。

---

introduce
[ˌɪntrə`djus]

v 介紹，納入，引進

The sunflower was introduced to Europe in the 1500's.

太陽花於 1500 年代引進歐洲。

記憶技巧　intro- 表示往內；duc- 表示拉；introduce 的意思是往內拉，引申為介紹、引進。

Part **2**

CH 1
CH 2
CH 3

齒間音、齒齦音、齒齦後音、硬顎音轉換

produce
[prə`djus]
v 生產

Red blood cells and most white blood cells are produced in the bone marrow.
紅血球細胞及大部分白血球細胞在骨髓中製造。

記憶技巧 　pro- 表示往前；duc- 表示拉；produce 的意思是往前拉，引申為把東西生產出來。

product
[`pradəkt]
n 產物，成果

This food product contains no animal fat or artificial flavors.
該食品不含動物脂肪或人工香料。

記憶技巧 　product 是 produce 的名詞。

相關字彙
產品

- brand 牌子
- brand leader 品牌領導者
- by-product 副產品
- commodity 商品
- derivatives 衍生性金融商品
- end product 成品
- producer goods 生產者物品
- soft goods 非耐用品

productive
[prə`dʌktɪv]
a 多產的，富創造力的

The productive capacity is the maximum amount of products and services that can be produced.
生產能力是指能夠生產的產品及服務的最大量。

記憶技巧 　-ive 為形容詞字尾。

reduce
[rɪ`djus]
v 減少，減價，還原

In order to reduce costs, the company decided to start layoffs next quarter.
為減少成本，公司決定下一季開始裁員。

記憶技巧 　re- 表示背後、回；duc- 表示拉；reduce 的意思是拉回，意即減少。

seduce
[sɪ`djus]
v 誘惑，使入歧途

Many people were seduced into pre-ordering the computer by the offer of a free flight ticket.
許多人受誘惑，衝著免費機票而預購電腦。

記憶技巧 　se- 表示離開；duc- 表示拉；seduce 的意思是拉離正軌，使人誤入歧途。

traduce
[trə`djus]
v 誹謗，詆毀

The panelist has shamelessly traduced the politician.
名嘴無恥地詆毀這名政治人物。

記憶技巧 　tra- 等同於 across，表示跨越；duc- 表示拉；traduce 的意思是拉到另一端，可以想像成顛倒事實，1580 年代才有詆毀的意思。

tree - dur

子音 t 和 d 互換、母音通轉，tree 現今意思是樹，但兩者原始意思皆表示穩固、堅固，可用樹的堅固形象來記憶。

---

duration
[dju`reʃən]
n 持續的時間

| 相關字彙 |
| 頻率、持續時間 |

The exchange student planned a stay of three years' duration.
交換學生計畫停留三年。

記憶技巧 dur-，表示穩固；-ation 為名詞字尾；duration 的意思是可以穩定持久，引申為持續的時間。

- frequency 頻率
- rate 速率
- irregularity 無規律
- length 期間
- come down 流傳下來
- drag on 拖延
- endure 時間持久
- linger 繼續逗留
- see out 持續到～結束
- run on 流逝

---

during
[`djurɪŋ]
prep 在～期間

Night shift workers have to work during the night and sleep by day.
夜班員工必須夜間工作，白天睡覺。

記憶技巧 dur- 表示穩固；during 表示持續的期間。

---

durable
[`djurəbḷ]
a 耐久的

Durable goods can be used for a period of time, usually three or more years.
耐久物品能使用一段時間，通常是至少三年。

記憶技巧 dur- 表示穩固；-able 為形容詞字尾；durable 的意思是可以持續撐很久的，引申為耐久的。

---

obdurate
[`ɑbdjərɪt]
a 倔強的

The manager remained obdurate that the project should be completed as scheduled.
經理堅持計畫必須如期完成。

記憶技巧 ob- 表示相對；dur- 表示穩固；-ate 為形容詞字尾；obdurate 的意思是穩定的對抗，引申為倔強的。

---

endure
[ɪn`djur]
v 忍耐

The passengers couldn't help but endure a six-hour delay at the airport.
乘客不得不待在機場，忍受六小時的班機延誤。

記憶技巧 en- 等同於 in，表示內；dur- 表示穩固；endure 的意思是內部穩固，可以撐很久，引申為忍耐。

Part
2

CH 1
CH 2
CH 3

齒間音、齒齦音、齒齦後音、硬顎音轉換

timid - dino

雖無明確字源上的關係，但可藉由子音 t 和 d 互換、母音通轉來記憶，兩者的意思皆是恐懼。

dinosaur

[ˋdaɪnəˏsɔr]

n 恐龍

Dinosaurs became extinct at the end of the Cretaceous Period.

恐龍於白堊紀末期絕跡。

> **記憶技巧** dino- 表示恐懼；saur- 表示類蜥蜴的爬行動物；dinosaur 指的是恐龍。

相關字彙 各種古生物

- archaeopteryx 始祖鳥
- pterodactyl 翼手龍
- triceratops 三角龍
- mammoth 毛象
- stegosaurus 劍龍

teach - doc

雖無明確字源上的關係，但可藉由子音 t 和 d 互換、母音通轉來記憶，兩者的意思皆是教。

doctor

n 醫師，博士

This afternoon, my assistant went to an eye doctor for a check-up.

今天下午，我的助理去找眼科醫師檢查眼睛。

> **記憶技巧** doc- 表示教；-or 表示人；doctor 的意思是教導者，特指教堂中的神職人員，14 世紀末時，才有大學最高學歷持有人的意思，後當博士解釋。

doctorate

[ˋdɑktərɪt]

n 博士學位

The deputy commissioner finally earned his doctorate degree in criminal psychology.

副局長終於獲得犯罪心理學博士學位。

> **記憶技巧** doctor 表示博士；-ate 為名詞字尾；doctorate 的意思是博士學位。

doctrine

[ˋdɑktrɪn]

n 教訓，教義，主義

The psychology professor is questioning the doctrines of Sigmund Freud.

心理學教授質疑弗洛依德學說。

> **記憶技巧** doc- 表示教；-or 表示人；-ine 為抽象名詞字尾；doctrine 是教導的意思，引申為教訓、教義。

document
[`dɑkjəmənt]
n 證件，公文，文書

Ironically, the public notary was charged with using forged documents.
很諷刺，公證人被控使用偽造文件。

記憶技巧 doc- 表示教；-ment 為名詞字尾；document 本意是教學，18 世紀才有證明文件的意思。

docile
[`dɑsḷ]
a 易於管教的，溫順的

相關字彙
難以馴服、管教近義字

Luckily, all my students are docile and eager to learn.
幸運地，我的學生都易於管教，而且熱衷學習。

記憶技巧 doc- 表示教；-ile 為形容詞字尾；docile 的意思是教得來的，引申為易於管教的。

- indocile 不順從的
- incorrigible 屢教不改的
- intractable 倔強的
- obstreperous 吵鬧的
- recalcitrant 頑強的
- undisciplined 不遵守紀律的

tear - derm
可藉由子音 t 和 d 互換，母音通轉來記憶，兩者的古義皆是剝皮，derm- 現今的意思是皮膚。

epidermis
[ˌɛpə`dɝmɪs]
n 表皮

相關字彙
皮膚生成物

The mountain guide was lucky to get away from the mountain lion with only a few scratches on his epidermis.
山林嚮導很幸運，只受一些表皮抓傷就擺脫山獅。

記憶技巧 epi- 表示在～上；derm- 表示皮膚；epidermis 的意思是上層皮膚，特指表皮。

- beauty spot 美人痣
- birthmark 胎記
- freckle 雀斑
- goose bumps 雞皮疙瘩
- mole 痣

dermatology
[ˌdɝmə`tɑlədʒɪ]
n 皮膚病學（科）

The dermatology department was well-known for diagnosing sources of skin rash.
皮膚科部門以診斷皮膚疹病原聞名。

記憶技巧 dermato- 表示皮膚；-logy 表示理論、學說；dermatology 的意思是皮膚科。

dermatologist
[ˌdɝmə`tɑlədʒɪst]
n 皮膚科醫師

After he saw a special dermatologist, Tom's burned skin was almost unnoticeable.
求診一名特別的皮膚科醫師之後，湯姆燙傷的皮膚幾乎看不出來。

記憶技巧 -ist 表示人；dermatologist 的意思是皮膚科醫師。

hypoderm [ˋhaɪpədɝm] **n** 皮下組織	The knife wound was certain to result in scarring, because the cut went deep into the hypoderm. 由於傷口深及皮下組織，刀傷一定會留下疤痕。 記憶技巧　hypo- 表示在～下；derm- 表示皮膚；hypoderm 的意思皮下。
dermatitis [͵dɝməˋtaɪtɪs] **n** 皮膚炎	The man was prescribed a special ointment to be applied twice daily for his dermatitis on his elbows. 男子被開立特殊藥膏，一天抹兩次治療手肘皮膚炎。 記憶技巧　dermat- 表示皮膚；-itis 表示發炎；dermatitis 即皮膚炎。

root - rad

可藉由子音 t 和 d 互換，母音通轉來記憶，兩者的意思皆是根。

radical [ˋrædɪk!] **a** 基本的，主要的，最初的	With nothing able to reduce the gap between rich and poor, the professor's radical economic ideas are becoming more attractive. 由於縮小貧富差距束手無策，教授的激進的經濟概念愈來愈吸引人。 記憶技巧　rad- 表示根；-ical 為形容詞字尾；radical 的意思是根本的、激進的。
radish [ˋrædɪʃ] **n** 蘿蔔	After dicing the white radish, you can boil it in a soup or simmer it in a stew. 白蘿蔔切丁後，可放進湯裡煮，或跟著燉菜一起慢煮。 記憶技巧　rad- 表示根；radish（蘿蔔）屬於根菜類。
eradicate [ɪˋrædɪ͵ket] **v** 根絕，消滅	While no one was looking, the legislators passed a series of laws designed to eradicate the protestors from the site. 立法委員趁隙通過一連串將抗議人士驅離現場的法案。 記憶技巧　e- 等同於 ex-，表示外面；rad- 表示根；-ate 為動詞字尾；eradictae 的意思是根除。

相關字彙
去除某物

- clear 清除
- dispose of 去除（或處理、捨棄）某人、物
- eliminate 消除
- displace（從原來的地方）移開
- disperse 將～安置在不同地點
- dissolve 分解
- remove 去掉

eradicable

[ɪˈrædɪkəbl]

a 可根除的，
可拔除的

It was proven that polio was a disease that was eradicable, but there have been a few recorded cases recently.

小兒麻痺症證實是可根除的疾病，但最近出現一些病例。

記憶技巧 -able 為形容詞字尾；eradicable 表示可以根除的。

rat - rod

可藉由子音 t 和 d 互換、母音通轉來記憶，有學者推測 rat（老鼠）和 rod- 有字源上的關係，兩者的意思皆是咬。

rodent

[ˈrodn̩t]

a 齧齒動物的

When the farmer believed there was a rodent problem, he adopted a dozen cats to live on his farm.

農夫發現齧齒動物問題後，領養 12 隻貓讓牠們住在農場。

記憶技巧 rod- 表示咬；-ent 為名詞字尾；rodent 表示齧齒動物。

相關字彙
吃東西的方式

- bite 咬
- bolt 吞吃
- champ 大聲地咀嚼
- chomp 大聲咀嚼
- crunch 嘎吱作響地咬嚼
- devour 狼吞虎嚥地吃
- gobble 狼吞虎嚥
- gulp 大口吞
- munch 津津有味地嚼
- nibble 一點點地咬

corrode

[kəˈrod]

v 侵蝕，腐蝕

There can be a problem with a city's drinking water when acidic rain corrodes old lead pipes.

酸雨侵蝕老舊鉛管的話，市區飲水就可能出現問題。

記憶技巧 cor- 等同於 com-，表示加強語氣；rod- 表示咬；corrode 的字面意思上是咬，引申為侵蝕、腐蝕。

corrosive

[kəˈrosɪv]

a 侵蝕的，腐蝕的

As the pH level of water lowers because there is more CO_2 in the air, the water becomes more corrosive.

空氣中的二氧化碳增加，水的酸鹼值下降，水變得較有腐蝕性。

記憶技巧 -ive 為形容詞字尾。

erode

[ɪˈrod]

v 侵蝕，腐蝕

Water and ice have eroded the area known as the Grand Canyon for the past 20 million years.

過去 2 千萬年以來，水和冰一直腐蝕大峽谷這個區域。

記憶技巧 e- 等同於 ex-，表示離開；rod- 表示咬；erode 字面上意思是咬掉，引申為侵蝕、腐蝕。

erosive

[ɪˈrosɪv]

a 侵蝕的，腐蝕的

The erosive effect of the Pacific waves created the spectacular coastline of eastern Taiwan.

太平洋波浪侵蝕效應造成台灣東海岸壯麗的海岸線。

記憶技巧 -ive 為形容詞字尾。

---

cut - cide

雖無明確字源上的關係，但可藉由子音 t 和 d 互換、母音通轉來記憶，兩者的意思皆是切。

---

decide

[dɪˈsaɪd]

v 決定，裁決，選定

The employee took a week off to conclusively decide which job offer he would accept.

員工請假一週，為接受哪一個工作機會做最後決定。

記憶技巧 de- 表示離開；cid- 表示切；decide 的字面意思是切開，引申為果斷決定。

---

decisive

[dɪˈsaɪsɪv]

a 決定性的，果決的

After returning to his office, the decisive manager chose to fire the staff member who was regularly late.

回到辦公室之後，果決的經理選擇辭掉經常遲到的員工。

記憶技巧 -ive 為形容詞字尾。

---

concise

[kənˈsaɪs]

a 簡潔的，概括的

I don't have time for a long explanation, so please give me a concise summary of what is going on.

我沒有時間聆聽冗長解釋，麻煩簡短說一下大概情形。

記憶技巧 con- 表示加強語氣；cis- 表示切；concise 的意思是切除乾淨，引申為簡潔的。

---

circumcise

[ˈsɝkəmˌsaɪz]

v 行割禮

The Jewish mother explained to her non-Jewish friend that her son was circumcised to follow their religious custom.

猶太母親向非猶太的友人說明她兒子行割禮是為了遵循宗教習俗。

記憶技巧 circum- 表示迴繞、圈；cis- 表示割；circumcise 即是割一圈下來，後來當做行割禮解釋。

相關字彙
摘除身體的某部分或器官

- amputate 截（肢）
- castrate 割去睪丸
- decapitate 斬首
- disembowel 除去～的內臟
- eviscerate 取出～的內臟
- mutilate 切斷（手足等）

precise

[prɪ`saɪs]

🅐 精確的，考究的

The steel sheet needed to be of a precise thickness, or it could become jammed in the roller.

鋼板厚度必須精確，否則可能會卡在滾軸。

記憶技巧　pre- 表示前面；cis- 表示切；precise 表示事先就想好要怎麼切割，下刀精準，引申為精確的。

---

precision

[prɪ`sɪʒən]

🄝 精確，嚴謹

The die casting company had a reputation for extreme precision when producing its molds.

壓鑄公司以製模極度精確著稱。

記憶技巧　-ion 為名詞字尾。

---

homicide

[`hɑmə͵saɪd]

🄝 殺人犯

The homocide detective worked overtime on the case, because the police chief demanded that it be solved quickly.

命案偵查員超時查案，因為警長要求快速破案。

記憶技巧　hom- 表示人；cid- 表示殺；homicide 是殺人案或殺人犯。

---

suicide

[`suə͵saɪd]

🄝 自殺

The hand-written note lay next to the body of a woman who apparently committed suicide.

手寫字條放在看似自殺的女子屍體旁邊。

記憶技巧　sui- 表示自己；cid- 表示殺；suicide 的意思是自殺。

---

herbicide

[`hɝbə͵saɪd]

🄝 除草劑

The scientist claimed that herbicide was not necessary to increase crop yields.

科學家聲稱要增加作物收成，除草劑並非必要的。

記憶技巧　herb- 表示草；cid- 表示殺；herbicide 的意思是除草劑。

---

insecticide

[ɪn`sɛktə͵saɪd]

🄝 殺蟲劑

The pest control company produced predatory ladybugs to release in the fields as a replacement for insecticide.

害蟲防治公司生產獵食性的瓢蟲，野放田裡以替代殺蟲劑。

記憶技巧　insect 表示昆蟲；cid- 表示殺；insecticide 的意思是殺蟲劑。

Part **2**

CH 1

CH 2

CH 3

齒間音、齒齦音、齒齦後音、硬顎音轉換

原來如此！

drop 意思是「掉落」或「落下」，母音通轉，同源字 droop 意思是「下垂」；drape 有垂掛的意思，雖不是同源字，但僅母音不同，可藉由 drop 及 droop 聯想學習。

eat - ed
可藉由子音 t 和 d 互換、母音通轉來記憶，兩者的意思皆是吃。

---

edible
[ˈɛdəbl̩]
a 可食用的

If you're camping in the forest, don't forget to consult your field guide to find out which mushrooms are edible.
樹林露營時，別忘了查閱野外指南以了解那些蘑菇可食用。

記憶技巧　ed- 表示吃；-ible 為形容詞字尾；edible 的意思可食用的。

---

inedible
[ɪnˈɛdəbl̩]
a 不可食用的

In the USA, the carp is considered an inedible fish because of too many fishbones, but it is widely consumed in Asia.
在美國，鯉魚因為多刺，一般認為不可食用，但是在亞洲很多人在吃。

記憶技巧　in- 為否定詞；inedible 表示不可食用的。

---

obese
[oˈbis]
a 肥胖的

Entering the airport for the first time in the USA, the Chinese student was amazed to see such an obese population.
首次踏入美國機場，中國學生看到這麼多肥胖的人，感到十分訝異。

記憶技巧　ob- 等同於 over，表示超過；es- 表示吃；obese 表示吃過多造成肥胖的。

---

obesity
[oˈbisətɪ]
n 肥胖

Chronic obesity is a major problem in American society, robbing the population of health and productivity.
長期肥胖是美國社會一大問題，剝奪民眾健康及生產力。

記憶技巧　ob- 等同於 over，表示超過；es- 表示吃；-ity 為名詞字尾；obesity 表示吃過多造成肥胖。

great - grand
可藉由子音 t 和 d 互換，母音通轉來記憶，兩者的意思皆是大。

---

grand
[grænd]
a 偉大的，高貴的，大的

The land developer chose to develop the riverside on a grand scale, to increase the potential for profit.
土地開發商選擇大規模開發河岸地區，以增加收益潛力。

記憶技巧　grand 即（偉）大的。

grandiose
[`ɡrændɪos]

a 宏偉的，誇大的

The wealthy tycoon's plans for a religious theme park were grandiose, but the ability to fund it was uncertain.
財力雄厚的商業鉅子的宗教主題公園計畫非常浩大，但是挹注資金的能力不明確。

記憶技巧 grand- 表示大；-ose 等同於 -ous，為形容詞字尾；grandiose 的意思是宏偉的。

相關字彙
藝術相關

- aesthetic 美學的
- lifelike 栩栩如生的
- artistic 藝術的
- pictorial 如畫的
- avant-garde 前衛的
- surrealistic 超現實主義的

grandeur
[`ɡrændʒɚ]

n 偉大，高貴

The Grand Cypress Ballroom exuded the grandeur and charm of a regal estate.
大柏舞廳散發出帝王豪邸的貴氣及魅力。

記憶技巧 grand- 表示大；-eur 為法文名詞字尾；grandeur 的意思是偉大。

grandparent
[`ɡrænd͵pɛrənt]

n 祖父、母

Harold was not prepared to be a grandparent when his son returned home from college with the surprising news.
兒子帶著意外消息從大學返家時，哈洛德還沒準備好要當阿公。

記憶技巧 grand- 表示大；parent 表示父母親之一；grandparent 指的是比父母親大一輩的人，即祖父母。

grandchild
[`ɡrænd͵tʃaɪld]

n 孫子

Holding his grandchild in his arms, the man warmed up to the idea of having a new addition to the extended family.
孫子抱在懷裡時，男子才開始喜歡大家庭增加一名新成員的想法。

記憶技巧 grand- 表示大；child 表示小孩；grandchild 的實際語意和字面上意思不同，在講輩分時，特指比小孩年輕一輩的，指孫子。

aggrandize
[ə`ɡræn͵daɪz]

v 增大

The man founded the non-profit organization to expand his social networks and aggrandize his family name.
為了擴展社交網絡及提高姓氏地位，男子創設該非營利組織。

記憶技巧 ag- 等同於 ab-，表示朝～方向；grand- 表示大；-ize 為動詞字尾；aggrandize 的意思是使～變大。

Part **2**
CH 1
CH 2
CH 3

齒間音、齒齦音、齒齦後音、硬顎音轉換

sit - sed

可藉由子音 t 和 d 互換、母音通轉來記憶，兩者的意思皆是坐。

---

sedative
[ˋsɛdətɪv]

n 鎮靜劑，止痛藥

Lavender is a flower that can be served in tea, and its oil can be inhaled as a natural sedative.

薰衣草是一種可當茶來泡的花，精油可吸入作為天然鎮靜劑。

記憶技巧　sed- 表示坐；-ate 為動詞字尾；-ive 為形容詞字尾；sedative 的意思是使人安靜坐下來的，後來亦作鎮定劑解釋。

---

sediment
[ˋsɛdəmənt]

n 沉澱物，沖積物

The muddy sediment was dredged out of the canal, so it could become deep enough to serve as a waterway for boats.

運河疏浚了淤泥沉澱，因此深度足以作為船隻水道。

記憶技巧　sed- 表示坐；-ment 為名詞字尾；sediment 的意思是（坐）落下來的沉澱物。

---

assiduous
[əˋsɪdʒuəs]

a 勤勉的

The man was assiduous in work to make sure his car was immaculately clean.

為了確定愛車無可挑剔也清潔，男子勤奮擦洗。

記憶技巧　as- 表示朝某方向；sid- 表示坐；-ous 為形容詞字尾；assiduous 表示可以坐下來鑽研學問，引申為勤勉的。

相關字彙
勤勉近義字

• sedulous 勤勉的　　　• conscientious 認真的　　　• industrious 勤奮的
• committed 盡心盡責的　• diligent 勤勉的

---

settle
[ˋsɛtl̩]

v 安頓，排解，定居，調停

The woman sued the political candidate, and settled out of court for half a million dollars.

女子控告參政候選人，並五十萬元庭外和解。

記憶技巧　set- 等同於 sed- / sit，表示坐；settle 表示坐落下來，引申為安頓、定居下來。

---

session
[ˋsɛʃən]

n 會議，開庭，授課時間，期間

During the therapy session, it was discovered that the woman was abused as a child.

治療期間，女子被發現童年遭虐。

記憶技巧　sess- 等同於 sit，表示坐；-ion 為名詞字尾；session 指的是坐下來的一段期間，後指開會、開庭的一段時間。

assess
[ə`sɛs]
V 評價，徵收，課稅

Ever year, the city property appraisers assess the values of all properties within city limits.
每年市不動產估價師會估算全市所有不動產價值。

記憶技巧 as- 等同於 ad-，表示往某方向；sess- 等同於 sit，表示坐；assess 的意思是坐下，特指以前坐法官旁邊確定罰金或稅金要繳多少錢的助理工作，後來才有評價、課稅等意思。

obsessive
[əb`sɛsɪv]
a 妄想的

The female celebrity was nervous seeing the obsessive fans outside of her apartment window.
看到公寓窗外妄想的粉絲，女星感到緊張。

記憶技巧 ob- 表示反對；sess- 表示坐；-ive 為形容詞字尾；obsessive 的本意是坐在~對面、包圍、佔據，表示只看的到，卻未必可以得到的，引申為妄想的。

possess
[pə`zɛs]
V 持有

When one possesses the power to influence the lives of millions of people, there is great pressure to be responsible.
擁有影響數百萬人性命的權力時，要負責任有很大的壓力。

記憶技巧 pos- 等同於 power，表示力量；sess- 等同於 sit，表示坐；possess 的意思是坐擁力量，引申為持有。

president
[`prɛzədənt]
n 總統，總裁，
（大學）校長

When you achieve the position of president in the company, you are entitled to use the company's executive jet.
登上公司總裁職位，你就有資格使用行政噴射機。

記憶技巧 pre- 表示前面；sid- 等同於 sit，表示坐；-ent 為名詞字尾，表示人；president 字面意思是坐在前面的人，引申為總裁、校長等。

reside
[rɪ`zaɪd]
V 住，居住

The Governors of the States are required to reside in the stately home across the street from the capitol building.
美國州長規定住在州議會大廈對面的豪華住宅。

記憶技巧 re- 表示回來；sid- 表示坐；reside 字面上的意思回來坐，表示即便每天外出，都還是會回家住，引申為住。

residue
[`rɛzədju]
n 殘餘

The investigator found gunpowder residue on the clothing of the shooting suspect.
調查人員發現槍擊嫌犯衣服上的火藥殘留。

記憶技巧 re- 表示後面；sid- 表示坐；residue 的意思是留在後面，引申為殘餘。

Part
2
CH 1
CH 2
CH 3

齒間音、齒齦音、齒齦後音、硬顎音轉換

subside
[səb`saɪd]
v 降落，平息

When the water levels subsided in the reservoir, a maintenance worker discovered a 600 year-old submerged statue of the Buddha.
水庫水位下降，維護工人發現一尊 600 年歷史泡在水裡的佛陀雕像。

記憶技巧 sub- 表示在～下面；sid- 表示坐；subside 的意思是坐下來，引申為降落、平息。

subsidy
[`sʌbsədɪ]
n 助學金，補助金，津貼

The green energy subsidy offered to homeowners encouraged them to purchase energy-saving devices.
提供給屋主的綠能津貼促使他們購置節能設施。

記憶技巧 sub- 表示在～下面；sid- 表示坐；-y 為名詞字尾；subsidy 的意思是讓～安定坐下來的助學金、補助金。

相關字彙
補助金和津貼

- allowance 零用錢
- annuity 年金
- bursary 大學獎學金
- fellowship（給研究生等的）獎學金
- grant 獎學金
- scholarship 獎學金
- stipend 津貼

subsidiary
[səb`sɪdɪˌɛrɪ]
n 附屬品，子公司

A subsidiary of the pharmaceutical company researched the natural medicinal cures known to indigenous peoples.
一家製藥公司的子公司研究原住民族才知道的天然藥物。

記憶技巧 sub- 表示在～下面；sid- 表示坐；-ary 為名詞字尾；subsidiary 的意思是（坐）在～下面的人、事、物、機構等，引申為附屬品、子公司。

besiege
[bɪ`sidʒ]
v 圍攻，困擾

During the Spanish Civil War, Madrid was a besieged city for two and a half years.
西班牙內戰時期，馬德里是一座遭到兩年半包圍的城市。

記憶技巧 be- 表示在附近；siege- 等同於 sit，表示坐；besiege 在附近坐下來，引申為包圍、圍攻。

猜猜看！

❶ 請從 triple / triangle / trinity 等單字猜出字根 tri- 所表示的單字？

❷「president（總裁，校長，總統）」是「坐在前面的人」，猜 sid- 所表示的單字？

答案：❶ three（三）　❷ sit（坐）

two - dia

可藉由子音 t 和 d 互換、母音通轉來記憶，dia- 的意思是「through（穿過、通過）」，字源學家推測，dia- 和 two 是同字源，或許是出自於穿透兩個端點。

diabetes
[ˌdaɪə`bitiz]
n 糖尿病

Diabetes mellitus is an increasingly common disease resulting in high blood sugar in the bloodstream.
糖尿病是一種日益普遍的疾病，會造成高血糖。

記憶技巧 dia- 表示穿透；betes 表示走；diabetes 字面的意思是走過，糖尿量的病症，其中一個是尿液多，會有大量尿液排出身體外。

相關字彙　常見病症
● allergy 過敏症
● amenorrhea 經痛
● amnesia 失憶
● aphasia 失語症
● arthritis 關節炎
● asthma 氣喘（病）
● atrophy 萎縮
● autism 自閉症
● Down syndrome 唐氏症
● epilepsy 癲癇
● gallstone 膽石
● halitosis 口臭
● heatstroke 中暑
● impotence 陽萎
● migraine 偏頭痛
● tennis elbow 肘部發炎

diagnose
[`daɪəgnoz]
v 診斷

The mechanic turned on the engine, pressed the gas pedal, and easily diagnosed the problem.
技術人員發動引擎，壓下油門踏板，輕鬆查出問題。

記憶技巧 dia- 表示穿透、徹底；gno- 等同於 know，表示知道；diagnose 字面意思是徹底知道，引申為診斷。

diameter
[daɪ`æmətɚ]
n 直徑

The gas pipeline with a 6-inch diameter ruptured, because its internal pressure was above its threshold.
直徑六吋的油管破裂，因為內部壓力超出限制。

記憶技巧 dia- 表示穿透；meter 表示測量；diameter 的意思是穿過圓心測量到的直徑。

dialect
[`daɪəlɛkt]
n 方言，土話

The Minnan language sounds similar to a dialect of Hakkanese spoken in Xiamen, China.
閩南語聽起來跟中國廈門地區所講的客家話相似。

記憶技巧 dia- 表示跨越、穿透；lect- 表示說；dialect 本指和人交談，後來特指某地區的方言、土話。

dialogue
[`daɪəˌlɔg]
n 對話，交談

The dialogue between two lovers should not be recorded and made public, but it should remain private.
男女交往時的談話不該錄音公開，而是要保有隱私。

記憶技巧 dia- 表示跨越；log- 表示說；dialogue 即交談。

diaphanous

[daɪˈæfənəs]

a 透明的

The award-winning celebrity surprised audiences with a white, diaphanous dress on top of a lacy, black bra.

得獎的名人穿著白色透明洋裝搭蕾絲黑色胸罩，觀眾驚呆了。

記憶技巧 dia- 表示穿透；phan- 表示顯示；-ous 為形容詞字尾；diaphanous 的意思是若隱若現、透露出來，引申為透明的。

Section 2

〔θ〕對應〔d〕

---

faith - fid

子音 th 和 d 互換，母音通轉，兩者的意思皆是相信。

---

fidelity

[fɪˈdɛlətɪ]

n 忠誠，傳真度

His fidelity to the cause of indigenous people helped him to gain widespread respect as an advocate.

他對原住民事業的赤誠使他博得提倡者的尊稱。

記憶技巧 fid- 表示相信；-ity 為名詞字尾；fidelity 即忠誠的意思。

---

confidence

[ˈkɑnfədəns]

n 信心，信任，大膽

The confidence the man exuded on the court contrasted with the quiet demeanor he showed off the court.

男子法庭上散發的自信與法庭外的安靜神情形成對比。

記憶技巧 con- 表示加強語氣；fid- 表示相信；-ence 為名詞字尾；confidence 的意思是信任、信心。

---

confidant

[ˌkɑnfɪˈdænt]

n 知己

The paranoid emperor trusted no one, except for a lone confidant, whom he made the Chief of Security.

疑心重的皇帝不信任任何人，除了一位孤鳥親信，親自拔擢為保安隊長。

記憶技巧 con- 表示加強語氣；fid- 表示相信；-ant 為名詞字尾，表示人；confidant 是可以相信的人，表示知己。

相關字彙
值得信賴的人
- right-hand man 左右手
- mainstay 支柱
- anchor 靠山
- trouper 臺柱演員

confidential

[ˌkɑnfəˋdɛnʃəl]

a 機密的，獲信任的

The office worker was asked to deliver the confidential papers personally to the office of the attorney.

辦公室員工被要求親自將機密文件送到律師事務所。

記憶技巧　con- 表示加強語氣；fid- 表示相信；-ence 為名詞字尾；-ial為形容詞字尾；confidential指的是機密的、可信任的。

---

defy

[dɪˋfaɪ]

v 蔑視，藐視，公然反抗

The survivor of the shipwreck defied the odds and survived on a deserted island for two months.

船難生還者不向命運低頭，在荒島求生了兩個月。

記憶技巧　de- 表示離開；-fy 等同於 faith，表示信念；defy 的意思是放棄信念，引申為藐視、公然反抗。

---

defiant

[dɪˋfaɪənt]

a 大膽的，反抗的

The defiant prisoner did not reveal the location of the rebel base and resisted until his last breath.

頑強的囚犯不供出叛軍基地，一直抗拒到死。

記憶技巧　-ant 為形容詞字尾；defiant 是 defy 的形容詞。

---

diffident

[ˋdɪfədənt]

a 無自信的，謙遜的

The diffident youngster sat in the back of the class, wanting to avoid the attention of his teacher.

缺乏自信的年輕人坐在教室後面，想要避開老師的注意。

記憶技巧　dif- 等同於 dis-，表示離開；fid- 表示相信；-ent 為形容詞字尾；diffident 的意思是不相信自己，引申為無自信的。

---

perfidy

[ˋpɝfədɪ]

n 背信，出賣

No one trusted the hermit, because of the perfidy that was trademark of his dark past.

沒人相信那名隱士，因為背信是他黑暗過往的特性。

記憶技巧　per- 表示穿透、藉由；fid- 表示相信；perfidy 的意思是藉由別人信任來欺騙，引申為背信。

Part

2

CH 1

CH 2

CH 3

齒間音、齒齦音、齒齦後音、硬顎音轉換

Section **3**

〔d〕對應〔t〕

end - ante

子音 d 和 t 互換、母音通轉，end 現今意思是結束，古義是在～之前或相對，和 ante（在～之前）系出同源、兩者同源並不難理解，我們常說在～之前結束，結束的概念是建立在某個時間點之前。

---

antebellum
[ˈæntɪˋbɛləm]
n 戰爭前的

The antebellum period before the American Civil War was marked by a large expansion of territory in the West.
美國南北戰爭前的時期特徵為西方領土大擴張。

> 記憶技巧 ante- 表示在～之前；bell- 表示戰爭；antebellum 即戰前。

---

antecedent
[ˌæntəˋsidənt]
n 前事，前情

The Agricultural Revolution, which led to great population growth, was an antecedent of the Industrial Revolution.
造成人口爆炸的農業革命是工業革命的前哨。

> 記憶技巧 ante- 表示在～之前；ced- 表示走；-ent 為名詞字尾；antecedent 的意思是前情。

---

antediluvian
[ˌæntɪdɪˋluvɪən]
a 大洪水前的，早已過時的

The unicorns were believed to be antediluvian creatures that didn't survive the Great Flood.
一般相信獨角獸是大洪水時期未能存活下來的大洪水前的生物。

> 記憶技巧 ante- 表示在～之前；di- 表示離開；luv- 表示沖洗；-ian 為形容詞字尾；antediluvian 的意思是在洪水來臨之前的。

相關字彙
老舊過時的
- old-fashioned 過時的
- obsolete 過時的
- archaic 古老的
- primitive 原始的
- dated 陳舊的

---

antemeridian
[ˌæntɪməˋrɪdɪən]
a 上午的

The lieutenant preferred to complete his daily tasks during antemeridian time, so he could go fishing in the afternoons.
陸軍中尉偏好上午完成日常工作，這樣下午就能去釣魚。

> 記憶技巧 ante- 表示在～之前；meridian 表示子午線；antemeridian 指子午線之前的，即上午的。

anticipate
[æn`tɪsə,pet]

v 預期，期望，預料

The investor anticipated an increase in the stock price after the company was bought by a technology giant.
公司被科技大廠收購後，投資者預期股價上漲。

記憶技巧 　anti- 等同於 ante-，表示在～之前；cip- 等同於 cap-，表示拿；-ate 為動詞字尾；anticipate 的字面意思是事先拿，直到 1749 年才有預期的意思。

end - anti

子音 d 和 t 互換，母音通轉，end 現今意思是結束，古義是在～之前或相對，anti- 的意思即保留相對這個古義。

antidote
[`æntɪ,dot]

n 解毒藥，解毒劑

Once the patient was diagnosed with the dangerous disease, they administered an antidote immediately.
病患一旦診斷出危險疾病，他們隨即給予一帖解藥。

記憶技巧 　anti- 表示對抗；dot- 表示給；antidote 表示給～人對抗的力量，引申為解毒劑。

antagonism
[æn`tægə,nɪzəm]

n 對抗，敵對，對立，敵意

Every time Tim reached out to his brother, he was met with unwavering antagonism.
每次提姆向弟弟伸出援手時，碰到的都是強硬的敵意。

記憶技巧 　ant- 表示對抗；agon- 表示競爭；-ism 為名詞字尾；antagonism 的意思是競爭、對抗。

antibody
[`æntɪ,badɪ]

n 抗體

The human body is a powerful fighter of disease, producing antibodies that attack invading germs.
人體是一個強大的疾病戰士，能夠製造攻擊入侵細菌的抗體。

記憶技巧 　anti- 表示對抗；body 表示身體；antibody 即抗體。

相關字彙
感染和對抗感染

- contagion 感染
- cross-infection 交叉感染
- defence 防禦
- fester 化膿
- histamine 組織胺
- immune system 免疫系統
- inflammation 發炎
- quarantine 隔離
- septic 化膿的

antipathy
[æn`tɪpəθɪ]

n 反感，厭惡

The leader revived the historical antipathy among his citizens against the neighboring countries.
領導人重新挑起公民對鄰國的歷史反感。

記憶技巧 　anti- 表示對抗；path- 表示感覺；-y 為名詞字尾；antipathy 即反感。

under - intra

雖無明確字源關係，但可藉由子音 d 和 t 互換、母音通轉來記憶，under 是在～之下，intra- 則是在～之內。

intramural
[ˌɪntrə`mjurəl]
a 同一校內的，內部的

Within the walls of this corporate complex, employees are provided with a variety of intramural recreational activities.
集團企業提供員工各式各樣的內部休閒活動。

記憶技巧　intra- 表示在～之內；mural 表示牆壁的；intramural 指的是在牆內，引申出校內的意思。

intravenous
[ˌɪntrə`vinəs]
a 靜脈內的

The runner was so dehydrated that paramedics needed to provide an intravenous injection of fluids.
跑者脫水嚴重，急救護理人員必須給予流體靜脈注射。

記憶技巧　intra- 表示在～之內；ven- 等同於 vein，表示靜脈；-ous 為形容詞字尾；intravenous 的意思是靜脈內的。

intrinsic
[ɪn`trɪnsɪk]
a 本身的，固有的，內在的

Every infant has an intrinsic need to feel the warm embrace of his or her mother.
每一嬰兒都有感覺母親溫暖擁抱的內在需求。

記憶技巧　intra- 表示在內；intrinsic 即內在的。

mind - ment

子音 d 和 t 互換，母音通轉，兩者皆表示心。

mental
[`mɛntl]
a 精神的，智力的，心理的

The man's potential was not limited by his physical body, but it was his mental state that stopped him.
這名男子的潛力不受生理限制，羈絆他的是心理狀態。

記憶技巧　ment- 表示心；-al 為形容詞字尾；mental 即心理的。

mention
[`mɛnʃən]
v 提到，記載，提名表揚

I am sorry if you missed the meeting, because I failed to mention it to you during breakfast.
早餐時我未向您提到這個會議，若是讓您錯過了，我很抱歉。

記憶技巧　ment- 表示心；-ion 為名詞字尾；mention 的意思是將～放心上，1520 年代才有動詞意思，引申為提及。

commentary

[`kɑmən‚tɛrɪ]

n 註解，評論，紀事

When the student returned to the class after a long absence, his classmate provided commentary on what he had missed.

學生長期缺席後回到班上，同學評論了他錯過的事情。

記憶技巧 com- 表示加強語氣；ment- 表示心；-ary 為名詞字尾；commentary 的意思是將～記在心裡，引申為註解。

dementia

[dɪ`mɛnʃɪə]

n 早發性癡呆

When the woman's children returned to visit her at the nursing home, dementia prevented her from recognizing them.

孩子回到安養院看望時，婦人的癡呆症狀讓她認不出他們。

記憶技巧 de- 表示離開；ment- 表示心；-ia 表示疾病；dementia 即心理無法正常運作的疾病，當作癡呆解釋。

amentia

[ə`mɛnʃɪə]

n 精神錯亂

Patients in varying states of amentia were cared for in a nursing facility staffed by healthcare practitioners.

各種精神錯亂的病患在配備照護人員的安養機構中受到照顧。

記憶技巧 a- 表示離開；ment- 表示心；-ia 表示疾病；amentia 是心理無法正常運作的症狀，引申為精神錯亂。

remind

[rɪ`maɪnd]

v 提醒，使想起

Please remind me where I placed the car keys, so that we won't be late for school.

麻煩提醒一下我把汽車鑰匙放到哪裡，我們上學才不會遲到。

記憶技巧 re- 表示再一次；mind 表示心；remind 字面上意思是再一次回到心上，引申為提醒。

---

draw - tract

子音 d 和 t 互換，母音通轉，兩者皆表示拖、拉。

---

contract

[`kɑntrækt]

n 合約

The meeting resulted in the signing of a contract whereby the supplier guaranteed its price for the next 12 months.

會議使合約順利簽妥，藉此廠商保證未來 12 個月的價格。

記憶技巧 con- 表示加強語氣；tract- 表示脫、拉；contract 即把大家拉在一起，引申為彼此同意的合約。

Part **2**

CH 1
CH 2
CH 3

齒間音、齒齦音、齒齦後音、硬顎音轉換

attractive
[əˋtræktɪv]
🄰 有吸引力的，
嫵媚的

The players were distracted by the attractive cheerleaders during the game.
比賽期間，選手受到吸睛的啦啦隊員影響而分心。

記憶技巧 at- 等同於 ad-，表示朝～；tract- 表示拉；-ive 為形容詞字尾；attractive 的意思是拉往某方向的，即某對象有吸引力，拉住其他人注意力。

abstract
[ˋæbstrækt]
🄰 抽象的，空想的

Although "love" is an abstract concept, the child had no problem helping her classmates to understand it.
儘管「愛」是一個抽象概念，那名孩子還是能夠幫助同學體會。

記憶技巧 abs- 表示離開；tract- 表示拉；abstract 的意思是拉開，遠離務實的想法，因此愈來愈抽象的。

detraction
[dɪˋtrækʃən]
🄝 減除，誹謗

The bad deeds of the son was not a detraction from the reputation of the father, who was considered a war hero.
兒子的不良行為無損被視為戰爭英雄的父親英名。

記憶技巧 de- 等同於 down，表示下；tract- 表示拉；-ion 為名詞字尾；detraction 的意思是往下拉，引申出詆毀人名譽的意思。

detractor
[dɪˋtræktɚ]
🄝 誹謗者

相關字彙
涉及爭吵、打架的人

The detractors of the new World Trade Center project say that the old facilities are still more than adequate.
貶低新建世貿中心計畫的人說老舊設施仍然堪用。

記憶技巧 -or 表示人。

● opponent 對手　　　● objector 反對者　　　● warrior 戰士
● fighter 戰士　　　● dissenter 持異議者

distractive
[dɪˋstræktɪv]
🄰 分心的

The low-cut red dress of the young woman in the audience was distractive to the guest speaker.
聽眾中的年輕女子的低胸大紅洋裝讓來賓講者分心。

記憶技巧 dis- 表示離開；tract- 表示拉；-ive 為形容詞字尾；distractive 的意思是將別人專注力拉走，引申為分心的。

extract
[ɪkˋstrækt]
🄥 抽離，蒸餾，
摘要，引用

The process extracts sap from the rubber trees to be purified and processed into commercial-grade rubber.
工序是自橡膠樹汁液抽取汁液，提煉、加工為商業等級的橡膠。

記憶技巧 ex- 表示外面；tract- 表示拉；extract 的意思是往外拉，因此有抽離、摘要的意思。

protract
[pro`trækt]

v 拖長，延長

The college student couldn't decide on a major and protracted his college education into an eight-year endeavor.

這名大學生無法決定一門主修，就把大學教育延長到八年。

記憶技巧　pro- 表示往前；tract- 表示拉；protract 的意思是往前拉，引申為延長。

retract
[rɪ`trækt]

v 撤回，收回

The principal had wanted to acknowledge the actions of the fire chief during her speech, but retracted that part.

校長原本想在演講時感謝消防隊長的付出，但是收回了這部分。

記憶技巧　re- 表示回來；tract- 表示拉；retract 即撤回、收回。

subtract
[səb`trækt]

v 減去，扣除

The accountant calculated the net profit by subtracting the expenses from the gross profit.

會計從總利潤扣除支出藉以計算淨利潤。

記憶技巧　sub- 表示在～下面；tract- 表示拉；subtract 字面上意思是往下拉，引申為減去。

track
[træk]

n 痕跡，路程，
跑道，徑賽，軌道

The sales recruit impressed everyone and was on track to break the monthly sales record.

新進行銷人員令大家印象深刻，他正在打破月銷售紀錄之路邁進。

記憶技巧　track 疑似和 tract 同源，tract 即跑步時拉長的路徑、軌跡。

---

murder-mort

子音 d 和 t 互換，母音通轉，兩者原始意思皆表示死。

---

amortize
[ə`mɔrtaɪz]

v 分期償還

The expense for the expensive copy machine was amortized over a five-year period.

昂貴的影印機費用以五年期限分期償還。

記憶技巧　a- 等同於 -ad，表示朝～方向；mort- 表示死亡；-ize 為動詞字尾；amortize 字面意思是使某人死亡，後衍伸出消滅的意思，更明確的意思是消滅債務，引申為分期償還。

相關字彙
償還與拖欠

- clear 償清（債務）
- default 違約
- discharge 清償
- liquidate 償付
- redeem 償還
- square up 付帳

齒間音、齒齦音、齒齦後音、硬顎音轉換

immortal [ɪˋmɔrtl̩] a 不朽的， 流芳百世的	Not only was the vampire a powerful adversary, but it was an immortal creature. 吸血鬼不僅是一個強大對手，也是一個不死的生物。 記憶技巧 im- 為否定詞；mort- 表示死亡；-al 為形容詞字尾；immortal 的意思是不死的。
moribund [ˋmɔrəˏbʌnd] a 垂死的	The stock market was facing a drastic decline and approached a moribund state. 股市面臨重挫，逼近垂死狀態。 記憶技巧 mori- 表示死亡；-bund 為拉丁形容詞字尾，類似 -ing；moribund 即 dying，表示垂死的。
mortgage [ˋmɔrgɪdʒ] n 抵押	The couple took out a 30-year mortgage with the bank to buy the house of their dreams. 為了買下夢想的房子，夫婦背負 30 年的銀行抵押貸款。 記憶技巧 mort- 表示死；gage 表示發誓；mortgage 即死誓，用死來做擔保，引申為抵押。
mortuary [ˋmɔrtʃʊˏɛrɪ] n 停屍間，太平間	The janitor dreaded working in the mortuary each night, especially when he heard unexplained noises. 管理員害怕每晚在停屍間工作，尤其是聽到不明的聲音時。 記憶技巧 mort- 表示死；-ary 為名詞字尾；mortuary 是死者的遺體停放之處，即太平間。

Section 4

〔l〕對應〔t〕

roll - rot

子音 l 和 t 互換，母音通轉，兩者原始意思皆表示輪子、滾動。

---

rotate

[ˋrotet]

v 旋轉，輪流，交替

The restaurant on top of Sydney Tower rotates slowly to give patrons a 360-degree view.
為提供顧客 360 度景觀，雪梨塔頂部餐廳緩慢旋轉。

記憶技巧　rot- 表示輪子；-ate 為動詞字尾；rotate 的意思是輪流、旋轉。

---

rotation

[roˋteʃən]

n 旋轉，交替，循環

The rate of rotation for the revolving restaurant on top of the tower is once every thirty minutes.
塔樓最高處的旋轉餐廳旋轉速率是每三十分鐘轉一圈。

記憶技巧　-ion 為名詞字尾。

---

rotary

[ˋrotərɪ]

a 旋轉的，輪流的

The nostalgic woman still used an old rotary dial phone; you need to use your fingers to turn the dial of it.
懷舊的婦人仍使用舊式旋轉撥號電話，就是要用手指轉撥號盤的那種。

記憶技巧　rot- 表示輪子；-ary 為形容詞字尾；rotary 的意思是輪流的。

原來如此！

相較於 short，long 表示「長」：名詞是與 long 的同源字 length；動詞是 length 的衍生字 lengthen。linger 意思是拖延或徘徊，是 long 的同源字，母音通轉、黏接字尾 -er 衍生而成。

Section **5**

〔s〕對應〔t〕

plus - plut

兩者雖無字源上的關係，但可藉由子音 s 和 t 互換、母音通轉來記憶，plus 的意思是更多，plut 是財富，可想像成財富是累積來的、愈來愈多。

plutocracy

[plu`takrəsɪ]

n 富豪統治，財閥政治

It's not hard to believe that plutocracies exist, given that the wealthy have an immense level of influence.
鑒於富人極大的影響力，不難相信富豪統治是存在的。

記憶技巧 pluto- 表示財富；-cracy 表示統治；plutocracy 即有錢人統治。

相關字彙
各類型統治
- autocracy 獨裁
- kleptocracy 竊盜統治
- democracy 民主制度
- monarchy 君主政治
- oligarchy 寡頭政治
- protectorate 攝政政體

measure - meter

子音 s 和 t 互換，母音通轉，兩者古義皆表示測量。

meter

[`mitɚ]

n 測量器，公尺

The electic meter box measures the monthly electricity use for the house.
電表箱測量屋子每月用電。

記憶技巧 meter 表示測量或測量的單位——公尺。

centimeter

[`sɛntəˌmitɚ]

n 公分

The boy had grown to an astonishing 184 centimeters before his 15th birthday.
這名男孩在 15 歲生日之前長到 184 公分高，令人驚訝。

記憶技巧 cent- 表示百分之一；meter- 表示公尺；centimeter 即一公分。

相關字彙
長度單位
- bore（槍砲、管道等的）口徑
- cubit 腕尺
- foot 英尺
- inch 英吋
- micron 微米
- millimeter 公釐
- nanometer 奈米
- yard 碼

kilometer
[ˋkɪləˏmitɚ]
n 公里

The engineer chose to live in the small town, because it was only 12 kilometers from his office.
工程師選擇住在小鎮，因為距離辦公室僅 12 公里。

記憶技巧　kilo- 表示千；meter- 表示公尺；kilometer 即一千公尺。

---

geometry
[dʒɪˋɑmətrɪ]
n 幾何學

It seems that knowledge in geometry is a requisite for excellence in physics and engineering.
幾何學知識似乎是精通物理及工程學所必需的。

記憶技巧　geo- 表示土地；meter- 表示測量；-y 為名詞字尾；geometry 原本是丈量土地之學，後作幾何學解釋。

相關字彙
各類型數學

- algebra 代數學
- arithmetic 算術
- calculus 微積分
- topology 拓撲數學
- trigonometry 三角學

---

symmetry
[ˋsɪmɪtrɪ]
n 對稱，調和

The 1,000-year-old classical Roman sculpture showed remarkable symmetry in the facial features.
千年歷史的古典羅馬雕像的臉貌明顯對稱。

記憶技巧　sym- 表示一起；meter- 表示測量；-y 為名詞字尾；symmetry 意思是一起測量發現比例對稱。

---

thermometer
[θɚˋmɑmətɚ]
n 溫度計

A food thermometer was inserted into the turkey to measure the internal temperature.
食物溫度計被插入火雞裡面測量內部溫度。

記憶技巧　thermo- 表示熱；meter- 表示測量；thermometer 即測量熱度的溫度計。

---

seismometer
[saɪzˋmɑmətɚ]
n 地震儀

The seismometer at the geological center near Oklahoma City measured an unusually large tremor.
奧克拉荷馬市附近的地質中心的地震儀測得一異常大震動。

記憶技巧　seismo- 表示地震；meter- 表示測量；seismometer 即測量地震強度、方位的地震儀。

Part
2
CH 1
CH 2
CH 3

齒間音、齒齦音、齒齦後音、硬顎音轉換

Section **6**

〔θ〕對應〔t〕

thin - ten

子音 th 和 t 互換，母音通轉，兩者皆表示薄。

---

tenuity

[tɛn`juətɪ]

n 稀薄，貧乏

There was a barrier between them, but the tenuity was enough for them to stand each other.

他們之間有嫌隙，但還不至於無法彼此忍受。

記憶技巧　ten- 表示薄；-ity 為名詞字尾；tenuity 即稀薄。

---

tenuous

[`tɛnjuəs]

a 稀薄的，薄弱的

The friendship between them was made tenuous by the fact that one of them owed the other a lot of money.

欠款未還，雙方的友誼因而變淡。

記憶技巧　ten- 表示薄；-ous 為形容詞字尾；tenuous 即稀薄的。

相關字彙　無法持久、短促

- brevity 短暫
- impermanence 暫時性
- transience 稍縱即逝
- mutability 易變性

---

attenuate

[ə`tɛnjuˌet]

v 使稀薄，減弱

The cement seawall was attenuated by the constant pounding of the waves.

水泥海堤因長期遭受海浪擊打而變小。

記憶技巧　at- 等同於 ad-，表示朝～方向；ten- 表示薄；-ate 為動詞字尾；attenuate 的意思是使稀薄。

相關字彙　減少、減輕

- lessen 減輕
- reduce 降低
- subside 消退
- chip away 小塊小塊地弄掉
- weaken 削弱
- erode 腐蝕
- undermine 暗中破壞

---

extenuation

[ɪk`stɛnjuˌeʃən]

n 減輕，偏袒的辯護

During the father's conversation with the judge, he appealed for an extenuation of his son's criminal act.

父親與法官談話時，央求對自己兒子的犯行從輕發落。

記憶技巧　ex- 表示外面；ten- 表示薄；-ate 為動詞字尾；-ion 為名詞字尾；extenuation 的意思是愈變愈薄，引申為減輕。

three - tri / ter

子音 th 和 t 互換，母音通轉，兩者皆表示三。

---

triple
[`trɪp!]
a 三倍

The name-brand medicine was more than triple the cost of the generic brand.

原廠藥是非專利藥的三倍價錢。

記憶技巧 tri- 表示三；pl- 表示折；triple 即三折，引申為三倍。

---

triangle
[`traɪæŋg!]
n 三角形

The percussion musical instrument is in the shape of a triangle, and is, in fact, named a "triangle."

打擊樂器是三角形狀，事實上，就稱作「三角鐵」。

記憶技巧 tri- 表示三；angle 表示角；triangle 即三角形。

---

trilogy
[`trɪlədʒɪ]
n 三部曲

The Lord of the Rings trilogy of novels was made into a movie trilogy directed by Peter Jackson.

魔戒三部曲小說被拍成彼得‧傑克森執導的電影三部曲。

記憶技巧 tri- 表示三；-logy 表示故事；trilogy 即三部曲。

相關字彙
書籍相關

- almanac 年鑑
- autobiography 自傳
- best-seller 暢銷書
- booklet 小冊子
- cookbook 食譜
- encyclopedia 百科全書
- memoirs 自傳
- reprint 再版（本）

---

tribe
[traɪb]
n 部落，種族

Some Indonesian islands are still populated by tribes that have not changed the way they live for a thousand years.

一些印尼島嶼仍住著一千年從未改變生活方式的部族。

記憶技巧 tri- 表示三；tribe 本是羅馬三大部族：拉丁人、薩賓人和伊特魯裡亞人。

相關字彙
群聚

- colony 殖民地
- community 社區
- population 人口，（特定）居民

---

tertiary
[`tɝʃɪɛrɪ]
a 第三的

A college education is often referred to in some countries as tertiary, or third-level, education.

一些國家中，大學教育常被稱為 tertiary，亦即第三層級的教育。

記憶技巧 ter- 表示第三；-ary 為形容詞字尾；tertiary 即第三的。

Part **2**

CH 1
CH 2
CH 3

齒間音、齒齦音、齒齦後音、硬顎音轉換

thumb - tum

子音 th 和 t 互換，母音通轉，兩者皆表示腫脹的，thumb 現今意思是大拇指，即最腫脹的手指。

---

tumid
[ˋtjumɪd]
a 腫脹的，浮誇的

The area on the side of the woman's neck appeared tumid, and it was a swollen lymph node.
女子頸部側邊出現腫脹，是個腫大的淋巴結。

記憶技巧 tum- 表示腫；-id 為形容詞字尾；tumid 即腫脹的。

---

tumescence
[tjuˋmɛsn̩s]
n 腫脹

The proboscis monkey is named for the surprising tumescense on its nose.
長鼻猴因鼻子突兀腫脹而得名。

記憶技巧 tum- 表示腫；-escence 表示名詞字尾，指變化的過程；tumescence 即變腫。

---

tumor
[ˋtjumɚ]
n 腫瘤

There was a lump on the man's jawbone that turned out to be a tumor.
男子頷骨出現腫塊，後來變成一處腫瘤。

記憶技巧 tum- 表示腫；-or 為名詞字尾；tumor 即腫瘤。

---

tumult
[ˋtjumʌlt]
n 喧囂，騷動

The tumult of the chaotic classroom was too much for the teacher to handle.
教室太亂，一片喧囂，老師控制不了。

記憶技巧 tum- 表示腫；tumult 的意思是整個氣氛熱絡，像是發酵後膨脹起來，引申為喧囂、騷動。

---

tumultuous
[tjuˋmʌltʃʊəs]
a 喧囂的，騷動的

After his parents died, the teenager lived a few tumultuous years on the streets of Manila.
雙親過世後，該名青少年流落馬尼拉街頭，在不安中度過幾年。

記憶技巧 -ous 為形容詞字尾。

---

contumacious
[͵kɑntjuˋmeʃəs]
a 抗拒的，不服從的

The court ordered that the man stay under house arrest, but he soon left his home in a contumacious act.
法院命令男子在家拘禁，但他很快抗拒而外出。

記憶技巧 con- 表示加強語氣；tum- 表示腫；-ous 為形容詞字尾；contumacious 亦即自我膨脹、自大，引申為抗拒的、不服從的。

thrust - trud

子音 th 和 t 互換，母音通轉，兩者皆表示戳、刺、推。

---

intrude

[ɪn`trud]

v 闖入，侵擾

The housekeeping maid apologized for walking into the wrong room and intruding on the couple's private moments.

家事女僕為走錯房間，侵擾夫婦隱私時間而道歉。

記憶技巧　in- 表示內；trud- 表示刺；intrdue 即刺入，引申為闖入。

---

obtrude

[əb`trud]

v 侵入，強迫

The sound of the marching band practicing outside obtruded into the teacher's classroom instruction.

外面操演的軍樂隊聲響侵擾到老師的課堂教學。

記憶技巧　ob- 表示前面；trud- 表示刺；obtrude 的意思是往前刺入，引申為侵入、強迫。

---

extrude

[ɛk`strud]

v 擠出，逐出，
　　使流出

The drunken man collapsed in front of the toilet, and his partially-digested dinner extruded from his mouth.

酒醉男子在廁所前摔倒，消化一半的晚餐從嘴巴吐出來。

記憶技巧　ex- 表示外面；trud- 表示刺；extrude 的意思是刺出，引申為擠出。

---

abstruse

[æb`strus]

a 深奧的，難解的

The psychotic patient mumbled abstruse phrases as he twiddled his thumbs incessantly.

精神病患不斷撫弄大拇指，含糊地唸一些別人聽不懂的話。

記憶技巧　ab- 表示離開；trus- 等同於 trud-，表示刺、推；abstruse 字面意思是推開，衍生出無法理解，離知識愈來愈遠，因此有深奧的意思。

---

protrusive

[pro`trusɪv]

a 突出的

The dentist recommended that the child wear braces to correct her front teeth, which were too protrusive.

牙醫師建議孩童戴上牙套以矯正太突出的前排牙齒。

記憶技巧　pro- 表示前；trus- 表示戳、推；-ive 為形容詞字尾；protrusive 的字面意思是往前推出的，引申為突出的。

---

thrust

[θrʌst]

v 猛推，插入

The female supervisor thrust a large pile of paperwork towards the clerk's face and said his work was not complete.

女主管將一大疊文件堆往職員面前，並說他工作還沒完成。

記憶技巧　thrust 即戳、刺。

| 相關字彙
推擠 | • push
• shove 推 | • heave 舉起
• prod 刺 | • jab 戳
• shoulder 用肩推 |

---

threat
[θrɛt]
n 恐嚇，威脅，凶兆

In desperate times, governments target certain ethnic groups as a serious threat to national security.
危急時期，政府將一些少數民族組織列為國家安全的嚴重威脅。

記憶技巧　threat 源自於戳、刺，因帶有威脅性，故有恐嚇等意思產生。

| 相關字彙
威脅、危險 | • danger 危險
• endangerment 危險
• hazard 危害 | • menace 威脅
• peril 危險 |

---

thunder - ton

子音 th 和 t 互換，母音通轉，兩者皆表示打雷。

---

astonish
[əˈstɑnɪʃ]
v 使驚訝

The violinist astonished the audience members, including the Queen, who was in attendance.
小提琴家令觀眾驚豔，包括在場的女王。

記憶技巧　as- 等同於 ad-，表示朝～方向；ton- 表示雷；-ish 為動詞字尾；astonish 的意思是打雷使人震驚。

---

detonate
[ˈdɛtə‿net]
v 爆裂

The trained dolphin detonated the floating mine, saving the lives of passengers on the cruise ship.
受過訓練的海豚引爆漂浮水雷，救了遊輪乘客性命。

記憶技巧　de- 表示下；ton- 表示打雷；-ate 為動詞字尾；detonate 的意思是爆破，因其聲響像打雷。

---

detonator
[ˈdɛtə‿netɚ]
n 炸藥，雷管

The desperate man kept the police at bay by holding a detonator and threatening to blow himself up.
絕望的男子握著炸藥，以炸掉自己為要脅，要求警方不要逼近。

記憶技巧　-or 為名詞字尾。

| 相關字彙
炸藥一部分 | • fuse 導火線
• nitroglycerine 硝化甘油
• shrapnel 砲彈碎片 | • warhead 彈頭 |

thwart - tort

子音 th 和 t 互換，母音通轉，兩者皆表示扭曲。

---

torture
[ˈtɔrtʃɚ]
v 拷問，使痛苦

An ancient means of torture was to tie down a prisoner and drip water on his or her forehead.
一種古老折磨方式是綑綁囚犯，並將其前額浸泡在水裡。

記憶技巧　tort- 表示扭曲；-ure 為名詞字尾；torture 的意思是因遭受折磨，而身體扭曲，本是名詞，後轉當動詞用。

---

tortuous
[ˈtɔrtʃuəs]
a 彎曲的，不正直的

The dangerous mountain pass was a tortuous route not often chosen by tourists.
這危險的山路很蜿蜒，旅客不常走。

記憶技巧　tort- 表示扭曲；-ous 為形容詞字尾；tortuous 即彎曲的。

---

torment
[tɔrˈmɛnt]
v 使苦惱，拷問

The soldier was not heard from after the war, tormenting his mother and father.
士兵戰後音訊全無，父母非常煎熬。

記憶技巧　tor- 表示扭曲；-ment 為動詞字尾；torment 的意思是因苦惱、痛苦身體扭曲變形，引申為使苦惱。

---

tortoise
[ˈtɔrtəs]
n 龜

The Galapagos tortoise is a species that is known to have a life expectancy of over 100 years.
大家都知道加拉帕戈斯象龜是一種壽命超過一百年的物種。

記憶技巧　tort- 表示扭曲，有字源學家推測 tortoise 這個字，是因烏龜的腳形狀扭曲而來的。

---

torch
[tɔrtʃ]
n 火把，火炬

The survivors lit their torches and explored the caverns to find suitable shelter.
為了找合適的棲身地點，生還者點燃火把探索各個洞穴。

記憶技巧　字源學家推測火把上沾蠟的麻布的形狀扭曲。

---

distort
[dɪsˈtɔrt]
v 使歪扭，曲解

The public relations agency was hired to produce video footage to distort the truth about the conflict.
為扭曲衝突真相，公關公司受雇製作影片。

記憶技巧　dis- 表示完全；tort- 表示扭曲；distort 的意思是曲解。

Part
2
CH 1
CH 2
CH 3

齒間音、齒齦音、齒齦後音、硬顎音轉換

extort

[ɪkˈstɔrt]

v 強奪，勒索

The reporter extorted a payment from the mayor in exchange for not reporting the incident.

記者以不爆料為條件向市長強索一筆金錢。

記憶技巧　ex- 表示外面；tort- 表示扭曲；extort 的意思是強行從人身上扭出東西來，引申為強奪、勒索。

---

retort

[rɪˈtɔrt]

n 反擊，反駁，
反唇相譏

During the retiree's farewell speech, his longtime secretary offered a clever retort that made everyone laugh.

退休人員惜別演說中，跟隨他很久的祕書巧妙挖苦，每個人都會心一笑。

記憶技巧　re- 表示回去；tort- 表示扭曲；retort 的意思是扭回去，引申為反擊、反駁。

---

through - trans

子音 th 和 t 互換，母音通轉，兩者皆表示跨越。

---

transition

[trænˈzɪʃən]

n 過渡期，演變

The young man's transition between being a student and being a responsible adult was difficult.

年輕人從學生到一名負責任的成年人的歷程是艱辛的。

記憶技巧　trans- 表示跨越；it- 表示走；-ion 為名詞字尾；transition 的意思是跨越過去，引申為過渡期、演變。

---

translate

[trænsˈlet]

v 翻譯

The most skilled and highly-paid interpretors can simultaneously translate while they are listening to a speech.

技巧最熟練的高薪口譯者能夠聽講時同時翻譯。

記憶技巧　trans- 表示跨越；lat- 表示攜帶；translate 的意思是攜帶過去，後來作翻譯解釋。

---

transmit

[trænsˈmɪt]

v 傳送

The weather station in Greenland constantly transmits weather data through its antenna.

格陵蘭氣象站一直都是由天線傳送天氣資料。

記憶技巧　trans- 表示跨越；mit- 表示送；transmit 的意思是送過去，引申為傳送。

transportation

[ˌtrænspɚˋteʃən]

n 運輸，運輸工具

The general manager hired a logistics company to provide ongoing transportation services for his products.

總經理雇請物流公司持續提供產品運送服務。

記憶技巧 trans- 表示跨越；port- 表示攜帶；-ation 為名詞字尾；transportation 表示將人或物帶往某地的運輸工具。

transpire

[trænˋspaɪr]

v 蒸發，發汗，透露，發生

The pilot was afraid to discuss what transpired during his flight over the Bermuda Triangle.

飛行員害怕談論自己飛越百慕達三角洲發生的狀況。

記憶技巧 trans- 表示跨越；spir- 表示呼吸；transpire 即水份轉成氣體從皮膚蒸發掉，後又作發汗解釋。

transcribe

[trænsˋkraɪb]

v 謄寫，記錄，改編

A professional was paid to transcribe the speeches at the conference in order to publish the content in a newsletter.

一名專業人士受雇紀錄會議中的發言內容，要將內容刊登於業務通訊。

記憶技巧 trans- 表示跨越；scrib- 表示寫；transcribe 即寫過去，引申為謄寫、紀錄等意思。

thatch - tect

子音 th 和 t 互換，母音通轉，thatch 現今的意思是蓋屋頂的茅草，兩者皆表示覆蓋。

detect

[dɪˋtɛkt]

v 偵查，發現

The latest ultrasound technology clearly detects any damage to muscle tissue.

最新超音波科技能清楚偵測肌肉組織的任何損傷。

記憶技巧 de- 表示離開；tect- 表示覆蓋；detect 表示拿掉覆蓋物，引申為偵查、發現。

detective

[dɪˋtɛktɪv]

n 偵探

After his father lost his wallet, Jeff played detective to look for clues.

老爸弄丟錢包，傑夫為了尋找線索而扮起了偵探。

記憶技巧 -ive 為形容詞字尾；detective 本當形容詞用，後轉當名詞用，作偵探解釋。

相關字彙
私家調查員

• investigator 探員
• private eye 私家偵探
• dick 偵探

Part **2**

CH 1
CH 2
CH 3

齒間音、齒齦音、齒齦後音、硬顎音轉換

protect
[prə`tɛkt]

v 保護，防護

When visiting Finland, the visitor wore long thermal underwear to protect against the harsh cold.
觀光客造訪芬蘭時穿上厚重衣物禦寒。

> 記憶技巧　pro- 表示在～前面；tect- 表示覆蓋；protect 的意思是在前面擋住，即保護的意思。

protective
[prə`tɛktɪv]

a 保護的，防護的

The boss was extremely protective of his secretary, taking the blame for the communication error.
老闆百般護著私人祕書，自己擔起聯繫差錯的責任。

> 記憶技巧　-ive 為形容詞字尾。

protectionism
[prə`tɛkʃənɪzəm]

n 保護政策

The national leader adopted a policy of blatant protectionism to avoid growing external threats.
為避免日益嚴重的外部威脅，國家領導人採取明顯的保護政策。

> 記憶技巧　protect 表示保護；-ion 為名詞字尾；-ism 表示教條、系統，為名詞字尾；protectionism 即保護政策。

protégé
[`protə‚ʒe]

n 受保護者

Sam studied for years under the veteran actor, becoming quite the talented protégé.
山姆在老練的演員門下學習多年後成為一名才華洋溢的弟子。

> 記憶技巧　pro- 表示在～前面；tégé 等同於 tect-，表示保護；protégé 源自法語，是保護者的意思。

throw - trit / trib

子音 th 和 t 互換，母音通轉，兩者的古義都是磨擦，throw 的現今的意思是拋，可想像成東西拋出來，和外物產生摩擦。

trite
[traɪt]

a 陳腐的

The author's story was rejected by the publisher, being accused of containing trite material.
作者的故事遭出版社退稿，還被指責內容陳腐。

> 記憶技巧　trit- 表示摩擦；trite 即東西不停摩擦，東西變老舊，引申出陳腐的意思。

相關字彙
描述一個人的言語

- acid 尖酸刻薄的
- astringent 嚴厲的
- bland 溫和的
- defamatory 誹謗的
- insightful 有深刻見解的
- pungent 尖刻的
- tart 辛辣的

attrition

[əˋtrɪʃəl]

n 摩擦，磨損

After competing against ten different tea shops on the same street, the original tea shop won the war of attrition.

與同一條街上的不同茶店一番較勁之後，老店在消耗戰中勝出。

記憶技巧 at- 等同於 ad-，表示朝～方向；trit- 表示摩擦；-ion 為名詞字尾；attrition 即摩擦的意思。

contrite

[ˋkɑntraɪt]

a 悔恨的

During the trial, the bank manager offered a contrite opening statement in front of the jury.

審判期間，銀行經理向陪審團提出一份充滿悔意的公開陳述。

記憶技巧 con- 表示一起；trit- 表示摩擦；contrite 的意思是一起摩擦，可想像成被過往的事情折磨著。

detriment

[ˋdɛtrəmənt]

n 損害

The Dean of the university cut the budget to the regrettable detriment of staff salaries.

大學院長刪減預算而損及職員薪資，令人遺憾。

記憶技巧 de- 表示離開；tri- 表示摩擦；-ment 為名詞字尾；detriment 的意思是被磨損，引申為損害。

detrition

[dɪˋtrɪʃəl]

n 消耗，磨損

In the mining operation, the rock grinders were the first to suffer from equipment detrition.

採礦作業中，磨石機是最先耗損的機具。

記憶技巧 de- 表示離開；trit- 表示摩擦；-ion 為名詞字尾；detrition 的意思是磨掉，引申為消耗、磨損。

---

thirst - terr

子音 th 和 t 互換，母音通轉，兩者的意思是乾燥，thirst 是口乾舌燥，terr 則是乾燥的土地。

---

terrace

[ˋtɛrəs]

n 一排房屋，臺地，梯田

The ancient rice terraces in the Northern Philippines are considered an architectural wonder.

一般認為菲律賓北方的古代稻米梯田是一項建築奇觀。

記憶技巧 terr- 表示土地；terrace 現指臺地、梯田。

Part 2

CH 1
CH 2
CH 3

齒間音、齒齦音、齒齦後音、硬顎音轉換

territory

[ˋtɛrəˏtorɪ]

n 領土，版圖，範圍

The Unites States owns several island territories in the Pacific and Caribbean.

太平洋及加勒比海上的數座島嶼屬於美國領土。

記憶技巧 terr- 表示土地；-ory 為名詞字尾，表示地方；territory 指領土。

相關字彙
國家疆域

- airspace 領空
- borderland 國境
- enclave 飛地

Mediterranean

[ˏmɛdətəˋrenɪən]

a 地中海的

Latakia is an important port city for Syria on the Eastern Mediterranean Sea.

拉塔基亞是敘利亞位於地中海東岸的重要港市。

記憶技巧 medi- 表示在～之間；terr- 表示土地；-ean 為形容詞字尾；Mediterranean 字面意思是在土地之間的，後來亦可當名詞用，指在歐洲和北非之間的海域。

相關字彙
國家、文化相關

- Anglo 美國西南部北歐裔英語系美國人
- Asiatic 亞洲的
- Caribbean 加勒比人的
- Celtic 凱爾特（語）的
- Gaelic 蓋爾（人）語
- Nordic 北歐人的
- Scandinavian 斯堪的納維亞的
- Yiddish 意第緒語的

neither - neutr

子音 th 和 t 互換，母音通轉，兩者系出同源，neither 指兩者皆不，neutr 也表兩者皆不，但後來衍生出中立的意思。

neutral

[ˋnjutrəl]

a 中立的，公平的

When two of your friends disagree, it is a smart bet to remain neutral.

你有兩位朋友意見不合時，保持中立是明智選擇。

記憶技巧 neutr- 表示中立；-al 為形容詞字尾；neutral 表示中立的。

neutron

[ˋnjutrɑn]

n 中子

A common neutron has no observable electric charge and accounts for most of an atom's mass.

一般的中子沒有明顯電荷，而且占有原子大部份的質量。

記憶技巧 neutr- 表示中立；-on 為名詞字尾，表示亞原子粒子；neutron 即中子。

相關字彙
和原子相關

- anion 陰離子
- cation 陽離子
- electron 電子
- ion 離子
- molecule 分子
- nucleus（原子）核
- valence 原子價

myth - myst

兩者雖無字源關係，但可藉由子音 th 和 t 互換，母音通轉來記憶，myth 是神話，myst 則是神祕。

mystical [`mɪstɪk!] a 神祕的	Although dragons are considered to be mystical creatures, you can see creatures similar to them on Komodo Island. 儘管龍被視為神祕生物，你可以在科摩多島上看得到相似的生物。 記憶技巧　myst- 表示神祕；-ical 為形容詞字尾；mystical 的意思是神祕的。
mystery [`mɪstərɪ] n 神祕， 　不可思議（的事）	Research into metaphysics has solved some of the greatest mysteries of the universe. 形而上學的研究解開一些宇宙最大的謎團。 記憶技巧　myst- 表示神祕；-ery 為名詞字尾；mystery 即神祕。

Section 7

〔ð〕對應〔t〕

other - alter / ali

子音 th 和 t 互換，母音通轉，兩者的核心意思皆是兩者當中的第二個或其他，但 alter 又衍生出改變的意思。

alter [`ɔltɚ] v 改變，更改	Providing a Christmas bonus can radically alter the morale of the employees. 發放耶誕紅利能使員工士氣完全改變。 記憶技巧　alter 表示改變。

alias
[`elɪəs]
n 化名，假名

相關字彙
姓名、稱呼

The writer wanted to retain her privacy, so she used an alias on her work.
作者想保有隱私，因此化名發表作品。

記憶技巧 alias 即其他名字，如：化名、假名等。

- appellation 名稱
- designation 命名
- epithet 稱號
- forename 在姓前面的名
- family name 姓
- first name 西方人名的第一個字
- moniker 名字
- nickname 綽號
- pseudonym 假名
- sobriquet 綽號

alibi
[`ælə,baɪ]
n 不在場證明，藉口

The passenger provided the taxi driver with an indisputable alibi during the time of the crime.
乘客提供計乘車司機案發時明確的不在場證明。

記憶技巧 alibi 即不在事發現場，而在其他地方，引申為不在場證明。

alien
[`elɪən]
a 外國人的，相反的

The perfect metal sphere discovered in the 2,000-yr-old temple seemed alien in origin.
在 2000 年歷史的古廟發現的完美金屬球體似乎是來自外國。

記憶技巧 ali- 表示其他；-en 為形容詞字尾；alien 本是其他的，引申為外國人的。

alienable
[`eljənəb!]
a 可讓渡的

In order to ensure ongoing revenues, the lawmakers made property tax alienable to new land owners.
為確保歲收，立法委員讓房屋稅得以轉讓給土地新持有人。

記憶技巧 ali- 表示其他；-en 為形容詞字尾；-able 為形容詞字尾；alienable 表示可讓給其他人的，引申為可讓渡的。

altercate
[`ɔltɚ,ket]
v 爭論，口角

The attorneys eventually altercated after passionately negotiating a new contract for the athlete.
幾位律師激烈協商運動員新合約後，終於爆發口角。

記憶技巧 alter- 表示其他；-ate 為動詞字尾；altercate 表示和他人爭辯。

adultery
[ə`dʌltərɪ]
n 通姦

Sam never imagined that his wife of 20 years would have committed adultery with his tax accountant.
山姆從未想像自己 20 年的妻子會與他的稅務會計師有染。

記憶技巧 ad- 表示往～方向；ulter- 等同於 alter-，表示其他；-y 為名詞字尾；adultery 指和其他人有染。

Section **8**

〔t〕對應〔n〕

put - pon

雖無字源關係，但可藉由子音 t 和 n 互換，母音通轉來記憶，兩者皆表示放。

---

component
[kəm`ponənt]
n 成分

The electronic component gave the monitor the most vivid colors in the market.
這個電子零件讓監視器擁有市面上最鮮明的顏色。

記憶技巧　com- 表示一起；pon- 表示放；-ent 為名詞字尾；component 的意思是組成成分，因為把成分放一起，可以做出成品。

---

opponent
[ə`ponənt]
n 反對者，敵手

The Chess Master made quick work of his first opponent during the national tournament.
棋王在全國賽中很快擊敗第一位對手。

記憶技巧　op- 表示在～之前；pon- 表示放；-ent 為名詞字尾；opponent 的是擋在某人面前，引申為敵手。

---

proponent
[prə`ponənt]
n 提議者，支持者

The city councillors were vocal proponents of the mayor's new smoking ordinances.
市議員是市長新禁菸令的積極支持者。

記憶技巧　pro- 表示前面；pon- 表示放；-ent 為名詞字尾；proponent 是把東西放到前面的人，引申為提倡者。

---

compound
[`kɑmpaʊnd]
a 混合的，合成的，複合的

The compound interest on the loan quickly put the borrower in serious debt.
貸款複利迫使借款人快速背負沉重債務。

記憶技巧　com- 表示一起；pound 等同於 put，表示放；compound 是把東西放一起，引申為合成的。

---

expound
[ɪk`spaʊnd]
v 闡述，解釋

The sales manager was asked to expound on his promise to break the annual sales record.
業務經理被要求說明他對打破年度行銷紀錄的承諾。

記憶技巧　ex- 表示往前；pound 等同於 put，表示放；expound 是把東西往前放讓人看清楚，引申為解釋。

postpone

[post`pon]

v 使延期

The department store indefinitely postponed their grand opening until they could pass the safety inspection.

百貨公司盛大開幕式一直延至安檢通過才舉行。

記憶技巧 post- 表示後面；pon- 表示放；postpone 即往後放，引申為延期。

Section **9**

〔r〕對應〔l〕

---

star - stell

子音 r 和 l 互換，母音通轉，兩者皆表示星星。

---

stellar

[`stɛlɚ]

a 星星的，
星星繁多的，
第一流的

In a stellar performance for the ages, the baseball player hit four home runs in a game.

最高水準的賽事中，這名棒球選手一場比賽就擊出四支全壘打。

記憶技巧 stell- 表示星星；-ar 為形容詞字尾；stellar 即星星的意思。

---

interstellar

[ˌɪntɚ`stɛlɚ]

a 星際的

The private aerospace company's founder touted the goal of interstellar travel by the end of the century.

私人航太公司創辦人宣傳本世紀末星際旅行的目標。

記憶技巧 inter- 表示介於～之間的；stell- 表示星星；-ar 為形容詞字尾；interstellar 即星際的。

---

constellation

[ˌkɑnstə`leʃən]

n 星座，群聚

The Southern Cross is a famous constellation that can only be seen in the southern hemisphere.

南十字星座是一個南半球才看得見的知名星座。

記憶技巧 con- 表示一起；stell- 表示星星；-ation 為名詞字尾；constellation 的意思是群星聚集，當成星座解釋。

相關字彙

天文相關

- asteroid 小行星
- black hole 黑洞
- comet 彗星
- exoplanet 外部行星
- the Galaxy 星系
- the Milky Way 銀河
- nebula 星雲
- satellite 衛星
- white dwarf 白矮星
- supernova 超新星

Section 10
〔n〕對應〔r〕

cancer - carcin

子音 n 和 r 互換，母音通轉，兩者皆表示腫瘤、癌症。

carcinogen

[karˋsɪnədʒən]

n 致癌物質

The food safety department was tasked with finding known carcinogens in processed food products.

食安部門受命查察加工食品中的已知致癌物質。

記憶技巧　carcin- 表示癌；gen- 表示生長；carcinogen 即致癌物。

carcinoma

[ˌkarsɪˋnomə]

n 癌

It was ascertained that the dark spots on the patient's face were actually early stages of carcinoma.

病人臉上的黑點確診為早期癌症。

記憶技巧　carcin- 表示癌；-oma 表示腫瘤，為醫學名詞字尾；carcinoma 為癌症。

Section 11
〔l〕對應〔r〕

silk - seri

子音 l 和 r 互換，母音通轉，兩者皆表示蠶絲。

sericultural

[ˌsɛrɪˋkʌltʃərəl]

a 養蠶的

The International Sericultural Commission welcomed its 18th member silk-producing country in 2016.

國際養蠶委員會於 2016 年歡迎他們第 18 個產蠶會員國。

記憶技巧　seri-，蠶，culture，培養，-al，形容詞字尾，sericultural 即養蠶的。

wall - mur

兩者雖無字源關係，但可藉由子音 l 和 r 互換，母音通轉來記憶，兩者皆表示牆壁。

mural [ˋmjurəl] **n** 壁畫，壁飾	The creative mural on the wall of the cafeteria offers a festive tropical atmosphere to the room. 餐廳牆上的創意壁畫帶給房子歡樂的熱帶氣氛。 記憶技巧　mur- 表示牆；-al 為名詞字尾；mural 指牆壁上的畫。
immure [ɪˋmjur] **v** 監禁	As a punishment for failing the exam, the student was immured in his room without access to a computer. 學生被監禁在自己房間，不得接觸電腦，作為考試不及格的處罰。 記憶技巧　im- 等同於 in-，表示在～之內；mur- 表示牆壁；immure 有「被牆壁圍起來」的意思，指監禁的意思。
extramural [ˌɛkstrəˋmjurəl] **a** 校外的，城牆外的	The assistant professors performed extramural duties in remote villages for field research. 助理教授在偏鄉進行校外田野研究。 記憶技巧　extra- 表示外面；mur- 表示牆壁；-al 為形容詞字尾；extramural 指「牆壁外的」，引申為校外的。
intramural [ˌɪntrəˋmjurəl] **a** 校內的，城牆內的	Most unversities offer a selection of intramural activities for their athletic students. 大部分大學會提供運動員學生一些校內活動。 記憶技巧　intra- 表示內部；mur- 表示牆壁；-al 為形容詞字尾；intramural 指「牆壁內的」，引申為校內的。

Section 12

〔ʃ〕對應〔s〕

---

sugar - sacchar

子音 sh 和 s 互換，母音通轉，兩者皆表示糖。

saccharin

[ˋsækərɪn]

n 糖精

The artificial sweetener, known as saccharin, is the oldest known substitute for sugar.

人工增甜劑，也就是糖精，是流傳最久的糖替代品。

> 記憶技巧　sacchar- 表示糖；-in 為名詞字尾，表示化學物質；saccharin 指糖精。

相關字彙
食物飲料成分

- additive 添加物
- aspartame 阿斯巴甜
- caffeine 咖啡因
- carbohydrate 碳水化合物
- fat 脂肪
- flavoring 調味料
- glucose 葡萄糖
- preservative 防腐劑
- starch 澱粉
- trans fat 反式脂肪

---

shine - scinti

子音 sh 和 s 互換，母音通轉，兩者皆表示火花、發光、閃亮。

scintilla

[sɪnˋtɪlə]

n 火花，閃爍

Is there any scintilla of doubt that protecting sources of clean water should be a priority?

應該將保護乾淨水資源列為優先考量，有沒有任何一點點質疑？

> 記憶技巧　scinti- 表示火花；scintilla 即火花或閃亮。

scintillate

[ˋsɪntˌlet]

v 發出火花

Seen from the mountaintop, the lights of the ski resort scintillated brightly below.

山頂俯瞰，底下的滑雪場燈光明亮閃耀。

> 記憶技巧　-ate 為動詞字尾。

相關字彙
火

- blaze 火焰
- conflagration 大火
- combustion 燃燒
- flame 火焰
- inferno 熊熊烈火
- ignition 燃燒
- wildfire（毀滅性的）大火災

🎧 189

Section **13**

〔d〕對應〔θ〕

death - thanas

兩者雖無字源關係，但可藉由子音 d 和 th 互換，母音通轉，兩者皆表示死亡，Thanatos 是希臘故事中的死亡之神。

euthanasia
[ˌjuθəˈneʒɪə]
n 安樂死（術）

The couple made the difficult decision to resort to euthanasia to end the suffering of their old, lame dog.
夫婦做出安樂死結束瘸腿老狗痛苦的困難決定。

記憶技巧 eu- 表示優的、好的；thanas- 表示死亡；-ia 為名詞字尾；euthanasia 的意思是安詳死亡，指安樂死。

door - thyr

子音 d 和 th 互換，母音通轉，兩者皆表示門，thyr 又有盾甲的意思。

thyroid
[ˈθaɪrɔɪd]
n 甲狀腺，甲狀軟骨

It was suggested that the woman consume seaweed to treat her swollen thyroid.
有人建議婦人吃海帶治療甲狀腺腫。

記憶技巧 thyr- 表示盾甲；-oid 表示似～的；thyroid 是人類的甲狀腺，因其外形猶如盾甲。

do - thet

子音 d 和 th 互換，母音通轉，本意都是放，可用做完後排放（整齊）來記憶。

thesis
[ˈθisɪs]
n 論文，論點，主題

The topic of the Chairman's MBA thesis was the effect of the microfinance industry on African Economic Community.
主席的 MBA 論文主題是微經濟產業對非洲經濟共同體的衝擊。

記憶技巧 thet- 等同於 thes-，表示放；thesis 要到 1650 年代才有論文的意思，論文是將研究有系統排列、有組織地放一起。

antithesis
[æn`tɪθəsɪs]
n 對照，對句

After the election, the President's decisions were the antithesises of his campaign promises.
贏得選戰，總統的決策與選舉活動的承諾形成對照。

記憶技巧 anti- 表示相反；thes- 表示放；antithesis 的意思是放在相對的地方，指對照、對句。

hypothesis
[haɪ`pɑθəsɪs]
n 假設，前提

The detective offered a highly-improbable hypothesis for the death, but there was no other explanation available.
偵探提出很不可能的死因假設，但是沒有其他的解釋。

記憶技巧 hypo- 表示在～之下；thes- 表示放；hypothesis 的意思是放在～之下的，即形成理論之前的假設。

parenthesis
[pə`rɛnθəsɪs]
n 插入句，圓括弧

When writing text inside of parentheses, you should only use a period if the text is a complete sentence.
括弧內寫字時，只有是完整句子，才應該句號。

記憶技巧 par- 等同於 para-，表示在～旁邊；en- 等同於 in，表示在～之內；thes-，表示放；parenthesis 即放到～之中的插入詞、句，後作插入句、圓括弧解釋。

Part **2**
CH 1
CH 2
CH 3

齒間音、齒齦音、齒齦後音、硬顎音轉換

Section **14**

〔s〕對應〔θ〕

ascetic - ath

兩者雖無字源關係，但可藉由子音 s 和 th 互換，母音通轉來記憶，ascetic 是禁慾的、苦行的，和運動競賽有關，因為運動員須能刻苦耐勞、自律性高才能完成訓練，而 ath 是（運動）競賽的意思。

athlete
[`æθlit]
n 運動員

The highly-paid athlete raised funds for an orphanage to deflect criticism about his salary.
為轉移外界對薪水的批評，高薪運動員為一家孤兒院募款。

記憶技巧 ath- 表示運動競賽；athlete 是運動員。

pentathlon

[pɛnˋtæθlən]

n 五項運動

In the 2016 Summer Olympics, running, swimming, fencing, horse riding and shooting made up the pentathalon.

2016 年夏季奧運，跑步、游泳、擊劍、馬術及射箭組成五項運動。

記憶技巧　pent- 表示五；ath- 表示運動競賽；pentathlon 即五項運動。

---

decathlon

[dɪˋkæθˏlɑn]

n 十項運動

American Dan O'Brian was one of the most recognized Olympic decathalon champions in history.

美國選手丹・布萊恩是史上最受公認的奧運十項運動冠軍之一。

記憶技巧　dec- 表示十；ath- 表示運動競賽；decathlon 即十項運動。

相關字彙
田徑運動

- discus 鐵餅
- field event 田賽項目
- high jump 跳高
- hurdle 跨（欄）
- javelin 標槍
- long jump 跳遠
- track and field 田徑運動
- weightlifting 舉重

Section **15**

〔t〕對應〔s〕

put - pos

兩者雖無明確字源關係，但可藉由子音 t 和 s 互換，母音通轉來記憶，兩者皆作放的意思，以下所列單字雖皆含 pos-，但來源並不同，一個是來自拉丁文中的 pausare，和現代英語中的 pause 同源，另一個是拉丁文中的 positus，為了方便記憶，就不再細分。

pose

[poz]

v 擺姿勢，假裝

Amazingly, the male model held a steady pose for a good hour for the class of art majors.

令人驚訝的是，男模特兒為了美術主修生課程而維持了一個小時的固定姿勢。

記憶技巧　pos- 表示放；pose 的意思是將動作放到定點，即擺姿勢。

齒間音、齒齦音、齒齦後音、硬顎音轉換

compose

[kəm`poz]

v 組成，作曲，
寫作，使平靜

The best man elegantly composed a memorable poem to wish the newlyweds a happy marriage.

為了祝福新人新婚愉快，伴郎優雅地做了一首令人難忘的詩。

記憶技巧 com- 表示一起；pos- 表示放；compose 即把東西放在一起，引申為作曲、寫作。

composition

[ˌkɑmpə`zɪʃən]

n 組成，作文，
作曲，混合物

The elemental composition of the sun is almost wholly hydrogen and helium.

太陽的元素組成幾乎都是氫和氦。

記憶技巧 com- 表示一起；pos- 表示放；-ion 為名詞字尾；composition 的意思是作文、作曲。

composer

[kəm`pozɚ]

n 作曲家

Educated in London, Fela Sowande became one of the best-known African composers of classical music.

曾於倫敦受教育，索旺德成為最知名的非裔的古典音樂作曲家之一。

記憶技巧 com- 表示一起；pos- 表示放；-er 為名詞字尾，表示人；composer 即作曲家。

相關字彙
音樂家或表演者

- accompanist 伴奏者
- bandsman 樂隊隊員
- cellist 大提琴手
- organist 風琴手
- one-man band 獨角樂隊
- pianist 鋼琴家
- piper 風笛手
- soloist 獨奏者
- virtuoso 音樂名手

dispose

[dɪ`spoz]

v 處置，處理

The clerk was scolded because he carelessly disposed of the copy machine's toner cartridge.

店員遭到責罵，因為沒有小心處理影印機碳粉匣。

記憶技巧 dis- 表示分開；pos- 表示放；dispose 的意思是把東西分開放、排列整齊，引申為處理。

deposit

[dɪ`pɑzɪt]

n 存款，押金，
沉澱物

The restaurant's nightly deposit of cash into its bank account was handled by armed guards.

餐廳由武裝警衛處理夜間現金存放銀行帳戶的作業。

記憶技巧 de- 表示離開；pos- 表示放；deposit 的意思是放到一旁，引申為存款、押金。

discompose

[ˌdɪskəm`poz]

v 使不安

The scene at the car accident was so horrible that even the emergency workers were discomposed.

車禍現場過於驚悚，連急救人員都感到不安。

記憶技巧 dis- 表示離開；com- 表示一起；pos- 表示放；discompose 的意思是不使～聚在一起，引申為使不安。

disposable

[dɪ`spozəbl]

a 可任意處置的，用完即丟的

The supervisor refused to use disposable pens, opting instead to use those with replaceable ink cartridges.
主管不願使用拋棄式的筆，而選用可換墨水筆心的筆。

記憶技巧　dis- 表示離開；pos- 表示放；-able 為形容詞字尾；disposable 的意思是可以放到一邊去的，引申為用完即丟棄的。

expose

[ɪk`spoz]

v 暴露，揭露

The investigative journalist took a risk to expose the food industry scandal involving three countries.
查訪的記者冒險揭發牽連三個國家的食品產業醜聞。

記憶技巧　ex- 表示外面；pos- 表示放；expose 的意思是放到外面去，引申作暴露。

exposition

[ˌɛkspə`zɪʃən]

n 博覽會，展覽，解說

The Violin Museum in Cremona, Italy, held an important exposition of rare Stradivarius violins.
義大利克雷莫納小提琴博物館舉辦一場稀有斯特拉迪瓦里小提琴的重要展覽。

記憶技巧　ex- 表示外面；pos- 表示放；-ion 為名詞字尾；exposition 的意思是放到外面去，引申為展覽。

impose

[ɪm`poz]

v 強加（負擔、懲罰），課稅

The government imposed a 20% tax on all cigarettes in hope of reducing smoking among minors.
政府課徵所有菸品 20% 稅金以期降低吸菸的未年成人。

記憶技巧　im- 表示內；pos- 表示放；impose 的意思是放到～裡面，引申為強加（負擔、懲罰）。

opposition

[ˌɑpə`zɪʃən]

n 反對，反對黨，對立

There was no opposition to the proposed legislation to create a national holiday honoring the deceased leader.
新增一個紀念已逝領導人的國定假日的立法提案未遭反對。

記憶技巧　op- 等同於 ob-，表示放～前面；pos- 表示放；-ion 為名詞字尾；opposition 指擋在～前面，引申為反對。

suppose

[sə`poz]

v 推測，假定，認為

Where do you suppose the proceeds from the sales of lottery tickets go?
你認為彩券銷售收益去了哪裡？

記憶技巧　sup- 表示下面；pos- 表示放；suppose 指放在論點下面、用以支撐論點，引申為假設。

propose

[prə`poz]

v 提議，計劃

When the governor proposed to curb the use of oil pipelines, there was strong backlash from the oil companies.

州長打算管制油管使用時，石油公司強力反對。

> **記憶技巧** pro- 表示往前；pos- 表示放；propose 的意思是把～往前放，引申為提議。

purpose

[`pɝpəs]

n 目的，宗旨，決心，效果

The company's mission statement prevented policy makers from pursuing profit without a benevolent purpose.

公司的企業宗旨防止決策者一味追求利益而缺乏良善目的。

> **記憶技巧** pur- 表示往前；pos- 表示放；purpose 的意思是置於行動之前的目標。

Section **16**

〔s〕對應〔r〕（r 音化）

---

onus - oner

子音 s 和 r 轉換，母音通轉，兩者皆表示負擔。

exonerate

[ɪg`zanə‚ret]

v 使免受指控，證明～無罪

The judge exonerated the convicted criminal after DNA evidence cleared him of the crime.

DNA 證據澄清該名罪犯未涉案，法官免除其刑。

> **記憶技巧** ex- 表示去除；oner- 表示負擔；-ate 為動詞字尾；exonerate 的意思是免於負擔，引申出使免受指控。

onerous

[`anərəs]

a 繁重的，麻煩的

The mechanic was happy to get hired, but he regretted it when he realized how onerous the job was.

技工高興被錄用，但是了解工作多麼繁重後就後悔了。

> **記憶技巧** oner- 表示負擔；-ous 為形容詞結尾；onerous 的意思是繁重的。

plus - plur
子音 s 和 r 轉換，母音通轉，兩者皆表示更多。

plus [plʌs] **conj** 加上	The temperature on the mountain top was 13 degrees, plus it felt like 7 degrees when the wind was blowing. 山頂溫度是 13 度，另外，起風時感覺只有 7 度。 記憶技巧 plus 表示更多，引申為加。
surplus [ˋsɝpləs] **n** 剩餘	When the occupying forces returned home, they left behind a surplus of vehicles for the locals to use. 佔領軍撤回時，將剩餘的車輛留給當地居民使用。 記憶技巧 sur- 表示超過；plus- 表示多出來；surplus 的意思是因超過而多出來，引申為剩餘。
plural [ˋplʊrəl] **n** 複數	Some plural words, such as "fish," don't need "s" or "es" at the end. 一些複數形單字不須字尾加上「-s」或「-es」，例如「魚」這個字。 記憶技巧 plur- 表示更多；-al 為形容詞字尾；plural 的意思是多於一個，引申為複數。

原來如此！

spider 蜘蛛是一吐絲織網的生物，宛如紡紗工人或是紡織機一樣。因此，spider 源自於單字 spinner；當然，spin ——紡、吐絲，是 spinner 的字幹，以 spider 聯想 spin 及 spinner 二字，有如蜘蛛吐絲，字彙自然擴展。

Chapter 4
硬顎音、軟顎音、喉門音轉換
〔g〕、〔k〕、〔h〕、〔dʒ〕、〔tʃ〕、〔ŋ〕、〔j〕

〔k〕對應〔g〕

sect - seg

子音 k 和 g 互換，母音通轉，兩者原意皆表示切，sect 現指派別。

section [`sɛkʃən] **n** 部門，區域，地段	The pie chart showed five colored sections to indicate areas of expense. 圓餅圖以五個顏色區塊顯示經費用途。 記憶技巧 sect- 表示切；section 是切下來的部分，衍生出部門的意思。
insect [`ɪnsɛkt] **n** 昆蟲	The resourceful Chinese have established farms to grow insects to supply pharmaceutical companies. 資源豐富的中國人設立昆蟲養殖農場以供應製藥公司。 記憶技巧 in- 表示進入；sect- 表示切；在此當「節」；insect 是身體分節的昆蟲。
segment [`sɛgmənt] **n** 部分，片段	When attacked by the bird, the lizard lost a segment of its tail and ran away. 遭受鳥類襲擊時，這隻蜥蜴丟掉了一部份的尾巴，然後逃跑。 記憶技巧 seg- 表示切；-ment 為名詞字尾；segment 即切下來的片段。

acre - agri

子音 c 和 g 互換，母音通轉，兩者皆表示田地，acre 在今日英語中的意思是英畝，agri- 還可指農業，兩者系出同源。

agriculture [`ægrɪkʌltʃɚ] **n** 農業	There has been a trend of chemical companies getting into the agriculture business. 有一個化學公司跨足農產業的趨勢。 記憶技巧 agri- 表示農地；culture 表示培養；agriculture 的意思是農業。

agricultural

[͵ægrɪ`kʌltʃərəl]

a 農業的

Development of agricultural and transportation infrastructure will ensure the country can feed its population.

農業及運輸基礎設施發展將確保該國人民糧食無虞。

記憶技巧 -al 為形容詞字尾。

agronomy

[ə`grɑnəmɪ]

n 農業經濟學

Agronomy has been a catalyst for the growth of great civilizations, including the ancient Egyptian Kingdoms.

農業經濟一直是古埃及王國等偉大文明的成長助力。

記憶技巧 agr- 表示農業；-nomy 為名詞字尾，表示經營法則；
agronomy 指的是經營農業的法則，引申為農業經濟學。

Part 2 CH 1 CH 2 CH 3 CH 4

硬顎音、軟顎音、喉門音轉換

corn - gran

子音 c（發〔k〕的音）和 g 互換，母音通轉，兩者皆表示穀物。

granary

[`grænərɪ]

n 穀倉，
穀產豐富的地區

The villagers built an elevated granary on poles to prevent rats from pillaging the grain.

為防止老鼠掠奪穀糧，村民在桿子上蓋高架穀倉。

記憶技巧 gran- 表示穀物；-ary 為名詞字尾，表示地方；granary 即
穀倉。

granular

[`grænjələ]

a 顆粒的

In the factory, granular salt was refined from rock salt that was mined within the mountain.

工廠裡，粒狀鹽是由採自山區的礦鹽精煉而成。

記憶技巧 gran- 表示穀物；-ar 為形容詞字尾；granular 即穀粒的。

know - gn

子音 k 和 g 互換，母音通轉，兩者皆表示知道。

diagnose

[`daɪəgnoz]

v 診斷，分析

After the patient was diagnosed with having an ulcer, he was warned not to eat spicy foods.

診斷出潰瘍之後，病患被警告不要吃辛辣食物。

記憶技巧 dia- 表示分開；gn- 表示知道；diagnose 的意思是分析、
辨明，引申為診斷。

相關字彙
護理人員的工作

- confine 使臥床
- cure 治療
- examine 診察
- hospitalize 使住院治療
- prescribe 開（藥方）
- prognosis 預後、病情發展預測
- treat 治療

---

ignore
[ɪgˋnor]
v 忽視，不理會

The factory ignored the water rationing limits and was imposed a fine of $100,000.
工廠未注意水的配量限制，遭罰款十萬元。

記憶技巧　i- 等同於 in-，表示不；gn- 表示知道；ignore 字面上的意思是不知道，引申為忽略、不理會。

---

ignorant
[ˋɪgnərənt]
a 無知的，無學識的

The sales clerk was not excused for breaking the company regulation just because he was ignorant of the rules.
銷售員違反公司規定一事，沒有因為不知道規則而被原諒。

記憶技巧　-ant 為形容詞字尾；ignorant 即無知的。

---

recognize
[ˋrɛkəgˏnaɪz]
v 辨識，承認

Sudan was the first country to recognize South Sudan as an independent nation.
蘇丹這國家首先承認南蘇丹是獨立國家。

記憶技巧　re- 表示再一次；co- 等同於 com-，表示一起；gn- 表示知道；-ize 為動詞字尾；recognize 字面上的意思是再一次知道，引申為辨識。

---

notorious
[noˋtorɪəs]
a 惡名昭彰的

Every resident knew that the southwest corner of the city was notorious for drug trafficking activity.
每個居民都知道城市西南邊因為運毒活動而惡名昭彰。

記憶技巧　no- 等同於 know；-ous 為形容詞字尾；notorious 的意思是大家都知道的，但這個字具有負面語意，作惡名昭彰解釋。

---

crowd - greg
兩者雖無字源關係，但可藉由子音 c 和 g 互換，母音通轉來記憶，兩者皆作群聚解釋。

---

aggregate
[ˋægrɪˏget]
a 總計的

The aggregate demand for all products and services in Norway increased dramatically after its discovery of oil.
挪威發現石油之後，所有產品及服務的需求總額急遽攀升。

記憶技巧　ag- 等同於 ad-，表示朝～方向；greg- 表示聚集；-ate 為動詞字尾；aggregate 的意思是聚集，形容詞的意思是總計的。

congregation
[͵kɑŋgrɪˋgeʃən]
n 聚集，集會

The church congragation grew faster than its competitors because its members were more active in recruiting.

這個教堂會眾較競爭者成長快速，因為教友較積極招募新成員。

記憶技巧 con- 表示一起；greg- 表示聚集；-ation 為名詞字尾；congregation 即聚會。

Part
2
CH 1
CH 2
CH 3
CH 4
硬顎音、軟顎音、喉門音轉換

segregation
[͵sɛgrɪˋgeʃən]
n 隔離，種族隔離

The factory no longer allowed segregation of male and female workers in separate work areas.

工廠不再允許將男女員工隔離在分開的作業區域工作。

記憶技巧 se- 表示分開；greg- 表示聚集；-ation 為名詞字尾；segregation 指隔離。

相關字彙
種族隔離、宗教仇恨

- anti-Semite 反猶太分子
- apartheid（南非）種族隔離政策
- Islamophobia 伊斯蘭恐懼症
- the Ku Klux Klan 三 K 黨
- pogrom 集體屠殺
- supremacist 至上主義者
- white supremacy 白人至上
- xenophobia 對外國的無理仇視（或畏懼）

---

lax - langu
子音 k（x 發〔k〕和〔s〕兩個音）和 g 互換，母音通轉，兩者的意思皆是鬆。

---

languid
a 軟弱無力的，倦怠的

Lying in his hammock on the beach, the man was in a languid mood during his vacation trip.

躺在沙灘吊床上，男子度假期間心情慵懶。

記憶技巧 langu- 表示鬆；-id 為形容詞字尾；languid 的意思是鬆軟無力的。

相關字彙
身體虛弱

- enfeebled 虛弱的
- frail 身體虛弱的
- feeble 無力的
- infirm 體弱的
- malnourished 營養失調的
- sickly 不健壯的
- unsteady 不穩固的
- vulnerable 脆弱的
- weak 衰弱的

languish
[ˋlæŋgwɪʃ]
v 凋萎，衰弱

Demoted and shamed, the manager languished in his new position as the janitor.

降職又遭羞辱，經理了無活力委身於管理員這個新職務。

記憶技巧 langu- 表示鬆；-ish 為動詞字尾；languish 的意思是變鬆，引申為凋萎。

ache - alg

兩者雖無字源關係，但可藉由子音 ch（發〔k〕）和 g 互換，母音通轉來記憶，兩者皆作疼痛解釋。

---

arthralgia
[ɑrˋθrældʒə]
n 關節痛

Crippled with chronic arthralgia after the accident, the athlete could no longer compete.
意外後，慢性關節炎導致不良於行，運動員不能再參與比賽。

（記憶技巧） arthr- 表示關節；-algia 表示疼痛；arthralgia 即關節痛。

---

analgesic
[ˏænælˋdʒizɪk]
n 止痛藥

The bark of the willow tree provides a strong, natural analgesic when ingested.
柳樹皮被吸收了便是強效的天然止痛藥。

（記憶技巧） an- 表示不；alg- 表示疼痛；-ic 為形容詞字尾；analgesic 的意思是使～不痛的，後轉當名詞用，意思是止痛藥。

---

neuralgia
[njuˋrældʒə]
n 神經痛

The debilitating neuralgia in the clerk's forearm forced him to take an early retirement.
辦事員的前臂肌肉無力的神經痛迫使他提早退休。

（記憶技巧） neur- 表示神經；-algia 表示疼痛；neuralgia 的意思是神經痛。

---

nostalgia
[nɑsˋtældʒɪə]
n 鄉愁，念舊

The distinguished woman regularly watches old black and white movies for the nostalgia they offer.
這名傑出的女子經常觀看黑白舊電影，沉浸其中的懷舊思情。

（記憶技巧） nost- 和 nest（巢穴）同源，意思是平安回家；-algia 表示疼痛；nostalgia 的意思是想要平安回家的思鄉之痛，引申為鄉愁、念舊。

---

eke - aug

子音 k 和 g 互換，母音通轉，兩者皆表示增加。

---

augment
[ɔgˋmɛnt]
v 擴編，增加

The popular smart phone game augments reality with cute animated characters that users can catch.
人氣手機遊戲用玩家抓得到的可愛動畫角色擴增實境。

（記憶技巧） aug- 表示增加；augment 即是增加。

auction

[`ɔkʃən]

n 拍賣，標售

The highlighted auction at Sotheby's featured authentic costumes from famous movies.

本次蘇富比眾人矚目的拍賣會的亮點是知名電影的真實戲服。

記憶技巧 -ion 為名詞字尾；auction 即拍賣喊價過程中，價格不停攀升增加。

---

author

[`ɔθɚ]

n 作者，作品，發起人

The author of the adventure novel signed autographs at Big City Bookstore over the weekend.

冒險小說作者週末在 Big City 書店為讀者簽名。

記憶技巧 auth- 等同於 aug-，表示增加；-or 表示人；author 字面上的意思是創造者、增加者，引申為作者。

---

authority

[ə`θɔrətɪ]

n 權威，權力，許可權

After the war, survivors were confused as to which group was the rightful authority.

戰爭過後，倖存者對於哪一組織才是合法政權感到困惑。

記憶技巧 -ity 為名詞字尾；authority 即創造者所擁有的無上權威。

---

cleave - glyph

子音 k 和 g 互換、v 和 ph 互換，母音通轉，兩者皆表示切、分開、刻。

---

hieroglyph

[`haɪərə‚glɪf]

n 象形符號，象形文字

The ancient 2,000-year-old stone calendars of Taiwan's Bunun Tribe feature remarkable hieroglyphs.

台灣布農族兩千年歷史的古老曆法石以顯著的象形符號為特色。

記憶技巧 hiero- 表示神聖的；-glyph 表示刻；hieroglyph 即刻出來的象形文字。

猜猜看！

廚房 kitchen 是烹煮的地方，kitch- 猜一單字？

答案：cook（煮）

carve - graph

子音 k 和 g 互換，母音通轉，兩者系出同源，carve 表示刻、刮，-graph 表示寫，可用古代寫字是用刻的來聯想。

---

graph

[græf]

V 用圖表表示

If one could graph man-made production of CO_2 gas globally, it would show a rapid acceleration.

若能畫出全球人為二氧化碳成長的圖表，會顯示出急遽增快。

記憶技巧　graph 的字面意思是寫，後引申為圖表，動詞當用圖表表示。

---

photograph

[ˋfotəˌgræf]

n 照片

After paying a lot to open his deceased father's safe, the son discovered only old photographs.

付出高額費用打開已故父親的保險箱，兒子只發現一些老照片。

記憶技巧　photo- 表示光；-graph 表示寫；photograph 是用光寫下的紀錄，引申作照片解釋。

---

calligraphy

[kəˋlɪgrəfɪ]

n 書法，筆跡

The student was enrolled in a calligraphy class to learn patience and appreciation for culture.

為了學習耐心及文化賞析，該名學生報名書法課程。

記憶技巧　calli- 表示漂亮；-graphy 表示寫；calligraphy 是漂亮的書寫文字，引申為書法。

相關字彙
手寫和拼字

- cursive 草寫的字母
- handwriting 手寫，筆跡
- orthography 拼字法
- penmanship 書法
- scrawl 潦草地寫
- stenography 速記

---

geography

[ˋdʒɪˋɑgrəfɪ]

n 地理學，地勢

The diverse geography of the peninsula and its natural resources historically attracted many invaders.

半島上多樣的地勢及天然資源歷代以來招致許多入侵者。

記憶技巧　geo- 表示土地；-graphy 表示寫、紀錄；geography 是紀錄土地的學問，當地理學解釋。

---

orthography

[ɔrˋθɑgrəfɪ]

n 正確拼法，拼字法

The linguist studied the orthography of a language in order to master its use.

為了精通該語言的用法，語言學家研究它的正確拼字。

記憶技巧　ortho- 表示正確的；-graphy 表示寫；orthography 的意思是正確的拼字。

choreography

[ˌkɔrɪ`ɑgrəfɪ]

n 編舞

The pop concert was so grand that organizers had to hire eight directors to manage the choreography.

流行音樂會非常盛大，策劃人員必須雇請八名指導人員處理編舞事項。

記憶技巧 choreo- 表示舞；-graphy 表示寫；choreography 的字面意思是寫舞，亦即編舞。

Part

2

CH 1
CH 2
CH 3
CH 4

硬顎音、軟顎音、喉門音轉換

---

ankle - angl

子音 k 和 g 互換，母音通轉，兩者系出同源，皆表示彎曲，ankle 是可彎曲的踝關節，angl- 是角，亦是彎曲之處。

---

angle

[`æŋgl̩]

n 角度，觀點，方面

By studying the angle of entry and following the trajectory, the detective could determine the location of the shooter.

藉由研究入角並追蹤彈道，偵探得以決定槍手位置。

記憶技巧 angle 即角度，引申為觀點。

---

angular

[`æŋgjələ]

a 有角的，笨拙的

The model was glorified for his strong, angular jaw and high cheekbones.

模特兒下顎豐腴有角，顴骨又高，非常亮眼。

記憶技巧 angl- 表示角；-ar 為形容詞字尾；angular 即有角的。

---

triangular

[traɪ`æŋgjələ]

a 三角形的，三重的，三方的

Triangular street signs warn drivers of upcoming obstacles or dangers.

三角形街道標示警告駕駛人前方有障礙或危險。

記憶技巧 tri- 表示三；angular 表示有角的；triangular 即三角的。

---

rectangle

[rɛk`tæŋgl̩]

n 矩形，長方形

The coach drew two rectangles on the parking lot with chalk, so that the children could play dodgeball.

教練用粉筆在停車場畫二個長方形，這樣孩童便能玩躲避球。

記憶技巧 rect- 表示正當的、正的；angle 表示角；rectangle 即有四個直角的長方形。

相關字彙
多角形

- hexagon 六角形
- heptagon 七角形
- octagon 八角形
- chevron V 形臂章
- diamond 菱形
- oblong 長方形
- square 正方形
- trapezoid 梯形

work - erg
子音 k 和 g 互換，母音通轉，兩者皆表示工作。

---

erg
[ɝg]
n 爾格（功的單位）

The efficiency of the new machines can be measured in the ergs of work produced per hour.
每小時產生的功爾格數可用來測量新機器的效能。

> 記憶技巧　erg 的字面意思是做工、工作，其定義是 1 達因（dyne）的力使物體在力的方向上移動一厘米所作的功。

---

allergic
[əˈlɝdʒɪk]
a 過敏的

The mother asked the chef if the soup contained any shrimp or crab, beause her son was allergic to shellfish.
因為兒子對帶殼海鮮過敏，母親問主廚湯有沒有蝦子或螃蟹。

> 記憶技巧　all- 等同於 other，表示其他；erg- 表示工作；-ic 為形容詞字尾；allergic 的意思是異物在某對象上工作，引申為過敏的。

---

energy
[ˈɛnɚdʒɪ]
n 活力，能力，能量

When all energy sources are renewable, the world can have fewer security issues.
所有能源都可再生時，世界的安全議題就會減少。

> 記憶技巧　en- 表示在～上；erg- 表示工作；-y 為名詞字尾；energy 即能量。

---

energetic
[ˌɛnɚˈdʒɛtɪk]
a 精力充沛的

The team leader was chosen for her energetic personality, in order to raise morale in the office.
為了提振辦公室士氣，小組領導人充滿活力的特質讓他當選。

> 記憶技巧　-ic 為形容詞字尾。

---

act - ag
子音 k 和 g 互換，母音通轉，兩者皆表示驅使、行動、做。

---

action
[ˈækʃən]
n 動作，行動，作用，訴訟

The punitive action taken by the supervising committee was regarded as a slap on the wrist.
監督委員會採取的懲罰行動被視為輕輕放下。

> 記憶技巧　act- 表示行動；-ion 為名詞字尾；action 即行動。

activate

[`æktə‚vet]

v 刺激（，活化）

The chemical compound will remain inert until it is activated by a catalyst.

這個化學化合物受到觸媒活化之前都是惰性。

記憶技巧 act- 表示行動；-ive 為形容詞字尾；-ate 為動詞字尾；activate 的意思是使～動起來，引申為刺激。

actual

[`æktʃuəl]

a 真實的，實際的

The actual sales growth figures and the projection differed by only a few percentage points.

實際銷售成長數字與預測僅一些百分比的差距。

記憶技巧 act- 表示驅使、行動；-al 為形容詞字尾；actual 的意思是行動的，引申為真實的。

enact

[ɪn`ækt]

v 頒布，扮演

相關字彙
制定、廢除、修訂法規

The general established a military committee that enacted martial law upon the citizens.

將軍設置一個對市民實施軍法的軍事委員會。

記憶技巧 en- 為動詞字首；act- 表示行動；enact 的意思是在表演中擔任某一角色，在 15 世紀中葉後才有頒布法令的意思。

- abolish 廢除
- amend 修訂
- codify 將～編成法典
- decriminalize 除罪化
- legislate 制定（或通過）法律
- reading（議案的）宣讀
- revoke 廢除
- come into effect 生效

transaction

[træn`zækʃən]

n 交易，處理，執行

The ATM machines charge a fee of $NT15 for every financial transaction.

每筆金融轉帳自動提款機收取台幣 15 元費用。

記憶技巧 trans- 表示跨越；act- 表示驅使；-ion 為名詞字尾；transaction 的意思是驅使某對象，使其從甲地移動到乙地，引申出交易的意思。

agent

[`edʒənt]

n 代理人，動作者，仲介

The legislature became a change agent for good within the mental health industry.

立法委員成為心理衛生產業好轉的推手。

記憶技巧 ag- 表示動作；-ent 表示人；agent 即動作者，引申出代理人的意思。

agile

[`ædʒaɪl]

a 活潑的，敏捷的

The agile gymnast could climb buildings, and was recruited by the mob boss to be a thief.

矯健的體操選手能夠攀爬建築物，被犯罪組織首腦吸收為竊賊。

記憶技巧 ag- 表示動作；-ile 為形容詞字尾；agile 的意思是動作敏捷的。

Part **2**

CH 1
CH 2
CH 3
CH 4

硬顎音、軟顎音、喉門音轉換

act - agon

子音 k 和 g 互換，母音通轉，兩者皆表示驅使、行動，agon- 指情緒受到驅使，特指因競賽而呈現出痛苦的狀態。

agony [ˋægənɪ] n 極大的痛苦	The agony of defeat motivated the athlete to train harder, so as not to repeat being a loser. 落敗的痛苦燃起運動員加倍苦練的動機，不要再當魯蛇。 **記憶技巧** agon- 表示痛苦；-y 為名詞字尾；agony 即極大的痛苦。
antagonist [ænˋtægənɪst] n 敵對者，反對者	The new president mended relations with the former antagonist nation. 新任總統修正與前敵對國家的關係。 **記憶技巧** anti- 表示對抗；agon- 表示競賽；-ist 為名詞字尾，表示人；antagonist 的意思是競賽中的敵對者。
protagonist [proˋtægənɪst] n 領導者，主角	In the popular children's novel, the spider is the protaganist. 受歡迎的兒童小說中，蜘蛛是主角。 **記憶技巧** proto- 表示第一；agon- 表示競賽；-ist 為名詞字尾，表示人；protagonist 是競賽中的領導者，亦作戲劇中的主角解釋。

猜猜看！

pass 表示「通過，經過」，猜 pass- 為首，表示經過一個地方的人？

答案：passer-by（過路者）

Section 2

〔h〕對應〔g〕

硬顎音、軟顎音、喉門音轉換

heavy - grav

兩者雖無字源關係，但可藉由子音 h 和 g 互換，母音通轉來記憶，兩者皆表示重。

---

grave
[grev]
a 重要的，嚴重的

The investment strategist made a grave error in judgment, leading to his firm going bankrupt.
投資策略家犯下一個嚴重的判斷錯誤，導致公司破產。

記憶技巧 grave 即嚴重的。

---

gravity
[ˈgrævətɪ]
n 莊重，嚴重性，
地心引力

Not aware of the gravity of the situation, the vacationers ignored official warnings to avoid visiting the island.
未察覺局勢嚴重，度假人群忽略避免造訪該島嶼的官方警示。

記憶技巧 grav- 表示重；-ity 是名詞字尾；gravity 可作莊重、地心引力等意思解釋。

相關字彙
程度劇烈

- acuteness 劇烈
- austerity 嚴厲
- extremity 極度
- severity 嚴厲
- seriousness 嚴重性
- savageness 兇猛
- starkness 嚴酷

---

aggravate
[ˈægrəˌvet]
v 加重（病情），
使惡化

Only a month after knee surgery, the coach aggravated his knee injury by trying to dunk a basketball.
教練膝蓋手術後僅一個月便因嘗試灌籃而傷勢惡化。

記憶技巧 ag- 等同於 ad-，表示往～方向；grav- 表示重；-ate 為動詞字尾；aggravate 的意思是加重。

---

grief
[grif]
n 悲傷，不幸

It is said that there is no grief like that of a mother who has lost her child.
據說，沒有傷痛能比擬母親喪子的悲傷。

記憶技巧 grief 等同於 grav-，指情緒沉重，引申作悲傷。

〔g〕對應〔k〕

grow - cre
兩者雖無字源關係，但可藉由子音 g 和 c 互換，母音通轉，兩者皆表示成長。

---

creature
[ˋkritʃɚ]
n 人類，生物，動物

An unusual creature discovered on the beach renewed speculation that mermaids actually existed.
海灘上發現的奇特生物再度引發美人魚確實存在的猜測。

記憶技巧　crea- 表示成長；-ure 為名詞字尾；creature 的意思是會成長的生物。

---

creativity
[ˌkrieˋtɪvətɪ]
n 創造力

The child, endowed with boundless creativity, was enrolled in a special academy for the gifted.
創意無限的孩子就讀適合資優學生的特殊學院。

記憶技巧　creative 表示有創意的；-ity 為名詞字尾；creativity 即創造力。

---

concrete
[ˋkɑnkrit]
a 具體的

The incoming executive vowed concrete measures to reduce expenses and increase the bottom line of profitability.
新任主管鄭重宣布刪減經費及增加利潤的具體措施

記憶技巧　con- 表示一起；cre- 表示成長；concrete 的意思是一起成長，彼此鞏固，引申出固體的、具體的意思。

---

decrease
[dɪˋkris]
v 減少

The decrease in tuition rates also meant a decrease in revenues for the school.
學費減少同時意味著學校收入減少。

記憶技巧　de- 表示離開；cre- 表示成長；decrease 的意思是愈長愈偏，引申為減少。

---

increase
[ɪnˋkris]
v 增加

Effective on January 1, the pay rate of every employee of this company will increase by 10%.
元月一日生效，該公司每名員工薪資調升 10%。

記憶技巧　in- 表示內；cre- 表示成長；increase 表示在內部成長，引申為增加。

recreation

[ˌrɛkrɪˈeʃən]

n 娛樂，消遣

Some fishing vessel owners have begun to offer fishing trips for pleasure and recreation.

一些漁船船東開始提供休閒娛樂目的的捕魚行程。

> **記憶技巧** re- 表示再一次；cre- 表示成長；-ation 為名詞字尾；recreation 的字面上意思是再一次成長，後有使人有活力、再生的意思，後來引申為娛樂（因為娛樂可使人放鬆、恢復活力）。

crew

[kru]

n 全體工作人員

The night crew of the hospital received a surprise visit from a celebrity.

醫院夜班員工意外遇上一位知名人士到訪。

> **記憶技巧** crew 等同於 cre-，表示增加；指招募而來逐漸增加的人員，當全體工作人員解釋。

相關字彙
船員、機組員

- captain 船長
- docker 碼頭工人
- ferryman 渡船夫
- helmsman 舵手
- sailor 水手
- submariner 潛水艇人員

recruit

[rɪˈkrut]

v 招募

In an effort to recruit more officers into the police force, scholarships for college tuition were offered.

為了招募更多新人投入警界，因此提供了大學學費獎學金。

> **記憶技巧** re- 表示再一次；cruit 等同於 cre-，表示增加；recruit 的字面意思是再增加，引申為招募，因為招募會增加新成員。

---

gall - chol

子音 g 和 k 互換，母音通轉，兩者皆表示膽汁。

cholesterol

[kəˈlɛstərol]

n 膽固醇

Patients with serious heart conditions are advised to reduce cholesterol intake.

建議心臟症狀嚴重的病患應減少膽固醇攝取量。

> **記憶技巧** chole- 表示膽；ster- 等同於 stereo-，表示堅固；-ol 等同於 oil，表示油；cholesterol 的意思是膽固醇。

chololith

[ˈkoləˌlɪθ]

n 膽石

The world record holder for eating the most eggs in one sitting developed a large, painful chololith.

一口氣吃下最多蛋的世界紀錄保持人長出一顆又大又痛的膽結石。

> **記憶技巧** chol- 表示膽；lith- 表示石頭；chololith 的意思是膽石。

Part **2**
CH 1
CH 2
CH 3
CH 4

硬顎音、軟顎音、喉門音轉換

211

cholera
[`kɑlərə]
n 霍亂

The sewage of aid workers drained into the source of drinking water, causing an outbreak of cholera.
救援人員的汙水排入飲用水源，結果爆發霍亂。

記憶技巧　霍亂，是一種急性腹瀉疾病，古人相信是由膽汁所造成的。

---

egalitarian - equ / equi
子音 g 和 q 互換，母音通轉，兩者皆表示平等。

---

equal
[`ikwəl]
a 相等的，勝任的

The group of women demanded equal pay for comparable employment responsibilities.
婦女團體要求職責相當的平等薪資。

記憶技巧　equ- 表示平等；-al 為形容詞字尾；equal 的意思是相等的。

---

equator
[ɪ`kwetɚ]
n 赤道

Much of the land on the equator is uninhabitable by humans, being dry deserts or dangerous jungles.
赤道上許多陸地是乾旱沙漠或危險叢林，不適合人類居住。

記憶技巧　equ- 表示平等；-ate 為動詞字尾；-or 為名詞字尾；equator 是均分南北半球的赤道。

相關字彙　世界地理

- Antarctic 南極地區
- Arctic 北極地區
- Atlantic Rim 環大西洋
- Australasia 澳大拉西亞
- East Asia 東亞
- Oceania 大洋洲
- Southeast Asia 東南亞
- the subtropics 亞熱帶
- the tropics 熱帶

---

equity
[`ɛkwətɪ]
n 公正，財產淨值

With real estate prices plummeting, they decided to sell their home while there was still equity available.
房地產價格崩跌，他們決定趁仍有資產淨值的時候售出自用住宅。

記憶技巧　equ- 表示平等；-ity 為名詞字尾；equity 即公平、公正。

---

equivalent
[ɪ`kwɪvələnt]
a 相等的，相同的

After passing the GED exam, equivalent to having a high school diploma, the young man enrolled in a community college.
通過美國高中同等學歷測驗，等同於擁有中學文憑的年輕人註冊進入社區大學。

記憶技巧　equi- 表示平等；val- 表示價值；-ent 為形容詞字尾；equivalent 即等價的、對等的。

equivocal
[ɪˈkwɪvək!]
a 含糊的，不確定的

The father was equivocal in expressing what he hoped would be his son's future career.
父親含糊表達對兒子未來職業的希望是什麼。

記憶技巧　equi- 表示平等；voc- 表示聲音；-al 為形容詞字尾；equivocal 的意思是兩個相同的聲音，引申出含糊的、不確定的意思。

equilibrium
[ˌikwəˈlɪbrɪəm]
n 平衡

The coffee became creamy brown throughout the cup, when all of the ingredients achieved equilibrium.
咖啡所有成分達到平衡時，整個杯子變成乳棕色。

記憶技巧　equi- 表示平等；libr- 表示秤；-ium 為名詞字尾；equilibrium 的意思是（秤子）平衡。

equinox
[ˈikwəˌnɑks]
n 春分，秋分，晝夜平分點

The school traditionally broke on the Spring Equinox for a one week break.
傳統上，春分時學校會放假一星期。

記憶技巧　equi- 表示平等；nox- 等同於 night，表示晚上；equinox 的意思是等夜，即春分、秋分兩個時間點。

相關字彙　一年四季

● midsummer 仲夏
● summer solstice 夏至
● winter solstice 冬至
● in the dead of winter 寒冬

adequate
[ˈædəkwɪt]
a 適當的，充分的，勝任的

The interviewee displayed fairly adequate skills, but the HR manager was seeking someone exceptional.
面試者展示相當勝任的技能，但是人資經理物色的是特殊人才。

記憶技巧　ad- 表示朝～方向；equ- 表示平衡；-ate 為形容詞字尾；adequate 即平衡的，引申為適當的、充分的。

Part **2**
CH 1
CH 2
CH 3
CH 4

硬顎音、軟顎音、喉門音轉換

猜猜看！

「ankle（腳踝）」是彎曲有角度的部分，猜一單字？

答案：angle（角度）

Section **4**

〔h〕對應〔k〕

（拉丁文的 c 發〔k〕的音，在現代英語中，有些已改發〔s〕的音）

heart - cord

子音 h 和 c 互換，母音通轉，兩者皆表示心。

accord [əˈkɔrd] **v**（使）一致， （使）調和，給予	The vice president was accorded the powers of the president while he was away on vacation. 總統外出度假時，副總統被賦予總統權力。 記憶技巧　ac- 等同於 ad-，表示朝～方向；cord- 表示心；accord 的意思是讓心思集中，引申為（使）一致、（使）調和。
concordant [kənˈkɔrdənt] **a** 一致的，和諧的	The statement of the witness interviewed by the police was concordant with the claims of the victim. 警方約談的目擊者的陳述與受害人供詞一致。 記憶技巧　con- 表示一起；cord- 表示心；-ant 為形容詞；concordant 的意思是心思一致的。
cordial [ˈkɔrdʒəl] **a** 誠懇的，友善的	The diplomat had a cordial demeanor in front of the assembly at the United Nations. 這名外交官在聯合國與會者面前舉止誠懇。 記憶技巧　cord- 表示心；-ial 為形容詞字尾；cordial 是出自內心的，表示誠懇的。
record [ˈrɛkəd] **n** 紀錄，履歷	It was public record that the legislator consistently voted for tax rate increases. 這名立法委員一直投票贊成增稅，這已列入公開紀錄。 記憶技巧　re- 表示恢復；cord- 表示心；record 的意思是恢復記憶，record 引申為紀錄。
discordant [dɪsˈkɔrdn̩t] **a** 不一致的， 不和諧的	His experience with his recently purchased car was discordant with the promises of the used car salesman. 他最近購買的車子開起來和二手車業務承諾的有出入。 記憶技巧　dis- 表示分開；cord- 表示心；-ant 為形容詞字尾；discordant 的意思是不同心的，引申為不一致的。

core
[kor]
n 核心，果核

Reputed to be rotten to the core, the criminal didn't care about the consequences of his actions.
惡名昭彰的罪犯泯滅人性，不在意所作所為的後果。

記憶技巧 core 等同於 cord-，表示心；core 是核心。

courageous
[kəˋredʒəs]
a 勇敢的

The courageous captain secured the release of his crewmen after pirates hijacked his ship.
船隻遭海盜劫持後，英勇的船長讓船員獲釋。

記憶技巧 cour- 等同於 cord-，表示心；-age 為名詞字尾；-ous 為形容詞字尾；在中世紀時 courage 可指內心的各種想法、感受，因此有驕傲、憤怒、信心、慾望、勇敢等意思，後來語意變窄，courageous 專指勇敢的。

encourage
[ɪnˋkɝɪdʒ]
v 鼓勵，助長

Parents should encourage teenagers to stay in school, instead of going to work at a young age.
家長應鼓勵青少年孩子就學，不要年紀輕輕就去工作。

記憶技巧 en- 等同於 in-，表示放入，讓名詞轉動詞；cour- 等同於 cord-，表示心；-age 為名詞字尾；encourage 的意思是給人內心注入勇氣，引申為鼓勵。

discourage
[dɪsˋkɝɪdʒ]
v 勸阻，使沮喪

A sharp increase in shipping rates discouraged many factories from sourcing materials from overseas.
運費飆漲讓許多工廠不從國外進口原料。

記憶技巧 dis- 表示離開；courage 表示勇氣；discourage 的意思是沒了勇氣，即使沮喪的意思。

---

horn - corn

corn 的兩大主要意思：穀物／玉米、雞眼／硬皮，語意之所以落差這麼大，主要是來源不同。表示穀物的 corn 和 grain 同源，可用格林法則 g、c 互換、母音通轉來記憶，至於表示雞眼的 corn 則是和 horn 同源，可用格林法則 c、h 互換、母音通轉來記憶，horn 是角，古義尚有頭、身體最外面的（突出）部分，雞眼是皮膚上的突起物。

Capricorn
[ˋkæprɪkɔrn]
n 摩羯座，山羊座

The thoughtful author was born in January, and his star sign was Capricorn.
一月份出生，心思細膩的作家的星座是魔羯座。

記憶技巧 Capr- 表示山羊；corn- 表示角；Capricorn 即山羊座。

cornucopia
[ˌkɔrnəˋkopɪə]
n 豐盛

The harvest season in the village provided visitors with a cornucopia of vegetables to choose from.
村莊於採收季節提供豐盛蔬菜供訪客選擇。

> **記憶技巧** corn- 表示角；copia 即「copious（富饒的）」；cornucopia 是希臘神話中哺育宙斯的那頭羊的角，引申作豐饒的象徵。

---

hundred - cent
子音 h 和 c 互換，母音通轉，兩者皆表示百，cent- 亦作百分之一。

---

century
[ˋsɛntʃʊrɪ]
n 世紀，百碼賽跑

According to the science magazine, the last century saw great leaps forward in medical technology.
根據科學雜誌，上一世紀經歷醫藥科技大幅躍進。

> **記憶技巧** cent- 表示百；century 即一百年。

---

centennial
[sɛnˋtɛnɪəl]
a 百年（一次）的

In 2015, Webster University had a street party to kick off its centennial celebration.
2015 年，韋伯斯特大學舉辦街頭派對為創校百年慶揭開序幕。

> **記憶技巧** cent- 表示百；enn- 等同於 ann-，表示年；-ial 為形容詞字尾；centennial 的意思是百年一次的。

---

centimeter
[ˋsɛntəˌmitɚ]
n 公分

In most countries, accumulated rainfall is measured in centimeters instead of inches.
大多數國家以公分作為累積雨量測量單位，不是英吋。

> **記憶技巧** cent- 表示百分之一；-meter 表示公尺；centimeter 即公分。

---

centipede
[ˋsɛntəˌpid]
n 蜈蚣

Some centipedes are so ferocious and poisonous that they can defeat scorpions and spiders in battle.
一些蜈蚣凶殘又具有毒性，戰鬥中能夠擊退蠍子及蜘蛛。

> **記憶技巧** cent- 表示百；ped- 表示腳；centipede 即百足蟲、蜈蚣。

相關字彙
蟲

- bedbug 臭蟲
- beetle 甲蟲
- black widow 黑寡婦
- bumblebee 熊蜂
- cicada 蟬
- cricket 蟋蟀
- firefly 螢火蟲
- fruit fly 果蠅
- locust 蝗蟲
- termite 白蟻
- woodworm 木蛀蟲

percent

[pɚˋsɛnt]

n 百分比

It's not easy to find a safe investment that can provide a return of over six percent annually.

要找到能夠提供年收益超過百分之六的投資不容易。

記憶技巧 per- 表示每一；cent- 表示百；percent 即百分比。

Part 2
CH 1
CH 2
CH 3
CH 4
硬顎音、軟顎音、喉門音轉換

horse - equ

兩者雖無字源關係，但可藉由子音 h 和 q（發〔k〕的音）互換，母音通轉來記憶，兩者皆表示馬。

equestrian

[ɪˋkwɛstrɪən]

a 馬的

Jill joined the equestrian club to improve her horseback riding as well as to meet a wealthy, single man.

為了增進騎馬技術，遇上多金單身男子，吉兒加入馬術俱樂部。

記憶技巧 equ- 表示馬；-ian 為形容詞字尾；equestrian 的意思是馬的、騎馬者的。

hound - cyn / can

子音 h 和 c 互換，母音通轉，兩者皆表示犬。

canine

[ˋkenaɪn]

a 犬的，似犬的

The father brought his son to the canine kennel to find a cute puppy to adopt.

為了找到一隻領養的可愛小狗，父親帶兒子到養狗場。

記憶技巧 can- 表示犬；-ine 為形容詞字尾；canine 即犬的。

cynic

[ˋsɪnɪk]

n 憤世嫉俗者，玩世不恭者

With so many broken campaign promises, most voters in that country have become cynics.

很多競選活動承諾未兌現，那國家的選民變得憤世忌俗。

記憶技巧 cyn- 表示犬；cynic 的意思是像犬的，一般認為犬儒學派是蘇格拉底的弟子安提斯泰尼所創立的。早期的犬儒主義是根據自身的道德原則去蔑視世俗的觀念，後期卻轉變成玩世不恭。

相關字彙
不開心、不友善、對人生無望的人

• pessimist 悲觀者
• defeatist 失敗主義者
• misery【英】老發牢騷的人
• Cassandra 凶事預言家

cynical
['sɪnɪkl̩]
a 憤世嫉俗的，悲觀的

The executive was cynical about the sales manager's promise to increase company sales by 12 percent.
主管對於業務經理增加一成二公司銷售額的承諾不抱希望。

記憶技巧 -al 為形容詞字尾。

---

have - cap
子音 h 和 c 互換，母音通轉，兩者原始意思皆表示抓、握。

---

capture
['kæptʃɚ]
v 捕獲，奪取

The new Canon cameras offer the ability to capture your life's important moments in 30 megapixels.
新款佳能相機能夠以三千萬畫素捕捉生活重要時刻。

記憶技巧 capt- 表示抓；-ure 為名詞字尾；capture 即抓取的意思，本為名詞，後亦可當動詞用。

---

captive
['kæptɪv]
n 俘虜，受迷惑者

The uncooperative captive was placed in the isolation cell for a week as punishment.
俘虜不配合，被關進隔離牢房一周作為懲罰。

記憶技巧 capt- 表示抓；-ive 為形容詞字尾；captive 字面上的意思是被抓走的，引申做被迷惑的，名詞當俘虜、受迷惑者解釋。

相關字彙
牢獄

- condemned 被判罪的
- custodial 監禁的
- detention 拘留
- internment 拘留
- incarceration 監禁
- lockdown 把犯人關入牢房
- term 期限

---

captivate
['kæptə͵vet]
v 迷惑

The Chinese dance troupe has captivated audiences around the world for the past ten years.
中國舞蹈團過去十年來在世界各地觀眾魅力不減。

記憶技巧 -ate 為動詞字尾；captivate 指迷惑。

---

caption
['kæpʃən]
n 標題

The travel article included beautiful photography with descriptive captions underneath.
旅遊文章包括底下有說明文字的美麗照片。

記憶技巧 cap- 表示抓；-ion 為名詞字尾；caption 指的是能夠抓住讀者注意力的標題。

house - eco

兩者雖無字源關係，但可藉由子音 h 和 c 互換，母音通轉來記憶，兩者皆表示家。

ecology
[ɪˈkɑlədʒɪ]

n 生態學

Jill studied ecology in college so that she could one day help to protect the habitats of endangered species.
吉兒大學研讀生態學，以便有一天能夠協助保護瀕臨絕種動物棲息地。

記憶技巧 eco- 表示家；-logy 表示研究；ecology 即研究生物和其所處環境的一門學問，即生態學。

economy
[ɪˈkɑnəmɪ]

n 經濟，節約

The economies of nations can be significantly influenced by the hopes and fears of investors.
各國的經濟深受投資者看多或看空的影響。

記憶技巧 eco- 表示家；-nomy 表示管理、法規；economy 的意思是管理家裡的法則，後引申為經濟、節約。

economic
[ˌikəˈnamɪk]

a 經濟學的，經濟上的，實用的

An economic collapse may be devastating, but it offers opportunistic investors a chance for profit.
經濟崩盤或許是一場災難，但會讓投機的投資客有機會獲利。

記憶技巧 -ic 為形容詞字尾；economic 指經濟學上的。

economical
[ˌikəˈnamɪkl̩]

a 經濟的，節儉的

The decision to outsource customer service to a foreign firm was purely economical.
客服業務外包給國外公司的決定純粹是經濟考量。

記憶技巧 -al 為形容詞字尾；economical 指節儉的、經濟的。

hearth - carbo

子音 h 和 c 互換，母音通轉，兩者原意皆表示火、熱、燃燒；hearth 指壁爐；carbo 是碳。

carbon
[ˈkɑrbən]

n 碳

The development of fine carbon fibers is a major advancement in energy storage technology.
細碳纖維研發是能量儲存技術的重大進展。

記憶技巧 carbon 即是碳。

Part **2**

CH 1
CH 2
CH 3
CH 4

硬顎音、軟顎音、喉門音轉換

carbohydrate
[ˌkɑrbəˈhaɪdret]
n 碳水化合物

Wheat bread offers an abundant source of carbohydrates, but it doesn't provide many important nutrients.
小麥麵包提供豐富的碳水化合物來源，但是重要營養成分不多。

記憶技巧 carbo- 表示碳；hydr- 表示水；-ate 為名詞字尾，表示化學物質；carbohydrate 即碳水化合物。

carboholic
[ˌkɑrbəˈhɔlɪk]
n 好吃甜食的人

The bakery worker became an eventual carboholic after eating bread almost every day.
幾乎天天吃麵包，麵包店員工後來變成一個愛吃甜食的人。

記憶技巧 carbo- 表示碳，在此指 carbohydrate；-(a)holic 表示喜愛～的人或致力於～的人；carboholic 指喜愛攝取碳水化合物（醣類）的人。

hour - chron

兩者雖無字源關係，但可藉由子音 h 和 ch（發〔k〕的音）互換，母音通轉來記憶。hour 表示小時，chron- 可以是年、月、日內的任一時段，因此 chron- 亦蘊含小時的意思。

chronic
[ˈkrɑnɪk]
a 慢性的，長期的

Chronic knee pain prevented the grandfather from joining his son's family on weekly hikes.
慢性膝蓋疼痛讓祖父無法與兒子的家人去每週的健行。

記憶技巧 chron- 表示時間；-ic 為形容詞字尾；chronic 指持續很長久的，引申為慢性的、長期的。

chronology
[krəˈnɑlədʒɪ]
n 年表

The chronology of the Ancient Eyptian Civilizations spans over 3,000 years, ending with the death of Cleopatra.
古埃及文明的年表跨越三千多年，結束於克麗巴特拉女王之死。

記憶技巧 chrono- 表示時間；-logy 表示說、研究；chronology 指按時間編排的年表。

anachronism
[əˈnækrəˌnɪzəm]
n 年代錯誤

A careful viewer spotted a passing airplane in the movie about Jesus, which was an obvious anachronism.
一名細心的觀眾注意到關於耶穌的電影畫面中出現一架飛機飛過，這是明顯的年代錯置。

記憶技巧 ana- 表示相反；chron- 表示時間；-ism 為名詞字尾；anachronism 指逆時，引申做年代錯誤。

synchronize

[`sɪŋkrənaɪz]

v 同時發生，校準

The team of divers synchronized their watches and agreed to return to the surface at two o'clock sharp.
潛水團隊校準手錶，約定兩點整回到水面。

> 記憶技巧　syn- 表示相同；chron- 表示時間；-ize 為動詞字尾；synchronize 指使時間相同，亦即校準、同時發生。

synchronous

[`sɪŋkrənəs]

a 同時的

After finishing his test, Fred tapped his pencil on the desk in synchronous timing to the ticking of his watch.
寫完考卷，弗瑞德和著手錶滴答聲用鉛筆輕輕敲著桌子。

> 記憶技巧　-ous 為形容詞字尾；synchronous 指同時的。

相關字彙
同步、同時

- at the same time 同時
- in the meantime 同時
- concurrent 同時發生的
- meanwhile 同時
- simultaneous 同步的

hurry - celer

兩者雖無字源關係，但可藉由子音 h 和 c，母音通轉來記憶，兩者皆表示快速移動。

celerity

[sə`lɛrɪtɪ]

n 快速，敏捷

As the train started to pull away from the station, the celerity of her pace quickened in an effort to catch it.
火車啟動駛離車站時，她加快步伐努力趕上。

> 記憶技巧　celer- 表示快速移動；-ity 為名詞字尾；celerity 的意思是快速、敏捷。

accelerate

[æk`sɛləˌret]

v 加速，促進

The politician's speech about closing the borders only accelerated the influx of illegal immigrants.
政治人物關閉邊境的演說只加速非法移民的湧入。

> 記憶技巧　ac- 表示朝～方向；celer- 表示速度；-ate 為動詞字尾；accelerate 的意思是加速。

decelerate

[di`sɛləˌret]

v 減速，減緩

The country could not decelerate the flight of its educated workforce to other countries.
這個國家無法減緩高學歷人力外流其他國家。

> 記憶技巧　de- 表示相反；celer- 表示速度；-ate 為動詞字尾；decelerate 即減速。

Part **2**

CH 1
CH 2
CH 3
CH 4

硬顎音、軟顎音、喉門音轉換

heat - cal

兩者雖無字源關係，但可藉由子音 h 和 c，母音通轉來記憶，兩者皆表示熱。

---

calorie

[ˋkælərɪ]

n 卡路里

The diet soda advertised that it contained only one calorie, but its artifical sweetener may be dangerous.

低糖汽水廣告宣稱僅含一卡路里，但其中的人工甜味劑可能危害身體。

記憶技巧　calorie 是計算食物所含的熱量的單位。

---

nonchalant

[ˋnɑnʃələnt]

a 冷淡的

It is an extremely strange scene in the movie when the woman buries her son in a nonchalant manner.

電影中極為怪異的一幕是婦人冷漠埋葬自己兒子。

記憶技巧　non- 表示缺乏；chal- 等同於 cal-，表示熱；-ant 為形容詞字尾；nonchalant 字面上的意思是沒有熱度，引申為冷淡的。

---

head - cap

子音 h 和 c 互換，母音通轉，兩者皆表示頭。

---

cap

[kæp]

n 帽子，蓋子

The apprentice frantically searched under the table for the cap to his new pen.

實習生在桌子底下拼命找尋新鋼筆的筆蓋。

記憶技巧　cap 即戴在頭上的帽子。

---

capital

[ˋkæpət!]

n 大寫字母，資本，首都

An injection of capital was necessary to pay the salaries of the school staff for another semester.

為了支付學校員工另一學期的薪資，資金挹注有其必要。

記憶技巧　capit- 表示頭；-al 為名詞字尾；capital 的意思是頭部，引申為首都、大寫字母等意思，亦可當形容詞用。

---

capitalism

[ˋkæpət!ˏɪzəm]

n 資本主義

China has gradually introduced capitalism into its Communist-run economy.

中國逐漸將資本主義引進共產主義支配的經濟中。

記憶技巧　-ism 為名詞字尾。

相關字彙　
經濟體制

- communism 共產主義
- corporatism 集團主義
- industrialism 工業主義
- knowledge economy 知識經濟
- macroeconomy 總體經濟
- market economy 市場經濟
- sharing economy 共享經濟

captain

[`kæptɪn]

n 警長，機長，船長

The captain announced on the intercom for passengers to return to their seats and fasten their seatbelts.

機長透過機艙通訊系統告知乘客回到座位，繫上安全帶。

記憶技巧 capt- 表示頭；captain 即領頭者，引申為警長、船長等意思。

capitulate

[kə`pɪtʃə‚let]

v 投降

The Qing Empire capitulated by giving up Taiwan, the Pescadores and Liaodung Peninsula.

清廷投降，割讓台灣、澎湖及遼東半島。

記憶技巧 capit- 表示頭，此處當章節、標題解釋；-ate 為動詞字尾；capitulate 本來的意思是草擬章節標題，後來指擬定（投降）協定，引申為投降。

decapitate

[dɪ`kæpə‚tet]

v 斬首

School officials were seriously concerned when they interviewed a student known for decapitating dolls.

學校主管訪談一名以斬首洋娃娃著稱的學生時，甚感不安。

記憶技巧 de- 表示離開；capit- 表示頭；-ate 為動詞字尾；decapitate 的意思是頭離開身體，引申為斬首。

precipitate

[prɪ`sɪpə‚tet]

v 猛然落下

Diplomats scrambled to call a meeting to prevent the conflict from precipitating into a full-blown war.

為了防止突如其來的衝突演變成全面戰爭，外交人員緊急召開會議。

記憶技巧 pre- 表示前；cipit- 等同於 cap-，表示頭；-ate 為動詞字尾；precipitate 的意思是頭往前倒（倒栽蔥），引申為猛然落下。

---

horse - cur

子音 h 和 c 互換，母音通轉，兩者原意皆表示跑，可用馬擅長跑步來記憶。

current

[`kɝənt]

n 潮流，電流

The Gulf Stream is an important current that brings warm waters to the North Atlantic.

墨西哥灣流是將暖水流引至北大西洋的重要潮流。

記憶技巧 cur- 表示跑；-ent 為形容詞字尾；current 的意思是跑動的或流通的，後轉當名詞用，意思是潮流、電流。

Part **2**

CH 1
CH 2
CH 3
CH 4

硬顎音、軟顎音、喉門音轉換

currency
[`kɝənsɪ]
n 流通，貨幣，通貨

In the tiny Pacific island, the only currency used by local villagers is a type of rare seashell.
此太平洋小島上，當地村民唯一使用的貨幣是一種稀有貝殼。

記憶技巧 -ency 為名詞字尾。

concurrent
[kən`kɝənt]
a 同時的，一致的，和諧的

Different departments are working on concurrent projects that address the shortfall in revenues.
各部門一直進行同期的計畫，要處理收益赤字。

記憶技巧 con- 表示一起；cur- 表示跑；-ent 為形容詞字尾；concurrent 字面上意思是一起跑的，引申為同時的、一致的等意思。

excursive
[ɛk`skɝsɪv]
a 漫遊的，離題的

While the main group surrounded the city, a small excursive group went north to scout for supplies.
主力圍城時，一支小規模的游擊部隊往北移動搜索補給物資。

記憶技巧 ex- 表示外面；cur- 表示跑；-ive 為形容詞字尾；excursive 的意思是跑到外面去的，引申為離題的、漫遊的。

incursive
[ɪn`kɝsɪv]
a 入侵的

The soldiers made incursive challenges to the front line to test the invading army for weaknesses.
為測試入侵部隊的弱點，士兵對前線進行入侵挑戰。

記憶技巧 in- 表示內；cur- 表示跑；-ive 為形容詞字尾；incursive 的意思是跑到裡面的，引申為入侵的。

occur
[ə`kɝ]
v 發生，使想起

An eclipse of the moon during the Winter Solstice is an event that occurs only once every 500 years.
冬至期間月蝕是每五百年才發生一次的事情。

記憶技巧 oc- 等同於 ob-，表示相對、朝～方向；cur- 表示跑；occur 是朝某方向跑過去，引申為發生。

recurrent
[rɪ`kɝənt]
a 循環的，週期的

The janitor preferred nighttime work to avoid having recurrent nightmares about his wartime experiences.
為擺脫揮之不去的戰時經歷的夢魘，管理員偏好值夜班。

記憶技巧 re- 表示回來；cur- 表示跑；-ent 為形容詞字尾；recurrent 字面上的意思是跑回來的，引申為循環的、週期的。

course
[kors]
n 路線，跑道，課程，一道菜

The teachers were required to take continuing education courses in order to keep their jobs.
教師被要求修讀進修教育課程以保住飯碗。

記憶技巧 course 等同於 cur-，表示跑；course 即路線、跑道。

curriculum

[kə`rɪkjələm]

n 課程

The educational curriculum of every public school changed after the progressive President took over.

改革派總統就任之後，每一所公立學校的教育課程改變了。

記憶技巧　cur- 表示跑；-um 為名詞字尾；curriculum 的意思是跑出來的流程，引申為課程。

---

concourse

[`kɑnkors]

n 群眾，合流
　　（，大廳）

Every December, the main concourse of the city train station features colorful Christmas displays.

每年十二月，城市火車站中央大廳的特色是五彩繽紛的耶誕展示。

記憶技巧　con- 表示一起；course 表示跑；concourse 大家一起跑，引申為群眾、合流、大廳。

相關字彙
建築物及內部設施

- auditorium 禮堂
- departure lounge 候機室
- front desk 服務台
- green room 演員休息室
- locker room 置物櫃室
- lounge 會客廳
- reception 接待處
- smoking room 吸菸室
- transit lounge 轉機候機室

---

intercourse

[`ɪntɚ͵kors]

n 交際，交流，交媾

The students were forbidden to use foul language and discuss intercourse on campus.

校園內禁止學生出現不雅語言及討論交媾。

記憶技巧　inter- 表示在～之間；course 表示跑；intercourse 的意思是在～之間跑，引申為交際、交流。

---

recourse

[rɪ`kors]

n 求助，請求保護，
　　償還要求

There will be no legal recourse if one becomes injured using the product in a reckless manner.

若是不慎使用產品而導致受傷則無法索賠。

記憶技巧　re- 表示回來；course 表示跑；recourse 的意思是跑回來，引申為求助。

---

hill - cel

子音 h 和 c 互換，母音通轉，兩者皆表示山丘、高。

---

excel

[ɪk`sɛl]

v 勝過，優於

The experienced attorney earned a seven-figure salary, because he excelled at mergers and acquisitions.

經驗豐富的律師精通企業合併及收購，薪水達七位數字。

記憶技巧　ex- 表示外面；cel- 表示山丘；excel 指的是比山丘還要高，引申為勝過。

excellent
[ˋɛksḷənt]
a 出色的，傑出的，
優等的

The engineer had an excellent credit rating, so his low-interest loan was approved quickly.
工程師信用評等良好，低利貸款很快通過。

記憶技巧 -ent 為形容詞字尾。

heaven - cel

兩者雖無字源關係，但可藉由子音 h 和 c 互換，母音通轉來記憶，兩者皆表示天空。

ceiling
[ˋsilɪŋ]
n 天花板

The housing prices in Taipei will reach their ceiling in a few years, and may drop drastically in a correction.
台北房價幾年內達到天花板，而可能暴跌修正。

記憶技巧 ceil- 等同於 cel-，表示天；-ing 為名詞字尾；ceiling 是天花板。

celestial
[sɪˋlɛstʃəl]
a 天空的，天國的

The black hole is a celestial body that can only be seen when a bright object passes behind it.
黑洞是一個天體，只有在明亮物體從後面通過時才看得見。

記憶技巧 cel- 表示天；-ial 為形容詞；celestial 的意思是天空的。

hand - chiro

兩者雖無字源關係，但可藉由子音 h 和 ch（發〔k〕的音）互換，母音通轉來記憶，兩者皆表示手。

chirography
[Ʌkaɪˋrɑgrəfɪ]
n 筆跡，書寫

The English teacher admired good chirography, so she required handwritten reports from her students.
英文老師讚賞工整筆跡，因此要求學生繳交手寫報告。

記憶技巧 chiro- 表示手；-graphy 表示寫；chirography 的意思是手寫，引申為筆跡、書寫。

chiropractor
[ˋkaɪrəͺpræktɚ]
n 按摩師

The talented rider needed to visit a chiropractor for six months after falling off her racehorse.
從賽馬摔下之後，天賦聰穎的騎士必須找按摩師調理六個月。

記憶技巧 chiro- 表示手；pract- 表示方法、實施；-or 表示人；chiropractor 的意思是按摩師。

heap - cumul

兩者雖無字源關係，但可藉由子音 h 和 c 互換，母音通轉來記憶，兩者皆表示堆積。

accumulate

[əˋkjumjəˌlet]

v 累積，積聚，積攢

The family had to remove the huge piles of newspapers accumulated by the deceased.

家人必須清除已故親人堆積的大量報紙。

記憶技巧 ac- 等同於 ad-，表示朝～方向；cumul- 表示堆積；-ate 為動詞字尾；accumulate 的意思是堆積。

---

cumulus

[ˋkjumjuləs]

n 積雲，堆積

The pilot flew a course around the dark cumulus clouds to avoid the thunderstorm.

為避開雷雨，飛行員航行繞過黑色積雲的航道。

記憶技巧 cumul- 表示堆積；-us 為名詞字尾；cumulus 指積雲、堆積。

相關字彙
水氣、雲、天氣

- cirrocumulus 捲積雲
- cirrostratus 捲層雲
- cumulonimbus 積雨雲
- fogbound 被霧籠罩的
- mist 薄霧
- nimbus 雨雲
- storm cloud 暴風雲
- thundercloud 雷雨雲

Part **2**

CH 1
CH 2
CH 3
CH 4

硬顎音、軟顎音、喉門音轉換

hole - cav

兩者雖無字源關係，但可藉由子音 h 和 c 互換，母音通轉來記憶，兩者皆表示中空。

cave

[kev]

n 洞穴，地窖

Shards of pottery and arrowheads from the Stone Age were found in a cave in France.

一些石器時代陶器碎片及箭頭鏃在法國一處洞穴被發現。

記憶技巧 cav- 表示中空；cave 是洞穴的意思。

---

cavern

[ˋkævən]

n 大穴，大洞

Son Doong in Vietnam has the distinction of being the largest cavern in the world.

越南韓松洞以世界最大洞穴著稱。

記憶技巧 cav- 表示中空；cavern 是大穴的意思。

---

cavernous

[ˋkævənəs]

a 多洞穴的，凹陷的

The bombing of the military base left a cavernous hole in the side of the mountain.

對軍事基地的轟炸在山邊留下一個凹洞。

記憶技巧 -ous 為形容詞字尾。

cavity

[ˋkævətɪ]

n 穴，凹處，腔

If there is reasonable suspicion of drugs being transported at the airport, a person may receive a cavity search.

在機場，如果被合理懷疑運毒，可能就得接受體腔搜查。

> 記憶技巧　cav- 表示中空；-ity 為名詞字尾；cavity 即穴、凹處。

---

concave

[ˋkɑnkev]

a 凹的，凹面的

A concave mirror will make reflected objects seem smaller than they actually are.

凹面鏡會使反射物體看起來較實際來得小。

> 記憶技巧　con- 表示加強語氣；cav- 表示中空；concave 的意思是凹的。

---

excavate

[ˋɛkskəˌvet]

v 挖掘，開鑿

The government gave archeologists approval to excavate artifacts from the site before construction resumed.

政府允許考古學家在建築工程持續之前，在場址挖掘手工藝品。

> 記憶技巧　ex- 表示外；cav- 表示中空；-ate 為動詞字尾；excavate 的意思是使～中空，引申為挖掘。

---

hide - cel / ceal

兩者雖無字源關係，但可藉由子音 h 和 c 互換，母音通轉來記憶，兩者原意皆表示覆蓋，hide 的意思是被蓋起來，引申為躲藏。

---

cell

[sɛl]

n 細胞，電池，電腦元件

The chicken egg is actually a large cell that needs to be fertilized to divide and reproduce.

事實上，雞蛋是一個需要受孕以分裂複製的巨大細胞。

> 記憶技巧　cel- 表示覆蓋；cell 本意是隱士的住所、修道院的房間，後來才有細胞、電池等意思。

---

cellar

[ˋsɛlɚ]

n 地窖

The estate includes ten acres of land, a swimming pool, two tennis courts, a three-car garage, and a large wine cellar.

這筆房屋包括十英畝土地、一座游泳池、兩座網球場、停放三部車的車庫及一間大酒窖。

> 記憶技巧　cellar 本是儲存物品的房間，後作地窖解釋。

conceal

[kən`sil]

v 隱瞞，隱藏，埋伏

If everyone in the community had concealed weapons when they went out, they would feel very insecure.

社區每個人外出時若都隨身攜帶藏著的武器，則會很沒安全感。

記憶技巧 con- 表示加強語氣；ceal- 表示覆蓋；conceal 的意思是隱藏。

harvest - carp

子音 h 和 c 互換，母音通轉，兩者皆表示採收，carp- 現今的意思是果實。

carpogenic

[͵karpə`dʒɛnɪk]

a 結果實的

The bees are an important carpogenic factor in the rate of fruit production in the orchard.

對於果園水果生產率，蜜蜂是結果實的重要因素。

記憶技巧 carpo- 表示果實；gen- 表示生；-ic 為形容詞字尾；carpogenic 的意思是結果實的。

carpophagous

[kar`pafəgəs]

a 食果實的

The largest bats, known as flying foxes, are fortunately carpophagous creatures.

體型最大的蝙蝠稱為飛狐，還好只是食果實動物。

記憶技巧 carpo- 表示果實；phag- 表示吃；-ous 為形容詞字尾；carpophagous 的意思是食果實的。

hew - cuss

兩者雖無字源關係，但可藉由子音 h 和 c 互換，母音通轉來記憶，兩者原始意思皆表示敲，hew 現今的意思是砍，cuss- 的意思是敲。

discuss

[dɪ`skʌs]

v 討論，辯論，
對債務人起訴

A meeting was called to discuss the employee reaction to the new company policies.

召開了一場會議，以討論員工對公司新政策的反應。

記憶技巧 dis- 表示分開；cuss- 表示敲；discuss 本意是敲碎，後來當討論解釋。

percussion

[pə`kʌʃən]

n 打擊樂器，衝擊，
震動

The African tribal troupe played ten different types of percussion instruments.

非洲部落劇團演奏十種不同類型的打擊樂器。

記憶技巧 per- 表示從頭到尾；cuss- 表示敲；-ion 為名詞字尾；percussion 即敲擊、衝擊。

| 相關字彙
樂器 | • stringed instrument 弦樂器   • brass instrument 銅管樂器
• wind instrument 管樂器 |

---

repercussion
[ˌripɚˋkʌʃən]
n 反射，彈回

The company's decision to move its factories overseas had major repercussions for local economy.
公司的工廠外移決策衝擊當地經濟。

> 記憶技巧 re- 表示後；percussion 表示敲擊；repercussion 即敲回去，當反射、彈回解釋。

---

concussion
[kənˋkʌʃən]
n 震動，衝擊，
腦震盪

The Austrian skiier remained in the hospital during the entire competition after suffering from a concussion.
腦部遭受重擊之後，奧地利滑雪選手整個比賽期間都在醫院。

> 記憶技巧 con- 表示一起；cuss- 表示敲；-ion 為名詞字尾；concussion 的意思是一起敲，1540 年代才有腦震盪的意思。

---

white - cand

兩者雖無字源關係，但可藉由子音 h 和 c 互換，母音通轉來記憶，兩者原始意思皆表示白色、發光。

---

candle
[ˋkændl]
n 蠟燭，燭光

The elderly woman kept a cabinet stocked with wax candles as a precaution for power outages.
老婦人存了一櫃子的蠟燭作為停電的預防措施。

> 記憶技巧 cand- 表示發光；candle 的意思是會發光的蠟燭。

---

candor
[ˋkændɚ]
n 正直，坦白

It was disappointing when the candidate who displayed the most candor was ignored by the media.
表現最正直的候選人不受媒體青睞，真是令人失望。

> 記憶技巧 cand- 表示白；-or 為名詞字尾；candor 的意思是坦白。

---

candid
[ˋkændɪd]
a 正直的，坦白的

During the TV interview, the famous boxer offered a candid account of his troubled childhood.
電視訪談中，知名拳擊手坦白地透露自己紛擾的童年。

> 記憶技巧 cand- 表示白；-id 為形容詞字尾；candid 的意思是正直的、坦白的。

incandescent
[ˌɪnkænˈdɛsn̩t]
a 熾熱的，閃亮的

The city government invested millions to replace inefficient incandescent light bulbs with LED light bulbs.
市政府投資數百萬元以 LED 燈泡替換效率差的熾熱燈泡。

記憶技巧　in- 表示在～裡面；cand- 表示白、發光；-escent 表示變；incandescent 的意思是內部變白，引申做發白光、閃亮的、熾熱的。

---

candidate
[ˈkændədet]
n 候選人，候補人

The executive announced that employees who reached their sales goals would be considered candidates for promotion.
主管宣布達到銷售目標的員工將列入升遷名單中。

記憶技巧　cand- 表示白；candidate 以前欲求公職的古羅馬人所穿的寬外袍，現今代指候選人。

相關字彙
候選人
- front runner 領先的人
- running mate 競選伙伴

Part
2
CH 1
CH 2
CH 3
CH 4
硬顎音、軟顎音、喉門音轉換

hub - centr
兩者雖無字源關係，但可藉由子音 h 和 c 互換，母音通轉來記憶，兩者皆表示中心。

---

center
[ˈsɛntɚ]
n 中央，中心，起源

The historic city of Tashkent was once considered a center of commerce on the Great Silk Road.
歷史古城塔什干曾被視為偉大絲綢之路的商業中心。

記憶技巧　center 即中心。

---

central
[ˈsɛntrəl]
a 中央的，主要的，重要的

The central authority has been known to be a bureacratic barrier to progress in the country.
中央政府官僚體制已被認為是國家進步的障礙。

記憶技巧　-al 為形容詞字尾。

---

centripetal
[sɛnˈtrɪpətl̩]
a 向心的

In the movie, the spaceship plotted a course around the planet to use the centripetal force of gravity to accelerate.
電影中，太空船劃出一條繞過行星的路線，以運用重力的向心力加速。

記憶技巧　centr- 表示中心；pet- 表示追尋；-al 為形容詞字尾；centripetal 的意思是往中心走去，引申作向心的。

231

centrifugal
[sɛn`trɪfjugl]
a 離心的

The test tubes spun in the machine, using centrifugal force to separate the heavier elements from the lighter ones.
試管在機器中旋轉，利用離心力分離較重與較輕的成分。

記憶技巧　centr- 表示中心；fug- 表示逃；-al 為形容詞字尾；centrifugal 的意思是逃離中心的，引申作離心的。

concentrate
[`kɑnsɛnˌtret]
v 專注，集中，濃縮

The father locked himself in his study to concentrate on the report that was due the next day.
為了專注於明天到期的報告，父親將自己鎖在書房中。

記憶技巧　con- 表示一起；centr- 表示中心；-ate 為動詞字尾；concentrate 的意思是到中心去，引申為集中。

Section **5**

〔tʃ〕對應〔k〕

chaste - cast

子音 ch 和 c 互換，母音通轉，兩者核心意思皆表示切除、純潔的，切除不必要的部分，是為了讓某對象更純淨、純潔。

caste
[kæst]
n 種姓，（印度社會的）種姓制度，等級制度

The Rukai tribe was organized into caste groups and ruled by a royal family.
魯凱族由不同等級的族群所組成，統治者是貴族。

記憶技巧　cast- 表示切；caste 的意思是切割不純淨的種族，讓特定種族變得純淨，一般相信印度種姓制度原是為了確保雅利安人的執政權和保持各種工作都有一定的人數，而創立的社會制度和規範。

castigate
[`kæstəˌget]
v 申斥，懲罰

The manager was publicly castigated by his assistant before she tendered her resignation.
遞辭呈之前，助理公開狠批經理一頓。

記憶技巧　cast- 表示純潔的；-ate 為動詞字尾；castigate 這個字背後的概念是透過斥責和矯正，讓人變的純潔。

castration
[kæsˋtreʃən]
n 去勢

The mental patients were once forced into castration before being admitted into the institution.
精神病患獲准進入該機構之前曾被迫去勢。

> **記憶技巧** cast- 表示切除；-ation 為名詞字尾；castration 的意思是切除男人的生殖器官。

相關字彙
動物醫療

- dock 剪短（尾巴等）
- neuter（委婉語）閹割
- put something to sleep 被處以安樂死
- spay 割除卵巢
- vaccinate 接種疫苗
- veterinarian 獸醫

chastise
[tʃæsˋtaɪz]
v 懲戒，責罰，鞭打

For fear of being chastised, the student avoided bringing his report card home.
害怕受到責罰，學生避免將成績單拿回家。

> **記憶技巧** chast- 等同於 cast-，表示純潔；-ise 為動詞字尾；chastise 原意是使純潔，後作懲罰、譴責，背後的概念是：懲罰、罵人是為了去除不好的行為，變的純潔。

chasten
[ˋtʃesn̩]
v （為了使人改正或變好而）懲罰（人），磨鍊

The young man stopped bragging about his superiority after being soundly chastened and defeated on the court.
法庭上受到嚴厲懲戒和挫敗後，年輕人不再誇耀自己的優越。

> **記憶技巧** chast- 等同於 cast-，表示純潔的；-en 為動詞字尾，原意是使純潔，後作懲罰、譴責，背後的概念是：懲罰某人是為了讓他更好，能去除不好的行為，變的純潔。

chamber - camer
子音 ch 和 c 互換，母音通轉，兩者核心意思皆是室、房間。

bicameral
[baɪˋkæmərəl]
a 兩院制的

The bicameral legislative body of the American Congress is emulated in many other democratic countries.
美國國會兩院制立法體制受到許多其他民主國家的效仿。

> **記憶技巧** bi- 表示二；camer- 表示室；-al 為形容詞字尾；bicameral 字面上意思是兩室的，後指國家的立法機構是由兩個獨立運作的議院所組成。

相關字彙
政府制度

- autocratic 專制的
- autonomous 自治的
- collectivism 集體主義
- federal 聯邦（制）的
- imperial 帝國的
- totalitarian 極權主義的
- unitary 單一制的
- theocratic 神權政治的

Part 2
CH 1
CH 2
CH 3
CH 4

硬顎音、軟顎音、喉門音轉換

camera
[ˋkæmərə]
n 照相機，電影攝影機，電視攝像機

It was difficult to find instant film cameras in the digital age, but they are making a comeback.
拍立得相機在數位時代幾乎絕跡，但是即將捲土重來。

記憶技巧　18 世紀初，camera 是「camera obscura（暗箱）」的縮寫形式，為歷史上最早出現的元祖攝影器材，意思是就是「暗室」。

---

arch - arc

子音 ch 和 c 互換，母音通轉，兩者核心意思皆是弓形、拱形。

---

arcade
[ɑrˋked]
n 拱廊，騎樓

The popular arcade offered patrons video games and games of chance to win prizes.
人氣遊樂場提供顧客電玩及贏得獎品的賭盤遊戲。

記憶技巧　arc- 表示拱形；-ade 為名詞字尾；arcade 的意思是拱廊。

---

chant - cant

子音 ch 和 c 互換，母音通轉，兩者核心意思皆是唱歌。

---

accent
[ˋæksɛnt]
n 腔調，重音

The Norwegian was not hired by the English language school because of his heavy, Nordic accent.
這名挪威人因濃濃北歐腔而不為英國語言學校聘用。

記憶技巧　ac- 等同於 ad-，表示朝～方向；cent- 等同於 cant-，表示唱歌；accent 的意思是在講話時加入歌唱，後指腔調、重音。

---

cant
[kænt]
n 行話，術語

The citizens were frustrated by the accusatory cant of the politicians during this year's election.
今年選舉期間，市民對政治人物的謾罵言語感到失望。

記憶技巧　cant- 表示唱歌，1680 年後才有乞丐、罪犯黑話、術語等意思。

---

enchant
[ɪnˋtʃænt]
v 蠱惑，施行魔法

The foreigner was hired by the Chinese firm to enchant visitors to its trade show booth.
外籍人士受雇於中國公司，負責將參觀人潮拉到商展攤位。

記憶技巧　en- 表示內；chant- 等同於 cant-，表示唱歌；enchant 即用歌聲來蠱惑人。

chariot - car

子音 ch 和 c 互換，母音通轉，兩者核心意思皆是車子。

Part

2

CH 1
CH 2
CH 3
CH 4

硬顎音、軟顎音、喉門音轉換

cargo
[ˋkɑrgo]

n 貨物，負荷，荷重

In a surprising development, the company donated its cargo containers to the charity that built affordable housing.

在一項令人驚訝的發展中，公司捐贈自家貨櫃給興建平價住屋的慈善團體。

記憶技巧 cargo 是車上所裝載的貨物。

carry
[ˋkærɪ]

v 搬運，攜帶，傳達

It makes no sense to carry your bags to your room when there are porters here to do that job.

現場有門房代勞時，自己將袋子提到房間毫無意義。

記憶技巧 car- 表示車；carry 即用車子裝載、搬運。

career
[kəˋrɪr]

n 職業，生涯，履歷

The worker planned a stable career in manufacturing, but ended up managing a small flower shop.

工人原打算在製造業謀個穩定職業，後來卻經營一家小花店。

記憶技巧 car- 表示車；career 是車行走的軌跡，引申為職業、生涯等。

touch - tact

子音 ch 和 c 互換，母音通轉，兩者核心意思皆是碰觸。

intact
[ɪnˋtækt]

a 未受損的，
原封不動的

Keeping his pride intact, the fired laborer was eventually recognized for his skill and hired for a better job.

豪氣絲毫不減，遭解職的勞工的技術終於受到認定，得到一份較好的工作。

記憶技巧 in- 表示否定字；tact- 表示碰觸；intact 字面上的意思是沒有碰觸的，亦即未受損的，原封不動的。

tactile
[ˋtæktɪl]

a 觸覺的，有觸覺的

The blind worshippers use tactile reading methods to study the Bible.

視障信徒運用觸覺閱讀法學習聖經。

記憶技巧 tact- 表示碰觸；-ile 為形容詞字尾；tactile 的意思是觸覺的。

contact
[kənˋtækt]

v 接觸，聯繫，交涉

The successful salesman makes it a point to contact each person the day after he gets their business card.
成功的銷售員會在拿到名片的隔天就聯繫本人。

記憶技巧 con- 表示一起；tact- 表示碰觸；contact 的意思即接觸。

---

tangent
[ˋtændʒənt]

a 切線，正切，
接觸的，相切的

The architect placed the antenna on a tangent to the curved rooftop.
建築師將天線置於圓弧屋頂的正切方向。

記憶技巧 tang- 等同於 tact-，表示碰觸；-ent 為形容詞字尾；tangent 的意思是切線。

相關字彙
測量描述角度

- cosine 餘弦
- cotangent 餘切
- degree 度數
- oblique 非直角的
- orthogonal 直角的
- tangent 正切
- sine 正弦

---

intangible
[ɪnˋtændʒəb!]

a 無實體的，模糊的

There were intangible reasons why the coach was able to win the championship with a team lacking superstars.
沒有具體理由說明教練怎麼讓缺乏明星選手的隊伍贏得比賽，理由還是眾說紛云。

記憶技巧 in- 表示否定字；tang- 等同於 tact-，表示碰觸；-ible 為形容詞字尾；intangible 的意思是碰觸不到的，引申為無實體的。

相關字彙
未知、神祕的

- hidden 隱藏的
- mysterious 神祕的
- obscure 隱匿的
- private 隱蔽的
- secret 機密的
- unknown 未知的
- uncertain 不明確的

---

contingent
[kənˋtɪndʒənt]

a 偶發的，有條件的

The sale of the old building was contingent on its passing the safety inspection.
老舊建物是安檢通過後才脫手。

記憶技巧 con- 表示一起；ting- 等同於 tact-，表示碰觸；-ent 為形容詞字尾；contingent 的字面上意思是碰觸的，從碰觸聯想到發生的，最後語意更窄化到偶發的、有條件的等意思。

---

contagious
[kənˋtedʒəs]

a 傳染病的，
有感染力的

The contagious pathogen was locked up in a secure medical facility for further study.
具感染力的病原體被鎖在安全的醫療機構中以供進一步研究。

記憶技巧 con- 表示一起；tag- 表示碰觸；-ous 為形容詞字尾；contagious 引申為有傳染力的。

contiguous
[kənˋtɪgjʊəs]

a 接觸的，鄰近的

Nepal is contiguous with both India and China, and has a culture that is influenced by both countries.
尼泊爾與印度及中國接壤，擁有受兩國影響的文化。

記憶技巧　con- 表示一起；tig- 等同於 tag-，表示碰觸；-ous 為形容詞字尾；contiguous 的意思是接觸的。

integral
[ˋɪntəgrəl]

a 整數的，積分的，必要的

In Bhutan, religion, government and education are integral institutions.
在不丹，宗教、政治及教育都是不可或缺的體制。

記憶技巧　in- 表示否定字；teg- 等同於 tact-，表示碰觸；-al 為形容詞字尾；integral 指沒受汙染的，仍保持完整的，引申為整數的。

integrate
[ˋɪntəˌgret]

v 使成整體，結合

The Supreme Court case integrated black students and white students in the same schools.
高等法院案例使黑人及白人學生在同一學校就學。

記憶技巧　in- 表示否定字；teg- 表示碰觸；-ate 為動詞字尾；integrate 原本意思是使不受汙染，使之保持完整，1802 後才有使成整體、結合的意思。

attain
[əˋten]

v 達到，獲得

Thirty minutes of meditation per day can help one attain a more peaceful attitude and health benefits.
每天靜坐三十分鐘能使人獲得平和的態度和健康的好處。

記憶技巧　at- 等同於 ad-，表示朝～方向；tain 等同於 touch，表示碰觸；attain 引申為達到。

taint
[tent]

n 汙點，腐敗

The taint of oil lingered in the water supply of the region for more than five years.
油汙積在此區的水源五年多了。

記憶技巧　taint 等同於 touch，表示碰觸；可以想像成玷汙，名詞是汙點的意思。

Part
2

CH 1
CH 2
CH 3
CH 4

硬顎音、軟顎音、喉門音轉換

〔g〕對應〔h〕

garden - horti

子音 g 和 h 互換，母音通轉，兩者核心意思皆是包圍，garden 是圍起來的花園，horti- 亦是花園，和 yard 也是同源。

horticulture
['hɔrtɪ͵kʌltʃɚ]
n 園藝，園藝術

The Japanese facility focused on a highly-specialized type of horticulture growing seaweed.
該日本機構專注於一種高度專業的昆布培植園藝形式。

記憶技巧　horti- 表示花園；culture 表示栽培；horticulture 的意思是園藝。

相關字彙
園藝

- bonsai 種植盆景的藝術
- compost 堆肥
- earth up 用土掩蓋
- fertilize 使肥沃，施肥
- graft 嫁接用的嫩枝
- hedge 用樹籬笆圍住
- pollinate 給～授花粉
- propagate 繁殖
- transplant 移植

guest - host / hosp

子音 g 和 h 互換，母音通轉，兩者核心意思皆是主、客，「host（主）」、「guest（客）」同源。

hospital
['hɑspɪtl]
n 醫院

Doctors Without Borders is a group of doctors who volunteer to work in hospitals in conflict zones.
無國界醫師是一群自願赴衝突地區醫院工作的醫師。

記憶技巧　hosp- 表示客人；hospital 是接待病人的場所。

hospitality
[͵hɑspɪ'tælətɪ]
n 好客，殷勤招待

Hotels train their staff to show their guests great hospitality, providing for all of their needs.
飯店訓練員工殷勤接待賓客，提供他們所有需求。

記憶技巧　hosp- 表示客人；hospitality 的意思是好客。

hotel
[hoˋtɛl]
n 旅館，飯店

They became a reliable vendor for the hotel chain, cleaning all of their blankets and linens.
他們是飯店集團的可靠配合廠商，洗淨所有毯子及亞麻製品。

記憶技巧 hotel 是招待客人住宿的地方。

Part
2
CH 1
CH 2
CH 3
CH 4
硬顎音、軟顎音、喉門音轉換

get - prehend
子音 g 和 h 互換，母音通轉，兩者核心意思皆是拿、抓。

apprehend
[ˌæprɪˋhɛnd]
v 逮捕，理解，憂慮

The investigators of the white-collar crime unit apprehended a wide money laundering network.
負責白領犯罪集團的調查人員破獲一個大的洗錢網絡。

記憶技巧 ap- 等同於 ab-，表示朝～方向；prehend- 表示抓；apprehend 有逮捕的意思，以學習而言，當理解來解釋。

comprehend
[ˌkɑmprɪˋhɛnd]
v 理解，領悟，包含

Even though their countries are far apart, people in Austronesian tribes can comprehend each other.
儘管國家相距甚遠，南島部落民族也能彼此了解。

記憶技巧 com- 表示完全；prehend- 表示抓；comprehend 的意思是完全抓住，以學習來說，當理解、領悟來解釋。

comprehensive
[ˌkɑmprɪˋhɛnsɪv]
a 有理解力的，廣泛的

The district attorney presented a comprehensive timeline of events to prosecute the defendent.
為了起訴被告，地方檢察官提出一份清晰的事件時間表。

記憶技巧 -ive 為形容詞字尾。

comprehensible
[ˌkɑmprɪˋhɛnsəbl̩]
a 能理解的

Researchers have been recording whale songs for decades to determine if they have a comprehensible language.
為了推斷是否擁有可理解的語言，數十年來研究人員不斷錄下鯨魚的歌聲。

記憶技巧 -ible 為形容詞字尾，表示可以～的；comprehensible 是能理解的。

comprise
[kəm`praɪz]
v 包括，由～組成

Tonight's concert will comprise of eight performances by two different music groups.
今晚的音樂會包括兩支不同音樂團體的八個演出。

記憶技巧　com- 表示一起；pris- 等同於 prehend-，表示抓；comprise 的意思是抓一起，引申為包括。

---

prison
[`prɪzn]
n 監獄，監禁

A group of convicted felons discreetly gathered in the yard to discuss their prison break.
為了商討越獄行動，一群重刑犯小心翼翼地聚在庭院。

記憶技巧　pris- 表示抓；prison 即監獄。

---

imprison
[ɪm`prɪzn]
v 禁錮

The famous leader said that his opponent could imprison his body, but could not extinguish his spirit.
著名的領導人說，對手能禁錮他的肉身，但摧毀不了他的靈魂。

記憶技巧　im- 等同於 in-，表示在～之內；prison 表示監獄；imprison 的意思是囚禁。

---

grass - herb

兩者雖無字源關係，但可藉由子音 g 和 h 互換，母音通轉來記憶，兩者皆草。

---

herbicide
[`hɝbəˌsaɪd]
n 除草劑

The herbicide promised increased crop yield at a negligible risk to consumers.
這款除草劑能在對消費者幾乎無風險下增加作物產量。

記憶技巧　herb- 表示草；-cide 等同於 cut，表示切；herbicide 的字面意思是切除雜草，引申為除草劑。

---

herbivore
[`hɝbəˌvɔr]
n 草食性動物

Not all grazing herbivores are peaceful, as some larger ones are known to attack humans.
不是所有放牧的食草動物都很溫和，一些大型食草動物已知會攻擊人類。

記憶技巧　herb- 表示草；vor- 表示吃；herbivore 即草食性動物。

Section 7

〔k〕對應〔dʒ〕

硬顎音、軟顎音、喉門音轉換

carry - ger

兩者雖無字源關係，但可藉由子音 c（發〔k〕的音）和 g（發〔dʒ〕的音）互換，母音通轉來記憶，兩者皆表示攜帶。

belligerent
[bə`lɪdʒərənt]
a 好戰的，好鬥的

When ordered to the principal's office, the bully remained belligerent.
被叫到校長室時，霸凌學生仍是一副好鬥。

記憶技巧 bell- 表示戰爭；ger- 表示帶來；-ent 為形容詞字尾；belligerent 的意思是好戰的。

exaggerate
[ɪg`zædʒəˌret]
v 誇張，誇大

The retired policeman often exaggerated the size of his catches during his fishing outings.
退休警察時常誇大外出捕魚時的漁獲量。

記憶技巧 ex- 表示徹底地；ag- 等同於 ad-，表示往～方向；ger- 表示帶；-ate 為動詞字尾；exaggerate 字面上意思是徹底將東西帶往某地集中，引申出誇大的意思。

相關字彙
誇飾、強調
• aggrandize 誇張的
• magnify 誇大的
• overstate 誇大的
• overplay 過分強調

knee - genu

子音 k 和 g 互換，母音通轉，兩者的意思皆是膝蓋。

genuflection
[ˌdʒɛnjuˋflɛkʃən]
n 屈膝，屈服

To show his sincerity, the soldier went into genuflection when proposing marriage to his girlfriend.
為了展現誠意，軍人向女友求婚時屈膝告白。

記憶技巧 genu- 表示膝蓋；flect- 表示彎曲；-ion 為名詞字尾；genuflection 的意思是屈膝。

cold - gel
子音 k 和 g 互換，母音通轉，兩者的意思皆是冷、凍結。

gel [dʒɛl] n 膠體，凝膠	The waitress received a pair of shoe inserts filled with soft gel, which increased the comfort of her feet. 女服務生得到一雙填塞軟凝膠，能讓腳部更舒適的鞋墊。 記憶技巧　gel- 表示凍結；gel 當凝膠解釋。
gelid [ˋdʒɛlɪd] a 冰似的，冷的，極寒的	Below the snow-covered rooftop, gelid icicles hung from the gutters of the home. 覆蓋積雪的屋頂下方，冷冽的冰柱從屋子雨水槽垂懸而下。 記憶技巧　gel- 表示冷；-id 為形容詞字尾；gelid 即冷的。

kind - gen
子音 k 和 g 互換，母音通轉，兩者的意思皆是生（產）、種類。

gene
[dʒin]
n 基因

Gene therapy, combined with stem cell therapy, promises to reverse the effects of aging.
結合幹細胞療法的基因療法帶給人們延緩老化作用的希望。

記憶技巧　gen- 表示種類；gene 的意思是基因。

相關字彙
遺傳基因

- chromosome 染色體
- cloning 複製科技
- cross-fertilize 使異體受精
- deoxyribonucleic acid (DNA) 脫氧核糖核酸
- gene pool 基因庫
- genetic fingerprinting 基因指紋鑑別法
- genome 基因組
- mutation 突變

general
[ˋdʒɛnərəl]
a 一般的

It is general practice in Asia to take off your shoes before entering someone's home.
在亞洲，進到別人家之前大多會先脫鞋子。

記憶技巧　gen- 表示種類；-al 為形容詞字尾；general 是大家屬同一類，大家都一樣，引申為一般的。

generate
[ˋdʒɛnəˌret]
v 生殖，產生，導致

After the animated film is completed, selling the individual cells of the film as artworks can generate income.
完成動畫電影之後，將影片個別單元當作藝術品出售可產生收益。

記憶技巧　gen- 表示生；-ate 為動詞字尾；generate 即生殖、產生。

genuine
[ˋdʒɛnjuɪn]

a 真正的，真誠的，
純種的

It is hard to tell the difference between a genuine, natural diamond and one that is manufactured.

分辨真正的天然鑽石及人造鑽石的差別不容易。

記憶技巧　gen- 表示生；-ine 為形容詞字尾；genuine 是天生的，不是人工的，引申為真誠的、純種的。

genius
[ˋdʒinjəs]

n 天才，（精靈），
特徵

Steve Jobs was widely considered a genius for creating innovations in the tech industry.

普遍認為賈伯斯是科技業的創新天才。

記憶技巧　gen- 表示生；genius 即天生的特質，後作天才、天資解釋。

gentle
[ˋdʒɛntl̩]

a 溫和的

The gentle doe pleased many children at the petting zoo.

溫馴的雌鹿在觸摸動物園裡讓許多小朋友很開心。

記憶技巧　gen- 表示生；gentle 本指與生俱來的高貴特質，1550 年代後才有溫和的意思。

---

queen - gyn
子音 q（發〔k〕的音）和 g 互換，母音通轉，兩者的意思皆是女人。

---

gynecology
[ˌgaɪnəˋkalədʒɪ]

n 婦科

Karen visited the obstetrics and gynecology department often because of complications with her unborn child.

胎兒有些併發症，凱倫經常到婦產科部門。

記憶技巧　gyn- 表示女人；-logy 為名詞字尾；gynecology 研究女人疾病和健康的學問，作婦科解釋。

相關字彙
醫學分支

- cardiology 心臟病學
- cytology 細胞學
- dentistry 牙科醫學，牙醫業
- dietetics（用作單數）飲食學
- embryology 胚胎學
- geriatrics（用作單數）老人醫學
- hematology 血液學
- immunology 免疫學
- neurology 神經學
- pharmacology 藥理學
- radiology 放射學
- rheumatology 風濕病學

androgynous
[ænˋdradʒənəs]

a 雌雄同體的，
中性化的

The college student preferred wearing black clothes and sporting androgynous hairstyles.

這名大學生偏好黑色服飾，留中性髮型。

記憶技巧　andro- 表示男人；gyn- 表示女人；-ous 為形容詞字尾；androgynous 的意思是雌雄同體的。

Part **2**

CH 1
CH 2
CH 3
CH 4

硬顎音、軟顎音、喉門音轉換

Section **8**

〔j〕對應〔dʒ〕

young - juven / jun
子音 y 和 j 互換，母音通轉，兩者的意思皆是年輕。

juvenile
[ˋdʒuvən!]
a 青少年的

The national juvenile justice system works to treat and rehabilitate juvenile offenders.
國家青少年司法體系運作處理並矯正青少年犯。

記憶技巧 juven- 表示年輕；-ile 為形容詞字尾；juvenile 即青少年的意思。

junior
[ˋdʒunjɚ]
a 年少的，資淺的

The junior executive didn't expect a promotion within the company until he had a few years of experience.
資淺主管熬過幾年經驗後才期待公司內部升遷。

記憶技巧 jun- 表示年輕；junior 等同於 younger，意思是比較年輕的。

yoke - jug
子音 y 和 j 互換，母音通轉，兩者的意思皆是綁、聯結。

conjugate
[ˋkɑndʒɚˏget]
v 列舉

The lecturer conjugated a number of advantages of outsourcing, such as cheap costs, increased productivity and economies of scale.
演講者列舉許多外包的好處，例如降低成本、增加生產力及縮小編制。

記憶技巧 con- 表示一起；jug- 表示綁；-ate 為動詞字尾；conjugate 的意思是綁在一起，引申為動詞因人稱、時態、單複數、陰陽性產生的詞形變化。

subjugate
[ˋsʌbdʒɚˏget]
v 征服，制服，使屈從

The Japanese forces subjugated the indigenous tribes by hiring one to fight the other.
藉由雇用一方攻打另一方，日本軍隊降服了原住民部落。

記憶技巧 sub- 表示在～下；jug- 表示綁；-ate 為動詞字尾；subjugate 是把～綁起來，引申為征服。

Chapter 5
子音對應相同

母音可能產生音變、形變，並夾雜其他子音的音變、形變

Section **1**

〔b〕對應〔b〕

beautiful - bell
母音通轉，兩者的意思皆是美。

belle [bɛl] **n** 美女	The charming woman was a Southern belle that married into the family of the wealthy steel tycoon. 嬌媚的婦人是南方美人胚子，嫁入鋼鐵鉅子的豪門世家。 記憶技巧　bell- 表示美；belle 是美女的意思。
embellish [ɪmˈbɛlɪʃ] **v** 美化，潤飾	The military officer usually embellished the truth to get the reinforcements he wanted. 軍官經常渲染實情以獲得他要的支援。 記憶技巧　em- 等同於 en-，表示使～；bell- 表示美；-ish 為古法語動詞字尾；embellish 即美化、潤飾。

book - biblio
兩者雖無字源關係，但可藉由母音通轉來記憶，兩者皆表示書。

bibliography [ˌbɪblɪˈɑgrəfɪ] **n** 參考書目，書目	The bibliography of the book was surprisingly short, indicating very few outside resources were referenced. 書的參考書目出奇的簡短，顯示其他參考資源很少。 記憶技巧　biblio- 表示書；-graphy 表示寫；bibliography 是寫書的意思，1869 年之後才有參考書目的意思。
bibliophile [ˈbɪblɪəˌfaɪl] **n** 愛書者	The British bibliophile built a large library to house his extensive collection. 為了容納他的龐大藏書，這名英國愛書人士建了一間大圖書館。 記憶技巧　biblio- 表示書；-phile 表示喜歡～的人；bibliophile 即愛書者。

bibliomania
[ˌbɪblɪəˈmenɪə]
n 藏書狂

The literary convention was popular due to the bibliomania that was widespread throughout Europe.
由於遍及歐洲的藏書狂熱，文藝大會人氣鼎盛。

記憶技巧 biblio- 表示書；-mania 表示狂；bibliomania 即藏書狂。

---

beat - bat
母音通轉，兩者的意思皆是打擊。

Part 2 CH 1 CH 2 CH 3 CH 4 CH 5

子音對應相同

---

bat
[bæt]
n 球棒，球拍

Cricket is a popular sport where a hard ball is hit by a flat-edged bat.
板球是一項熱門運動，比賽中，一顆硬球以扁形邊緣的球棒打擊。

記憶技巧 bat 即打擊用的球棒或球拍。

---

battle
[ˈbætl̩]
n 戰鬥，戰役，競爭

The Battle of Leyte Gulf was considered the largest naval battle during World War II.
雷伊泰灣海戰被認為是二次大戰期間規模最大的海軍戰役。

記憶技巧 bat- 表示打擊；battle 即戰鬥。

---

abate
[əˈbet]
v 減輕，中止

After the high tide abated, the family sifted through the mud for a harvest of clams.
漲潮退後，全家人為了採收蛤蜊而篩過泥土。

記憶技巧 ab- 等同於 ad-，表示朝～方向；-ate 為動詞字尾；abate 的意思是往～方向打下去，引申為減輕。

---

combative
[kəmˈbætɪv]
a 好鬥的

After growing up to be a teenager, the son became the most combative member of the family.
長大成為青少年之後，兒子成了家中最好鬥的一員。

記憶技巧 com- 表示一起；bat- 表示打擊；-ive 為形容詞字尾；combative 的意思是大家打成一塊，引申為好鬥的。

---

debate
[dɪˈbet]
n 討論，辯論

There is growing debate as to whether or not the government's new labor laws will help the country.
關於政府的新勞工法令是否對國家有益，爭辯愈發激烈。

記憶技巧 de- 表示完全；bat- 表示打擊；debate 的意思是完全打擊對方，引申為辯論。

bind - band

母音通轉，兩者的意思皆是綁。

bandage

[`bændɪdʒ]

n 繃帶

As the soldiers returned home, many were missing limbs or were covered with bloody bandages.
軍人們返鄉後，許多人失去手腳，或者包覆著沾血汙的繃帶。

> 記憶技巧 band-表示綁；-age 為名詞字尾；bandage 的意思是繃帶。

bond

[band]

n 結合物，結盟，束縛，契約，債券，保證人

The bond between brothers and sisters should be unbreakable, but often the contrary is true.
手足連結應該牢不可破，但事實往往相反。

> 記憶技巧 bond 等同於 band-，表示綁，後引申為結盟、束縛等意思。

Section 2

〔p〕對應〔p〕

---

people - popul

母音通轉，兩者的意思皆是人。

popular

[`papjələ]

a 大眾的，受歡迎的

The factory manager brought the buyers from America to the most popular restaurant in the city.
工廠經理帶來自美國的買家到市區最受歡迎的餐廳。

> 記憶技巧 popul- 表示人；-ar 為形容詞字尾；popular 即大眾的，後引申出受大眾歡迎的。

populous

[`papjələs]

a 人口稠密的

Shanghai has long held the distinction of being China's most populous city.
長久以來，上海一向有中國人口最稠密都市的名聲。

> 記憶技巧 popul- 表示人；-ous 為形容詞字尾；populous 的意思是充滿著人，引申為人口稠密的。

population

[ˌpɑpjəˈleʃən]

n 人口

It is uncertain how long the Earth can sustain unchecked population growth.

人口成長不受抑制，地球還能撐多久實在不確定。

記憶技巧　popul- 表示人；-ation 為名詞字尾；population 的意思是人口。

overpopulated

[ˌovəˈpɑpjəˌletɪd]

a 人口（或生物）過多的

When an area becomes overpopulated with deer, they can quickly decimate their food supply.

一個地區的鹿過多時，牠們的食物供給很快就會大幅減少。

記憶技巧　over- 表示超過；popul- 表示人；-ate 為動詞字尾；overpopulated 的意思即人口過多的。

pig - porc / pork

兩者雖無字源關係，但可藉由子音 g 和 k 互換，母音通轉來記憶，兩者皆表示豬。

porcine

[ˈpɔrsaɪn]

a （像）豬的

In the bush, the tiger eyed the family of porcine creatures as potential snacks.

灌木叢中，老虎注視著一家子豬類動物，把牠們看作可能的點心。

記憶技巧　porc- 表示豬；-ine 為形容詞字尾；porcine 即（像）豬的。

porpoise

[ˈpɔrpəs]

n 海豚；鼠海豚

The diver was relieved when he realized the shadow was from a porpoise above and not a shark.

潛水夫知道影子是來自上方的海豚而不是鯊魚時，鬆了一口氣。

記憶技巧　porc- 表示豬；poise 表示魚；porpoise 字面意思是豬魚，因其口鼻和豬的口鼻形似。

猜猜看！

「appreciate（欣賞）」表示去賦予價值，猜 preci- 是哪一單字？

答案：price（價格）

push - pel
母音通轉，兩者的意思皆是推、驅使。

---

appeal
[ə`pil]

v 呼籲，懇求

A flyer was circulated among the talent pool in the city to appeal to workers for the newly-opened positions.
為了招募新職缺員工，傳單在全市人才庫之間流傳。

> 記憶技巧　ap- 等同於 ad-，表示朝～方向；peal- 等同於 pel-，表示推；appeal 的字面意思是朝～推進，引申為呼籲、懇求。

---

compel
[kəm`pɛl]

v 強迫，使不得不

相關字彙
強制、強迫

Aside from offering a pay raise, the company recruiter didn't know how to compel the employee to stay.
除了加薪，公司招聘人員不知道如何讓這名員工留下來。

> 記憶技巧　com- 表示一起；pel- 表示推；compel 的意思是一起將～推到某地，引申為強迫。

- bulldoze 強行通過
- badger 糾纏
- coerce 強制
- compel 強迫
- pester 糾纏
- threaten 威脅

---

dispel
[dɪ`spɛl]

v 驅散（雲等）；消除（煩惱等）

To dispel rumors of corruption, the director released his tax returns of the last ten years.
為了消除貪汙傳言，主管公開近十年的個人稅務申報書。

> 記憶技巧　dis- 表示離開；pel- 表示推；dispel 的意思是推開，引申為驅散。

---

expel
[ɪk`spɛl]

v 驅逐，趕走

After a long discussion with the parents, the principal decided to expel the troublesome student.
與家長長談之後，校長決定開除令人頭痛的學生。

> 記憶技巧　ex- 表示外面；pel- 表示推；expel 的意思是推到外面，引申為驅逐。

---

repellent
[rɪ`pɛlənt]

a 擊退的，抵禦的，排斥的

The repellent nature of the man's personality came from his distrust of others.
男子個性上的排斥性來自對人不信任。

> 記憶技巧　re- 表示回去；pel- 表示推；-ent 為形容詞字尾；repellent 的意思是擊退的。

please - plac

母音通轉，兩者的意思皆是舒緩、安靜。

---

placate

[`plek*e*t]

v 安撫，撫慰，使和解

The busy mother usually bought toys or candy to placate her crying toddler.

忙碌的母親經常為了撫慰哭鬧的學步兒而購買玩具或糖果。

記憶技巧　plac- 表示舒緩；-ate 為動詞字尾；placate 的意思是撫慰。

---

placebo

[plə`sibo]

n 安慰劑

相關字彙
普遍的藥物名稱

Research participants who took the placebos showed the same positive results as those taking the new drug.

服用安慰劑的研究參與者出現和服用新藥者相同的陽性結果。

記憶技巧　placebo 是安慰劑，可舒緩症狀，但卻無藥效。

- cure-all 萬靈藥
- panacea 萬能藥
- pharmaceutical 藥物
- remedy 藥物、療法

---

complacent

[kəm`plesn̩t]

a 自滿的

The reason why the manager in Hawaii wouldn't accept a promotion was that he grew complacent in his position.

夏威夷區經理不接受升遷是因為自滿於現有的職位。

記憶技巧　com- 表示加強語氣；plac- 表示舒緩；-ent 為形容詞字尾；complacent 的意思是讓人舒緩、取悅人的，18 世紀才有自滿的意思。

---

paint - pict

母音通轉，兩者的意思皆是畫。

---

picture

[`pɪktʃɚ]

n 圖畫，相片，化身

The doctor declared that the retired teacher was a picture of good health.

醫生宣布該名退休教師健康良好。

記憶技巧　pict- 表示畫；-ure 為名詞字尾；picture 即圖畫。

---

picturesque

[ˌpɪktʃə`rɛsk]

a 栩栩如生的

Every view of the fishing village on the Greek island was as picturesque as a postcard.

希臘島嶼漁村的每一景象有如明信片一樣別緻。

記憶技巧　picture 表示畫；-esque 為形容詞字尾，相似的意思；picturesque 指藝術作品相當逼真。

Part **2**

CH 1
CH 2
CH 3
CH 4
CH 5

子音對應相同

depict
[dɪ`pɪkt]
v 描述

The memoirs from a Japanese soldier found on Iwo Jima depicted the immense struggles faced by the defeated side.
硫磺島發現的日本兵所寫的回憶錄描述敗退的一方面臨的慘烈戰鬥。

記憶技巧 　de- 表示下面；pict- 表示畫；depict 字面意思是畫下去，引申為描述。

pigment
[`pɪgmənt]
n 顏料，色素

The local tribe produced a natural dark blue pigment from the indigofera tinctoria plant.
當地部落從木藍類植物製造出天然的深藍色顏料。

記憶技巧 　pig- 等同於 pict-，表示畫；-ment 為名詞字尾；pigment 是顏料的意思。

---

pray - prec
母音通轉，兩者的意思皆是懇求、要求。

---

precarious
[prɪ`kɛrɪəs]
a 危險的

Starting a business with a large loan puts the company in a precarious position to start with.
高額借貸創業使公司一開始就陷入困境。

記憶技巧 　prec- 表示懇求；-ous 為形容詞字尾；precarious 的意思是藉由懇求來獲得事物，引申為有風險的、有危險的。

相關字彙
危險、不安全的

- disastrous 災難性的
- hazardous 有危險的
- ruinous 毀滅性的
- perilous 危險的
- injurious 致傷的

precatory
[`prɛkə͵torɪ]
a 懇求的

The wife of the deceased read his precatory statement to endow the university with 50% of his estate.
死者的妻子讀了將個人一半財產捐贈給大學的請求聲明。

記憶技巧 　prec- 表示懇求；-ory 為形容詞字尾；precatory 即懇求的。

deprecation
[͵dɛprə`keʃən]
n 反對，駁斥

The priest declared a firm deprecation of the youngsters who vandalized the statue of the Virgin Mary.
牧師嚴厲譴責破壞聖母瑪利亞雕像的青年人。

記憶技巧 　de- 表示離開；prec- 表示要求；-ation 為名詞字尾；deprecation 的意思是要求離開，引申為反對。

imprecate

[ˋɪmprɪ͵ket]

v 詛咒

How awful the taste of being imprecated is, especially when it comes from one's mother.
受詛咒的滋味很可怕，尤其是來自親生母親。

記憶技巧 im- 表示內；prec- 表示祈求；-ate 為動詞字尾；imprecate 的意思是祈求惡靈降禍，引申為詛咒。

Part 2
CH 1
CH 2
CH 3
CH 4
CH 5
子音對應相同

power - potent

母音通轉，兩者的意思皆是力量。

potential

[pəˋtɛnʃəl]

a 有潛力的

The potential client was wined and dined in order to obtain his approval.
為了獲得青睞，於是招待潛在客戶飲酒用餐。

記憶技巧 potent- 表示力量；-ial 為形容詞字尾；potential 即有潛力的。

impotent

[ˋɪmpətənt]

a 虛弱的

Not having the ability to offer a solution, the clerk felt she was an impotent bystander.
職員沒有能力提供解決方案，感覺自己是無能的旁觀者。

記憶技巧 im- 為否定字；potent- 表示力量；impotent 的意思是無力的、虛弱的。

peace - pac

母音通轉，兩者的意思皆是和平。

pacify

[ˋpæsə͵faɪ]

v 安撫，恢復和平

The manufacturing company offered an extra payment to pacify the aggressive creditors.
為了安撫咄咄逼人的債權人，製造公司額外支付款項。

記憶技巧 pac- 表示和平；-fy 為動詞字尾；pacify 的意思是恢復和平、安撫。

pacifier

[ˋpæsə͵faɪɚ]

n 調停者，奶嘴

Brand-new cars have often been used as pacifiers to reduce tensions between gang leaders.
全新汽車常當作調停物，用以降低幫派頭子之間的緊張關係。

記憶技巧 -er 為名詞字尾，做出動作者；pacifier 即調停者、奶嘴。

pacific
[pə`sɪfɪk]
a 平靜的，和平的

The negotiator used his pacific demeanor to reduce the tensions in the room.
談判人員以冷靜態度減低房間裡的緊張氣氛。

> 記憶技巧　pac- 表示和平；fic- 等同於 fac-，表示做；pacific 的意思是締造和平，引申為平靜的。

---

price - prec
母音通轉，兩者的意思皆是價格、價值。

---

precious
[`prɛʃəs]
a 貴重的，珍貴的，講究的

The precious minerals produced by the mines of Myanmar boosted the economy in the impoverished region.
緬甸礦區產出的珍貴礦物提升窮困地區的經濟。

> 記憶技巧　prec- 表示價格；-ous 為形容詞字尾；precious 的意思是珍貴的、貴重的。

---

appreciate
[ə`priʃɪet]
v 感謝，欣賞，升值

When the manager appreciates the subordinates, his actions can boost morale and productivity.
經理賞識部屬時，所做的就會提振士氣及生產力。

> 記憶技巧　ap- 等同於 ad-，表示朝～方向；prec- 表示價格；-ate 為動詞字尾；appreciate 的意思是增加價格，亦有欣賞、感謝等意思。

---

depreciate
[dɪ`priʃɪet]
v 減價，貶值，輕視

The value of the company declined slightly because of the value of their fleet of taxis depreciated by 20%.
因為所屬計程車隊市值跌了 20%，公司市值也稍微下降。

> 記憶技巧　de- 表示往下；prec- 表示價格；-ate 為動詞字尾；depreciate 的意思是價格往下跌，亦有輕視的意思。

---

praise
[prez]
v 稱讚，讚美

The congregation of followers fervently praised their deity and studied their scriptures.
一群信眾熱切讚揚他們的神，研讀經文。

> 記憶技巧　praise 即看中別人的價值而讚美、稱讚他。

---

appraise
[ə`prez]
v 鑑定，估價

The deceased woman's estate was recently appraised at two million dollars.
已逝婦人財產最近估價為兩百萬美元。

> 記憶技巧　ap- 等同於 ad-，表示朝～方向；praise 等同於 prec-，表示價格；appraise 的意思是給某物估價。

pure - purg
母音通轉，兩者的意思皆是清潔、清除。

purge
[pɝdʒ]

v 使清淨，清除，刪除

A special computer security company was hired to purge the infected files from the mainframe computer.
特殊電腦安全公司受雇刪除主機遭病毒感染的檔案。

記憶技巧 purge 即清除、使清淨。

purgative
[`pɝgətɪv]

a 通便的，淨化的

Eating fruits high in fiber content gives people a healthy purgative effect on their digestive systems.
食用富含纖維物質的水果對人們消化系統有健康淨化的效果。

記憶技巧 purg- 表示清除；-ive 為形容詞字尾；purgative 的意思是淨化的，引申為通便的。

相關字彙
各種藥物

- anaesthesia 麻醉
- analgesic 止痛劑
- antibiotic 抗生素
- antidote 解毒劑
- contraceptive 避孕藥
- depressant 鎮靜劑
- enema 灌腸劑
- hypnotic 安眠藥
- painkiller 止痛劑
- steroid 類固醇
- tranquilizer 鎮定劑
- vaccine 疫苗

expurgate
[`ɛkspɝ͵get]

v 刪除，修訂

The expurgated content of the song was found to be too vulgar for young audiences.
歌曲遭刪的內容發現對年輕聽眾太過粗俗。

記憶技巧 ex- 表示外面；purg- 表示清除；-ate 為動詞字尾；expurgate 即將～清除出去，引申為刪除、修訂。

punish - pen
母音通轉，兩者的意思皆是付錢、補償、懲罰。

penalty
[`pɛn͵tɪ]

n 刑罰，懲罰，罰款，罰球

The soccer player was awarded a 12-yard penalty kick to make a goal after he was tripped by the opposing player.
被對手球員絆倒之後，足球選手獲得一次 12 碼罰球得分機會。

記憶技巧 pen- 表示付錢、賠償；-al 為形容詞字尾；-ty 為名詞字尾；penalty 即懲罰、罰款。

相關字彙
懲罰一般用語

- punishment 懲罰
- retribution 報應
- reprisal 報復
- comeuppance 罪有應得

Part
2
CH 1
CH 2
CH 3
CH 4
CH 5

子音對應相同

punitive
[`pjunɪtɪv]
a 刑罰的，懲罰的

The large fine imposed on the bank did not satisfy the senator, who felt the punitive measure was weak.
對銀行徵收高額罰款未讓參議員感到滿意，他覺得懲罰措施沒什麼作用。

記憶技巧 puni- 等同於 pen-，表示處罰；-ive 為形容詞字尾；punitive 即懲罰的。

repentant
[rɪ`pɛntənt]
a 懊悔的

The repentant taxi driver offered to take care of the widow's family after he caused the fatal accident.
闖下致死意外之後，懊悔的計程車司機表示願意照顧寡婦的家庭。

記憶技巧 re- 表示加強語氣；pen- 表示懲罰，後作後悔解釋，-ant，形容詞字尾，repentant 的意思是懊悔的。

penitence
[`pɛnətəns]
n 懺悔，後悔

In a public display of penitence, the student was required to write an apology 100 times on the blackboard.
為了公開表示後悔，學生被要求在黑板上寫一百遍道歉。

記憶技巧 pen- 表示懲罰，在這裡當「後悔」解釋；-ence 為名詞字尾；penitence 的意思是懺悔。

appear - par
母音通轉，兩者的意思皆是顯現、出現。

apparent
[ə`pærənt]
a 明顯的，明白的，顯而易見的，不言自明的

The eldest son was the apparent heir to the throne, even though others in line were also prepared for royal duty.
長子顯然是王位繼承人，即使其他候補者也在為皇室職位作預備。

記憶技巧 ap- 表示朝～方向；par- 表示顯現；-ent 為形容詞字尾；apparent 的意思是明顯的。

transparent
[træns`pɛrənt]
a 透明的，透徹的，坦率的

The NGO was required to make its financial records transparent in order to qualify for tax advantages.
非政府組織被要求財務紀錄透明化，以符合稅務優惠資格。

記憶技巧 trans- 表示跨越、穿越；par- 表示顯現；-ent 為形容詞字尾；transparent 即透徹的、坦率的。

prey - preda

母音通轉,兩者的意思皆是抓取、獵取。

---

predator

[`prɛdətɚ]

n 掠奪者,肉食動物

The honey badger can defend itself against lions, earning the reputation of being the fiercest predator pound-for-pound.

蜜獾能夠擊退獅子,贏得以體重比例的最兇猛掠食者稱號。

> **記憶技巧** preda- 表示獵取;-or 指做出動作者;predator 即掠奪者。

相關字彙
根據飲食分類動物

- cannibal 同類相食者
- carnivore 肉食性動物
- feeder 進食的人(或動物)
- herbivore 草食性動物
- insectivore 食蟲者
- omnivore 雜食性動物
- ruminant 反芻動物
- scavenger 食腐動物

---

predatory

[`prɛdəˌtorɪ]

a 掠奪的,肉食的,壓榨他人的

Predatory lenders use high interest rates and late fees to keep borrowers in debt indefinitely.

嗜血的放款人利用高利息及高滯納金讓借款人陷入債務深淵。

> **記憶技巧** -ory 為形容詞字尾。

---

depredation

[ˌdɛprɪ`deʃən]

n 掠奪

Reforms in the consumer loan industry aims at protecting inexperienced borrowers from depredation.

消費者融資業改革目標是保護沒經驗的借款人不遭掠奪。

> **記憶技巧** de- 表示徹底地;preda- 表示獵取;-ion 為名詞字尾;depredation 的意思是掠奪。

Part
2
CH 1
CH 2
CH 3
CH 4
CH 5

子音對應相同

〔m〕對應〔m〕

man - mas

兩者雖無明確字源關係，但可透過母音通轉來記憶，兩者的意思皆是男性。

masculine [`mæskjəlɪn] **a** 男性的，男子的	Through his action movies, the star developed the reputation of being the ideal masculine stereotype. 藉由動作片，這位明星以完美的陽剛路線塑造口碑。 **記憶技巧** mascul- 表示男性；-ine 為形容詞字尾；masculine 即男性的。
emasculate [ɪˋmæskjəˌlet] **v** 給～去勢， 使（男人）柔弱	The wife dominated the family, often emasculating the husband in order to assert her authority. 為了顯示權威，妻子把持整個家庭，時常讓丈夫毫無地位。 **記憶技巧** e- 等同於 ex-，表示離開；mascul- 表示男性；-ate 為動詞字尾；emasculate 即去勢。

market - merc

母音通轉，兩者的意思皆是交易、交易報酬。

commercial [kəˋmɝʃəl] **n** 商業廣告	Some television commercials focus on emotional response, making it difficult to discern what product is being sold. 一些電視廣告聚焦於情感反應，模糊了主打商品。 **記憶技巧** com- 表示一起；merc- 表示交易；-ial 為形容詞字尾；commercial 的意思是和商業相關的，1935 年後才有電視廣告的意思。
merchant [ˋmɝtʃənt] **n** 商人	The wine merchant will continue to do free tastings at the winery near the vineyard. 酒商將繼續在葡萄園附近的釀酒廠做免費品酒活動。 **記憶技巧** merch- 等同於 merc-，表示交易；-ant 為名詞字尾；merchant 即商人。

Part 2
CH 1
CH 2
CH 3
CH 4
CH 5

子音對應相同

merchandise

[ˈmɝtʃənˌdaɪz]

n 商品

The game show provided clever ways for contestants to win desirable merchandise.

電視遊戲節目提供巧妙方式讓比賽者贏得想要的商品。

記憶技巧 -ise 一般為動詞字尾，在此當名詞字尾用；merchandise 即商品。

---

mercy

[ˈmɝsɪ]

n 恩惠，幸運

After falling behind by ten runs, the visiting team was shown mercy when the umpire ended the game.

落後十分之後，客隊在裁判結束比賽時獲得幸運之神的眷顧。

記憶技巧 merc- 表示交易；-y 為名詞字尾；mercy 本是交易所得、報酬，引申為恩惠、幸運。

---

merciful

[ˈmɝsɪfəl]

a 慈悲的

The tyrant considered himself merciful to anyone who would pledge their loyalty to him.

暴君覺得自己對於任何宣誓效忠他的人都算慈悲了。

記憶技巧 -ful 為形容詞字尾；merciful 當「慈悲」解釋。

---

mercenary

[ˈmɝsnˌɛrɪ]

n 雇傭兵

Covert international mercenaries were hired to assist government forces to tackle the kidnapping case.

祕密國際傭兵受雇協助政府軍處理該起綁架案。

記憶技巧 merc- 表示交易；-ary 為形容詞字尾；mercenary 是交易獲利的，引申為圖利的，名詞當作為了金錢工作的（外國）雇傭兵。

---

mix - misc

母音通轉，兩者的意思皆是混合。

---

miscellaneous

[ˌmɪsɪˈlenjəs]

a 混雜的，五花八門的

The pawn shop sold miscellaneous goods of value at a small discount.

當鋪小折扣販賣五花八門的珍貴商品。

記憶技巧 misc- 表示混合；-ous 為形容詞字尾；miscellaneous 的意思是混雜的。

---

miscellany

[mɪˈsɛlənɪ]

n 混合物，混雜

The army consisted of conscripts with a miscellany of backgrounds and skills.

部隊由背景及技術混雜的受徵召的士兵所組成。

記憶技巧 misc- 表示混合；-y 為名詞字尾；miscellany 的意思是混合物。

promiscuous

[prə`mɪskjuəs]

a 雜亂的，
男女亂交的

The female staff member warned the HR manager of a male employee who was overly promiscuous.

女職員告知人事經理一名男員工男女關係過於複雜。

記憶技巧 pro- 表示前面；misc- 表示混和；-ous 為形容詞字尾；promiscuous 即雜亂的、男女亂交的。

---

move - mot

母音通轉，兩者的意思皆是移動。

---

motor

[`motɚ]

n 發動機，汽車

An electric motor is basically a reversal of an electric generator.

基本上，電動馬達是電動發電機的相反。

記憶技巧 mot- 表示移動；-or 為做出動作者；motor 的意思是發動機、汽車。

---

motif

[mo`tif]

n 主題，動機

The Chinese company designed their lobby in a Ming dynastic motif to show their cultural pride.

為了彰顯文化尊榮，中國公司以明朝的主題設計大廳。

記憶技巧 mot- 表示移動；motif 即動機。

---

commotion

[kə`moʃən]

n 暴動，騷動

There was a commotion in the concourse when a hot dog vendor there offered his remaining stock for half-price.

熱狗攤半價販售存貨時引發車站大廳一陣騷動。

記憶技巧 com- 表示徹底地；mot- 表示移動；-ion 為名詞字尾；commotion 的意思是徹底變動，引申為暴動、騷動。

---

emotional

[ɪ`moʃənl]

a 感情的，易激動的

Japanese soccer fans were clearly emotional when their national team fell short in the world championships.

日本國家隊在世界冠軍賽中未達期待，該國球迷情緒十分激動。

記憶技巧 e- 等同於 ex-，表示外面；mot- 表示移動；-ion 為名詞字尾；-al 為形容詞字尾；emotional 的意思是易激動的，或當「感情的」來解釋。

---

locomotive

[ˌlokə`motɪv]

n 火車頭

The railway invested heavily to upgrade their network to use electric-powered locomotives.

為了使用電力火車頭，鐵路公司重金投資提升網絡。

記憶技巧 loc- 表示地方；mot- 表示移動；-ive 為形容詞字尾；locomotive 即移動的，名詞意思是火車頭。

promote
[prə`mot]
v 促進，推廣，擢陞

The junior executive, known as a brown noser, would do anything to get his boss to promote him.

大家都知道資淺主管是個阿諛奉承的人，會極盡所能爭取老闆拔擢。

記憶技巧　pro- 表示往前；mot- 表示移動；promote 的意思是往前移動，引申為促進。

remote
[rɪ`mot]
a 遙遠的，遠親的

In the remote, snowy regions of Greenland, monitoring stations measure the depth of the permafrost ice.

在格陵島上遙遠又覆雪的地區，監測站測量永久凍層的冰塊深度。

記憶技巧　re- 表示離開；mot- 表示移動；remote 的意思是移出去，引申為遙遠的。

motivate
[`motə,vet]
v 引發動機，激發

The coach motivated his players through a combination of reward and punishment.

教練獎勵及處罰並用激勵選手。

記憶技巧　mot- 表示移動；-ive 為形容詞字尾；-ate 為動詞字尾；motivate 的意思是引發動機。

motivation
[,motə`veʃən]
n 動機，刺激，動力

Successful sales managers were given a week of training in Hawaii as extra motivation to meet their goals.

成功的業務經理得到夏威夷一周訓練，作為達成目標的額外動力。

記憶技巧　-ion 為名詞字尾。

---

machine - mechan

母音通轉，兩者的意思皆是機械、機器。

---

mechanic
[mə`kænɪk]
n 技工，機械工

An automobile mechanic typically earns more than teachers and professors in the USA.

在美國，汽車技師的收入通常較教師及教授來得高。

記憶技巧　mechan- 表示機械；-ic 為形容詞字尾；mechanic 的意思是機械的，後當名詞使用，意思是機械工。

Part **2**

CH 1
CH 2
CH 3
CH 4
CH 5

子音對應相同

mechanics
[məˋkænɪks]
n 機械學，力學

New theories in quantum mechanics improve our understanding of how gravity affects light.
量子力學新理論使我們更加了解重力是如何影響光的。

記憶技巧 -ics 表示～學；mechanics 即是機械學。

相關字彙
物理學

- aerodynamics 航空動力學
- dynamics 動力學
- particle physics 粒子物理學
- thermodynamics 熱力學

mechanical
[məˋkænɪkḷ]
a 機械的，自動的

The mechanical engineer developed methods of reducing friction between moving parts.
機械工程師開發減少活動零件之間摩擦力的方法。

記憶技巧 -al 為形容詞字尾。

mechanism
[ˋmɛkəˌnɪzəm]
n 機械，結構，機制

The complex hemoglobin protein provides a natural mechanism for the transfer of oxygen.
複合血紅素蛋白質提供輸送氧氣的天然機制。

記憶技巧 -ism 為名詞字尾；mechanism 的意思是機械、機制。

---

mind - mania

母音通轉，兩者的原意都是思考，mania 是現今的意思是狂躁、瘋狂，亦即認知思考發生問題。

maniac
[ˋmenɪˌæk]
n 瘋子，入迷者

The business tycoon was considered a maniac, but his ruthless style made him a fortune.
商業鉅子被認為是瘋子，但是他的狠心的風格使他致富。

記憶技巧 maniac 即瘋子。

megalomania
[ˌmɛgələˋmenɪə]
n 誇大狂

It is not out of the realm of possibility that some world leaders suffer from megalomania.
不無可能的是，一些世界領袖患有誇大狂。

記憶技巧 megalo- 表示大；mania 表示狂躁；megalomania 即誇大狂。

pyromania
[ˌpaɪrəˋmenɪə]
n 縱火狂

The twin brothers were constantly at odds, with one being a fireman and the other being fascinated with pyromania.
雙胞胎兄弟一向各自發展，一個當消防隊員，一個著迷於縱火狂。

記憶技巧 pyro- 表示火；mania 表示狂躁；pyromania 即縱火狂。

mold - mod

母音通轉，兩者的意思皆是模子、模型、模式等。

---

model

[`madl̩]

n 模型，模範

The retired mechanic passed much of his time building scale models of World War Two aircraft.

退休技工在建造二戰比例模型飛機中度過一些時間。

記憶技巧　mod- 表示模型；model 即模型。

---

modern

[`madɚn]

a 現代的

The artist was commissioned by the insurance company to produce a modern sculpture for the front entrance.

藝術家接受保險公司委託，在前門入口建一座現代雕塑。

記憶技巧　mod- 表示模型；-ern 為形容詞字尾；modern 的意思是現今可見的模式，引申為現代的。

---

moderate

[`madərɪt]

a 適度的，穩健的

These countries have experienced moderate inflation in recent years.

這些國家最近幾年經歷適度通貨膨脹。

記憶技巧　mod- 表示模式；-ate 為形容詞字尾；moderate 的意思是受既定的模式限制，引申為適度的。

---

modest

[`madɪst]

a 謙遜的，簡樸的，有節制的

The successful accountant lived in a modest home, spending most of his income on his personal travels.

成功的會計師住在簡樸的房子，大多數收入都花在個人旅遊上。

記憶技巧　mod- 表示模子；modest 即被既定模式規範住，引申為有節制的。

---

modification

[ˌmadəfəˈkeʃən]

n 修飾，變更

The specialized shop makes modifications to automobile engines to increase power and efficiency.

這間專門店改造汽車引擎，以增加動力及效能。

記憶技巧　mod- 表示模子；fic- 表示做；-ation 為名詞字尾；modification 原指做出模子，因此有限制的意思，引申為修飾。

---

modulate

[`madʒəˌlet]

v 調整，輪調

The military transmitter modulated its frequency to prevent eavesdropping.

軍事發報機調整頻率以防竊聽。

記憶技巧　mod- 表示模子；-ate 為動詞字尾；modulate 原指被模子給框住，引申為調整。

accommodation

[ə‚kɑmə`deʃən]

n 調節，便利，膳（住）宿

The medical department provided each research volunteer basic accommodation near the campus.
醫學系提供每位研究志工校園附近的基本住宿。

記憶技巧　ac- 等同於 ad-，表示朝～方向；com- 表示加強語氣；mod- 表示模式；-ation 為名詞字尾；accommodation 的意思是順應模式調整。

commodious

[kə`modɪəs]

a 便利的，適宜的

The senior professors were provided with more commodious living space than the assistant professors.
相較於助理教授，校方提供資深教授的居住空間更為寬敞。

記憶技巧　com- 表示加強語氣；mod- 表示模式；-ous 為形容詞字尾；commodious 指吻合模式，引申為適宜的。

remember - memor

母音通轉，兩者的意思皆是記得、記憶。

memory

[`mɛmərɪ]

n 記憶，記憶力，紀念

Even though it happened 15 years ago, the Spring Break trip was still a fond memory for the deliveryman.
儘管是 15 年前的往事，那趟春季旅行仍是送貨員的一段愉快記憶。

記憶技巧　memor- 表示記得；-y 為名詞字尾；memory 的意思是記憶。

memorial

[mə`morɪəl]

n 紀念碑

The town built a bronze memorial for a dog named Hachiko, which was known as the Most Loyal Dog in History.
小鎮為一隻名叫小八的狗立一尊紀念銅像，牠以史上最忠心的狗著稱。

記憶技巧　memor- 表示記得；-ial 為形容詞字尾；memorial 的意思是紀念的，名詞的意思是紀念碑。

memorable

[`mɛmərəbl]

a 難忘的，著名的

The New Year's Party was a memorable affair for all staff members who attended.
新年派對對所有出席員工來說是一場難忘盛會。

記憶技巧　memor- 表示記憶；-able 為形容詞字尾；memorable 即難忘的。

memoir

[ˋmɛmwɑr]

n 回憶錄，自傳

After her death, the memoirs of the starlet became a best-selling book.

這名未成名的年輕女演員，她的回憶錄成了暢銷書。

記憶技巧 memoir 是古法文字，意思是回憶錄。

memento

[mɪˋmɛnto]

n 紀念品

Every sales trainee took home a small wooden tiki as a unique momento of their conference in Hawaii.

每一名銷售受訓者都帶一座木刻提基像回家，作為夏威夷大會獨特紀念品。

記憶技巧 memento 是可以保存記憶的紀念品。

相關字彙
紀念品

• keepsake 紀念品
• souvenir 紀念品

commemorable

[kəˋmɛmərəbl]

a 值得紀念的，慶祝的

The reuniting of North and South Vietnam in 1976 was hailed as a commemorable event.

大家認定南越北越 1976 年再度統一是值得紀念的事件。

記憶技巧 com- 表示加強語氣；memor- 表示記得；-able 為形容詞字尾；commemorable 即值得紀念的。

small - min

兩者雖無字源關係，但可藉由母音通轉來記憶，兩者的意思皆是小。

minister

[ˋmɪnɪstɚ]

n 部長，牧師

The American minister traveled to Ethiopia, where ancient Christian traditions could be found.

美籍牧師走訪擁有基督教古老傳統的衣索匹亞。

記憶技巧 mini- 表示小；-ster 表示人；minister 的意思是位階稍低的人，原指國王底下的臣子，後指部長，另有牧師的意思。

minimize

[ˋmɪnəˏmaɪz]

v 減至最少量

The captain of the team tried to minimize the loss in his speech, but the disappointed fans would have none of it.

隊長演講中儘量減少損失，但是失望的粉絲不接受。

記憶技巧 mini- 表示小；-ize 為動詞字尾；minimize 的意思是減至最少量。

Part

2

CH 1
CH 2
CH 3
CH 4
CH 5

子音對應相同

minimal [ˋmɪnəməl] **a** 最小的， 　　最低限度的	Investors are invited to the first round of capital funding with a minimal investment of one million dollars. 投資者受邀參與首輪資金募集，每筆投資金額最少一百萬美元。 **記憶技巧** mini- 表示小；-al 為形容詞字尾；minimal 的意思是最小的。
minor [ˋmaɪnɚ] **a** 較小的	There was a minor incident in the staff lounge, so we recommend everyone to go out for lunch today. 員工休息室有個小狀況，建議大家今天外出中餐。 **記憶技巧** minor 是較小的、較少的。
diminish [dəˋmɪnɪʃ] **v** 貶損，減少	The discovery of the politician's infidelity did little to diminish the people's fervor for him. 發現政治人物出軌幾乎不減人們對他的好感。 **記憶技巧** di- 表示完全；min- 表示小；-ish 為動詞字尾；diminish 的意思是減少。

small - micro

兩者雖無字源關係，但可藉由母音通轉來記憶，兩者的意思皆是小、微。

microwave [ˋmaɪkroˌwev] **n** 微波	Percy Spencer discovered the technology used in microwave ovens by accident. 培西・史賓賽意外發現運用於微波爐的技術。 **記憶技巧** micro- 表示微；wave 表示波；microwave 的意思是微波。
microbiology [ˌmaɪkrobaɪˋɑlədʒɪ] **n** 微生物學	The well-funded microbiology department studied how cancer cells were affected by different chemical compounds from plants. 資金雄厚的微生物學部門探討不同植物化學複合物如何影響癌細胞。 **記憶技巧** micro- 表示微；biology 表示生物學；microbiology 即微生物學。
microscope [ˋmaɪkrəˌskop] **n** 顯微鏡	The view in the microscope revealed that the patient's red blood cells were flowing too slowly. 顯微鏡影像顯示病患紅血球細胞流動太慢。 **記憶技巧** micro- 表示微；scope 表示觀測鏡；microscope 即顯微鏡。

microeconomics [͵maɪkrə͵ikə`nɑmɪks] **n** 個體經濟學， （微觀經濟學）	The field workers in the field of microeconomics studied fascinating activities in African villages. 個體經濟學領域的田野工作者研究非洲村落裡很有趣的活動。 記憶技巧　micro- 表示微；economics 表示經濟學；microeconomics 即微觀經濟學、個體經濟學。

many - multi

兩者雖無字源關係，但可藉由母音通轉來記憶，兩者皆表示多。

multitude [`mʌltə͵tjud] **n** 多數，群眾	Elvis Presley was heaped with a multitude of posthumous awards and accolades. 貓王埃爾維斯．普雷斯利獲得許多身後獎項及讚揚。 記憶技巧　multi- 表示多；-tude 為抽象名詞字尾；multitude 即多數。
multiply [`mʌltəplaɪ] **v** 乘，增加，繁殖	The investor made small investments in a number of tech companies, expecting to multiply his money. 投資客小額投資數家科技公司，期待財富倍增。 記憶技巧　multi- 表示多；-ply 表示折；multiply 的意思是對折多次，引申為乘、繁殖。
multimedia [mʌltɪ`midɪə] **a** 多媒體的	The real estate company presented prospective investors with a polished multimedia presentation. 不動產公司向潛在投資客呈現精美多媒體簡報。 記憶技巧　multi- 表示多；media 表示媒體；multimedia 的意思是多媒體。
multicultural [͵mʌltɪ`kʌltʃərəl] **a** 多種文化的	The university organized a multicultural event to give international students a chance to express their pride. 為了提供國際學生表達自豪的機會，大學規劃一項多文化活動。 記憶技巧　multi- 表示多；cultural 表示文化的；multicultural 即多種文化的。
multiparous [mʌl`tɪpərəs] **a** 多產的	The country of Benin in Africa has the highest rate of multiparous births in the world. 非洲國家貝南一胎多產的比率全世界最高。 記憶技巧　multi- 表示多；par- 表示生產；-ous 為形容詞字尾；multiparous 即多產的。

multifarious
[ˌmʌltəˈfɛrɪəs]
a 各式各樣的

The crime family carried out multifarious operations, making it hard for the police to investigate its activities.
犯罪集團從事各種行動，讓警方難以查察他們的活動。

記憶技巧 multi- 表示多；-farious 表示以多種方式表達；multifarious 即各式各樣的。

---

month / moon - men
母音通轉，兩者皆表示月亮。

---

menstruate
[ˈmɛnstruˌet]
v 月經來潮

Most mothers have discussions with their daughters before they begin to menstruate to prevent fear and confusion.
為避免恐慌及困惑，大多數母親會在女兒初經前和她們有所討論。

記憶技巧 men- 表示月；-ate 為動詞字尾；menstruate 的意思是月經來潮。

---

menopause
[ˈmɛnəˌpɔz]
n 停經

Grace was sad on her 40th birthday, stating all she had to look forward to was menopause and retirement.
格瑞絲四十歲生日那天很傷心，說著自己面臨的是停經及退休。

記憶技巧 meno- 表示月；pause 表示停止；menopause 即停經。

相關字彙
生理期

- amenorrhoea 閉經症
- cramps 痙攣
- menstrual cycle 月經週期
- ovulate 排卵
- period pain 經痛
- postmenopausal 停經後
- premenstrual 經前
- sanitary towel 衛生棉
- tampon 衛生棉條

---

mouse - myo
母音通轉，兩者皆表示老鼠，亦可做肌肉解釋，因肌肉形狀像老鼠。

---

myocardium
[ˌmaɪəˈkɑrdɪəm]
n 心肌

Regular exercise and endurance training strengthen the myocardium, reducing the risk of heart attack.
規律運動及耐力訓練能強化心肌，降低心臟病發作的風險。

記憶技巧 myo- 表示肌肉；card- 表示心；-ium 為名詞字尾；myocardium 即心肌。

myosin

[ˋmaɪəsɪn]

n 肌凝蛋白

The scientists conducted myosin research to find better ways to improve the strength of muscle filaments.

為了找到增進肌絲的更佳方法，科學家進行肌凝蛋白研究。

記憶技巧 myo- 表示肌肉；-in 表示化合物；以前的科學認為肌凝蛋白只有在肌肉上才有。

myocarditis

[ˌmaɪokɑrˋdaɪtɪs]

n 心肌炎

Showing symptoms of myocarditis, Jeremy was put on a strict, low-salt diet to reduce the risk of heart failure.

出現心肌炎症狀，傑若米得控制低鹽飲食，以降低心臟衰竭的風險。

記憶技巧 myo- 表示肌肉；card- 表示心；-itis 表示炎；myocarditis 的意思是心肌炎。

Part 2
CH 1
CH 2
CH 3
CH 4
CH 5
子音對應相同

---

mid - meso

母音通轉，兩者皆表示中間。

---

middle

[ˋmɪdḷ]

a 中部的，中間的

The couple sat in the middle rows of the auditorium to get the best view.

夫婦坐在禮堂中央幾排以取得最佳視線。

記憶技巧 mid- 表示中間；middle 即中間的。

Mesopotamia

[ˌmɛsəpəˋtemɪə]

n 美索不達米亞

Mesopotamia was the center of Western civilization during the Bronze Age.

美索不達米亞是銅器時代西方文明中心。

記憶技巧 Meso- 表示中間；potamia 表示河流；Mesopotamia 即兩河之間的美索不達米亞。

猜猜看！

measure 表示「測量」，猜由它衍生出的長度單位的單字？

答案：meter（公尺）

miss - mut

母音通轉，子音 s 和 t 互換，兩者的核心意思皆表示改變、移動，miss 是朝錯誤的方向改變、移動，衍生出錯過的意思。

---

amiss
[ə`mɪs]

a 錯誤的，不見的，丟失的

He paused when he felt something was amiss, and then realized he had left his briefcase in his office.

他感到有什麼東西不見時，暫停下來，發現是公事包留在辦公室裡了。

記憶技巧　a- 等同於 on，表示在～上；miss 表示朝錯誤的方向改變、移動，引申為錯誤的。

---

mutual
[`mjutʃuəl]

a 相互的，共有的

I discovered that the woman I was going to meet was a mutual friend of yours.

我發現我即將見面的女子是你們的共同朋友。

記憶技巧　mut- 表示移動、改變；-al 為形容詞字尾；mutual 本是移動的，引申為共有的。

---

mutable
[`mjutəbl]

a 易變的，三心二意的

The mutable nature of the football game made it hard to predict the outcome.

橄欖球比賽瞬息萬變，結果難以預測。

記憶技巧　mut- 表示改變；-able 為形容詞字尾；mutable 即易變的。

---

mutation
[mju`teʃən]

n 變異，突變種，讓受

The gamma radiation caused an observable mutation in 10% of the fish.

伽瑪射線導致 10% 魚類顯著突變。

記憶技巧　mut- 表示改變；-ation 為名詞字尾；mutation 的意思是變異。

---

commuter
[kə`mjutɚ]

n 通勤者

The commuter spent half an hour on the train and twenty minutes on the bus to get to work.

該名通勤族上班要花半小時搭火車，接著花二十分鐘搭公車。

記憶技巧　com- 表示加強語氣；mut- 表示改變；commute 是改變（方向），1889 年起才有通勤的意思，commuter 是通勤者。

Part
2
CH 1
CH 2
CH 3
CH 4
CH 5
子音對應相同

Section 4

〔f〕對應〔f〕

flow - flu

兩者雖無字源關係，但可藉由母音通轉來記憶，兩者皆表示流。

---

fluency

[ˋfluənsɪ]

n 流暢，流利

The reading fluency rate is low in poor countries, making it difficult to find educated professionals to work there.

貧窮國家閱讀流暢度低，不易找到高學歷專業人士前往工作。

記憶技巧 flu- 表示流；-ent 為形容詞字尾；-cy 為名詞字尾；fluency 的意思是流利。

---

confluent

[ˋkɑnfluənt]

a 匯集的

The rise of the digital age and the expansion of the surveillance industry are confluent forces that erode privacy.

數位時代的崛起與監控產業的擴張結合成侵犯隱私的力量。

記憶技巧 con- 表示一起；flu- 表示流；-ent 為形容詞字尾；confluent 指匯集在一起的。

---

fluid

[ˋfluɪd]

n 流體

Mercury is a metal that is in a fluid form under normal room temperature conditions.

水銀是一種金屬，在常溫中是流體。

記憶技巧 flu- 表示流；fluid 的意思是流體。

---

influence

[ˋɪnfluəns]

n 影響力，影響

This year saw the passing of a comedic actor who had a great influence on our generation.

今年發生了影響我們世代甚鉅的喜劇演員殞落。

記憶技巧 in- 表示內；flu- 表示流；-ence 為名詞字尾；influence 的意思是流進去，引申為造成影響。

---

influenza

[ˌɪnfluˋɛnzə]

n 流行性感冒

The Spanish influenza pandemic of 1918 took the lives of over 20 million people globally.

1918 年西班牙流感大流行，奪走全世界超過兩千萬人的性命。

記憶技巧 flu- 表示流；influenza 指流感。

fiber - fibr

fiber 省略母音字母，兩者皆表示纖維。

fibroid
['faɪbrɔɪd]
a 纖維的

Fibroid degeneration usually represents a process in which a fibroid tumor starts to collapse and calcium deposits build up.
纖維退化經常表示纖維瘤開始萎縮，鈣沉澱物擴增。

記憶技巧　fibr- 表示纖維；-oid 為形容詞字尾；fibroid 即纖維的。

fibrosis
[faɪ`brosɪs]
n 纖維化

The man developed asthma-like symptoms because of the lung tissue damage caused by pulmonary fibrosis.
因為肺纖維化引起組織傷害，男子出現類似氣喘的症狀。

記憶技巧　fibr- 表示纖維；-osis 為名詞字尾，當「疾病」解釋；fibrosis 即纖維化。

face - fic

母音通轉，兩者皆表示臉、面。

facial
['feʃəl]
a 臉部的，表面的

Protective facial masks are worn by almost every commuter in the polluted city.
遭受汙染城市，幾乎每一位通勤族都戴著防護口罩。

記憶技巧　fac- 表示臉；-ial 為形容詞字尾；facial 的意思是臉部的。

facade
[fə`sad]
n 建築物正面

The man's reputation as a generous philanthropist was a facade. In fact, he had never made a donation.
男子大慈善家的名聲只是個幌子，事實上從未捐過錢。

記憶技巧　fac- 表示面；-ade 為名詞字尾；facade 指建築物的正面，是法文借字。

相關字彙
建築結構

- alcove 壁龕
- balcony 陽臺
- catacomb 地下墓穴
- corridor 走廊
- foundation stone 基石
- garage 車庫
- hallway 玄關
- wing 側廳

superficial
['supɚ`fɪʃəl]
a 表面的，膚淺的

The repairs to the school were merely superficial, as the roof leaked again in a matter of weeks.
屋頂幾周內再度漏水，學校修繕僅是草率了事。

記憶技巧　super- 表示在～之上；fic- 表示面；-ial 為形容詞字尾；superficial 即表面上的，引申為膚淺的。

fight - flict

兩者雖無字源關係，但可藉由母音通轉來記憶，兩者皆表示打擊。

conflict

[ˋkɑnflɪkt]

n 衝突，鬥爭

The Congo has been a region with massive conflict ever since it was ruled as a Belgian colony.
比利時殖民統治以來，剛果一直是大規模的衝突地區。

記憶技巧 con- 表示一起；flict- 表示打擊；conflict 一起打架，引申出衝突、鬥爭的意思。

afflict

[əˋflɪkt]

v 使痛苦

In 2015, an unusually large number of Tainan City residents were afflicted with Dengue Fever.
2015 年，台南市遭受登革熱之苦的人數出奇地高。

記憶技巧 af- 等同於 -ad，表示朝～的；flict- 表示打擊；afflict 本指去攻擊別人，引申出讓人痛苦的意思。

afflictive

[əˋflɪktɪv]

a 痛苦的，苦惱的

The man's body odor was an afflictive condition, which disgusted and repulsed everyone around him.
男子的體味是個苦惱狀況，令周圍的每個人作噁及反感。

記憶技巧 -ive 為形容詞字尾。

free - franc

兩者雖無字源關係，但可藉由母音通轉來記憶，兩者皆表示自由。

frankly

[ˋfræŋklɪ]

ad 坦白地

The chairman was frankly unwilling to cancel his golf outing to attend the meeting.
主席明白表示不願取消高爾夫球行程而去開會。

記憶技巧 frank 等同於 franc-，表示自由；-ly 為副詞字尾；frankly 指無拘束的，說話可以坦白。

franchise

[ˋfrænˌtʃaɪz]

n 經銷權，特權

In the mold of a famous American company, Mr. Donut has become a popular doughnut franchise in Asia.
循著美國知名公司模式，Mr. Donut 成為亞洲地區人氣甜甜圈特許經營店。

記憶技巧 franch- 等同於 franc-，表示自由；franchise 本指的是自由權，到 1959 年才有經銷權的意思。

Part **2**

CH 1
CH 2
CH 3
CH 4
CH 5

子音對應相同

disenfranchise

[ˌdɪsɪnˋfræntʃaɪz]

v 剝奪（～的公民）
權力

The central government disenfranchised the tribal peoples by taking away their voting rights.
中央政府取消原住民族投票權而剝奪他們的權利。

記憶技巧 dis- 為否定字首，表示分開；franch- 表示自由；-ise 為動詞字尾；disfranchise 本指剝奪自由權，後指剝奪權力。

enfranchise

[ɪnˋfræntʃaɪz]

v 賦予權力

Women's suffrage succeeded in giving women the rights to vote and instantly enfranchised half of the population.
女性選舉權成功賦予她們投票權，半數人口立即獲得此一權力。

記憶技巧 en- 等同於 in-，表示內；franch- 表示自由；-ise 為動詞字尾；enfranchise 字面上意思給予自由，後作賦予權力。

相關字彙
選舉

- by-election 遞補選舉
- direct elections 直接選舉
- Gallup poll 蓋洛普民意調查
- platform（政黨等的）政綱或宣言
- referendum 公民投票
- suffrage 投票
- gerrymander 選區不公正的重新劃分

freeze - frig

兩者雖無字源關係，但可藉由母音通轉來記憶，兩者皆表示冷（凍）。

frigid

[ˋfrɪgɪd]

a 寒冷的，嚴寒的

Some of the survivors of the sunken ship were immersed in the frigid North Atlantic until they suffered from hypothermia.
一些沉船生還者泡在嚴寒的北大西洋，直到失溫。

記憶技巧 frig- 表示冷；-id 為形容詞字尾；frigid 的意思是寒冷的。

相關字彙
冷的

- arctic 極寒的
- bitter 極冷的
- chilly 冷颼颼的
- freezing 凍結的
- glacial 冰的

refrigerator

[rɪˋfrɪdʒəˌretə]

n 冰箱，雪櫃，
冷藏室，冷凍庫

The large food container truck is practically a giant mobile refrigerator unit on wheels.
這輛大型食品貨櫃卡車事實上是一台有輪子可移動的大冷藏裝置。

記憶技巧 re- 表示再一次；frig- 表示冷；-ate 為動詞字尾；-or 表示做出～動作者；refrigerator 是可使東西降溫變冷的機器，即冰箱。

相關字彙
冷凍、冷藏設備

- cooler 冷藏箱
- deep freeze 冰櫃
- fridge 電冰箱
- icebox 冷藏庫

fire - flam

兩者雖無字源關係，但可藉由母音通轉來記憶，兩者皆表示火。

Part

2

CH 1
CH 2
CH 3
CH 4
CH 5

子音對應相同

flame

[flem]

n 火焰，燃燒

The flames of hell licked at the heels of the hero as he barely escaped the clutches of the demon.
主角就要逃離魔掌時，地獄火焰竄燒到他的腳跟。

記憶技巧　flam- 表示火；flame 即火焰。

flammable

[`flæməbl]

a 易燃的，可燃的

There are large warning signs on trucks and containers that transport flammable liquids.
運送可燃液體的卡車及容器都有大型警告標示。

記憶技巧　flam- 表示火；-able 為形容詞字尾；flammable 即易燃的。

相關字彙
燃燒

• combustible 可燃的
• inflammable 易燃的
• non-flammable 不易燃的

aflame

[ə`flem]

a 燃燒的

The vacation home was aflame, because the vacationers forgot to turn off the stove.
因為度假民眾忘了關掉火爐，所以度假屋起火燃燒。

記憶技巧　a- 表示在～之上；flam- 表示火；aflame 即燃燒的。

inflammation

[͵ɪnflə`meʃən]

n 激昂，發炎

The man was required to stop eating spicy chili peppers, because he suffered from inflammation of his esophagus.
男子食道發炎，被要求別吃辛辣的辣椒。

記憶技巧　in- 表示內；flam- 表示火；-ation 為名詞字尾；inflammation 的意思是內部燃燒，引申為發炎。

相關字彙
疾病及健康

• antibody 抗體
• biosecurity 生物安全
• defense mechanism（心理）防禦機制

• immune 免疫的
• quarantine 隔離

flamingo

[flə`mɪŋgo]

n 紅鶴

The plastic pink flamingo adorned the lawn of the artist's home in the desert.
塑膠粉紅火鶴椿是這名藝術家在沙漠的家的草皮。

記憶技巧　flam-，火焰，flamingo 是紅鶴，因其羽毛火紅。

相關字彙
住在河邊、湖邊的鳥類

• coot 大鷭
• crane 鶴
• kingfisher 翠鳥

• osprey 魚鷹
• plover 千鳥
• swan 天鵝

flee - fug

兩者雖無字源關係，但可藉由母音通轉來記憶，兩者皆表示逃。

refuge [ˋrɛfjudʒ] **n** 庇護，庇護者， 避難所	The City of Boulder, Colorado, voted to be a refuge for immigrants. 科羅拉多伯爾德城投票成為移民的一處庇護所。 記憶技巧 re- 表示回來；fug- 表示逃；refuge 指可以逃回來尋求庇護的場所，即庇護所、避難所。
refugee [ˌrɛfjuˋdʒi] **n** 難民，逃亡者	The conflicts in the Middle East led to an influx of homeless refugees into Europe. 中東衝突導致無家可歸的難民湧向歐洲。 記憶技巧 re- 表示回來；fug- 表示逃；-ee 表示人；refugee 是逃回來的人，指難民。
vermifuge [ˋvɝməˌfjudʒ] **n** 驅蟲藥	The dog was given vermifuge cream to ingest after parasitic worms were found in its stool. 發現便便有寄生蟲之後，狗狗被給予驅蟲藥膏讓牠吸收體內。 記憶技巧 verm- 等同於 worm，表示蟲；fug- 表示逃；vermifuge 即可驅趕蟲蟻，讓蟲蟻逃跑的驅蟲藥。

fear - phob

兩者雖無字源關係，但可藉由母音通轉來記憶，兩者皆表示恐懼。

phobia [ˋfobɪə] **n** 恐懼症	The hypnotist is specialized in treatment of patients with debilitating phobias. 催眠師專於治療衰弱恐懼症病患。 記憶技巧 phob- 等同於 fear，表示恐懼；-ia 表示疾病症狀；phobia 是恐懼症。
acrophobia [ˌækrəˋfobɪə] **n** 懼高症	Just the thought of bungee jumping or skydiving made the man with acrophobia extremely nervous. 光想到高空彈跳或跳傘就讓懼高症男子極度緊張。 記憶技巧 acro- 表示頂部、最高；-phobia 表示恐懼症；acrophobia 即懼高症。

hydrophobia
[ˌhaɪdrəˈfobɪə]
n 狂犬病

Hydrophobia patients acquire their disease from rabid animals and refuse water, because it hurts for them to swallow it.

狂犬病患者病源是患有狂犬病的動物，會抗拒喝水，因為一吞水就痛。

記憶技巧 hydro- 表示水；-phobia 表示恐懼症；hydrophobia 即恐水症、狂犬病。

photophobia
[ˌfotəˈfobɪə]
n 畏光症

The old man with photophobia never left his room, because even the smallest amount of light hurt his eyes.

畏光症的老先生絕不踏出房間，因為即使是最微量的光線都會讓他眼睛疼痛。

記憶技巧 photo- 表示光；-phobia 表示恐懼症；photophobia 即畏光症。

Section 5

〔v〕對應〔v〕

---

void - vac / van
母音通轉，兩者皆表示空、缺乏。

avoid
[əˈvɔɪd]
v 避免，使無效，撤銷

The commuter drove around the outskirts of the town to avoid the heavy traffic.

通勤族開車繞道城市外圍以避開繁忙車潮。

記憶技巧 a- 等同於 ex-，表示外面；void- 表示空；avoid 的意思是清空，引申為避免、使無效等。

devoid
[dɪˈvɔɪd]
a 缺乏的

The island provided safety for the shipwreck survivor, but it was devoid of life.

島嶼提供船難生還者安全庇護，但島上沒有生物。

記憶技巧 de- 表示離開；void- 表示空；devoid 的意思是把東西搬出去，淨空某空間，引申為缺乏的。

vacuum
['vækjuəm]
n 真空

In the early days of radios, vacuum tubes were used to control electric signals.
早期收音機使用真空管控制電訊號。

記憶技巧　vacu- 表示空；-um 為名詞字尾；vacuum 即真空。

相關字彙
空

- emptiness 空虛
- space 空間
- lacuna 空白
- blankness 空白

vanish
['vænɪʃ]
v 消失，消滅

The new cleaning fluid guarantees to make stains vanish with one application.
新清潔液保證一抹就能去除髒汙痕跡。

記憶技巧　van- 表示空；-ish 為動詞字尾；vanish 的意思是清空，引申為消失、消滅。

vital - viv
母音通轉，兩者皆表示生命。

vivid
['vɪvɪd]
a 活潑的，鮮豔的，栩栩如生的

The special digital camera captured extremely vivid photos because of its sensitive light sensor chip.
因為有敏銳感光晶片，所以這台特殊數位相機拍攝極為鮮豔的相片。

記憶技巧　viv- 表示生命；-id 為形容詞字尾；vivid 指的是活生生的，引申為活潑的、鮮豔的。

vivacious
[vaɪ'veʃəs]
a 活潑爽朗的

At the class reunion, most attendees flocked around a vivacious woman, who was the former cheerleading captain.
同學會，大多數出席同學往一位活潑女子四周擠，她是前啦啦隊長。

記憶技巧　viv- 表示生命；-ous 為形容詞字尾；vivacious 是指人活潑爽朗的。

vivisection
[ˌvɪvə'sɛkʃən]
n 活體解剖

The animal rights activist protested in front of the medical reseach facility against their use of vivisection on cats and dogs.
動物權擁護份子在醫學研究機構前面抗議用貓、狗做活體解剖。

記憶技巧　viv- 表示生命；sect- 表示切割；-ion 為名詞字尾；vivisection 的意思是切割活生生的生物，即活體解剖。

相關字彙
科學相關研究

- anatomize 解剖
- chromatography 色層分析
- dissect 解剖
- double-blind 雙盲的
- laboratory 實驗室
- specimen 樣品
- in vitro 在試管內

revival [rɪ`vaɪvl̩] **n** 甦醒，回復	Winning their first championship in 95 years, the football team brought a revival of civic pride to their city. 95 年來首次奪冠，橄欖球隊喚回當地市民的驕傲。 記憶技巧 re- 表示再一次；viv- 表示生命；-al 為名詞字尾；revival 即復甦。
survive [sɚ`vaɪv] **v** 生還	If your small business can survive its first five years, there is more than a 50/50 chance of success. 你的小公司若能撐過前五年，成功機會就超過 50%。 記憶技巧 sur- 等同於 super-，表示在～之上；viv- 表示生命；survive 字面意思是活在～之上，引申為生還、倖存。

Section 6

〔d〕對應〔d〕

down - de
兩者雖無字源關係，但可藉由母音通轉來記憶，兩者皆表示往下。

decadence [`dɛkədəns] **n** 衰微，墮落	The Roaring 20's refers to the decade in America, when the wealthy recklessly pursued a life of decadence. 咆哮的 20 年代是指美國富人盲目追求頹廢生活的十年。 記憶技巧 de- 表示往下；cad- 表示落；-ence 為名詞字尾；decadence 字面意思是往下落，引申為墮落、衰微。
deciduous [dɪ`sɪdʒʊəs] **a** 脫落性的， 落葉性的	Tourists flocked to Vermont in autumn to view the colorful leaves of maple and other deciduous trees. 秋天時，遊客湧向佛蒙特觀看楓樹和其他落葉木五顏六色的葉子。 記憶技巧 de- 表示往下；cid- 等同於 cad-，表示落；-ous 為形容詞字尾；deciduous 是落葉性的。

相關字彙 樹的種類	• coniferous 結毬果的 • softwood 針葉樹材 • evergreen 常綠的

---

degenerate
[dɪˋdʒɛnəˌret]

v 衰退的，墮落的

As he was confined to a wheelchair, his life degenerated into a lonely, monotonous one.
限制於輪椅上，他的生活落至孤獨單調。

記憶技巧   de- 表示往下；gen- 表示生；-ate 為動詞字尾；degenerate 字面意思是往下生長，引申為衰退的、墮落的。

---

depend
[dɪˋpɛnd]

v 相信，信賴

The company's profitability depends on its ability to provide enough value to enough people at the right price.
公司盈利能力取決於以適當價格為足夠的人提供足夠價值的能力。

記憶技巧   de- 表示下面；pend- 表示掛著；depend 的意思是在下方掛著，引申為依賴。

---

depose
[dɪˋpoz]

v 免職，作證，放置

In a dramatic military coup, the patriotic general deposed the corrupt president.
一場戲劇性的軍事政變中，愛國的將軍將貪腐的總統免職。

記憶技巧   de- 表示下面；pos- 表示放；depose 的意思是放到下面，引申為免職。

---

day - di
兩者雖無字源關係，但可藉由母音通轉來記憶，兩者皆表示日子。

---

diary
[ˋdaɪərɪ]

n 日記，日誌，日記簿

The "*Diary of a Wimpy Kid*" book series follows the life experiences of a boy named Greg Heffley.
《遜咖日記》系列叢書是以一位名叫格雷格·赫弗利的男孩的生活經驗為主。

記憶技巧   di- 表示日；-ary 為名詞字尾；diary 的意思是日記。

---

dismal
[ˋdɪzm̩l]

a 憂鬱的，沉悶的，淒涼的

The manager refused to pay bonuses to the sales staff after a dismal 4th quarter performance.
第四季慘澹的業績後，經理拒絕向銷售人員支付獎金。

記憶技巧   dis- 表示日；mal- 表示不好的；dismal 的字面意思是不好的日子，引申為憂鬱的、淒涼的。

diurnal
[daɪˈɝnl̩]
a 每日的，一日間的

Most flowering plants have a diurnal cycle of opening and closing its petals each day.
大多數開花植物有每天打開和闔上花瓣的晝夜循環。

記憶技巧 di- 表示日；-al 為形容詞字尾；diurnal 的意思是每日的。

---

meridian
[məˈrɪdɪən]
n 子午線，經線

The Prime Meridian, located at 0 degrees longitude, runs through Europe and Africa.
本初子午線，位於 0 度經線，穿過歐洲和非洲。

記憶技巧 meri- 等同於 mid-，表示中間；di- 表示日；meridian 本指正中午，後來當子午線解釋。

相關字彙
地表上想像的線

- the Antarctic Circle 南極圈
- the Arctic Circle 北極圈
- the equator 赤道
- the international date line 國際換日線
- latitude 緯線
- longitude 經線
- tropic 回歸線
- the Tropic of Capricorn 南迴歸線
- the Tropic of Cancer 北迴歸線

---

quotidian
[kwoˈtɪdɪən]
a 每日的，平凡的，司空見慣的

In the quotidian rush to get to work, masses of people crowd into buses and commuter trains.
每天匆忙趕去上班，大量人群擠進公共汽車和通勤火車。

記憶技巧 quot- 表示數量、順序；di- 表示日；-an 為形容詞字尾；quotidian 指每日的，引申為平凡的。

---

direct - dress
母音通轉，兩者皆表示直。

---

address
[əˈdrɛs]
n 地址，演講，致辭

This misprinted address caused the package to arrive at the wrong destination.
錯誤地址導致包裹送到不對的地點。

記憶技巧 ad- 表示往～方向；dress- 等同於 direct-，表示直；address 的意思是弄直，要 15 世紀後才衍生出地址、演講、致辭等意思。

---

redress
[rɪˈdrɛs]
v 矯正，改正

The new hearing was held to redress the unjust ruling of the previous trial.
新庭訊是為了矯正前次審理的不公裁決而舉行的。

記憶技巧 re- 表示再一次；dress- 表示直；redress 字面上的意思是將～弄直，引申為矯正、改正。

Part 2
CH 1
CH 2
CH 3
CH 4
CH 5
子音對應相同

order - ordin
母音通轉，兩者皆表示順序。

---

ordinance
['ɔrdɪnəns]

n 法令，條例

The street vendor received a $50 fine for breaking the city ordinance banning food sales without a license.
路邊攤販違反禁止無照販售食品的城市法令而受到50元罰款。

記憶技巧 ordin- 表示順序；-ance 為名詞字尾；ordinance 字面上意思是使有～次序，引申為法令，因為法令的目的是維持秩序。

---

ordinary
['ɔrdn͵ɛrɪ]

a 普通的，正常的

The advertising agency's campaign turned an ordinary food item into an expensive, luxury brand.
廣告代理商的活動使普通食品成為昂貴奢侈品牌。

記憶技巧 ordin-，順序，-ary，形容詞字尾，ordinary 是指按照一般順序的，引申為普通的、正常的。

---

coordination
[ko͵ɔrdn͵eʃən]

n 協調

The successful product launch took coordination between the production and marketing departments.
成功產品的推出需要生產部門和行銷部門的協調。

記憶技巧 co- 表示一起；ordin- 表示順序；-ation 為名詞字尾；coordination 按順序把東西排在一起，引申為協調。

---

coordinator
[ko'ɔrdn͵etɚ]

n 協調者

The event coordinator frantically searched for a replacement emcee for the upcoming awards ceremony.
為了即將到來的頒獎典禮，活動協調員全力尋找一位替代主持人。

記憶技巧 -or 為做出動作者。

---

extraordinary
[ɪk'strɔrdn͵ɛrɪ]

a 特別的，臨時的，非常的

The double rainbow is a good omen, indicating it is going to be an extraordinary day.
兩道彩虹是一個好兆頭，表示將有特別的一天。

記憶技巧 extra- 表示外面、離開；ordinary 表示普通的；extraordinary 的意思是離開普通的狀況，引申為特別的。

---

subordinate
[sə'bɔrdn͵ɪt]

a 部下級的，次要的，服從的

The police chief called a meeting of his subordinate officers to discuss new policies.
警察局長召集部屬開會討論新措施。

記憶技巧 sub- 表示在～之下；ordin- 表示順序；-ate 為形容詞字尾；subordinate 的意思是排在下面的，引申為次要的、服從的。

Part
2
CH 1
CH 2
CH 3
CH 4
CH 5

子音對應相同

Section 7

〔t〕對應〔t〕

time - tempo

兩者雖無字源關係，但可藉由母音通轉來記憶，兩者皆表示時間。

---

temporal

[ˋtɛmpərəl]

a 時間的，世俗的，現世的

Some religious leaders may have temporal motivations instead of spiritual ones.

一些宗教領袖可能有世俗而非精神方面的動機。

記憶技巧　tempo- 表示時間；-al 為形容詞字尾；temporal 是時間的，引申出世俗的、現世的等意思。

---

temporary

[ˋtɛmpəˏrɛrɪ]

a 臨時的，一時的

The judge granted a temporary injunction to prevent the developer from building in the national park.

法官頒發臨時禁令，防止開發商在國家公園內大興土木。

記憶技巧　tempo- 表示時間；-ary 為形容詞字尾；temporary 的意思是臨時的。

---

contemporary

[kənˋtɛmpəˏrɛrɪ]

n 同時代的人

Although Benjamin Franklin was not president, he was a famous contemporary of George Washington.

雖然班傑明・富蘭克林不是總統，但他是喬治・華盛頓同時代的名人。

記憶技巧　con- 表示一起；tempo- 表示時間；-ary 為形容詞字尾；contemporary 指的是同時間的；當名詞用時，指的是同時代的人。

---

extemporaneous

[ɛkˏstɛmpəˋrenɪəs]

a 即席的

After being surprised with an award, the designer gave an extemporaneous speech to thank the academy.

設計師驚喜獲獎後，即席發表演說感謝學會。

記憶技巧　ex- 表示離開；tempo- 表示時間；-ous 為形容詞字尾；extemporaneous 的意思是沒時間可準備，引申為即席的。

相關字彙　未經計劃

- accidental 偶然的
- coincidental 巧合的
- instinctive 本能的
- random 隨機的
- spontaneous 自發的

turn - turb

兩者雖無字源關係，但可藉由母音通轉來記憶，兩者皆表示翻轉。

---

disturb
[dɪs`tɝb]
v 擾亂，打擾

Exhausted from preparing the annual report, the director instructed the assistant to keep anyone from disturbing him.
準備年度報告精疲力盡，主管指示助理不要讓任何人打擾他。

記憶技巧　dis- 表示完全；turb- 表示翻轉；disturb 的意思是完全翻轉，引申為擾亂。

---

disturbance
[dɪs`tɝbəns]
n 騷動，擾亂

Greg didn't believe in ghosts, but he could not explain the nightly disturbances in the unoccupied apartment.
格雷格不信鬼，但無法解釋空盪公寓夜晚的騷動。

記憶技巧　-ance 為名詞字尾。

---

turbulent
[`tɝbjələnt]
a 騷動的，動亂的

The 1960's was a turbulent time, when civil society was actively calling for the end of the Vietnam war.
1960 年代是一個動盪時期，民間社會積極要求終止越戰。

記憶技巧　turb-，翻轉，-ent，形容詞字尾，turbulent 的意思是翻轉過來的，引申為騷動的。

---

troublesome
[`trʌbl̩səm]
a 麻煩的

The couple agreed to adopt the troublesome twin girls, even though they didn't have much of a home to offer.
即使他們能給得不太算是個家，夫婦同意領養那對令人頭痛的雙胞胎女孩。

記憶技巧　trouble 等同於 turb-，表示翻轉；-some 為形容詞字尾；troublesome 指的是去擾亂人家，讓其生活產生麻煩。

---

intestine - entero

母音通轉，兩者皆表示腸子。

---

enteritis
[ˌɛntə`raɪtɪs]
n 腸炎

The paramedics rushed the teenager to the emergency room, but instead of appendicitis, he had only enteritis.
醫務人員將青少年緊急送進急診室，但不是盲腸炎，只是腸炎。

記憶技巧　entero- 表示腸子；-itis 表示發炎；enteritis 即腸炎。

Part

2

CH 1
CH 2
CH 3
CH 4
CH 5

子音對應相同

| 相關字彙
特殊疾病 | ● Alzheimer's disease
　阿茲海默症
● anorexia 厭食
● anthrax 炭疽（病）
● beriberi 腳氣病 | ● cystitis 膀胱炎
● dengue fever 登革熱
● hemophilia 血友病
● Parkinson's disease
　帕金森氏病 | ● scurvy 壞血病
● silicosis 矽肺病
● yellow fever 黃熱病 |

enterotomy

[͵ɛntəˋrɑtəmɪ]

n 腸切開術，
腸解剖學

The doctor performed an enterotomy to release the swelling in the patient's intestines.

為了消除患者腸腫脹，醫生進行腸切除術。

記憶技巧 enter- 表示腸子；-tomy 表示切；enterotomy 即腸切開術。

turn - tour

母音通轉，兩者皆表示轉。

tour

[tʊr]

n 旅行，巡迴演出，
巡迴醫療

While the lower-level employees were being trained, the executives were given a personal tour of a winery.

低階員工受訓時，主管被招待到一處釀酒廠進行私人旅遊。

記憶技巧 tour 表示轉，意思是出去轉一圈，引申為旅行。

tourism

[ˋtʊrɪzəm]

n 觀光業

The island in the South Seas relies on tourism to attract most of its foreign capital.

這個南海島嶼依賴旅遊業吸引大部分的外資。

記憶技巧 -ism 為名詞字尾。

tourist

[ˋtʊrɪst]

n 觀光客

The hotel manager instructed his employees to put themselves in the shoes of the tourists when handling a complaint.

酒店經理指示員工處理客訴時要設身處地為遊客著想。

記憶技巧 tour 表示轉；-ist 表示人；tourist 即觀光客。

tournament

[ˋtɝnəmənt]

n 錦標賽

The schools organized a basketball tournament fielding teams from throughout the country.

這些學校規劃一場籃球錦標賽，讓全國各地的隊伍參加。

記憶技巧 tourn- 等同於 turn，表示轉；-ment 為名詞字尾；
tournament 本指在馬背上的騎士，騎著馬繞圈進行決鬥，
1761 年才有錦標賽的意思。

detour

[`ditur]

v 迂迴，繞道

There was an accident in the tunnel, so traffic was detoured to an adjacent bridge.

隧道發生車禍，因此車輛繞道至鄰近橋樑。

> **記憶技巧** de- 表示旁邊；tour 表示轉；detour 的字面上意思是轉到旁邊，引申為繞道。

---

turn - trop

兩者雖無字源關係，但可藉由母音通轉來記憶，兩者皆表示轉。

---

tropical

[`trɑpɪkl]

a 熱帶的

Indonesia is a tropical country that has a wealth of resources and the largest population of Muslims in the world.

印尼是一個熱帶國家，擁有豐富資源和世界最大穆斯林人口。

> **記憶技巧** trop- 表示轉；tropic 本指太陽在天空南、北兩個端點間移動，太陽走到某一端點，就折返、轉回去；tropical 到 1837 年才有熱帶的引申義。

相關字彙
溫暖、熱的

- burning 火熱的
- boiling 沸騰的
- balmy 溫和的
- mild 溫和的
- overheated 過熱的
- scorching 灼熱的
- scalding 滾燙的

---

subtropical

[sʌb`trɑpɪkl]

a 亞熱帶的

Taiwan sits in the subtropical zone, having an ideal climate to grow peaches and papayas.

台灣坐落在亞熱帶地區，擁有種植桃子和木瓜的理想氣候。

> **記憶技巧** sub- 表示在～之下；subtropical 即亞熱帶的。

---

heliotropism

[ˌhiliˋɑtrəpɪzm̩]

n 向日性

During the winter months, it is easier to see the heliotropism exhibited by sunflowers.

冬季時，較容易看到向日葵呈現的向日性。

> **記憶技巧** helio- 表示太陽；trop- 表示轉；-ism 為名詞字尾；heliotropism 的意思是轉向太陽，即向日性。

---

hydrotropism

[haɪˋdrɑtrəˌpɪzəm]

n 向水性

Due to the hydrotropism of the cactus roots, one can follow them to the source of water.

仙人掌根擁有向水性，可以跟著它們找到水源。

> **記憶技巧** hydro- 表示水；trop- 表示轉；-ism 為名詞字尾；hydrotropism 的意思是轉向水，即向水性。

trophy

[`trofɪ]

n 獎品,戰利品

The woman was 20 years younger than her husband and was considered by many to be a trophy wife.

女子比丈夫年輕 20 歲,許多人認為是一個花瓶妻子。

記憶技巧 troph- 表示轉;trophy 本來的意思是敵人戰敗,轉頭就逃所遺留下的東西,後當戰利品解釋。

Part 2
CH 1
CH 2
CH 3
CH 4
CH 5
子音對應相同

Section **8**

〔n〕對應〔n〕

---

no - ne / neg

母音通轉,兩者皆表示非、不、無。

negative

[`nɛɡətɪv]

a 消極的,陰性的

If you want a promotion, it is best to avoid having a negative attitude about your job.

如果想升遷,最好避免對工作有負面的態度。

記憶技巧 neg- 表示不;-ive 為形容詞字尾;negative 的意思不是正向的,而是消極的。

neglect

[nɪɡ`lɛkt]

n 疏忽,忽略,怠慢

After years of neglect and disrepair, the old school was overrun by wild plant and animal life.

多年的忽略和失修,老學校到處可見野生植物及動物。

記憶技巧 neg- 表示不;lect- 表示挑選;neglect 的字面意思是不挑選,引申為忽略。

negligence

[`nɛɡlɪdʒəns]

n 怠慢

Their child was hit by truck, and the parents were punished for their negligence.

小孩被卡車撞上,家長因疏忽而受到懲罰。

記憶技巧 neg- 表示不;lig- 等同於 lect-,表示挑選;-ence 為名詞字尾;negligence 的意思是不挑選,引申為怠慢。

相關字彙
專注、不專注

- absent 心不在焉的
- inattentive 不注意的
- preoccupied 全神貫注的
- neglectful 不注意的

neglectful
[nɪgˋlɛktfəl]
a 疏忽的，冷淡的

The toddler was locked in the apartment for the entire day by his neglectful parents.
孩子被疏忽的父母鎖在公寓一整天。

記憶技巧　neg- 表示不；lect- 表示挑選；-ful 為形容詞字尾；neglectful 意思是沒挑到的，引申為疏忽的。

negligible
[ˋnɛglɪdʒəbḷ]
a 可忽視的，
　　不足取的

The survey results had a sample size of 10,000, providing a negligible margin of error.
調查結果的樣本量為 10,000，誤差幅度可忽略。

記憶技巧　neg- 表示不；lig- 等同於 lect-，表示挑選；-ible 為形容詞字尾；negligible 字面上意思是沒挑到的，引為可忽視的。

negotiation
[nɪͺgoʃɪˋeʃən]
n 交涉，商議

The business negotiation began with each party stating their demands within the contract.
商業談判在各方陳述對合同的要求中展開序幕。

記憶技巧　neg- 表示不；oti- 表示輕鬆；-ation 為名詞字尾；negotiation 的字面上意思是缺乏輕鬆，引申為交涉、商議這些不輕鬆的事情。

---

no - nihil
母音通轉，兩者皆表示非、不、無。

---

nihilistic
[ͺnaɪəˋlɪstɪk]
a 虛無論的

The nihilistic man lay in a coma after drinking and driving off a bridge.
虛無主義的男子酒駕落下一座橋之後，陷入昏迷。

記憶技巧　nihil- 表示無；-ist 表示主義；-ic 為形容詞字尾；nihilistic 即虛無主義的。

相關字彙
無宗教信仰或不神聖

- secular 世俗的
- agnostic 不可知論的
- unorthodox 非正統的
- atheist 無神論者
- heretic 異教徒

annihilate
[əˋnaɪəͺlet]
v 毀滅，消滅

The movie centers around a plot in which an alien race prepares to annihilate all human beings.
電影繞著外星人準備消滅全人類的情節打轉。

記憶技巧　an- 等同於 ad-，表示朝～方向；nihil- 表示無；-ate 為動詞字尾；annihilate 的意思是使一切化為虛無，引申為毀滅。

no - null
母音通轉，兩者皆表示非、不、無。

null
[nʌl]
a 無效的

If there is a null value in the database field, there will be no data displayed in the program.
如果數據庫欄位出現一個空值，程式將不顯示任何數據。

記憶技巧 null 的意思是無效的。

nullify
[ˋnʌləˏfaɪ]
v 取消，使無效

The committee voted to nullify the results of the election after evidence was found of vote tampering.
發現投票篡改的證據後，委員會投票決定選舉結果無效。

記憶技巧 null- 表示無效；-fy 為動詞字尾；nullify 的意思是使無效。

annul
[əˋnʌl]
v 取消，作廢

After getting married over the weekend to a total stranger, the young man returned to Las Vegas to annul the marriage.
周末和一個完全陌生的人結婚後，年輕人回到拉斯維加斯取消婚姻。

記憶技巧 an- 等同於 ad-，表示往～方向；nul- 表示無；annul 的意思是使～空無，引申為作廢。

name - nomin
母音通轉，兩者皆表示名字。

cognomen
[kɑgˋnomən]
n 姓氏，綽號

In ancient Rome, several notable figures were named Brutus, which was a cognomen of the Roman family, Junia.
古羅馬時代，幾位著名的人物被命名為布魯圖斯，這是羅馬家族，朱尼亞的姓氏。

記憶技巧 cog- 等同於 con-，表示一起；omen- 等同於 nomin-，表示名字；cognomen 的意思是和名字放在一起的姓氏。

misnomer
[ˏmɪsˋnomɚ]
n 誤稱

The word "starfish" is a misnomer, the creature neither being a heavenly body nor a fish.
「海星」這個詞是一個誤稱，該生物既不是星體，也不是魚。

記憶技巧 mis- 表示錯誤；misnomer 即錯誤的稱呼。

Part
2
CH 1
CH 2
CH 3
CH 4
CH 5

子音對應相同

ignominious

[ˌɪgnə`mɪnɪəs]

a 不名譽的

When the bold, polarizing leader won the election, the opposition party supporters wallowed in ignominious defeat.

大膽又極端派的領導人贏得選舉時，反對黨支持者陷入敗選的恥辱中。

記憶技巧　ig- 等同於 in-，表示不；nomin- 表示名字；-ous 為形容詞字尾；ignominious 的意思是不名譽的、沒有好名聲的。

相關字彙　令人尷尬、羞愧

- awkward 尷尬的
- embarrassing 令人尷尬的
- humiliating 恥辱的
- shameful 可恥的

nominate

[`namə,net]

v 提名，任命，指派

The raucous crowd cheered as the popular politician was nominated to run as the presidential candidate.

因受歡迎的政治人物被提名為總統候選人時，喧囂的群眾一陣歡呼。

記憶技巧　nomin- 表示名字；-ate 為動詞字尾；nominate 的意思是提名。

nominal

[`namən!]

a 名義上的

The salesman explained that a protective sealant can be sprayed on the bottom of the car for a nominal fee.

銷售員說明保護密封劑可噴灑在汽車底部，只收取象徵性的費用。

記憶技巧　nomin- 表示名字；-al 為形容詞字尾；nominal 的意思是名義上的。

nominator

[`namə,netɚ]

n 提名人，任命人，推薦人

The nominator of every class leader is always the homeroom teacher.

每位班長的提名者一向都是導師。

記憶技巧　-or 表示做出動作者；nominator 即提名人。

nominee

[,namə`ni]

n 被提名人，被任命人

Senator Bernie Sanders was a popular Democratic Party nominee in the 2016 Presidential Election.

參議員伯尼‧桑德斯是 2016 年總統選舉中受歡迎的民主黨被提名人。

記憶技巧　-ee 表示動作接受者；nominee 即被提名人。

相關字彙　各種活動參與者、競爭者

- candidate 候選人
- competitor 競爭者
- contestant 角逐者
- contender 競爭者
- rival 敵手
- runner-up（競賽中的）第二名
- teammate 隊友
- underdog 競爭失敗的人

name - onym

母音通轉，添加母音，兩者皆表示名字。

---

anonymous

[əˋnɑnəməs]

a 匿名的，假名的

The donor who made the generous donation that saved the orphanage chose to remain anonymous.

慷慨捐款拯救孤兒院的捐贈者選擇保持匿名。

記憶技巧 an- 表示無；onym- 表示名字；-ous 為形容詞字尾；anonymous 的意思是不顯露名字的，即匿名的。

---

pseudonym

[ˋsudn̩͵ɪm]

n 假名，筆名

J. K. Rowling is the pseudonym used by Joanne Rowling, the author of the "*Harry Potter*" series.

J. K. 羅琳是喬安妮・羅琳使用的筆名——《哈利波特》系列的作者。

記憶技巧 pseudo- 表示假；-onym 表示名字；pseudonym 即假名。

相關字彙 姓名稱呼
- appellation 名稱
- designation 命名
- epithet 稱號
- forename 在姓前面的名
- nickname 渾名
- surname 綽號

---

antonym

[ˋæntə͵nɪm]

n 反義詞

The retired banker was extremely greedy, the antonym of generous.

退休銀行家極度貪婪，是慷慨的相反。

記憶技巧 anti- 表示相反；-onym 表示名字；antonym 做反義詞解釋。

---

synonym

[ˋsɪnə͵nɪm]

n 同義詞

The man gave compliments to the woman, describing her as pretty, beautiful, and other synonyms.

男子讚美女子，形容她是漂亮、美麗和其他同義詞。

記憶技巧 syn- 表示相同；-onym 表示名字；synonym 的意思是同義詞。

---

acronym

[ˋækrənɪm]

n 頭字詞

The space agency in China is CNSA, which is an acronym for China National Space Agency.

中國太空部門是 CNSA，中國國家太空總署的首字母縮寫。

記憶技巧 acro- 表示尖、高、最突出的；-onym 表示名字；acronym 的意思是由數個單詞的第一個字母合併而成，即頭前詞。

相關字彙 常見縮寫
- BAU = business as usual 一切正常
- cf. = compare with〔拉〕參見
- cont. = continue 繼續
- dept. = department 科系
- e.g. = exempli gratia〔拉〕例如
- esp. = especially 尤其
- ibid. = ibidem〔拉〕出處同上
- Rep. = representative 代表

number - numer

母音通轉，子音省略，兩者皆表示數字。

---

numeral

[ˋnjumərəl]

a 數字的

The Hindu numeral system uses a symbolic representation of numbers developed in India.

印度數字系統使用印度發展出來的數字符號圖像。

記憶技巧 numer- 表示數字；-al 為形容詞字尾；numeral 即數字的。

---

numerous

[ˋnjumərəs]

a 眾多的

The chief executive resigned under the pressure of numerous accusations of infidelity.

執行長在許多不忠誠的指控壓力下辭職。

記憶技巧 numer- 表示數字；-ous 為形容詞字尾；numerous 表示眾多的意思。

---

supernumerary

[ˌsupəˋnjuməˌrɛrɪ]

n 冗員，臨時人員

With an unusually small body, the man was often cast as a supernumerary in sci-fi movies.

男子身軀異常的瘦小，經常被選派為科幻電影臨時演員。

記憶技巧 super- 表示超過；numer- 表示數字；-ary 為形容詞字尾；supernumerary 本指多於出來的，1630 年代之後才有名詞用法。

nose - nas

母音通轉，兩者皆表示鼻子。

---

nasal

[ˋnezl]

a 鼻腔的，鼻音的

The taste tester could not perform his duties on days when his nasal cavities were congested.

味道測試者鼻塞的那幾天無法執行職務。

記憶技巧 nas- 表示鼻子；-al 為形容詞字尾；nasal 即鼻腔的、鼻音的。

---

nostril

[ˋnɑstrɪl]

n 鼻孔

The agent identified the rebel as the one brandishing a silver ring in his pierced nostril.

密探認出叛亂者是一個鼻孔穿閃亮亮銀戒的人。

記憶技巧 nos- 表示鼻子；tril- 表示穿孔；nostril 即鼻孔。

naked - nud

母音通轉，兩者皆表示裸的。

Part

2

CH 1
CH 2
CH 3
CH 4
CH 5

子音對應相同

nude
[njud]
a 裸的，與生俱有的

When nude photos of the candidate's wife were revealed to the press, his chances of winning the election dwindled.

妻子裸照被爆料時，候選人勝選的機會變小了。

記憶技巧 nude 即裸的。

nudophobia
[ˌnjudoˈfobɪə]
n 裸體恐懼症

Mark never attended in PE class, because his nudophobia prevented him from taking showers at school.

馬克從未上體育課，因為他的裸體恐懼症讓他無法在學校洗澡。

記憶技巧 nud- 表示裸的；-phobia 表示恐懼症；nudophobia 即裸體恐懼症。

相關字彙
恐懼
- apprehension 恐懼
- alarm 恐懼
- fright 恐怖
- horror 震驚
- panic 恐慌

night - noct

母音通轉，兩者皆表示夜。

nocturnal
[nakˈtɝnl̩]
a 夜晚的，夜行性的

The woman enjoyed a nocturnal lifestyle, choosing night shifts throughout her career.

女子享受夜生活，整個職業生涯中都選擇夜班工作。

記憶技巧 noct- 表示夜；-al 為形容詞字尾；nocturnal 的意思是夜行的。

equinox
[ˈikwəˌnɑks]
n 春分

The vernal and autumnal equinoxes are the two times of the year when day and night are approximately equal in length everywhere on earth.

春分和秋分是一年中白天和黑夜在地球各地長度大約相等的兩個時期。

記憶技巧 equi- 表示相等；nox- 表示夜；equinox 的意思是日夜等長，即春分、秋分。

noctambulist

[nɑkˋtæmbjəˌlɪst]

n 夢遊者

The woman, who was a known noctambulist, was not allowed to sleep on the second floor of the house.

這名女子已知是夢遊者，不准睡在房子二樓。

記憶技巧　noct- 表示夜；ambul- 表示走路；-ist 表示人；noctambulist 的意思是夜間起來走路的人，即夢遊者。

noctilucent

[ˌnɑktəˋlusənt]

a 夜間發光的

The campers knew sunrise was coming soon, because the clouds in the horizon became noctilucent.

露營者知道日出即將到來，因為地平線上的雲在夜間發光。

記憶技巧　noct- 表示夜；luc- 表示光；-ent 為形容詞字尾；noctilucent 的意思即是夜間發光的。

相關字彙　各種光

- candlelight 燭光
- gaslight 瓦斯燈
- glow 白熱光
- lamplight 燈光
- spotlight 聚光燈
- sunbeam 日光
- torchlight 火炬光

---

nine - non

母音通轉，兩者皆表示九。

nonagon

[ˋnɑnəˌgɑn]

n 九邊形，九角形

A company called "Cloud Nine" made a unique umbrella in the shape of a nonagon.

一家名為「樂不可支」的公司造出一個獨特的九邊形雨傘。

記憶技巧　non- 表示九；gon- 表示角；nonagon 即九角形。

---

nine - novem

母音通轉，兩者皆表示九。

November

[noˋvɛmbɚ]

n 十一月

November is not a bad time to visit Orchid Island, because it isn't too cold and the typhoon season is over.

11 月是到蘭嶼玩的好時節，不會太冷，颱風季節也結束。

記憶技巧　novem- 表示九；-ber 表示月份；November 是羅馬舊曆中的九月，曆法改革後往後延兩個月，在新曆中變成十一月。

nine - ennea

母音通轉，添加母音，兩者皆表示九。

---

enneagon

[ˋɛnɪəˏgɑn]

n 九角形

Another name for a nine-sided shape, or nonagon, is enneagon.

九個邊的形狀或九邊形另一名稱是九角形。

記憶技巧 ennea 表示九；gon- 表示角；enneagon 即九角形。

---

enneahedron

[ˏɛnɪəˋhidrən]

n 九面體

The natural blue diamond was found in the shape of an enneahedron, or a shape with nine planar faces.

天然藍鑽石被發現是九面體，就是有九個平面的形狀。

記憶技巧 ennea-表示九；-hedron 表示面；enneahedron 即九面體。

---

nurture - nutri

rt 音素互換，兩字母順序對調變成 tr，因此 nurt 變成 nutr，兩者皆表示營養。

---

nutrient

[ˋnjutrɪənt]

n 營養物

Seafood farms are booming as more people seek iodine, an important nutrient, in their diets.

海鮮養殖場蓬勃發展，因為更多人尋求飲食中的碘，一種重要營養素。

記憶技巧 nutri- 表示營養；nutrient 即營養物。

---

nutrition

[njuˋtrɪʃən]

n 營養，營養學

Some believe that all health professionals should be required to have a better understanding of nutrition.

有些人認為應該要求所有健康專業人員更加了解營養學。

記憶技巧 nutri- 表示營養；-ion 為名詞字尾；nutrition 即營養。

---

malnutrition

[ˏmælnjuˋtrɪʃən]

n 營養不良

While you sit there eating steak and lobster, you should think of the millions of children who suffer from malnutrition.

你坐在那裡大啖牛排和龍蝦時，應該想到數百萬營養不良的兒童。

記憶技巧 mal- 表示不好的、壞的；nutrition 表示營養；malnutrition 即營養不良。

Part 2

CH 1
CH 2
CH 3
CH 4
CH 5

子音對應相同

nutritious

[njuˋtrɪʃəs]

a 營養的

It is believed that the people of a Japanese island live long lives because of their nutritious plant-based diets.

普遍相信，一座日本島嶼上的人民長壽的原因是營養的植物性飲食。

> **記憶技巧** -ous 為形容詞字尾；nutritious 即營養的。

Section **9**

〔1〕 對應 〔1〕

---

light - lumin

母音通轉，兩者皆表示光、明亮。

---

illuminate

[ɪˋlumə͵net]

v 照明

The LED projector displayed the Powerpoint presentation on the screen and illuminated the colleagues' faces.

LED 投影機在螢幕上顯示 Powerpoint 簡報，同時照亮同事們的面部。

> **記憶技巧** il- 等同於 in-，lumin- 表示光；-ate 為動詞字尾；illuminate 即內部發光，引申為照明、說明。

相關字彙
散發光芒

- shine 發光
- glow 發白熱光
- flash 使閃光
- flare 閃亮
- gleam 發微光
- sparkle 閃耀
- glare 眩目地照射
- blaze 閃耀

---

luminiferous

[͵luməˋnɪfərəs]

a 發光的

The full moon cast a luminiferous shine on the meadow, making it easy to see the deer.

滿月在草地上發出光芒，讓鹿容易被看到。

> **記憶技巧** lumin- 表示光；fer- 表示帶來；-ous 為形容詞字尾；luminiferous 指帶來光亮的。

---

luminescence

[͵luməˋnɛsn̩s]

n 螢光

Strolling at night on Green Island, the man and his wife marveled at the luminescence in the surf.

夜裡漫步在綠島，男子和妻子對螢光的海浪驚嘆不已。

> **記憶技巧** lumin- 表示光；-escence 表示狀態；luminescence 的意思是發光的狀態，現指螢光。

light - luc

母音通轉，兩者皆表示光、明亮。

Part
2
CH 1
CH 2
CH 3
CH 4
CH 5

子音對應相同

---

lucid
[`lusɪd]
a 透明的，清楚的

The man was convinced he saw an oasis, but it was only a lucid mirage.
男子相信自己看到一片綠洲，但只是一個清晰的海市蜃樓。

> **記憶技巧** luc- 表示發光；-id 為形容詞字尾；lucid 的意思是發光的，引申為清楚的。

---

elucidate
[ɪ`lusə‚det]
v 說明，闡明

It is important to attend this meeting to elucidate the reasoning behind closing the company.
參加這次會議來說明公司結束經營的背後理由，這很重要。

> **記憶技巧** e- 等同於 ex-，表示外面；lucid 表示清楚的；-ate 為動詞字尾；elucidate 即闡明。

---

translucent
[træns`lusn̩t]
a 半透明的

The new species of fish found in the dark cave was translucent, so it is amazing that the fish were spotted.
黑暗洞穴中發現的新魚種是半透明的，因此這種魚被看見真是十分驚奇。

> **記憶技巧** trans- 表示穿透；luc- 表示光；-ent 為形容詞字尾；translucent 的意思是光能穿透的，引申為半透明的。

---

illustrious
[ɪ`lʌstrɪəs]
a 顯著的

The Major didn't have the illustrious career that his superior had, but he earned the loyalty of his subordinates.
少校沒有上司的傑出職業生涯，但贏得下屬的忠誠。

> **記憶技巧** il- 等同於 in-，表示內；lustr- 表示光；-ous 為形容詞字尾；illustrious 的意思是內部有光，引申出顯著的意思。

---

illustrate
[`ɪləstret]
v 圖解，舉例說明

If you're an author, it is important to choose the right artist to illustrate your book.
如果你是一位作家，應該要選擇適合的藝術家幫你的書插畫。

> **記憶技巧** il- 等同於 in-，表示內；lustr- 表示光；-ate 為動詞字尾；illustrate 即內部照光，使之可以看清楚，引申為舉例說明。

相關字彙
描述
- describe 描述
- delineate 畫～的輪廓
- exemplify 例示
- profile 給～畫側面像

leaf - libr

母音通轉，兩者皆表示書頁、書。

---

library
[ˋlaɪͺbrɛrɪ]
n 圖書館，書房

The retired professor buried himself in his personal library for days at a time.
退休教授埋首在個人圖書館裡，一次長達好幾天。

記憶技巧 libr- 表示書；-ary 為名詞字尾；library 即圖書館。

---

librarian
[laɪˋbrɛrɪən]
n 圖書館員

Fascinated by factual and fictional stories, the woman had a satisfying career as a librarian.
著迷於真實和虛構故事，女子有一份令她滿意的圖書館員職業。

記憶技巧 -an 表示人。

---

libretto
[lɪˋbrɛto]
n 歌劇劇本

The songwriter took up the challenge of writing a libretto for a new modern opera production.
歌曲作家接受挑戰，為一齣新現代歌劇作品寫歌劇劇本。

記憶技巧 libr- 表示書；libretto 是歌劇劇本。

---

libel
[ˋlaɪbḷ]
n 誹謗，諷刺

The presidential candidate sued the famous newspaper for libel, after it published a story he claimed to be false.
總統候選人在知名報社發表其聲稱為子虛烏有的報導後，提起誹謗告訴。

記憶技巧 lib- 表示書；libel 原本是原告書面上的指控，後當毀謗解釋。

相關字彙
各種犯罪行為
- bigamy 重婚（罪）
- blackmail 敲詐
- fraud 騙局
- human trafficking 人口販賣
- slander 誹謗罪
- smuggling 走私
- solicitation 教唆罪
- treason 謀反罪
- recidivism 再犯

猜猜看！

「biology（生物學）」中的 logy 表示「學說」，猜一相關單字？

答案：logic（邏輯）

loose - lax

兩者雖無字源關係，帶可藉由母音通轉來記憶，兩者皆表示鬆。

lax

[læks]

ⓐ 鬆弛的，含糊的，放縱的

After a series of acts of vandalism, the principal met with the teachers to declare that the school rules were too lax.

一連串故意破壞公物的行為之後，校長會見老師，宣布校規太寬鬆。

記憶技巧　lax 即鬆的。

relax

[rɪˋlæks]

ⓥ 放鬆，減輕，緩和

The spa offered a sauna and massage package designed to help customers to relax and rejuvenate.

SPA 提供設計專為幫助客人緩壓及回復青春的三溫暖及按摩套裝服務。

記憶技巧　re- 表示後面；lax- 表示鬆；relax 即放鬆。

loose - lys

母音通轉，兩者皆表示鬆。

analysis

[əˋnæləsɪs]

ⓝ 分解，分析，解析

The analysis presented by the analyst showed that the company health insurance expenditures were extremely high.

分析師提出的分析顯示，公司的醫療保險支出非常高。

記憶技巧　ana- 即從頭到尾；lys- 表示鬆開；analysis 的意思是將內部結構鬆解，引申為分析。

analyze

[ˋænlͺaɪz]

ⓥ 分解，分析，解析

The lie detector machine helped investigators to analyze patterns in the voice to detect stress.

測謊機協助調查人員分析聲音模式偵測壓力。

記憶技巧　analyze 是 analysis 的動詞。

analytical

[ͺænlˋɪtɪkl̩]

ⓐ 分解的，分析的

The woman told the man that he was being too analytical about her invitation to attend a movie with her.

女子告訴男子，對於她要他一起看電影的邀約，他想太多了。

記憶技巧　-al 為形容詞字尾。

Part

2

CH 1
CH 2
CH 3
CH 4
CH 5

子音對應相同

paralysis
[pə`ræləsɪs]
n 麻痺，中風，無力

The sting from a box jellyfish is severe enough to cause temporary paralysis, which can drown swimmers.
箱形水母的蜇刺劇毒足以造成暫時麻痺，會使被蜇的泳者溺水。

記憶技巧　para- 表示旁邊；lys- 表示鬆；paralysis 即周身無力，引申為麻痺、中風。

---

lean - climo
母音通轉，添加子音，兩者皆表示傾斜、倚靠。

---

climax
[`klaɪmæks]
n 頂點，高潮

In the climax of the movie, the hero is surrounded by an army of robots before the commandos arrive.
這部電影最高潮處，主角在突擊隊員到達之前被機器人軍隊包圍。

記憶技巧　climo- 表示倚靠，在此當靠在牆上的梯子解釋；climax 本指一步一步沿著梯子往上爬，爬到最高點，引申為高潮。

相關字彙　轉折點
- highlights 最突出（或最精彩）的部分
- milestone 劃時代的事件
- peak 最高點
- turning point 轉折點
- watershed 轉折點

---

climate
[`klaɪmɪt]
n 氣候，風土

The rare cigars are safe within the glass humidor, which contains a carefully-controlled climate.
稀有雪茄在玻璃保濕盒內是安全的，內置精控保濕空調。

記憶技巧　climo- 表示傾斜；climate 本指傾斜的平面，早期地理學家用太陽照在地球表面的角度來劃分不同氣候區，後指氣候。

相關字彙　天候
- meteorology 氣象學
- spell（某種天氣的）一段持續時間
- temperate 溫和的
- weather forecast 氣象預報

---

climatology
[ˌklaɪməˋtɑlədʒɪ]
n 氣候學

The climatology experts study many natural and man-made factors that affect the Earth's environment.
氣候學專家研究許多影響地球環境的自然和人為因素。

記憶技巧　-logy 表示學；climatology 即氣候學。

length - long
母音通轉，兩者皆表示長。

longitude
[`lɑndʒəˌtjud]
n 經線，經度

The International Date Line is located at 180 degrees longitude, which is on the opposite side of the Prime Meridian.
國際換日線位於 180 度經度，本初子午線對面。

記憶技巧 long- 表示長；-tude 為名詞字尾；longitude 指的是經線。

longevity
[lɑn`dʒɛvətɪ]
n 長壽，資歷

Galapagos turtles are known for their size as well as their longevity.
加拉帕戈斯龜以體型及長壽聞名。

記憶技巧 long- 表示長；ev- 表示年紀；-ity 為名詞字尾；longevity 的意思是長壽。

along
[ə`lɔŋ]
prep 順著，沿著

Over 14 dams have been constructed along the path of the Yellow River in China.
中國黃河沿岸建造了超過 14 座水壩。

記憶技巧 a- 是 ante- 表示前面；long- 表示長；along 的本意是前面的長度，衍生意思有沿著、成一行地等意思。

belong
[bə`lɔŋ]
v 屬於

The police were called to the library to find out who the abandoned baby belonged to.
警方被叫到圖書館，要找出棄嬰是誰的。

記憶技巧 be- 表示加強語氣；long- 表示長，在此有 along（一起的意思）；belong 的字面意思是伴隨著某人，引申為屬於。

elongate
[ɪ`lɔŋˌget]
v 拉長，伸長，延長

The entertainer elongated three balloons and twisted them together to form the shape of a giraffe.
藝人拉長三個氣球，扭曲在一起，形成長頸鹿的形狀。

記憶技巧 e- 等同於 ex-，表示外面；long- 表示長；-ate 為動詞字尾；elongate 的意思是往外伸長。

oblong
[`ɑblɔŋ]
a 長方形的，橢圓形的

In the early 20th Century, oblong airships transported people through the skies in luxury.
20 世紀初，長方形飛艇豪奢地載著客人飛過天空。

記憶技巧 ob- 表示加強語氣；long- 表示長；oblong 的原始語意是很長，語意轉變，後來才作長方形的、橢圓形的來解釋。

Part **2**
CH 1
CH 2
CH 3
CH 4
CH 5

子音對應相同

prolong
[prə`lɔŋ]

v 延長，引伸

The television program was cut off prematurely, prolonging the suspense until the next broadcast.

電視節目提前中斷，延長懸疑至下一集。

記憶技巧 pro- 表示往前；long- 表示長；prolong 的意思是往前延長。

---

language - lingu

母音通轉，兩者皆表示語言。和 tongue 亦是同源字，藉由子音 d 和 t 互換，母音通轉，即可記憶 lingu 這個字根。

---

bilingual
[baɪ`lɪŋgwəl]

a 雙語的

The family moved overseas to give their children the ability to become truly bilingual students.

為了給孩子成為真正雙語學生的能力，全家移居海外。

記憶技巧 bi- 表示雙；lingu- 表示語言；-al 為形容詞字尾；bilingual 即雙語的。

---

linguist
[`lɪŋgwɪst]

n 語言學家，通曉多種外國語的人

The linguist noticed similarities in the phonetics and language patterns of the Taiwanese and Filipino tribes.

語言學家注意到台灣人和菲律賓部落在語音和語言模式的相似之處。

記憶技巧 lingu- 表示語言；-ist 為做～者；linguist 是語言學家。

---

monolingual
[ˌmɑnə`lɪŋgwəl]

a 單語言的

The foreign national refused to learn the native language, holding on to his monolingual preferences.

外籍人士拒絕學習本土語言，堅持自己的單語偏好。

記憶技巧 mono- 表示單一；lingu- 表示語言；-al 為形容詞字尾；monolingual 即單語言的。

相關字彙
語言的使用

- fluency 流暢
- polyglot 通曉多種語言的
- trilingual 能講三種語言的

---

multilingual
[`mʌltɪ`lɪŋgwəl]

a（會）多種語言的

With a rich variety of languages in Taiwan, its citizens are most likely to be multilingual.

台灣語種多樣，民眾很有可能會說多語。

記憶技巧 multi- 表示許多；lingu- 表示語言；-al 為形容詞字尾；multilingual 是多種語言的。

line - lin
母音通轉，兩者皆表示（亞麻）線。

linen
[`lınən]
n 亞麻布

The girl lay on the cool, soft linens on her bed in the British summer cottage.
在英國夏季別墅，女孩躺床上的涼爽柔軟的亞麻布上。

記憶技巧　lin- 表示亞麻線；linen 即亞麻布。

linoleum
[lı`nolıəm]
n 油布

The builder chose linoleum flooring for the home because of its durability and relative affordability.
因為耐久性和相對便宜，建商為房子選用油布地板材料。

記憶技巧　lin- 表示亞麻；-oleum 表示油；linoleum 是油布。

linseed
[`lın‚sid]
n 亞麻子

The retiree followed a daily regimen of consuming linseed oil in order to reduce cholesterol levels.
為了降低膽固醇，退休者遵循每日服用亞麻子油的養生之道。

記憶技巧　lin- 表示亞麻；seed 表示種子；linseed 即亞麻子。

limit - limin
母音通轉，兩者皆表示門檻、限制。

eliminate
[ı`lımə‚net]
v 排除

Many older people eat kale and drink its nutritious juice to eliminate feces in the bowels.
為了消除腸子糞便，許多老年人吃羽衣甘藍並喝它的營養湯汁。

記憶技巧　e- 等同於 ex-，表示外面；limin- 表示門檻；-ate 為動詞字尾；eliminate 的意思是屏除在門檻之外，引申為排除。

elimination
[ı‚lımə`neʃən]
n 排除，淘汰，預賽

The elimination of his political opponents was the top priority of the incoming leader.
消除政治反對派是新任領導人的最優先要務。

記憶技巧　-ion 為名詞字尾。

Part **2**

CH 1
CH 2
CH 3
CH 4
CH 5

子音對應相同

preliminary

[prɪˈlɪməˌnɛrɪ]

a 初步的，預備的

The preliminary report from headquarters indicated that there would be a reduction in the company's workforce.

總部的初步報告指出，公司人力將減少。

> 記憶技巧　pre- 表示在～之前；limin- 表示門檻；-ary 為形容詞字尾；preliminary 的意思是在門檻之前，引申為初步的。

---

letter - liter
母音通轉，兩者皆表示文字。

---

literal

[ˈlɪtərəl]

a 文字的，
逐字逐句的

There is a literal war occurring over the ownership of the Middle Eastern oil fields.

關於中東油田所有權的筆戰正炒得沸沸揚揚。

> 記憶技巧　liter- 表示文字；-al 為形容詞字尾；literal 即文字的、逐字的。

---

literally

[ˈlɪtərəlɪ]

ad 照字義，逐字地，
實在地

There are literally millions of users logging into the social networking web site every day.

每天確實有數百萬用戶登錄社交網站。

> 記憶技巧　-ly 為副詞字尾。

---

literary

[ˈlɪtəˌrɛrɪ]

a 文學的，著作的

Long before they became popular movies, the "*Lord of the Rings*" series of books were considered literary gems.

拍成賣座電影很久以前，《魔戒》系列書就被認為是文學珍寶。

> 記憶技巧　liter- 表示文字、文學；-ary 為形容詞字尾；literary 是文學的。

---

illiterate

[ɪˈlɪtərɪt]

a 未受教育的，
文盲的

Where there are a large number of illiterate citizens, there is usually a wide income gap.

文盲公民人數眾多的國家，收入差距通常很大。

> 記憶技巧　il- 為否定字首；liter- 表示文字；-ate 為形容詞字尾；illiterate 的意思是不識字的，即文盲的。

相關字彙
缺乏經驗、教育水平低的

- inexperienced 不熟練的
- uneducated 未受教育的
- untrained 未受訓練的
- unskilled 不熟練的

transliterate
[træns`lɪtə‚ret]
v 音譯，直譯

Many Chinese language instruction books transliterate Chinese text into pinyin writing to aid foreign students.

為了幫助外國學生，許多中文教學書籍將中文課文直譯成拼音。

記憶技巧　trans- 表示跨越；liter- 表示文字；-ate 為動詞字尾；transliterate 是將文字從來源語直譯或音譯到目標語。

相關字彙
翻譯
- interpret 口譯
- target language 目標語言
- transcribe 抄寫
- translate 轉譯
- source language 來源語言

island - insul
兩者並無字源關係，但可藉由母音通轉來記憶，兩者皆表示島嶼。

peninsula
[pə`nɪnsələ]
n 半島

Parts of the Shandong Peninsula of China were controlled by Germany and were handed over to Japan after the war.

中國山東半島部分受德國控制，戰後交給日本。

記憶技巧　pen- 表示幾乎；insul- 表示島嶼；peninsula 的意思是幾乎是島嶼，引申為半島。

insular
[`ɪnsələ]
a 島嶼的，偏狹的

Due to the insular nature of the country of Bhutan, its people know very little of the outside world.

不丹地處偏僻，人民對外部世界幾乎一無所知。

記憶技巧　insul- 表示島嶼；-ar 為形容詞字尾；insular 即島嶼的，引申為偏狹的。

insulate
[`ɪnsə‚let]
v 絕緣，隔離

Even though they were poor, the parents did their best to insulate their children from the hardships of the ghetto.

即使貧窮，父母盡力讓孩子不受貧民區種種困苦的影響。

記憶技巧　insul- 表示小島；-ate 為動詞字尾；insulate 即是像小島一般，與外界世界隔絕，引申為隔離。

isolate
[`aɪsḷ‚et]
v 使孤立，使隔離

After chemists were able to isolate the active chemical compound from the plant, they were able to mass produce a drug.

化學家有能力從這種植物分離活性化合物之後，他們能夠大量製造藥物。

記憶技巧　isol- 等同於 insul-，表示島嶼；-ate 為動詞字尾；isolate 與 insulate 同義，指使孤立、使隔離。

isolation

[ˌaɪsl̩ˈeʃən]

n 孤立，隔離

The police intimidated the protestor and held him in an isolation cell for the remainder of his jail term.

警察恐嚇抗議者，監禁餘期都將他關在隔離牢房。

記憶技巧 -ion 為名詞字尾。

---

league - lig

母音通轉，兩者皆表示綁。

---

oblige

[əˈblaɪdʒ]

v 迫使，施惠於

Thank you for obliging me on this hot day by offering a cool glass of lemonade.

在這個炎熱日子裡給我一杯清涼檸檬汁，真是感激。

記憶技巧 ob- 表示朝～方向；lig- 表示綁；oblige 的意思是綁住某對象，使其往某方向走，引申為迫使。

---

obligation

[ˌabləˈgeʃən]

n 義務，證券，債務，恩惠

Applicants were given a free one-night stay at the resort with no obligation to purchase anything.

申請人獲得度假村免費一晚住宿，且不承擔購物義務。

記憶技巧 ob- 表示朝～方向；lig- 表示綁；obligation 的意思是綁往，引申為義務。

---

obligatory

[əˈblɪgəˌtorɪ]

a 義務上的，必須的

The Generals made the obligatory offer of congratulations to the new President, but were not supportive of him.

將軍們必須向新總統表示祝賀，但不支持他。

記憶技巧 -ory 為形容詞字尾。

---

religion

[rɪˈlɪdʒən]

n 宗教，信仰

The entrepreneurs decided to capitalize on the power of religion and formed their own church.

企業家們決定利用宗教力量成立自己的教會。

記憶技巧 re- 表示加強語氣；lig- 表示綁；-ion 為名詞字尾；religion 即宗教，因為宗教的教義往往有將信徒緊密綁在一塊的功能。

相關字彙
宗教信仰和典故

- absolution 罪之赦免
- archangel 天使長
- blasphemous 褻瀆的
- chastity 貞潔
- conversion 改變信仰
- incarnation（神靈等的）化身
- the Last Judgment 最後的審判
- monotheism 一神論
- pantheism 泛神論
- polytheism 多神論
- sectarian 宗派的
- taboo 禁忌

religious

[rɪˋlɪdʒəs]

a 宗教的，虔誠的

In the Dark Ages, men hid behind their religious affiliation to commit horrendous crimes against humanity.

黑暗時代，人們躲在宗教信仰背後，犯下違反人道的可怕罪行。

記憶技巧 -ous 為形容詞字尾。

Part **2** CH 1 CH 2 CH 3 CH 4 CH 5

子音對應相同

lean - clin

母音通轉，兩者皆表示傾斜、傾向於，lean 是 clin 中的子音脫落所形成。

decline

[dɪˋklaɪn]

n 下降，衰退，婉拒

The decline of the Roman empire was preceded by its treasury being depleted to fund its military expansion.

羅馬帝國衰落之前，其財政因資助軍事擴張而耗盡。

記憶技巧 de- 表示從；clin- 表示傾斜；decline 的意思是從～傾斜，衍生出下降、衰退等意思。

disincline

[ˌdɪsɪnˋklaɪn]

v 使厭惡

Your child's petulant behavior disinclines me to volunteer to babysit for you.

你孩子任性的行為令我幫你當保姆一事視為畏途。

記憶技巧 dis- 表示不；incline 表示傾向；disincline 的字面意思是不傾向於，引申為使厭惡。

incline

[ɪnˋklaɪn]

v 傾斜，傾向

The teacher was inclined to believe her honor students over those whose grades were poor.

老師傾向於相信成績優秀的學生，而不相信成績差的。

記憶技巧 in- 表示內；clin- 表示傾向；incline 的意思是傾向。

inclination

[ˌɪnkləˋneʃən]

n 傾斜度，趨勢

There is an inclination for female judges to award child custody to mothers in divorce cases.

離婚案件中，女法官傾向將子女監護權判給母親。

記憶技巧 -ation 為名詞字尾。

recline

[rɪˋklaɪn]

v 斜倚，倚靠

The female patrons sipped on wine and reclined in massage chairs while their fingernails were trimmed.

修剪指甲時，女顧客啜著酒，斜倚在按摩椅上。

記憶技巧 re- 表示後面、靠著；clin- 表示傾斜；recline 即斜倚。

mutation - migr

母音通轉，兩者皆表示移動、改變。

---

migrate
[ˈmaɪˌgret]
v 遷移，移居，洄游

Wildebeest migrate by the millions each year in the epic search for food and water.

為了尋找食物和水，每年數百萬隻牛羚壯觀地遷徙。

記憶技巧 migr-表示移動；-ate 為動詞字尾；migrate 即遷徙、移居。

---

migratory
[ˈmaɪgrəˌtorɪ]
a 移居的，漂泊的

Some birds are migratory creatures, living in multiple parts of the world, while others prefer to stay in one area.

有些鳥是遷徙生物，生活在世界各地，有些鳥偏好停留在一個地區。

記憶技巧 -ory 為形容詞字尾。

相關字彙
描述鳥類
- fledged（幼鳥）能飛翔的
- fully-fledged（指幼鳥）羽毛豐滿的
- gregarious 群居性的
- webbed 有蹼的
- web-footed 蹼足的

---

emigrate
[ˈɛməˌgret]
v 移居外國，遷出

Nearly half of the population emigrated from the war-torn country within a ten-year period.

近半數人口在十年內從戰爭蹂躪的國家移居國外。

記憶技巧 e- 等同於 ex-，表示外面；migr- 表示移動；-ate 為動詞字尾；emigrate 是移出去。

相關字彙
移居
- asylum 避難
- exile 流放
- expatriate 移居國外
- refugee 難民

---

emigration
[ˌɛməˈgreʃən]
n 移民（行為），移居

The last great emigration forced the government to recruit doctors and other professionals from other countries.

上一次大移民迫使政府招聘其他國家的醫生和其他專業人員。

記憶技巧 -ion 為名詞字尾。

---

immigrant
[ˈɪməgrənt]
n 移民（者）

Millions of illegal immigrants will be deported soon after the new president takes office.

新任總統一上任，數百萬非法移民將立即遭到驅逐。

記憶技巧 im- 等同於 in-，表示內；migr- 表示移動；-ant 為名詞字尾；immigrant 是移入境內的移民。

---

transmigrate

[træns`maɪgret]

v 移居，遷徙，輪迴

A documented case involved a young woman from Kinmen transmigrating to a woman in Taichung after death.

有一份檔案是關於，一名金門年輕女子死後轉世為台中的一名女子。

記憶技巧 trans- 表示跨越；migr- 表示移動；-ate 為動詞字尾；transmigrate 即移居、遷徙、輪迴等。

Part

2

CH 1
CH 2
CH 3
CH 4
CH 5

子音對應相同

---

old - al / ul

母音通轉，兩者皆表示成長、營養。

---

alimentary

[͵ælɪ`mɛntərɪ]

a 營養的

The alimentary canal of a plant-eater is typically longer than that of a carnivore.

草食動物消化道通常比肉食動物的道長。

記憶技巧 al- 表示養分；-ment 為名詞字尾；-ary 為形容詞字尾；alimentary 的意思是營養的。

---

alimony

[`ælə͵monɪ]

n 贍養費，撫養費，生活費

相關字彙
離婚和分開

The divorced woman relied on the monthly alimony from her ex-husband to raise her children.

離婚婦人靠前夫每月贍養費撫養孩子。

記憶技巧 al- 表示養分；-mony 為表狀態的名詞字尾；alimony 是給予養分的意思，引申為離婚後的贍養費、撫養費。

- decree absolute 絕對判決
- dissolution 解除（婚約）
- joint custody 對子女的共同監護
- palimony 贍養費
- split up 分離
- tug-of-love 爭奪監護權的

---

adolescent

[͵ædl̩`ɛsn̩t]

n 青少年

Acne is more common on the facial skin of adolescents because of hormones and other factors.

因為賀爾蒙和其他因素，青春痘較常出現在青少年臉部皮膚。

記憶技巧 ad- 表示朝～方向；ol- 等同於 al-，表示成長；-escent 表示變化；adolescent 是成長中的青少年。

---

adult

[ə`dʌlt]

n 成人

The mature content of the movie made it ideal for adults only.

電影的成熟內容使其只適合成年人觀看。

記憶技巧 ad- 表示朝～方向；ul- 表示成長；adult 是已長大成熟的人，做成人解釋。

prolific [prəˋlɪfɪk] **a** 多產的	The prolific artist produced at least one fantastic oil painting per week. 多產的藝術家每週至少完成一幅精彩油畫。 記憶技巧 pro- 表示往前；ol- 表示成長；-fic 表示做；prolific 的意思是往前長，引申為多產的。
proliferate [prəˋlɪfəˌret] **v** 增加，大量生產	The Chinese leader vowed to prevent nuclear weapons from proliferating to other Asian countries. 中國領導人誓言阻止核武擴展到其他亞洲國家。 記憶技巧 pro- 表示向前；ol- 表示成長；fer- 表示攜帶；-ate 為動詞字尾；proliferate 的意思是大量生產。

Section **10**

〔g〕對應〔g〕

gorge - gurg

母音通轉，gorge 是喉嚨，而 gurg- 是吞，可用「喉嚨吞食東西」記憶。

regurgitate [rɪˋgɝdʒəˌtet] **v** 流回，反芻	The robin regurgitated the partially digested worms to feed its three chicks. 知更鳥反芻部分消化的蟲餵養牠的三隻幼鳥。 記憶技巧 re- 表示回來；gurg- 表示吞；-ate 為動詞字尾；regurgitate 即反芻。

原來如此！

grass（草），自地面迸出，生長於地面，「草地」也就是 grass。grass 源自 sprout（新芽）或 young shoot（幼苗），與 grow（生長）同源，母音通轉。草幾乎都是綠色，grass 便借用表示 green（綠色）。

〔k〕對應〔k〕

Part **2**

CH 1
CH 2
CH 3
CH 4
CH 5

子音對應相同

cause - cus
母音通轉，兩者皆表示原因、理由。

cause
[kɔz]
n 理由，事業

When able-bodied men have the free time and free will, they have the ability to take up a cause.
體格健壯的男人時間及意志自由時，他們有能力承擔一個事業。

記憶技巧 cause 即理由。

excuse
[ɪk`skjuz]
n 藉口

His excuse worked the first time, but the teacher did not believe it the second time.
他的藉口第一次有用，第二次老師就不相信了。

記憶技巧 ex- 表示離開；cus- 表示理由；excuse 即找個理由替自己開脱，名詞當藉口解釋。

accuse
[ə`kjuz]
v 指控，控告

The disabled child was often wrongly accused of breaking items in the classroom.
殘障兒童常被誤指在教室裡打破物品。

記憶技巧 ac- 等同於 ad-，表示和～相關；cus- 表示理由；accuse 即找個相關的理由來指控某人。

cross - cruc
母音通轉，兩者皆表示十字。

cruciform
[`krusə,fɔrm]
a 十字形的

In the national cemetery, visitors can see rows of cruciform tombstones stretching as far as the eye can see.
在國家公墓，遊客可以看到視線所及之處都是成排的十字形墓碑。

記憶技巧 cruc- 表示十字；form- 表示形狀；cruciform 即十字形的。

crucifix
[ˋkrusəˌfɪks]
n 十字架

The ancient Romans often punished criminals and political opponents by nailing them to a crucifix.
古羅馬人常將罪犯和政敵釘上十字架以示懲罰。

> 記憶技巧　cruc-表示十字；fix表示釘牢；crucifix是釘犯人的十字架。

crusade
[kruˋsed]
n 十字軍，改革運動

The energetic leader knocked on every door in the neighborhood to ask people to join his crusade against gang violence.
精力充沛的領袖敲打附近每一扇門，要求人們參加他的反幫派暴力的運動。

> 記憶技巧　crus- 等同於 cruc-，表示十字；-ade 為名詞字尾；crusade 即十字軍。

相關字彙	• bandwagon 得勢派，風潮	• juggernaut 駭人的毀滅力量
運動、浪潮	• blitz 閃電戰	• movement 運動
	• campaign 運動	

cruiser
[ˋkruzɚ]
n 巡邏車，巡洋艦

Two cruisers joined the naval task force to prevent the aggressive nation from imposing a blockade.
兩艘巡洋艦加入海軍特遣部隊，防止侵略國家強行封鎖。

> 記憶技巧　cruise 等同於 cruc- / cross，表示十字，另有跨越的意思；-er指做出動作者；cruiser的意思有巡邏艦、巡邏車。

crucial
[ˋkruʃəl]
a 關鍵的，極重要的

When the oil prices dropped, the revenues, which were crucial to the economy of the oil producer, evaporated.
油價下跌時，對於石油生產國經濟至關重要的收益蒸發就不見了。

> 記憶技巧　cruc- 表示十字；-ial 為形容詞字尾；crucial 即十字的，可想像成站在十字路口上，面臨關鍵抉擇，因此衍生出極重要的意思。

clear - clar
母音通轉，兩者皆表示清楚。

clarify
[ˋklærəˌfaɪ]
v 澄清，淨化

The attorney clarified the government's position during the negotiations over retirement benefits.
退休福利協商期間，律師澄清政府的立場。

> 記憶技巧　clar- 表示清楚；-fy 為動詞字尾；clarify 的意思是弄清楚，引申為澄清。

clarity

[`klærətɪ]

n 清楚，清澈

The Native Americans consumed a hallucinogenic plant to gain clarity when seeking answers from the spirit world.

尋求靈界的答案時，美洲原住民過去會食用一種迷幻植物以獲得心靈透澈。

記憶技巧 clar- 表示清楚；-ity 為名詞字尾；clarity 即清楚。

declare

[dɪ`klɛr]

v 宣佈，發表，聲明，申報

When the customs checkpoint officers asked if he had anything to declare, the man revealed his gun collection.

海關檢查站人員問他是否有物品申報時，男子出示他的槍枝收藏。

記憶技巧 de- 表示加強語氣；clar- 表示清楚；declare 即說清楚，引申為聲明。

declaration

[ˌdɛklə`reʃən]

n 宣言

In a bold public declaration, the chairman said his company would put humans on Mars within 100 years.

一份大膽的公開聲明中，董事長表示公司將在 100 年之內送人類上火星。

記憶技巧 -ion 為名詞字尾。

Part **2**

CH 1
CH 2
CH 3
CH 4
CH 5

子音對應相同

---

call - claim

兩者並無字源關係，但可藉由母音通轉來記憶，兩者皆表示喊叫。

claim

[klem]

n 主張，要求，權利

In no way can you seriously claim to have eaten one hundred hot dogs in under a minute.

你決不能認真聲稱一分鐘內吃了一百支熱狗。

記憶技巧 claim 本意是喊叫，衍生出主張、要求等意思。

acclaim

[ə`klem]

v 喝采，歡呼

The volunteers were publicly acclaimed for their contribution to the community.

志工們對社區的貢獻獲得大眾的喝采。

記憶技巧 ac- 等同於 ad-，表示朝～方向；claim- 表示喊叫；acclaim 的字面意思是朝～喊叫，引申為歡呼、喝采。

exclamation
[ˌɛksklə`meʃən]
n 呼喊，感嘆

The slam dunk at the end of the game was the superstar's exclamation of dominance.
比賽結束時的灌籃是超級巨星呈現優勢的驚嘆。

> **記憶技巧** e- 等同於 ex-，表示外面；clam- 表示喊叫；-ation 為名詞字尾；exclamation 的意思是叫出來，引申出感嘆的意思。

proclaim
[prə`klem]
v 聲明，公佈

The oil company proclaimed the regulations to be invalid and had a chance to make their case in the federal court.
石油公司宣布規章無效，有機會在聯邦法院贏得訴訟。

> **記憶技巧** pro- 表示向前；claim- 表示喊叫；proclaim 的意思是向前喊叫，引申為聲明、公布。

proclamation
[ˌprɑklə`meʃən]
n 宣言，公布

Wearing a clown suit, the boss made a proclamation that on Fridays, staff could wear whatever they wanted.
穿著小丑西裝，老闆宣布員工星期五可以穿任何想要穿的衣服。

> **記憶技巧** -ion 為名詞字尾。

reclaim
[rɪ`klem]
v 矯正，教化，開墾

A wall was built around the city and water was pumped out to reclaim more land from the sea.
城市週圍建一座牆，然後把水抽出去，以從海上開墾更多的土地。

> **記憶技巧** re- 表示回來；claim- 表示喊叫；reclaim 的意思是叫回來，引申為矯正、開墾等。

相關字彙
環保議題

- biodegradable 生物所能分解的
- conservation（對自然資源的）保護
- deforestation 砍伐森林
- eco-friendly 環保的
- preservation 維護
- reforestation 重新造林
- unsustainable 無法維持的，不永續的

cook - coct
母音通轉來記憶，兩者皆表示煮。

decoct
[`dɪ`kɑkt]
v 熬，煎（藥）

The pine needles were decocted in boiling water to brew a nutritious tea for the hunters.
松針在沸水中煎煮，以釀造營養的茶給獵人。

> **記憶技巧** de- 表示下面；coct- 表示煮；decoct 即熬煮。

concoct
[kən`kakt]
v 調製，虛構

The first pizzas were concocted by people who threw together their leftovers to make a new dish.
早期的披薩是將剩菜丟在一起做成一道新菜的人做出來的。

記憶技巧 con- 表示一起；coct- 表示煮；concoct 的意思是一起煮，引申為調製。

precocity
[prɪ`kasətɪ]
n 早熟

The young autistic child exhibited a precocity for mathematical equations.
年輕自閉症兒在數學方程式方面表現早熟。

記憶技巧 pre- 表示前面；coc- 表示煮；-ity 為名詞字尾；precocity 的意思是早熟。

precocious
[prɪ`koʃəs]
a 早熟的，過早的

The precocious four-year-old musician walked onto the stage in a tuxedo and sat behind the piano.
早熟的四歲音樂家著燕尾服走上舞台，坐在鋼琴後面。

記憶技巧 -ous 為形容詞字尾。

相關字彙
人的聰明才智

- genius 天資
- intelligent 聰明的
- wise 有智慧的
- brilliant 才華橫溢的
- clever 伶俐的
- bright 聰穎的
- brainy 腦筋好的

---

care - cur

兩者雖無字源關係，但可藉由母音通轉來記憶，兩者皆表示留意、照料、小心，cur- 另有治療等意思。

---

incurable
[ɪn`kjurəbl]
a 不可治療的

When learning he had incurable cancer, the employee quit his job and planned his travels around the world.
得知罹患不治的癌症時，員工辭職並計劃環遊世界。

記憶技巧 in- 為否定字首；cur- 表示治療；-able 為形容詞字尾；incurable 即不可治療的。

curiosity
[ˌkjurɪ`asətɪ]
n 好奇心，求知慾

Armed with a strong sense of curiosity and a desire to solve problems, the young man chose to be an inventor.
滿懷強烈好奇心和解決問題的渴望，年輕人選擇成為一名發明家。

記憶技巧 cur- 表示小心；-ous 為形容詞字尾；-ity 為名詞字尾；curiosity 的本意是小心，特別是在求知上，後來衍生出好奇心等意思。

Part **2**
CH 1
CH 2
CH 3
CH 4
CH 5

子音對應相同

accurate
[ˋækjərɪt]
a 準確的，正確的

The Doppler radar system has improved the weather forecaster's ability to make accurate predictions.
都普勒雷達系統提升預報員準確預報天氣的能力。

記憶技巧　ac- 等同於 ad-，表示朝～方向；cur- 表示留意、小心；-ate 為形容詞字尾；accurate 的意思是留意的，衍生出準確的、正確的等意思。

procurement
[proˋkjurmənt]
n 獲得，採購

Check out the clerk at the office supply department and submit the procurement form to request more copy paper.
找辦公用品部門辦事員，然後提交採購表格，以申請更多複印紙。

記憶技巧　pro- 指代表；cur- 表示小心、留意；-ment 為名詞字尾；procurement 本指小心，到 14 世紀末，才有獲得的意思。

secure
[sɪˋkjur]
v 使安全，擔保

The strategist's main priority was to secure the beach, so that more reinforcements could land at a later time.
戰略家主要優先守住海灘，如此一來更多增援部隊稍後就能登陸。

記憶技巧　se- 表示免於；cur- 表示留意、小心；secure 的意思是因為安全無虞，因此免於掛慮。

security
n 安全，保證，擔保，抵押品

The security network included monitoring stations, video cameras and motion sensors.
安全網絡包括監控站、攝影機和動作偵測器。

記憶技巧　-ity 為名詞字尾。

citizen - civi
母音通轉，兩者皆表示公民的。

civics
[ˋsɪvɪks]
n 公民課

The civics education regulation requires all students to know basic facts about the US government and history.
公民教育法規要求所有學生對美國政府和歷史有基本認知。

記憶技巧　civi- 表示公民的；-ics 表示學科；civics 是公民科。

civil
[ˋsɪvl̩]
a 民事的，公民的，文明的

Unable to pursue a sports career, the disabled athlete chose to study to become a civil servant.
無法追求運動職業，殘障運動員選擇苦讀拼公務員。

記憶技巧　civ- 表示公民的；civil 衍生出文明的、民事的等意思。

civilian

[sɪˋvɪljən]

n 市民，平民，
民法學者

During wartime conflicts, the civilians usually bear the brunt of the damage and suffering.
戰爭衝突期間，平民通常首當其衝遭受損害和痛苦。

記憶技巧　civil 表示公民的；-ian 為形容詞字尾；civilian 是平民的，
亦可當名詞用。

civilization

[ˌsɪvḷəˋzeʃən]

n 文明，文明世界，
教化，教育

The ancient civilizations of Central America and South America knew much about the sun, stars and the moon.
中美洲和南美洲的古代文明非常了解太陽，星星和月亮的知識。

記憶技巧　civil 表示公民的；-ize 為動詞字尾；-ation 為名詞字尾；
civilization 即教化。

相關字彙
社會、文化、文明

- civilization 文明
- ethnic 民族的
- future shock 未來衝擊
- patrimony 繼承的遺產
- primitive 原始的
- heritage 繼承物

---

color - chromo

兩者並無字源關係，但可藉由子音 l 和 r 互換，母音通轉來記憶，兩者皆表示顏色。

chromatic

[kroˋmætɪk]

a 彩色的

Vivid colors like red, green and blue are chromatic colors, while white, grey and black are achromatic.
紅色、綠色和藍色等鮮豔色是彩色，而白色、灰色和黑色是非彩色。

記憶技巧　chroma- 表示顏色；-ic 為形容詞字尾；chromatic 是彩色的。

chromosome

[ˋkroməˌsom]

n 染色體

The patient with Down syndrome was given a new type of chromosome therapy.
唐氏症患者接受一種新型染色體治療。

記憶技巧　chromo- 表示顏色；-some 表示體；chromosome 即染色體。

monochromatic

[ˌmɑnəkrəˋmætɪk]

a 單色的

The special LED lamp provides a monochomatic red light that helps plants to thrive.
特別的 LED 燈提供單色紅光，有助於植物茁壯成長。

記憶技巧　mono-，單一；chroma-，顏色；-ic，形容詞字尾；
monochromatic 即單色的。

polychromatic
[pɑlɪkroˋmætɪk]
a 多色的

The polychromatic light bulb emits a variety of blended colors that appear white or yellow.
多色燈泡發出呈現白色或黃色的多種混合色。

記憶技巧　poly- 表示多；chroma- 表示顏色；-ic 為形容詞字尾；polychromatic 即多色的。

---

common - commun
母音通轉，兩者皆表示共同的、普遍的、公眾的。

---

commune
[ˋkɑmjun]
n 社區，社區居民

The early settlers lived in small communes where they shared land ownership and responsibilities.
早期移民住在小公社，共享土地所有權和責任。

記憶技巧　commun- 等同於 common，表示共同的；commune 是大家所共同居住的社區。

---

communication
[kəˏmjunəˋkeʃən]
n 傳播，通訊，溝通

The cornerstone of good communication is making the time and effort to listen to others well.
良好溝通的基礎是花時間用心傾聽他人。

記憶技巧　commun- 等同於 common，表示共同的；-ation 為名詞字尾；communication 的意思是共同分享、交流，引申為傳播、溝通。

相關字彙　
溝通過程

- contact 聯繫
- correspondence 通信
- discourse 談話
- interaction 互動
- liaison 聯絡

---

community
[kəˋmjunətɪ]
n 社區，團體

The young woman founded a newsletter to let local businesses advertise to the community.
年輕女子創辦了一份商務通訊，以便當地企業向社區做廣告。

記憶技巧　commun 表示共同；-ity 為名詞字尾；community 即大家一起生活的社區。

---

communism
[ˋkɑmjuˏnɪzəm]
n 共產主義

The leader instituted martial law and suspended certain rights to prevent communism from spreading.
領導人制定戒嚴法，並暫停某些權利，以防止共產主義擴散。

記憶技巧　commun- 表示共同；-ism 表示主義；communism 即共產主義。

quarrel - quer

母音通轉，兩者皆表示埋怨。

querimonious
[ˌkwɪrɪˈmonɪəs]
a 愛抱怨的

The aunt was known to throw the occasional querimonious tantrum.
大家都知道姑姑偶爾愛抱怨耍脾氣。

記憶技巧 queri- 表示埋怨；moni- 表示狀態；-ous 為形容詞字尾；querimonious 是愛抱怨的。

querulous
[ˈkwɛrələs]
a 愛發牢騷的，易怒的，愛挑剔的

Never satisfied with her husband's income or profession, she always spoke to him in a querulous tone.
對丈夫的收入或職業從不滿意，她總是用牢騷的語氣和丈夫說話。

記憶技巧 querul- 表示埋怨；-ous 為形容詞字尾；querulous 是愛發牢騷的。

calm - qui

兩者雖無字源關係，但可用母音通轉來記憶，兩者皆表示安靜。

quiet
[ˈkwaɪət]
a 安靜的，鎮靜的

The successful auctioneer booked a short getaway to the country cottage to enjoy a quiet weekend.
成功的拍賣商訂一個鄉村別墅，短暫遠離塵囂，享受一個安靜的周末。

記憶技巧 qui- 表示安靜；quiet 即安靜的。

quietude
[ˈkwaɪəˌtjud]
n 寂靜，鎮靜

Taking slow, deep breaths and letting go of all thoughts, the disciple achieved a state of quietude.
緩慢深呼吸，放開所有意念，門徒達到一種寧靜的狀態。

記憶技巧 quiet 表示安靜；-tude 為抽象名詞字尾；quietude 即寂靜。

quiescence
[kwaɪˈɛsn̩s]
n 寂靜

After what seemed like three years of quiescence, the bamboo shoots grew at a crazy rate.
休眠了似乎有三年的時間之後，竹筍以瘋狂速度生長。

記憶技巧 qui- 表示安靜；-escence 為名詞字尾，表示狀態；quiescence 是寂靜。

Part
2
CH 1
CH 2
CH 3
CH 4
CH 5

子音對應相同

acquiesce

[ˌækwɪˈɛs]

v 默許，勉於同意

The native residents did not want any bloodshed, so they acquiesced to the occupying forces.
當地居民不要任何流血衝突，因此默許佔領軍的行動。

記憶技巧 ac- 等同於 ad-，表示朝～方向；qui- 表示安靜；acquiesce 是保持沉默，且同意他人所作所為，引申為默許。

相關字彙 同意做某事
- undertake 同意
- consent 贊成
- yield 屈從
- accede 答應
- agree 同意

Section **12**

〔h〕對應〔h〕

---

whole - holo

兩者並無字源關係，兩者皆表示全部。

---

holocaust

[ˈholəˌkɔst]

n 大屠殺

The United States Holocaust Museum memorializes the victims of the Nazi Final Solution.
美國大屠殺博物館紀念納粹最終解決方案受害者。

記憶技巧 holo- 表示全部；caust- 表示燃燒；holocaust 本意是全部燒掉，後當作種族大屠殺解釋。

相關字彙 軍事活動
- overwatch 看守
- battle 戰鬥
- campaign 戰役
- struggle 競爭
- mission 作戰任務
- combat 戰鬥
- assault 攻擊

---

holoscopic

[ˌholəˈskɔpɪk]

a 綜觀全局的

The new medical machine produces 3D holoscopic imaging of scanned areas of the body.
新醫療機器產生身體掃描區域 3D 立體影像。

記憶技巧 holo- 表示全部；scop- 表示看；-ic 為形容詞字尾；holoscopic 的意思是全部都看到，引申為綜觀全局的。

相關字彙 觀、看
- kaleidoscopic 千變萬化的
- macroscopic 宏觀的
- microscopic 微觀的
- stereoscopic 有立體感的

heir - her
母音通轉，兩者皆表示繼承。

heir
[ɛr]
n 繼承人

The archduke is one of the heirs to the House of Habsburg estate.
大公是哈布斯堡莊園之家的繼承人之一。

記憶技巧 heir 即繼承人。

---

heiress
[ˈɛrɪs]
n 女繼承人

The heiress to the fashion empire was a glamorous and talented young designer.
時尚帝國的女繼承人是一個迷人而且才華洋溢的年輕設計師。

記憶技巧 heir- 表示繼承人；-ess 表示女性；heiress 即女繼承人。

相關字彙
獲得一筆錢財、收集物品的人

- beneficiary 受益人
- recipient 受領者
- magpie 有收集零碎東西癖好的人
- addressee 收信人
- inheritor 繼承人

---

inherit
[ɪnˈhɛrɪt]
v 繼承，遺傳

Believing he will inherit his grandfather's fortune, the boy never plans to study seriously for a career.
男孩相信將繼承祖父財富，從未打算認真學習一個職業。

記憶技巧 in- 等同於 en-，表示使～；her- 表示繼承人；inherit 的意思是使成為繼承人，引申為繼承。

---

heredity
[həˈrɛdɪtɪ]
n 遺傳

Some people believe heredity is an important factor in the athletic abilities of human beings.
有些人認為遺傳是人類運動能力的一個重要因素。

記憶技巧 her- 表示繼承；-ity 為名詞字尾；heredity 是遺傳。

---

hereditary
[həˈrɛdəˌtɛrɪ]
a 祖傳的，世襲的

Finding a Chinese girl with blue eyes, the talent scout knew he had discovered a rare hereditary trait.
找到一個藍眼睛的中國女孩，星探知道他發掘了一個罕見的祖傳特徵。

記憶技巧 -ary 為形容詞字尾。

---

heritage
[ˈhɛrətɪdʒ]
n 遺產

The driver was proud of his Italian heritage, which included famous cars like Ferrari and Lamborghini.
司機為義大利傳統感到自豪，這包括像法拉利和藍寶堅尼等名車。

記憶技巧 her- 表示繼承；-age 為名詞字尾；heritage 是所繼承之物，即遺產。

Part 2

CH 1
CH 2
CH 3
CH 4
CH 5

子音對應相同

321

human - homo
母音通轉，兩者皆表示人類。

homage
[ˋhɑmɪdʒ]

n 尊敬，敬意，崇敬

Thousands visited the home of the deceased filmmaker, to pay homage to the man who forever changed the industry.
數千人參觀已故製片人的住宅，向這位永遠改變這個行業的人致敬。

記憶技巧 hom- 表示人類；-age 為名詞字尾；homage 的意思是對人產生的敬意。

相關字彙
敬佩、稱讚
- admiration 欽佩
- credit 讚揚
- compliment 敬意
- regard 尊敬
- acclaim 稱讚

homicide
[ˋhɑməˌsaɪd]

n 殺人（案）

After the bloody footprints were discovered, it was determined that the cause of death was a homicide.
血跡被發現腳印之後，確定死因是殺人事件。

記憶技巧 hom- 表示人類；cid- 表示殺；homicide 即殺人。

Section **13**

〔dʒ〕對應〔dʒ〕

jet - jac / ject
母音通轉，兩者皆表示丟、投擲。

reject
[rɪˋdʒɛkt]

v 拒絕，抵制，駁回，否決

After being rejected for the seventh time, she was finally successful in landing a job.
七次被拒絕後，她終於成功找到工作。

記憶技巧 re- 表示回去；ject- 表示丟；reject 的意思是丟回去，引申為拒絕、駁回。

abject

[`æbdʒɛkt]

a 卑鄙的，不幸的

The children of the garbage mountain in Manila live in abject poverty.

住在馬尼拉垃圾山的孩子生活困頓。

記憶技巧　ab- 表示離開；ject- 表示丟；abject 的意思是丟棄，1510 年代才有卑鄙的、不幸的等衍生意思產生。

conjecture

[kən`dʒɛktʃə]

n 推想，臆測

To say the CEO could be guilty of bribery is just conjecture at this point.

說執行長可能涉及賄賂在目前只是猜測。

記憶技巧　con- 表示一起；ject- 表示丟；conjecture 的意思是丟在一起，演變為做出結論的意思，引申為推想、臆測。

dejected

[dɪ`dʒɛktɪd]

a 沮喪的，
　情緒低落的

The fan sat dejected after failing to get his football autographed by his favorite player.

球迷沒請他最喜歡的球員在他的足球簽名，沮喪地坐著。

記憶技巧　de- 表示下面；ject- 表示丟；-ed 為過去分詞字尾；dejected 的意思是被丟到下面的，引申為情緒低落的。

ejection

[ɪ`dʒɛkʃən]

n 噴出，噴出物，
　逐出

The ejection of the basketball player in the second half was a turning point in the game.

下半場籃球員被逐出場是比賽的一個轉振點。

記憶技巧　e- 等同於 ex-，表示外面；ject- 表示丟；-ion 為名詞字尾；ejection 是丟到外面，引申為噴出、逐出。

ejaculate

[ɪ`dʒækjəˌlet]

v 射出，突然喊叫

The sperm bank asks donors to ejaculate into a test tube in a private room.

精子銀行要求捐精者在一個隱密房間射精到試管內。

記憶技巧　e- 等同於 ex-，表示外面；jac- 表示丟；-ate 為動詞字尾；ejaculate 的意思是丟到外面，引申為射出。

inject

[ɪn`dʒɛkt]

v 注入，注射，加入

The patient sat for his weekly IV treatment to inject antibiotics into his bloodstream.

患者坐著接受每週靜脈注射治療，要注射抗生素到血液。

記憶技巧　in- 表示內；ject- 表示丟；inject 是丟入，引申為注射。

interjection

[ˌɪntə`dʒɛkʃən]

n 感嘆詞，插入語

The bowler uttered proud interjections after every strike or spare that he made.

保齡球選手打出全倒或補中後，發出驕傲的感嘆聲。

記憶技巧　inter- 表示在～之間；ject- 表示丟；-ion 為名詞字尾；interjection 的意思是丟在～之間，引申為插入語，另有感嘆詞的意思。

Part

2

CH 1

CH 2

CH 3

CH 4

CH 5

子音對應相同

objection
[əb`dʒɛkʃən]
n 反對，異議

With no objection offered by the attendees, the wedding proceeded.
出席者未提出反對，婚禮持續進行。

> 記憶技巧　ob- 表示朝～方向；ject- 表示丟；-ion 為名詞字尾；objection 是往某方向丟東西以表示反對之意。

objective
[əb`dʒɛktɪv]
n 目標，實體

The stated objective of the annual report was to balance the need for profit with the desire to serve.
年度報告的既定目標要平衡利潤的需求和服務的渴望。

> 記憶技巧　ob- 表示朝～方向；ject- 表示丟；-ive 為形容詞字尾；objective 是瞄準～方向丟東西，本當形容詞，後當名詞用，引申為目標。

project
[`pradʒɛkt]
n 計畫，專案

The draftsman was recruited to join the project planning team to build new retail space.
製圖人員受聘加入專案規畫團隊，來建設新的零售空間。

> 記憶技巧　pro- 表示往前；ject- 表示丟；project 本意是往前丟、往前拋，17 世紀後才有計畫的意思。

subject
[`sʌbdʒɪkt]
a 受支配的，從屬的

The proposed increase in salaries was subject to review by the board of directors.
加薪建議案須經董事會審核。

> 記憶技巧　sub- 表示下面；ject- 表示丟；subject 是丟到下面的，引申為受支配。

---

joy - jubil
兩者並無字源關係，但可藉由母音通轉記憶，兩者皆表示喜悅。

---

jubilant
[`dʒublənt]
a 喜氣洋洋的，令人喜悅的

The crowd was jubilant, as the prince and princess were paraded down the boulevard in a spectacular motorcade.
民眾歡騰，王子和公主在大道上壯觀車隊中遊行。

> 記憶技巧　jubil- 表示喜悅；-ant 為形容詞字尾；jubilant 是令人喜悅的。

相關字彙
感到開心

- content 滿足的
- happy 開心的
- pleased 高興的
- satisfied 滿足的
- exuberant 興高采烈的

join - junct
母音通轉，兩者皆表示連結。

junction
[`dʒʌŋkʃən]

n 連接，交叉點，匯合處

The wiring of the office building met at a junction box, where one could find fuses and switches.
辦公大樓線路在接線盒相接，那裡可找到保險絲和開關。

記憶技巧 junct- 表示連結；-ion 為名詞字尾；junction 是連結、交叉點。

conjunction
[kən`dʒʌŋkʃən]

n 聯合，連接詞

In conjunction with celebrations throughout the island, the government sponsored a concert.
連結整個島嶼的慶祝活動，政府贊助了一場音樂會。

記憶技巧 con- 表示一起；junct- 表示連結；-ion 為名詞字尾；conjunction 的意思是連結在一起。

disjunction
[dɪs`dʒʌŋkʃən]

n 分離，分裂

The parents were disappointed by the disjunction between their son's promises and his obvious failures.
父母感到非常失望，因為兒子的承諾和明顯失敗有落差。

記憶技巧 dis- 表示分開；junct- 表示連結；-ion 為名詞字尾；disjunction 的意思是沒有連結在一起，即分離。

Part **2**

CH 1
CH 2
CH 3
CH 4
CH 5

子音對應相同

extra - ultra
兩者並無字源關係，但可藉由母音通轉記憶，兩者皆表示超越。

ultra
[`ʌltrə]

n 極端主義者

There is a growing movement of ultras leading the call for secession.
極端主義者領導要求，這國家分裂運動愈來愈壯大。

記憶技巧 ultra 的本意為超越，後作極端主義者解釋。

ultrared
[ˌʌltrə`rɛd]

a 紅外線的

The ultrared scanner is used by the military to see living targets in the dark.
紅外線掃描器被軍方用於在黑暗中看見活目標。

記憶技巧 ultra- 表示超越；red 表示紅色；ultrared 是紅外線。

相關字彙
用以描述各種光

- candlelit 燭光的
- fluorescent 發螢光的
- moonlit 月光照耀的
- phosphorescent 發出磷光的
- starlit 星光照耀的
- sunlit 陽光照射的
- twilit 微明的
- spotlit 用聚光照明的

ultraviolet

[͵ʌltrə`vaɪəlɪt]

a 紫外線的

The ultraviolet light bulb did not light up the room, but it made phosphorescent colors glow brightly.

紫外燈泡沒有照亮房間，但使磷光顏色發光明亮。

> 記憶技巧　ultra- 表示超越；violet 表示紫色；ultraviolet 即紫外線。

eight - octo

母音通轉，子音 g（雖沒發音）和 k 互換，兩者皆表示八。

octopus

[`ɑktəpəs]

n 章魚

The popular sushi restaurant offered raw octopus, otherwise known as "tako."

人氣壽司餐廳提供生章魚，也稱為「tako」。

> 記憶技巧　octo- 表示八；pus- 表示腳；octopus 即所謂的八爪章魚。

October

[ɑk`tobɚ]

n 十月

In October, the chain store opened three new locations in New York State.

十月份時，連鎖店在紐約州開了三家新店。

> 記憶技巧　Octo- 表示十；-ber 表示表月份字尾；在古羅馬舊曆中是八月，儒略曆和現代陽曆中是十月。

octogenarian

[͵ɑktədʒə`nɛrɪən]

a 八十幾歲的

My uncle achieved octogenarian status because he ate well and exercised regularly.

我叔叔飲食適當且定期運動，活到八十幾歲。

> 記憶技巧　octo- 表示八；-genarian 表示十倍的；octogenarian 的意思是八十幾歲的。

Part

2

CH 1
CH 2
CH 3
CH 4
CH 5

子音對應相同

Section 14

〔r〕對應〔r〕

ray‧radi

母音通轉，兩者皆表示光線、輻射線。

---

radio

[`redɪo]

n 無線電，
無線電廣播，
收音機

It is harder to find radios in homes and offices, but they are still commonplace inside automobiles.
現在較難在家庭和辦公室看到收音機，但汽車內部仍然常見。

記憶技巧 radio 本指光線，後有無線電的意思。

---

radioactive

[ˌredɪoˈæktɪv]

a 放射性的，
有輻射能的

A trace amount of radioactive isotope was found in a dead killer whale in Alaska.
在阿拉斯加，一隻死亡的殺人鯨體內發現微量放射性同位素。

記憶技巧 radio- 表示輻射線；active 指在活動中的；radioactive 即有輻射能的。

---

radius

[`redɪəs]

n 半徑，半徑範圍

The radius of the new coins are larger than that of previous coins, so they do not fit into the vending machines.
新製硬幣半徑大於舊硬幣，自動販賣機不適用。

記憶技巧 radius 除了有輻射線的意思外，亦有半徑的意思，因半徑是從圓心放射出去的。

---

radiation

[ˌredɪˈeʃən]

n 放射，輻射

The workers sued the power company for not adequately protecting them against radiation poisoning.
工人提告電力公司，因其未充分保護他們免於輻射中毒。

記憶技巧 radi- 表示輻射線；-ation 為名詞字尾；radiation 是輻射。

相關字彙
放射（線）

- alpha particle α 粒子
- carbon dating 碳 -14 年代測定（法）
- cosmic rays 宇宙射線
- gamma rays γ 射線（伽瑪射線）
- half-life 半衰期
- plutonium 鈽
- X-ray X 射線，X 光

raw - rud

兩者雖無字源關係，但可藉由母音通轉來記憶，兩者皆表示未加工的。

rude
[rud]
a 粗糙的，粗暴的

If you think your boss will give you a raise just because you were polite, you are in for a rude awakening.
如果覺得只因你有禮貌老闆給你加薪，你要準備猛然醒悟了。

記憶技巧 rud- 表示未加工的；rude 有粗糙的、粗暴的等意思。

rudimentary
[ˌrudə`mɛntəri]
a 基礎的，初期的

The electrician had a rudimentary knowledge of math, but it was enough for him to do his job.
電工對數學有只有基本知識，但足以將工作做好。

記憶技巧 rud- 表示未加工的；-ment 為名詞字尾；-ary 為形容詞字尾；rudimentary 即未加工的原始狀態，引申為基礎的，初期的。

erudite
[`ɛrʊˌdaɪt]
a 博學的

Visiting the academic conference, one could expect to hear an erudite discussion at any time.
參加學術會議時，可以期待隨時聽到博學的討論。

記憶技巧 e- 等同於 ex-，表示外面；rud- 表示未加工的；-ite 為形容詞字尾；erudite 的意思是離開未加工的原始狀態。用來形容一個人很有學問，已脫離懵懂無知狀態。

rule - reg

母音通轉，兩者原始意思皆表示直、統治、領導。亦可用 right（直接地），藉由母音通轉來記憶。

regal
[`rigl̩]
a 帝王的，堂皇的，豪華的

The palace hosted a regal affair once a year to raise money for charity.
王宮每年舉辦一次王室慈善籌款宴會。

記憶技巧 reg- 表示統治；-al 為形容詞字尾；regal 是統治的，引申為帝王的。

regime
[rɪ`ʒim]
n 政權，政體

The popularly elected leader was replaced in an unexpected and unwanted regime change.
普選選出的領導人在一場意外且無必要的政權更替中遭到替換。

記憶技巧 reg- 表示統治；regime 是政體。

region
[ˈridʒən]
n 區域，領域

The Bordeaux region of France is famous for its varieties of red and white wines.
法國波爾多地區以多種紅葡萄酒和白葡萄酒聞名。

記憶技巧 reg-，統治，-ion，名詞字尾，region 是統治的區域，後作區域、領域解釋。

realm
[rɛlm]
n 領域，王國

相關字彙
研究領域的一般說法

The life coach transformed his students' lives, creating new realms of possibility for them.
人生教練改變學生的人生，為他們創造嶄新的潛力領域。

記憶技巧 realm 是 reg- 的變體，表示領域。

- area 領域
- field 領域
- domain 領域
- specialism 專門研究
- speciality 專長
- scene 活動領域
- territory 領域

Part 2
CH 1
CH 2
CH 3
CH 4
CH 5

子音對應相同

reign
[ren]
n（君主）統治（時期）

The reign of the King John of England was notable for his signing of the Magna Carta.
英王約翰統治時期以簽署大憲章而著名。

記憶技巧 reign 等同於 reg-，表示統治。

regular
[ˈrɛgjələ]
a 規律的，常例的，定期的

The adults pay the regular bus fare, while their children are eligible for the half-priced fare.
成人付普通公車票價，孩子有資格享有半價優惠。

記憶技巧 reg- 表示統治；-ar 為形容詞字尾；regular 即藉由統治讓人民過著規律生活。

regulation
[ˌrɛgjəˈleʃən]
n 規定，條例

The new regulation requires a dress shirt and tie for men and aims to give the company a more professional image.
新規定要求男子穿著正式襯衫領帶，目的是使公司形象更專業。

記憶技巧 reg- 表示統治；-ation 為名詞字尾；regulation 是統治者所頒布的規定。

royal
[ˈrɔɪəl]
a 王室的，高貴的，莊嚴的

The royal insignia on the letterhead indicated that the invitation came directly from the palace.
信箋上方的皇家徽章表明邀請函直接來自皇宮。

記憶技巧 roy- 等同於 reg-，表示統治；-al 為形容詞字尾；royal 本指統治的，引申為王室的、高貴的。

right - rect

母音通轉，兩者原始意思皆表示直、統治、領導，rect- 和 reg- 實則系出同源。

direct

[dəˋrɛkt]

a 直接的，坦白的

The tradesman would only accept a direct answer when he asked vendors for pricing.
店主向供應商詢價時，只接受直接的回答。

> 記憶技巧　di- 等同於 dis-，表示分開；rect- 表示直；direct 的意思是直接的。

direction

[dəˋrɛkʃən]

n 指導，說明，方向

The limo driver waited for the passenger to tell him in which direction to go.
豪華轎車司機等候乘客告訴他開往哪個方向。

> 記憶技巧　di- 等同於 dis-，表示分開；rect- 表示直；-ion 為名詞字尾；direction 是弄直，引申為指導、說明。

erect

[ɪˋrɛkt]

v 豎立，建立

A statue of the deceased company founder was erected in front of the headquarters building.
已故公司創辦人雕像豎立在總部大樓前。

> 記憶技巧　e- 表示離開、上；rect- 表示直；erect 是直立起來。

rough - rug

兩者雖無明確字源關係，但可藉由母音通轉來記憶，兩者原始意思皆表示起皺紋。

corrugated

[ˋkɔrəˏgetɪd]

a 起皺的，波狀的

The corrugated tin roof provided shelter from the rain, but the patter of the raindrops on it was loud.
波紋錫屋頂阻隔雨水，但雨滴在上面的拍打聲很響亮。

> 記憶技巧　cor- 等同於 con-，表示加強語氣；rug- 表示起皺紋；-ate 為形容詞字尾；corrugated 即起皺的。

猜猜看！

「excuse（藉口）」表示說出來的原因，cuse 猜一相關單字？

（案答：cause（原因））

rip - rupt

母音通轉，兩者皆表示撕裂。

---

abrupt
[ə`brʌpt]
a 突然的，斷裂的

The news of the assassination caused an abrupt halt to trading on the stock exchange.
暗殺消息導致證券交易所的交易突然停止。

> **記憶技巧** ab- 表示離開；rupt- 表示破裂；abrupt 即裂開，到 1630 年代才有突然的意思。

---

bankrupt
[`bæŋkrʌpt]
a 破產的

相關字彙
破產

Having lost all of his savings in a bad investment, the bankrupt security guard considered a life of crime.
在一次失敗投資中失去了所有儲蓄，破產的保全人員，考慮犯罪。

> **記憶技巧** bank 表示銀行；rupt- 表示破裂；bankrupt 有破產的意思。

- go bust 破產
- discharged bankrupt 被免除債務的破產者
- liquidator 清算人
- official receiver 官方接管人
- undischarged bankrupt 未償清的破產者
- insolvency 無力償還
- go broke 破產

---

corrupt
[kə`rʌpt]
a 貪腐的，墮落的

The corrupt system made people believe that they could not survive by being honest.
腐敗制度使人們認為靠誠實無法生存。

> **記憶技巧** cor- 等同於 con-，表示加強語氣；rupt- 表示破裂；corrupt 的意思是破的徹底，引申為貪腐的、墮落的。

---

disrupt
[dɪs`rʌpt]
v 使分裂，使中斷

The blockage in the water main disrupted the flow of water throughout the apartment building.
總水管堵塞使整棟大樓的水流受阻。

> **記憶技巧** dis- 表示離開；rupt- 表示破裂；disrupt 即使分裂。

---

erupt
[ɪ`rʌpt]
v 爆發，噴出，出疹

When Mt. St. Helens erupted in 1980, it was the only major volcanic eruption in the USA after 1915.
聖海倫斯山在 1980 年爆發時，這是美國自 1915 年以來唯一的重大火山噴發。

> **記憶技巧** e- 表示外面；rupt- 表示破裂；erupt 有爆發、噴出意思。

---

interrupt
[ˌɪntə`rʌpt]
v 妨礙，插嘴，中斷

The stockbroker was often tired at work because his neighbor usually interrupted his sleep.
股票經紀人工作時常感到疲勞，因為鄰居經常打斷他的睡眠。

> **記憶技巧** inter- 表示在～之間；rupt- 表示破裂；interrupt 的字面意思是從中間撕裂，引申為妨礙、中斷等意思。

Part **2**

CH 1
CH 2
CH 3
CH 4
CH 5

子音對應相同

river - rrhea

兩者雖無字源關係，但可藉由母音通轉來記憶，river 的意思是大量水流、河流，rrhea- 則是流動。

---

diarrhea
[͵daɪəˋriə]
n 腹瀉

Unbelievably, many people in Third World countries still die from diarrhea, which is easily treatable.
令人難以置信的是，第三世界國家許多人仍死於腹瀉這種可輕易療癒的病。

記憶技巧　dia- 表示穿過；-rrhea 表示流；diarrhea 的本意是流過，引申為腹瀉。

---

hemorrhoids
[ˋhɛmə͵rɔɪdz]
n 痔瘡

When suffering from painful hemorrhoids, the teacher preferred to stand the entire day.
痔瘡痛苦時，老師寧願站一整天。

記憶技巧　hemo- 表示血；-rrhoids 表示流；hemorrhoids 即是流血，得痔瘡常會出血。

reason - rat

母音通轉，子音 s 和 t 互換，兩者的本意皆是考量、推理、理性。

---

ration
[ˋræʃən]
n 定額，定量，
　配給（量）

During the food shortage, citizens needed to wait in line to receive rations of rice and beans.
糧食短缺期間，人民需要排隊等米和豆子的配給。

記憶技巧　rat- 表示考量；-ion 為名詞字尾；ration 是思索計算出來的數量，引申為定額。

---

rationale
[͵ræʃəˋnæl]
n 基本原理，
　理論基礎

He couldn't understand the rationale behind his son's decision to join the military.
他不明白兒子決定從軍的背後理由。

記憶技巧　ration 表示考量、推理；rationale 是基本原理。

---

rational
[ˋræʃən!]
a 理性的，推理的，
　合理的

The kinsmen chose to take a rational approach to resolving the land dispute.
親戚選擇採取合理的方法解決土地糾紛。

記憶技巧　ration 表示理性；-al 為形容詞字尾；rational 即理性的。

ratify

['rætə,faɪ]

v 批准

The peace treaty was not valid until it could be ratified by two-thirds of the parliament.

和平條約直到國會三分之二席次批准才生效。

記憶技巧　rati- 表示考量；-fy 表示做；ratify 的意思是做了考量後允許。

ratio

['reʃo]

n 比率，比例

With the ratio of two females per male at the college, the men had a good chance of finding a date.

大學男女人數比例是 1 比 2，男生找到約會對象的機會很大。

記憶技巧　ratio 即考量計算，後當作比例、比率解釋。

Part 2
CH 1
CH 2
CH 3
CH 4
CH 5
子音對應相同

red - rub

母音通轉，兩者的意思皆是紅色。

ruby

['rubɪ]

n 紅寶石

Myanmar is the largest producer of rubies, producing about 90% of the world's supply.

緬甸是最大的紅寶石生產國，生產全世界大約 90% 供應量。

記憶技巧　rub- 表示紅色；ruby 是紅寶石。

相關字彙
寶石

- aquamarine 海藍寶石
- crystal 水晶
- diamond 鑽石
- emerald 祖母綠
- gemstone 寶石
- quartz 石英
- sapphire 藍寶石

rubric

['rubrɪk]

n （用紅字印刷的）題目，成規，提示，指示

Before accepting the new assignment, the intelligent man asked his boss for his rubric.

接受新任務之前，聰穎的男子向老闆請示作法。

記憶技巧　rub- 表示紅色；rubric 本是紅色印刷，後衍生出標題、成規等意思。

猜猜看！

hundred 是數字百，hund 猜一個字根？

答案：cent-（百）

ear - aur

母音通轉，兩者的意思皆是耳朵，aur- 亦有聽的意思。

auricle
[ˋɔrɪkḷ]
n 外耳

The auricle of the Short Island natives appears to have a pointed shape, similar to that of an elf.
肖特島原住民的耳廓形狀是尖的，就像精靈的耳廓。

記憶技巧　aur- 表示耳朵；-cle 表示小的字尾；auricle 的本意是小耳，後當外耳解釋。

aural
[ˋɔrəl]
a 聽覺的

The museum director was responsible for recording the aural tour information.
博物館館長負責錄製語音導覽資訊。

記憶技巧　aur- 表示聽；-al 為形容詞字尾；aural 是聽覺的。

相關字彙
聽力、耳朵

- anvil 砧骨
- deaf 聾的
- earlobe 耳垂
- earwax 耳垢
- hearing-impaired 聽覺受損的
- lip-reading 讀唇術

auscultation
[ˋɔskḷˋteʃən]
n 聽診

Concerned that the girl may have contracted tuberculosis, the doctor performed a thorough auscultation.
擔心女孩可能感染結核病，醫生進行徹底聽診。

記憶技巧　aus- 等同於 aur-，表示聽；-ation 為名詞字尾；auscultation 的意思是聽，引申為聽診。

order - orn

母音通轉，order 是次序，orn- 是裝飾，兩者系出同源。

ornament
[ˋɔrnəmənt]
n 裝飾

The retired toymaker handed the homeless boy a hand-painted Christmas ornament.
退休玩具工匠給無家可歸的男孩一個手繪的聖誕節裝飾品。

記憶技巧　orn- 表示妝飾；-ment 為名詞字尾；ornament 即裝飾。

ornamental
[ˌɔrnəˋmɛntḷ]
a 裝飾的

The walls of the old temple were lined with ornamental handmade figurines of Taoist characters.
古廟牆壁排滿裝飾性的道教人物手工小雕像。

記憶技巧　-al 為形容詞字尾。

adorn
[əˋdɔrn]
v 裝飾

The warrior's earlobes were adorned with painted pieces of bone.
戰士的耳垂用彩繪骨頭裝飾著。

記憶技巧 ad- 表示朝～方向；orn- 表示裝飾；adorn 的意思是裝飾。

---

air - aer
母音通轉，兩者皆表示空氣。

---

aerial
[ˋɛrɪəl]
a 空氣的，航空的

The documentary film used stunning aerial video to show the beauty of the island.
紀錄片使用驚人的空拍錄影展示島嶼之美。

記憶技巧 aer- 表示空氣；-al，為形容詞字尾；aerial 即空氣的、航空的。

---

aerobatics
[ˌɛərəˋbætɪks]
n 特技飛行

The Black Falcons is a team that performs breathtaking aerobatics in New Zealand.
黑隼是一個紐西蘭表演驚人特技飛行的團隊。

記憶技巧 aero- 表示空氣；aerobatics 是仿造 acrobatics（雜技）所造出來的單字，表示特技飛行。

---

aerobics
[ˌɛəˋrobɪks]
n 有氧運動

The secretary joined an aerobics class twice a week to manage her weight.
祕書每週兩次上有氧運動課來控制體重。

記憶技巧 aero- 表示空氣；-ics 表示科學、學科；aerobics 是有氧運動。

相關字彙
運動

- aquarobics 水上增氧健身操
- body building 健美運動
- callisthenics 健美體操
- isometrics 定肌收縮運動
- pushup 伏地挺身
- sit-up 仰臥起坐
- weight training 重量訓練

---

aeronautics
[ˌɛərəˋnɔtɪks]
n 航空學

One of the pioneers of aeronautics was Michelangelo, who designed flying machines hundreds of years ago.
航空學先驅之一是米開朗基羅，他在數百年前設計飛行機器。

記憶技巧 aero- 表示空氣；naut- 表示航行；-ics 表示學問；aeronautics 是航空學。

Part
2
CH 1
CH 2
CH 3
CH 4
CH 5

子音對應相同

> ## arise - ori
> 母音通轉，兩者皆表示上升，ori- 又有誕生的意思。

---

oriental
[ˌorɪˈɛntl̩]
a 東方的

There is a store in Chinatown in San Francisco that sells oriental antiques and oddities.
舊金山的唐人街有一家賣東方古董和奇物的商店。

> **記憶技巧** ori- 表示上升；-al 為形容詞字尾；oriental 是太陽上升的方位，即東方的。

---

orientation
[ˌorɪənˈteʃən]
n 朝東，定位，指導，傾向，取向

Human resources managers were told that they were not allowed to base hiring decisions on sexual orientation.
人力資源經理被告知不得根據性取向決定僱用。

> **記憶技巧** ori- 表示上升；-ation 為名詞字尾；orientation 的意思是引導到太陽上升的方位，即東方，因此有朝東、定位等意思。

---

origin
[ˈɔrədʒɪn]
n 起源，出處

A crude drawing on a napkin was the origin of the concept of the new spacecraft.
餐巾上的簡略畫是新太空船概念的起源。

> **記憶技巧** ori- 表示上升；origin 引申為起源。

相關字彙
某人出處

- birthplace 出生地
- fatherland 祖國
- homeland 祖國
- mother country 祖國
- old country 故國

---

originate
[əˈrɪdʒəˌnet]
v 創始

Scientists have long debated the question of where life originated on our planet.
科學家長期爭論生命起源於我們星球上的何處這問題。

> **記憶技巧** -ate 為動詞字尾。

---

abortion
[əˈbɔrʃən]
n 墮胎，流產

Many religious groups fight for the rights of the unborn by trying to discourage abortions.
許多宗教團體試圖阻止墮胎以捍衛未出生嬰兒的權利。

> **記憶技巧** ab- 表示離開，在此當錯誤解釋；or- 等同於 ori-，表示上升，在此當出生；-tion 為名詞字尾；abortion 指的是未能出生，即墮胎。

相關字彙
生育控制

- birth control 避孕
- cap 避孕用的子宮帽
- condom 保險套
- contraceptive 避孕劑，避孕用具
- IUD (intrauterine device) 子宮內避孕器具
- morning-after pill 事後避孕藥
- oral contraceptive 口服避孕劑
- rhythm method 週期避孕法
- rubber 避孕套

aboriginal

[ˌæbəˈrɪdʒənl]

a 原始的，土著的

The Siraya Street is named after an aboriginal tribe in the Tainan area of Taiwan.

西拉雅大道以台灣台南地區原住民部落命名。

記憶技巧 ab- 表示從～離開；ori- 表示上升，在此當源頭；-al 為形容詞字尾；aboriginal 即出自於源頭，引申為原始的。

Part
2
CH 1
CH 2
CH 3
CH 4
CH 5

子音對應相同

Section **15**

〔s〕對應〔s〕

sue -sequ

母音通轉，兩者原意皆表示跟隨，sue 到 14 世紀末才有控告的意思。

pursue

[pɚˈsu]

v 追求，追趕，
實行，繼續

The young man left college early to pursue a business opportunity with a startup company.

為了用新創公司尋求商機，年輕人提早離開大學。

記憶技巧 pur- 等同於 pro-，表示往前；sue 表示跟隨；pursue 的意思是跟隨著往前走，引申為追趕、追求等。

相關字彙
追求、跟隨

- chase 追求
- come after 追趕
- go after 追求
- in hot pursuit 窮追不捨
- run after 追求

ensue

[ɛnˈsu]

v 隨後發生

A prolonged fight ensued between the couple after a disagreement could not be resolved.

意見不合無法解決之後，夫婦間的長期對抗接踵而至。

記憶技巧 en- 等同於 in-，表示隨即；sue 表示跟隨；ensue 是隨後發生。

pursuit

[pɚˈsut]

n 追求，實行，經營

His lifelong pursuit of perfection proved to be worthwhile when he led his basketball team to championship.

當他領導籃球隊獲得冠軍，他終身追求對於完美的證明是值得的。

記憶技巧 pursuit 是 pursue 的名詞。

suitable

[`sutəbl]

a 合適的

Army planners spent two weeks searching for suitable landing point for the invading forces.

陸軍策劃人員花兩星期尋找入侵部隊的適當著陸點。

記憶技巧 suit- 表示跟隨；-able 為形容詞字尾；suitable 的意思是跟隨合適的人，引申為合適的、可匹配的。

---

sequence

[`sikwəns]

n 連續，順序，結果

The new program allows researchers to visualize DNA sequences on a computer screen.

新程式能讓研究人員在電腦螢幕上看見 DNA 序列。

記憶技巧 sequ- 表示跟隨；-ence 為名詞字尾；sequence 指的是一個跟著一個的順序。

---

subsequent

[`sʌbsɪˌkwɛnt]

a 後來的，附隨的

After the war ended, notable advances were made in the Arts in the subsequent period of peace.

戰爭結束後，藝術在隨後的和平時期顯著進步。

記憶技巧 sub- 在此當緊密的意思；sequ- 表示跟隨；-ent 為形容詞字尾；subsequent 的意思是緊跟在後，引申為後來的。

---

consequence

[`kɑnsəˌkwɛns]

n 結果，影響，重要（性）

You'd better believe that there will be consequences to your decision to start smoking.

你最好相信，決定開始吸菸會有後續影響。

記憶技巧 con- 表示一起；sequ- 表示跟著；-ence 為名詞字尾；consequence 的意思是緊跟在後，引申出結果的意思。

---

consecutive

[kən`sɛkjutɪv]

a 連續的

There were six consecutive months without rain, so water rationing was put into effect.

連續六個月沒有下雨，因此開始定量配水。

記憶技巧 con- 表示一起；secu- 表示跟著；-ive 為形容詞字尾；consecutive 的意思是大家一起跟著，引申為連續的。

---

same - simil

母音通轉，兩者出自同源，same 是相同的，simil- 是相同的、相似的。

---

simile

[`sɪməˌli]

n 直喻，明喻

He offered a simile to describe his best friend, declaring that he was as dependable as a brother.

他用比喻描述自己最好的朋友，說他像兄弟一樣可靠。

記憶技巧 simil- 表示相似的；simile 是一種修辭手法，藉由觀察兩者相似的地方，將某對象比喻成另一對象。

similarity
[ˌsɪməˈlærətɪ]

n 相似，相似處

There was a striking similarity between the candidate's speech and the speech of the previous president.
候選人的演講和前總統的演講有著明顯的相似之處。

記憶技巧　simil- 表示相似的；-ar 為形容詞字尾；-ity 為名詞字尾；similarity 即相似之處。

---

simulate
[ˈsɪmjəˌlet]

v 假裝，類似，模擬

The video game simulates the places and events of Shanghai in the 1920's.
電動遊戲模擬上海 1920 年代的場景和事件。

記憶技巧　simul- 等同於 simil-，表示相似的；-ate 為動詞字尾；simulate 即調整自己，讓自己像他者，因此有假裝的意思。

---

simultaneous
[ˌsaɪmlˈtenɪəs]

a 同時發生的，同時存在的

As the frame travels down the assembly line, the motor is assembled in a simultaneous process.
框架在組裝線移動時，電動機同時在組裝的工序中。

記憶技巧　simul- 等同於 simil-，表示相似的、相同的；-ous 為形容詞字尾；simultaneous 指的是同時發生的。

---

assimilate
[əˈsɪmlˌet]

v 同化，融入

The student didn't quite assimilate into the academic cram school because of its strict methods.
由於方法嚴格，學生無法完全融入學科補習班。

記憶技巧　as- 等同於 ad-，表示朝～方向；simil- 表示相似的；-ate 為動詞字尾；assimilate 的意思是使～相似、相同，引申為同化。

---

dissimilation
[dɪsˌɪməˈleʃən]

n 異化

After diverse migrants arrived, the population underwent a process of dissimilation in regards to appearance.
不同移民到達後，人口在外觀上經歷了異化過程。

記憶技巧　dis- 表示相反；simil- 表示相似的；-ation 為名詞字尾；dissimilation 即不相像，引申為異化解釋。

---

resemble
[rɪˈzɛmbl̩]

v 相像，相似

It is questionable that she could be your child, because she resembles no one in your family.
很懷疑她怎麼會是你的孩子，因為她根本不像你家裡的任何人。

記憶技巧　re- 表示加強語氣；semble 等同於 simil-，表示相似的；resemble 的意思是相像。

相關字彙
相似

- take after 相似
- be the image of【口】極像某人／某事物
- be every inch something 像極了某類型的人

facsimile

[fækˋsɪməlɪ]

n 傳真，複製

The British fooled the advancing German army by placing a large number of fascimiles of tanks on the battlefield.

英國人在戰場放置大量逼真坦克騙過向前行進的德軍。

> **記憶技巧** fac- 表示做；simil- 表示相似的；facsimile 的意思是做出類似的東西，引申為複製。

---

stand - sist

母音通轉 sist- 中的 st 即 stand，兩者皆表示站。

---

assist

[əˋsɪst]

v 援助

The aide was hired to assist the legal team to deal with the complicated case.

助理受聘協助法律團隊處理複雜案件。

> **記憶技巧** as- 等同於 ad-，表示朝～方向；sist- 表示站；assist 的意思是去站～旁邊，引申為協助參加。

---

consistent

[kənˋsɪstənt]

a 一致的，不變的

Both parents discussed punishment with each other before facing the child, in order to offer consistent reasoning.

面對孩子前，父母先彼此討論如何處罰，以使理由一致。

> **記憶技巧** con- 表示一起；sist- 表示站；-ent 為形容詞字尾；consistent 的意思是站在一起，引申出穩固的，現今的意思是一致的。

---

insistent

[ɪnˋsɪstənt]

a 堅持的，顯著的

The parents were insistent that the Dean of the school give their child a makeup exam.

父母堅持學校教務長要讓他們的孩子補考。

> **記憶技巧** in- 表示在～之上；sist- 表示站；-ent 為形容詞字尾；insistent 的意思是站在～之上，引申出堅持的、顯著的等意思。

---

persist

[pɚˋsɪst]

v 堅持，固執

The girl quickly learned that persisting in her demands would lead to the desired result.

女孩很快學到，堅持要求將導致期望的結果。

> **記憶技巧** per- 表示徹底地；sist- 表示站；persist 的意思是一直站著，引申出堅持、固執的意思。

resistance

[rɪ`zɪstəns]

n 抵抗

The woman put up little resistance to her boss, but filed a lawsuit afterwards.

女子對老闆幾乎沒有反抗，但之後有提告。

記憶技巧 re- 表示抵抗；sist- 表示站；-ance 為名詞字尾；resistance 的意思即抵抗。

subsistence

[səb`sɪstəns]

n 生存，
賴以活命的東西

The family packed light in order to experience living in subsistence in the forest during their vacation.

為了在度假期在森林中體驗生存，這家庭輕裝打包行李。

記憶技巧 sub- 表示在～下面；sist- 表示站；-ence 為名詞字尾；subsistence 指在底下站著，引申出支持著的意思，因此有生存、生計等意思。

exist

[ɪg`zɪst]

v 存在，生存

The only way to know that black holes exist is to study their effects on objects near them.

知道黑洞存在的唯一方法是研究它對附近物體的影響。

記憶技巧 ex- 表示往前；sist- 表示站；exist 的意思是往前站，引申出生存的意思。

Part 2 CH 1 CH 2 CH 3 CH 4 CH 5 子音對應相同

---

sopor - somn

兩者系出同源，藉由子音 p 和 m 互換，母音通轉，soper 表示酣睡，somn- 表示睡。

soporific

[͵sopə`rɪfɪk]

a 催眠的

The student had to be alert for her exam, so she consumed warm milk for its soporific effects.

學生必須為考試保持警醒，所以她喝了有助睡眠的溫牛奶。

記憶技巧 sopor- 表示熟睡；-ic 為形容詞字尾；soporific 的意思是熟睡的，引申為催眠的。

insomnia

[ɪn`sɑmnɪə]

n 失眠，失眠症

The security guard suffered from insomnia every night, so he chose to work the night shift.

保全人員每晚都失眠，所以選擇夜班工作。

記憶技巧 in- 表示否定字首；somn- 表示睡眠；-ia 表示疾病；insomnia 的意思是睡不著的疾病，即失眠症。

相關字彙
醒著沒睡著

- awake 醒著的
- sleepless 失眠的
- wakeful 不眠的
- wide awake 完全醒著的
- toss and turn 輾轉反側

somnambulism
[sɑmˋnæmbjəlɪzəm]
n 夢遊症

The patient attended a session with a hypnotist to treat her persistent somnambulism.
患者去看了一次催眠師，以治療持續的夢遊。

> **記憶技巧** somn- 表示睡覺；ambul- 表示走路；-ism 為名詞字尾；somnambulism 的意思是夢遊症。

somnolent
[ˋsɑmnələnt]
a 嗜睡的，催眠的

The somnolent office worker could be seen nodding with his eyes closed during the meeting.
會議期間，可以看到嗜睡的辦公室員工閉著眼睛打瞌睡。

> **記憶技巧** somn- 表示睡覺；-olent 為形容詞字尾，表示充滿的；somnolent 的意思是嗜睡的、催眠的。

suck - succ
兩者皆表示吸。

succulent
[ˋsʌkjələnt]
a 多水分的

We couldn't wait to taste the succulent meat of the suckling pig roasting over the coals.
我們迫不及待要品嚐炭烤乳豬鮮美多汁的肉。

> **記憶技巧** succ- 表示吸；-ulent 為形容詞字尾，表示充滿的；succulent 的意思是多水分的。

seed - semin
母音通轉，兩者皆原始意思皆表示播種，亦有種子的意思。

seminar
[ˋsɛməˌnɑr]
n 研討會

With the 5-day seminar on personal transformation, you may totally change your life.
參加為期 5 天個人改造研討會中，你可能完全改變人生。

> **記憶技巧** semin- 表示播種；-ar 為名詞字尾；seminar 的意思是苗圃，研討會的意思在 1944 年始見於紀錄。

相關字彙
會議

- appointment（尤指正式的）約定會面
- assembly 集會
- audioconferencing 音訊會議
- briefing 簡報
- conference call 電話會議
- congress 會議
- convention 會議
- consultation（磋商）會議
- convocation（尤指宗教或學術上的）會議
- forum 討論會
- session（議會等的）開會
- symposium 座談會
- videoconference 視訊會議
- workshop 專題討論會

seminal

[ˋsɛmən!]

a 種子的，有潛力的，開創性的

Marie Curie's seminal work with radioactive chemicals influences the work of oncologists today.

瑪麗·居禮在放射性化學物質的開創性工作影響了今日腫瘤學家的工作。

記憶技巧 semin- 表示種子；-al 為形容詞字尾；seminal 即種子的。

---

seminary

[ˋsɛməˌnɛrɪ]

n 神學院，溫床

Th man attended a seminary, so his mother could be proud to have a minister in the family.

男子就讀神學院，因此他母親可能為家中有一位神職人員而感到驕傲。

記憶技巧 semin- 表示種子；-ary 表示地方；seminary 本指苗圃，1580 年代後才有神學院的意思。

---

disseminate

[dɪˋsɛməˌnet]

v 傳播，散佈

With social media, it is much easier to disseminate unbiased news, as well as gossip.

因為有社交媒體，傳播公允的消息及八卦容易多了。

記憶技巧 dis- 表示各個方向；semin- 表示種子；-ate 為動詞字尾；disseminate 的意思是散播種子，引申為傳播、散佈。

---

serum - sero / seri
母音通轉，兩者皆表示血清。

serous

[ˋsɪrəs]

a 血清的

The researchers spun test tubes containing a serous mixture of snake venom and chemical preservatives.

研究人員轉動試管，裡面含有蛇毒和化學防腐劑的血清混合物。

記憶技巧 ser- 表示血清；-ous 為形容詞字尾；serous 的意思是血清的。

---

sound - son
母音通轉，兩者皆表示聲音。

sonorous

[səˋnorəs]

a 響亮的

The voice actor was very popular with advertising agencies because of the sonorous tone of his voice.

配音員因為聲音響亮，頗受廣告公司歡迎。

記憶技巧 son- 表示聲音；-ous 為形容詞字尾；sonorous 是聲音響亮的。

Part 2

CH 1
CH 2
CH 3
CH 4
CH 5

子音對應相同

consonance
[ˋkɑnsənəns]

n 一致，和諧

There was a definite consonance between the increase in productivity and the rise in wages.
提高生產力和升高工資之間有明確一致性。

記憶技巧 con- 表示一起；son- 表示聲音；-ance 為名詞字尾；consonance 的意思是一起發出聲音，引申為一致、和諧。

dissonant
[ˋdɪsənənt]

a 刺耳，不一致，不和諧的

The coffeeshop was usually chaotic scene because of the barista and his dissonant team members.
因為這位店員和他不和的團隊成員，咖啡店經常場面混亂。

記憶技巧 dis- 表示分開；son- 表示聲音；-ant 為形容詞字尾；dissonant 的意思是聲音不一致，因此有刺耳的意思。

supersonic
[ˌsupɚˋsɑnɪk]

a 超音波的，超音速的

With supersonic flight being a reality, man aimed to build aircraft capable of hypersonic flight.
超音速飛行已成真，人類以建造能夠特超音速飛行的飛機為目標。

記憶技巧 super- 表示超過；son- 表示聲音；-ic 為形容詞字尾；supersonic 的意思是超音速的。

ultrasonic
[ˌʌltrəˋsɑnɪk]

a 超音波的

Medical scanner can measure ultrasonic sound waves to produce ultrasound images.
醫療掃描器能夠測得超聲波以產生超聲波圖像。

記憶技巧 ultra- 表示超過；son- 表示聲音；-ic 為形容詞字尾；ultrasonic 即超音波的。

相關字彙
聲音

- acoustics 聲學
- audio 聽覺的
- decibel 分貝
- stereo 立體聲
- volume 音量
- loudness 響度

resonance
[ˋrɛzənəns]

n 共鳴，回響

The two musicians experienced a powerful resonance when they created music together.
兩位音樂家一起創作音樂時體驗到強大的共鳴。

記憶技巧 re- 表示回來、再一次；son- 表示聲音；-ance 為名詞字尾；resonance 即回響、共鳴。

unison
[ˋjunəsn̩]

n 一致，和諧

The trio sang in perfect unison to produce a beautiful harmony together.
三重唱完美一致，一起營造美麗和聲。

記憶技巧 uni- 表示一；son- 表示聲音；unison 的意思是一種聲音，引申為一致。

sonar

[`sonɑr]

n 聲納

Dolphins have a natural sonar system, which allows them to avoid hitting objects when they swim in the dark.

海豚有天然聲納系統，讓牠們在黑暗中游泳時不撞到物體。

記憶技巧 son- 表示聲音；-ar 為名詞字尾，表示做出動作者；sonar 是聲納，藉由發出音響訊號，由反射情況來得知其他事的方位、距離等。

相關字彙
航行、船上設備

- anchor 錨
- ballast 壓艙物
- buoy 救生圈
- lifebelt 救生帶
- lifejacket 救生衣
- oar 槳
- paddle（短而闊的）槳

Part

2

CH 1
CH 2
CH 3
CH 4
CH 5

子音對應相同

---

six - sex

母音通轉，兩者皆表示六。

---

sextet

[sɛks`tɛt]

n 六重奏

The group of ex-classmates formed a jazz sextet and perfomed at their high school class reunion.

一群老同學組成一個爵士六重奏，並在他們的高中同學會表演。

記憶技巧 sex- 表示六；sextet 是六重奏。

---

sexagenarian

[ˌsɛksədʒəˋnɛrɪən]

n 六十幾歲的人

The sexagenarian couple was remarkably active, dancing into the late hours on weekends.

這對六十幾歲的夫婦活力十足，週末跳舞到很晚。

記憶技巧 sex- 表示六；-genarian 表示十倍；sexagenarian 即六十幾歲的（人）。

---

sun - sol

子音 n 和 l 互換，母音通轉，兩者皆表示太陽。

---

solar

[`solɚ]

a 太陽的

Mobile solar generators are highly popular imported items in the Middle East.

活動太陽能發電機是中東地區非常受歡迎的進口項目。

記憶技巧 sol- 表示太陽；-ar 為形容詞字尾；solar 即太陽的。

insolation
[ˌɪnsəˋleʃən]
n 中暑，太陽曝曬

Planners studied the map looking for areas of high insolation in order to choose the ideal location for the solar farm.

計劃人員研究地圖，尋找高日照區域，以挑選太陽能發電場理想位置。

記憶技巧　in- 表示在～內；sol- 表示太陽；-ation 為名詞字尾；insolation 即曝曬在陽光中。

parasol
[ˋpærəˌsɔl]
n 陽傘

Distinguished ladies of society were holding parasols open to protect themselves from the sun.

社交名媛撐起陽傘保護自己不曬到太陽。

記憶技巧　para- 表示抵抗；sol- 表示太陽；parasol 即陽傘，可抵抗陽光直接曝曬。

相關字彙
戶外桌椅、遮蔽處

- bench 長凳
- chaise 躺椅
- deckchair 帆布摺椅
- sunbed 日光浴（或太陽燈浴）浴床
- sunshade 遮陽傘（篷）
- windbreak 風障

salt - sal
兩者皆表示鹽。

saline
[ˋselaɪn]
a 鹽的，含鹽的，鹹的

Drugs can be introduced into the bloodstream through an IV drip, but should be diluted with saline solution.

藥物可透過靜脈注射送至血液，但要用含鹽溶液稀釋。

記憶技巧　sal- 表示鹽；-ine 為形容詞字尾；saline 即鹽的。

salinity
[səˋlɪnətɪ]
n 鹽分，鹹度，含鹽量

The salinity of the Dead Sea is over 33%, so it is highly corrosive.

死海含鹽量超過 33%，因此腐蝕性頗高。

記憶技巧　sal- 表示鹽；-ine 為形容詞字尾；-ity 為名詞字尾；salinity 即鹽分。

saltern
[ˋsɔltɚn]
n 鹽田，製鹽廠

In southwestern Taiwan, people still use salterns to collect salt for sale.

在臺灣西南部，人們仍然運用鹽田收集鹽巴販售。

記憶技巧　salt- 表示鹽；saltern 是鹽田。

salad

[`sæləd]

n 沙拉，萵苣，生菜

Eating a green salad with each meal will ensure that you get enough fibre in your diet.

每餐食用蔬菜沙拉可確保從飲食攝取足夠纖維素。

記憶技巧　sal- 表示鹽；salad 本意是用鹽醃製的蔬菜，後來專指沙拉。

相關字彙
沙拉，沙拉醬

- Caesar salad 凱撒沙拉
- Greek salad 希臘沙拉
- green salad 蔬菜沙拉
- salad cream 一種放在沙拉上面的蛋黃醬
- salad dressing 生菜食品之調味汁
- coleslaw 涼拌卷心菜
- tabbouleh 麥粒番茄生菜沙拉
- Waldorf salad 沃爾多夫沙拉

salary

[`sæləɪ]

n 薪水

It wasn't the decent salary that was the deciding factor, but it was the amount of vacation time offered.

決定因素不是豐厚的薪水，而是所提供的假期天數。

記憶技巧　sal- 表示鹽；salary 是薪水，有一說法是發給羅馬士兵用來買鹽的薪水，後來這個字就專指薪水。

self - sui

母音通轉，兩者皆表示自己。

suicidal

[ˌsuəˋsaɪdl̩]

a 自殺的

You should reach out to your friends and family, if you ever have suicidal thoughts.

如果有自殺念頭，應該和家人及朋友聯繫。

記憶技巧　sui- 表示自己；cid- 表示殺；-al 為形容詞字尾；suicidal 即自殺的。

spy - spec

母音通轉，兩者的原意皆表示觀察、看。

expect

[ɪkˋspɛkt]

v 預期，期待

What did you expect to happen when you gave your credit card to your teenage daughter?

你把你的信用卡給十幾歲的女兒時，預料會發生什麼事？

記憶技巧　ex- 表示外面；spect- 表示看；expect 的意思是往外看，引申為期待。

相關字彙
預期、預料

- bargain on【口】預料
- count on 指望
- calculate on 指望
- plan on 打算
- reckon on 指望
- suppose 期望

Part **2**

CH 1
CH 2
CH 3
CH 4
CH 5

子音對應相同

aspect

[`æspɛkt]

n 方面，外觀，形勢

It is up to the readers to decide which aspect of the novel is most relevant to their lives.

是讀者決定小說的哪一方面跟他們的生活最有關聯。

記憶技巧　as- 等同於 ad-，表示朝～方向；spect- 表示看；aspect 的意思是朝～方向看，引申為看事情的方式，因此有方面的意思。

inspect

[ɪn`spɛkt]

v 檢查

The high speed railway trains were inspected for any defects, before they were approved and shipped abroad.

高速鐵路列車核准運送國外前，被檢查以找出任何的瑕疵。

記憶技巧　in- 表示內；spect- 表示看；inspect 的意思是往內看，引申為檢查。

perspective

[pɚ`spɛktɪv]

n 看法，觀點

In an unusual storytelling method, the film switches often between the perspectives of the killer and the victim.

電影以特殊的說故事方法，常在兇手和受害者的觀點之間做變換。

記憶技巧　per- 表示穿透；spect- 表示看；-ive 為形容詞字尾；perspective 的意思是透視、看法、觀點等。

prospective

[prə`spɛktɪv]

a 預期的，有希望的

The talent scout hosted a job fair to interview prospective candidates for the new trainee program.

星探主辦一場人才招募會，以面試可能的人選參加新培訓課程。

記憶技巧　pro- 表示往前；spect- 表示看；-ive 為形容詞字尾；prospective 的意思是往前看的，引申為預期的、有希望的。

respect

[rɪ`spɛkt]

n 尊重

The business owner showed no respect to the health inspector until he was forced to pay a fine.

業主對稽查員不敬，直到被迫付罰款。

記憶技巧　re- 表示回去；spect- 表示看；respect 的意思是回頭看，引申為尊敬。

suspect

[`sʌspɛkt]

n 嫌疑犯

When the petty cash box disappeared, all employees were suspects.

小現金盒不見時，所有員工都是嫌疑犯。

記憶技巧　sus- 等同於 sub-，表示下面；spect- 表示看；suspect 的意思是站在下面往上偷偷看，因此有懷疑意思，名詞當嫌疑犯解釋。

suspicious

[sə`spɪʃəs]

a 可疑的

New security cameras have been installed in the hallways to observe and record any suspicious activity.

新監視器已安裝在走廊,監視和記錄任何可疑活動。

記憶技巧 sus- 等同於 sub-,表示下面;spic- 等同於 spect-,表示看;-ous 為形容詞字尾;suspicious 的意思是在下面偷偷看,引申為可疑的。

specimen

[`spɛsəmən]

n 標本,樣品

Prospective employees were required to submit a stool specimen and a urine sample.

可能的員工被要求交糞便檢體及尿液採樣。

記憶技巧 spec- 表示看;-men 為名詞字尾;specimen 是供人欣賞的標本或樣品。

special

[`spɛʃəl]

a 特別的,專用的

In the airport VIP lounge, members were afforded special privileges while they waited.

機場貴賓室提供會員候機時的特殊禮遇。

記憶技巧 spec- 表示看;-ial 為形容詞字尾;special 的意思是看起來不同的,因此有特別的、專用的等衍生意思。

specific

[spɪ`sɪfɪk]

a 明確的

If there was a specific incident that turned his life around, it was when the late owner offered him a job.

如果有件明確的事翻轉他的人生,就是已故的老闆雇用他的時候。

記憶技巧 spec- 表示看(起來特別);fic- 表示做;specific 的意思是做出看起來很特別的事,至於明確的意思始見於 1740 年的紀載。

spectacular

[spɛk`tækjəlɚ]

a 壯觀的

New Year's celebration this year included a spectacular fireworks display and a special guest.

今年新年慶祝活動包含一場壯觀煙火秀和一位特別來賓。

記憶技巧 spect- 表示看;spectacle 是壯觀的場面;-ar 為形容詞字尾;spectacular 即壯觀的。

auspice

[`ɔspɪs]

n 前兆,吉兆

A flock of white doves flew over the wedding, an obvious auspice for a happy marriage.

一群白鴿飛過婚禮,顯然是幸福婚姻的吉兆。

記憶技巧 au- 等同於 av-,表示鳥;spic- 等同於 spect-,表示看;auspice 的意思是看鳥飛,古人藉由觀察鳥的飛行來占卜吉凶,引申為前兆、吉兆。

Part
2
CH 1
CH 2
CH 3
CH 4
CH 5

子音對應相同

despise

[dɪˋspaɪz]

v 輕視

The policeman despised the criminal who had killed his relative, but he still had to bring him in to face trial.
警察輕視殺害親屬的犯人，但仍然必須帶他去面對審判。

記憶技巧 de- 表示往下；spis- 等同於 spect-，表示看；despise 的意思是往下看，引申為輕視。

---

sister - soror

母音通轉，兩者皆表示姊妹。

sororal

[səˋrorəl]

a 姊妹的

During the sleepover, the friends braided each other's hair and participated in other sororal activities.
在過夜聚會中，這群朋友彼此編頭髮辮子，並參與其他姊妹活動。

記憶技巧 soror- 表示姊妹；-al 為形容詞字尾；sororal 即姊妹的。

---

sound - san

兩者雖無字源關係，但可藉由母音通轉來記憶，兩者皆表示健康的。

sane

[sen]

a 健全的，
神智正常的

Any sane father would have wanted his daughter to marry the generous tycoon.
任何正常的父親都會希望女兒嫁給這位慷慨的大亨。

記憶技巧 san- 表示健康的；sane 引申為神志正常的。

相關字彙
頭腦清楚的

- logical 合理的
- rational 理性的
- sensible 明智的

insane

[ɪnˋsen]

a 精神不健全的

It is incredible that they would let an insane person have access to the nuclear launch codes.
他們讓一個精神不健全的人使用核能啟動密碼，真是難以置信。

記憶技巧 in- 為否定字首；insane 即精神不健全的。

相關字彙
心理出狀況

- deranged 瘋狂的
- demented 精神錯亂狀態的
- hysterical 歇斯底里的

- melancholic 憂鬱的
- paranoid 屬於偏執狂的
- schizophrenic 精神分裂症的

stiff - stereo

兩者雖無字源關係，但可藉由母音通轉來記憶，兩者皆表示硬、挺，stereo- 衍生出立體的意思。

Part
2
CH 1
CH 2
CH 3
CH 4
CH 5

子音對應相同

stereo
[`stɛrɪo]
a 立體聲的

The music was broadcast to the audience with powerful speakers in stereo sound.
音樂被大功率立體聲喇叭傳送至聽眾。

（記憶技巧） stereo 即立體聲的。

stereotype
[`stɛrɪə,taɪp]
n 刻版印象

It is an unfair stereotype to consider computer programmers to be weak, antisocial people.
認為電腦程式設計師是體弱、不合群的人，是不公平的刻板印象。

（記憶技巧） stereo- 表示立體；type 表示類型；stereotype 的意思是由模板印出來的立體形式，引申為刻板印象。

相關字彙
典型（例子）
- archetype 原型
- prototype 原型
- template 樣板
- model 模範
- case 事例

star - aster

母音通轉，兩者皆表示星星。

asterisk
[`æstə,rɪsk]
n 星號

The asterisk next to the win-loss record indicated that the validity of the team's wins was questioned.
勝敗紀錄旁的星號顯示該隊獲勝的正確性遭到質疑。

（記憶技巧） aster- 表示星星；asterisk 是星號。

asteroid
[`æstə,rɔɪd]
n 小行星

The space agency planned to send a spaceship to collect samples from the passing asteroid.
太空部門計劃發送太空船，以從經過的小行星採集樣本。

（記憶技巧） aster- 表示星星；-oid 表示形狀；asteroid 的意思是星形的，名詞當小行星解釋。

astrology
[ə`strɑlədʒɪ]
n 占星術

Many housewives in the region turn to astrology to make decisions each day.
該地區許多家庭主婦每天靠占星術決定事情。

（記憶技巧） astro- 表示星星；-logy 表示學問；astrology 是占星學。

astronaut
[ˋæstrəˌnɔt]
n 太空人

The first astronaut to orbit the Earth, John Glenn, passed away on December 8, 2016.
第一位環繞地球的太空人約翰‧葛倫，於 2016 年 12 月 8 日逝世。

記憶技巧　astro- 表示星星；naut- 表示航員；astronaut 即在星際間航行的太空人。

astronomer
[əˋstrɑnəmɚ]
n 天文學家

Nicolaus Copernicus was the brilliant astronomer who proved that the Earth was not the center of the universe.
尼古拉斯‧哥白尼是證明地球不是宇宙的中心點的傑出天文學家。

記憶技巧　astro- 表示星星；nom- 表示規則；-er 為做出動作者；astronomer 是研究星象規則的天文學家。

disaster
[dɪˋzæstɚ]
n 災難

Facing certain disaster, the passengers of the stalled airplane began praying to their gods.
面臨必然的災難，熄火飛機的乘客開始祈求神明。

記憶技巧　dis- 在此有貶意；aster- 表示星星；disaster 即不好的星星，指凶星，古人相信會帶來災難。

---

strain - strict
母音通轉，兩者皆表示拉緊。

strain
[stren]
v 拉緊，壓力，緊張

I don't want you to strain your budget, so please allow me to pay for lunch today.
我不想要你荷包吃緊，因此請我付午餐錢。

記憶技巧　strain 即拉緊。

constrain
[kənˋstren]
v 強迫，約束，監禁

The junior executive felt constrained by his seniors, and demanded to be given more responsibilities.
初級主管感到被前輩約束，而要求被給予更多責任。

記憶技巧　con- 表示一起；strain- 表示拉緊；constrain 的意思是拉在一起，引申為強迫、約束。

相關字彙
限制、束縛

- control 克制
- fetter 束縛
- hamper 束縛
- limit 限制
- tie down 束縛

restrain

[rɪˋstren]

v 抑制，羈押

The father of the victim has to be restrained by the court police after the defendant was declared "not guilty."

宣布被告無罪後，受害者父親必須由法警壓制。

記憶技巧 re- 表示回來；strain- 表示拉緊；restrain 的意思是拉回來，引申為抑制、羈押等。

strict

[strɪkt]

a 嚴格的，嚴厲的

The Thai monk adhered to a strict routine of meditation, exercise and study.

這名泰國和尚遵守冥想、運動、研讀的嚴格作息。

記憶技巧 strict 表示拉緊，引申為嚴格的。

restrict

[rɪˋstrɪkt]

v 限制，約束

In order to restrict the intake of cholesterol, the dietician planned meals that did not include eggs.

為了限制膽固醇攝取量，營養師設計不含蛋的餐點。

記憶技巧 re- 表示回來；strict- 表示拉緊；restrict 的意思是拉回來，引申為限制。

distressful

[dɪˋstrɛsfəl]

a 悲慘的，
使人苦惱的

She couldn't bear the distressful news that her grandfather lost all of the money she was going to inherit.

她無法忍受祖父失去所有她原本要繼承的財產的悲慘消息。

記憶技巧 dis- 表示分開；stress- 表示拉緊；-ful 為形容詞字尾；distressful 字面上意思是拉開，有強迫、阻撓的意思，因此衍生出悲慘的、使人苦惱的等負面意思。

---

spars - spers

母音通轉，兩者皆表示撒、分散。

aspersion

[əˋspɝʒən]

n 中傷，誹謗

The mayor believed his falling popularity was a result of aspersions cast upon him by the opposition.

市長相信他的人氣下滑是在野黨造謠中傷毀謗的結果。

記憶技巧 a- 等同於 ad-，表示往～方向；spers- 表示撒；-ion 為名詞字尾；aspersion 字面上的意思是朝～撒東西，引申為毀謗。

相關字彙
毀人名譽

- discredit 敗壞～的名聲
- disgrace 使蒙受恥辱
- slander 詆毀
- stain 玷汙
- smear 誹謗
- taint 玷汙

Part 2
CH 1
CH 2
CH 3
CH 4
CH 5
子音對應相同

disperse [dɪˋspɝs] **v** 散布，分散	The Austronesian people are dispersed over a wide area from Taiwan to Hawaii to New Zealand. 南島族群分布區域廣大，從臺灣到夏威夷到紐西蘭。 記憶技巧 dis- 表示分開；spers- 表示撒；disperse 的意思是撒開，因此有散布、分散等意思。
sparse [spɑrs] **a** 稀疏的	Not having time to entertain guests, the grad student lived in an apartment with sparse furnishings. 沒時間招呼旅客，研究生住在家具稀少的公寓裡。 記憶技巧 spars- 表示撒；sparse 表示撒開的，引申為稀疏的。

原來如此！

一些字容易混淆，但若以音相近、意相連的原則處理，還是不難找出同源字及其語意傾向。就以 rise / arise / raise / rouse / arouse 這幾個動詞來說：rise / arise / raise 發音相近，同源，都與上升的動作有關；arouse 是 rouse 的衍生字（a + rouse = on + rouse），都與醒來或激起行動有關。

rise 意思是上升，動詞變化 rose - risen 都是母音通轉；

arise 意思是上升或出現，動詞變化與 rise 的母音通轉形式一致；

raise 意思是舉起，源自 rise，規則動詞變化；

rouse 意思是叫醒或喚起，而 arouse 也有這些語意。

Chapter 6
〔h〕變化

Section 1

〔s〕對應〔h〕

（拉丁語、英語字母「s」，對應希臘語字母「h」）

---

six - hexa

子音 s 和 h 對應，母音通轉，兩者皆表示六。

---

hexagram
[ˋhɛksəˏɡræm]
n 六角星形

The witches and warlocks performed incantations standing on a hexagram drawn on the floor.
女巫和術士站在畫在地板上的六角星形上施咒語。

> 記憶技巧　hexa- 表示六；-gram 為名詞字尾，表示圖案或寫；hexagram 即六角星形。

---

hexapod
[ˋhɛksəˏpɑd]
n 昆蟲類，
六足（動物）

The machine that won the science fair was a walking hexapod robot that resembled a bettle.
贏得科學展覽的機器是一個像甲蟲走路的六足機器人。

> 記憶技巧　hexa- 表示六；pod- 等同於 ped-，表示腳；hexapod 即六足動物。

---

sun - helio

子音 s 和 h 對應，母音通轉，兩者皆表示太陽。

---

helioscope
[ˋhiliəˏskop]
n 觀日望遠鏡

The first helioscope used to view the sun was invented by Benedetto Castelli over 350 years ago.
第一個用於觀看太陽的觀日望遠鏡是貝內代卡斯泰利於超過 350 年前發明的。

> 記憶技巧　helio- 表示太陽；scope 表示看；helioscope 是觀日的望眼鏡。

相關字彙
看東西時可以讓物體放大的設備

- eyepiece 接目鏡
- field glasses 望遠鏡
- periscope 潛望鏡
- spyglass 小望遠鏡
- telescope（單筒）望遠鏡

heliocentric
[͵hilɪoˋsɛntrɪk]
a 以太陽為中心的

In the heliocentric model of our solar system, our sun is positioned in the center.
太陽中心的太陽系模型中，太陽位於中心。

記憶技巧 helio- 表示太陽；center 表示中心；-ic 為形容詞字尾；heliocentric 即以太陽為中心的。

heliotropic
[͵hilɪəˋtrɑpɪk]
a 向日性的

As the sun moves towards the horizon, the heliotropic sunflowers follow the sun's movement.
太陽朝向地平線移動時，趨光性的向日葵隨著太陽轉動。

記憶技巧 helio- 表示太陽；trop- 表示轉；-ic 為形容詞字尾；heliotropic 即向日性的。

helium
[ˋhilɪəm]
n 氦

Helium replaced hydrogen as the gas used in ballons, because it is non-flammable.
由於不可燃特性，氦取代氫氣作為氣球使用的氣體。

記憶技巧 天文學家於 1868 年研究太陽光譜時所發現的元素，因為起先是在太陽上發現，接著才在地球上發現，故以「hel-（太陽）」來命名，-ium 是表示金屬的化學元素，但氦並非金屬元素，被視為誤用。

相關字彙
各種氣體

- ammonia 氨
- argon 氬
- ethane 乙烷
- fluorine 氟
- hydrogen 氫
- laughing gas 笑氣
- oxygen 氧氣
- shale gas 頁岩氣
- tear gas 催淚瓦斯
- water vapor 水蒸汽

---

seek - hegemon
子音 s 和 h 對應，k 和 g 互換，母音通轉，兩者皆表示追求。

---

hegemony
[hiˋdʒɛmənɪ]
n 霸權，領導權

The Baltic country of Latvia separated from Russian hegemony in 1990.
拉脫維亞這個波羅的海國家於 1990 年自俄國霸權分離。

記憶技巧 hegemon- 表示追求；-y 為名詞字尾，可藉由「擁有領導權是許多人想追求的」來聯想。

相關字彙
政府系統

- banana republic【貶】香蕉共和國
- caretaker government 看守政府
- e-government e 化政府
- martial law 戒嚴令
- power-sharing 權力分享
- self-determination 民族自決

Part **2**

CH 1
CH 2
CH 3
CH 4
CH 5
CH 6

〔h〕
變化

sleep - hypno

子音 s 和 h 對應，母音通轉，兩者皆表示睡眠。

---

hypnosis
[hɪpˋnosɪs]
n 催眠術，催眠狀態

The sleepwalker overcame his condition after a week of hypnosis sessions.

一週催眠治療後，夢遊者克服自己的病情。

記憶技巧 hypno- 表示睡眠；-osis 為名詞字尾，表示狀態或情況；hypnosis 即催眠術。

---

hypnotize
[ˋhɪpnʌˏtaɪz]
v 催眠

The patron felt hypnotized by the barmaid's eyes, and didn't hear her asking for his order.

顧客因女酒保雙眼而感到催眠，聽不到她要求點餐的聲音。

記憶技巧 hypno- 表示睡眠；-ize 為動詞字尾；hypnotize 即催眠。

---

hypnotherapy
[ˏhɪpnoˋθɛrəpɪ]
n 催眠療法

The therapist offers hypnotherapy as an option for patients to quit smoking.

治療師提供催眠療法做為病患戒菸的一種選擇。

記憶技巧 hypno- 表示睡眠；therapy 表示治療；hypnotherapy 是催眠治療法。

相關字彙
催眠、沉思

- meditation 沉思
- trance 催眠狀態

---

sweet - hedon

子音 s 和 h 對應，t 和 d 互換，母音通轉，兩者皆表示甜。

---

hedonism
[ˋhidnˏɪzəm]
n 快樂主義

The popular resort for newly-wed couples is an island known for beauty and hedonism.

受新人歡迎的度假勝地是一座以美景及享樂主義聞名的島嶼。

記憶技巧 hedon- 表示甜；-ism 為名詞字尾；hedonism 是喜歡甜頭的，引申為享樂主義。

相關字彙
縱情享樂

- epicurean 愛奢侈享受的
- extravagance 奢侈
- indulgence 放縱
- sybaritic 奢侈淫逸的

serpent - herp

子音 s 和 h 對應，母音通轉，兩者皆表示爬蟲類動物，特指蛇。

---

serpent

[ˋsɚpənt]

n 蛇（尤指大蛇、毒蛇）

The caduceus medical symbol contains two serpents wrapping around a winged staff.

雙蛇醫學標記包含兩條纏繞一支展翼權杖的蛇。

記憶技巧 serpent 即蛇。

---

serpentine

[ˋsɚpənˌtin]

a 蜿蜒的，彎彎曲曲的

相關字彙 線條形式

The pipeline had a serpentine appearance as it snaked its way through the hills and valleys.

輸送管線蜿蜒穿過山丘和山谷，因此有彎曲的外貌。

記憶技巧 serpent- 表示蛇；-ine 為形容詞字尾，表示像～；serpentine 指像蛇的爬行動作，引此有蜿蜒、彎曲等意思。

- linear 直線的
- longitudinal 縱向
- oblique 傾斜的
- parallel 平行的
- tangential 切線的
- wavy 起伏的

---

herpetology

[ˌhɚpəˋtɑlədʒɪ]

n 爬蟲學

Having been fascinated with snakes since watching a Harry Potter movie, the young man chooses to study herpetology.

看了哈利波特電影後對蛇深感迷惑，年輕人選擇研究爬蟲學。

記憶技巧 herp- 表示爬蟲類動物；-logy 為名詞字尾，表示學問；herpetology 即爬蟲學。

---

salt - hal

子音 s 和 h 對應，母音通轉，兩者皆表示鹽。

---

halogen

[ˋhælədʒən]

n 鹵素

相關字彙 化學元素

The car was customized with LED lights because the halogen lights were not as bright or energy-efficient.

車子客製化，裝有 LED 燈，因為鹵素燈沒有那麼明亮或節能。

記憶技巧 鹵素元素家族的四個元素氟、氯、溴、碘，與金屬形成化合物以後，會產生「gen-（氯化鈉）」，氯化鈉是「salt（鹽巴）」的主要成分。

- arsenic 砷
- cadmium 鎘
- fluorine 氟
- magnesium 鎂
- sulfur 硫
- titanium 鈦
- uranium 鈾

［h］變化

sit - hedron

子音 s 和 h 對應，子音 t 和 d 互換，母音通轉，兩者皆表示基座，-hedron 衍生出「面體」的意思。

polyhedron
[ˌpɑlɪˈhidrən]

n 多面體，多角體

Most natural gemstones are found in a rough polyhedron shape, and need to be cut and polished to shine.

大多天然寶石以粗糙多角體形成，需要切割拋光才會光亮。

(記憶技巧) poly- 表示多；-hedron 表示面體；polyhedron 是多面體。

seven - hepta

子音 s 和 h 對應，子音 v 和 p 互換，兩者皆表示七。

heptahedron
[ˌhɛptəˈhidrən]

n 七面體

The rare emerald was cut to take on a stunning hetpahedron shape.

罕見的翡翠切割成迷人的七面體形狀。

(記憶技巧) hepta- 表示七；-hedron 表示面體；heptahedron 即七面體。

heptagon
[ˈhɛptəˌgɑn]

n 七角形

In 2011, England had two coins with a heptagon shape, incuding the 20-pence and 50-pence coins.

2011 年，英國兩種七角形硬幣，包含 20 便士和 50 便士的硬幣。

(記憶技巧) hept- 表示七；-gon 表示角；heptagon 即七角形。

猜猜看！

sit 坐在座位上，猜一四字母的單字？

答案：seat（座位）

same - homo
子音 s 和 h 對應，母音通轉，兩者皆表示相同。

Part 2
CH 1
CH 2
CH 3
CH 4
CH 5
CH 6
〔h〕變化

homogeneous
[ˌhoməˈdʒinɪəs]
a 相似的，同類的

The Japanese population is almost entirely homogeneous, while that in the USA represents a melting pot.
日本人口非常相似，而美國人口則代表一個大熔爐。

記憶技巧 homo- 表示相同；gen- 表示生；-ous 為形容詞字尾；homogeneous 表示有相同出身的，引申為同類的。

homosexual
[ˌhoməˈsɛkʃʊəl]
a 同性戀

The homosexual man hid his sexual preference for many years, although some of his friends already knew.
男同性戀者隱瞞性偏好許多年，即便一些友人早就知情。

記憶技巧 homo- 表示相同；sex 表示性；-ual 為形容詞字尾；homosexual 的意思是同性戀的。

相關字彙
性向
• bisexual 雙性戀的
• gay 同性戀的
• lesbian 女同性戀者
• pansexual 泛性戀的
• queer（男）同性戀的
• sapphic 同性戀女子

homophile
[ˈhoməˌfaɪl]
n 同性戀者

The man had a fear of homophiles and encouraged others to hate them.
男子恐懼並鼓勵他人憎恨同性戀者。

記憶技巧 homo- 表示相同；-phile 表示愛；homophile 是愛好相同性別的人，即同性戀者。

super - hyper
子音 s 和 h 對應，母音通轉，兩者皆表示超過。

hypertrophy
[haɪˈpɝtrəfɪ]
n 營養過剩

The weightlifter's muscles were impressive, due to the hypertrophy caused by his weight training.
因為重量訓練造成的肥大，這名舉重選手肌肉令人印象深刻。

記憶技巧 hyper- 表示超過；-trophy 表示營養物的字尾；hypertrophy 即營養過剩。

相關字彙
醫學症狀
• alcoholism 酗酒
• allergy 過敏症
• amenorrhoea 閉經症
• catalepsy 僵強症
• colitis 結腸炎
• diabesity 肥糖病

hypercritical
[ˋhaɪpɚˋkrɪtɪkl̩]
a 吹毛求疵的

The man refused to allow his mother-in-law to move into his house because she was hypercritical of him.
男子不許岳母搬進住處，因為她對他吹毛求疵。

記憶技巧　hyper- 表示超過；critical 表示批評的、批判的；hypercritical 的意思是吹毛求疵的。

hypertension
[ˌhaɪpɚˋtɛnʃən]
n 高血壓

The overweight man suffered from hypertension, which made him a candidate for a heart attack.
過重的男子罹患高血壓，這使他成為心臟病潛在患者。

記憶技巧　hyper- 表示超過；tension 表示拉緊；hypertension 是高血壓。

相關字彙
心、血液

- aorta 主動脈
- blood clot 血栓
- blood pressure 血壓
- capillary 毛細血管
- coronary 冠狀動脈
- infarction 梗塞
- leukocyte 白血球
- plasma 血漿
- platelet 血小板
- white blood cell 白血細胞

---

sacred - hagio
兩者並無字源關係，但可藉由子音 s 和 h 對應、c 和 g 互換、母音通轉來記憶，兩者皆表示神聖。

---

hagiarchy
[ˋhæɡɪˌɑrkɪ]
n 神權統治，聖徒統治

The novel is set in the mythical hagiarchy of Fethoria, which is ruled by several religious Houses.
小說背景是菲索利亞的神祕神權統治，該地由數個修道院統治。

記憶技巧　hagio- 表示神聖的；-archy 表示統治；hagiarchy 即是神權統治。

hagiolatry
[hæɡɪˋɑlətrɪ]
n 聖徒崇拜

A shrine in St. Paul's cathedral is an example of hagiolatry of the well-known patron saint.
聖保羅大教堂神殿是對於這位知名聖徒的崇拜的一個例子。

記憶技巧　hagio- 表示神聖的；-latry 表示崇拜的字尾；hagiolatry 的意思是聖徒崇拜。

hagiology
[ˌhæɡɪˋɑlədʒɪ]
n 聖徒文學

An old book popular with animal lovers is a hagiology about St. Francis of Assisi.
有一本受動物愛好者歡迎的老書，是關於亞西西城聖方濟的聖徒文學。

記憶技巧　hagio- 表示神聖的；-logy 表示學問；hagiology 是聖徒文學。

sew - hymen

子音 s 和 h 對應，母音通轉，兩者皆表示縫，亦有膜的意思，hymen 是處女膜。

hymen
[ˋhaɪmən]
n 處女膜

The doctors checked the rape victim's hymen for any sign of forced entry to help the police with their case.
為幫助警方辦案，醫生檢查性侵受害者處女膜，找尋任何強迫侵入的徵狀。

記憶技巧　hymen 即處女膜。

相關字彙
性器官、生殖器官

- cervix 子宮頸
- clitoris 陰蒂
- genitals 生殖器
- labia 陰脣
- ovary 卵巢
- penis 陰莖
- testicle 睪丸
- vagina 陰道
- womb 子宮

Part 2
CH 1
CH 2
CH 3
CH 4
CH 5
CH 6
〔h〕變化

same + other - hetero

hetero-（其他）、homo- 及 same 皆系出同源，可利用子音 s 和 h 對應、母音通轉來記憶。hetero 中的 he 是 homo- 的意思，-ter 則是 other，可用 t 和 th 通轉來記憶。hetero 本指的是兩個相同事物中的另一個，後來單純用以表達另一個事物，引申為不同、其他的。

heterodox
[ˋhɛtərəˌdɑks]
a 異端的

With the main economic system putting pressure on the citizens, many turned to heterodox economics for solutions.
主要經濟體對人民產生壓力，許多人轉往非主流經濟求尋解決。

記憶技巧　hetero- 表示其他；dox- 表示意見；heterodox 的意思是其他意見，引申為異端的。

heterogeneous
[ˌhɛtərəˋdʒinɪəs]
a 異類的，不同的

The heterogeneous population of New York City gives it a truly international character.
紐約市不同的種族賦予該城市道地的國際特性。

記憶技巧　hetero- 表示其他；gen- 表示生；-ous 為形容詞字尾；heterogeneous 的意思出生時就和同類有別，引申為異類的。

heterosexual
[ˌhɛtərəˋsɛkʃʊəl]
n 異性戀

The macho man boasted about being the ultimate heterosexual because of his many conquests.
因為擄獲不少芳心，陽剛男子吹噓自己是終極異性戀。

記憶技巧　hetero- 表示其他；sex 表示性；-al 為形容詞字尾；heterosexual 即異性戀的，亦可當名詞用。

Section 2

有〔h〕對應沒〔h〕

haughty - alt

有 h 對應沒 h，母音通轉，兩者皆表示高。

---

altitude

[ˋæltəˌtjud]

n 高度，海拔

The captain announced that the airplane had reached cruising altitude and turned off the seat belt sign.

機長宣布飛機達到的飛行高度，並關掉安全帶警示燈。

記憶技巧　alt- 表示高；-tude 為抽象名詞字尾；altitude 是高度。

---

exalt

[ɪgˋzɔlt]

v 提高，讚揚

The congregation sang joyous songs and exalted the name of their Lord and Savior.

會眾唱著歡樂的歌曲，讚揚他們的主與救贖者之名。

記憶技巧　ex- 表示外面；alt- 表示高；exalt 即提高。

---

alto

[ˋælto]

n 男高音

The thin young man was invited to join the choir because they needed an alto.

消瘦的年輕男子受邀加入合唱團，因為有一個男高音的缺。

記憶技巧　alto 是男高音的意思。

相關字彙
歌手

- baritone 男中音
- bass 男低音
- choir 唱團
- contralto 女低音
- countertenor 高男中音
- prima donna（歌劇中的）女主角
- soprano 女高音
- tenor 男高音，次中音
- treble 最高聲部的

原來如此！

hunt 意思是「打獵（獵人打獵時要躲著）」，有如提示（hint）從後面提供訊息，因此可記得 hunt 與 hint 是同源字。

Part

2

CH 1
CH 2
CH 3
CH 4
CH 5
CH 6

〔h〕
變
化

原來如此！

shell 是貝殼或果殼，功用是保護裡面的生物或是果實；shelter 是庇護所，兩字功用一樣，彼此同源。另外，shield（盾牌）功用是保護戰士，與 shell 及 shelter 三字同源。

shelter 及 shield 源自 shell，反映出人類生活經驗是先接觸或使用 shell，而後 shelter 或 shield。值得一提的是，辨識同源字應該向前看，不能從後找，因為同源衍生通常是黏接字尾，拼字差異在字尾部分。

例如，shelter 的字尾 -er 是指器具，衍生詞綴；shelter 及 shield 的 t 及 d 則是語音考量而附加的。另外，世界石油大廠 Shell 想必是因 shell 與 shale oil（頁岩油）的 shale 是同源字，希望品牌與產品緊密連結而以 Shell 命名。

猜猜看！

❶ 小孩子吃 food 需餵食，猜一動詞？

❷ 古時候 bank 是擺放長凳子的地方，請將 bank 換成另一單字。

❸ 成人 adult 表示變老了，請問 ult 是哪一單字？

❹ 咖啡因是因為去哪裡喝了什麼？

❺ 停止 quit 之後當然就靜止了，猜一字？

答案：❶ feed（餵）　❷ bench（長板凳）　❸ old（老的）　❹ 咖啡店 café／咖啡 coffee　❺ quiet（安靜的）

Part ③
字根對應字根
（含少數字首、字尾）
Grimm's Law

唇舌之間，透過子音轉換操弄，連結兩組、甚或多組詞素，化繁為簡，以簡入繁，練就單字學習新工法。

Chapter 1
雙唇音、唇齒音轉換

〔b〕、〔p〕、〔m〕、〔f〕、〔v〕

〔p〕對應〔b〕

pot - bib

子音 p 和 b 互換，母音通轉，兩者皆表示喝。

---

potable
[`potəbḷ]
a 適於飲用的

Many have sought to find creative and inexpensive ways to provide potable water to desert communities.
許多人尋求創意且廉價方式提供沙漠群落飲用水。

記憶技巧　pot- 表示喝；-able 為形容詞字尾；potable 的意思是適合飲用的。

---

bib
[bɪb]
n 圍兜

A friend gave the pregnant woman a blue bib, as she expected a baby boy.
一位朋友送懷孕婦女一個藍色圍兜，因為她懷的是男嬰。

記憶技巧　bib 表示喝，引申為喝東西時圍在胸口的圍兜。

相關字彙
衣物配件

- bow 蝴蝶結
- cap 無邊便帽
- earrings 耳環
- gloves 手套
- hair band 髮帶
- mittens 連指手套
- scarf 圍巾
- tie 領帶
- wig 假髮

---

bibulous
[`bɪbjələs]
a 酗酒的

The bartender became bibulous after his divorce.
酒保離婚後酗酒成性。

記憶技巧　bib- 表示喝；-ous 為形容詞字尾；bibulous 的意思是喝～的，引申為酗酒的。

---

beverage
[`bɛvərɪdʒ]
n 飲料

The popular alcoholic beverage is produced from yeast-fermented apple juice.
人氣酒精飲料是酵母發酵的蘋果汁製成的。

記憶技巧　bever- 等同於 bib-，表示喝；-age 為名詞字尾；beverage 即飲料。

相關字彙
各式飲料

- soft drink 汽水
- alcoholic drink 酒精飲料
- carbonic acid drink 碳酸飲料
- diet drink 消脂飲料
- function drink 機能性飲料
- sports drink 運動飲料
- pick-me-up 提神的飲食

nup - nub

子音 p 和 b 互換，母音通轉，兩者皆表示結婚。

---

nuptial

[`nʌpʃəl]

a 婚姻的

The couple made their nuptial vows to each other in the wedding ceremony.

新人在婚禮中彼此立下婚約。

記憶技巧　nupt- 表示結婚；-ial 為形容詞字尾；nuptial 是婚姻的。

---

prenuptial

[pri`nʌpʃəl]

a 婚前的

The actress asked her fiancé to sign a prenuptial agreement when they got engaged.

女演員與未婚夫訂婚時，要求他簽訂婚前契約。

記憶技巧　pre- 表示前；nup- 表示結婚；-ial 為形容詞字尾；prenuptial 是婚前的。

---

connubial

[kə`njubiəl]

a 婚姻的

The couple celebrated half a century of connubial bliss in an island resort.

夫婦在一處度假島嶼慶祝金婚。

記憶技巧　con- 表示一起；nub- 表示結婚；-ial 為形容詞字尾；connubial 即婚姻的。

相關字彙
婚姻常見字

- bigamy 重婚罪
- polygamy 多配偶
- marital 婚姻的
- premarital 婚前的
- conjugal 結婚的
- spouse 配偶

Part 3

CH 1

雙唇音、唇齒音轉換

原來如此！

birth 意指 bear，出生的意思，字尾 -th 表示過程，bath 及 death 也是。-th 轉換為 -d，母音通轉，黏接字尾 -en，形成 burden（負擔）這單字：生、養、教一個孩子都是負擔及責任。

Section **2**

〔m〕對應〔p〕

crim - culp
兩者雖無字源關係，子音 m 和 p 互換，母音通轉，兩者皆表示罪。

---

decriminalize
[diˋkrɪmənəˌlaɪz]
v 使不算非法或犯罪

After several states decriminalized the use of marijuana, the rest of the states followed suit.
幾州將吸食大麻除罪化後，其餘各州也跟進。

記憶技巧 de- 表示離開；crim- 表示罪；-al 為形容詞字尾；-ize 為動詞字尾；decriminalize 即除罪化。

---

culpable
[ˋkʌlpəbl̩]
a 該受譴責的，有罪的

Although the man was drunk when he hit the pedestrian, he was going to be held fully culpable.
男子毆打行人時雖是酒醉，但要擔起全部責任。

記憶技巧 culp- 表示罪；-able 為形容詞字尾，即有罪的。

---

culprit
[ˋkʌlprɪt]
n 罪犯，刑事被告

It was decided that the mentally ill person was the culprit in the horrendous crime.
這名患有心理疾病的人是這起恐怖案件的罪犯。

記憶技巧 culp- 表示罪；culprit 即是罪犯。

相關字彙
罪犯

- criminal 罪犯
- delinquent 違法者
- gang（歹徒等的）一幫
- lowlife 罪犯
- accomplice 共犯
- ringleader 首惡

---

exculpate
[ˋɛkskʌlˌpet]
v 辯解，脫罪

Although he owned the gun, a security video exculpated the man from wrongdoing.
男子雖然擁有該槍枝，但監視影片為他脫罪。

記憶技巧 ex- 表示外；culp- 表示罪；-ate 為動詞字尾；exculpate 的意思是脫罪。

相關字彙
證明無罪、脫罪

- vindicate 證明～無辜
- absolve 赦（罪）
- exonerate 證明～無罪
- get off 逃脫處罰

inculpate

[ˋɪnkʌˏpet]

v 指責，控告，牽連

An effective judicial system should be able to ensure the innocent will not be inculpated.

一個有效的司法制度應能確保無辜者不致入罪。

> 記憶技巧 in- 表示內；culp- 表示罪；-ate 為動詞字尾；inculpate 的意思是歸罪在～上，引申為指控。

Section 3

〔b〕對應〔f〕

ambi - amphi

子音 b 和 ph 互換，母音通轉，兩者皆表示雙、環繞。

---

ambidextrous

[ˏæmbəˋdɛkstrəs]

a 雙手靈巧的

The ambidextrous baseball player was able to pitch right-handed and left-handed.

雙手靈敏的棒球選手左右投俱佳。

> 記憶技巧 ambi- 表示雙；dextr- 表示右（手）；-ous 為形容詞字尾；ambidextrous 的意思是兩隻手皆是右手，古人認為右手往往比左手靈巧。

---

amphibian

[æmˋfɪbɪən]

n 兩棲動物

The white salamander was the most popular amphibian in the Vancouver aquarium.

白色蠑螈是溫哥華水族館最受歡迎的兩棲動物。

> 記憶技巧 amphi- 表示雙；bi- 表示生物；amphibian 是兩棲動物。

---

amphitheater

[ˏæmfɪˋθɪətə]

n 圓形劇場

No trip to Rome can be complete without a tour of the ancient amphitheaters.

未到古羅馬圓形劇場一遊談不上玩遍羅馬。

> 記憶技巧 amphi- 表示環繞；theater 表示戲院；amphitheater 即圓形劇場。

相關字彙 提供休閒娛樂的地區和建築		
• arena 競技場	• concert hall 音樂廳	• health spa 減肥俱樂部
• auditorium 禮堂	• finess center 健身中心	• opera house 歌劇院
• cinema 電影院	• gym 體育館	• stadium 體育場

Section 4

〔p〕對應〔f〕

opt - ophthalm

子音 p 和 ph 互換，母音通轉，兩者皆表示眼睛。

optician [ɑpˋtɪʃən] n 光學儀器商，眼鏡商，配鏡師	If you want to wear corrective contact lenses, you need to visit an optician. 如果要戴矯正隱形眼鏡片，找配鏡師是必要的。 記憶技巧 opt- 表示眼睛；-ic 為形容詞字尾；-ian 表示人；optician 即眼鏡商。
ophthalmology [͵ɑfθælˋmɑlədʒɪ] n 眼科醫學	The boy was hit in the eye with a baseball and was taken to the ophthalmology department. 男孩被棒球打到眼睛，被送去眼科診所。 記憶技巧 ophthalm- 表示眼睛；-logy 為名詞字尾；ophthalmology 是眼科醫學。
ophthalmologist [͵ɑfθælˋmɑlədʒɪst] n 眼科醫師	Only a licensed ophthalmologist is qualified to perform surgery on eyes. 只有執照的眼科醫生才能進行眼睛手術。 記憶技巧 -ist 表示人；ophthalmologist 即眼科醫生。

猜猜看！

blow 表示吹，猜一個與 blow 同字源的樂器名稱？

答案：flute（長笛）

Section **5**

〔f〕對應〔v〕

phag - vor

兩者並無字源關係，但可用子音 ph 和 v 互換，母音通轉來記憶，兩者皆表示吃。

zoophagous
[zoˋɑfəgəs]
a 肉食的

Contrary to people's beliefs, chickens can be quite zoophagous.
與人們所相信的大不同，雞可以是很肉食性的。

記憶技巧　zoo- 表示動物；phag- 表示吃；-ous 為形容詞字尾；zoophagous 即肉食的。

devour
[dıˋvaur]
v 吞食，毀滅

The woman devoured half a case of oranges in an hour, seeking the Vitamin C.
女子一小時內吞下半盒橘子攝取維他命 C。

記憶技巧　de- 等同於 down；vour- 等同於 vor-，表示吃；devour 的意思是吃下去，引申為吞食、毀滅。

carnivorous
[karˋnıvərəs]
a 肉食性的

There aren't many carnivorous animals in New Zealand, and one of them is the snail.
紐西蘭肉食性動物不多，蝸牛是其中一種。

記憶技巧　carn- 表示肉；vor- 表示吃；-ous 為形容詞字尾；carnivorous 是肉食性的。

herbivorous
[həˋbıvərəs]
a 草食性的

Tortoises are usually herbivorous creatures, eating fruit and vegetation.
陸龜通常是吃蔬果的草食動物。

記憶技巧　herb- 表示草；vor- 表示吃；-ous 為形容詞字尾；herbivorous 是草食性的。

omnivorous
[amˋnıvərəs]
a 雜食的

Bears are the largest omnivorous animals and can adapt to different environments.
熊是體型最大的雜食動物，能夠適應不同環境。

記憶技巧　omni- 表示全部；vor- 表示吃；-ous 為形容詞字尾；omnivorous 是不分動植物，全都吃，即雜食的。

Section 6

〔p〕對應〔v〕

---

rap - rav

子音 p 和 v 互換，母音通轉，兩者皆表示抓走。

---

enrapture

[ɪn`ræptʃɚ]

v 使著迷

The girl was enraptured with the puppy sleeping on her chest.

女孩很喜歡睡在她懷裡的幼犬。

記憶技巧　en- 等同於 in-，表示放～內，為動詞字首；rapt- 表示抓；-ure 為名詞字尾；enrapture 是抓走目光、專注力，引申為使著迷。

相關字彙
喜悅

- delight 喜悅
- ecstasy 狂喜
- euphoria 興奮
- elation 興高采烈
- happiness 愉快
- joy 喜悅
- jollity 歡鬧
- pleasure 愉快
- nirvana 涅槃

---

rapacious

[rə`peʃəs]

a 強取的，貪婪的，捕食性的

I cannot understand why such a rich man can be such a rapacious landlord.

這麼有錢的人會是一名貪婪地主，真是無法理解。

記憶技巧　rap- 表示抓；-acious 為形容詞字尾；rapacious 的意思是抓取的，引申為貪婪的。

相關字彙
貪婪、自私

- cynical 憤世嫉俗的
- greedy 貪婪的
- inward-looking 更關心自己的
- selfish 自私的
- self-centred 自我中心的
- self-seeking 追逐私利
- self-absorbed 專心於自己的事務（或利益）的
- ungenerous 胸襟狹窄的

---

ravenous

[`rævɪnəs]

a 餓極了的，狼吞虎嚥的

The attorney has a ravenous appetite, consuming an entire rack of lamb at one sitting.

律師胃口大開，一口氣吃掉整塊小羊肋排。

記憶技巧　rav- 表示抓；-ous 為形容詞字尾；ravenous 的意思是大量抓取，引申為狼吞虎嚥。

相關字彙
飢餓

- appetite 胃口
- hunger 飢餓
- starvation 飢餓
- famine 饑荒
- peckish 肚子有些餓的

Chapter 2
雙唇音、唇齒音轉換

〔w〕、〔v〕（含 w / u / v 字母通轉）

Section 1　字母「u」對應字母「v」

字母「u」對應字母「v」

au - av

u 和 v 互換，母音通轉，兩者皆表示鳥。

---

auspicious
[ɔˋspɪʃəs]
a 吉祥的

The parents were excited because the baby was expected to be born in the auspicious Year of the Dragon.
父母非常興奮，因為孩子預計在吉祥龍年出生。

> 記憶技巧 au- 表示鳥；spic- 等同於 spect-，表示看；-ous 為形容詞字尾；auspicious 是看鳥飛行來斷吉凶，後特指好的徵兆，引申為吉祥的。

相關字彙
很有可能會成功

- bright 光明的
- feasible 可實行的
- likely 很可能的
- promising 有前途的
- propitious 順利的
- rosy 美好的

---

inaugurate
[ɪnˋɔgjəˌret]
v 開創，就任

The new leader was inaugurated in front of the military, economic and religious leaders of the country.
新領導者在國家軍隊、經濟及宗教領袖面前就任。

> 記憶技巧 in- 表示內；augur 是古羅馬的占兆官，藉由觀察鳥的飛行來斷吉凶；-ate 為動詞字尾；inaugurate 是觀察鳥飛行來斷定是否適合上任、動工等意思。

---

avian
[ˋevɪən]
a 鳥類的

The large mounds of mud on the side of the walls were, in fact, avian dwellings.
牆邊一大泥巴塚事實上是鳥類住處。

> 記憶技巧 av- 表示鳥；-an 為形容詞字尾；avian 即鳥類的。

---

aviary
[ˋevɪˌɛrɪ]
n 鳥籠

The mistress kept a dazzling collection of tropical birds in the aviary in the back yard.
女主人在後院鳥籠養很多炫目的熱帶鳥類。

> 記憶技巧 av- 表示鳥；-ary 為名詞字尾；aviary 是鳥籠。

aviation
[ˌevɪˋeʃən]
n 航行

Millionaire Howard Hughes was an avid fan of aviation and founded an aircraft company.
百萬富翁霍華德‧休斯是飛機迷，並創立了一家飛機公司。

記憶技巧 av- 表示鳥，在此作飛行；-ation 為名詞字尾；aviation 是航行。

相關字彙
飛行
- automatic pilot 自動駕駛儀
- manned 由人駕駛的
- navigation 航行
- take-off 起飛
- touchdown 降落

lau - lav
u 和 v 互換，母音通轉，兩者皆表示洗。

laundry
[ˋlɔndrɪ]
n 洗衣店，送洗衣物

The hotel relied on a vendor to handle all of its laundry needs.
旅館仰賴一家供應商處理所有洗衣需求。

記憶技巧 lau- 表示洗；laundry 是洗衣店或送洗衣物。

lavish
[ˋlævɪʃ]
a 過多的

He resided in Las Vegas in a lavish penthouse suite adorned with marble tiles and gold trim.
他住在位於拉斯維加斯的一間鑲飾大理石磚及黃金鑲邊的闊氣套房。

記憶技巧 lav- 表示洗；-ish 為形容詞字尾；lavish 是用大量的水沖洗，引申為過多的。

lava
[ˋlɑvə]
n 熔岩

On the big island of Hawaii, lava flows can be seen moving slowly towards the ocean.
在夏威夷大島嶼看得到岩漿緩緩流向海洋。

記憶技巧 lav- 表示洗；lava 指的是從火山口噴發後，流動下來的熔岩。

相關字彙
火山
- crater 火山口
- active 活躍的
- dormant 休眠的
- extinct 熄滅了的，死（火山）的
- eruption（火山）爆發

lavatory
[ˋlævəˌtorɪ]
n 盥洗室

There were concerns that there weren't enough lavatories at the popular wedding venue.
超人氣婚宴會場的廁所不足，令人堪憂。

記憶技巧 lav- 表示洗；-ory 為名詞字尾；lavatory 即盥洗室，1864 年才有廁所的意思。

nau - nav

u 和 v 互換，母音通轉，兩者皆表示船。

---

aquanaut
[ˋækwəˌnɔt]
n 潛水員

The women were trained to be aquanauts in order to harvest oysters and the famed black pearls.
為了採收牡蠣及有名的黑珍珠，婦人接受訓練成為潛水員。

> **記憶技巧** aqua- 表示水；naut- 表示航行者；aquanaut 是潛水員。

---

nausea
[ˋnɔʃɪə]
n 噁心，暈船

The woman complained of nausea and cravings for certain foods, and then was diagnosed with pregnancy.
女子抱怨自己噁心想吐，很想吃某些食物，隨後被診斷出懷孕。

> **記憶技巧** naus- 等同於 nau-，表示船；nausea 是暈船、噁心的意思。

相關字彙
不舒服、想吐

- bilious 噁心的
- chuck up 嘔吐
- disgorge 嘔出
- puke 嘔吐
- spew 嘔吐
- vomit 嘔吐
- upset someone's stomach 胃部不適

---

navy
[ˋnevɪ]
n 海軍，海軍官兵

The Philippines has a sizeable navy but doesn't have enough boats to patrols its many islands.
菲律賓海軍頗具規模，但沒有足夠的船隻巡邏其眾多島嶼。

> **記憶技巧** nav- 表示船；navy 是海軍。

相關字彙
軍事武力

- air force 空軍
- army 陸軍
- commander in chief 總司令
- cavalry 騎兵
- fleet 艦隊
- ground forces 地面部隊
- yeomanry 義勇騎兵隊

---

navigate
[ˋnævəˌget]
v 駕駛，導航，通過議案

The vessel's captain tried to use the stars to navigate during nighttime hours.
船長在夜晚時試著靠著星點導航。

> **記憶技巧** nav- 表示船；-ate 為動詞字尾；navigate 的意思是開船前進，即駕駛。

---

circumnavigation
[ˌsɝkəmˌnævəˋgeʃən]
n 環遊世界

Early aviators tried to make a name for themselves through circumnavigation of the globe.
早期飛行員試著藉由環遊世界而成名。

> **記憶技巧** circum- 表示環繞；navigation 表示駕駛；circumnavigation 即環遊世界的意思。

相關字彙
航行、航海

- anchor 拋錨泊船
- berth 使停泊
- castaway 遭船難者
- cruise 巡航
- sailing 航行
- yachting 駕遊艇
- seasickness 暈船

neur - nerv
u 和 v 互換，母音通轉，兩者皆表示神經。

neurology
[njuˋrɑlədʒɪ]
n 神經病學，神經學

The researcher studied neurology for years and was hired to treat victims of paralysis.
研究員鑽研神經病學多年，應聘治療癱瘓病患。

記憶技巧 neur- 表示神經；-logy 表示學；neurology 是神經學。

neuralgia
[njuˋrældʒə]
n 神經痛

The woman was on disability because her neuralgia was severe enough to prevent her from working.
女人殘障，因為神經痛太過嚴重而無法工作。

記憶技巧 neur- 表示神經；-algia 表示痛；neuralgia 是神經痛。

nervous
[ˋnɝvəs]
a 神經的，緊張的

The groom was nervous during the ceremony, wondering if he had made the right choice.
典禮期間新郎非常緊張，不知道自己是否做了正確選擇。

記憶技巧 nerv- 表示神經；-ous 為形容詞字尾；nervous 是神經緊繃的，即緊張的。

solu - solv
u 和 v 互換，母音通轉，兩者皆表示鬆。

solution
[səˋluʃən]
n 解決，溶解，溶液

In an act that was deemed the final solution for his allergy symptoms, the man got rid of his cat.
男子解決過敏症狀的最後方式是把貓送走。

記憶技巧 solu- 表示鬆；-ion 為名詞字尾；solution 字面意思是鬆掉，引申為解決。

resolution
[ˌrɛzəˋluʃən]
n 決心，解決，決議

The committee drafted a resolution to require its staff to have a passing score on the TOEIC exam.
委員會起草一項決議要求員工擁有多益及格成績。

記憶技巧 re- 表示加強語氣；solu- 表示鬆；-ion 為名詞字尾；resolution 的字面意思是鬆掉，有把某物分解的意思，1780 年代才有決心的意思。

Part
3

CH 1
CH 2

雙唇音、唇齒音轉換

absolute

[`æbsəˌlut]

a 絕對的，專制的，無條件的

The decision of the Supreme Court was absolute, leaving the defendant with no other recourse.

最高法院的判決是絕對性的，被告沒有其他轉圜餘地。

記憶技巧　ab- 表示離開；solu- 表示鬆；absolute 是鬆開，表示沒有限制的，但語意後來有了大幅度改變，1610 年代產生專制的意思。

solve

[salv]

v 解決，溶解，償債

The investigator solved the puzzling crime, when he studied the victim's phone records.

調查員研究受害者電話通聯記錄時破了膠著刑案。

記憶技巧　solve 是 solution 的動詞。

absolve

[əb`salv]

v 解除，赦免

The widow's grief was palpable after the man that had been sentenced to death for murder was absolved of his crime.

因謀殺而判死的男子被赦免後，寡婦的悲傷很明顯。

記憶技巧　ab- 表示離開；solv- 表示鬆；absolve 是鬆開，引申為赦免、解除。

dissolve

[dɪ`zalv]

v 溶解，分解，撤消，解散

The attorney advised the executives to go bankrupt and dissolve the company.

律師建議行政主管們宣布破產並解散公司。

記憶技巧　dis- 表示分開；solv- 表示鬆；dissolve 是鬆開的意思，引申為解除、赦免。

insolvency

[ɪn`salvənsɪ]

n 破產，無力償付債務

The groups of investors sought answers as to why their new startup faced insolvency so soon.

一群投資者正琢磨著為何他們新創立的公司會如此快速地面臨破產。

記憶技巧　in- 為否定字首；solv- 表示鬆；-ency 為名詞字尾；insolvency 指無法從債務的束縛中鬆開來，引申為破產。

相關字彙
破產

- bankrupt 破產的
- bust 使破產
- liquidator 清算人
- official receiver（負責處理破產事務的）官方接管人
- go broke 破產

resolve

[rɪ`zalv]

v 決定，分解，決議，解決

Peace was made and the dispute was resolved when the major shareholder gave up his resistance to the deal.

大股東不再抵抗協議時，大家相安無事，爭議平息。

記憶技巧　resolve 是 resolution 的動詞。

volu - volv

u 和 v 互換，母音通轉，兩者皆表示轉、滾。

---

volume

[`vɑljəm]

n 體積，音量，
書籍（冊），量

Consolidating the orders of small manufacturers, he leveraged the combined order volume to save money.

他合併小製造商的訂單，利用增加併單量以節省金錢。

記憶技巧　volu- 表示滾；volume 表示一卷書籍。

---

evolution

[ˌɛvəˋluʃən]

n 發展，演變，進化

The evolution of green technology is put at risk when the petroleum industry can influence government subsidies.

石油產業能夠左右政府補助時，綠科技發展陷入危機。

記憶技巧　e- 等同於 ex-，表示外面；volu- 表示滾；-ion 為名詞字尾；evolution 的意思是滾到外面，引申為發展。

相關字彙　演化

- Darwinism 達爾文主義
- intelligent design 神創論
- natural selection 天擇
- survival of the fittest 適者生存

---

revolutionary

[ˌrɛvəˋluʃənˌɛrɪ]

a 革命的

The historic turnout at the polling stations was a response to the revolutionary rhetoric.

投票站的投票人數創歷史新高，回應那則革命性的言論。

記憶技巧　re- 表示後面；volu- 表示轉；-ion 為名詞字尾；-ary 為形容詞字尾；revolutionary 是將某～轉到後面去，引申為革命的。

---

evolve

[ɪˋvɑlv]

v 進展，進化

Researchers in Denmark claim that cows evolved from the ancestor of the orca.

丹麥研究員聲稱牛是從虎鯨的始祖演化而來。

記憶技巧　evolve 是 evolution 的動詞。

相關字彙　演化

- Darwinian 達爾文的
- intelligent design 神創論
- natural selection 天擇
- survival of the fittest 適者生存

---

involve

[ɪnˋvɑlv]

v 包括，涉及，
使專注

Parents wanted to know why a 50-year-old school official was involved in a child sex scandal.

家長想知道為什麼一個五十歲的學校主管會涉入孩童性醜聞案。

記憶技巧　in- 表示內；volv- 表示轉；involve 是將～捲入其中，引申為涉及。

Part
3
CH 1
CH 2

雙唇音、唇齒音轉換

revolve

[rɪ`vɑlv]

v 循環，公轉

The heiress treated her servants poorly and believed that their lives should completely revolve around her.

女繼承人惡待僕人，並認為他們的生活應當完全以她為中心。

記憶技巧 re- 表示再；volv- 表示轉；revolve 的意思是繞著～旋轉，天文學上當公轉解釋。

---

revolt

[rɪ`volt]

n 背叛，反抗

In many instances throughout history, people revolted against their leaders when taxes were raised.

歷史中有許多例子，加稅時人民便起身反抗領導者。

記憶技巧 re- 表示回去；volt- 等同於 volu-，表示轉；revolt 的意思是轉回去攻打自家人，引申為背叛。

原來如此！

wine 是葡萄酒，原料取自 vineyard（葡萄園）裡葡萄藤（vine）上的葡萄，所以 wine 與 vine 同源，v 及 w 轉音衍生。vinegar 是醋，拉丁文的意思是變酸的酒—— wine turned sour，-gar 就表示 sour。另外，紅酒—— red wine 和 vinegar 調成 red wine vinegar ——紅酒醋，不僅字源相伴，美食也相佐。

Chapter 3
齒間音、齒齦音、齒齦後音、硬顎音轉換

〔d〕、〔t〕、〔n〕、〔l〕、〔ʃ〕、〔r〕、〔z〕、〔s〕、〔θ〕、〔ð〕、〔ʒ〕

Section **1**

〔r〕對應〔d〕

acer - acid

r 和 d 互換，母音通轉，兩者皆表示尖銳。尖銳衍生酸、苦或刺等意涵的單字。

---

exacerbate
[ɪgˋzæsɚˏbet]
v 使惡化

I felt bad when you beat me in the game, and you exacerbated my mood when you laughed at me.
你在比賽中打敗讓我不好受，而且嘲笑我時，我的心情更糟。

記憶技巧 ex- 表示完全；acer- 表示刺；-ate 為動詞字尾；exacerbate 指拿東西刺，因此有挑釁、刺激等意思，引申為惡化。

相關字彙
情況加劇
• worsen 惡化
• escalate 使逐步上升
• aggravate 使惡化
• inflame 加劇

---

acid
[ˋæsɪd]
a 酸性的，刻薄的

The fermentation process can produce vinegar, which is basically acetic acid
發酵過程可以產生醋，基本上就是醋酸。

記憶技巧 acid 表示刺，衍生出尖酸刻薄等意思。

相關字彙
與酸相關的化學成份
• amino acid 氨基酸
• citric acid 檸檬酸
• hydrochloric acid 鹽酸
• lactic acid 乳酸
• nitric acid 硝酸
• prussic acid 氫氰酸
• sulphuric acid 硫酸

---

acidulous
[əˋsɪdʒələs]
a 微酸的，
尖酸刻薄的

The unripe passion fruit is exceedingly acidulous, so I avoid it.
未成熟的百香果太酸了，因此我儘量不吃。

記憶技巧 acid- 表示酸；-ous 為形容詞字尾；acidulous 的意思是微酸的、尖酸刻薄的。

---

acute
[əˋkjut]
a 敏銳的，深刻的

Bomb-sniffing dogs have saved many lives with their acute sense of smell.
嗅彈犬以敏銳嗅覺救了許多性命。

記憶技巧 acute 等同於 acid-，為母音通轉，t 和 d 互換，表示尖，引申為敏銳的。

---

acetic
[ə`sitɪk]

a 酸的，醋的

The old batteries leaked in the drawer, giving off an acetic smell.

抽屜裡的舊電池漏液，散發一股酸味。

> 記憶技巧　acet- 等同於 acid-，表示酸；-ic 為形容詞字尾；acetic 是酸的。

acupuncture
[`ækjuˌpʌŋktʃɚ]

n 針灸

The athlete visited the Chinese medicine doctor to use acupuncture to relax tightened muscles.

運動員去看中醫用針灸舒緩緊繃肌肉。

> 記憶技巧　acu- 等同於 acid-，表示尖；punct- 表示刺；-ure 為名詞字尾；acupuncture 是針灸的意思。

相關字彙
醫療

- acupressure 指壓按摩
- anaesthesia 麻醉（法）
- aromatherapy 芳香療法
- art therapy 藝術治療
- blood transfusion 輸血
- chemotherapy 化學療法
- homeopathy 順勢醫療論
- naturopath 運用自然療法者
- shiatsu 指壓

acumen
[ə`kjumən]

n 理智，敏銳

The business acumen of the famous investor is rarely questioned, as millions of people follow his advice.

幾乎人人相信知名投資家的商業敏銳度，數百萬人聽從他的看法。

> 記憶技巧　acu- 表示尖銳；acumen 是指思考敏銳。

相關字彙
聰明、睿智

- clarity 明晰
- brilliance 才智
- intuition 敏銳的洞察力
- intellect 理解力
- judgment 辨別力
- wisdom 智慧

acrid
[`ækrɪd]

a 刺鼻的，刻薄的

The acrid scent of littered corpses and spent artillery shells left a permanent impression on the soldier's mind.

棄屍刺鼻味及廢砲彈在士兵心中留下難以磨滅的印象。

> 記憶技巧　acr- 等同於 acer-，表示刺；-id 為形容詞字尾；acrid 是刺鼻的。

acrimony
[`ækrəˌmonɪ]

n 辛辣，尖銳

The relationship of the two competitive teachers was destroyed by acrimony and jealousy.

尖銳和妒忌毀了兩位好競爭老師之間的關係。

> 記憶技巧　acr- 表示尖銳；-mony 為名詞字尾，表示一種狀態、情況；acrimony 是辛辣、尖銳的意思。

相關字彙
恨意、怒氣

- asperity（聲音、語調、態度、脾氣的）粗暴
- annoyance 惱怒
- fury 暴怒
- irritation 慍怒
- mood 心情不好
- outrage 憤慨
- rage 狂怒

Part
3

CH 1
CH 2
CH 3

齒間音、齒齦音、齒齦後音、硬顎音轉換

Section **2**

〔z〕對應〔d〕

oz - odor

z 和 d 互換，母音通轉，兩者皆表示聞、味道。

ozone [ˋozon] **n** 臭氧	Cancer rates in the southernmost countries are high because of the depleted levels of ozone. 減少的臭氧量導致最南端國家高罹癌率。 （記憶技巧） oz- 表示味道；1840 年德國化學家發現臭氧，因其味道，故以 ozone 來命名。
odor [ˋodɚ] **n** 氣味，臭氣	The polo player checked under his arm for any bad odor before introducing himself to the ladies. 馬球選手向女子自我介紹前前先聞聞自己腋下是否有異味。 （記憶技巧） odor 表示味道。
malodorous [mælˋodərəs] **a** 臭的	The reason for the shoe being malodorous was because the cat defecated inside it. 鞋子會臭是因為貓排便在裡面。 （記憶技巧） mal- 表示壞的；odor- 表示味道；-ous 為形容詞字尾；malodorous 即是臭的。

猜猜看！

「emotion（情緒）」是向外移動的氣，猜 mot 所表示的單字？

答案：move（移動）

〔s〕對應〔d〕

cas - cad

s 和 d 互換，母音通轉，兩者皆表示落下。

casual
[ˋkæʒʊəl]
a 偶然的，碰巧的

Slacks and a polo shirt are considered casual wear at certain business functions.
休閒褲和 polo 衫在某些商務集會中被視為休閒服飾。

記憶技巧 cas- 表示掉落；-al 為形容詞字尾；casual 的意思是突然間掉落下來的，引申為偶然的、碰巧的。

---

casualty
[ˋkæʒjʊəltɪ]
n 意外，意外死傷者

相關字彙
傷者

Mr. Jackson, a longtime accountant with the firm, was the first casualty of the downsizing.
傑克先生長期擔任公司會計師，是第一位裁員受害者。

記憶技巧 casual 表示偶然的；-ty 為名詞字尾；casualty 是偶然發生的事件，引申為意外或意外事件中的傷者。

- victim 犧牲者
- the injured 傷者
- amputee 被截肢者

---

occasional
[əˋkeʒənḷ]
a 偶然的，應景的，臨時的

I wouldn't say I am an alcoholic because I only enjoy an occasional drink with colleagues.
我不會說自己是酒鬼，因為我只偶爾與同事小酌。

記憶技巧 oc- 等同於 ob-，表示下、旁邊；cas- 表示掉落；-ion 為名詞字尾；-al 為形容詞字尾；occasional 是突然掉落的，引申為偶然的。

---

cascade
[kæsˋked]
n 小瀑布，串聯

相關字彙
湖泊、溪流的一部分

She salivated at the sight of the melted chocolate cascade coming from the fountain.
看著融化的巧克力小瀑布從噴泉流下時，她流了口水。

記憶技巧 cas- 表示落下；-ade 為名詞字尾；cascade 是瀑布，和另一個表示瀑布的字 falls，有異曲同工之妙，都和落下有關。

- backwater 壩的迴水
- cataract 大瀑布
- confluence（河流的）匯合
- crosscurrent 橫流
- estuary 河口
- shallows 淺灘
- whirlpool 漩渦

cadaver
[kə`dævɚ]
n 屍體

The junior officer had the unenviable task of taking the refrigerated cadaver out to re-examine it.

新進警官將冷凍屍體領出再度檢驗的任務令人不敢恭維。

> 記憶技巧 cad- 表示落下；cadaver 的字面是落下，引申出衰亡、滅亡、死亡的意思，現作屍體解釋。

相關字彙 屍身、死亡	
• body（人、動物等的）屍體	• mummy 木乃伊
• body count 死亡人數統計	• toll 傷亡人數
• corpse 屍體	• the deceased 死者

decadent
[`dɛkədn̩t]
a 頹廢的

The chef baked an extremely decadent chocolate devil's food cake for the birthday girl.

主廚為女壽星烘一個極端縱情享樂的惡魔巧克力蛋糕。

> 記憶技巧 de- 表示往下；cad- 表示落；-ent 為形容詞字尾；decadent 是往下落的，引申為頹廢的。

相關字彙 逾越道德		
• deviant 越軌的	• immoral 傷風敗俗的	• wicked 邪惡的
• evil 罪惡的	• perverted 墮落的	• unethical 不道德的
• gross 下流的	• sordid 卑鄙的	

accident
[`æksədənt]
n 意外事件

During the dinner date, the couple believed that their meeting in the cab was no accident.

晚餐約會時，情侶相信在計程車上相遇非意外。

> 記憶技巧 ac- 等同於 ad-，表示往～方向；cid- 等同於 cad-，表示落；accident 即意外落下，引申為意外事件。

相關字彙 意外、事故	
• calamity 災難	• mishap 不幸事故
• catastrophe 大災難	
• disaster 災害	

incident
[`ɪnsədn̩t]
n 事件，財產附帶權利

In a well-documented incident, the foreign minister fell down the stairs onto the tarmac.

在一次有紀錄的事件中，外交部長從樓梯跌落飛機跑道。

> 記憶技巧 in- 表示內；cid- 表示落；incident 的意思是落在～內，引申為事件。

coincident
[ko`ɪnsədənt]
a 巧合的，同時發生的

The company going into debt was coincident with the firing of the original founder.

公司開始負債時恰巧與開除公司原始創立人同時。

> 記憶技巧 co- 等同於 com-，表示一起；coincident 字面意思是一起掉落，引申為同時發生的。

相關字彙 同時發生	
• accompany 伴隨	• go together 一起去
• concur 同時發生	• go hand in hand 相伴而行
• overlap 部分同時發生	

cess - ceed
子音 s 和 d 互換，母音通轉，兩者的意思皆是走。

---

access
[`æksɛs]
n 接近，入口，通路

The campaign manager threatened to restrict access to his candidate if the reporters were not more polite.
競選活動負責人威脅記者再不多注意禮貌的話就限制接近候選人。

記憶技巧　ac- 等同於 ad-，表示朝～；cess-，表示走；access 字面意思是朝～方向，引申為接近、入口。

---

concede
[kən`sid]
v 讓步，許可

After the first Sino Japanese War, China conceded defeat and turned over some territories.
第一次中日戰爭後，中國承認戰敗並移交一些領土。

記憶技巧　con- 表示加強語氣；-cede 表示走；concede 即讓人走，引申為讓步。

---

excess
[ɪk`sɛs]
n 過剩，超越

The excess of food from the wedding was offered to the homeless shelter across the street.
婚禮剩餘食物被提供給對街遊民收容所。

記憶技巧　ex- 表示外面；cess- 表示走；excess 的意思是走到外面，引申為超越。

---

process
[`prɑsɛs]
n 過程，手續，步驟，傳票

The process of reconciliation for past abuses started with the formation of an investigatory committee.
過去傷害的和解程序從組成一個調查委員會開始。

記憶技巧　pro- 表示前；cess- 表示走；process 是往前走，引申為過程、步驟。

---

success
[sək`sɛs]
n 成功，成功的人或事

The entrepreneur published a series of books on success, but ended up declaring bankruptcy.
企業家出版一系列關於成功的書籍，但是最後卻宣告破產。

記憶技巧　suc- 表示後面；cess- 表示走；success 是走在後面，指的是亦步亦趨走向目的地，引申為成功。

---

recession
[rɪ`sɛʃən]
n 衰退，撤退，凹處

After a period of strong growth, the economy struggled and then declined into a sustained recession.
一波大幅成長後，經濟開始困頓，然後陷入持續的衰退。

記憶技巧　re- 表示後面；cess- 表示走；-ion 為名詞字尾；recession 的意思是走到後面，引申為衰退。

accede
[æk`sid]
v 同意，就職，繼承

The parents did not accede to their daughter's demand for a new smart phone.
家長不同意女兒要有新智慧型手機的要求。

記憶技巧 ac- 等同於 ad-，表示朝～方向；ced- 表示走；accede 的意思是朝～走，引申為就職、同意等。

precede
[pri`sid]
v 領先，優於

The Jurassic Era, which saw the development of many land reptiles, preceded the Cretaceous Era.
侏儸紀時期有許多陸地爬蟲類的演化，發生在白堊紀時期之前。

記憶技巧 pre- 表示前；-cede 表示走；precede 指走在前方，即領先、優於。

unprecedented
[ʌn`prɛsəˌdɛntɪd]
a 史無前例的，
無先例的，空前的

In an unprecedented move, the department store offered a half price sale after Thanksgiving.
百貨公司史無前例在感恩節過後提出半價促銷活動。

記憶技巧 pre- 表示前；-cede 表示走；-ent 為名詞字尾；precedent 現今的意思是先例，17 世紀開始一度當動詞使用；-ed 為過去分詞字尾；un- 為否定字首；unprecedented 字面上意思是沒走在～之前的，亦即史無前例的。

相關字彙
新的

- fresh 新鮮的
- innovative 創新的
- latest 最新的
- new 新的
- novel 新穎的
- original 新穎的
- pioneering 首創的
- up-to-the-minute 最新式的

exceed
[ɪk`sid]
v 優於，勝過，超過

When the demand exceeds supply, there is certain to be a sharp rise in price.
需求超過供給時，價格必定大漲。

記憶技巧 exceed 是 excess 的動詞。

succeed
[sək`sid]
v 成功，繼承

The laborer moved to the big city, got an education, and succeeded in opening his own business.
勞工搬到大城市，接受教育並成功開創自己事業。

記憶技巧 succeed 是 success 的動詞。

原來如此！

beard 是鬍子，修剪鬍子的師傅是 barber，兩字語意關聯，當然是同源字。

clus - clud

子音 s 和 d 互換，母音通轉，兩者的意思皆是關閉。

---

conclusion
[kənˋkluʒən]

n 結論，結尾，決定

In conclusion, I would like the audience to consider that feathered dinosaurs were the ancestors of birds.

總之，我要聽眾將長羽毛的恐龍視為鳥類祖先。

> **記憶技巧** con- 表示一起；clus- 表示關；-ion 為名詞字尾；conclusion 將許多東西一起放進來做總結。

---

exclusive
[ɪkˋsklusɪv]

a 排外的，獨佔的

To close the deal, the salesman offered an exclusive leather golf bag to the purchaser of the luxury car.

為了成交，銷售員提供豪華名車買主獨家的皮革高爾夫球袋。

> **記憶技巧** ex- 表示外面；clus- 表示關；-ive 為形容詞字尾；exclusive 的意思是關到外面的，引申為排外的。

---

disclose
[dɪsˋkloz]

v 洩露，表明

The police investigator reminded the reporter that he was not allowed to disclose his sources.

警方調查員提醒記者不得洩漏資料來源。

> **記憶技巧** dis- 為否定字首；close 等同於 clus-，表示關；disclose 的意思是關不住，引申為洩漏。

相關字彙	
洩漏秘密、消息	

- give away 有意或無意地洩漏某事物（或出賣某人）
- let on 洩露
- leak（秘密等的）洩漏
- lay something bare 秘密暴露
- reveal 洩露
- spill the beans 泄露（尤指秘密的）信息

---

recluse
[rɪˋklus]

n 隱士

The famous composer bought a small island to live on because she enjoyed the life of a recluse.

知名作曲家買下一個小島居住，因為她是享受隱士的生活。

> **記憶技巧** re- 表示一起；clus- 表示關；recluse 的意思是將自己關起來、與世隔絕的人，即隱士。

相關字彙	
害羞、不愛與人接觸	

- loner 喜孤獨者
- hermit 隱士
- introvert 內向的人
- homebody 宅男

---

closet
[ˋklɑzɪt]

n 壁櫥，內室

The housewife was excited when she learned the new house had a large closet in her bedroom.

家庭主婦知道新屋臥房有個大衣櫥時，她很興奮。

> **記憶技巧** close 等同於 clus-，表示關；closet 本指密閉的空間，後亦作壁櫥解釋。

Part **3**

CH 1
CH 2
CH 3

齒間音、齒齦音、齒齦後音、硬顎音轉換

enclose
[ɪnˋkloz]
v 附寄，圍繞

Kindly enclose a check or money order with your registration form for the music camp.
麻煩將支票或現金匯票與音樂營報名表一起附上。

> **記憶技巧** en- 表示動詞的字首；close 等同於 clus-，表示關；enclose 的意思是關起來，因此有圍繞、附寄等衍生意思。

include
[ɪnˋklud]
v 包含，計入

If you're planning our vacation trip, please include a few days of inactivity to rest.
如果你正在規畫我們的度假行程，請加入幾天的放空休息。

> **記憶技巧** in- 表示內；clud- 等同於 clus-，表示關；include 的意思是關進去，引申為包含。

preclude
[prɪˋklud]
v 排除，妨礙

The involvement of the CIA precluded the case from public scrutiny.
中情局的涉入使案件無法受公眾監督。

> **記憶技巧** pre- 表示前；clud- 表示關；preclude 的意思是在進來之前，就關起門，引申為排除。

seclude
[sɪˋklud]
v 隱居

Our plan is to seclude our research and development team for a few days to brainstorm.
我們計劃隔離研發團隊幾天，以進行腦力激盪。

> **記憶技巧** se- 表示分開；clud- 表示關；seclude 的意思是分開關，引申為隱居。

---

vis - vid
子音 s 和 d 互換，母音通轉，兩者的意思皆是分開。

---

division
[dəˋvɪʒən]
n 分割，分配，除法，分店

The food company was actually a division of the multinational corporation.
食品公司其實是一家跨國公司的分公司。

> **記憶技巧** di- 等同於 dis-，表示離開；vis- 表示分開；-ion 為名詞字尾；division 的意思即分割。

indivisible
[͵ɪndəˋvɪzəbl̩]
a 不可分裂的，不可整除的

Even through the rough times, our family remained indivisible and supportive of each other.
即使在艱困時期，我們家依然不可分離，相互扶持。

> **記憶技巧** in- 表示不；di- 表示離開；vis- 表示分開；-ible 為形容詞字尾；indivisible 即不可分裂的。

individual

[ˌɪndə`vɪdʒuəl]

a 個人的，獨特的

The mother prepared individual servings and packaged them in a basket to take to the picnic.

母親準備一人一份餐，然後裝在一個籃裡以便帶去野餐。

> 記憶技巧 in- 表示不；di- 表示離開；vid- 表示分開；-al 為形容詞字尾；individual 即不可分割的個體。

dividend

[`dɪvə,dɛnd]

n 股息，附贈品

The client's investment preference was one that paid steady quarterly dividends.

客戶投資偏好每季支付穩定股息的標的。

> 記憶技巧 di- 表示離開；vid- 表示分開；dividend 是借貸或股票利息的其中一部分。

相關字彙 獲利	
• profit 利潤	• profit margin 利潤率
• earnings 利潤	• gross profit 毛利
• proceeds 收益	• gross margin 毛利

---

gress - grad

子音 s 和 d 互換，母音通轉，兩者的意思皆是走。

---

progressive

[prə`grɛsɪv]

a 進步的，發展的

The political candidate outlined his progressive platform to the voters.

政治候選人對選民概略說明他的進步的政綱。

> 記憶技巧 pro- 表示前；gress- 表示走；-ive 為形容詞字尾；progressive 的意思是往前走，引申為進步的。

相關字彙 發展	
• budding 萌芽的	• embryonic 初期的
• dynamic 動態的	• fledgling 剛開始的
• emerging 新興的	• incipient 剛開始的

aggressive

[ə`grɛsɪv]

a 侵略的，攻勢的，挑釁的

Aggressive housing lenders offered attractive incentives and low interest rates to borrowers.

積極的房貸業者提供貸款人吸引人的誘因及低利率。

> 記憶技巧 ag- 等同於 ad-，表示朝～方向；gress- 表示走；-ive 為形容詞字尾；aggressive 的意思是往～走，引申為侵略的。

congress

[`kɑŋgrəs]

n 國會，集會，交際

The Congress of Pet Pig Lovers held an annual event for pigs and their owners.

寵物豬愛好者協會為豬及飼主舉辦年度活動。

> 記憶技巧 con- 表示一起；gress- 表示走；congress 的意思是走到一塊，1775 年才指美國的國家立法機構。

digression
[daɪˋgrɛʃən]
n 離題，脫軌

The speaker addressed the crying child and then apologized for the brief digression.
講者跟哭鬧的小孩說了幾句話，然後為短暫離題而道歉。

> **記憶技巧** di- 等同於 dis-，表示離開；gress- 表示走；-ion 為名詞字尾；digression 的意思是偏離正軌，引申為離題。

retrogress
[ˌrɛtroˋgrɛs]
v 倒退，衰退，退化

After his injury, the professional athlete retrogressed to his previous talent levels.
受傷之後，職業運動員的能力退到之前的水平。

> **記憶技巧** retro- 表示倒回去；gress- 表示走；retrogress 的意思是往回走，引申為衰退、退化。

transgress
[trænsˋgrɛs]
v 侵越，違犯法律

The woman was overcome by passion and transgressed her marital vows.
女子被情慾征服，背離婚姻誓言。

> **記憶技巧** trans- 表示跨越；gress- 表示走；transgress 的意思是走到別人地盤，引申為侵犯、違反法律。

gradual
[ˋgrædʒʊəl]
a 逐漸的，傾斜度小的

The tennis player showed gradual improvement throughout the year, and earned the right to join a competition.
網球選手在這整年期間展現逐漸進步，獲得參賽資格。

> **記憶技巧** grad- 表示走；-al 為形容詞字尾；gradual 的意思是持續往前走的，引申為逐漸的。

ingredient
[ɪnˋgridɪənt]
n 成分，要素

The chemical ingredients of the explosive mixture were added under controlled conditions.
炸藥混合物的化學成分在安全控管情況下添加。

> **記憶技巧** in- 表示內；gred- 等同於 grad-，表示走；ingredient 是走到～內，可想像成是完成一道菜前，放入鍋子內一樣又一樣的成分。

猜猜看！

shot 是射擊的名詞，那射擊的動詞是什麼？猜一五字母的單字？

答案：shoot（射擊）

lus - lud

子音 s 和 d 互換，母音通轉，兩者的意思皆是玩弄。

---

illusion

[ɪˈljuʒən]

n 幻想，錯覺

He discovered that financial security was just an illusion when he lost his home and business.

他發現，失去家以及事業的時候，財務安全只是幻想。

記憶技巧 il- 等同於 in-，表示在～內、在～之上；lus- 表示玩弄；-ion 為名詞字尾；illusion 是玩弄某人的眼睛或欺騙某人想法，因此有幻想、錯覺等意思。

---

delusion

[dɪˈluʒən]

n 迷惑，欺騙

She was under no delusion that she would get rich overnight and instead, prepared for long-term success.

她不妄想於一夜致富，而為長期成功做準備。

記憶技巧 de- 表示往下；lus- 表示玩弄；-ion 為名詞字尾；delusion 的意思是玩弄某人的眼睛或欺騙某人想法，因此有迷惑、欺騙等意思。

---

elusive

[ɪˈlusɪv]

a 逃避的
（，難以捉摸的）

The Florida panther is an elusive species that has rarely been witnessed by humans.

佛羅里達黑豹是難以捉摸的物種，人們鮮少目擊。

記憶技巧 e- 等同於 ex-，表示外面；lus- 表示玩弄；-ive 為形容詞字尾；elusive 原本有取笑、嘲諷等意思，直到 1610 年代才作逃避的解釋。

---

prelude

[ˈprɛljud]

n 序幕，前奏曲

The prelude to the football championship was an event where fans could meet the athletes.

美式足球錦標賽序幕是一場粉絲與運動員相見歡的活動。

記憶技巧 pre- 表示在～前；lud- 表示玩；prelude 的意思是在正式的表演前的序幕、前奏。

猜猜看！

「similar（相似）」前三個字母意思同於哪一個四字母單字？

答案：same（相同的）

fens - fend

子音 s 和 d 互換，母音通轉，兩者的意思皆是攻擊。

---

fence

[fɛns]

n 柵欄，籬笆

相關字彙
藩籬、阻隔

I was sitting on the fence, thinking about whether or not I should buy the property.

我坐在圍籬，思考是否該買那筆地產。

記憶技巧　fens- 表示攻擊；fence 是柵欄，可用來抵禦攻擊。

- abuttals（用複數）地界
- barbed wire 有刺鐵絲網
- barricade 路障
- paling 柵柵
- palisade 柵欄
- windbreak 防風林

---

defensive

[dɪˋfɛnsɪv]

a 防守的，自衛的

The karate master took a defensive position and asked his student to attack him.

空手道師傅擺出防禦姿勢，要求學生出手。

記憶技巧　de- 表示離開；fens- 表示攻擊；-ive 為形容詞字尾；defensive 是驅離前來攻擊的敵人，以保護自己，現今的意思是防守的、自衛的。

---

offense

[əˋfɛns]

n 犯罪，違反，冒犯

When asked to share his winning strategy, the coach said there was no defense like having a good offense.

被問到獲勝策略時，教練說最好的防禦就是好的進攻。

記憶技巧　of- 等同於 ob-，表示在前面抵抗；fens- 表示攻擊；offense 引申為犯罪、違反。

---

defendant

[dɪˋfɛndənt]

n 被告

相關字彙
法庭用語

In the case of the missing wallet, the defendant pleaded innocent, having never met the accuser before.

遺失皮夾的案件中，被告因從未見過原告，而做無罪申辯。

記憶技巧　de- 表示離開；fend- 表示攻擊；-ant 表示人；defendant 是遭攻擊、被迫回擊的被告。

- the accused 被告
- alibi 不在場證明
- appellant 上訴人
- court 法院
- expert witness 專家證人
- petitioner 請願人
- plaintiff 原告
- witness 證人

---

offend

[əˋfɛnd]

v 冒犯，違反，觸怒

There was no intention to offend the student when the teacher announced his failing grade in class.

老師在課堂上宣布學生成績不及格，並非有意冒犯他。

記憶技巧　offend 是 offense 的動詞。

---

pens - pend

子音 s 和 d 互換，母音通轉，兩者的意思皆是掛、增加重量、衡量。

compensate
[`kɑmpən‚set]

v 償還，補償

There was an effort to compensate the farmer after the pesticides poisoned his flock of sheep.
殺蟲劑使農夫的羊群中毒之後，有試圖補償他。

> 記憶技巧 | com- 表示一起；pens- 表示增加重量；-ate 為動詞字尾；compensate 的字面意思是一起秤重，為了使天平兩端能夠平衡，需要在天平一端增加重量，引申為補償。

indispensable
[‚ɪndɪs`pɛnsəbl]

a 不可或缺的，
不可避免的

The computer programmer made himself indispensable, because he had access to all of the passwords.
因為電腦程式設計師可取得所有密碼，而讓他自己不可或缺。

> 記憶技巧 | in- 為否定字首；dis- 表示外面；pens- 表示秤重；-able 為形容詞字尾；indispensable 的意思是無法秤斤論兩賣給客人，代表這項事物是自己所需、不可或缺的。

dispensary
[dɪ`spɛnsərɪ]

n 藥局（，配藥室）

The pharmacist visited the dispensary to stock up on pharmaceuticals she needed.
藥劑師去了配藥室庫存所需藥品。

> 記憶技巧 | dis- 表示外；pens- 表示秤重；-ary 表示地方；dispensary 是秤重賣藥的藥局。

相關字彙 醫院部門、診所	
• consulting room 診察室	• intensive care unit 加護病房
• dispensary 藥劑部	• operating room 手術室
• emergency room 急診室	• pharmacy 藥局

plaus - plaud

子音 s 和 d 互換，母音通轉，兩者的意思皆是拍手。

applause
[ə`plɔz]

n 喝采，熱烈鼓掌

I would like to remind the audience to please hold all applause until the end of the performance.
在此提醒觀眾將所有掌聲留到表演結束。

> 記憶技巧 | ap- 表示朝～方向；plaus- 表示拍手；applause 的意思是拍手表示同意、讚賞，引申為喝采。

相關字彙 用以溝通的聲音	
• boo（表示不滿、輕蔑等）噓	• hiss（表示不滿、責備）發出噓聲
• clapping 鼓掌聲	• tut（表示不耐煩、指責等）嘖！噓！
• brrr 表示冷	

Part **3**

CH 1
CH 2
CH 3

齒間音、齒齦音、齒齦後音、硬顎音轉換

explosion
[ɪk`sploʒən]

n 爆炸，擴張

The horrible explosion at the coal mine happened because fine coal dust was ignited by a spark.
煤礦坑發生恐怖爆炸，因為煤塵被火花點燃。

記憶技巧　ex- 表示外；plos- 表示拍手；-ion 為名詞字尾；explosion 的意思是拍手來驅趕台上表演者，類似噓聲、喝倒采的功能，後來才有爆炸的意思。

explode
[ɪk`splod]

v 爆炸，爆破，迅速發展

相關字彙
爆炸

The coach grabbed his young player to stop him from shaking the bottle of cola before it exploded.
教練抓住年輕選手，在可樂瓶爆開之前阻止他繼續搖晃。

記憶技巧　explode 是 explosion 的動詞。

- blast 爆炸
- blow up 爆炸
- blow off 炸掉
- burst 爆炸

plausible
[`plɔzəbl]

a 似乎合理的，似乎真實的

Your excuse would be plausible, but you couldn't have been in both locations at one time.
你的說詞本來會是合理的，但那時候你不可能同時出現在兩個地點。

記憶技巧　plaus- 表示拍手；-ible 為形容詞字尾；plausible 的意思是拍手表示同意，1560 年代才有似乎合理的意思。

spons - spond
子音 s 和 d 互換，母音通轉，兩者的意思皆是承諾、保證。

sponsor
[`spansɚ]

n 發起者，主辦者，保證人，資助人

The company offered to be a sponsor for the marathon, as they wanted to encourage their staff to be more active.
公司提議要作為馬拉松贊助商，因為有意鼓勵員工多活動。

記憶技巧　spons- 表示保證、承諾；-or 為做出動作者；sponsor 的意思是保證人，後衍生出資助人、贊助商的意思。

spouse
[spaʊz]

n 配偶

相關字彙
夫妻、伴侶

The service offered single men the opportunity to find a lovely spouse from several foreign countries.
該機構提供單身男士自數個海外國家覓得美嬌娘的機會。

記憶技巧　spouse 等同於 spons-，即許下諾言、廝守終生的配偶。

- helpmate 配偶
- husband 丈夫
- life partner 終身伴侶
- wife 妻子

responsibility

[rɪˌspɑnsəˋbɪlətɪ]

n 責任，負擔

When no one adopted the litter of puppies, the farmer took responsibility for their care.

沒人領養那窩小狗時，農夫負起照顧責任。

記憶技巧　re- 表示回；spons- 表示承諾；-ible 為形容詞字尾；-ity 為名詞字尾；responsibility 是給承諾，引申為責任。

---

correspond

[ˌkɔrɪˋspɑnd]

v 相當，對應，一致，符合，通信

The change in your health and well-being may correspond with your recent emotional state.

你的健康及財富起伏可能對應於你最近的情緒狀態。

記憶技巧　cor- 等同於 com-，表示一起；respond 表示回應；correspond 的意思是一起回應，引此有對應、通信等意思。

---

respond

[rɪˋspɑnd]

v 回應，反應，承擔責任，賠償

The candidate was given ample opportunity to respond to the opponent's criticism of his performance.

候選人有充足機會回應對手對他表現的批評。

記憶技巧　re- 表示回；spond- 表示承諾；respond 即給人承諾，後衍生出回應、反應等意思。

---

despondent

[dɪˋspɑndənt]

a 失望的，垂頭喪氣的

The paramedics arrived at the widow's home, finding her despondent and hopeless.

護理人員抵達寡婦家時，發現她萬念俱灰。

記憶技巧　de- 表示離開；spond- 表示承諾；-ent 為形容詞字尾；despondent 的意思是承諾將～送人，引申為不得不放棄，引申為失望的。

---

scens - scend

子音 s 和 d 互換，母音通轉，兩者的意思皆是爬、跳。

---

condescension

[ˌkɑndɪˋsɛnʃən]

n 屈尊俯就

The occupying soldiers were often seen expressing condescension when talking to the locals.

占領的士兵與當地人談話時常表現得屈尊就卑。

記憶技巧　con- 表示一起；de- 表示下；scens- 表示爬；-ion 為名詞字尾；condescension 的意思是爬下去，引申為屈尊俯就。

相關字彙

自豪、自大、自戀

- arrogance 傲慢
- egotism 自負
- narcissism 自戀
- pride 得意
- snobbery 勢利眼
- vanity 自負

Part **3**

CH 1
CH 2
CH 3

齒間音、齒齦音、齒齦後音、硬顎音轉換

ascend
[əˋsɛnd]
v 攀登，登上

The hard-working golfer ascended to the top of the world rankings within a relatively short time.
努力的高爾夫球選手在相對較短的時間內登上世界排名第一。

記憶技巧 as- 等同於 ad-，表示朝～方向；cend- 表示爬；ascend 的意思是爬上去，因此有攀登、登上等衍生意思。

ascendant
[əˋsɛndənt]
a 優勢的

In the ascendant period of the monarch's reign, the queen played a vital role in gaining people's support.
君王統治的日益掌權的時期，皇后扮演攏絡人心的重要角色。

記憶技巧 as- 等同於 ad-，表示朝～方向；cend- 表示爬；-ant 為形容詞字尾；ascendant 指爬到前方的，引申為優勢的、上升的。

descendant
[dɪˋsɛndənt]
n 後代，弟子

It may be hard to believe, but the dog is a descendant of the walrus.
也許難以置信，但狗是海象的後裔。

記憶技巧 de- 表示下；scend- 表示爬；-ant 為名詞字尾；descendant 的意思是往下，引申為後代。

相關字彙
家族系譜

- ancestry 祖先
- antecedents 祖先
- family tree 家譜
- forefathers 祖先
- genealogy 家系
- lineage 世系
- progenitor 祖先

transcend
[trænˋsɛnd]
v 超越，凌駕

The work of the artist was exalted as being so superior, it transcended comparisons to other artists.
藝術家的這件作品被評為非常優越，其他藝術家無可比擬。

記憶技巧 trans- 表示跨越；cend- 表示爬；transcend 是爬過去，引申為超越。

ris - rid
子音 s 和 d 互換，母音通轉，兩者的意思皆是笑。

derisive
[dɪˋraɪsɪv]
a 可笑的，值得嘲笑的

The team leader declared that his team could win the championship, bringing about derisive laughter from the judges.
隊長自稱能夠拿下冠軍，這招致了裁判嘲笑。

記憶技巧 de- 表示下；ris- 表示笑；-ive 為形容詞字尾；derisive 的意思是可笑的。

ridiculous

[rɪˋdɪkjələs]

a 可笑的，荒謬的

The authorities first believed his theory about the Earth rotating around the sun was ridiculous.

有關當局一開始認為他關於地球繞行太陽的理論十分荒謬。

記憶技巧 rid- 表示笑；-ous 為形容詞字尾；ridiculous 的意思是可笑的。

---

deride

[dɪˋraɪd]

v 嘲笑，愚弄

Although the quarterback lost the game, the coach told his teammates not to deride him too much.

四分衛輸掉比賽，但教練叮囑隊員不能太嘲弄他。

記憶技巧 deride 是 derisive 的動詞。

相關字彙
批評譴責

- blame 指責
- criticize 批評
- denigrate 詆毀
- find fault with 找碴
- reproach 斥責
- reprimand 訓斥
- rebuke 指責
- remonstrate 反對

---

ras - rad

子音 s 和 d 互換，母音通轉，兩者的意思皆是刮除。

---

erasable

[ɪˋresəbl̩]

a 可擦掉的，
可抹去的

The erasable ink requires a special type of eraser and is wildly popular with students.

可擦拭墨水需要特別種類橡皮擦，並且廣受學生歡迎。

記憶技巧 e- 等同於 ex-，表示外面；ras- 表示刮；-able 為形容詞字尾；erasable 的意思是可刮除的、可抹去的。

---

rascal

[ˋræskl̩]

n 惡棍，流氓

The Southern belle scoffed at the suitor, and stated that she could never love an ill-mannered rascal like him.

南方美女不屑該名追求者，表明絕不會愛上像他這樣無禮的流氓。

記憶技巧 ras- 表示刮除；rascal 的本意是刮除的渣滓，即不為人所喜的無用事物，後作惡棍、流氓解釋。

---

abrade

[əˋbred]

v 擦掉，磨損，擦傷

The doctor delicately abraded the infected bone tissue with a sponge soaked in antibiotics.

醫生以浸泡抗生素的海綿仔細擦磨感染的骨組織。

記憶技巧 ab- 表示離開；rad- 表示刮除；abrade 即刮掉，引申出磨損、擦傷的意思。

Part **3**

CH 1
CH 2
CH 3

齒間音、齒齦音、齒齦後音、硬顎音轉換

razor

[ˋrezɚ]

n 剃刀，刮鬍刀

The gentleman preferred an old-fashioned shave with a single-edged razor and warm shaving cream.
這位紳士偏好用單邊剃刀及溫熱刮鬍泡得舊式刮鬍。

記憶技巧　raz- 等同於 ras-，表示刮除；-or 為做出動作者；razor 即剃刀、刮鬍刀。

相關字彙
剔除鬍子、毛髮

- depilatory 有脫毛作用的
- pluck 拔～的毛
- shave 剃去～上的毛髮
- wax 熱蠟除毛

Section **4**

〔θ〕對應〔d〕

---

anthrop - andr

子音 th 和 d 互換，母音通轉，anthrop- 意思是人類，andr- 特指男性。

---

anthropology

[ˌænθrəˋpɑlədʒɪ]

n 人類學

Susan earned her PhD in anthropology and lived among the tribal peoples for two years.
蘇珊獲得人類學博士學位，與不同部落族人一起生活兩年。

記憶技巧　anthrop- 表示人；-logy 表示學問；anthropology 即人類學。

---

philanthropy

[fɪˋlænθrəpɪ]

n 慈善

With an education system that encourages philanthropy, the country has no problems with homelessness.
因著鼓勵慈善的教育體制，國家沒有無家可歸的問題。

記憶技巧　phil- 表示愛；anthrop- 表示人類；-y 為名詞字尾；philanthropy 的意思是愛人類的，引申為慈善。

---

androgen

[ˋændrədʒən]

n 男性賀爾蒙

During the development of the embryo, an introduction of androgen can help it to become a male.
胚胎發育期間，置入雄性賀爾蒙有助於胚胎變成雄性。

記憶技巧　andro- 表示男性；gen- 表示生；androgen 是產生男性特徵的男性賀爾蒙。

- adrenalin 腎上腺素
- endorphin 腦內啡
- estrogen 雌激素
- growth hormone 生長激素
- insulin 胰島素
- serotonin 血清素
- testosterone 睪丸素

Section **5**

〔r〕對應〔t〕

Part **3**

CH 1
CH 2
CH 3

齒間音、齒齦音、齒齦後音、硬顎音轉換

amor - amat

子音 r 和 t 互換，母音通轉，兩者的意思皆是愛。

amorous [`æmərəs] ⓐ 多情的	The amorous cat howled all night, hoping to attract the attention of a tomcat. 發情的貓整晚嚎叫，希望吸引雄貓注意。 記憶技巧 amor- 表示愛；-ous 為形容詞字尾；amorous 是多情的意思。
amateur [`æmə‚tʃur] ⓝ 業餘者，愛好者，外行 相關字彙 不擅長做某事的人	The photography competition is open to both amateurs and professionals. 業餘及專業攝影師都可參加攝影比賽。 記憶技巧 amat- 表示愛；-eur 表示人；amateur 是愛做某事的人，特指業餘者。 • incompetent 無能力的人 • bungler 經驗不夠的人
amiable [`emɪəbl̩] ⓐ 和藹可親的 相關字彙 友善真誠的	The barber was an amiable fellow, keeping his customers loyal and making them come back for social interactions. 理髮師為人和藹，贏得顧客忠誠且讓他們回到店裡社交互動。 記憶技巧 ami- 表示愛；-able 為形容詞字尾；amiable 的意思是有愛的，引申為和藹可親的。 • bubbly 熱情活潑的 • friendly 友善的 • genuine 真誠的 • good-natured 和藹的 • pleasant 和藹可親的

enemy

[ˋɛnəmɪ]

n 敵人，危害物

The electric generator in the weapons factory was sabotaged by an unknown enemy.

兵工廠發電機遭不明敵人破壞。

記憶技巧 en- 等同於 in-，為否定字首；emy 等同於 ami-，表示愛，亦當作朋友解釋；enemy 的意思是非朋友或沒有愛，引申為敵人。

enmity

[ˋɛnmɪtɪ]

n 敵意，敵對

After decades of enmity between North and South Korea, the two nations finally opened peace talks.

南北韓歷經數十年敵對後，終於展開和平對談。

記憶技巧 en- 等同於 in-，為否定字首；ami- 表示愛；-ity 為名詞字尾；enmity 的意思是沒有愛，引申為敵對的。

amity

[ˋæmɪtɪ]

n 和睦，和好

The Baltic nations signed an economic cooperation agreement to bolster prosperity and amity between them.

波羅的海周邊國家簽訂經濟合作協議，以增進繁榮和彼此友好的關係。

記憶技巧 ami- 表示愛；-ity 為名詞字尾；amity 即友愛的，引申為和睦、和好。

Section **6**

〔s〕對應〔t〕

glos - glot

子音 s 和 t 互換，母音通轉，兩者的意思皆是舌頭、詞語。

glossary

[ˋglɑsərɪ]

n 詞彙表，術語（或特殊用語）彙編

At the end of the English training manual, students could find a glossary of terms for reference.

在英語培訓手冊結尾處，學生可找到參考詞彙表。

記憶技巧 gloss- 表示詞語；-ary 為名詞字尾；glossary 是收集詞語的詞彙表。

monoglot

[`manə،glat]

n 只熟悉一種語言
的人

The people of the tribe were monoglots because they did not yet have contact with the outside world.
部落族人只熟悉一種語言，因為他們尚未與外界接觸。

記憶技巧 mono- 表示單一；glot- 表示話語；monoglot 是單一的話語，指只熟悉一種語言的人。

polyglot

[`palɪ،glat]

n 精通數國語言的人

The professional linguist was a naturally-gifted polyglot, inheriting the talent from his father.
專業語言學家承襲父親才華，具有多語天賦。

記憶技巧 poly- 表示多；glot- 表示話語；polyglot 的意思是精通數種語言的人。

Part

3

CH 1
CH 2
CH 3

齒間音、齒齦音、齒齦後音、硬顎音轉換

dos - dat

子音 s 和 t 互換，母音通轉，兩者的意思皆是給。

dose

[dos]

n 一劑藥，一服藥

The container held a few doses of antidote for the serious communicable disease.
容器裝有幾劑傳染性重病的解藥。

記憶技巧 dos- 表示給；dose 是醫生開給病人的一服藥。

data

[`detə]

n 資料

相關字彙
電腦檔案與資料夾

Under the dry desert of southern Arizona sits a vast data center connected to the Internet.
亞利桑那州南部乾旱沙漠地底下有一座連接網路大面積的數據中心。

記憶技巧 dat- 表示給；data 是給出去的資料。

- archive 資料庫
- backup 備份
- big data 大數據
- cookie 訊錄，網路餅乾
- database 資料庫
- download 下載
- podcast 播客
- scratch file 臨時檔
- zip file 壓縮檔

antidote

[`æntɪ،dot]

n 解毒劑

相關字彙
藥物

The research team worked feverishly to develop an antidote for the disease that had a high mortality rate.
研究團隊致力研發此個高致死率疾病的解藥。

記憶技巧 anti- 表示抵抗；dot- 表示給；antidote 的意思是給人抗毒的藥物。

- amphetamine 安非他命
- anaesthetic 麻醉劑
- booster 輔助藥劑
- decongestant 解充血藥
- expectorant 祛痰的
- inhalant 吸入劑
- syrup 含藥糖漿
- tranquillizer 鎮靜劑

anecdote
[`ænɪk,dot]
n 軼事

The president amused the visiting dignitaries with a few interesting anecdotes about the previous leader.
總統以一些前領導人奇聞軼事取悅來訪政要。

記憶技巧　an- 等同於 in-，為否定字首；ec- 等同於 ex-，表示外面；dot- 表示給；anecdote 是沒有給出去的，特指未出版的書籍，現今的語意是軼事。

相關字彙　各種故事

- allegory 寓言
- adaptation 改編故事
- detective 偵探故事
- epic 史詩
- fable 寓言
- fairy tale 童話
- folk tale 民間故事
- ghost story 鬼故事
- mythology 神話
- parable 寓言故事
- thriller 驚悚小說

pardon
[`pardn]
v 寬恕

The parents wrote many letters to the governor, asking him to pardon their son who was in prison.
家長多次寫信給州長請求寬恕服刑中的兒子。

記憶技巧　par- 表示完全地；don- 表示給；pardon 的意思是全部給人，引申為寬恕。

donate
[`donet]
v 贈予，捐贈

The university named a building after a patron who donated a million dollars.
大學以捐獻一百萬元的贊助人為一棟建築物命名。

記憶技巧　don- 表示給；-ate 為動詞字尾；donate 是捐贈。

相關字彙　贈與

- endowment（基金、財產等的）捐贈
- patronise 資助
- relief 救濟物品
- tied aid 限制性援助

condone
[kən`don]
v 赦免，寬恕

The teacher told the student that he could not condone his behavior in the classroom.
老師告訴學生他無法原諒他在教室裡的行為。

記憶技巧　con- 表示加強語氣；don- 表示給；condone 的意思是給予寬恕。

miss - mit
子音 s 和 t 互換，母音通轉，兩者的意思皆是（發）送。

mission
[`mɪʃən]
n 任務，使節團

If you choose to take on this secret mission, you must promise never to reveal your identity.
如果選擇接下這項祕密任務，你必須承諾絕不洩漏身份。

記憶技巧　miss- 表示送；-ion 為名詞字尾；mission 的意思是送走，引申為任務。

admission

[əd`mɪʃən]

n 入學許可，入場，承認

The review board was responsible for interviewing and offering admission to qualified candidates.

審查委員會面試合格候選人並給予入學資格。

記憶技巧 ad- 表示朝～方向；miss- 表示送；-ion 為名詞字尾；admission 的意思是允許送來，因此有入學許可、承認等衍生意思。

demise

[dɪ`maɪz]

n 死亡

As the tyrant reached an old age, there was hope among the people for the eventual demise of his kingdom.

隨著暴君邁向晚年，人民寄望他的王國終結。

記憶技巧 de- 表示離開；mis- 表示送；demise 的意思是送走，1754 才有死亡的意思。

dismiss

[dɪs`mɪs]

v 解散，免職，駁回

The staff was dismissed from the office early to attend the Cinco de Mayo celebrations.

為了參加五月五日節慶祝活動，員工提前自辦公室解散。

記憶技巧 dis- 表示離開；miss- 表示送；dismiss 是送走，引申為解散、駁回等意思。

submissive

[sʌb`mɪsɪv]

a 服從的，謙恭的

Though people thought she was a submissive wife, she had influence on the husband's decision-making.

雖被認為是個服從的妻子，但她對丈夫的決定具有影響力。

記憶技巧 sub- 表示下面；miss- 表示送；-ive 為形容詞字尾；submit 的意思是把～往下送；submissive 是讓～屈服在下，因此有服從的、謙恭的等意思。

missile

[`mɪsḷ]

n 飛彈

North Korea claimed its newest missiles could reach the shores of North America.

北韓宣稱自家新型飛彈可抵達北美海岸。

記憶技巧 miss- 表示送；-ile 為名詞字尾；missile 即是往前拋的物件，現作飛彈解釋。

相關字彙
各種飛彈

- air-to-air missile 空對空飛彈
- air-to-surface missile 空對面飛彈
- anti-submarine missile 反潛飛彈
- surface-to-air missile 面對空飛彈
- cruise missile 巡弋飛彈
- ballistic missiles 彈道飛彈

commit

[kə`mɪt]

v 委託，犯罪（，使投入戰鬥）

The general had to make the difficult decision of whether or not to commit his soldiers to the battle.

是否將戰士送上戰場讓將軍難以決定。

記憶技巧 com- 表示加強語氣；mit- 表示送；commit 是全部送人，引申為委託。

Part 3
CH 1
CH 2
CH 3

齒間音、齒齦音、齒齦後音、硬顎音轉換

407

omit

[o`mɪt]

V 省略，遺漏

The editor was directed to omit any language that could be deemed offensive.

編輯受指示刪去任何可能被視為冒犯的言詞。

記憶技巧 o- 等同於 ob-，表示加強語氣；mit- 表示送；omit 的意思是送到一旁去，引申為省略、遺漏。

相關字彙	
不包括	• count out 不包括某人／某事物 • leave out 省去 • drop 省略 • miss out 遺漏 • exclude 排除～在外

permit

[pɚ`mɪt]

n 許可證

Please visit the clerk's office to register for a permit in order to hold the outdoor activity.

請到職員辦公室登記取得舉辦戶外活動的許可證。

記憶技巧 per- 表示穿透；mit- 表示送；permit 的意思是送過去，引申為許可。

---

sens - sent
子音 s 和 t 互換，母音通轉，兩者的意思皆是感覺。

---

sensitive

[`sɛnsətɪv]

a 敏感的，過敏的

Some said the sensitive man was weak, but he showed great reliability when he was needed.

有人說該敏感的男子懦弱，但別人需要他時他卻是十足可靠。

記憶技巧 sens- 表示感覺；-ive 為形容詞字尾；sensitive 是敏感的。

sensible

[`sɛnsəbḷ]

a 明理的，可感覺的

The treasurer questioned whether or not it was sensible to build such an expensive memorial to the late founder.

財務主管質疑建造如此昂貴的已故創始者紀念館是否明智。

記憶技巧 sens- 表示感覺；-ible 為形容詞字尾；sensible 的意思是可以感覺的到的。

consensus

[kən`sɛnsəs]

n （意見）一致，輿論

Unless you can reach a consensus, we will not change any of the regulations.

除非你們達成共識，否則我們無法改變任何規則。

記憶技巧 con- 表示相同；sens- 表示感覺；consensus 的意思是有同感，引申為一致。

相關字彙	
同意	• agreement 同意 • unanimity 一致同意 • accord 調和 • understanding 共識 • contract 訂（約）

consent
[kən`sɛnt]
n 同意，贊成

The attorney argued that it wasn't the behavior itself that was under scrutiny, but it was the lack of consent.
律師主張，要審視的不是行為本身，而是缺乏認同。

記憶技巧 con- 表示相同；sens- 表示感覺；consent 的意思是有同感，引申為同意。

sentimental
[͵sɛntə`mɛnt!]
a 感情的，感傷的

Whenever he saw a beach scene, the retiree became sentimental and missed his days as a lifeguard.
每次看見沙灘的場景，退休者就變得感傷，並懷念擔任救生員的日子。

記憶技巧 sent- 表示感覺；ment- 為名詞字尾；-al 為形容詞字尾；sentimental 的意思是感情的。

---

nas - nat
子音 s 和 t 互換，母音通轉，兩者的意思皆是生。

---

nascent
[`næsṇt]
a 新生的

After receiving their first orders, the startup company believed that their nascent technology would be successful.
拿到首批訂單後，新創公司相信自家剛研發的科技將會成功。

記憶技巧 nasc- 表示生；-ent 為形容詞字尾；nascent 是新生的。

native
[`netɪv]
a 天生的，本國的，本地的

The newly graduated botanist moved to Western Canada to study the native flora there.
剛畢業的植物學家移居加拿大，以研究當地的原生植物。

記憶技巧 nat- 表示生；-ive 為形容詞字尾；native 是天生的。

相關字彙 居民
- aboriginal 土著的
- community 社區
- dweller 居住者
- indigenous 本地的
- local 本地人
- resident 居民

naïve
[nɑ`iv]
a 純真的

It wasn't long before the naïve intern was tricked into getting coffee for everyone.
沒多久天真的實習生就被哄去為大家拿咖啡。

記憶技巧 naïve 為法文字，表示與生俱來的特質，不假人工雕琢，引申為純真的。

相關字彙 易受騙
- credulous 輕信的
- deluded 受矇騙的
- gullible 易受騙的
- trusting 輕易信任別人的
- unworldly 不諳世故的

Part **3**

CH 1
CH 2
CH 3

齒間音、齒齦音、齒齦後音、硬顎音轉換

oss - ost

子音 s 和 t 互換，母音通轉，兩者的意思皆是骨頭。

ossify
[`ɑsə͵faɪ]

v （使～）骨化，（使）硬化

The soft tissue at the top of an infant's skull usually ossifies at the age of one year.
嬰兒顱骨上方的軟組織通常在一歲時硬化。

記憶技巧　oss- 表示骨頭；-fy 為動詞字尾；ossify 指使～骨化。

osteoporosis
[͵ɑstɪopə`rosɪs]

n 骨質疏鬆症

The article stated that eating certain supplements may actually accelerate the development of osteoporosis.
文章指出，食用某些補給品其實可能加速骨質疏鬆症的發展。

記憶技巧　ost- 表示骨頭；por- 表示孔；-osis 表示疾病的狀態；osteoporosis 的字面意思是多孔的骨頭，即骨質疏鬆症。患者骨骼會變脆弱，容易骨折。

osteoarthritis
[͵ɑstɪoɑr`θraɪtɪs]

n 退化性關節炎

The residents of the nursing home were given regular massages to relieve their osteoarthritis.
照護中心的老人按時接受按摩以舒緩退化性關節炎。

記憶技巧　ost- 表示骨頭；arthritis 表示關節炎；osteoarthritis 是退化性關節炎。

ostracize
[`ɑstrə͵saɪz]

v （古希臘）按貝殼流放法放逐（，排斥）

The politician was hated by multinational corporations, so the media attacked him to ostracize him.
跨國公司痛惡該名政治人物，因此媒體為了排斥他而予以撻伐。

記憶技巧　ost- 表示骨骼，希臘文中亦作陶罐碎片、貝殼解釋；-ize 為動詞字尾；ostracize 是貝殼放逐法，古希臘的雅典人民可以投票強制將某個人放逐，投票者在陶罐碎片刻上應被放逐者的姓名，放逐時間為十年。

aesthes - aesthet

子音 s 和 t 互換，母音通轉，兩者的意思皆是感覺。

anesthesia
[͵ænəs`θiʒə]

n 麻醉

The woman opted for anesthesia when getting her root canal treatment, as she dreaded the sounds of the drill.
女子根管治療時選擇麻醉，因為懼怕鑽子聲音。

記憶技巧　an- 表示缺乏；esthes- 表示感覺；-ia 為名詞字尾；anesthesia 的意思是沒有感覺的，引申為麻醉。

aesthetic
[ɛs`θɛtɪk]
a 美學的

The designer was hired to add aesthetic touches to the brand of electric toothbrushes.
設計師應聘為品牌電動牙刷增加美感。

記憶技巧　aesthet- 表示感覺；-ic 為形容詞字尾；aesthetic 的意思是有感覺的，1821 年才有美學的意思。

相關字彙　吸引人
- appealing 有魅力的
- adorable 可愛的
- lovely 美的
- captivating 迷人的
- delightful 令人愉快的
- eye-catching 引人注目的
- nice-looking 好看的
- stunning 美得令人目瞪口呆的

polis - polit
子音 s 和 t 互換，母音通轉，兩者的意思皆是城市。

metropolis
[mə`trɑplɪs]
n 首都，主要都市

Tokyo is a modern metropolis and can be easily traversed with its public transportation system.
東京是一現代化大都會，藉由大眾運輸系統便能輕易橫越。

記憶技巧　metro- 表示母親；polis- 表示城市；metropolis 的意思是母親城市，即一國之首都或主要城市。

相關字彙　市鎮
- capital 首都
- conurbation 集合都市
- garden city 花園城市
- ghost town 被遺棄而無人煙之村鎮
- metropolis 大都市

political
[pə`lɪtɪkl̩]
a 政治的

The couple's differing political views caused some conflict, but it did not destroy their marriage.
夫婦不同政治觀點產生一些衝突，但這並不破壞婚姻。

記憶技巧　polit- 表示城市，在此衍生出市民的意思，亦有公眾的意思；-ical 為形容詞字尾；political 的意思是治理眾人、管理城市的意思，即政治的。

相關字彙　政治、政府
- administration 行政機構
- affair 事務
- government 政府
- politicization 政治化
- sociopolitical 社會與政治的
- representation 代表權

cosmopolitan
[ˌkɑzmə`pɑlətn̩]
a 四海為家的
　　（，國際性的）

With a highly sophisticated image and youthful energy, Berlin has become a model cosmopolitan city.
有高度發展的形象及年輕活力，柏林已成為一個國際城市典範。

記憶技巧　cosmo- 表示世界；polit- 表示城市，在此作人民；-an 為形容詞字尾；cosmopolitan 的意思是以世界為家的人，引申為四海為家的。

peps - pept

子音 s 和 t 互換，母音通轉，兩者的意思皆是消化。

---

pepsin
[`pɛpsɪn]
n 消化素

The man had poor digestion because his stomach did not produce enough pepsin to break down the food.

男子消化不良，因為胃無法產生足夠消化素來分解食物。

> **記憶技巧** peps- 表示消化；-in 表示化學物質；pepsin 是消化素。

---

dyspepsia
[dɪ`spɛpʃə]
n 消化不良

The doctor suspected dyspepsia, so he recommended the patient eat five small meals daily.

醫生懷疑是消化不良，所以建議病人一天吃五小餐。

> **記憶技巧** dys- 表示壞的；peps- 表示消化；-ia 表示疾病；dyspepsia 是消化不良。

相關字彙
食物處理或消化
- anus 肛門
- bowel 腸
- colon 結腸
- duodenum 十二指腸
- esophagus 食管
- intestine 腸

---

eupeptic
[ju`pɛptɪk]
a 消化良好的
（，快樂的）

He wanted to be a food blogger, because his idol was a eupeptic food taster on a cable TV show.

他想成為美食部落客，因為偶像是一名有線電視節目裡健康愉快的美食品嚐家。

> **記憶技巧** eu- 表示好的；pept- 表示消化；-ic 為形容詞字尾；eupeptic 是消化良好的。

相關字彙
消化
- digestive 消化的
- dyspeptic 消化不良的

---

us - uti

子音 s 和 t 互換，母音通轉，兩者的意思皆是使用。

---

usage
[`jusɪdʒ]
n 用法，習慣，習俗

He was surprised that his cell phone bill was so high, because his usage did not exceed the monthly limit.

未超出單月用量限制但手機帳單費用很高，讓他十分吃驚。

> **記憶技巧** us- 表示使用；-age 為名詞字尾；usage 的意思是用法、習俗。

相關字彙
派上用場
- application 應用
- consumption 消耗
- exploitation 利用
- implementation 完成
- upcycling 升級再造
- use 發揮

abusive
[ə`bjusɪv]
a 妄用的

The introverted girl never forgave her abusive parents and ran away from home when she was only 14 years old.
內向女孩無法原諒虐待她的父母，年僅十四歲便離家出走。

> **記憶技巧** ab- 表示離開；us- 表示使用；-ive 為形容詞字尾；abusive 的意思是不合乎常理的使用，引申為妄用的。

utilize
[`jutḷˌaɪz]
v 利用

The young relief pitcher was utilized in the ninth inning, after the game was well in hand.
年輕救援投手第九局比賽完全掌握時上場。

> **記憶技巧** util- 表示使用；-ize 為動詞字尾；utilize 的意思是利用。

utilitarian
[ˌjutɪləˈtɛrɪən]
a 功利主義的

He learned a lot from his utilitarian uncle, always working to maximize the overall good.
他從功利主義的叔叔身上學到很多，總是努力增進整體的福利。

> **記憶技巧** utility 表示功利；-arian 為形容詞字尾；utilitarian 即功利主義的。

相關字彙
工作有成效、效率

- efficient 效率高的
- effective 有效的
- operative 起作用的

utensil
[juˈtɛnsḷ]
n 器具，廚房用具

The ladle is one utensil you don't want to forget when you are serving a pot of soup.
勺子是煮一鍋湯時不會忘記的廚房器具。

> **記憶技巧** ut- 表示使用；utensil 的意思是廚房用具或器具。

Part **3**

CH 1
CH 2
CH 3

齒間音、齒齦音、齒齦後音、硬顎音轉換

〔θ〕對應〔t〕

urethr - ureter

子音 th 和 t 互換，母音通轉，兩者皆和尿液相關。

urethra
[juˋriθrə]
n 尿道

After he got a bladder infection, his urethra became inflamed and urination was painful.
他膀胱感染後，尿道發炎，排尿會痛。

記憶技巧　urethra 是尿道。

ureteritis
[ˌjutəˋraɪtɪs]
n 輸尿管炎

The doctor blamed the painful ureteritis on the woman's poor hygiene.
醫生將女子疼痛的輸尿管炎歸咎於衛生習慣不良。

記憶技巧　ureter- 表示輸尿管；-itis 表示發炎；ureteritis 是輸尿管炎。

〔t〕對應〔n〕

cert - cern

子音 t 和 n 互換，母音通轉，兩者皆表示分辨、過濾、決定。

concert
[ˋkɑnsɚt]
n 音樂會，一致

The benefit concert attracted twenty thousand fans and raised a million dollars for charity.
慈善募捐音樂會吸引兩萬粉絲，為慈善機構募得一百萬元。

記憶技巧　con- 表示一起；cert- 表示決定；concert 的意思是一起決定，因此有一致的意思，衍生意思有協奏曲、音樂會等。

concern
[kənˋsɝn]

n 關係，關心，掛念

The director of Disease Control Bureau has already expressed his concern over the epidemic situation.
疾病管制局長對疫情已表達關心之意。

記憶技巧 con- 表示一起；cern- 表示分辨；concern 的字面意思是分辨，引申出理解、察覺，也因此衍生出關心、掛念等意思。

discern
[dɪˋzɝn]

v 辨識

It is very difficult to discern the difference between the two light sources, so we use a light meter.
辨識這兩光源差別很難，因此我們運用測光計。

記憶技巧 dis- 表示離開；cern- 表示分辨；discern 的意思是辨識。

discreet
[dɪˋskrit]

a 謹慎的，深思的

The discreet celebrity went into the store wearing a hat and sunglasses, but that didn't help him.
謹慎的名人戴上帽子和太陽眼鏡走進店家，但沒有幫助。

記憶技巧 dis- 表示離開；creet- 表示分開、過濾；discreet 的意思是把雜質過濾掉、分開，引申出謹慎的、深思的等意思。

discrete
[dɪˋskrit]

a 分開的，個別的，離散的

The piano plays notes in discrete tones while the organ blends them together in a continuous tone.
鋼琴以離散音調彈奏音符，風琴以連續音調將音符混和在一起。

記憶技巧 dis- 表示離開；cret- 表示分開、過濾；discrete 的意思是分開的。

secret
[ˋsikrɪt]

n 祕密，祕訣

If there were a secret to eternal life, would you want to know it?
如果有永生的祕訣，你會想知道嗎？

記憶技巧 se- 表示自己；cret- 表示分開；secret 的意思是把自己和大眾分開，從中抽身，因此有祕密的意思。

相關字彙
保密
- confidentiality 機密
- stealth 鬼鬼祟祟
- secrecy 祕密狀態

Part **3**
CH 1
CH 2
CH 3

齒間音、齒齦音、齒齦後音、硬顎音轉換

〔s〕對應〔r〕（r 音化）

hes - her

子音 s 和 r 轉換，母音通轉，兩者皆表示黏。

---

hesitate
[`hɛzə͵tet]
ⅴ 猶豫，支吾

| 相關字彙 |
| 猶豫、延宕 |

If you have any further concerns, please don't hesitate to contact me.
您若有另外重要事情，請不要猶豫，跟我聯絡。

記憶技巧　hes- 表示黏；-ate 為動詞字尾；hesitate 的意思是黏著不動，引申為猶豫。

- delay 使延期
- hold off 延期
- prevaricate 支吾
- procrastinate 延遲
- sit on 擱置
- temporize 拖延

---

inhesion
[ɪn`hiʒən]
n 固有，天生

The Bill of Rights guarantees the inhesion of the universal rights and freedoms in the Constitution.
權利法案保障憲法中與生俱來的普世權利與自由。

記憶技巧　in- 表示在～內；hes- 表示黏；-ion 為名詞字尾；inhesion 的意思是黏在裡面，引申為固有、天生。

---

adhere
[əd`hɪr]
ⅴ 黏著，追隨，遵循

Wanting to adhere to the wishes of his late father, he traveled to the Pacific to place his ashes in the sea.
立願追隨先父遺願，他到太平洋將骨灰灑入大海。

記憶技巧　ad- 表示朝～方向；her- 表示黏；adhere 的意思是黏著，引申出追隨、遵循等意思。

---

coherent
[ko`hɪrənt]
a 一致的，連貫的，緊密結合的

The police evaluated the driver to be coherent, so they let him go.
警察評估駕駛人條理清楚的，所以對他放行。

記憶技巧　co- 等同於 com-，表示一起；her- 表示黏；-ent 為形容詞字尾；coherent 的意思是黏在一起，因此有緊密結合的、連貫的等意思。

---

inherent
[ɪnˋhɪrənt]

a 內在的，固有的，
與生俱來的

Cleaning up messes in an inherent part of the job of a nursery school teacher.

整理一團糟是托兒所老師既定工作的一部分。

記憶技巧 in- 表示內；her- 表示黏；-ent 為形容詞字尾；inherent 的意思是黏在裡面的，引申為內在的、固有的。

---

jus - jur
子音 s 和 r 轉換，母音通轉，兩者皆表示法律、發誓。

just
[dʒʌst]

a 公正的，正直的，
合法的

Harry gave up his career as a successful attorney to serve as an arbiter for a just cause.

為了正義緣故，哈利放棄成功律師職涯，成為仲裁人。

記憶技巧 jus- 表示法律；just 有合法的、公正的等意思。

---

injustice
[ɪnˋdʒʌstɪs]

n 不正義，不公正

So much injustice in the world is justified through religious or political reasons.

世界上很多不公義因為宗教或政治因素而被正當化。

記憶技巧 in- 為否定字首；just 表示公正；-ice 為名詞字尾；injustice 即不公正。

---

justify
[ˋdʒʌstəˌfaɪ]

v 辯護，證明為正當

The woman left her baby locked in her car and was admonished for trying to justify her actions.

女子將嬰兒鎖在車裡，又因為企圖為自己行為合理化而遭譴責。

記憶技巧 just- 表示公正；-fy 為動詞字尾；justify 即做出公正的事，引申出辯護、證明為正當等意思。

---

jury
[ˋdʒʊrɪ]

n 陪審團

It took a month for the jury selection and another month for the court case to begin.

挑選陪審團花一個月，又花一個月才讓案件開始審理。

記憶技巧 jur- 表示法律；jury 表示陪審團，是一個平民團體，其職責是判定事實或被告是否有罪。

相關字彙
官司訴訟

- aggrieved 權利受非法侵害的
- alibi 不在犯罪現場的證明（或申辯）
- appellant 上訴人
- appellee 被告
- complainant 原告
- defendant 被告
- eyewitness 目擊者
- plaintiff 原告

jurisdiction
[ˌdʒurɪsˋdɪkʃən]

n 裁判權，司法權，管轄權

A state policeman does not have jurisdiction for crimes committed by Indians on an Indian reservation.

州警對印地安保留區印地安人沒有刑案管轄權。

記憶技巧 jur- 表示法律；dict- 表示說；-ion 為名詞字尾；jurisdiction 即根據法律做出一個判決，引申為裁判權、司法權。

- act 法令
- admiralty law 海事法
- bill 議案
- bylaw 地方法則
- civil law 民法
- clause 條款
- commercial law 商法
- cyberlaw 網路法律
- inheritance law 繼承法
- loophole 漏洞
- labor law 勞工法
- provision 條款
- quasi-contract 準契約
- rider 附加條款
- statute 法規

abjure
[əbˋdʒur]

v 棄絕

The terrorists forced the men to abjure their allegiance to the government or risk being put to death.

恐怖份子脅迫這些男子放棄效忠政府，否則將有處死風險。

記憶技巧 ab- 表示離開；jur- 表示發誓；abjure 的意思是發誓要離開某對象，引申為棄絕。

adjure
[əˋdʒur]

v 嚴令，懇請

The Jewish parents adjured the young man to become Jewish if he wanted their blessing to marry their daughter.

迎娶他們女兒時若要獲得祝福，猶太父母央請年輕男子信奉猶太教。

記憶技巧 ad- 表示朝～方向；jur- 表示發誓；adjure 的意思是發誓，衍生出嚴令等意思。

- abandon 放棄
- chuck in 放棄
- give up 放棄
- grow out of 因長大而丟棄
- give in 放棄戰鬥
- kick 戒絕（惡習）

conjure
[ˋkʌndʒɚ]

v 召喚，施魔法

The fortune-teller peered into her crystal ball and conjured a vision of the future.

算命師凝視水晶球並召喚未來景象。

記憶技巧 con- 表示一起；jur- 表示發誓；conjure 本來的意思是一起發誓，衍生出召喚、施魔法等意思。

perjury
[ˋpɝdʒərɪ]

n 作偽證

The sworn testimony was determined to be false, so the court charged the witness with perjury.

經宣誓的證詞被判定是假的，因此法庭判定目擊者作偽證。

記憶技巧 per- 表示離開；jur- 表示發誓；perjury 即違背良心和正途而作偽證。

- child abuse 虐待兒童
- contempt of court 蔑視法庭
- false imprisonment 非法拘禁
- inchoate offence 不完整罪
- medical malpractice 醫學處置失當
- solicitation 誘惑
- recidivism 累犯（行為或傾向）

rus - rur

子音 s 和 r 轉換，母音通轉，兩者皆表示農村。

rustic

[ˋrʌstɪk]

a 農村的，純樸的

The old cottage next to the saw mill exuded a rustic charm that could rarely be found.

鋸木廠旁的老舊小屋散發罕見農村魅力。

記憶技巧　rus- 表示農村；-ic 為形容詞字尾；rustic 即農村的，引申為純樸的。

rural

[ˋrʊrəl]

a 農村的，鄉村的

After the man retired, he moved to a rural community, where he could enjoy life at a slower pace.

男子退休後，遷至一處鄉村社區，在那裡可以享受慢活。

記憶技巧　rur- 表示農村；-al 為形容詞字尾；rural 即農村的。

quis - quir

子音 s 和 r 轉換，母音通轉，兩者皆表示尋找。

acquire

[əˋkwaɪr]

v 獲得，學得
（，收購）

The company's president suggested that they acquire the vendor to reduce the price of purchasing materials.

為降低原料採購價格，公司總裁建議他們併購供應商。

記憶技巧　ac- 等同於 ad-，在此當加強語氣用；quir- 表示尋找；acquire 的意思是汲汲追尋，引申為獲得、學得。

require

[rɪˋkwaɪr]

v 要求，需要

Will you require us to a vaccine before we are allowed to go on the trip?

你會要求我們獲准旅行前要接種疫苗嗎？

記憶技巧　re- 表示重複；quir- 表示尋找；require 的意思是重複尋找，1751 年後才有要求的意思。

prerequisite

[ˌpriˋrɛkwəzɪt]

n 首要事物，
必要條件，前提

The data processing class was a prerequisite to taking the computer programming course.

資料處理課是修習電腦程式設計課程的前提。

記憶技巧　pre- 表示前面；re- 表示重複；quis- 表示尋找；-ite 為名詞字尾；prerequisite 的意思是事前重複尋找，引申為前提、必要條件。

Part **3**

CH 1
CH 2
CH 3

齒間音、齒齦音、齒齦後音、硬顎音轉換

os - or

子音 s 和 r 轉換，母音通轉，兩者皆表示嘴巴或說。

---

oscular

[`ɑskjulɚ]

a 嘴巴的，親吻的

The young man will never forget when he practiced oscular stimulation in the closet with a female.

年輕男子忘不了藏身櫥櫃與女孩熱吻的那一幕。

記憶技巧　os- 表示嘴巴；-ar 為形容詞字尾；oscular 的意思是嘴巴的。

---

oral

[`orəl]

a 口頭的，口述的

Several of the exceptions to an otherwise valid oral agreement are as follows.

與口頭協議同具效力的數項例外如下。

記憶技巧　or- 表示說；-al 為形容詞字尾；oral 即嘴巴的，引申為口頭的。

---

adorable

[ə`dorəb!]

a 值得崇拜的
　（，可愛的）

The baby tigers are as adorable as kitten, but you shouldn't keep them as pets.

老虎寶寶和小貓一樣可愛，但不該當成寵物飼養。

記憶技巧　ad- 表示朝～方向；or- 表示說；-able 為形容詞字尾；adore 的意思是對～說（好話）或對～讚美；adorable 引申為值得崇拜的、可愛的。

---

oracle

[`ɔrək!]

n 神諭

The journey to the top of the mountain to seek an oracle for the meaning of life proved to be fruitless.

前往山頂尋求人生意義的神諭，最後證實是徒勞無功。

記憶技巧　or- 表示說；oracle 是神所說的訊息，亦即神諭。

相關字彙
魔法、術法

- amulet 護身符
- crystal ball 水晶球
- elixir 鍊金藥
- mascot 吉祥物
- talisman 護身符

Chapter 4
硬顎音、軟顎音、喉門音轉換

〔g〕、〔k〕、〔h〕、〔dʒ〕、〔tʃ〕、〔ŋ〕、〔j〕

Section **1**

〔k〕對應〔g〕

fict - fig

子音 c 和 g 轉換，母音通轉，兩者皆表示形狀、塑形。

---

fictional
[ˈfɪkʃənḷ]
a 虛構的，小說的

Peter Pan is a fictional character that has been loved by children for generations.
彼得潘是幾個世代的孩子喜愛的虛構角色。

> 記憶技巧　fict- 表示塑形；-ion 為名詞字尾；-al 為形容詞字尾；
> fictional 即塑形的，因為是塑造出來的，引申為虛構的。

---

figure
[ˈfɪgjɚ]
n 形狀，圖形，
人物，數字，身材

He was asked to write a figure on a piece of paper to establish the asking price for his home.
他被要求在紙上寫下數字，以確認他房屋的開價。

> 記憶技巧　fig- 表示形體；-ure 為名詞字尾；figure 即形狀，引申為身
> 材、圖形等。

---

figment
[ˈfɪgmənt]
n 虛構，虛構事物

The parents couldn't bear to tell the child that Santa was only a figment of his imagination.
家長無法告訴孩子聖誕老公公只是他想像的虛構人物。

> 記憶技巧　fig- 表示塑形；-ment 為名詞字尾；figment 即塑造出來的
> 形體，引申為虛構。

| 相關字彙
虛假 | • falsehood 虛假
• fantasy 幻想
• fraud 欺騙 | • hallucination 幻覺
• illusion 假象
• imaginings 想像出來的東西 | • myth 虛構的人、事
• mirage 海市蜃樓
• optical illusion 視錯覺 |

---

feign
[fen]
v 假裝，偽造，捏造

It was known that the student often feigned illness to avoid taking tests.
大家都知道學生常假裝生病來避開考試。

> 記憶技巧　feign 等同於 fict-，表示塑形，引申為假裝、偽造。

| 相關字彙
假裝 | • assume 假裝
• affect 裝作
• fake 冒充 | • make believe 假裝
• simulate 假裝 |

lect - leg

子音 c 和 g 轉換，母音通轉，兩者皆表示選擇。

---

electorate
[ɪˋlɛktərɪt]
n 選民，選區

The opponent won a slight majority of the votes and won the election, so the electorate was disappointed.
對手以些微差距贏得選戰，選民都失望了。

> 記憶技巧　e- 等同於 ex-，表示外面；lect- 表示選擇；-or 指做出動作者；-ate 為名詞字尾；electorate 即選民、選區。

---

selection
[səˋlɛkʃən]
n 挑選，淘汰

The selection process for the study exchange program is quite rigid.
交換學生計畫的挑選程序非常嚴格。

> 記憶技巧　se- 表示分開；lect- 表示選擇；-ion 為名詞字尾；selection 的意思選擇拿走某樣東西，引申出挑選、淘汰等意思。

---

neglect
[nɪgˋlɛkt]
v 疏忽，忽略

The staff neglected the nursing home patient, and he suffered from bed sores.
員工輕忽療養院病患導致他得了褥瘡。

> 記憶技巧　neg- 為否定字首；lect- 表示選擇；neglect 的意思是不選擇，引申出疏忽、忽略的意思。

---

diligent
[ˋdɪlədʒənt]
a 勤勉的

The diligent guard dog stood watch for 12 hours and was rewarded with raw steak.
勤快的看門犬看守十二個小時，獲得一塊生牛肉當作獎賞。

> 記憶技巧　di- 等同於 dis-，表示離開；lig- 表示選擇；-ent 為形容詞字尾；diligent 的意思是將～挑出來，因為在這挑選過程需要專注，也引申出勤勉的的意思。

---

eligible
[ˋɛlɪdʒəbl]
a 適任的，合格的

Only college graduates are eligible to be English language school teachers.
只有大學畢業生適任英語語言學校老師。

> 記憶技巧　e- 等同於 ex-，表示外面；lig- 表示挑；-ible 為形容詞字尾；eligible 的意思是挑出來的，引申為合格的、適任的。

Part **3**

CH 1
CH 2
CH 3
CH 4

硬顎音、軟顎音、喉門音轉換

Section 2

〔g〕對應〔k〕

log - locu
兩者雖無字源關係，但可藉由子音 g 和 c 互換，母音通轉來協助記憶，兩者皆表示說。

---

catalog
[`kætəlɔg]
n 目錄

The clothing store mails out product catalogs to its customers twice a year.
服飾店將產品目錄寄給顧客，一年兩次。

> **記憶技巧** cata- 表示往下、完全；log- 表示說；catalog 的意思是全說出來，引申為目錄。

相關字彙
印刷品
- almanac 年曆
- autobiography 自傳
- booklet 小冊子
- calendar 日曆
- memoir 回憶錄
- yearbook 年鑑

---

dialogue
[`daɪəˌlɔg]
n 對話

Opponents of the debate competition began the day with a round of dialogue.
辯論比賽對手以一回合的對話開戰。

> **記憶技巧** dia- 表示跨越；log- 表示說；dialogue 的意思是對話。

---

eulogy
[`julədʒɪ]
n 頌詞，頌揚

The pastor leading the funeral gave a heartfelt eulogy to the deceased.
主持喪禮的牧師對死者發表衷心的頌詞。

> **記憶技巧** eu- 表示好的；-logy 表示說、話語；eulogy 即說好話，有頌詞的意思。

相關字彙
喪事
- bier 棺材架
- coffin 棺材
- dirge 輓歌
- epitaph 墓志銘
- funeral 喪葬
- mourner 送葬者
- sarcophagus 石棺

---

apologize
[əˈpɑləˌdʒaɪz]
v 道歉

The businessman boastfully claimed to have never apologized for anything he ever did.
商人誇稱從未對任何做過的事道歉過。

> **記憶技巧** apo- 表示離開；log- 表示說；-ize 為動詞字尾；apologize 的意思是找藉口為自己開脫，後來衍生出道歉的意思。

analogy
[əˋnælədʒɪ]
n 類推，相似

A prefect analogy for what happened is the story, "The Boy Who Cried Wolf."

對於先前發生的事，有個完美的類比就是「狼來了」這個故事。

記憶技巧 ana- 表示根據；log- 表示說；analogy 的意思是根據某個說法，後引出類推的意思。

eloquent
[ˋɛləkwənt]
a 雄辯的，
　 富於表情的

The popular candidate overwhelmed his opponents at the debate with his eloquent speaking style.

人氣候選人辯論時以雄辯風格完全壓制對手。

記憶技巧 e- 等同於 ex-，表示外面；loqu 表示說；-ent 為形容詞字尾；eloquent 的意思是說出來，引申為雄辯的。

circumlocution
[ˌsɝkəmloˋkjuʃən]
n 婉轉（話），遁辭

Asian professors tend to favor circumlocution when writing their English research papers.

亞裔教授撰寫英文研究報告時有偏好婉轉語的傾向。

記憶技巧 circum- 表示環繞；locu- 表示說；-ion 為名詞字尾；circumlocution 即繞著圈子說話，引申為婉轉、遁詞等。

interlocutor
[ˌɪntɚˋlakjətɚ]
n 對話者

Trying to work out the problems between his friends, Jim offered to be an unbiased interlocutor.

努力解決朋友之間問題，吉米自願充當中立的對話者。

記憶技巧 inter- 表示在～之間；locu- 表示說；-or 指做出某動作者；interlocutor 的意思是對話者。

Part 3
CH 1
CH 2
CH 3
CH 4

硬顎音、軟顎音、喉門音轉換

原來如此！

古時放牧盛行，牛羊等牲畜於草原盡情吃草，grass 也被借用為吃草或放牧的動作── graze，只是同源的名詞字尾子音通常是無聲，而動詞字尾子音則是有聲，這是子音變換原則（consonant mutation），其他常見的例子有 house、use、advice / advise 等。

大年初二早上好友開著 Volkswagen 新車前來拜年，得意洋洋直誇德國名車真好。

　　好友：Volkswagen、Volkswagen!（標準的自然發音）

　　老蘇：不是 Volkswagen，是 Folksvagen 啦。

　　好友：我兒子教我唸的，標準自然發音。

　　老蘇：v 在德文唸 f，w 唸 v。

好友一臉錯愕！

　　老蘇：volks 就是英文的 folks，wagen 就是 vehicle，Volkswagen 就是國民車的意思。

　　好友：好比台灣的裕隆汽車嗎？

　　老蘇：是的。

　　好友：怎麼是這樣發音？

　　老蘇：很多英文字源自德文，而且很多英文同義字來自 w / v / f 的互換。

　　好友：例如？

　　老蘇：葡萄酒 wine 和葡萄樹 vine，風 wind、通風口 vent、電扇 fan。

好友一臉狐疑。

bomb 是炸彈，炸彈爆炸響起巨大聲音；boom 是隆隆作響，引申為市況興榮或暴漲，兩字同源。m 與 b 字母同是雙唇音，不發音的 b 可省略。

Chapter 5
子音對應相同

母音可能產生音變、形變，並夾雜其他子音的音變、形變

Section **1**

〔p〕對應〔p〕

apt - ept
母音通轉，兩者皆表示合適。

---

aptitude
[ˈæptəˌtjud]
n 才能，癖性

Showing no aptitude for math, the employee chose to work in the customer service center.

沒有數學長才，員工選擇在客服中心工作。

> **記憶技巧** apt- 表示適合；-tude 為抽象名詞字尾；aptitude 即適合做某事的才能。

相關字彙
才幹
- ability 能力
- experience 經驗
- equipment 才能
- capacity 本領

---

adaptive
[əˈdæptɪv]
a 適應的

One of the most adaptive animal species is the lizard, which can be found almost everywhere.

適應力最好的動物之一是蜥蜴，幾乎到處都能見到。

> **記憶技巧** ad- 表示朝～方向；apt- 表示適合；-ive 為形容詞字尾；adaptive 即適應的。

相關字彙
形容人的個性
- babyish 孩子氣的
- clingy 黏人的
- flexible 柔順的
- outward 向外的
- predisposed 先有傾向的
- reactive 反動的
- snivelling 哭哭啼啼的
- thick-skinned 厚臉皮的
- wayward 剛愎的

---

adept
[əˈdɛpt]
a 熟練的

The young man was quite adept at riding bicycles and later became a professional racer.

年輕男子對騎單車非常熟練，後來成為職業車手。

> **記憶技巧** ad- 表示朝～方向；ept- 表示合適；adept 的意思是合適的，衍生出熟練的等意思。

相關字彙
熟練的
- capable 有能力的
- born 天生的
- expert 熟練的
- professional 專業的

Section 2

〔m〕對應〔m〕

mani - manu

母音通轉，兩者皆表示手。

---

manifest
[`mænə͵fɛst]
a 明確（顯）的

The man was hired for his manifest charm and wit, which always impressed the clients.
男子受雇，因為魅力及機智出眾，總是讓顧客印象深刻。

記憶技巧 mani- 表示手；-fest 表示攻擊；manifest 的意思是用手去攻擊某對象，引申出動作明確、明顯的等意思。

---

manipulate
[mə`nɪpjə͵let]
v 操縱，竄改，控制

相關字彙
利用〜來

The bankers and brokers were arrested for manipulating the price of precious metals.
銀行家和掮客因為操縱貴重金屬價格而被捕。

記憶技巧 mani- 表示手；pul- 表示滿；-ate 為動詞字尾；manipulate 的意思是手上抓滿了東西，引申為控制、操控等。

- adopt 採納
- base on 以〜為依據
- draw on 利用
- fall back on 求助於
- use 使用

---

manual
[`mænjuəl]
n 手冊，說明書

The training manual for the company was revised five times before it was approved.
公司訓練手冊獲得許可前修訂了五次。

記憶技巧 manu- 表示手；-al 為名詞字尾；manual 即手冊。

---

manacle
[`mænəkḷ]
n 手銬，束縛

相關字彙
囚禁

Bound in iron manacles and chained to the wall, the prisoner lost all hope for freedom.
被綁上鐵手銬鍊在牆壁，囚犯失去自由的希望。

記憶技巧 manu- 表示手；manacle 是手銬。

- fetters 腳鐐
- shackles 手銬
- irons 鐐銬
- visiting hours 探望時間

manufacturer
[͵mænjə`fæktʃərə]
n 製造商，製造廠

The automobile company would only buy materials from pre-approved manufacturers.
汽車公司只會從核可的製造商採買材料。

記憶技巧 manu- 表示手；fact- 表示做；-ure 為名詞字尾；-er 指做出動作者；manufacturer 用手工製作的人，後引申為製造商。

manuscript
[`mænjə͵skrɪpt]
n 原稿

The old German manuscript turned out to be an ancient recipe for beer.
這份年代久遠的德文手稿原來是古老的啤酒祕方。

記憶技巧 manu- 表示手；script 表示書寫；manuscript 即手稿、原稿。

mont - mount
母音通轉，兩者皆表示山、突起物。

promontory
[`pramən͵torɪ]
n 岬

The young couple hiked to the top of the promontory to enjoy a picnic with the best view of the lake.
年輕夫婦健行至山岬頂部，伴著最美湖景野餐。

記憶技巧 pro- 表示前面；mont- 表示突出物；-ory 為名詞字尾；promontory，指陸地突出的尖端，引申為岬。

相關字彙
河、海、湖地形

- basin 盆地
- bank 河岸
- beach 海灘
- cape 岬，海角
- delta 三角洲
- dune 沙丘
- seashore 海岸

mountainous
[`mauntənəs]
a 多山的

In the mountainous Caucasus region, early human settlements could be found in the caves.
在多山的高加索區域，洞穴裡可發現早期人類的住居。

記憶技巧 mount- 表示山；-ous 為形容詞字尾；mountainous 即多山的。

amount
[ə`maunt]
n 總數

For the right amount of money, the man could be hired to fix anything around the house.
價碼合理，男子可以受雇修理整間屋子的任何東西。

記憶技巧 a- 等同於 ad-，表示朝～方向；mount- 表示山；amount 指的是像山一樣隆起，成堆疊的樣貌，引申為總數。

paramount

[`pærə͵maunt]

a 主要的，卓越的，
最重要的

Getting a college degree is paramount these days if you want to get a decent job.
如果想謀得像樣的工作，拿到大學學歷很重要。

記憶技巧　para- 表示穿過；mount- 表示山；paramount 指的是爬上山，引申為卓越的。

surmountable

[sə`mauntəbl̩]

a 可克服的

Defeating the chess champion is a great challenge, but it is surmountable.
擊敗西洋棋冠軍是一大挑戰，但是可以克服的。

記憶技巧　sur- 表示超過；mount- 表示山；-able 為形容詞字尾；surmountable 的字面意思是超越山的高度，引申為可克服的。

---

mers - merg

母音通轉，兩者皆表示浸入。

immerse

[ɪ`mɝs]

v 浸入，使陷入

People immerse themselves in the muddy hot springs to enjoy the health benefits of the minerals.
人們泡在泥溫泉，享受礦物質的健康效益。

記憶技巧　im- 表示內；mers- 表示浸入；immerse 即浸入。

merge

[mɝdʒ]

v 吞沒，合併，
使結合

When two corporations merge, there is often downsizing of the staff to reduce redundancies.
兩間公司合併，經常會人員縮編以減少冗員。

記憶技巧　merg- 表示浸入；merge 在 1726 後才有合併的意思。

相關字彙
混和

- blend 使混和
- combine 使結合
- jumble 使混亂
- mingle 使混合
- mix 使混和
- stir in 把~攪進去

emergency

[ɪ`mɝdʒənsɪ]

n 突然事件，
緊急情況

In an emergency, flight attendants will guide passengers to the nearest exit.
緊急情況下，空服員會指引乘客到最近逃生口。

記憶技巧　e- 等同於 ex-，表示外面；merg- 表示浸入；-ency 為名詞字尾；emergency 本指離開浸泡的狀態，引申為突然事件、緊急情況等。

Part **3**

CH 1
CH 2
CH 3
CH 4
CH 5

子音對應相同

submerge
[səbˋmɝdʒ]
v 使浸在水中，淹沒

相關字彙
浸泡

The divers submerged their vessel into the depths of the Mariana Trench.
潛水員使他們的船沉到馬里亞納海溝深度。

記憶技巧 sub- 表示在～下面；merg- 表示浸入；submerge 的意思是使浸入水中。

- duck 將～按入（水中）
- go under 沈沒
- sink 沉入
- swim 浸

Section 3

〔v〕對應〔v〕

---

ovu - ovi
母音通轉，兩者皆表示卵、蛋。

---

ovum
[ˋovəm]
n 卵，卵細胞

The doctors removed the ovum to store for eventual fertilization within a test tube.
醫生取下卵子儲藏，希望日後能在試管內受精。

記憶技巧 ovum 表示卵。

oviduct
[ˋovɪˏdʌkt]
n 輸卵管

The woman had an operation to remove a cyst from the walls of her oviduct.
這位女性接受了移除在輸卵管上囊腫的手術。

記憶技巧 ovi- 表示卵；duct- 表示引導（管）；oviduct 是輸卵管。

ovary
[ˋovərɪ]
n 卵巢

The advanced stage of ovarian cancer forced doctors to remove her affected ovary.
卵巢癌晚期階段迫使醫生移除受影響的卵巢。

記憶技巧 ov- 表示卵；-ary 為名詞字尾，表地方；ovary 是卵巢。

相關字彙
性器官
- cervix 子宮頸
- clitoris 陰蒂
- fallopian tube 輸卵管
- foreskin 包皮
- intrauterine 子宮內的
- phallus 陰莖
- testicle 睪丸
- vagina 陰道
- womb 子宮

Part
3
CH 1
CH 2
CH 3
CH 4
CH 5

子音對應相同

Section **4**

〔d〕對應〔d〕

damn - demn

母音通轉，兩者皆表示罵、傷害。

---

damn

[dæm]

V 咒罵

The earth opened up and demons dragged the poor man to hell and damned him for eternity.

土地裂開，惡魔將窮人拖到地獄，永遠詛咒。

記憶技巧 　damn 即罵。

---

damage

[`dæmɪdʒ]

n 損壞

There was extensive damage caused by the tornado strewn across the Missouri countryside.

整個密蘇里鄉下都是龍捲風掃過而造成的大範圍損壞。

記憶技巧 　dam- 表示傷害；-age 為名詞字尾；damage 名詞意思是損害，後亦可當動詞用，表示使損壞。

相關字彙
破壞

- destruction 毀壞
- demolition 破壞
- decay 腐爛
- devastation 蹂躪
- harm 損傷
- havoc 浩劫
- ruin 毀滅
- sabotage 破壞

---

indemnify

[ɪn`dɛmnə͵faɪ]

V 賠償，保障

The insurance company will indemnify the insured, as long as it can be proven that the crash was not intentional.

保險公司將賠償被保險人，只要證明事故不是蓄意造成。

記憶技巧 　in- 為否定字首；demn- 表示損害；-fy 為動詞字尾；indemnify 的意思是使不受傷害，後來引申為賠償。

相關字彙
保險保障

- actuary 精算師
- assurance 保證
- coverage 保險項目
- health insurance 健康保險
- insurance premium 保險費
- insurer 保險公司
- reinsurance 再保險
- travel insurance 旅遊保險
- underwrite（在～之下）簽署

---

condemn

[kən`dɛm]

V 譴責，宣判，報廢

The city inspector condemned the old apartment building, and forced the residents to move out.

城市檢查員將老舊公寓建物報廢，強迫居民搬出。

記憶技巧 　con- 表示加強語氣；demn- 表示傷害；condemn 意思是傷害，引申為譴責、報廢。

Section **5**

〔t〕對應〔t〕

tac - tic
母音通轉，兩者皆表示安靜。

taciturn
[ˈtæsəˌtɜn]

a 沉默的

The autistic child was taciturn when he was brought into social situations.
自閉症小孩被帶到社交場合時會保持沉默。

記憶技巧　tac- 表示安靜；taciturn 即安靜的。

reticent
[ˈrɛtəsn̩t]

a 緘默的

The media knew very little of the foreign shipping mogul, as he was reticent about his personal life.
媒體對於該外國貨運大亨幾乎一無所知，因為他對私生活從不張揚。

記憶技巧　re- 表示加強語氣；tic- 表示安靜；-ent 為形容詞字尾；reticent 的意思是緘默的。

Section **6**

〔n〕對應〔n〕

negr - nigr
母音通轉，兩者皆表示黑。

negro
[ˈnigro]

n 黑人

Before the 1960's, it was common for African-Americans to be referred to as negroes.
1960 年代之前，非裔美國人被指為黑人很普遍。

記憶技巧　negr- 表示黑；negro 是黑人的意思。

denigrate

[`dɛnəˌgret]

v 使變黑，詆毀

Most people don't believe it is patriotic to denigrate the president in public.

大多數人認為公開抹黑總統不是愛國行為。

記憶技巧　de- 表示完全；nigr- 表示黑；-ate 為動詞字尾；denigrate 的意思是抹黑。

---

nounc - nunci

母音通轉，兩者皆表示大叫。

announce

[ə`naʊns]

v 宣布，發布

The television commercial announced the grand opening of an automobile dealership.

電視廣告宣布一家汽車經銷商的盛大開幕。

記憶技巧　an- 等同於 ad-，表示朝～方向；nounc- 表示大叫；announce 的意思是對～大叫，引申為宣布。

---

denounce

[dɪ`naʊns]

v 指責，譴責

The leader denounced the bullying tactics of the larger, neighboring country.

領導人譴責較大的鄰國的霸凌手法。

記憶技巧　de- 表示往下；nounc- 表示大叫；denounce 的意思是對著下面大叫，引申出指責、譴責。

相關字彙
公開批評

- bash 痛擊
- condemn 責備
- decry 責難
- pillory 使～受公眾嘲笑
- slate 抨擊

---

renounce

[rɪ`naʊns]

v 聲明放棄，拋棄

After his marriage to an Austrian woman, the man moved and renounced his American citizenship.

與奧地利女子結婚後，男子遷移並放棄美國公民身分。

記憶技巧　re- 表示反對；nounc- 表示大叫；renounce 的意思是大聲反對，引申為聲明放棄、拋棄。

相關字彙
不再擁有

- forfeit（因犯罪、失職、違約等）喪失（權利、名譽、生命等）
- forswear 發誓拋棄
- give up 放棄
- relinquish 棄絕
- sacrifice 犧牲

---

renunciation

[rɪˌnʌnsɪ`eʃən]

n 宣告放棄，拋棄

His experiences in the war led to the renunciation of his vows to defend the Constitution.

戰爭中的經歷促使他宣告放棄保護憲法的誓言。

記憶技巧　renunciation 是 renounce 的名詞。

ann - enn
母音通轉，兩者皆表示年。

---

annuity
[ə`njuətɪ]

n 養老金，
年金（保險）

The conservative investor bought an annuity that would pay $2,000 per month.
保守的投資者購買每月支付 2,000 元的年金保險。

記憶技巧 　ann- 表示年；-ity 為名詞字尾；annuity 是年金（保險）。

---

anniversary
[͵ænə`vɝsərɪ]

n 週年，週年紀念

相關字彙
紀念活動

There was a huge turnout for the couple who celebrated their 50th wedding anniversary.
很多人出席夫婦結婚五十周年活動。

記憶技巧 　ann- 表示年；vers- 表示轉；-ary 為名詞字尾；anniversary 的意思是轉了一圈回來，引申為周年紀念。

- bicentenary 二百年紀念
- birthday 生日
- diamond anniversary
  六十年（有時指七十五週年）結婚紀念
- golden anniversary 五十年結婚紀念
- silver anniversary 二十五年結婚紀念日
- wedding anniversary 結婚紀念日

---

biennial
[baɪ`ɛnɪəl]

a 兩年一次的

The international media conference is held on a biennial basis in a different host country each time.
國際媒體大會由不同主辦國每兩年舉行一次。

記憶技巧 　bi- 表示雙；enn- 表示年；-ial 為形容詞字尾；biennial 是兩年一次的。

---

perennial
[pə`rɛnɪəl]

n 多年生植物

Some plants are perennials in their native region, flowering year after year.
一些植物在原生地是多年生植物，年復一年地開花。

記憶技巧 　per- 表示穿透；enn- 表示年；-ial 為形容詞字尾；perennial 是終年的，後來衍生出多年生植物的意思。

〔k〕對應〔k〕

circ - cycl

兩者並無字源關係，但可藉由母音通轉來記憶，兩者皆表示（圓）圈、環繞。

---

circular
[ˋsɝkjələ]
a 圓形的，巡迴的，循環的

A circular saw is the tool of choice to make wooden planks in wood mills.
圓形鋸是木材廠製造木板的工具。

記憶技巧　cir- 表示圓圈；circle 表示圓形；-ar 為形容詞字尾；circular 是圓形的。

---

circulate
[ˋsɝkjəˏlet]
v 循環，散佈，巡迴

A rumor circulated around the office that the junior executive would resign.
初階主管要辭職的傳言在辦公室流傳。

記憶技巧　cir- 表示圓圈；circle 表示圓形；-ate 為動詞字尾；circulate 的意思是繞圓圈，引申為循環、散佈。

---

circuit
[ˋsɝkɪt]
n 環行，巡迴，電路

If one closes the circuit, the series of lights will flash on and off.
如果關閉該線路，這排燈泡會一開一關閃爍。

記憶技巧　circ- 表示環繞；-it 表示走；circuit 的意思是繞著走，引申為巡迴、環行等意思。

---

circuitous
[sɚˋkjuɪtəs]
a 迂迴的，繞行的

The small road made a circuituous route through the countryside.
小道迂迴穿越鄉下地區。

記憶技巧　circuit 的意思是環行；-ous 為形容詞字尾；circuitous 即繞行的。

---

circus
[ˋsɝkəs]
n 馬戲團，圓形競技場

A curious attraction at the circus was a bear that could ride a bicycle.
馬戲團令人好奇的賣點是有隻熊會騎腳踏車。

記憶技巧　circ- 表示環繞；circus 本是環形劇場，後來衍生出馬戲團的意思。

Part **3**

CH 1
CH 2
CH 3
CH 4
CH 5

子音對應相同

相關字彙	• amusement park 遊樂園	• theme park 主題樂園
遊樂場、馬戲團	• Disneyland 迪士尼樂園	• water park 水上樂園
	• fairground 露天馬戲團	

circumspect
[ˋsɝkəmˏspɛkt]
a 慎重的，精密的

To be circumspect, it may have been foolish to bring my child to work during the important meeting.
慎重起見，重要會議期間帶小孩去上班會是蠢事一椿。

記憶技巧 circum- 表示環繞；spect- 表示看；circumspect 的意思是環顧四周，引申出謹慎的意思。

cycle
[ˋsaɪkl̩]
n 週期，循環，自行車

It is an annual cycle to hire extra staff for the Christmas shopping season and then to fire them afterwards.
雇請耶誕購物季額外員工而隨後解雇，這是每年循環的事。

記憶技巧 cycl- 表示環繞；cycle 有週期、循環等意思。

cyclone
[ˋsaɪklon]
n 龍捲風，氣旋

The cyclone that hit Sri Lanka caused serious flooding and damage to thousands of homes.
襲擊斯里蘭卡的龍捲風造成嚴重洪水及數千房屋損毀。

記憶技巧 cycl- 表示環繞；cyclone 是氣旋。

encyclopedia
[ɪnˏsaɪkləˋpidɪə]
n 百科全書

The large set of encyclopedias on the bookshelf gathered dust because the Internet made them useless.
書架上大套百科全書沾滿灰塵，因為網路使這些書用處盡失。

記憶技巧 en- 等同於 in-，表示在～裡面；cycl- 表示圈；ped- 表示小孩，在此當教育、訓練小孩；-ia 為名詞字尾；encyclopedia 的意思是一輪完整的訓練，指的是通識教育，後當百科全書解釋。

〔r〕對應〔r〕

ory / ery - ary

母音通轉，皆表示地點。

Part **3**

CH 1
CH 2
CH 3
CH 4
CH 5

子音對應相同

armory

[`ɑrmərɪ]

n 兵工廠

When the rebels took over the base, they stole weapons from the armory.

叛軍接管基地，從兵工廠偷走武器。

記憶技巧 arm 表示武器；-ory 表示地方；armory 是兵工廠。

---

conservatory

[kən`sɜvə,torɪ]

n 溫室

They sat in the conservatory at the back of the home to enjoy a cup of tea among the flowers.

他們坐在房子後面的溫室，在花叢中享用一杯茶。

記憶技巧 con- 表示加強語氣；serv- 表示留意、保持；-ory 表示地方；conservatory 即種植植物時，可提供較好照顧的地方，不受氣候影響。

---

dormitory

[`dɔrmə,torɪ]

n 宿舍

The parents sent their child to attend the specialized high school and live in the dormitory on campus.

父母送孩子就讀專門高中並住在校園宿舍。

記憶技巧 dorm- 表示睡眠；-ory 表示地方；dormitory 的意思是宿舍。

---

observatory

[əb`zɜvə,torɪ]

n 天文台

For his 45th birthday, the man was taken to the observatory to view the star that was named after him.

45 歲生日，男子被帶到天文台觀看以他命名的星星。

記憶技巧 ob- 表示在～之前；serv- 表示看；-ory 為名詞字尾；observe 的意思是在～前看，引申為觀察；observatory 是天文台。

---

bakery

[`bekərɪ]

n 麵包店

The apprentice worked long, hard hours in the bakery, saving up to have his own business.

學徒在麵包店長工時辛苦工作，積蓄一些錢要自行創業。

記憶技巧 bake 表示烘焙；-ery 為名詞字尾，表示地方；bakery 是烘焙麵包的麵包店。

cemetery
[ˈsɛməˌtɛrɪ]
n 墓地

The police were called to investigate a disturbance at the cemetery, and they approached with apprehension.
警方被找來調查在墓地的騷動，他們戒慎恐懼地往墓地前進。

記憶技巧 -ery 表示地方；cemetery 是人安息之所，指墓地。

- grave 墓穴
- mausoleum 陵墓
- necropolis 大墓地
- resting place 安息地
- tomb 墳墓

brewery
[ˈbruərɪ]
n 釀酒廠

Tourists visit Weihenstephan Abbey to see the oldest continuously operating brewery in Germany.
遊客造訪唯森修道院，一睹德國最老的連續運作釀酒廠。

記憶技巧 brew 表示釀造；-ery 表示地方；brewery 即釀酒廠。

refinery
[rɪˈfaɪnərɪ]
n 煉油廠

The oil refineries in Romania were commonly targeted by Allied bombers during World War II.
第二次世界大戰期間，羅馬尼亞煉油廠常是盟軍轟炸機的目標。

記憶技巧 re- 表示加強語氣；fine 表示精緻的、無雜質的；-ery 表示地方；refinery 是將雜質去除，提煉油品的煉油廠。

nursery
[ˈnɝsərɪ]
n 托兒所，苗圃

Gardeners can visit plant nurseries to buy young flowers for their gardens.
園丁可以參訪苗圃為自家花園購買花苗。

記憶技巧 nurse 表示培育；-ery 表示地方；nursery 是托兒所、苗圃。

- kindergarten 幼稚園
- preschool 幼稚園
- playschool 遊戲學校（即幼兒園）
- reception class（為初次入學學齡兒童所設的）小班

library
[ˈlaɪˌbrɛrɪ]
n 圖書館

Growing up in a poor family, the child would escape to the library whenever he could.
成長於窮困家庭，這孩子一有機會就會往圖書館去。

記憶技巧 libr- 表示書、紙；-ary 表示地方；library 是圖書館。

granary
[ˈgrænərɪ]
n 穀倉，盛產糧食的地方

The villager was instructed to maintain the roof of the granary to keep moisture away from the corn.
為了讓玉米不受潮，有人指導村民維修穀倉屋頂。

記憶技巧 gran- 等同於 grain，表示穀物；-ary 表示地方；granary 是穀倉。

mortuary
[`mɔrtʃu⸴ɛrɪ]
n 停屍間

The city mortuary is definitely one of the places I would not want to visit after midnight.
市立停屍間一定是我半夜不想去的地方之一。

記憶技巧　mort- 表示死亡；-ary 表示地方；mortuary 是停屍間。

〔s〕對應〔s〕

Part **3**
CH 1
CH 2
CH 3
CH 4
CH 5
子音對應相同

salt - sult / sili
母音通轉，皆表示跳。

saltant
[`sæltənt]
a 跳躍的

The boy performed a saltant expression of joy upon hearing the news that he passed the exam.
聽到通過考試的消息時，男孩高興地雀躍著。

記憶技巧　salt- 表示跳；-ant 為形容詞字尾；saltant 即跳躍的。

exultation
[⸴ɛgzʌl`teʃən]
n 狂喜，歡欣鼓舞

There was a full day of exultation for all citizens after the peace treaty was signed.
簽署和平協議後，市民一整天欣喜若狂。

記憶技巧　ex- 表示外面；sult- 表示跳；-ation 為名詞字尾；exultation 的意思是心情雀躍，引申為狂喜。

insult
[ɪn`sʌlt]
v 侮辱

The heavy-set boy insulted the girl in front of her parents and ran away laughing.
體格魁武的男孩在女孩父母面前侮辱她，然後笑著跑走。

記憶技巧　in- 表示上面；sult- 表示跳；insult 的意思是跳到～上，引申為侮辱。

result
[rɪ`zʌlt]
n 結果，效果，成績

The results of the speech competition were posted on the bulletin board soon after lunch.
演講比賽結果在午餐後隨即公布在布告欄。

記憶技巧　re- 表示回來；sult- 表示跳；result 是跳回來，引申為結果。

resilient [rɪˋzɪlɪənt] **a** 有彈性的，活潑的	The resilient fishermen offered boat tours after their fishing grounds were depleted. 能適應的漁夫在魚場耗盡後推出小船旅遊行程。 **記憶技巧** re- 表示回來；sili- 表示跳；-ent 為形容詞字尾；resilient 是彈（跳）回來的，引申為有彈性的。
salient [ˋselɪənt] **a** 突出的，顯著的	The lecturer covered the salient points of his speech early, in case some attendees needed to leave. 萬一有些與會者須離席，講師提早提到演講亮點。 **記憶技巧** sali- 表示跳；-ent 為形容詞字尾；salient 是跳出來的，引申為顯著的、突出的。
assault [əˋsɔlt] **n** 攻擊，襲擊，威脅	The military assault on Sicily, near Salerno was key to invading Italy. 對薩勒諾附近的西西里島展開軍事攻擊是入侵義大利的關鍵。 **記憶技巧** as- 等同於 ad-，表示朝～方向；sault- 表示跳；assault 是朝～跳，引申為攻擊。

strat - stern
兩者皆表示攤開、分散。

stratified [ˋstrætəˏfaɪd] **a** 形成階層的， 　　分為不同等級的	The marching band members were stratified on the football field to form a moving pattern of colors. 軍樂隊成員在足球場形成分階隊伍，形成彩色的移動圖案。 **記憶技巧** strat- 表示分散；-fy 為動詞字尾；-ed 為過去分詞字尾；stratified 指的是分散，衍生出形成階級的等意思。
consternation [ˏkɑnstɚˋneʃən] **n** 驚愕，驚駭	The student faced the consternation of the principal after he was caught painting graffiti on the wall. 在牆壁塗鴉被抓後，學生面對校長的驚愕。 **記憶技巧** con- 表示加強語氣；stern- 表示攤開；-ation 為名詞字尾；consternation 指的是因驚駭而臥倒在地上，引申為驚愕。
相關字彙 焦慮緊張	● concern 擔心　　　● distress 苦惱 ● tension 緊張 ● anxiety 焦慮

Chapter 6
〔h〕變化

Section 1 〔s〕對應〔h〕
（拉丁語、英語字母「s」，對應希臘語字母「h」）

〔s〕對應〔h〕

（拉丁語、英語字母「s」，對應希臘語字母「h」）

semi - hemi

子音 s 和 h 對應，母音通轉，兩者皆表示一半。

---

semidiameter
[ˌsɛmaɪdaɪˈæmətɚ]
n 半徑

A circle's semidiameter is the same as a circle's radius.
「semidiameter」和「radius」是相同的。

記憶技巧　semi- 表示一半；dia- 表示跨越；meter- 表示測量；diameter是穿越圓心所測得的直徑，semidiameter即半徑。

---

hemicycle
[ˈhɛməˌsaɪkl̩]
n 半圓

Basketball players must stand outside the large hemicycle around the basket to shoot a three-point shot.
籃球選手要投三分球，必須站在籃框周圍的大半圓形之外。

記憶技巧　hemi- 表示一半；cycle 表示圓；hemicycle 是半圓。

---

hemisphere
[ˈhɛməsˌfɪr]
n 半球

People who live in the Southern Hemisphere see a completely different star pattern at night.
住在南半球的人夜晚會看到完全不同的星空圖形。

記憶技巧　hemi- 表示一半；sphere 表示球體；hemisphere 是半球。

相關字彙
圓形物

- balloon 氣球
- cone 圓錐體
- cylinder 圓柱
- hoop 環，圈
- oval 橢圓形的

---

hemiplegic
[ˌhɛmɪˈplidʒɪk]
a 半身不遂

She took care of his father after a stroke left him with a hemiplegic body.
父親因中風而半生不遂之後，她照顧著他。

記憶技巧　hemi- 表示一半；pleg- 表示癱瘓；-ic 為形容詞字尾；hemiplegic 即半身不遂。

相關字彙
身體殘疾

- challenged 殘障的
- disabled 有缺陷的
- impaired 受損的
- invalid 殘疾者
- paralysed 癱瘓的
- paraplegic 下身麻痺患者
- quadriplegic 四肢麻痺患者

sub - hypo

子音 s 和 h 對應，母音通轉（拉丁文 u 對應希臘文字母 y），兩者皆表示在～下面。

subaquatic [ˌsʌbə`kwætɪk] 🅐 水下的，水中的	Sea turtles have almost completely subaquatic lives, emerging only to lay their eggs. 海龜幾乎都生活在水面下，只有下蛋時才浮出水面。 記憶技巧 sub- 表示在～下面；aqua- 表示水；-ic 為形容詞字尾；subaquatic 是水下的。
hypodermis [ˌhaɪpə`dɝmɪs] 🄝 皮下組織	During the dissection of the mouse, the students peeled off the outer layer of skin to reveal the hypodermis. 解剖老鼠時，學生剝下外層皮膚以使皮下組織外露。 記憶技巧 hypo- 表示在～下面；derm- 表示皮膚；hypodermis 是皮下組織。
hypochondria [ˌhaɪpə`kɑndrɪə] 🄝 憂鬱症，臆想病	The traumatized woman suffered from hypochondria, worrying about illnesses that she didn't have. 受創女子罹患憂鬱症，擔心自己沒患的病。 記憶技巧 hypo- 表示在～之下；chondr- 表示肋骨；古希臘人認為肋骨下的位置是大部分病痛的源頭，後指憂鬱症。

Part
3
CH 1
CH 2
CH 3
CH 4
CH 5
CH 6

〔h〕變化

原來如此！

shade 意思是樹蔭，樹蔭投擲出陰影 —— shadow，兩字同源。shade 產生 shadow，同時成為動物在曠野中的遮陽庇護地方，因此可聯想 shelter 這單字（音相近，意相連）。另外，umbrella 的字根 umbr- 源自拉丁文的 umbra，就是 shade、shadow 的意思，產生陰影的器具就是雨傘。

原來如此！

轉音是英文字彙擴增的途徑，除了形成語意相關字，也常見反義字，例如：

goose 是雌鵝、gander 是雄鵝；

vote 意思是投票、veto 意思卻是否決；

host 意思是主人、招待，[h] 轉音為 [g]，guest 意思是客人。

另一方面，host 的衍生字 hostile 及 hostility 卻是與 enemy 有關，分別表示敵對的及敵意。轉音衍生不僅存在於單字，也常見於字首綴詞，例如：hypersonic 及 supersonic 的意思都是超音速，字首 hyper- 及 super- 是轉音同源，也與 over 同源。hypo- 意思是 under，hyper- 的反義字，雖無轉音淵源，但見轉音對應。

原來如此！

單字 camp 原意是軍隊暫時駐紮的空曠地方，現在是營地或是露營的意思，衍生字 campus 原指大學校園，現在泛指一般校園；另一衍生字 campaign 原指空曠地方上的軍事操演，現在是指競選活動或一般的活動。champion 是 camp 的同源字 [tʃ] 和 [k] 轉音，表示優勝者或戰士，與空曠地方上的競賽或戰鬥有關。

Chapter 7
因接黏字根而變形

Section 1　同化作用（assimilation）

Section **1**

同化作用（assimilation）

com - cog / col / con / cor / co
全部皆表示一起，有時用來加強語氣。

---

compromise
[`kɑmprəˌmaɪz]
v 妥協，損害

The secret to a long, happy marriage lies in improving one's ability to compromise.
長久又快樂的婚姻祕訣在於增進妥協的能力。

記憶技巧　com- 表示一起；promise 表示承諾；compromise 的意思是大家一起承諾，引申出妥協、損害的意思。

---

cognition
[kɑg`nɪʃən]
n 認知，知識

The traditional methods of child cognition were not effective in preparing children for a life of creativity.
孩童認知的傳統方式對於訓練創意的生活毫無效果。

記憶技巧　co- 表示一起；gn- 表示知道；-ition 為名詞字尾；cognition 的意思是認知。

---

colloquial
[kə`lokwɪəl]
a 口語的，會話的

The exchange student found it difficult to follow conversations because of the use of colloquial language.
交換學生發現要跟上會話很難，因為使用的是口語形式。

記憶技巧　col- 表示一起；loqu- 表示說；-ial 為形容詞字尾；colloquial 的意思是一起說的，引申為會話的。

---

condominium
[`kɑndəˌmɪnɪəm]
n 各戶有獨立產權的公寓

There was an oversupply of condominiums built in Miami, so one could be purchased at a bargain.
邁阿密建造的公寓供過於求，每戶都可低價購得。

記憶技巧　con- 表示一起；domin- 表示房子；-ium 為名詞字尾；condominium 的意思大家所共有的房子，後來語意產生改變，表示各戶有獨立產權的公寓。

相關字彙
住所

- apartment building 公寓大樓
- chateau 別墅
- cottage 小屋，度假別墅
- dormitory 宿舍
- hostel 青年旅社
- villa 別墅

corrigible

[ˈkɔrədʒəb!]

a 可改正的，
　有待修正的

The father hoped his son's defect be corrigible when he went to military training camp.

父親希望兒子的缺點在他進入軍事訓練營區後能有所改正。

記憶技巧　cor- 表示加強語氣；rig- 等同於 rect-，表示直；-ible 為形容詞字尾；corrigible 的意思是可弄直的，引申為可改正的。

---

coerce

[koˈɝs]

v 強制，迫使

The woman smiled and subtly coerced the policeman into letting her go with just a warning.

女子微笑，巧妙促使警察僅予以警告即讓她離開。

記憶技巧　co- 表示一起；erc- 表示限制；coerce 是指大家一起限制，引申為強迫。

---

en - em
兩者皆表示在～裡面或在～上。

enthusiasm

[ɪnˈθjuzɪˌæzəm]

n 熱心，熱情，熱忱

After the first week of training, most of the workers lost their enthusiasm for their new jobs.

第一周訓練後，大多數員工即失去新工作的熱忱。

記憶技巧　en- 表示在～內；thus- 等同於 theo-，表示神；enthusiasm 的意思是內心受到神的啟發，引申出熱心、熱忱等意思。

---

embark

[ɪmˈbark]

v 上船，從事，著手

They said goodbye to their beloved daughter, who was about to embark on a four-year journey.

他們對心愛的女兒道別，因為她要展開為期四年的旅程。

記憶技巧　em- 表示在～上；bark 表示小船；embark 即上船。

---

syn - sym / syl / sy
皆表示一起的意思。

synthesis

[ˈsɪnθəsɪs]

n 綜合體，綜合

The botanists studied the jungle flora to aid in the biochemists' synthesis of pharmaceuticals.

植物學家研究叢林植物以協助生化學家藥品合成。

記憶技巧　syn- 表示一起；thes- 表示放；synthesis 的意思是放一起，引申為綜合。

Part **3**

CH 1
CH 2
CH 3
CH 4
CH 5
CH 6
CH 7

因接黏字根而變形

asymmetry

[eˋsɪmɪtrɪ]

n 不對稱

The asymmetry in the woman's face distinguished her from the other models in her agency.

女子不對稱的臉型讓她和經紀公司其他模特兒有所區別。

> 記憶技巧　a- 為否定字首；sym- 表示一起；metr- 表示測量；-y 為名詞字尾；asymmetry 的意思是一起測量時不對稱。

syllabus

[ˋsɪləbəs]

n 教學大綱，
課程大綱

When the principal took over, she promised to change the syllabus to include more national history.

校長接任時，她承諾改變課程大綱以涵蓋更多本國史。

> 記憶技巧　syl- 表示一起；syllabus 是將許多事項條列在一起的課程大綱。

systematic

[ˌsɪstəˋmætɪk]

a 有系統的，
成體系的

There was a systematic takeover after the democratic election in the country.

國內民主選舉後，有一個接任的系統性。

> 記憶技巧　sy- 表示一起；st- 表示站；-atic 為形容詞字尾；systematic 的意思是很多事物站一起形成一體系或系統。

---

ex - ef / ec / es / e

皆表示外面、離開、完全。

---

expropriate

[ɛksˋproprɪˌet]

v 徵用，沒收

When the robbers attempted to flee, the off-duty policeman expropriated a car to give chase.

搶匪企圖逃走時，下勤務的警察徵用一輛車子追逐搶匪。

> 記憶技巧　ex- 表示離開；propr- 表示自己（財物）；-ate 為動詞字尾；expropriate 的意思是拿走自己的財物，引申為徵收、沒收等。

相關字彙
奪取、收取

- attach 查封
- confiscate 徵收
- deprive 剝奪
- encroach 侵佔
- impound 扣押
- rob 劫掠
- repossess 收回
- requisition 徵用
- seize 奪取
- snatch 奪得

effective

[ɪˋfɛktɪv]

a 有效的

The staff pinned their hopes on the new CEO to come up with an effective solution.

員工將希望寄託在新任執行長，希望他能想出一個有效的解決方案。

> 記憶技巧　ef- 表示外面；fect- 表示做；-ive 為形容詞字尾；effective 的意思是做出來的，引申為有效的。

eccentric

[ɪkˈsɛntrɪk]

a 偏執的，離心的

The eccentric woman decorated her home with an outlandish display of wealth.

古怪的婦人以怪異風格的財富展示裝飾住家。

> 記憶技巧 ec- 等同於 ex-，表示離開；centr- 表示中心；-ic 為形容詞字尾；eccentric 的意思是離心的。

evaporate

[ɪˈvæpəˌret]

v （使）蒸發，
（使）揮發

The spilt milk eventually evaporated, leaving behind a congealed white crust.

溢出的牛奶最後蒸發，留下凝結的白色硬皮。

> 記憶技巧 e- 等同於 ex-，表示外面；vapor 表示蒸氣；-ate 為動詞字尾；evaporate 的意思是蒸氣跑出來，引申為使蒸發。

egregious

[ɪˈgridʒəs]

a 非常的，
震驚（人）的

The band of thieves committed egregious acts of violence upon the families they stole from.

竊盜集團對遭竊家庭施加駭人聽聞的暴力行徑。

> 記憶技巧 e- 等同於 ex-，表示外面；greg- 表示群體；-ous 為形容詞字尾；egregious 的字面意思是離開群眾的，引申出震驚的等意思。

in - im / il / ir / ig

母音通轉，表示否定或在～裡面的意思。

indisposed

[ˌɪndɪˈspozd]

a 不願的，厭惡的
（，微恙的）

Please don't seek the indisposed chairman, as you should respect his privacy during his bathroom break.

請不要去找身體微恙的主席，因為你應該尊重他上廁所時的隱私。

> 記憶技巧 in- 為否定字首；dis- 表示離開；pos- 表示放；-ed 為過去分詞字尾；dispose 的是將東西擺好，引申為安排，indisposed 的意思是安排得不好、無序的，引申為微恙、不願的。

imbibe

[ɪmˈbaɪb]

v 飲，喝

The birthday boy imbibed far too many shots of whiskey and found himself in a stranger's bed the next morning.

男壽星喝下太多杯威士忌，隔天早上發現自己躺在一位陌生人的床上。

> 記憶技巧 im- 表示裡面；bib- 表示喝；imbibe 是喝進去，即飲用。

相關字彙
喝

- consume 喝光
- drink 喝
- drink up 喝完
- drain 喝乾
- quench 解（渴）

Part
3

CH 1
CH 2
CH 3
CH 4
CH 5
CH 6
CH 7

因接黏字根而變形

illuminate

[ɪˈlumənet]

v 照亮，照射

The park became safer at night when it became illuminated by LED lamps.

公園以 LED 燈照明後晚上變得較安全。

記憶技巧 il- 表示在～內；lumin- 表示照光；-ate 為動詞字尾；illuminate 的意思是照亮。

irrigate

[ˈɪrəˌget]

v 灌溉

The Japanese built an impressive network of canals that still irrigates much of Taiwan's farmland.

日本人建造令人印象深刻的渠道網路，至今仍然灌溉許多台灣農地。

記憶技巧 ir- 表示在～內；rig- 表示使潮濕、澆水；-ate 為動詞字尾；irrigate 的意思是灌溉。

相關字彙 農業

- cultivate 耕種
- furrow 犁溝
- glean 拾（落穗）
- harvest 收穫
- plough 犁
- spray 噴霧器
- till 耕作

ignominy

[ˈɪgnəˌmɪnɪ]

n 恥辱

The protestors were forced to endure the ignominy of being strip-searched and jailed in outdoor cages.

抗議者被迫忍受脫衣搜身和拘禁於戶外籠子的恥辱。

記憶技巧 ig- 為否定字首；nomin- 表示名字；-y 為名詞字尾；ignominy 的意思名聲不好，引申為恥辱。

---

sub - suc / suf / sug / sum / sup / sur / sus

皆表示在～下面。

---

succumb

[səˈkʌm]

v 屈服，委棄，聽任

The peasant family were heavily taxed and eventually succumbed to starvation.

農家被課重稅，最後死於飢餓。

記憶技巧 suc- 表示在～下面；cumb- 表示躺；succumb 的意思是躺在～下面，引申為屈服。

相關字彙 屈服

- acquiesce 默從
- submit 使服從
- comply 順從
- yield 讓於

suffuse

[səˈfjuz]

v 遍布，充滿

The man accidentally walked into the occupied bathroom stall, and the boy's cheeks suffused with red color.

男子意外闖進使用中的淋浴間，男孩的臉頰就變得通紅。

記憶技巧 suf- 表示下面；fus- 表示倒；suffuse 的意思是倒到～下面，引申出遍布、充滿的意思。

suggest

[sə`dʒɛst]

v 建議，提議

What do you suggest we do with the leftover turkey after our feast?

宴席過後，剩下的火雞你會建議我們怎麼處理？

記憶技巧　sug- 表示在～下面；gest- 表示拿、攜帶；suggest 的意思是從下面拿出來，引申出提議的意思。

sumptuous

[`sʌmptʃuəs]

a 奢侈的，豪華的，昂貴的

As a reward for graduating from high school, the family treated him to a sumptuous four-course meal.

家人招待他享用一頓四道菜的佳餚作為高中畢業的獎勵。

記憶技巧　sum- 表示在～下面；-(e)mpt 表示拿；-ous 為形容詞字尾；sumptuous 的意思是從底下拿出來，毫無節制，引申為奢侈的、豪華的。

相關字彙　昂貴

- costly 貴重的
- expensive 貴的
- extravagant 奢侈的
- luxurious 奢華的
- pricey 貴的

suppression

[sə`prɛʃən]

n 壓制，鎮壓，禁止

The government banned media from covering the protest to hide the police's suppression of the protestors.

以掩蓋警方對於抗議者的鎮壓，政府禁止媒體報導抗議行動。

記憶技巧　sup- 表示在～下面；press- 表示壓；-ion 為名詞字尾；suppression 的意思是壓在下面，引申為鎮壓。

surrogate

[`sɝəgɪt]

n 代理者，代理人

In a surprising development, the dog accepted role of surrogate mother for the baby pig.

發展令人驚訝，狗狗接受豬仔代理母親的角色。

記憶技巧　sur- 表示在～下面，在此當替代；rog- 表示問；-ate 為動詞字尾；surrogate 的意思是替別人問，名詞的意思是代理人。

相關字彙　替代

- assignee 受託人
- alternate 交替的
- replacement 代替品、人
- substitute 代替人
- standby 備用物
- successor 繼任者
- substitute 代用品，替代者

susceptible

[sə`sɛptəbl]

a 易被感動的，易受～影響的

The lodge sold medicine to skiiers at the resort, as they were susceptible to colds and flus.

渡假勝地看守小屋販賣藥品給滑雪者，因為他們易受到感冒或流感影響。

記憶技巧　sus- 表示在～下面；cept- 表示拿；-ible 為形容詞字尾；susceptible 的意思是可以拿走的，引申為易受～影響的。

Part **3**

CH 1
CH 2
CH 3
CH 4
CH 5
CH 6
CH 7

因接黏字根而變形

> # ad - ac / af / ag / all / an / ap / ar / as / at
> 皆表示朝～方向、和～相關、加強語氣。

---

adjourn
[əˋdʒɝn]

v 使中止，使延期，休（會）

The judge called for the courtroom to be adjourned for lunch for two hours.
法官要求法庭暫停兩小時中午用餐。

`記憶技巧` ad- 表示朝～方向；journ- 表示日；adjourn 的意思是到另一日，引申為使延期。

---

accord
[əˋkɔrd]

v 符合，調和

The witness's account of the incident accords with the evidence from the scene.
目擊者對事件的陳述與現場取得的證據相符。

`記憶技巧` ac- 表示朝～方向；cord- 表示心；accord 指的是心向著心，兩心一致，引申為符合。

---

affidavit
[ˌæfəˋdevɪt]

n 宣誓書，口供書

The man signed an affidavit of support as required by the judge in the paternity lawsuit.
親子訴訟案中，男子在法官要求下簽署扶養宣誓書。

`記憶技巧` af- 表示朝～方向；fid- 表示信任；affidavit 是信任～的意思，引申為宣誓書、口供書。

---

agglomeration
[əˌɡlɑməˋreʃən]

n 結塊，堆，附聚（作用）

Arizona is home to the world's largest aircraft cemetery, with an incredible agglomeration of planes.
亞利桑那是世界最大的飛機墳場，成堆的飛機令人不可思議。

`記憶技巧` ag- 表示朝～方向；glomer- 表示球狀、團；-ation 為名詞字尾；agglomeration 是結塊、堆的意思。

---

alluvium
[əˋluvɪəm]

n 沖積層，沖積土

The annual flooding cycle flooded the plains with fresh alluvium, to the delight of the farmers.
農夫很高興，一年一度的洪水循環讓新沖積土湧入平原。

`記憶技巧` al- 表示朝～方向；luv- 表示沖洗；-ium 為名詞字尾；alluvium 是沖積層。

---

annex
[əˋnɛks]

v 附加，增添（，併吞）

Before World War II started, Germany annexed the neighboring territory known as Rhineland.
第二次世界大戰開打前，德國併吞了被稱為萊茵蘭的鄰近領土。

`記憶技巧` an- 表示朝～方向；nex- 表示綁；annex 的意思是綁住，引申為附加、增添及併吞。

appetite
[ˈæpəˌtaɪt]

n 食慾，胃口

The more foes the emperor vanquished, the greater his appetite for territory and power grew.

愈多敵人被皇帝征服，皇帝對領土及權力的胃口就變得愈大。

記憶技巧　ap- 表示朝～方向；pet- 表示尋找；-ite 為名詞字尾；appetite 的意思是去尋找，引申成渴望，特別是在找食物上，因此有食慾的意思。

相關字彙
飢餓

- hunger 飢餓
- famine 饑荒
- ravenous 狼吞虎嚥的
- starvation 飢餓

arrest
[əˈrɛst]

n 逮捕，拘留

The highly-publicized arrest of the star basketball player was on the front page of every newspaper.

籃球明星被逮一事各報紙頭版皆大幅報導。

記憶技巧　ar- 表示朝～方向；rest 表示維持；arrest 的意思是維持不動，引申出逮捕的意思。

assuage
[əˈswedʒ]

v 緩和，
減輕（病痛等）

The teacher accompanied the student to the speech competition to assuage her fears.

為了舒緩緊張，老師陪學生出席演講比賽。

記憶技巧　as- 表示朝～方向；suag- 表示甜；assuage 即給甜頭，藉以緩和或減輕不開心、壓力、疼痛的情況。

attorney
[əˈtɜnɪ]

n 律師

The divorce attorney enjoyed brisk business during the holiday season.

離婚律師假期期間業務興旺。

記憶技巧　at- 表示朝～方向；torn- 等同於 turn-，表示轉；attorney 的意思是轉向～人（求助），引申成遇到法律上問題可以尋求協助或打官司的人。

Part
3
CH 1
CH 2
CH 3
CH 4
CH 5
CH 6
CH 7

因接黏字根而變形

ob - oc / of / op / o
兩者皆表示朝向、相反的意思。

obsequious
[əbˈsikwɪəs]

a 諂媚的，奉承的

The students seemed too obsequious to their professor, raising the suspicion of coercion.

學生對教授似乎太奉承了，提高了強迫的嫌疑。

記憶技巧　ob- 表示朝向，在此作在～後；sequ- 表示跟隨；-ous 為形容詞字尾；obsequious 的意思是跟在某人身後的，引申為諂媚的、奉承的。

offer
[`ɔfə]

v 給予，提供，
拿出，出示

The competing bidders offered their bids in quick succession at the automobile auction.
汽車拍賣會中，競標者連續快速投標。

> 記憶技巧　of- 表示朝向；fer- 表示帶；offer 的意思是帶給某人，引申為給予、提供等意思。

oppose
[ə`poz]

v 反對，反抗，妨礙

Those who opposed bailing out the bankrupt financial institutions took to the streets in force.
反對為破產金融機構紓困的人大批走上街頭抗議。

> 記憶技巧　op- 表示相反；pos- 表示放；oppose 的意思是放到對面擋住某人，引申為反對。

omission
[o`mɪʃən]

n 省略，刪除

When he was not announced as a serious candidate for the job, he believed the omission was a mistake.
他未被發布為這個工作認真的應徵者，他相信略過他是個錯誤。

> 記憶技巧　o- 在此可能是加強語氣；miss- 表示送；-ion 為名詞字尾；omission 的意思是送走，引申為省略。

dis - dif / di
皆表示缺乏、離開、相反。

differentiate
[ˌdɪfə`rɛnʃˌet]

v 使有差異，
構成～間的差別

The new line of shoes used yellow shoelaces to differentiate it from the previous lines.
為了區別舊款鞋子，新款鞋子採用黃色鞋帶。

> 記憶技巧　dif- 表示離開；fer- 表示帶；-ate 為動詞字尾；differentiate 的意思是帶開，以示區別。

diversion
[daɪ`vɝʒən]

n 轉向，轉移，轉換

The accountant played chess with his colleagues online as a diversion from his monotonous job.
會計師在線上和同事下西洋棋，作為單調工作的消遣。

> 記憶技巧　di- 表示離開；vers- 表示轉；-ion 為名詞字尾；diversion 的意思是轉開、轉移。

原來如此！

年初四晚間與幾位友人到山區一間三代傳承的山產店用餐。

老楊：This is a century-old restaurant!

友人：餐廳和世紀什麼關係？

老楊：cent 表示 100，世紀是 100 年，century-old store 是老店的意思。

友人欣喜！

野味上桌，香酥蜈蚣。

友人：這道菜應該是 cent 什麼的吧？

老楊：沒錯！這是 centipede，pede 就是 foot！

友人食指大動，品嘗美味！

第二道菜上桌，清蒸章魚，八隻腳盤在盤子上！

友人：這道菜該不會是什麼 pede 吧？

老楊：octopus，octo- 表示八，pus 和 pede 都是腳，同字源！

友人：了解！繼續享用美食！

第三道菜上桌，一隻兩腳野味！

友人：我猜這也是 pede 什麼的！

老楊：正是！名稱與單車有關！

友人放下筷子，頭腦轉了一下，說 biped！

老楊：去掉字尾 e，biped 兩足動物！

友人大啖，野味及英語一起下肚！

Part 3
CH 1
CH 2
CH 3
CH 4
CH 5
CH 6
CH 7
因接黏字根而變形

猜猜看！

❶ 戰役 battle 就是相互打擊，猜一四字母的單字？

❷ 考試中的 question，猜 ques 所代表的單字？

答案：❶ beat（打擊）　❷ query（問）

我的格林法則心智圖

（詳細範例請見書籍前方的拉頁。）

STEP 1

圓心｜兩音的轉換

先在中央畫一個圓，
然後填入兩音的轉換。

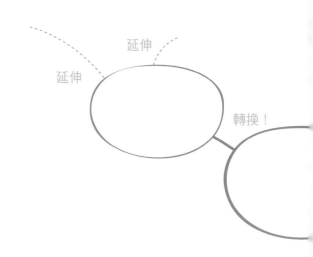

延伸

延伸

轉換！

STEP 2

第一層｜簡單字

第一層圓圈填入有簡單字
及其中文意思、詞性。

STEP 3

第二層｜轉音後的字根

填入轉音後的字根及其中文
意思、詞性。

STEP 4

第三層｜字根的衍生字

第三層圓圈要填入字根的衍
生字及其中文意思、詞性。

相關

我的格林法則心智圖

（詳細範例請見書籍前方的拉頁。）

STEP 1

圓心｜**兩音的轉換**

先在中央畫一個圓，
然後填入兩音的轉換。

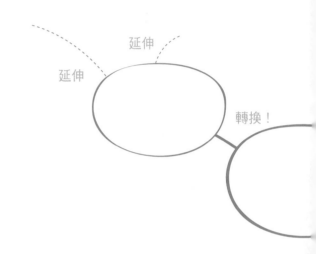

延伸

延伸

轉換！

STEP 2

第一層｜**簡單字**

第一層圓圈填入有簡單字
及其中文意思、詞性。

STEP 3

第二層｜**轉音後的字根**

填入轉音後的字根及其中文
意思、詞性。

STEP 4

第三層｜**字根的衍生字**

第三層圓圈要填入字根的衍
生字及其中文意思、詞性。

相關

國家圖書館出版品預行編目（CIP）資料

地表最強英文單字：不想輸，就用「格林
法則」背10,000個英文單字／楊智民、蘇
秦 著 -- 初版. -- 臺北市：我識，2017. 05
　　面；　公分

978-986-94501-3-3（平裝附光碟）
1. 英語 2. 詞彙
805.12　　　　　　　　　　106004385

地表最強英文單字

不想輸，就用「格林法則」
背10,000個英文單字

書名 / 地表最強英文單字：不想輸，就用「格林法則」背10,000個英文單字

作者 / 楊智民、蘇秦

發行人 / 蔣敬祖

專案副總經理 / 廖晏婕

副總編輯 / 劉俐伶

主編 / 謝昀蓁

校對 / 王傳明

視覺指導 / 黃馨儀

美術設計 / 李宜璟

內文排版 / 張靜怡

法律顧問 / 北辰著作權事務所蕭雄淋律師

印製 / 金濤印刷事業有限公司

初版 / 2017年05月

初版十刷 / 2019年02月

出版單位 / 我識出版教育集團——我識出版社有限公司

電話 / (02) 2345-7222

傳真 / (02) 2345-5758

地址 / 台北市忠孝東路五段372巷27弄78之1號1樓

郵政劃撥 / 19793190

戶名 / 我識出版社

網址 / www.17buy.com.tw

E-mail / iam.group@17buy.com.tw

facebook網址 / www.facebook.com/ImPublishing

定價 / 新台幣 399 元 / 港幣 133 元（附光碟）

總經銷 / 我識出版社有限公司業務部

地址 / 新北市汐止區新台五路一段114號12樓

電話 / (02) 2696-1357　傳真 / (02) 2696-1359

地區經銷 / 易可數位行銷股份有限公司

地址 / 新北市新店區寶橋路235巷6弄3號5樓

港澳總經銷 / 和平圖書有限公司

地址 / 香港柴灣嘉業街12號百樂門大廈17樓

電話 / (852) 2804-6687　傳真 / (852) 2804-6409

I'm 我識出版集團
I'm Publishing Group
www.17buy.com.tw

2011 不求人文化

2009 懶鬼子英日語

2005 意識文化

2005 易富文化

2003 我識地球村

2001 我識出版社

2011 不求人文化

2009 懶鬼子英日語

I'm 我識出版集團
I'm Publishing Group
www.17buy.com.tw

2005 意識文化

2005 易富文化

2003 我識地球村

2001 我識出版社